1.
WHAT IT MEANS

NEW ORLEANS
1917

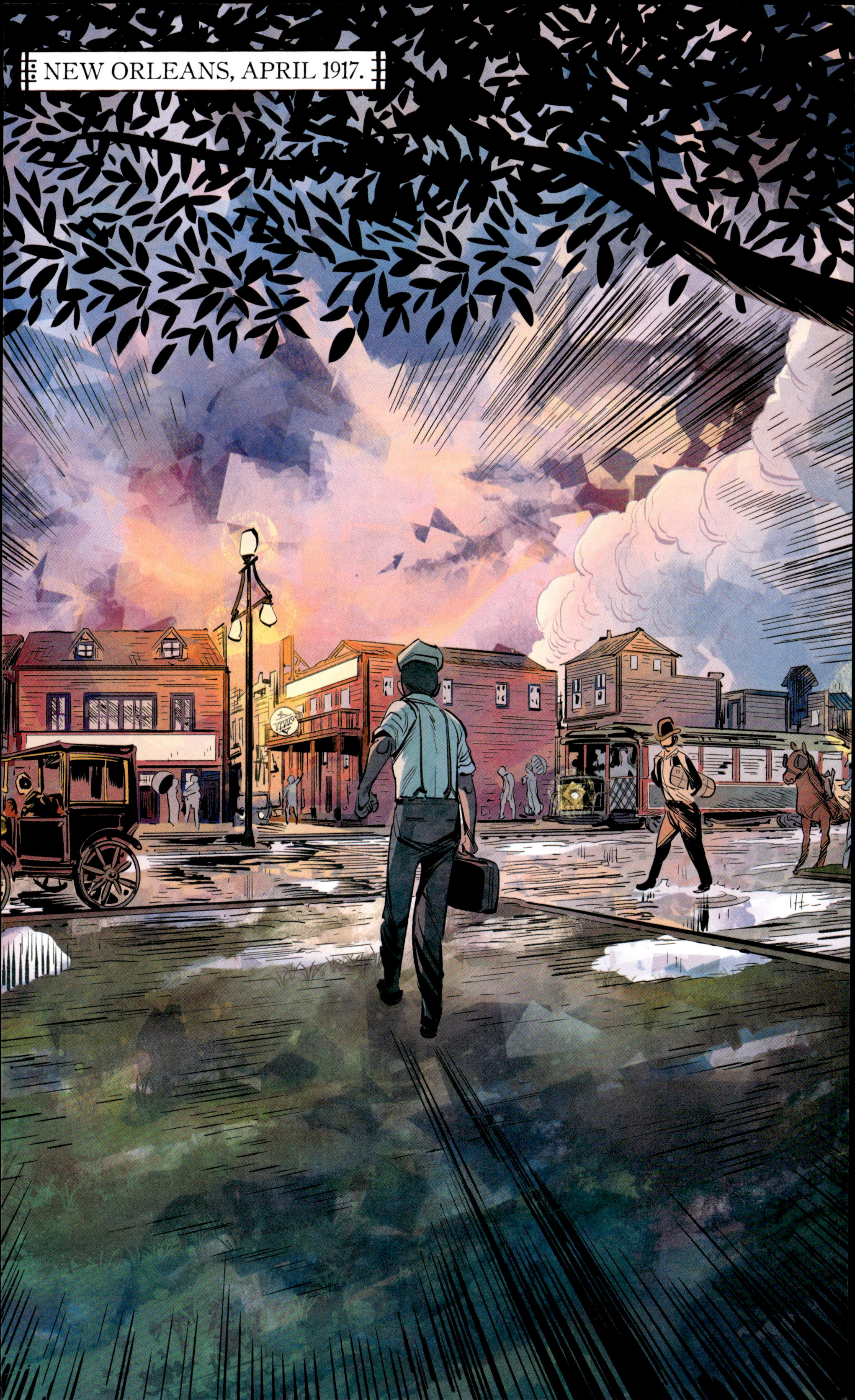
NEW ORLEANS, APRIL 1917.

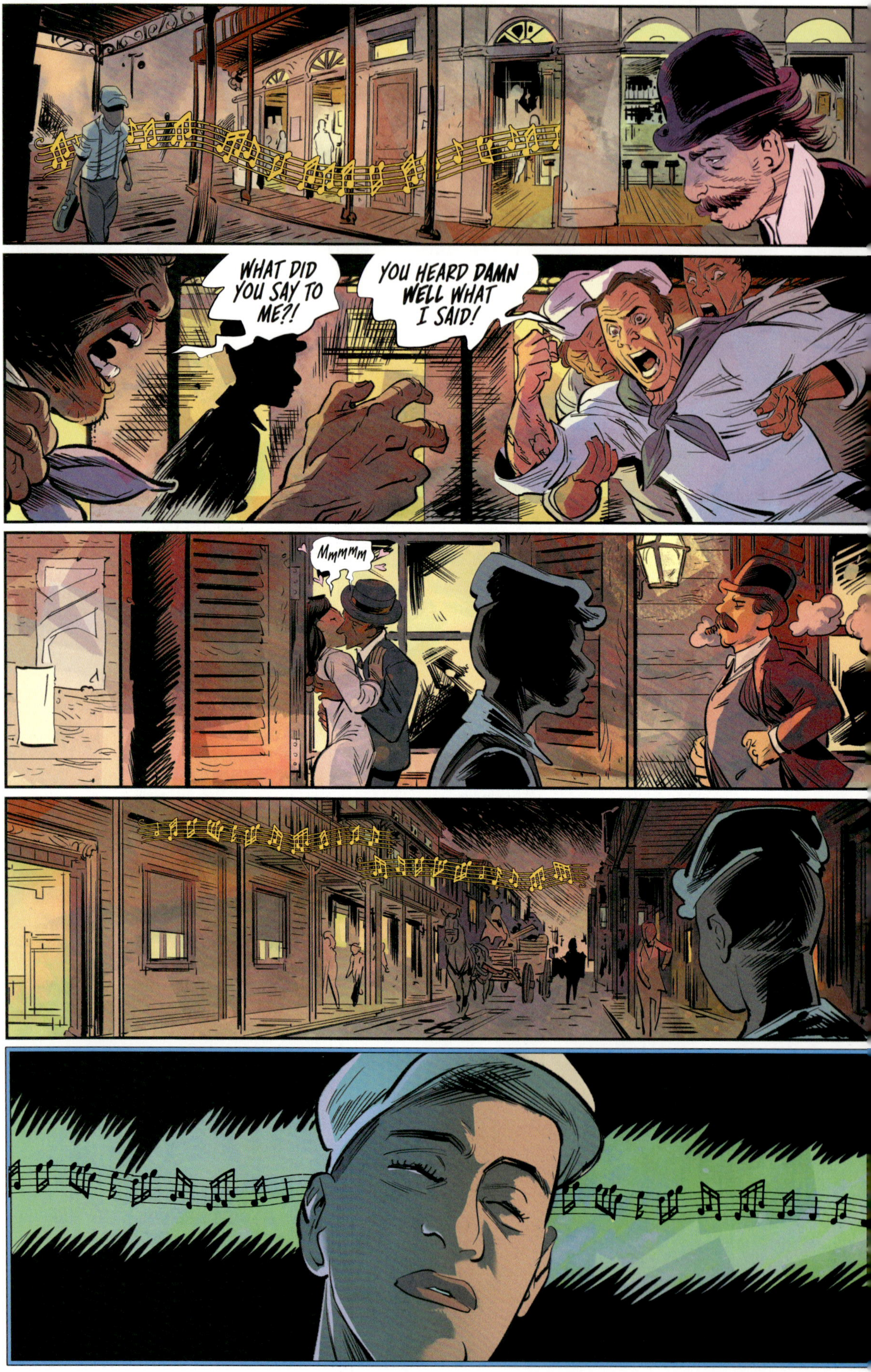
WHAT DID YOU SAY TO ME?!
YOU HEARD DAMN WELL WHAT I SAID!
Mmmmm

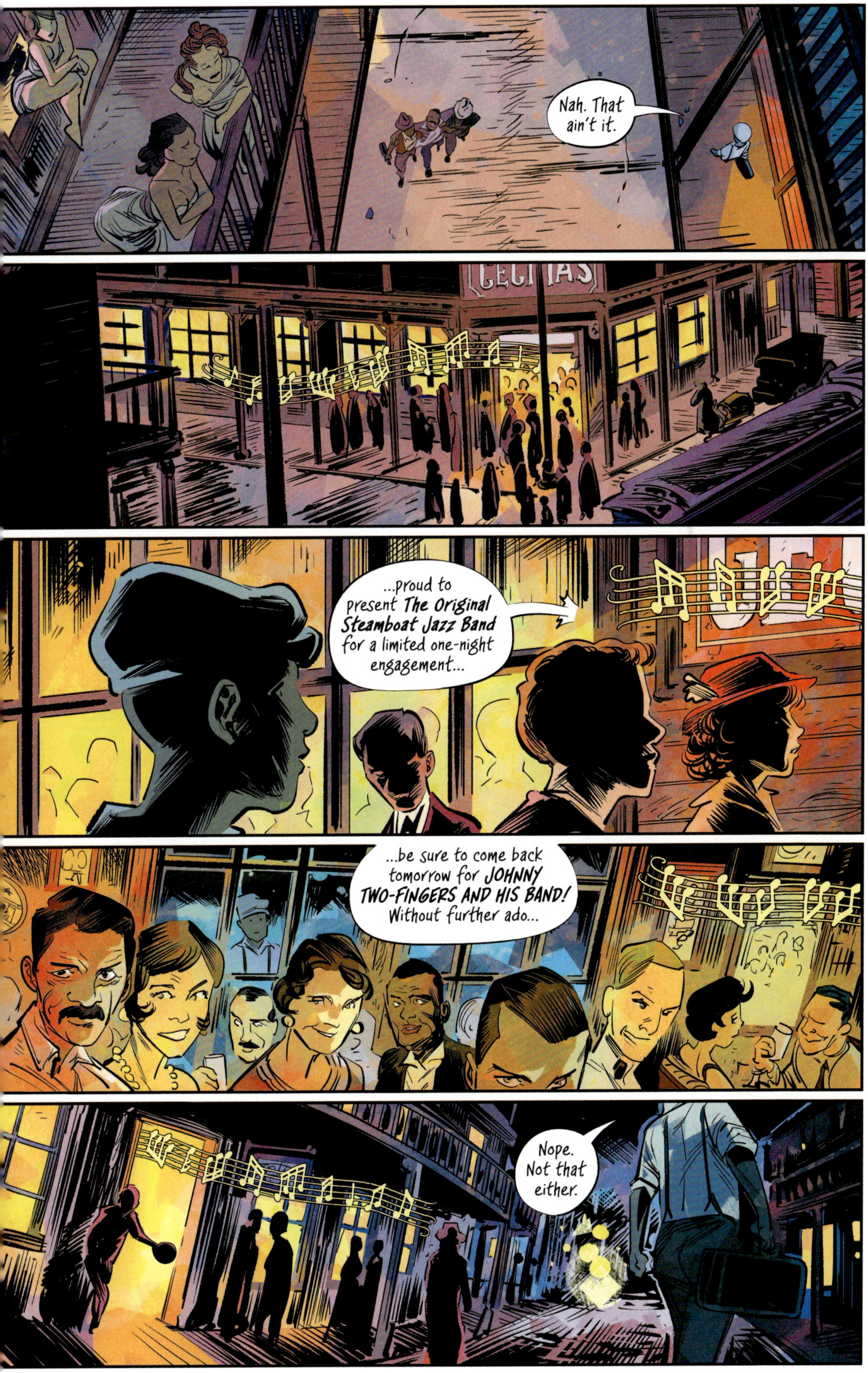
Nah. That ain't it.
...proud to present The Original Steamboat Jazz Band for a limited one-night engagement...
...be sure to come back tomorrow for JOHNNY TWO-FINGERS AND HIS BAND! Without further ado...
Nope. Not that either.

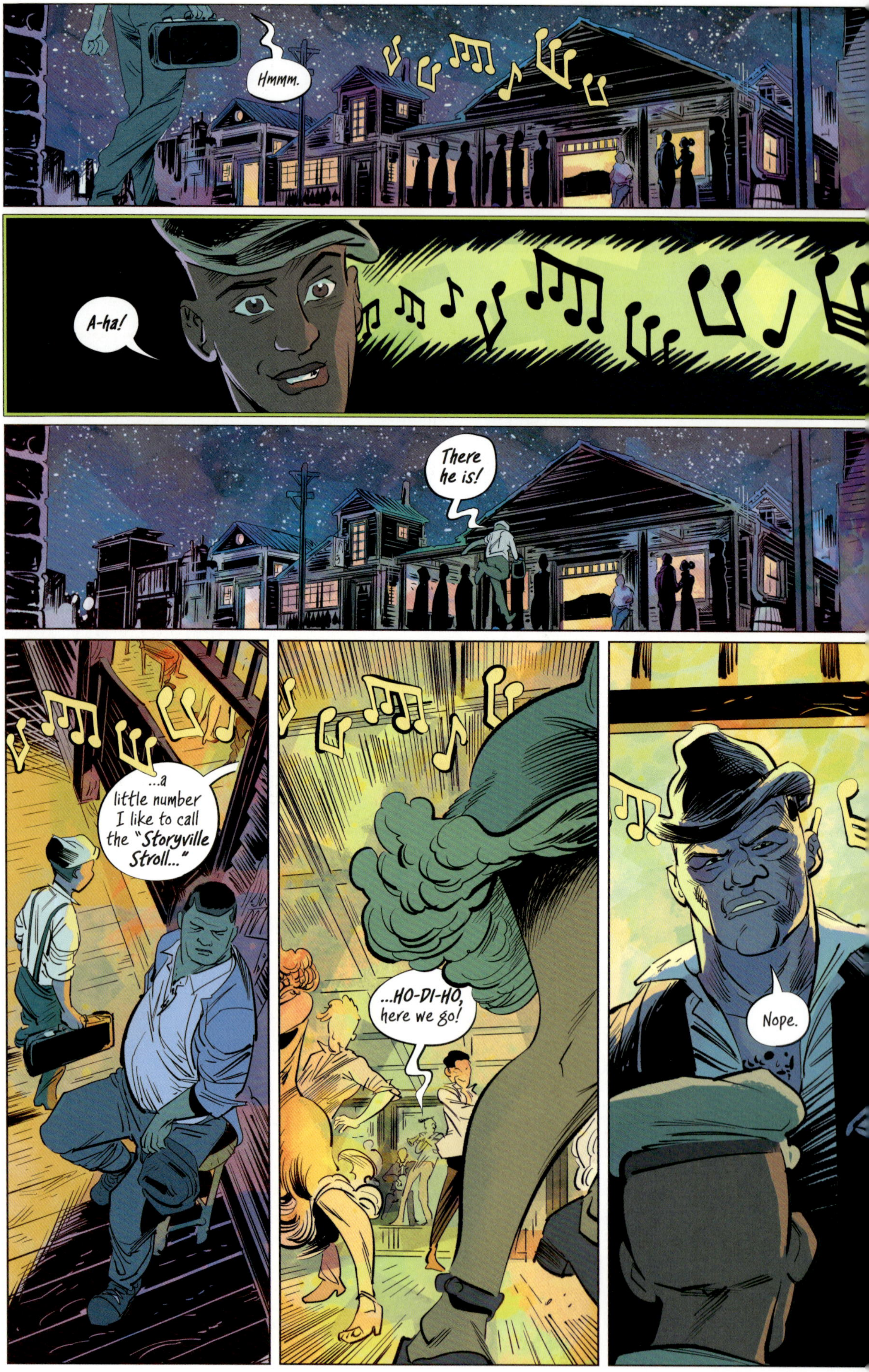
Hmmm.
A-ha!
There he is!
...a little number I like to call the "Storyville Stroll..."
...HO-DI-HO, here we go!
Nope.

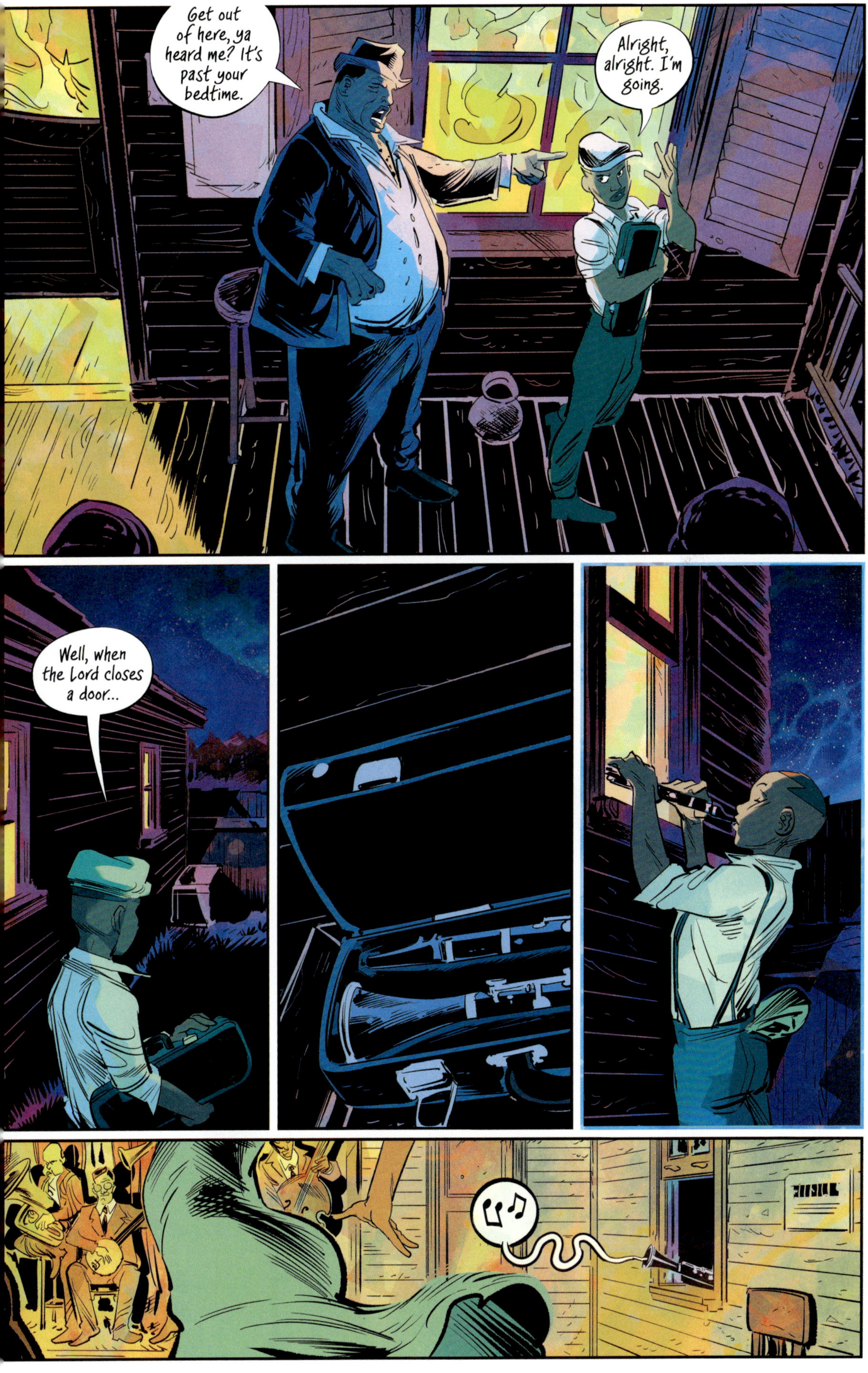
Get out of here, ya heard me? It's past your bedtime.
Alright, alright. I'm going.
Well, when the Lord closes a door...

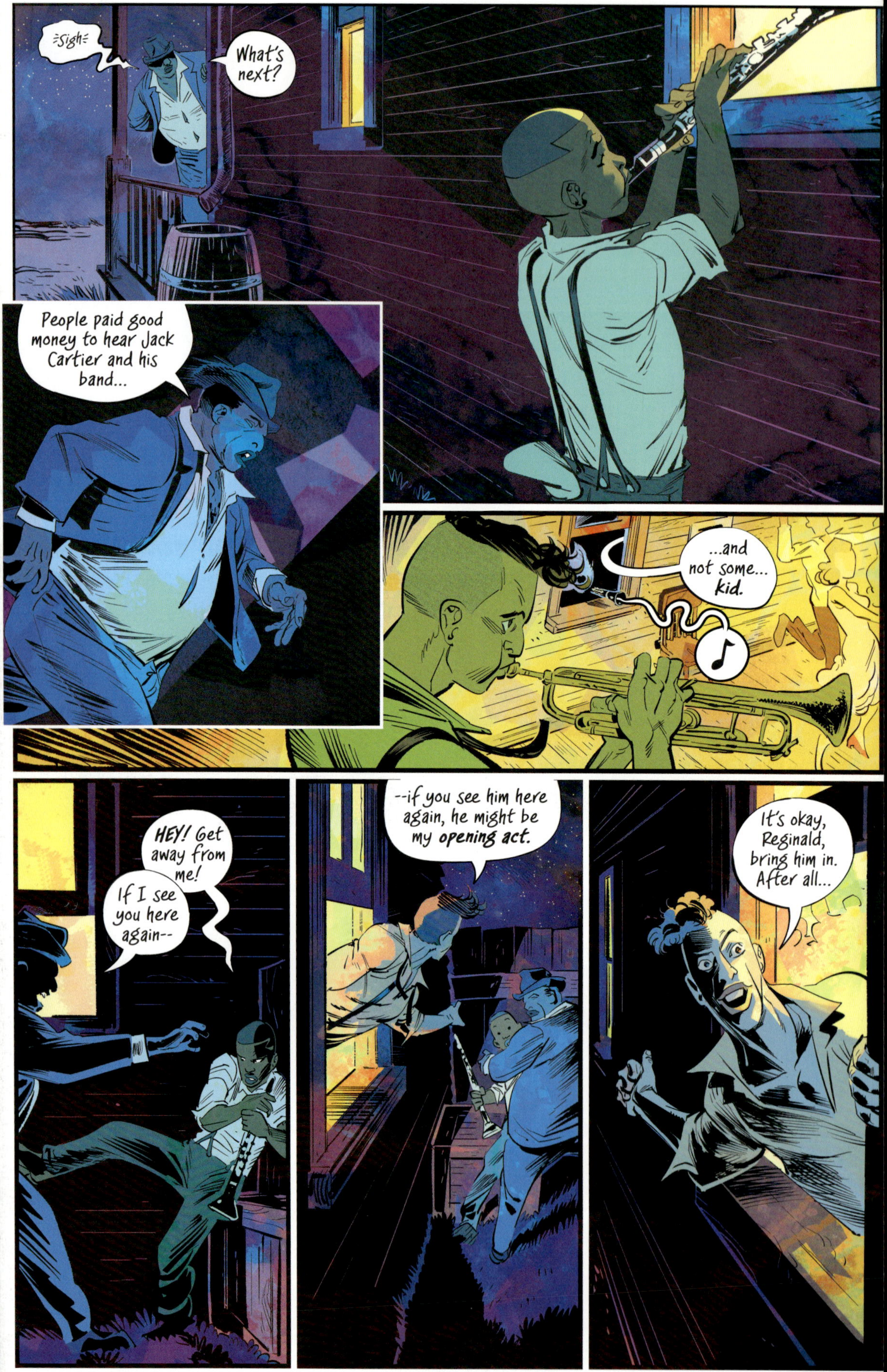
Sigh
What's next?
People paid good money to hear Jack Cartier and his band...
...and not some... kid.
HEY! Get away from me!
If I see you here again--
--if you see him here again, he might be my opening act.
It's okay, Reginald, bring him in. After all...

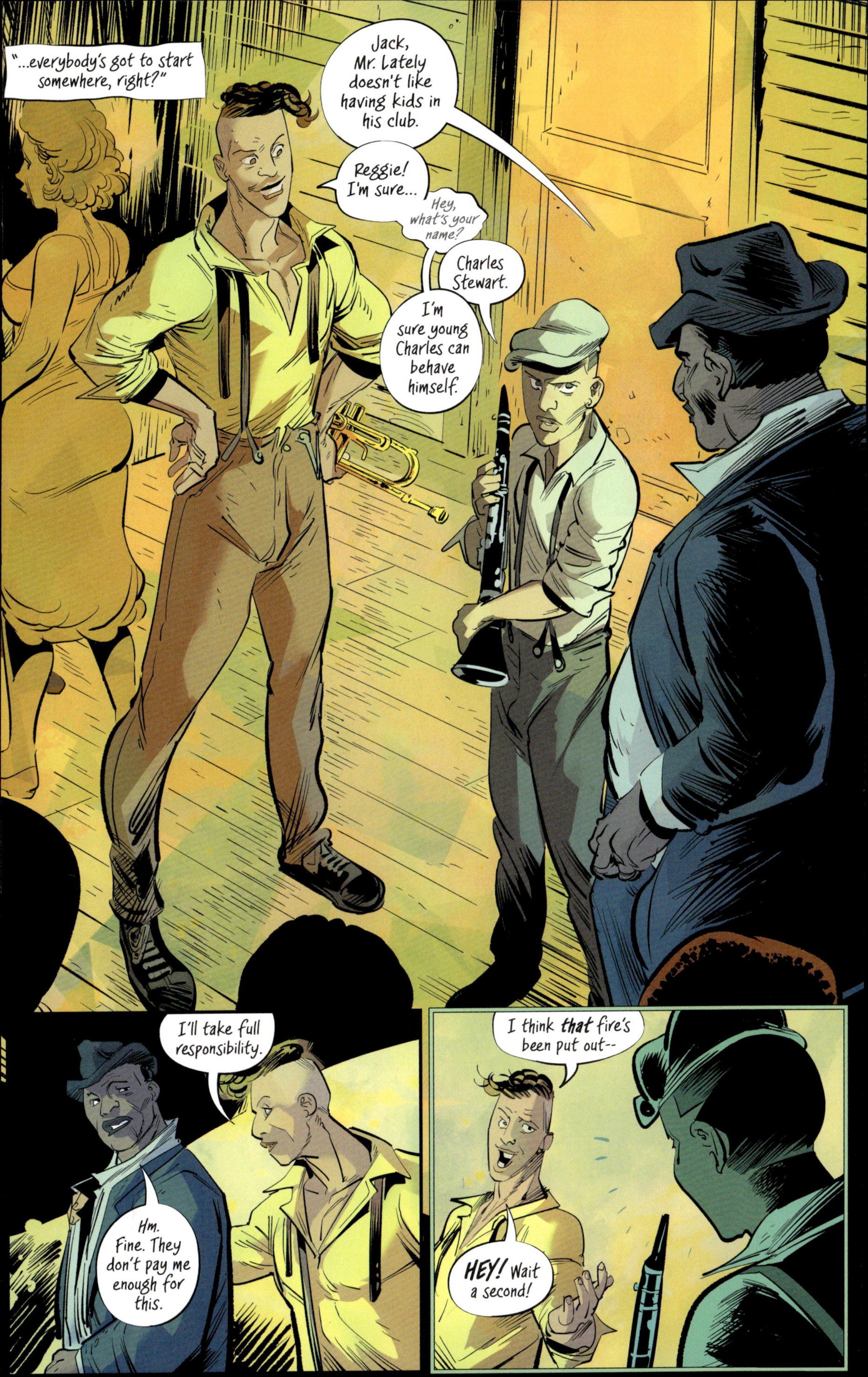

"...everybody's got to start somewhere, right?"
Jack, Mr. Lately doesn't like having kids in his club.
Reggie! I'm sure...
Hey, what's your name?
Charles Stewart.
I'm sure young Charles can behave himself.
I'll take full responsibility.
Hm. Fine. They don't pay me enough for this.
I think *that* fire's been put out--
HEY! Wait a second!

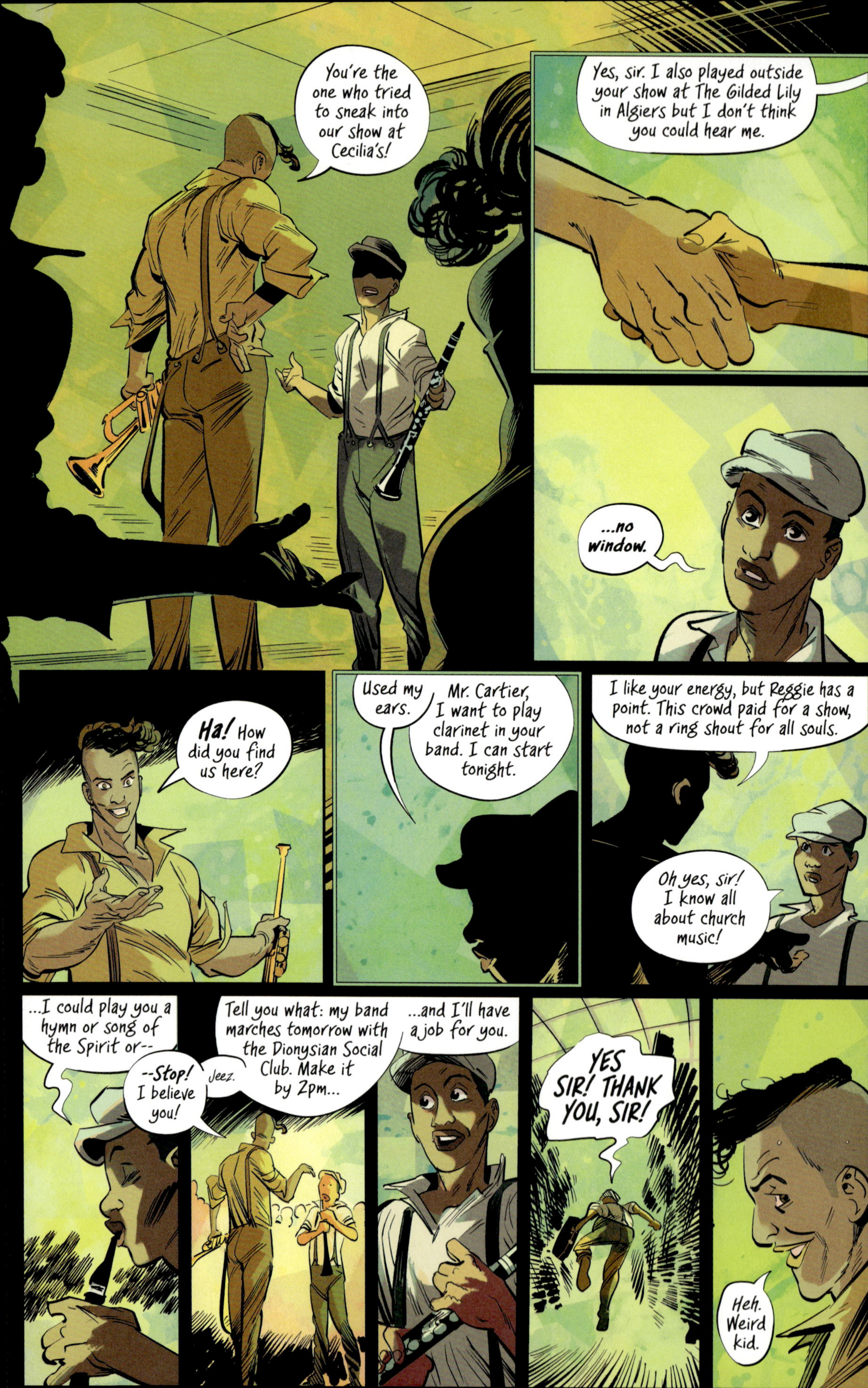
You're the one who tried to sneak into our show at Cecilia's!
Yes, sir. I also played outside your show at The Gilded Lily in Algiers but I don't think you could hear me.
...no window.
Ha! How did you find us here?
Used my ears.
Mr. Cartier, I want to play clarinet in your band. I can start tonight.
I like your energy, but Reggie has a point. This crowd paid for a show, not a ring shout for all souls.
Oh yes, sir! I know all about church music!
...I could play you a hymn or song of the Spirit or--
--Stop! I believe you!
Jeez.
Tell you what: my band marches tomorrow with the Dionysian Social Club. Make it by 2pm...
...and I'll have a job for you.
YES SIR! THANK YOU, SIR!
Heh. Weird kid.

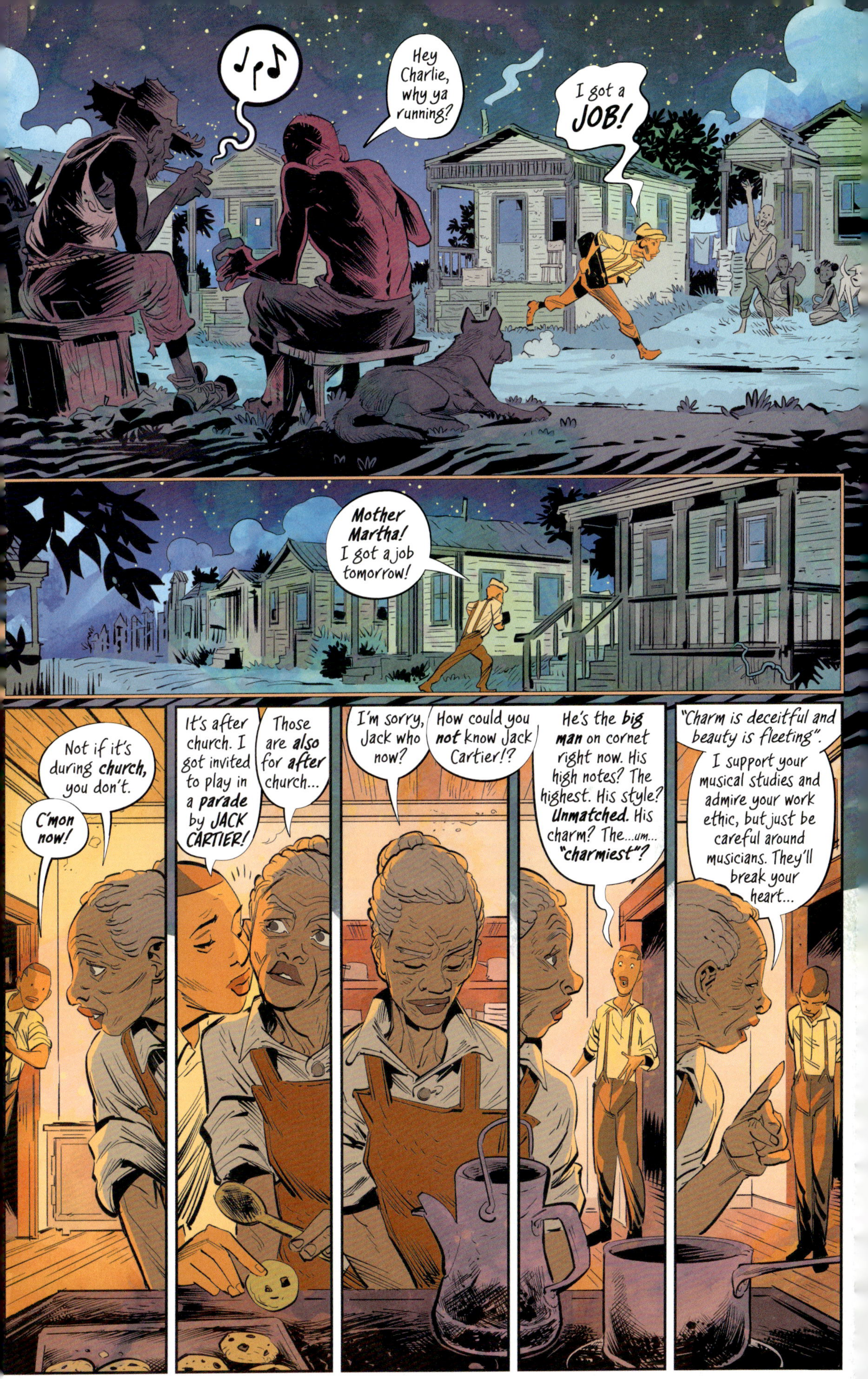

♪♪
Hey Charlie, why ya running?
I got a **JOB!**
Mother Martha! I got a job tomorrow!
Not if it's during **church,** you don't.
C'mon now!
It's after church. I got invited to play in a **parade** by **JACK CARTIER!**
Those are **also** for **after** church...
I'm sorry, Jack who now?
How could you **not** know Jack Cartier!?
He's the **big man** on cornet right now. His high notes? The highest. His style? **Unmatched.** His charm? The...um... **"charmiest"?**
"Charm is deceitful and beauty is fleeting".
I support your musical studies and admire your work ethic, but just be careful around musicians. They'll break your heart...

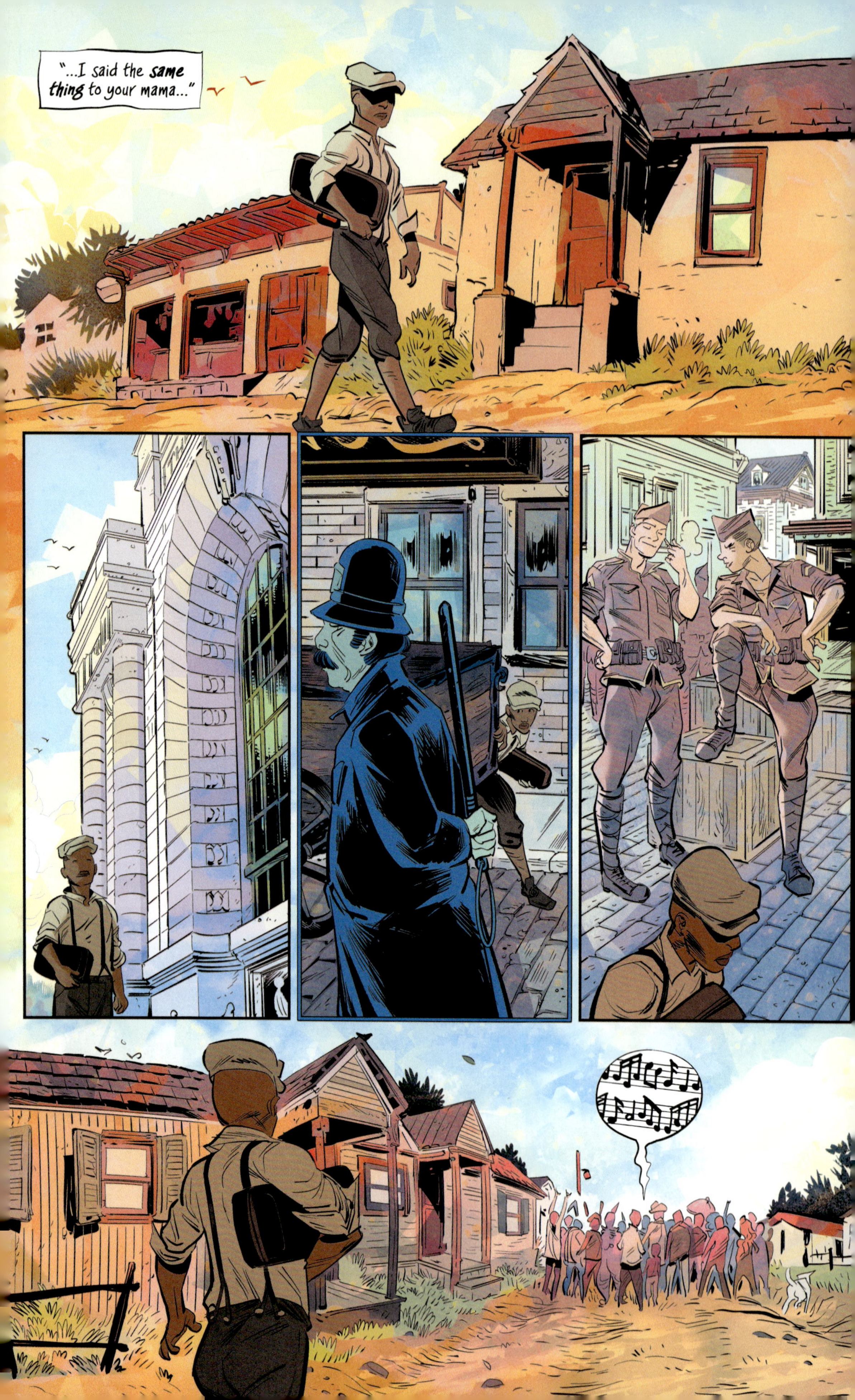
"...I said the **same thing** to your mama..."

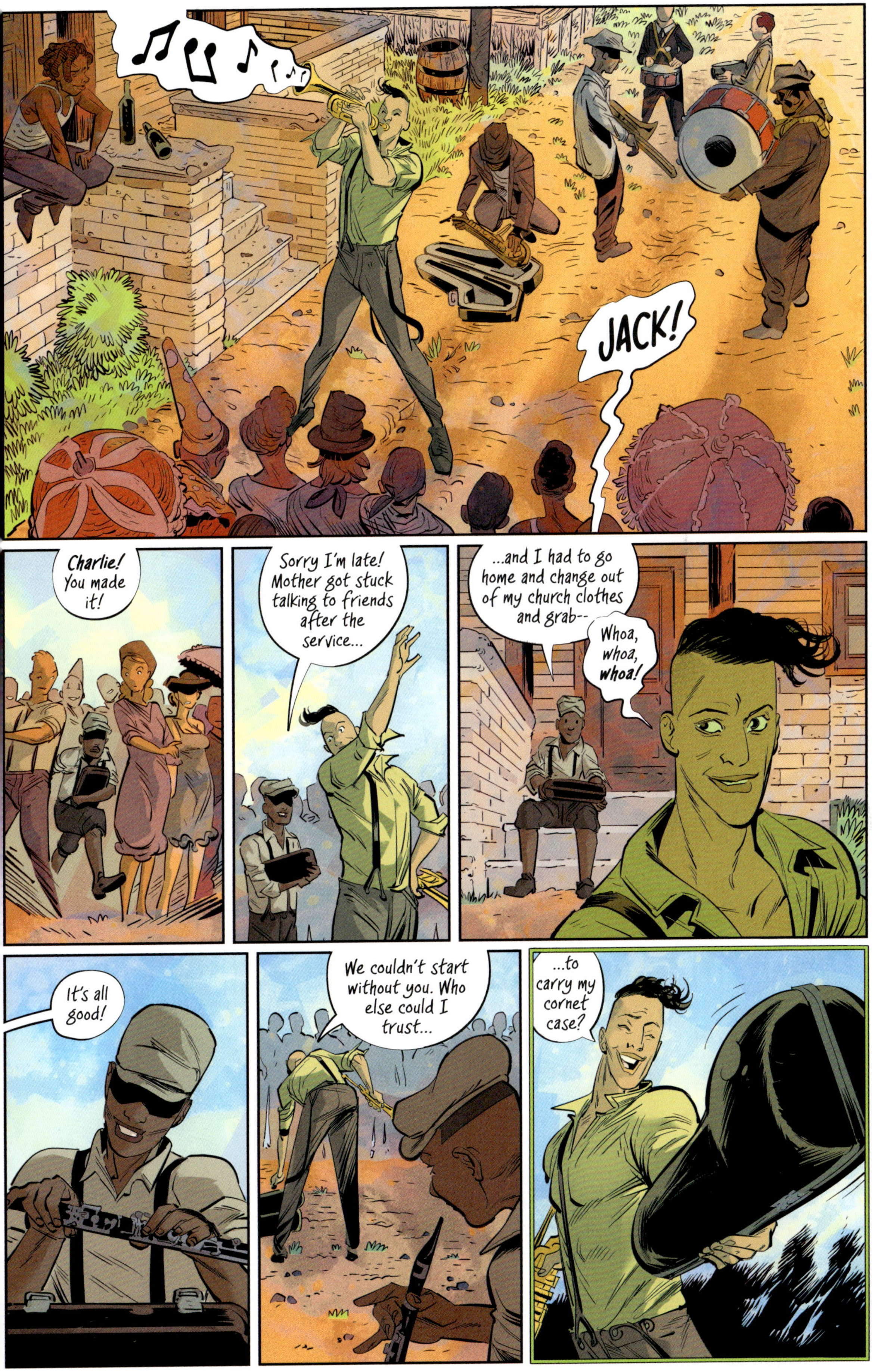
JACK!
Charlie! You made it!
Sorry I'm late! Mother got stuck talking to friends after the service...
...and I had to go home and change out of my church clothes and grab--
Whoa, whoa, whoa!
It's all good!
We couldn't start without you. Who else could I trust...
...to carry my cornet case?

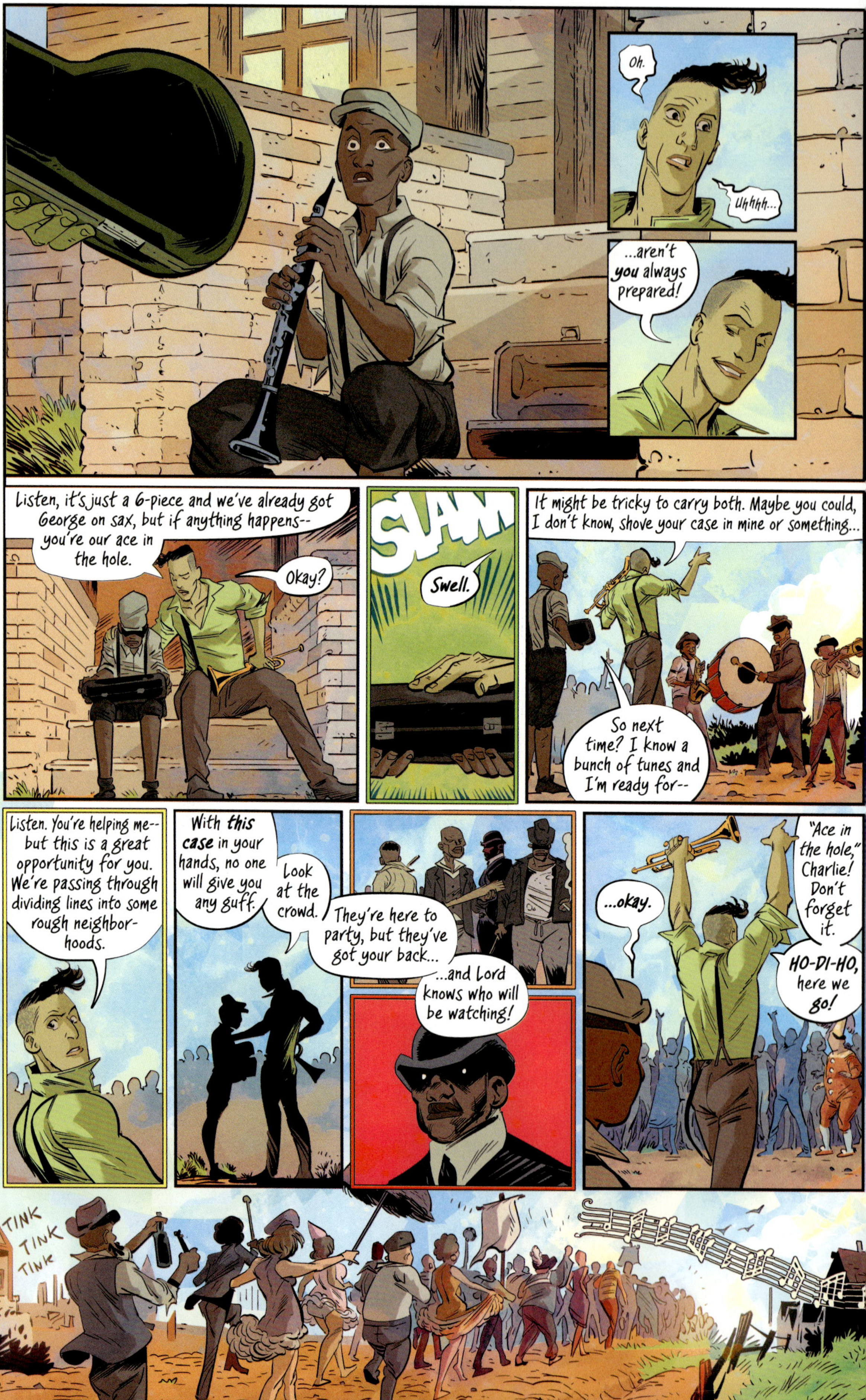
Oh.
Uhhhh...
...aren't *you* always prepared!
Listen, it's just a 6-piece and we've already got George on sax, but if anything happens--
you're our ace in the hole.
Okay?
SLAM
Swell.
It might be tricky to carry both. Maybe you could, I don't know, shove your case in mine or something...
So next time? I know a bunch of tunes and I'm ready for--
Listen. You're helping me--but this is a great opportunity for you. We're passing through dividing lines into some rough neighbor-hoods.
With *this case* in your hands, no one will give you any guff.
Look at the crowd.
They're here to party, but they've got your back...
...and Lord knows who will be watching!
...okay.
"Ace in the hole," Charlie! Don't forget it.
HO-DI-HO, here we go!
TINK TINK TINK

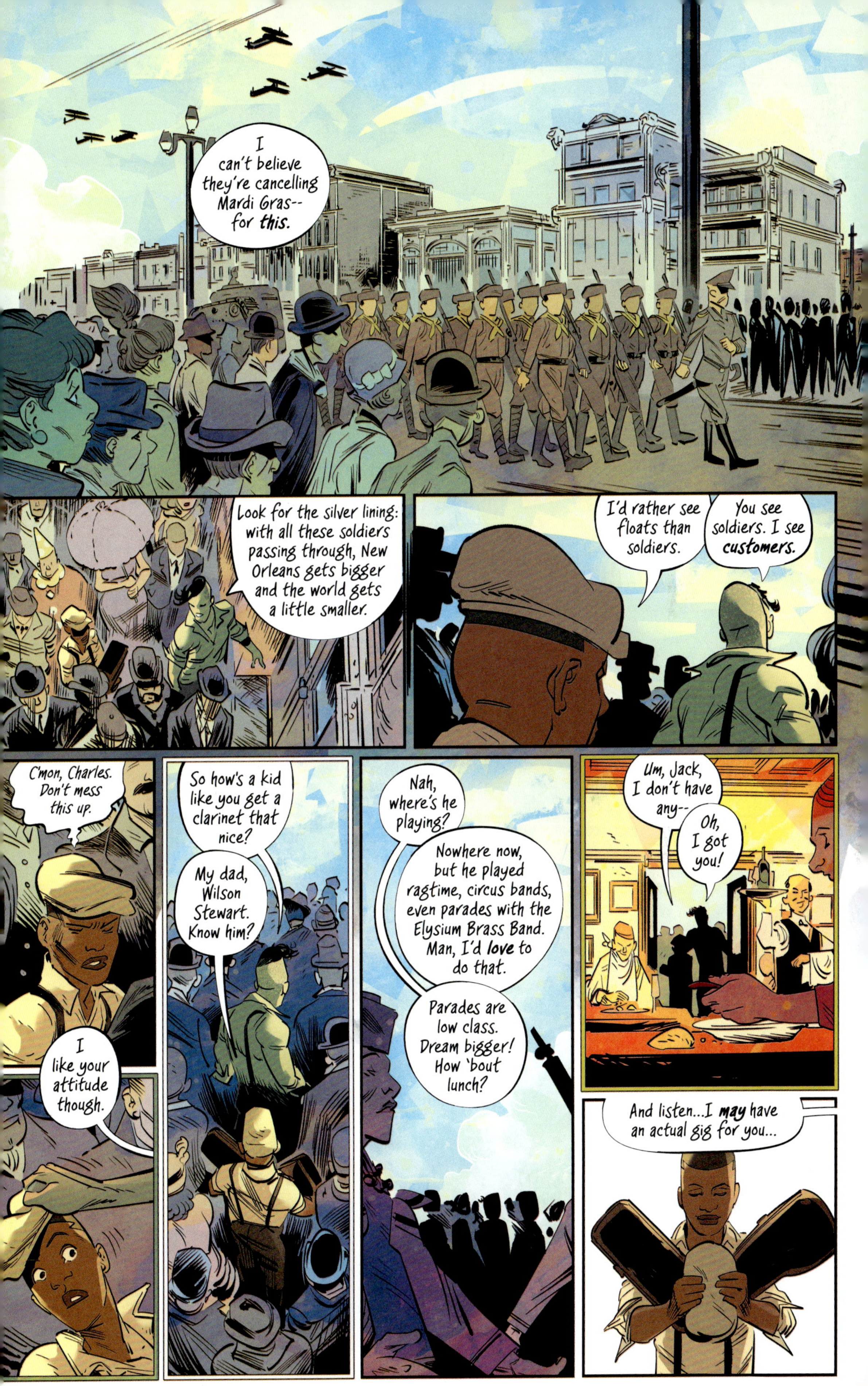
I can't believe they're cancelling Mardi Gras-- for *this.*
Look for the silver lining: with all these soldiers passing through, New Orleans gets bigger and the world gets a little smaller.
I'd rather see floats than soldiers.
You see soldiers. I see *customers.*
C'mon, Charles. Don't mess this up.
I like your attitude though.
So how's a kid like you get a clarinet that nice?
My dad, Wilson Stewart. Know him?
Nah, where's he playing?
Nowhere now, but he played ragtime, circus bands, even parades with the Elysium Brass Band. Man, I'd *love* to do that.
Parades are low class. Dream bigger! How 'bout lunch?
Um, Jack, I don't have any--
Oh, I got you!
And listen...I *may* have an actual gig for you...

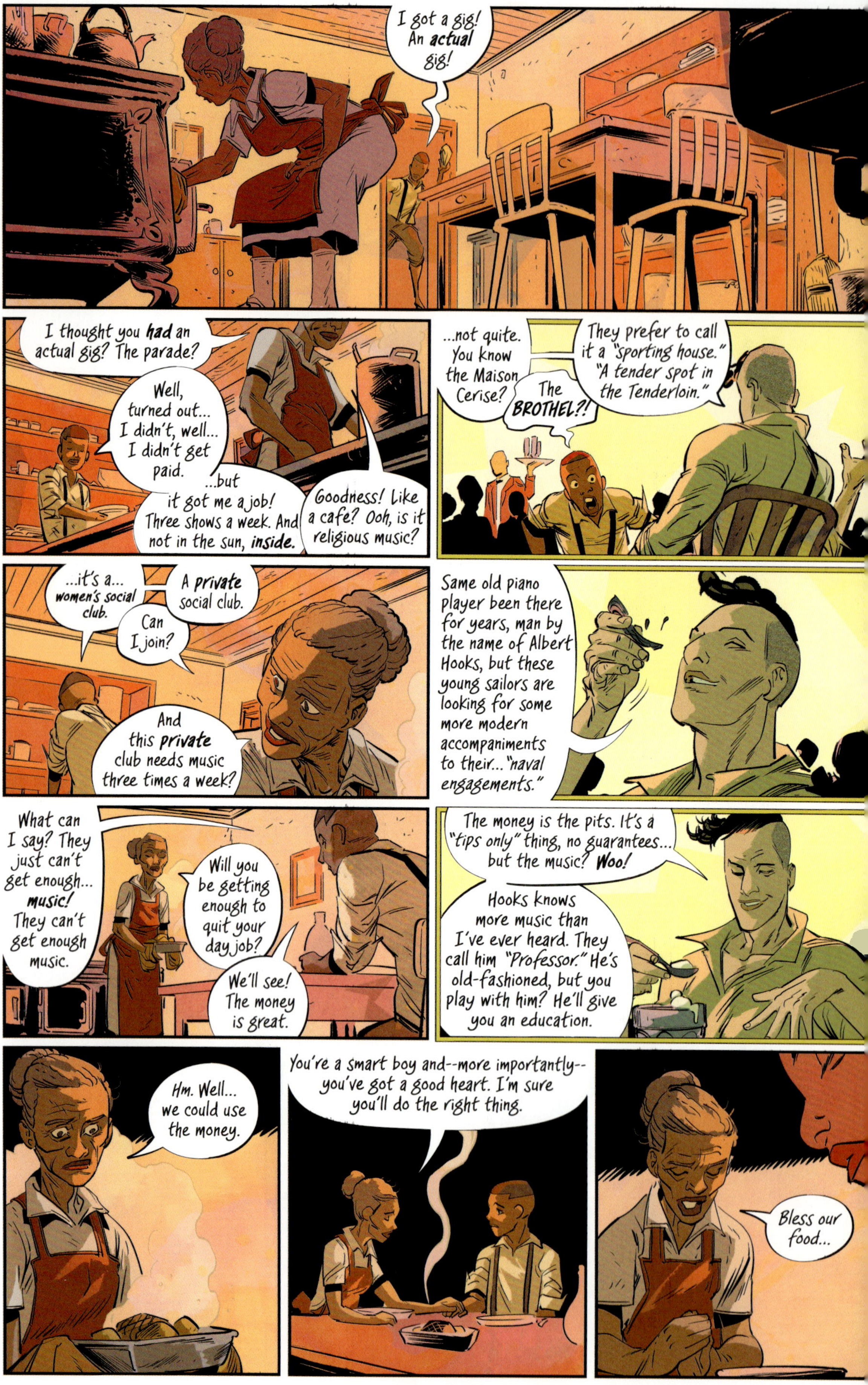
I got a gig! An **actual** gig!
I thought you **had** an actual gig? The parade?
Well, turned out... I didn't, well... I didn't get paid.
...but it got me a job! Three shows a week. And not in the sun, **inside.**
Goodness! Like a cafe? Ooh, is it religious music?
...not quite. You know the Maison Cerise?
The **BROTHEL?!**
They prefer to call it a "sporting house." "A tender spot in the Tenderloin."
...it's a... women's social club.
A **private** social club.
Can I join?
And this **private** club needs music three times a week?
Same old piano player been there for years, man by the name of Albert Hooks, but these young sailors are looking for some more modern accompaniments to their... "naval engagements."
What can I say? They just can't get enough... **music!** They can't get enough music.
Will you be getting enough to quit your day job?
We'll see! The money is great.
The money is the pits. It's a "tips only" thing, no guarantees... but the music? **Woo!**
Hooks knows more music than I've ever heard. They call him "Professor." He's old-fashioned, but you play with him? He'll give you an education.
Hm. Well... we could use the money.
You're a smart boy and--more importantly--you've got a good heart. I'm sure you'll do the right thing.
Bless our food...

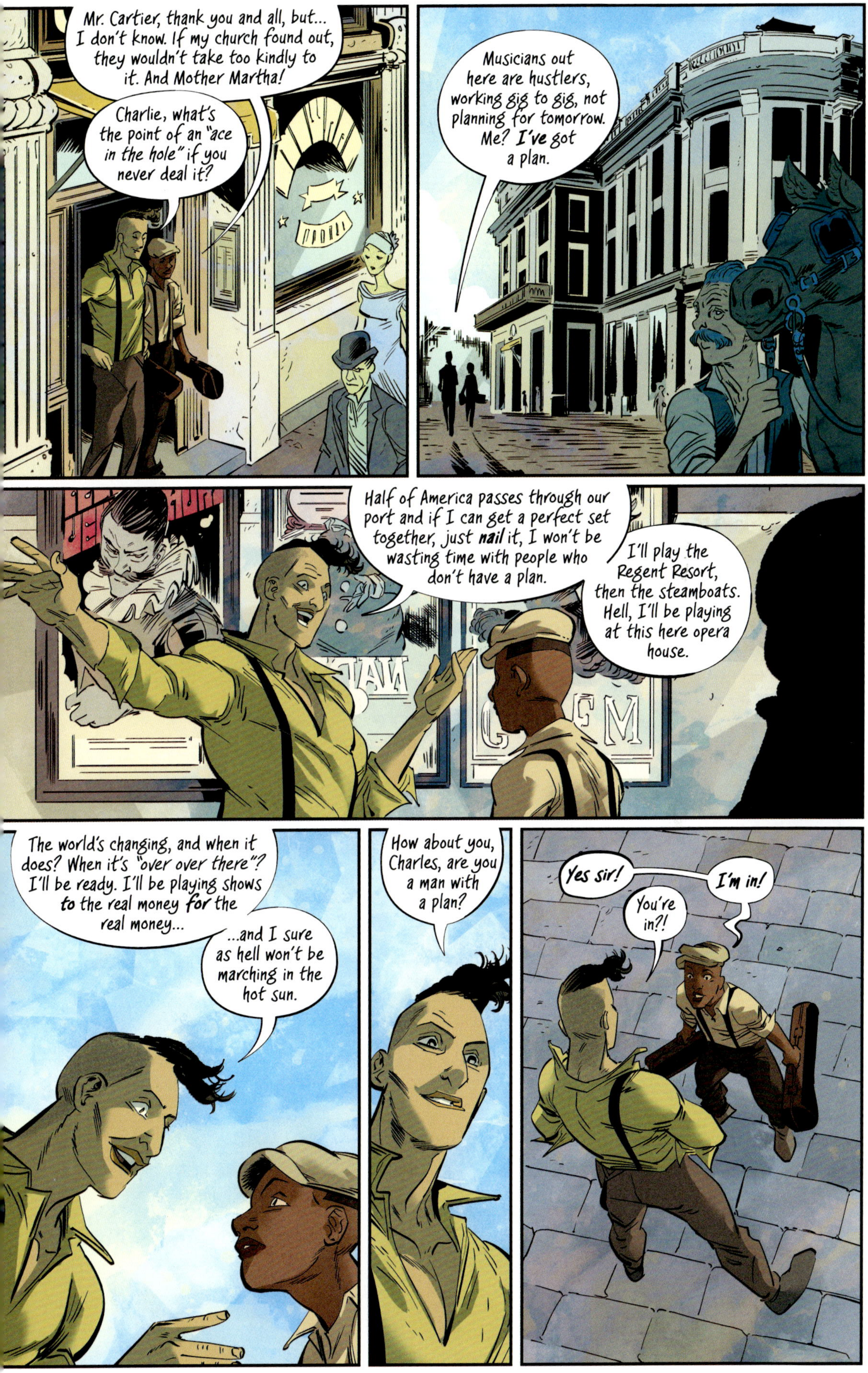
Mr. Cartier, thank you and all, but... I don't know. If my church found out, they wouldn't take too kindly to it. And Mother Martha!
Charlie, what's the point of an "ace in the hole" if you never deal it?
Musicians out here are hustlers, working gig to gig, not planning for tomorrow. Me? I've got a plan.
Half of America passes through our port and if I can get a perfect set together, just nail it, I won't be wasting time with people who don't have a plan.
I'll play the Regent Resort, then the steamboats. Hell, I'll be playing at this here opera house.
The world's changing, and when it does? When it's "over over there"? I'll be ready. I'll be playing shows to the real money for the real money...
...and I sure as hell won't be marching in the hot sun.
How about you, Charles, are you a man with a plan?
Yes sir!
I'm in!
You're in?!

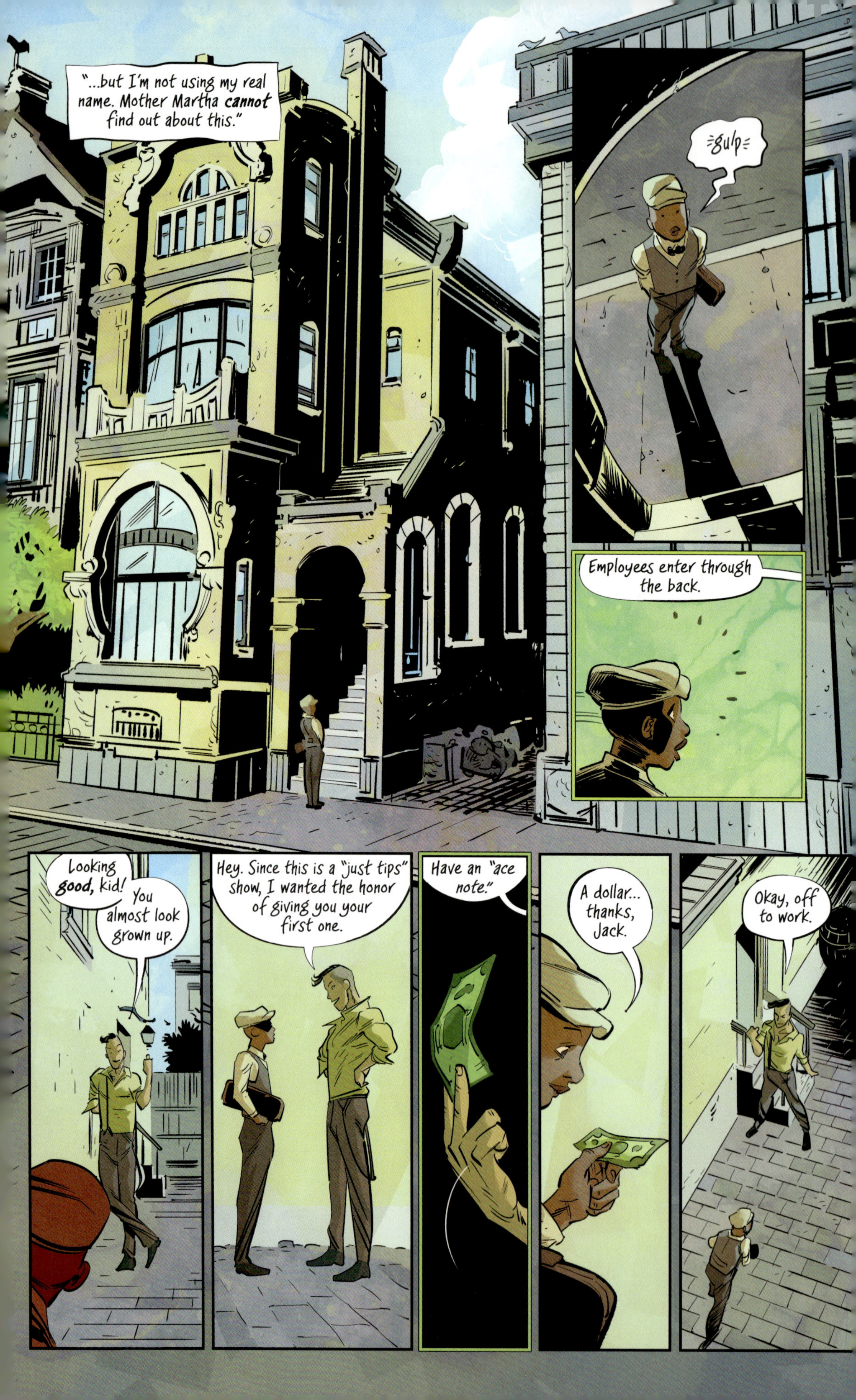
"...but I'm not using my real name. Mother Martha **cannot** find out about this."
gulp
Employees enter through the back.
Looking **good**, kid!
You almost look grown up.
Hey. Since this is a "just tips" show, I wanted the honor of giving you your first one.
Have an "ace note."
A dollar... thanks, Jack.
Okay, off to work.

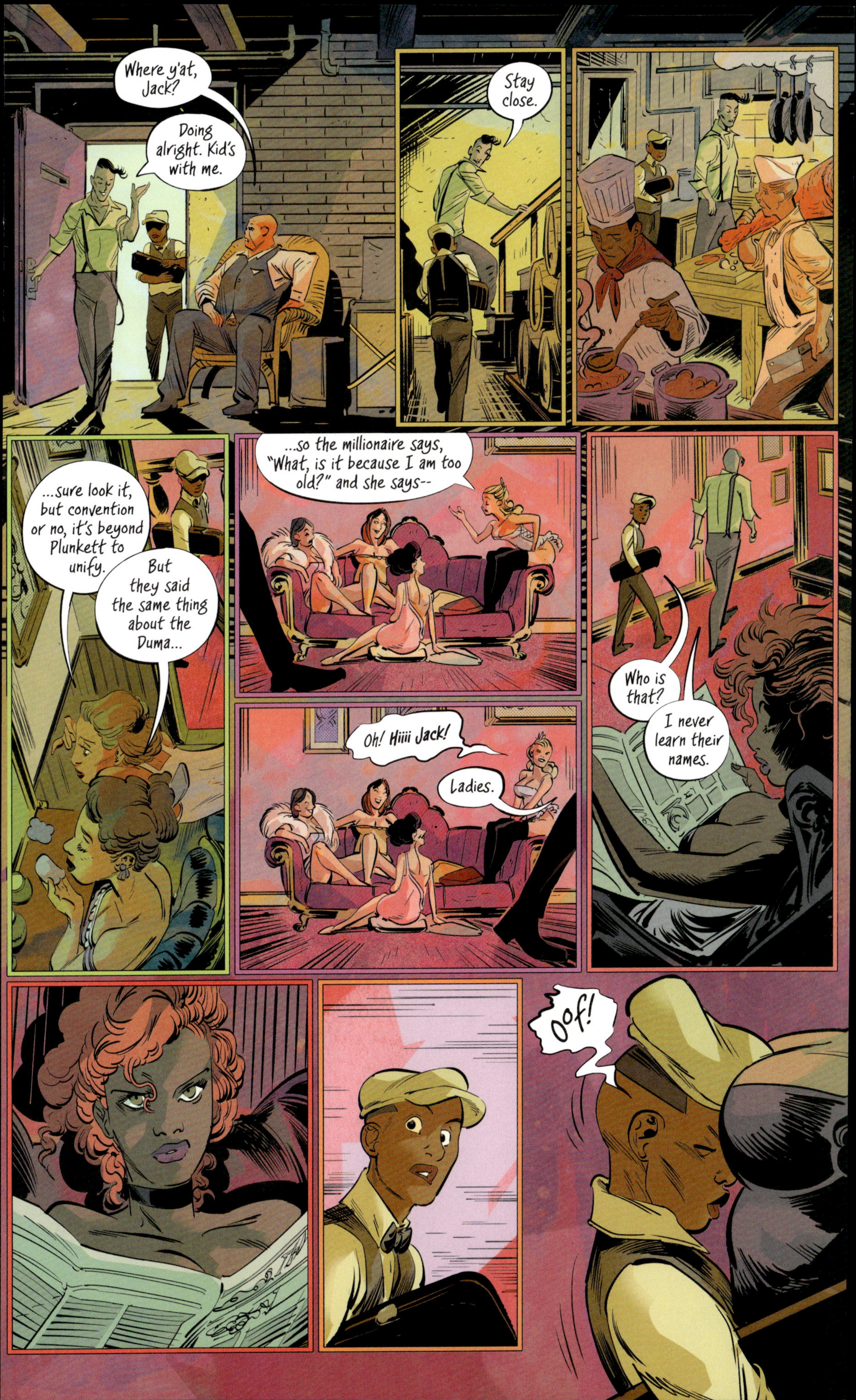
Where y'at, Jack?
Doing alright. Kid's with me.
Stay close.
...sure look it, but convention or no, it's beyond Plunkett to unify.
But they said the same thing about the Duma...
...so the millionaire says, "What, is it because I am too old?" and she says--
Oh! Hiiii Jack!
Ladies.
Who is that?
I never learn their names.
oof!

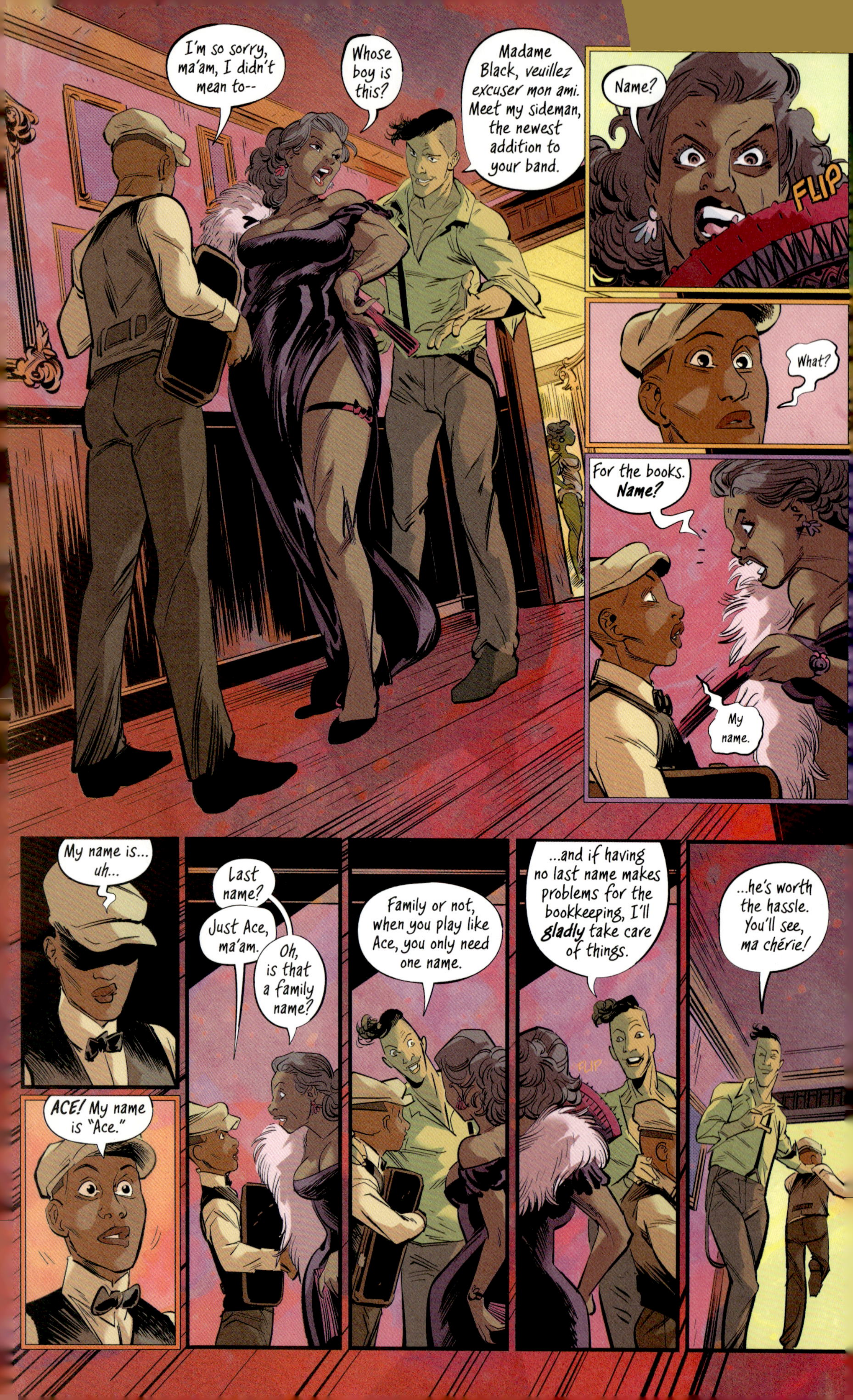

I'm so sorry, ma'am, I didn't mean to--
Whose boy is this?
Madame Black, veuillez excuser mon ami. Meet my sideman, the newest addition to your band.
Name?
FLIP
What?
For the books. **Name?**
My name.
My name is... uh...
ACE! My name is "Ace."
Last name?
Just Ace, ma'am.
Oh, is that a family name?
Family or not, when you play like Ace, you only need one name.
...and if having no last name makes problems for the bookkeeping, I'll *gladly* take care of things.
FLIP
...he's worth the hassle. You'll see, ma chérie!

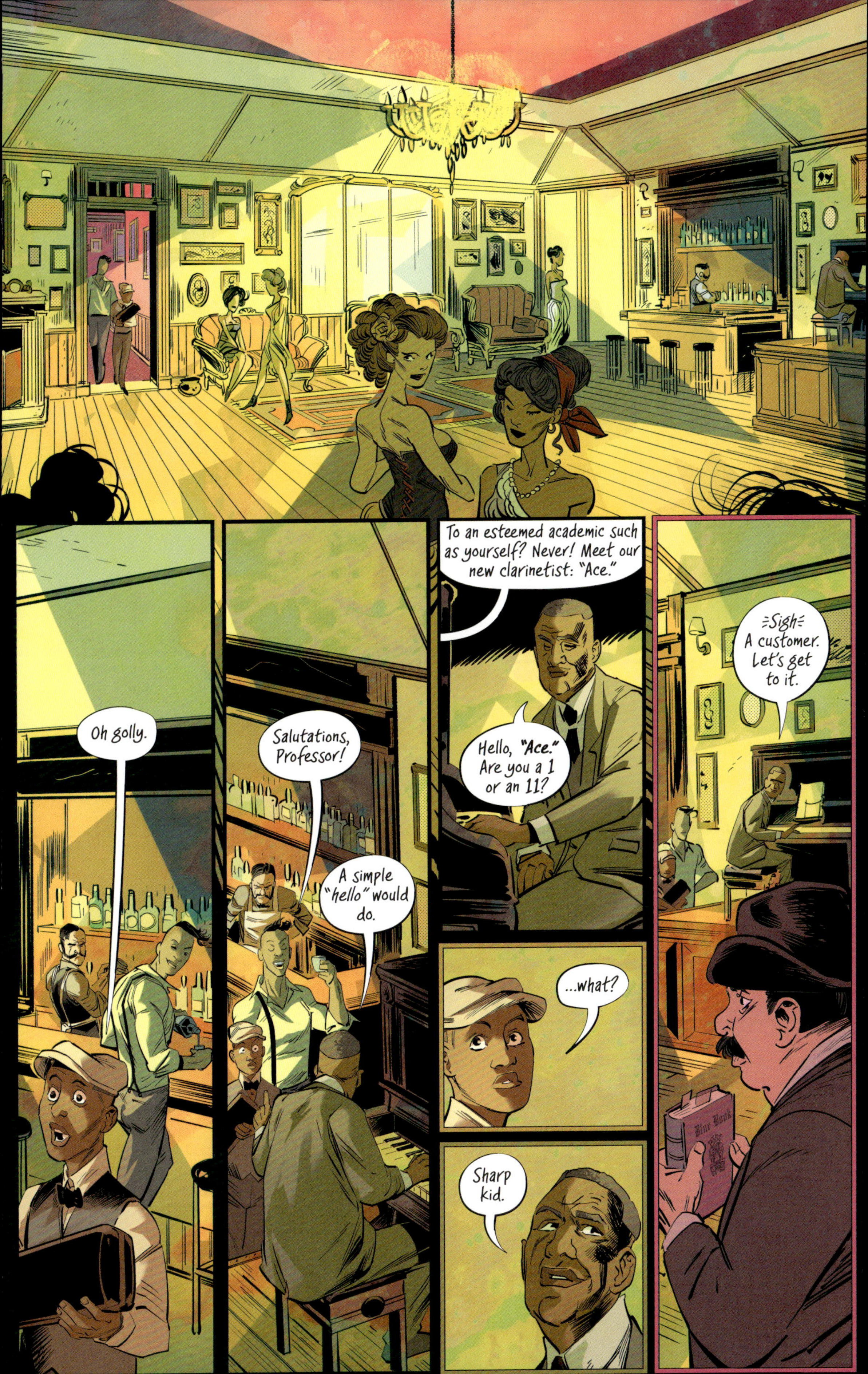
Oh golly.
Salutations, Professor!
A simple "hello" would do.
To an esteemed academic such as yourself? Never! Meet our new clarinetist: "Ace."
Hello, **"Ace."** Are you a 1 or an 11?
...what?
Sharp kid.
=Sigh= A customer. Let's get to it.
Blue Book

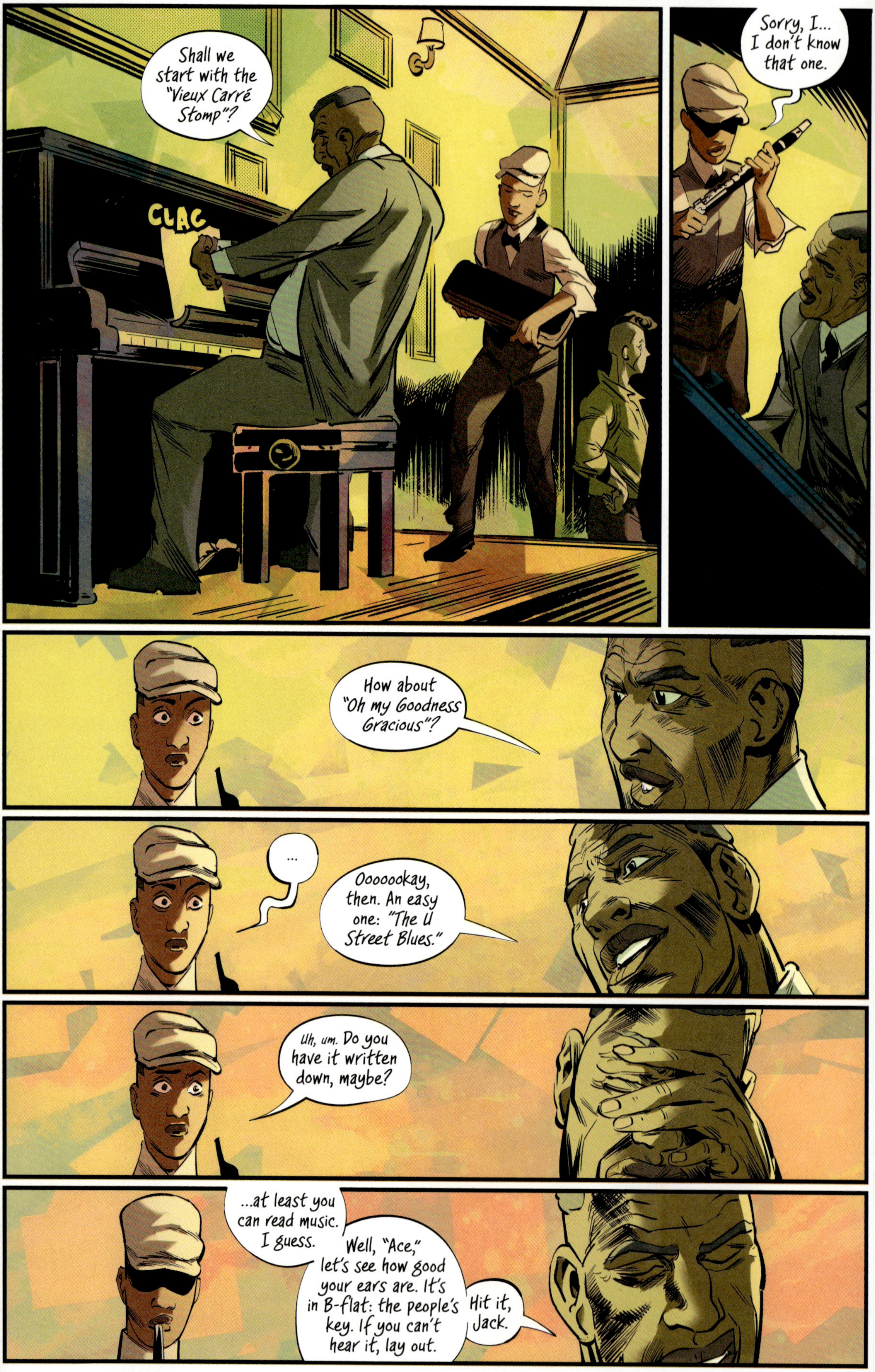
Shall we start with the "Vieux Carré Stomp"?
CLAC
Sorry, I... I don't know that one.
How about "Oh my Goodness Gracious"?
...
Ooooookay, then. An easy one: "The U Street Blues."
Uh, um. Do you have it written down, maybe?
...at least you can read music. I guess.
Well, "Ace," let's see how good your ears are. It's in B-flat: the people's key. If you can't hear it, lay out.
Hit it, Jack.

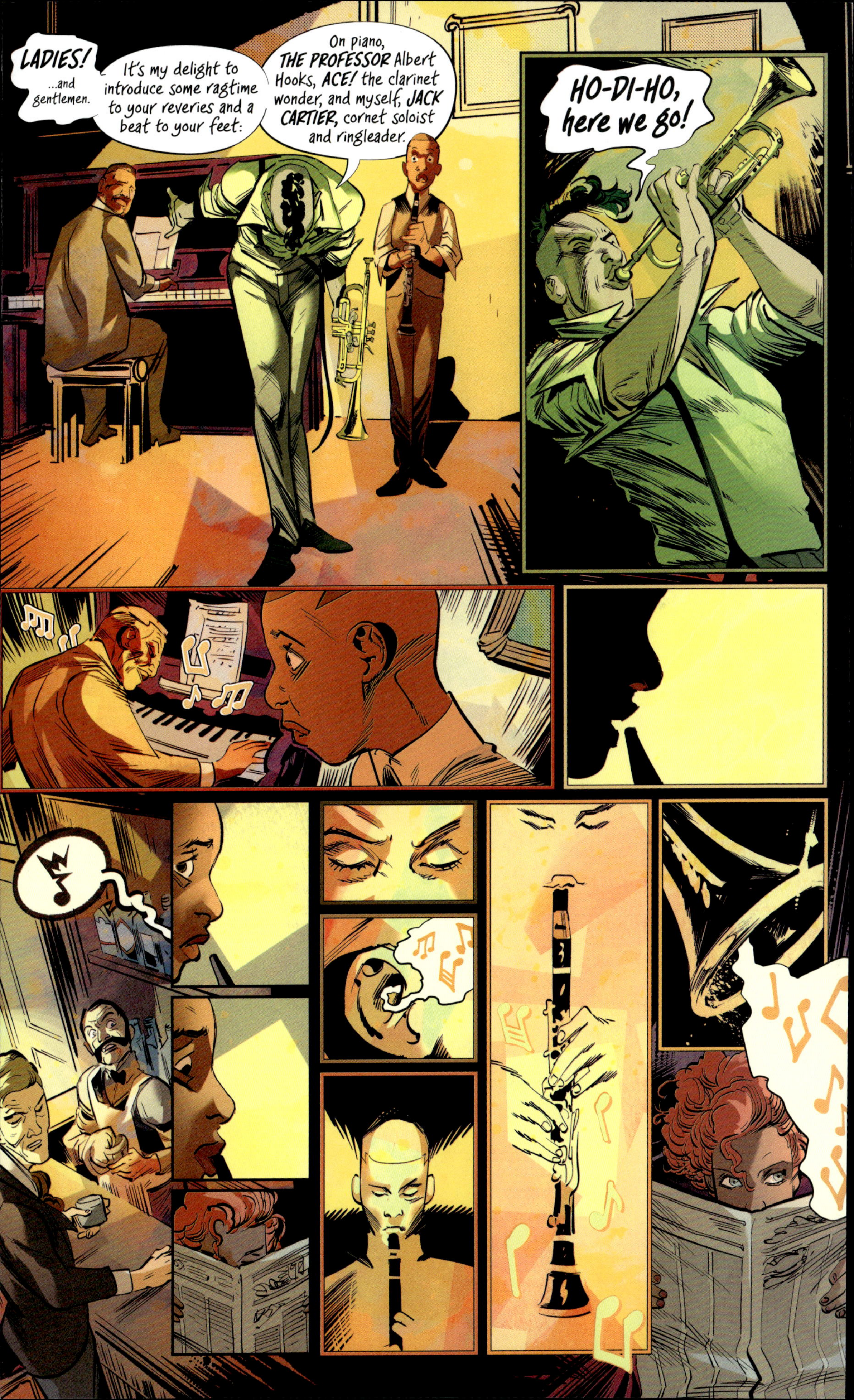
LADIES!
...and gentlemen.
It's my delight to introduce some ragtime to your reveries and a beat to your feet:
On piano, THE PROFESSOR Albert Hooks, ACE! the clarinet wonder, and myself, JACK CARTIER, cornet soloist and ringleader.
HO-DI-HO, here we go!

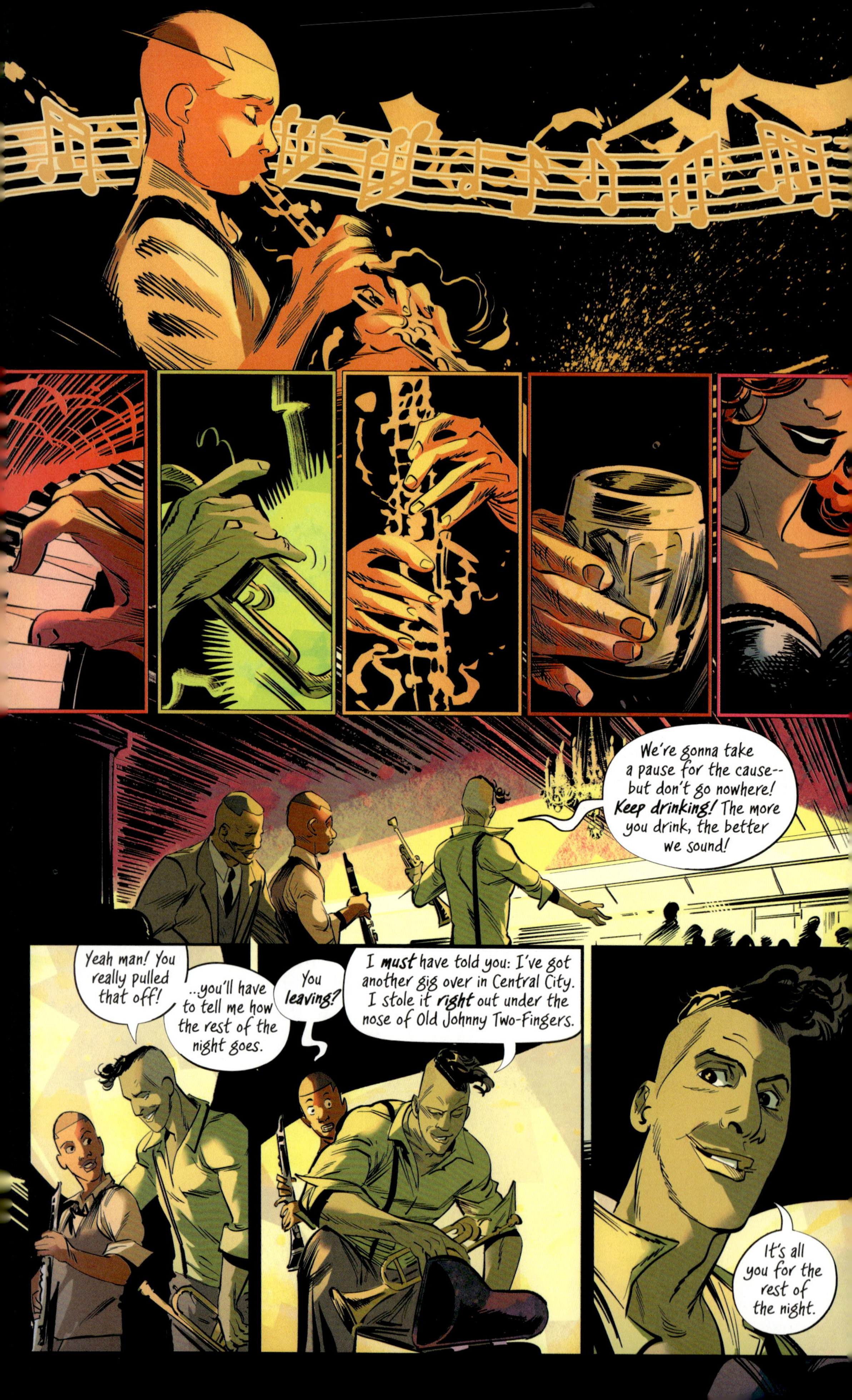
We're gonna take a pause for the cause--but don't go nowhere! **Keep drinking!** The more you drink, the better we sound!
Yeah man! You really pulled that off!
...you'll have to tell me how the rest of the night goes.
You **leaving?**
I **must** have told you: I've got another gig over in Central City. I stole it **right** out under the nose of Old Johnny Two-Fingers.
It's all you for the rest of the night.

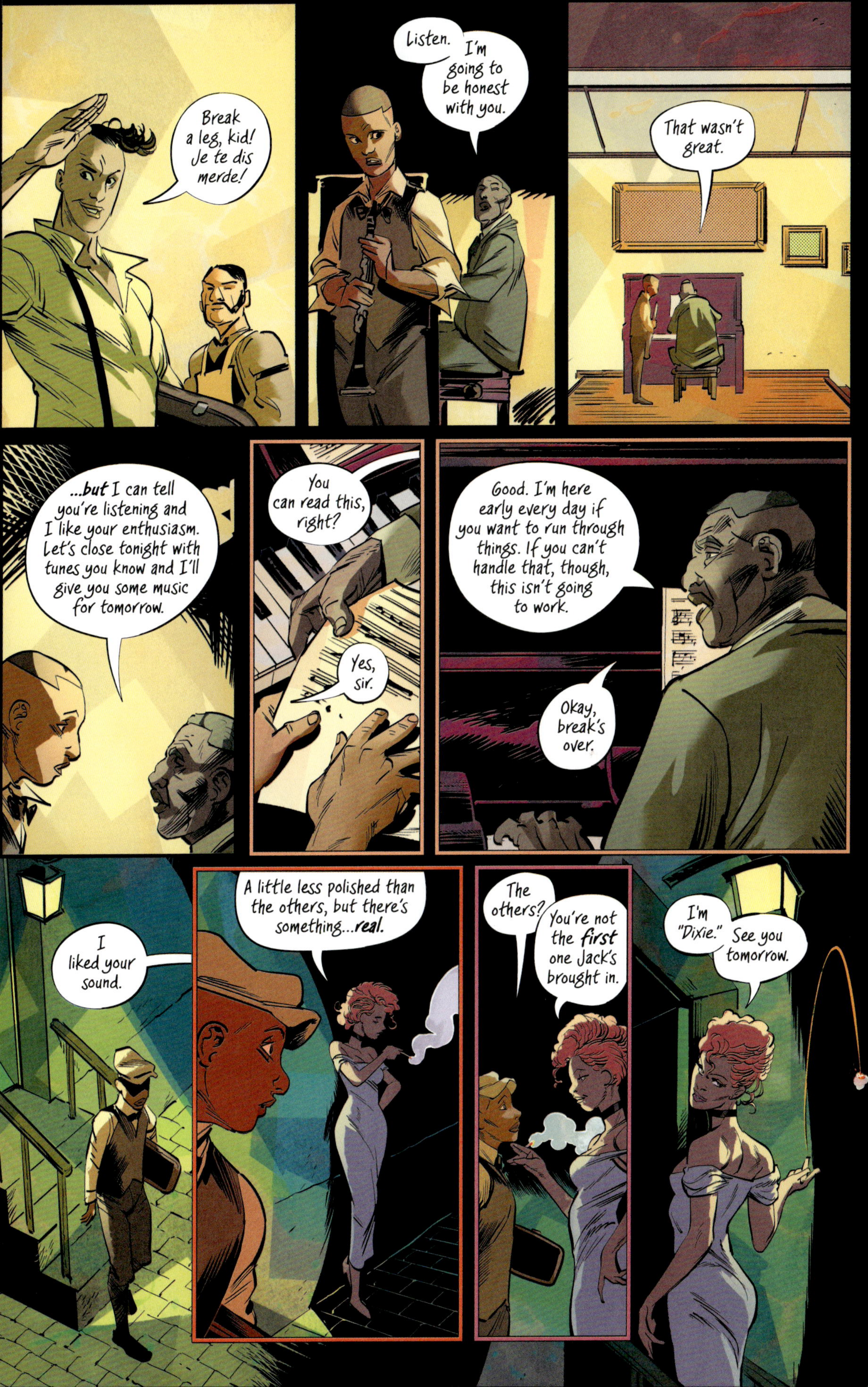
Break a leg, kid! Je te dis merde!
Listen.
I'm going to be honest with you.
That wasn't great.
...but I can tell you're listening and I like your enthusiasm. Let's close tonight with tunes you know and I'll give you some music for tomorrow.
You can read this, right?
Yes, sir.
Good. I'm here early every day if you want to run through things. If you can't handle that, though, this isn't going to work.
Okay, break's over.
I liked your sound.
A little less polished than the others, but there's something...real.
The others?
You're not the first one Jack's brought in.
I'm "Dixie."
See you tomorrow.

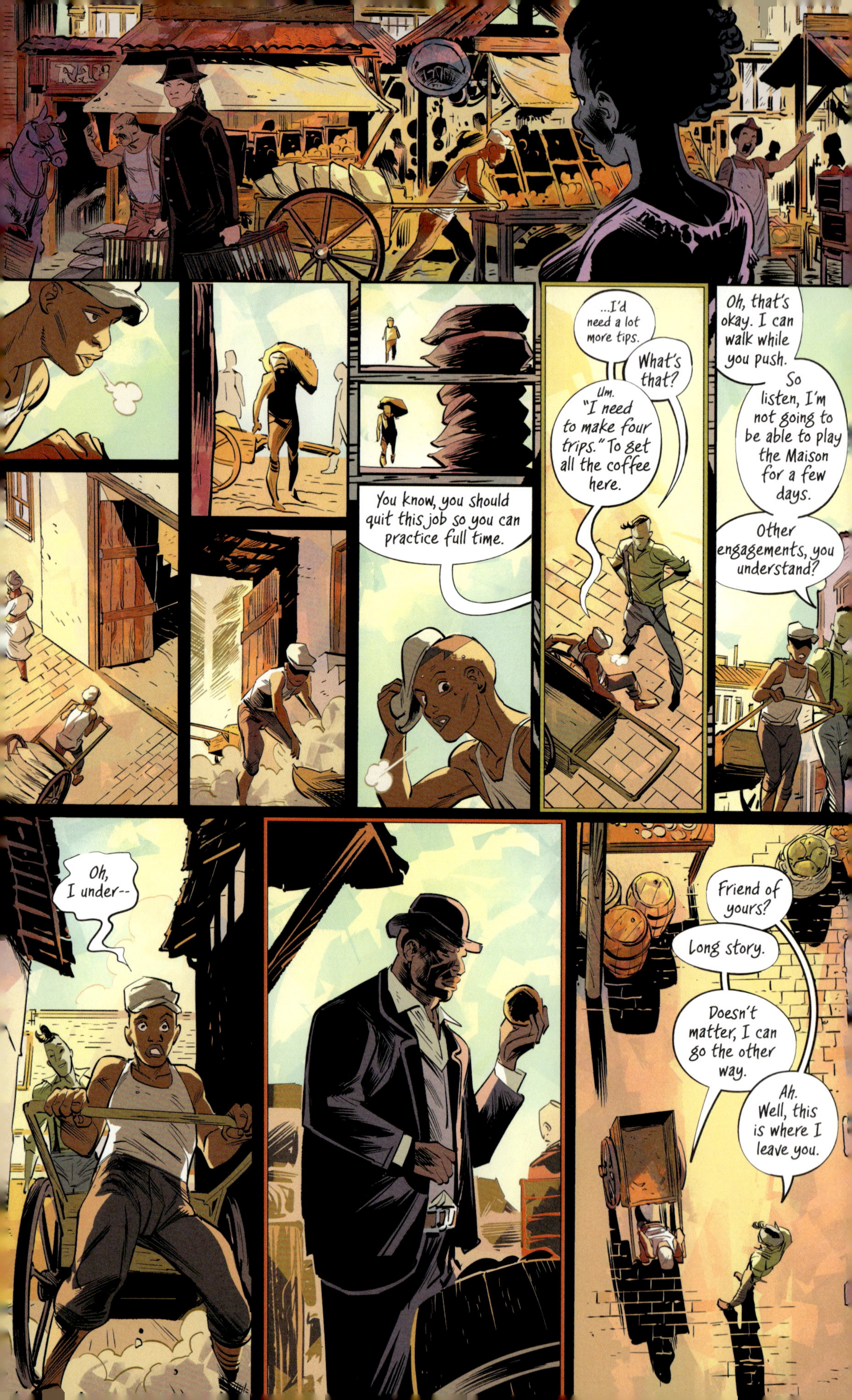
...I'd need a lot more tips.
What's that?
Um. "I need to make four trips." To get all the coffee here.
You know, you should quit this job so you can practice full time.
Oh, that's okay. I can walk while you push.
So listen, I'm not going to be able to play the Maison for a few days.
Other engagements, you understand?
Oh, I under--
Friend of yours?
Long story.
Doesn't matter, I can go the other way.
Ah. Well, this is where I leave you.

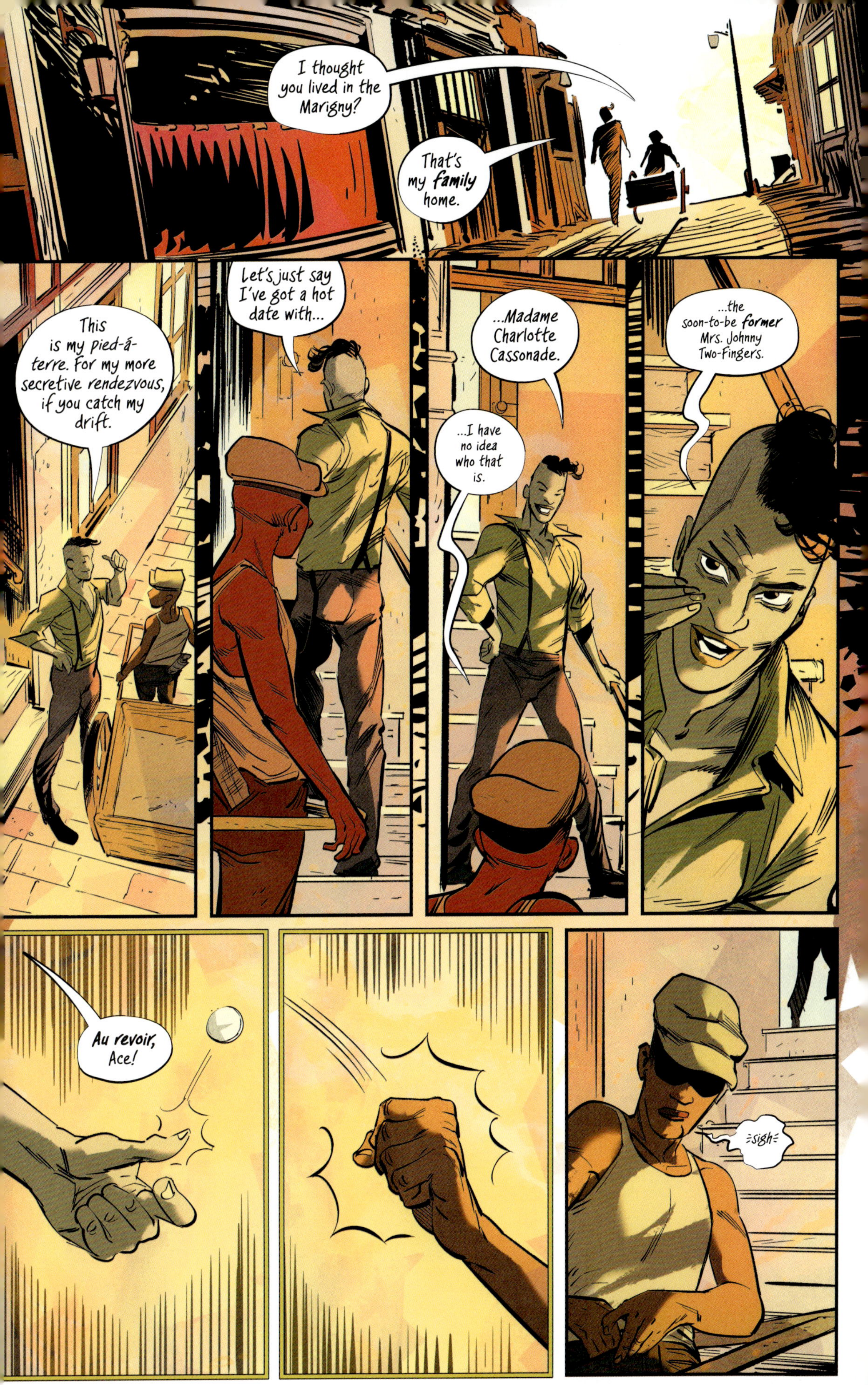
I thought you lived in the Marigny?
That's my *family* home.
This is my pied-à-terre. For my more secretive rendezvous, if you catch my drift.
Let's just say I've got a hot date with...
...Madame Charlotte Cassonade.
...I have no idea who that is.
...the soon-to-be *former* Mrs. Johnny Two-Fingers.
Au revoir, Ace!
sigh

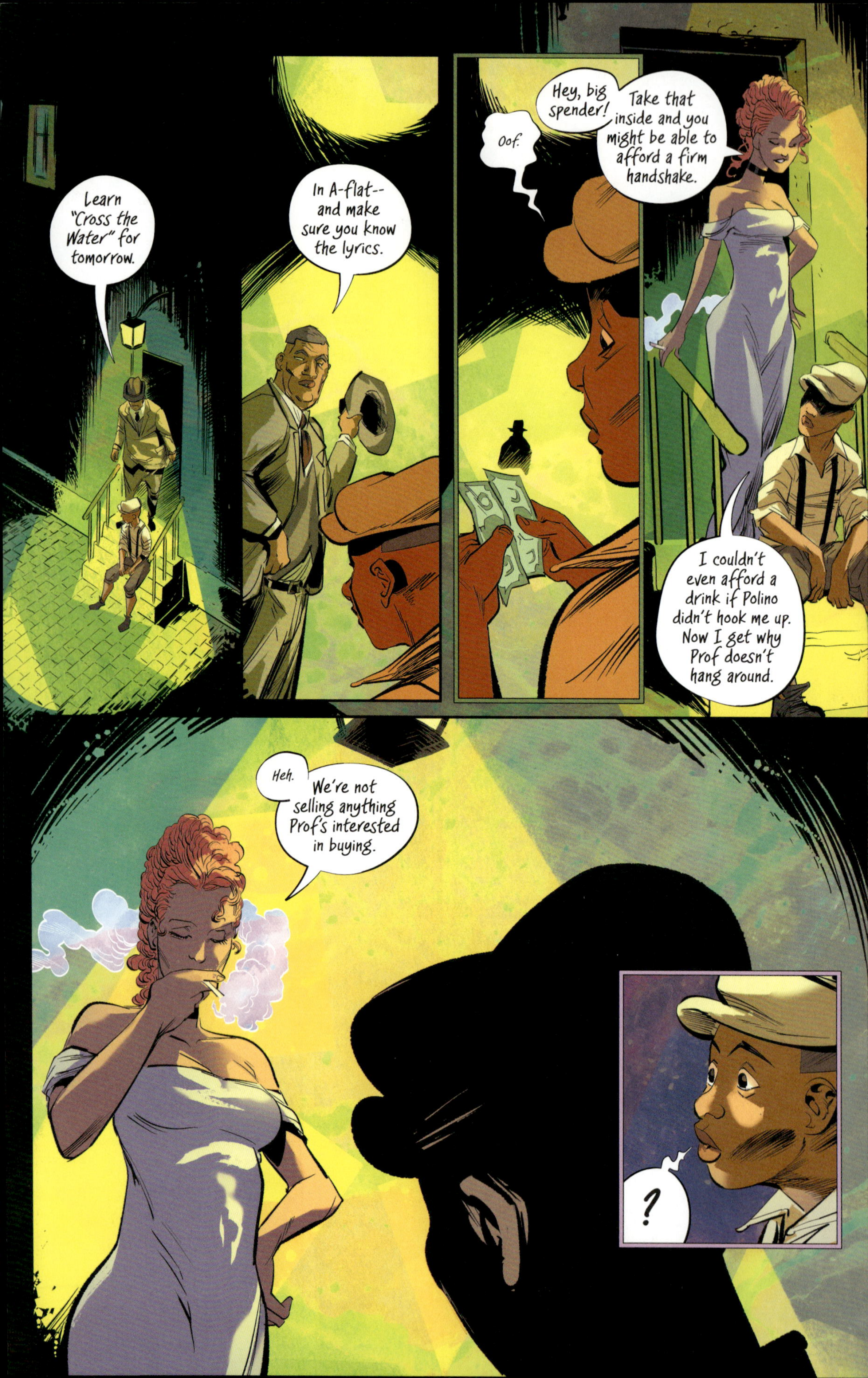
Learn "Cross the Water" for tomorrow.
In A-flat-- and make sure you know the lyrics.
Oof.
Hey, big spender!
Take that inside and you might be able to afford a firm handshake.
I couldn't even afford a drink if Polino didn't hook me up. Now I get why Prof doesn't hang around.
Heh.
We're not selling anything Prof's interested in buying.
?

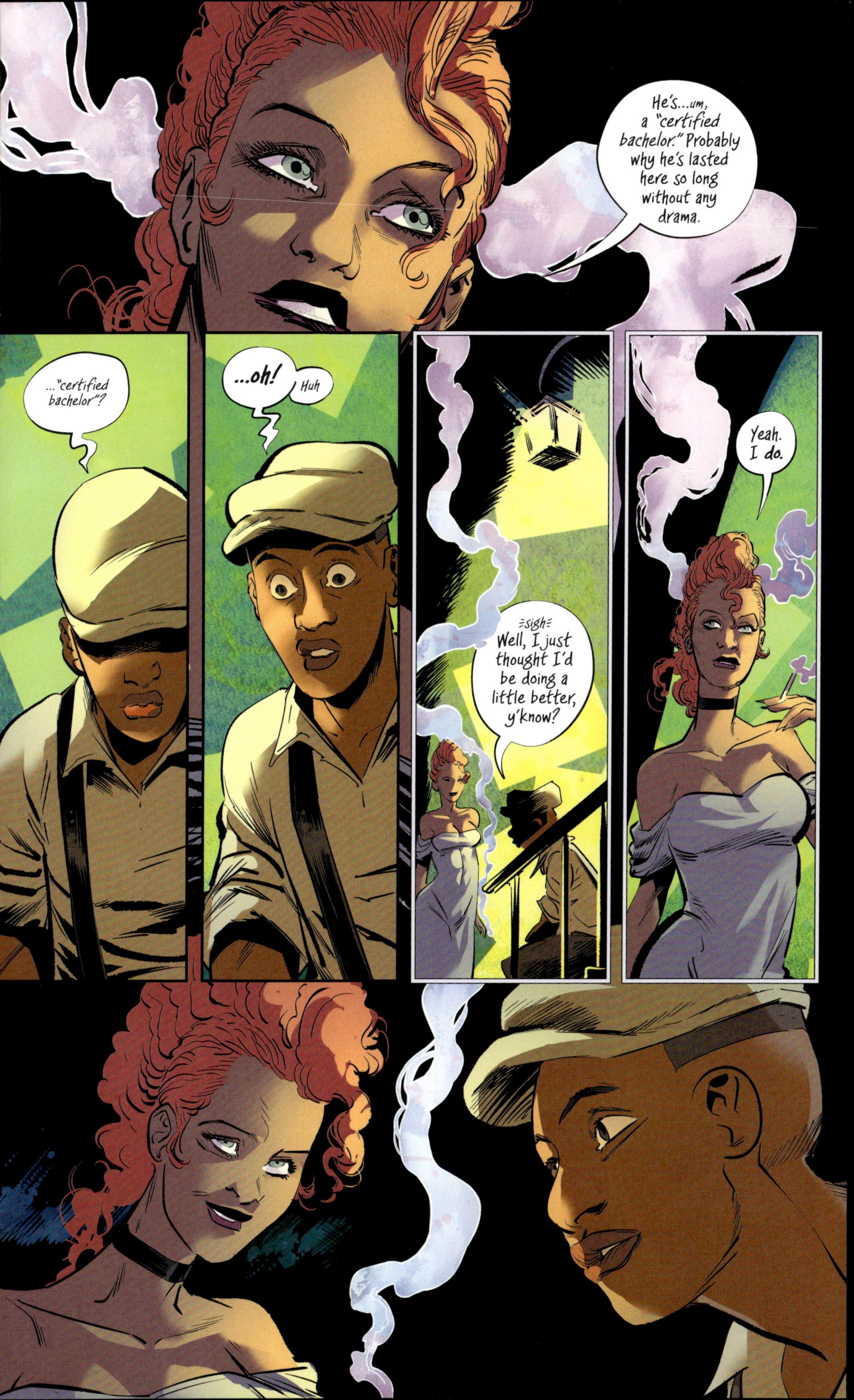
He's...um, a "certified bachelor." Probably why he's lasted here so long without any drama.
..."certified bachelor"?
...oh!
Huh
≈sigh≈
Well, I just thought I'd be doing a little better, y'know?
Yeah. I do.

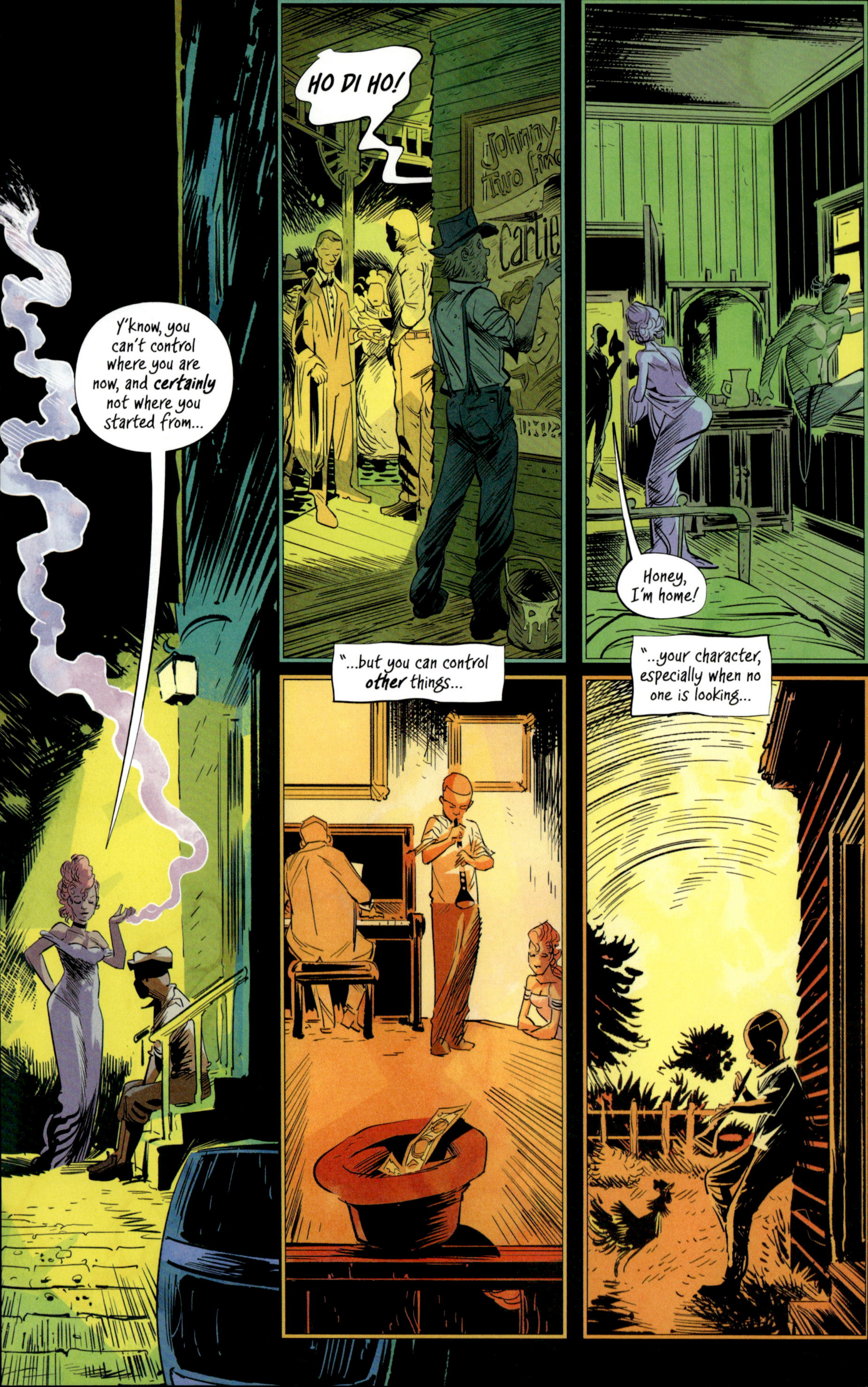
Y'know, you can't control where you are now, and **certainly** not where you started from...
HO DI HO!
Honey, I'm home!
"...but you can control **other** things...
"...your character, especially when no one is looking...

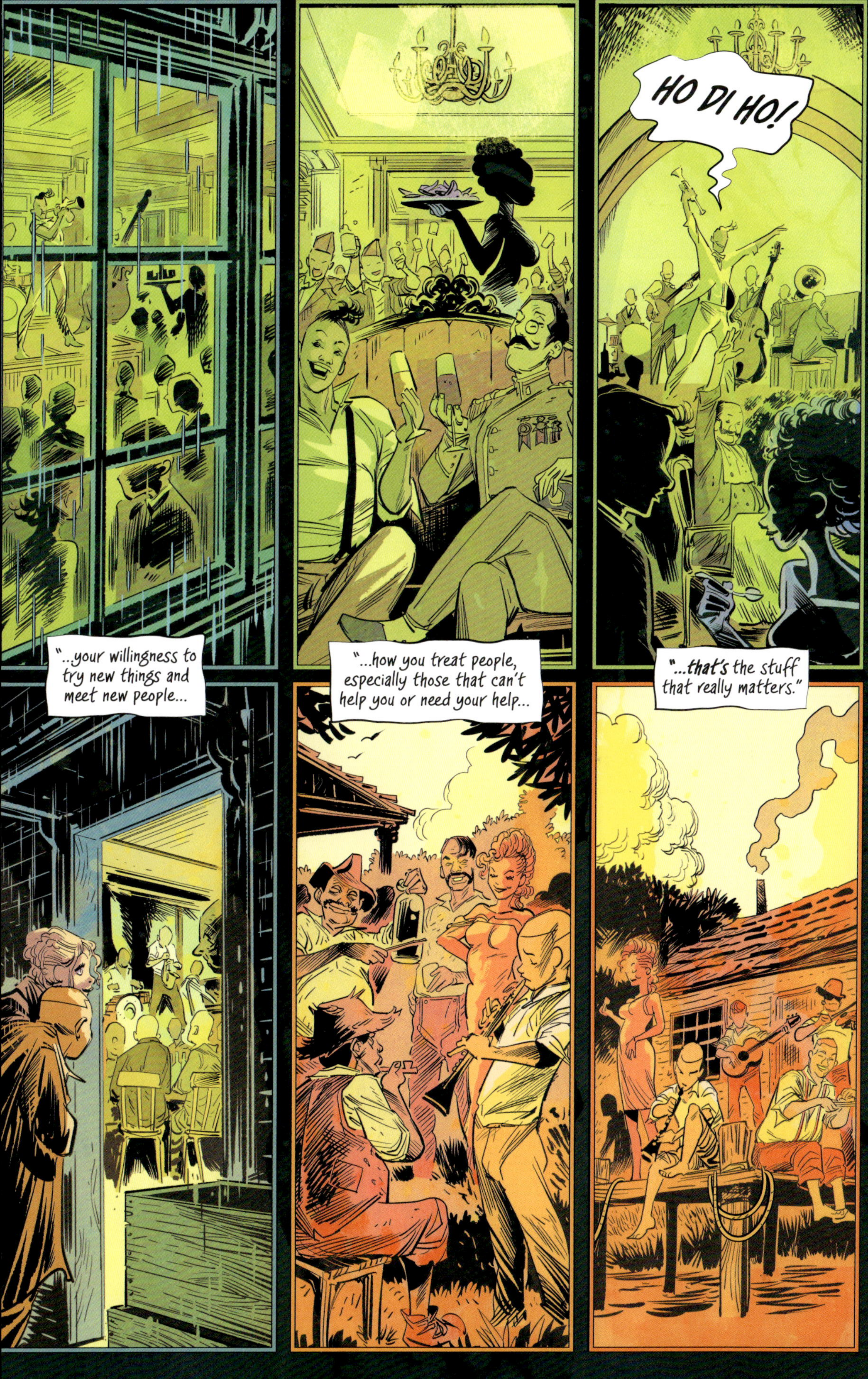
HO DI HO!
"...your willingness to try new things and meet new people...
"...how you treat people, especially those that can't help you or need your help...
"...that's the stuff that really matters."

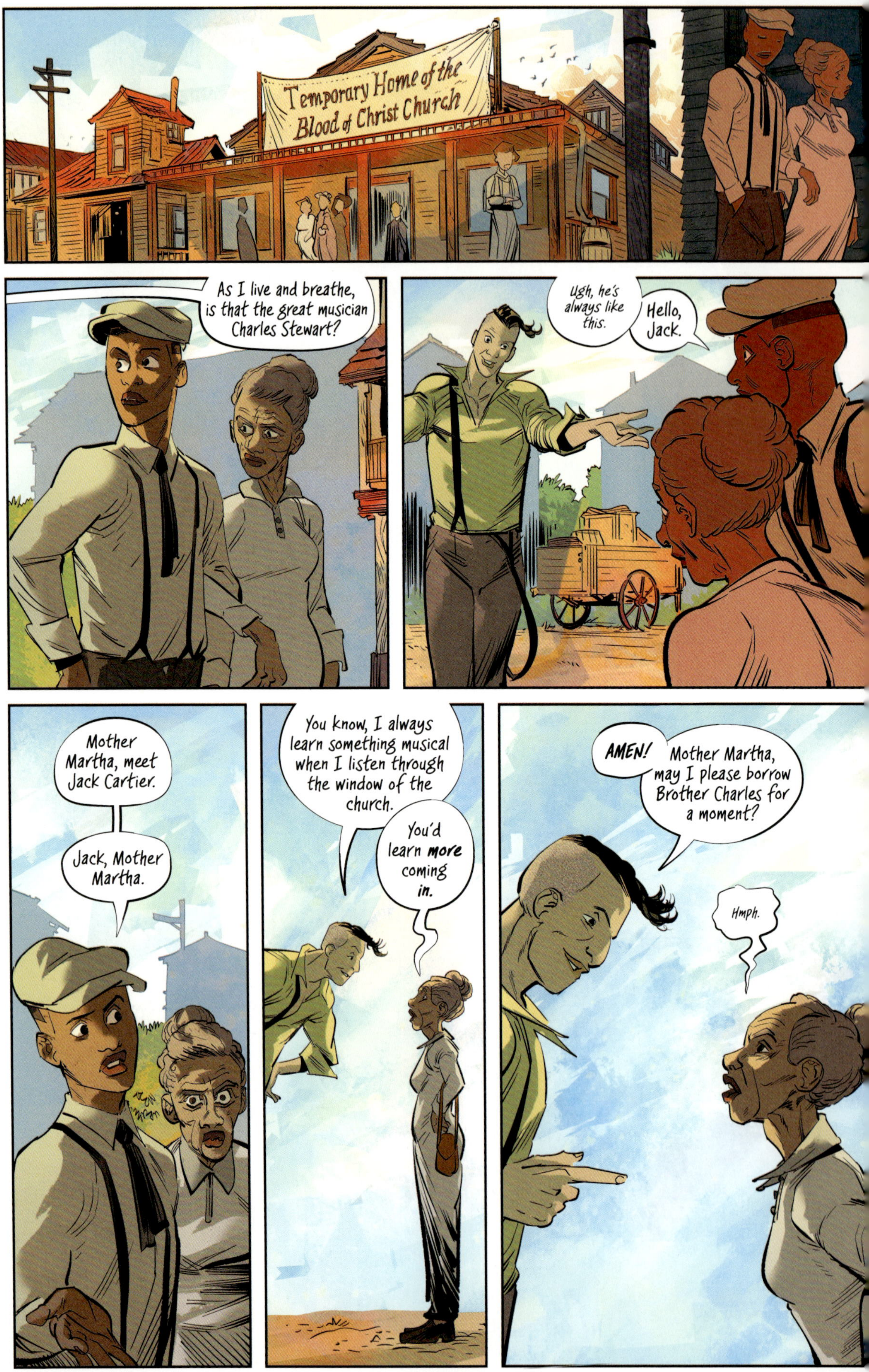
Temporary Home of the Blood of Christ Church
As I live and breathe, is that the great musician Charles Stewart?
Ugh, he's always like this.
Hello, Jack.
Mother Martha, meet Jack Cartier.
Jack, Mother Martha.
You know, I always learn something musical when I listen through the window of the church.
You'd learn **more** coming **in.**
AMEN!
Mother Martha, may I please borrow Brother Charles for a moment?
Hmph.

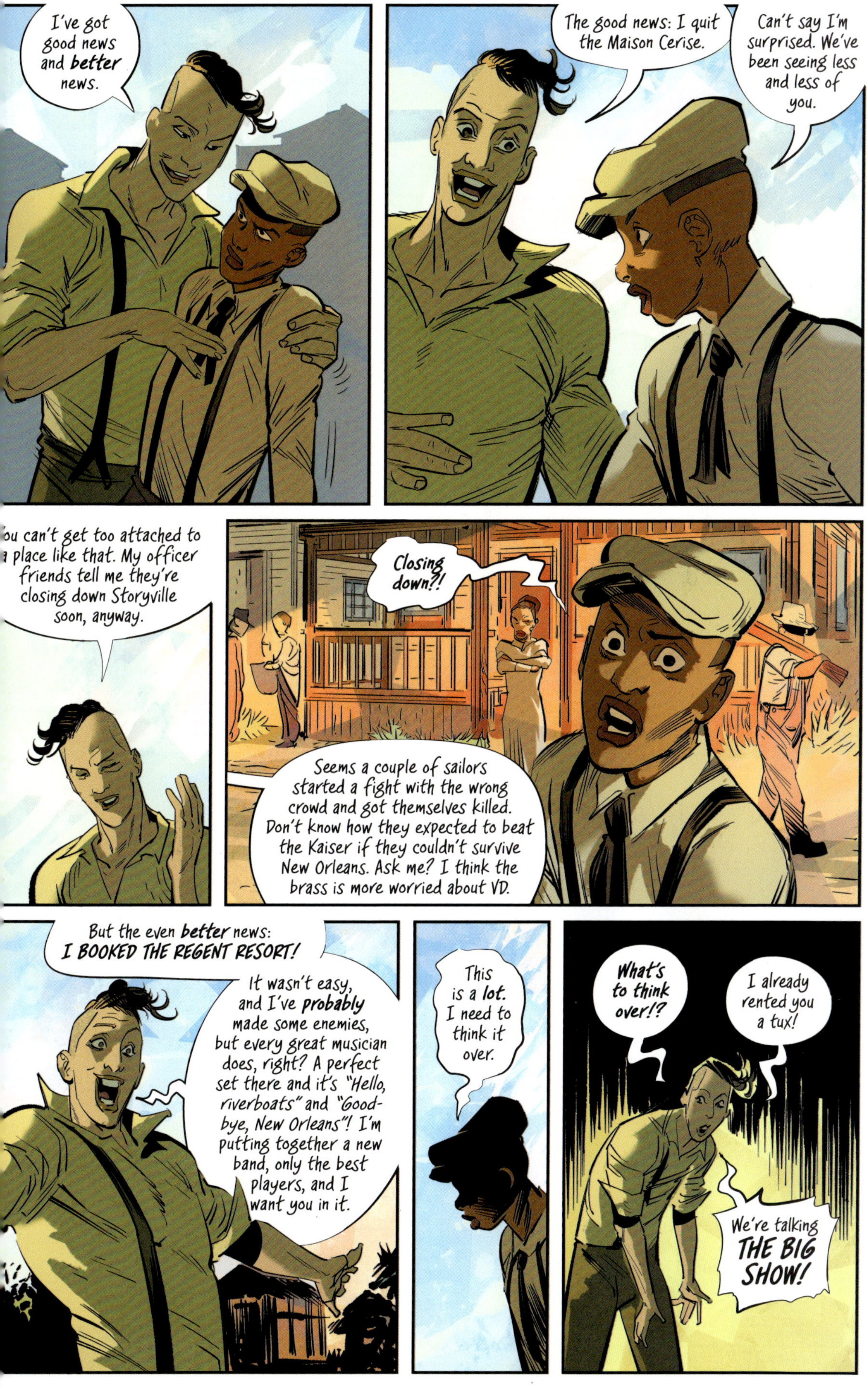

I've got good news and **better** news.
The good news: I quit the Maison Cerise.
Can't say I'm surprised. We've been seeing less and less of you.
ou can't get too attached to a place like that. My officer friends tell me they're closing down Storyville soon, anyway.
Closing down?!
Seems a couple of sailors started a fight with the wrong crowd and got themselves killed. Don't know how they expected to beat the Kaiser if they couldn't survive New Orleans. Ask me? I think the brass is more worried about VD.
But the even **better** news: **I BOOKED THE REGENT RESORT!**
It wasn't easy, and I've **probably** made some enemies, but every great musician does, right? A perfect set there and it's "Hello, riverboats" and "Good-bye, New Orleans"! I'm putting together a new band, only the best players, and I want you in it.
This is a **lot**. I need to think it over.
What's to think over!?
I already rented you a tux!
We're talking **THE BIG SHOW!**

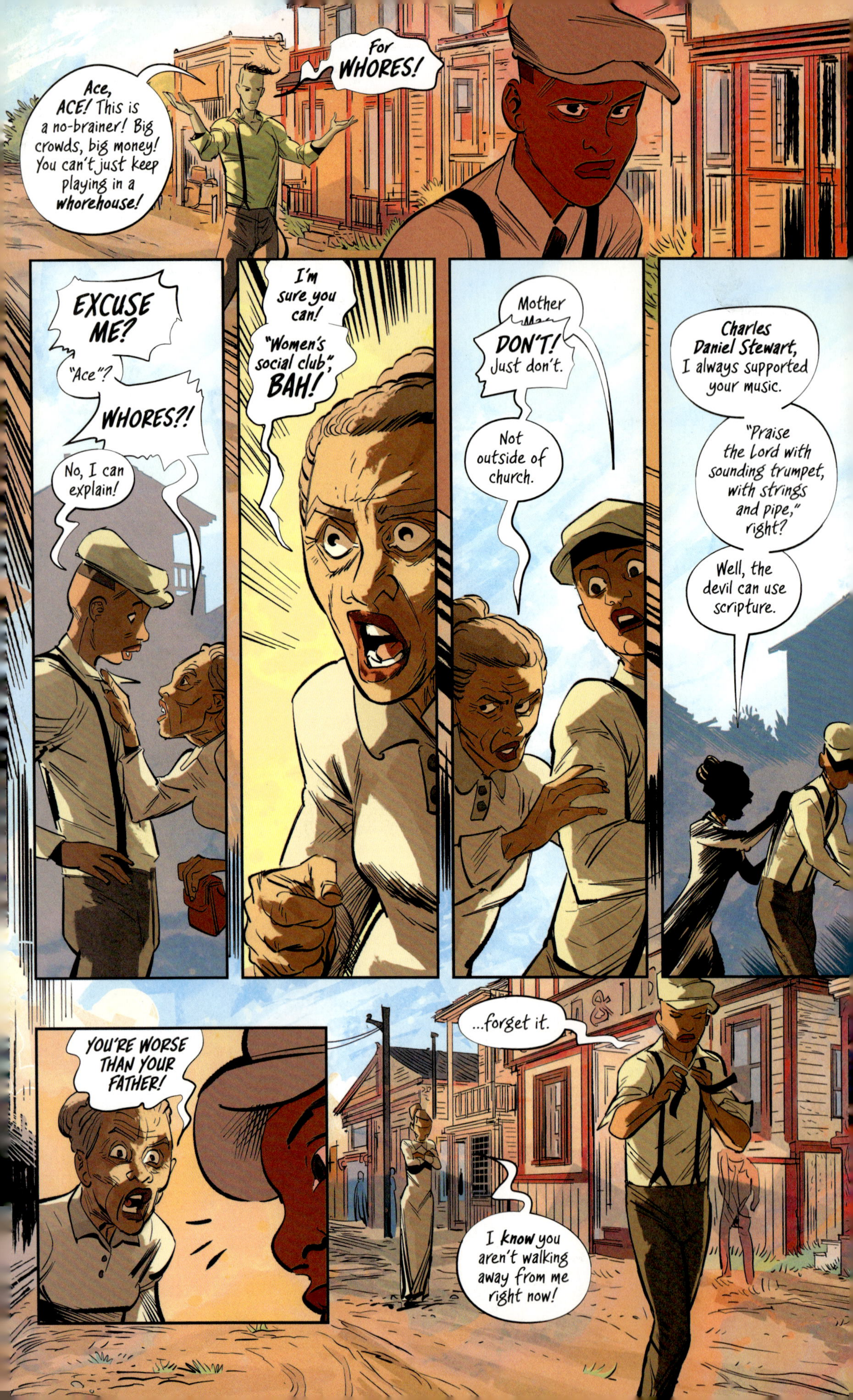
Ace, ACE! This is a no-brainer! Big crowds, big money! You can't just keep playing in a whorehouse!
For WHORES!
EXCUSE ME?
"Ace"?
WHORES?!
No, I can explain!
I'm sure you can!
"Women's social club", BAH!
Mother
DON'T! Just don't.
Not outside of church.
Charles Daniel Stewart, I always supported your music.
"Praise the Lord with sounding trumpet, with strings and pipe," right?
Well, the devil can use scripture.
YOU'RE WORSE THAN YOUR FATHER!
...forget it.
I know you aren't walking away from me right now!

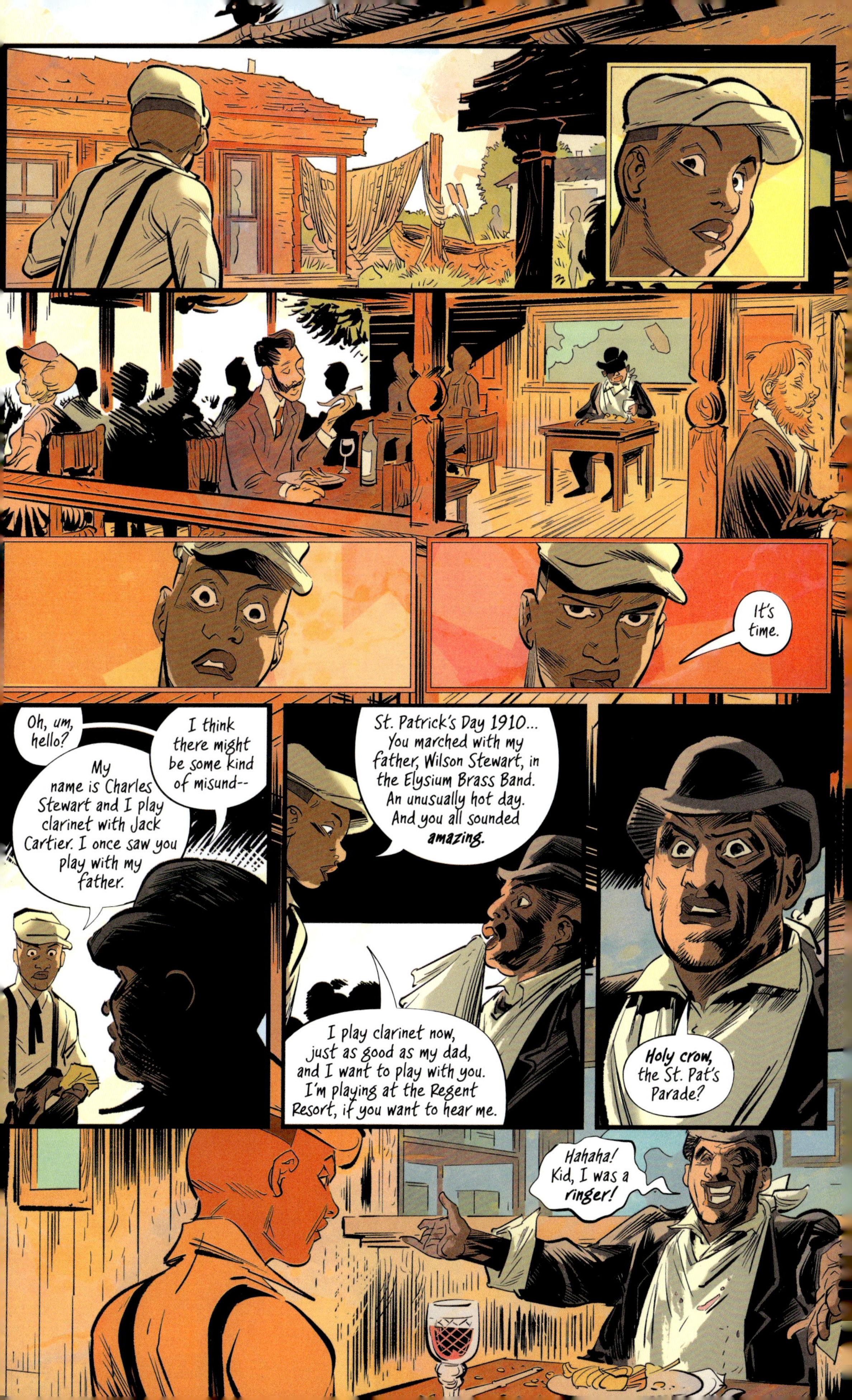
It's time.
Oh, um, hello?
I think there might be some kind of misund--
My name is Charles Stewart and I play clarinet with Jack Cartier. I once saw you play with my father.
St. Patrick's Day 1910... You marched with my father, Wilson Stewart, in the Elysium Brass Band. An unusually hot day. And you all sounded **amazing.**
I play clarinet now, just as good as my dad, and I want to play with you. I'm playing at the Regent Resort, if you want to hear me.
Holy crow, the St. Pat's Parade?
Hahaha! Kid, I was a **ringer!**

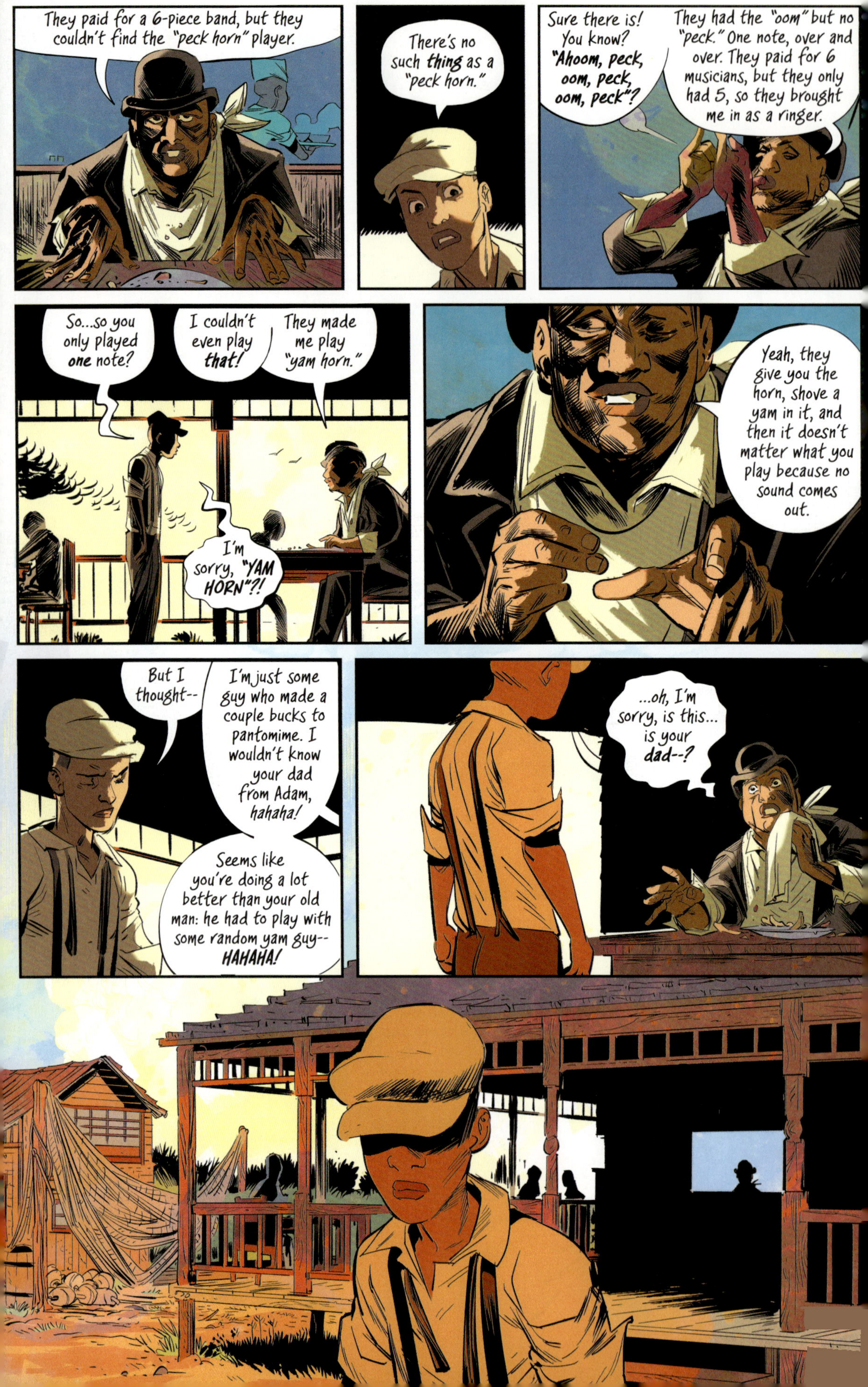
They paid for a 6-piece band, but they couldn't find the "peck horn" player.
There's no such *thing* as a "peck horn."
Sure there is! You know? **"Ahoom, peck, oom, peck, oom, peck"?**
They had the "oom" but no "peck." One note, over and over. They paid for 6 musicians, but they only had 5, so they brought me in as a ringer.
So...so you only played **one** note?
I couldn't even play **that!**
They made me play "yam horn."
I'm sorry, **"YAM HORN"?!**
Yeah, they give you the horn, shove a yam in it, and then it doesn't matter what you play because no sound comes out.
But I thought--
I'm just some guy who made a couple bucks to pantomime. I wouldn't know your dad from Adam, hahaha!
Seems like you're doing a lot better than your old man: he had to play with some random yam guy-- **HAHAHA!**
...oh, I'm sorry, is this... is your **dad--?**

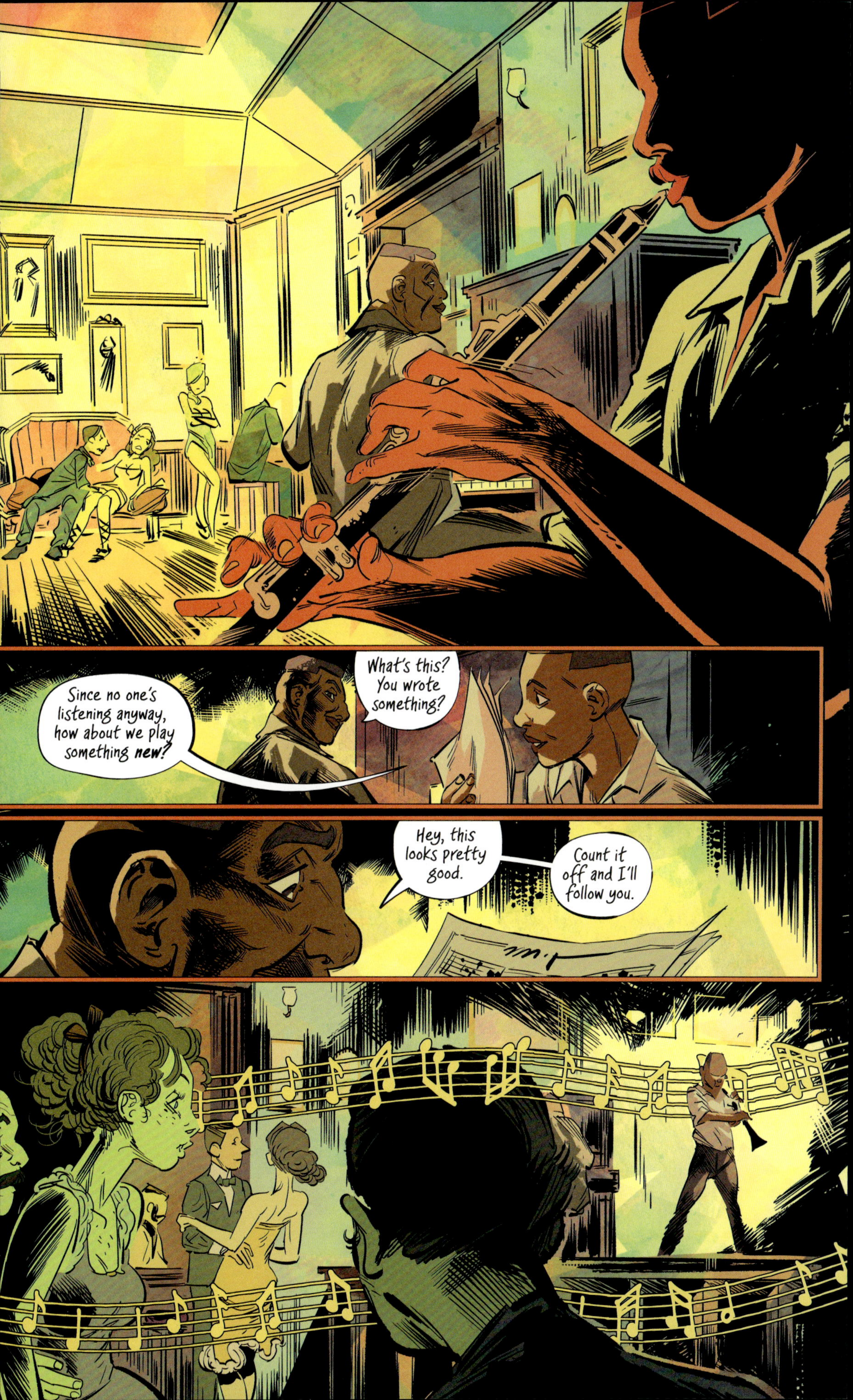
Since no one's listening anyway, how about we play something **new**?
What's this? You wrote something?
Hey, this looks pretty good.
Count it off and I'll follow you.

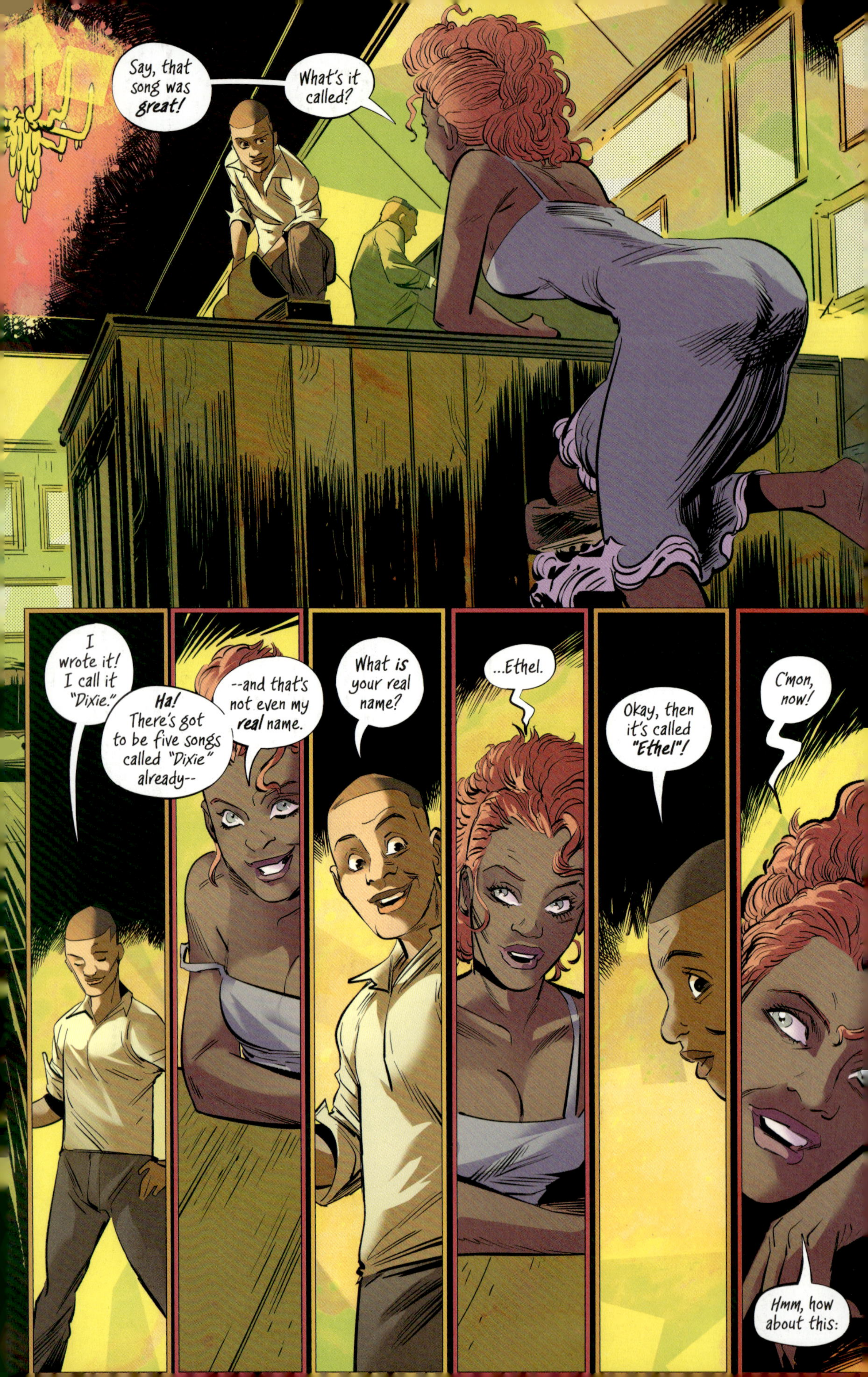
Say, that song was great!
What's it called?
I wrote it! I call it "Dixie."
Ha! There's got to be five songs called "Dixie" already--
--and that's not even my real name.
What is your real name?
...Ethel.
Okay, then it's called "Ethel"!
C'mon, now!
Hmm, how about this:

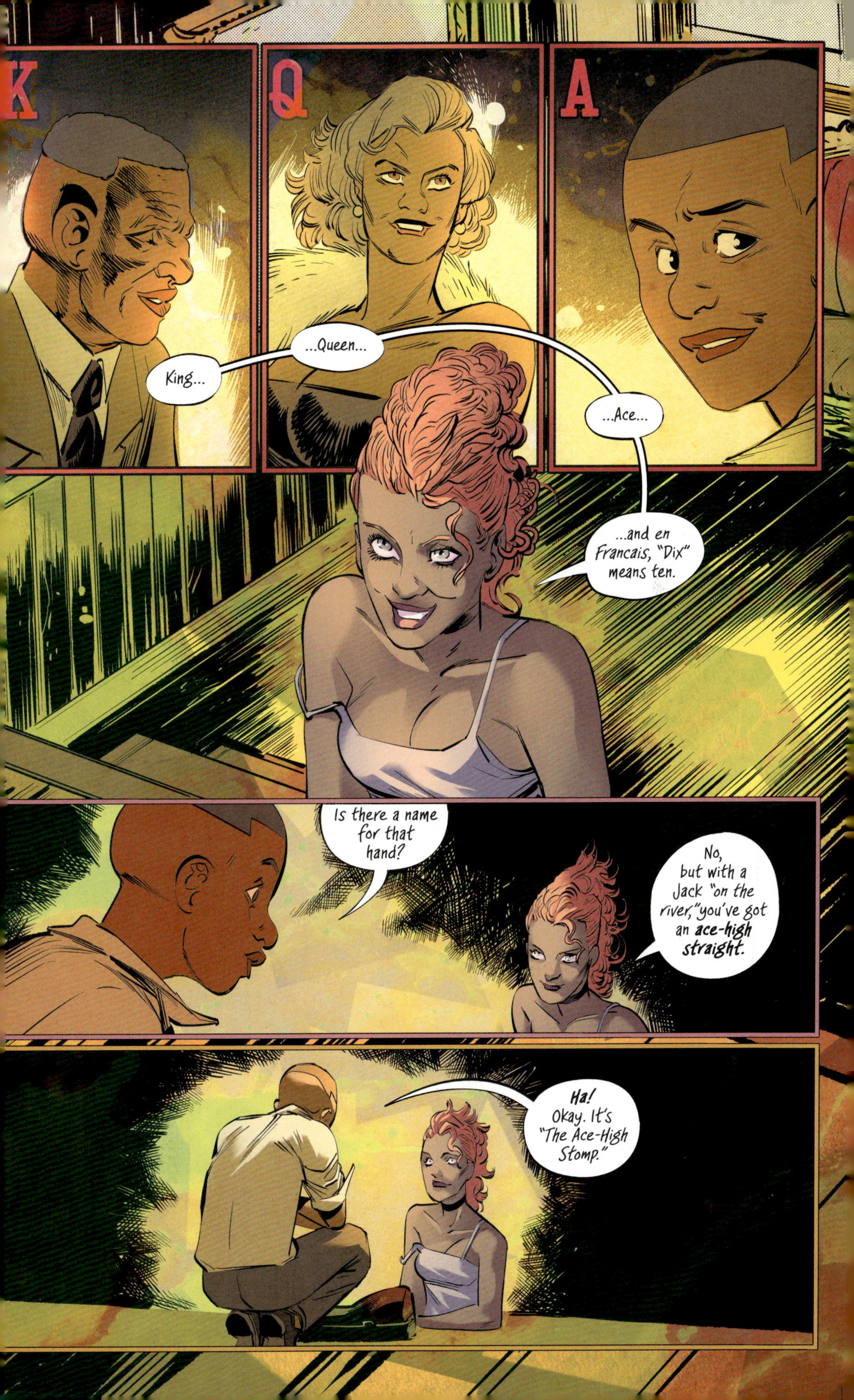
K
Q
A
King...
...Queen...
...Ace...
...and en Francais, "Dix" means ten.
Is there a name for that hand?
No, but with a Jack "on the river," you've got an **ace-high straight**.
Ha! Okay. It's "The Ace-High Stomp."

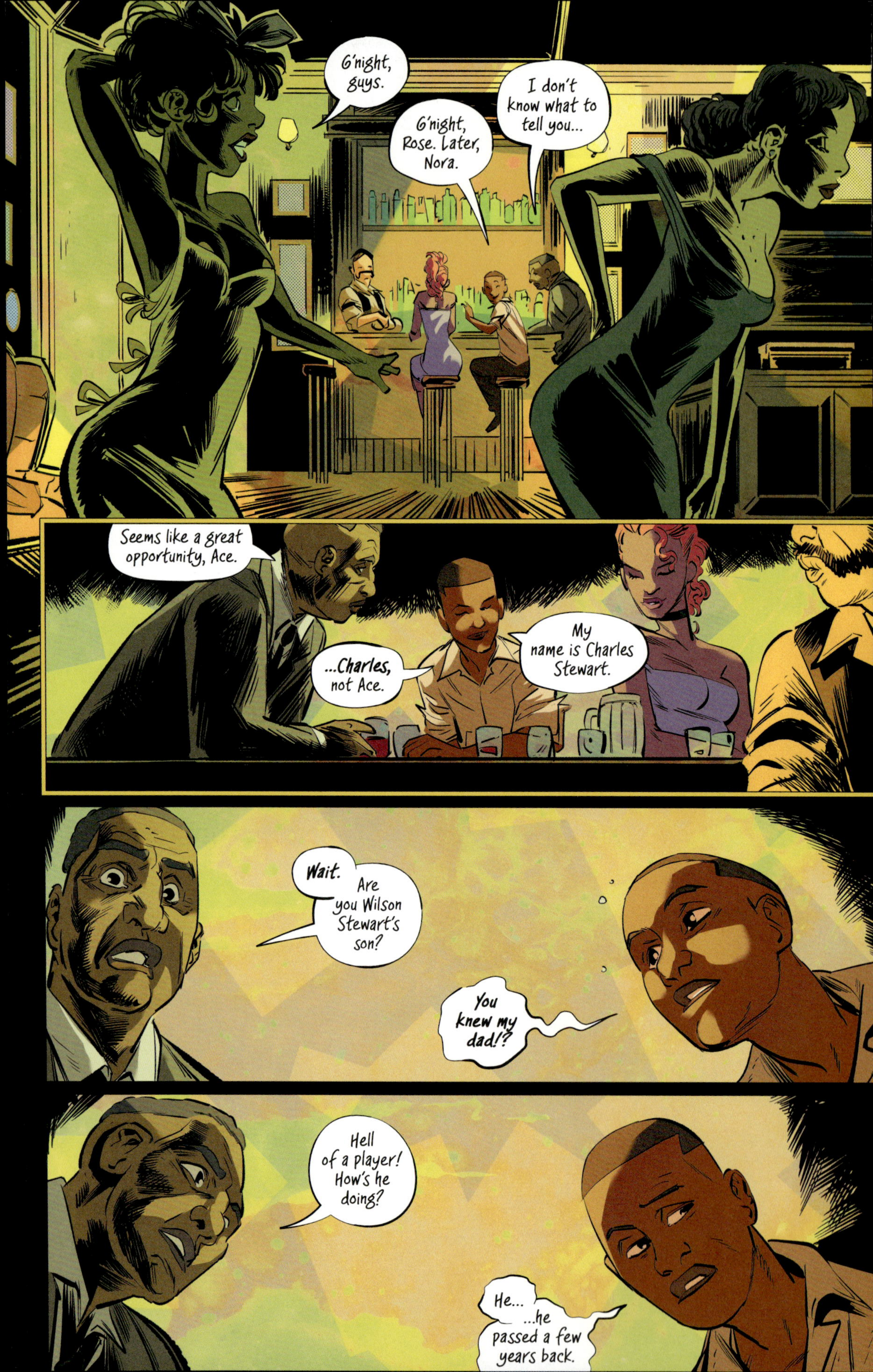
G'night, guys.
G'night, Rose. Later, Nora.
I don't know what to tell you...
Seems like a great opportunity, Ace.
...Charles, not Ace.
My name is Charles Stewart.
Wait. Are you Wilson Stewart's son?
You knew my dad!?
Hell of a player! How's he doing?
He... ...he passed a few years back.

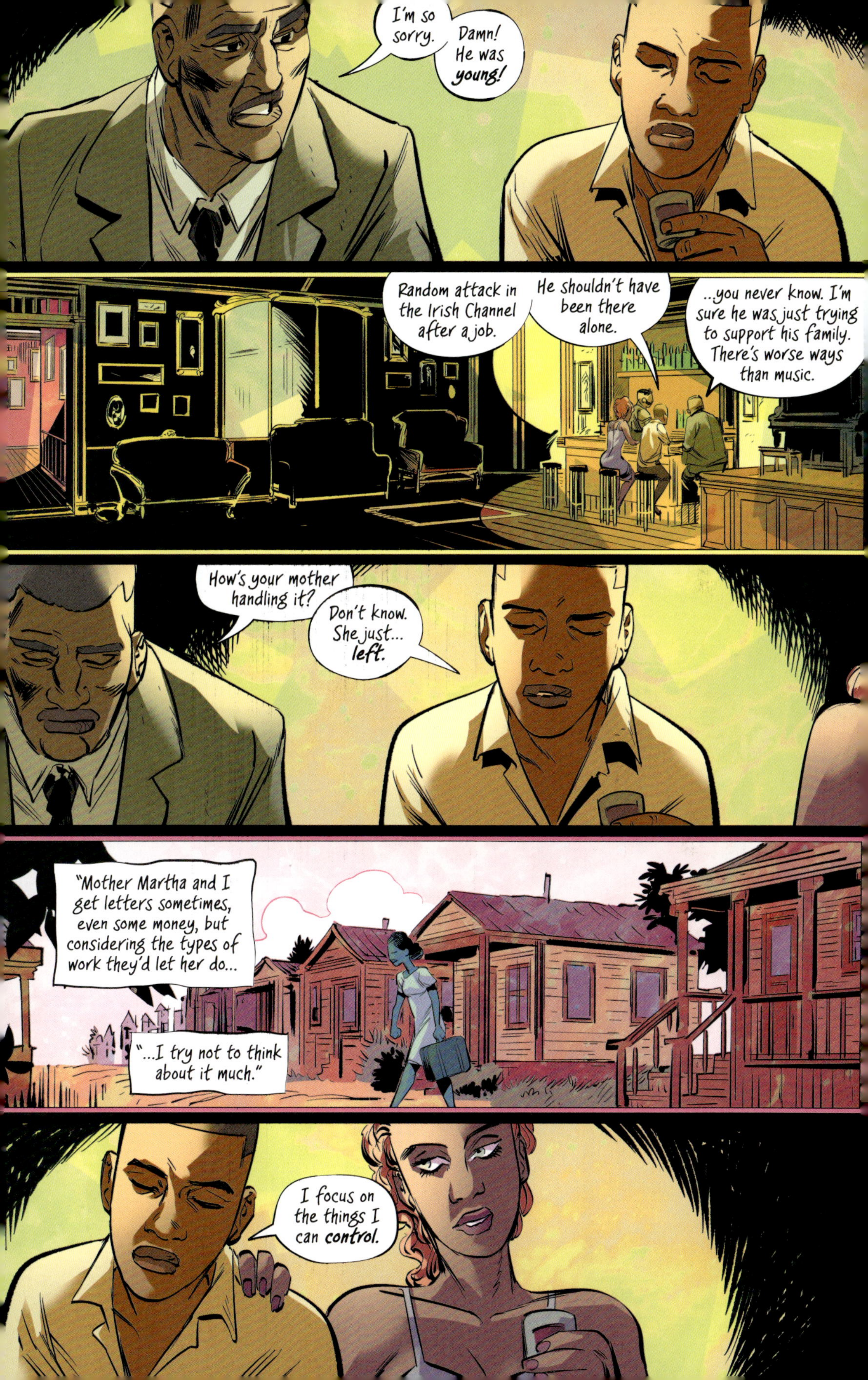
I'm so sorry.
Damn! He was *young!*
Random attack in the Irish Channel after a job.
He shouldn't have been there alone.
...you never know. I'm sure he was just trying to support his family. There's worse ways than music.
How's your mother handling it?
Don't know. She just... *left.*
"Mother Martha and I get letters sometimes, even some money, but considering the types of work they'd let her do...
"...I try not to think about it much."
I focus on the things I can *control.*

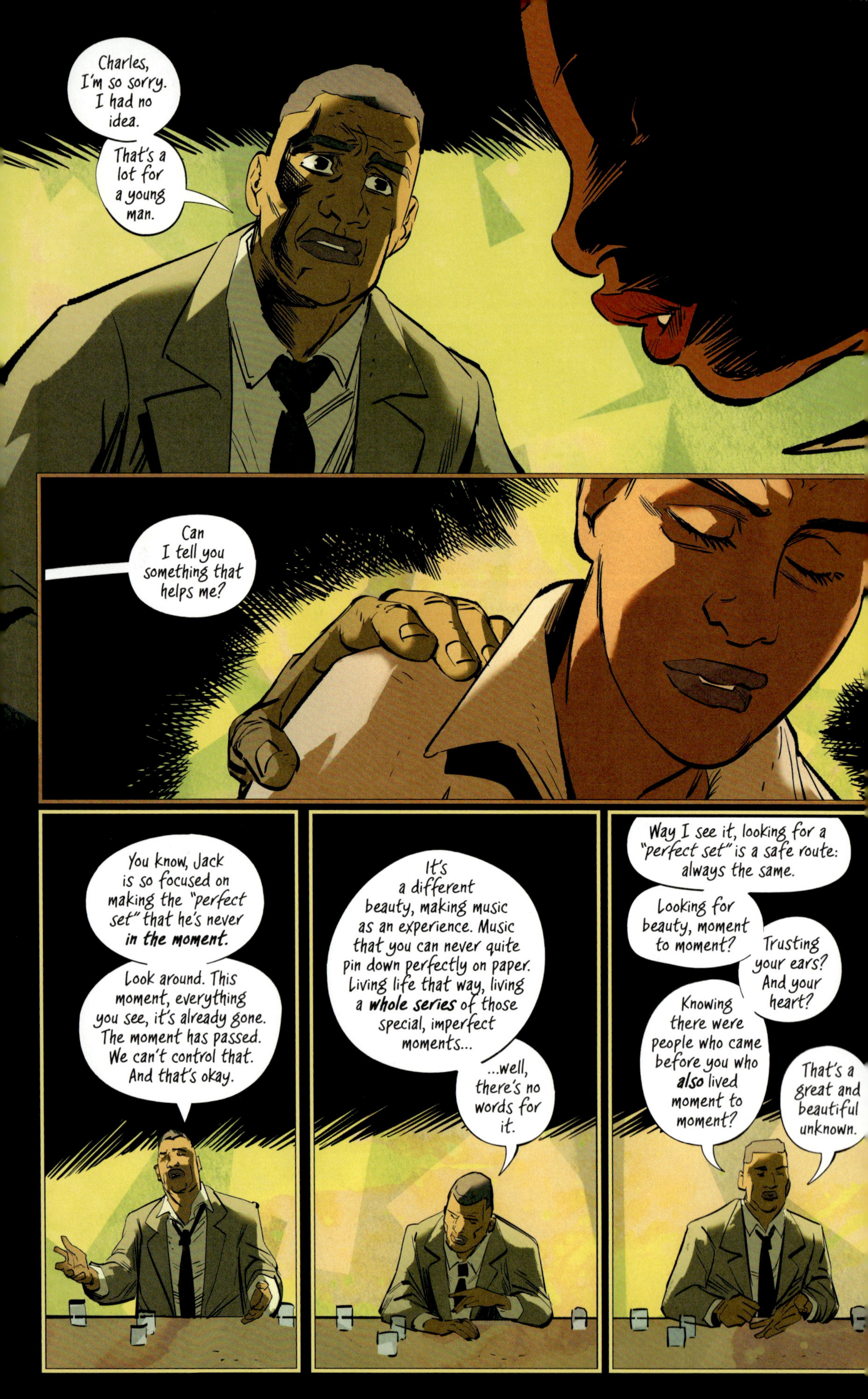
Charles, I'm so sorry. I had no idea.
That's a lot for a young man.
Can I tell you something that helps me?
You know, Jack is so focused on making the "perfect set" that he's never **in the moment.**
Look around. This moment, everything you see, it's already gone. The moment has passed. We can't control that. And that's okay.
It's a different beauty, making music as an experience. Music that you can never quite pin down perfectly on paper. Living life that way, living a **whole series** of those special, imperfect moments...
...well, there's no words for it.
Way I see it, looking for a "perfect set" is a safe route: always the same.
Looking for beauty, moment to moment?
Trusting your ears? And your heart?
Knowing there were people who came before you who **also** lived moment to moment?
That's a great and beautiful unknown.

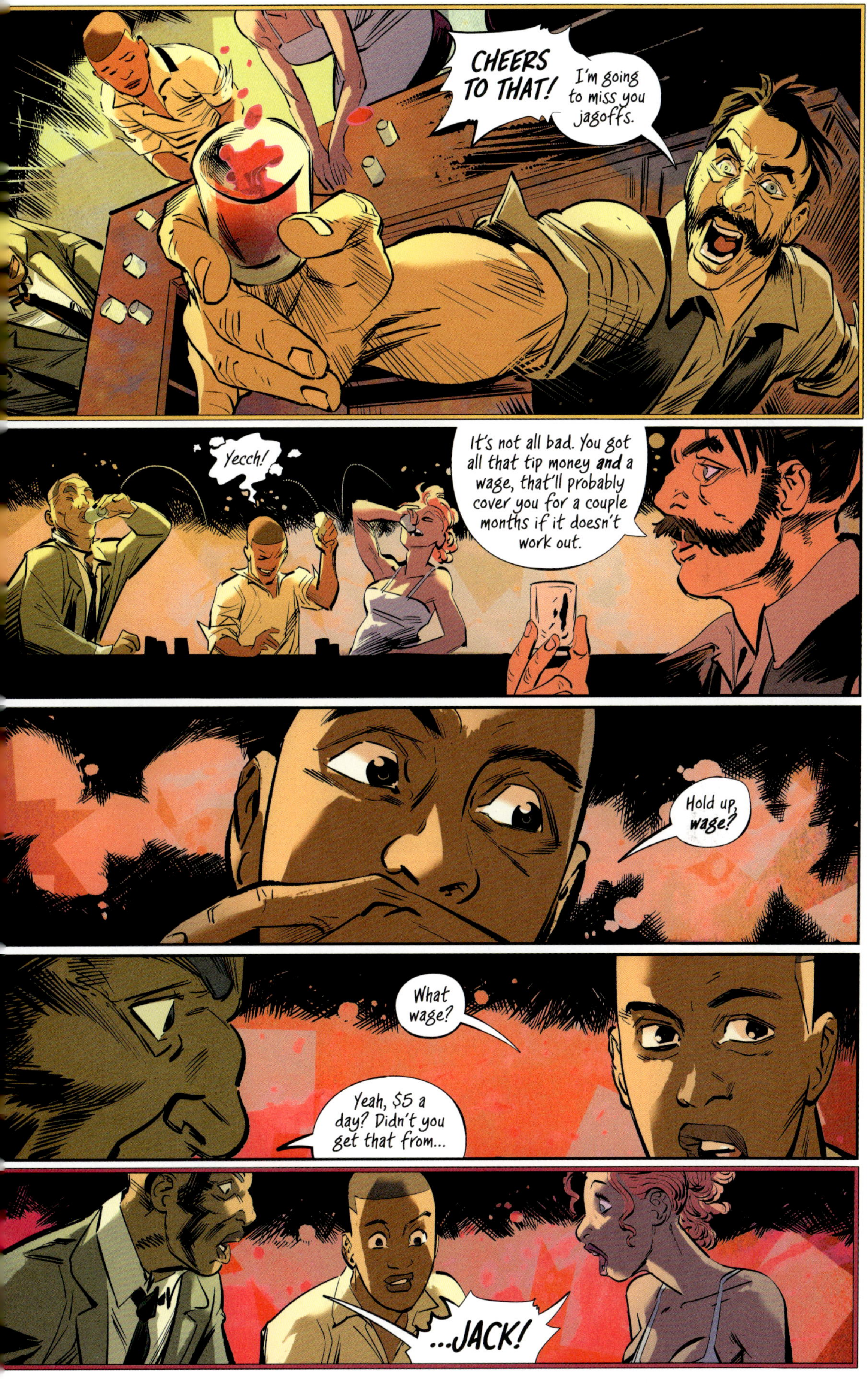
CHEERS TO THAT!
I'm going to miss you jagoffs.
Yecch!
It's not all bad. You got all that tip money **and** a wage, that'll probably cover you for a couple months if it doesn't work out.
Hold up, **wage?**
What wage?
Yeah, $5 a day? Didn't you get that from...
...JACK!

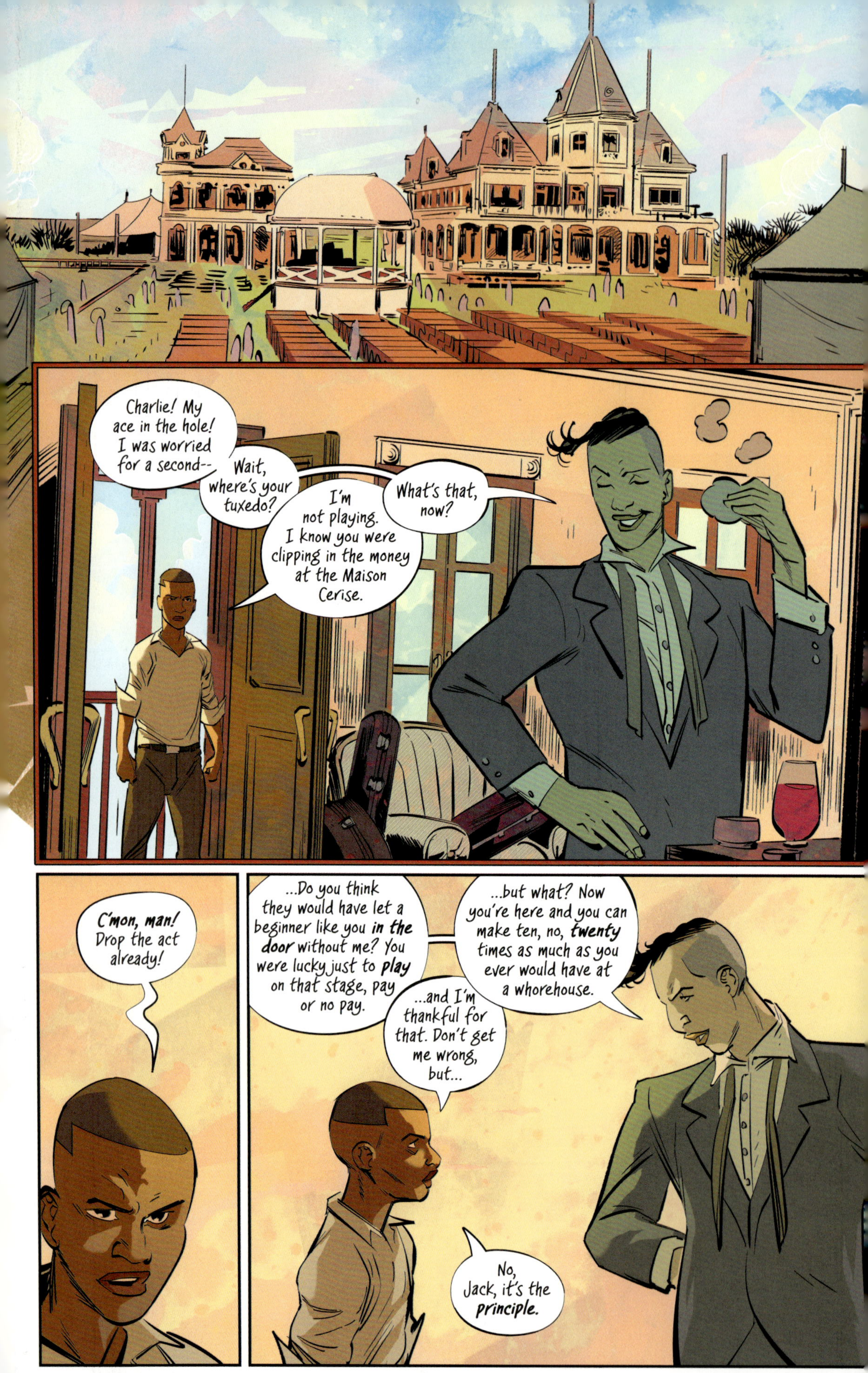

Charlie! My ace in the hole! I was worried for a second--
Wait, where's your tuxedo?
What's that, now?
I'm not playing. I know you were clipping in the money at the Maison Cerise.
C'mon, man! Drop the act already!
...Do you think they would have let a beginner like you in the door without me? You were lucky just to play on that stage, pay or no pay.
...and I'm thankful for that. Don't get me wrong, but...
...but what? Now you're here and you can make ten, no, twenty times as much as you ever would have at a whorehouse.
No, Jack, it's the principle.

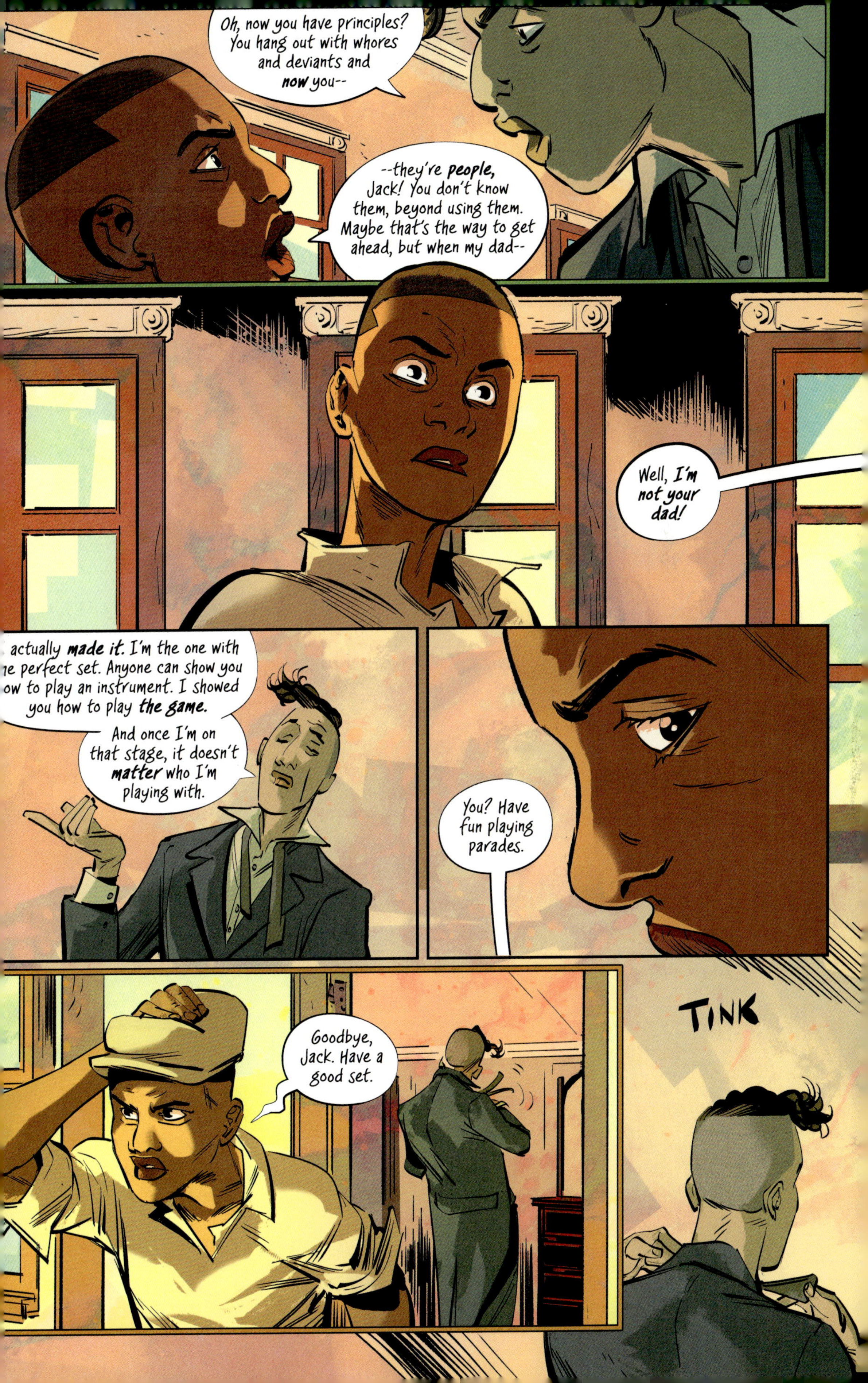
Oh, now you have principles? You hang out with whores and deviants and **now** you--
--they're **people,** Jack! You don't know them, beyond using them. Maybe that's the way to get ahead, but when my dad--
Well, **I'm not your** dad!
actually **made it**. I'm the one with he perfect set. Anyone can show you ow to play an instrument. I showed you how to play **the game.**
And once I'm on that stage, it doesn't **matter** who I'm playing with.
You? Have fun playing parades.
Goodbye, Jack. Have a good set.
TINK

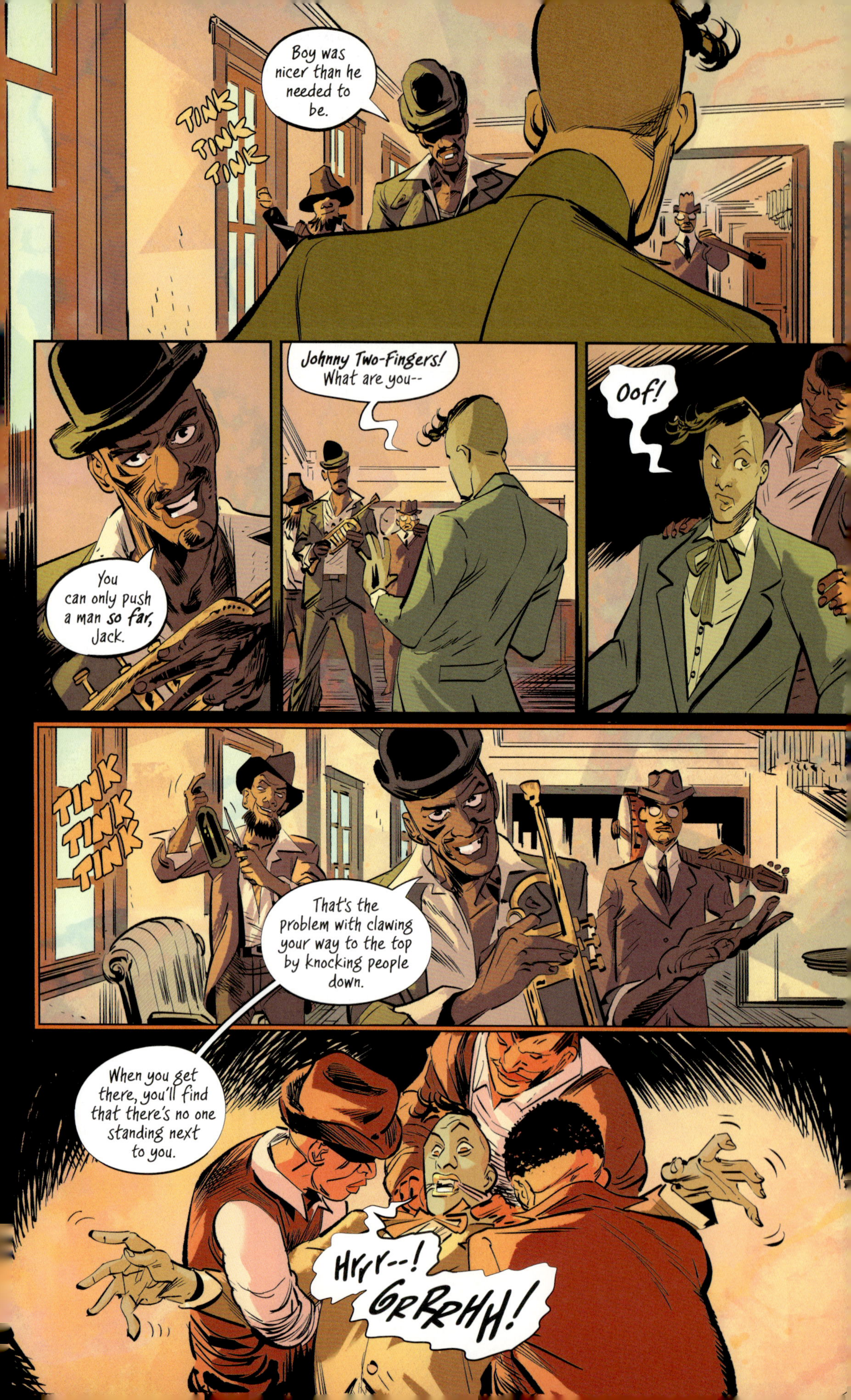
Boy was nicer than he needed to be.
TINK TINK TINK
You can only push a man **so far**, Jack.
Johnny Two-Fingers! What are you--
Oof!
TINK TINK TINK
That's the problem with clawing your way to the top by knocking people down.
When you get there, you'll find that there's no one standing next to you.
Hrrr--! GRRRHH!

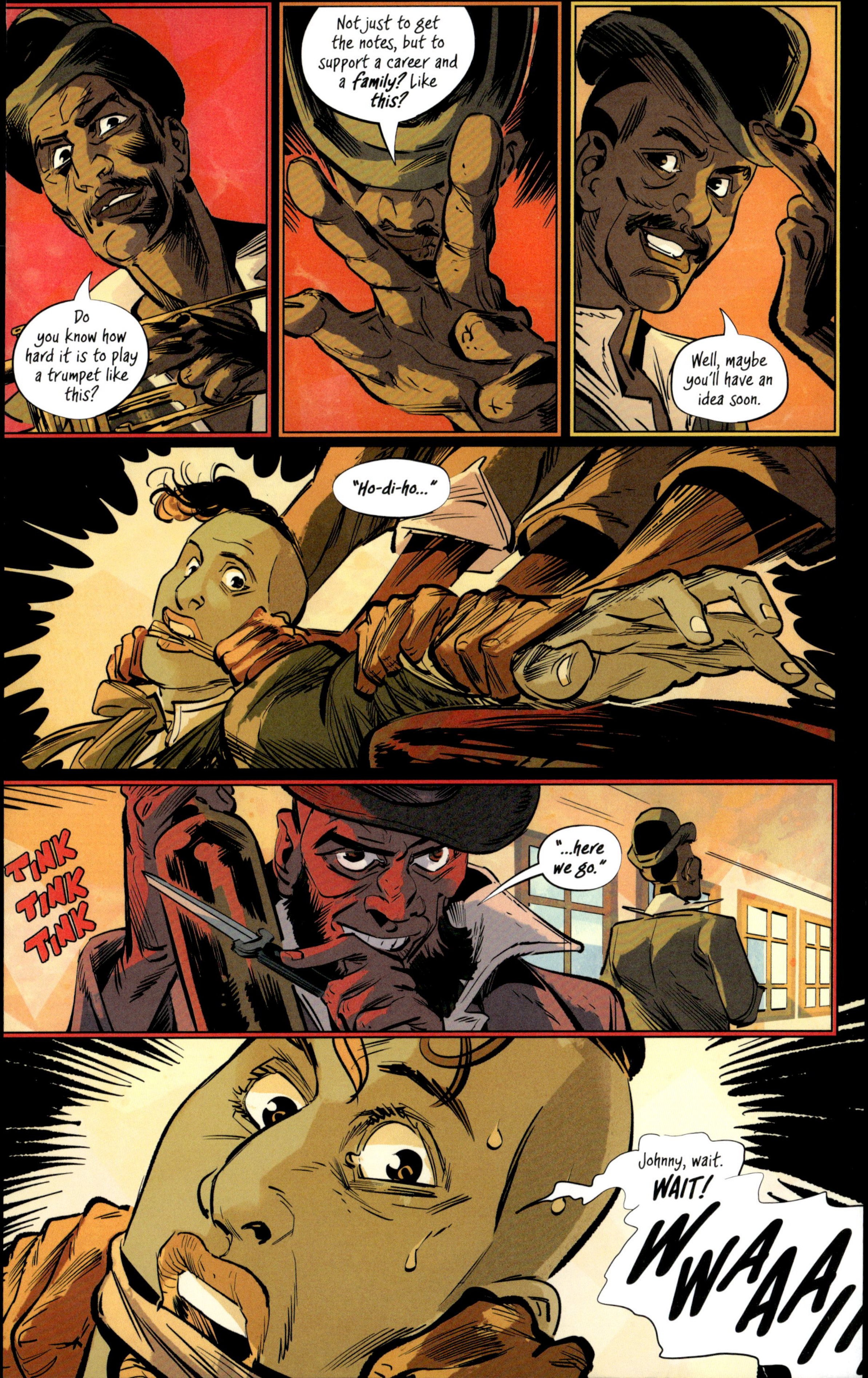

Do you know how hard it is to play a trumpet like this?
Not just to get the notes, but to support a career and a family? Like this?
Well, maybe you'll have an idea soon.
"Ho-di-ho..."
TINK TINK TINK
"...here we go."
Johnny, wait. WAIT!
WWAAAI

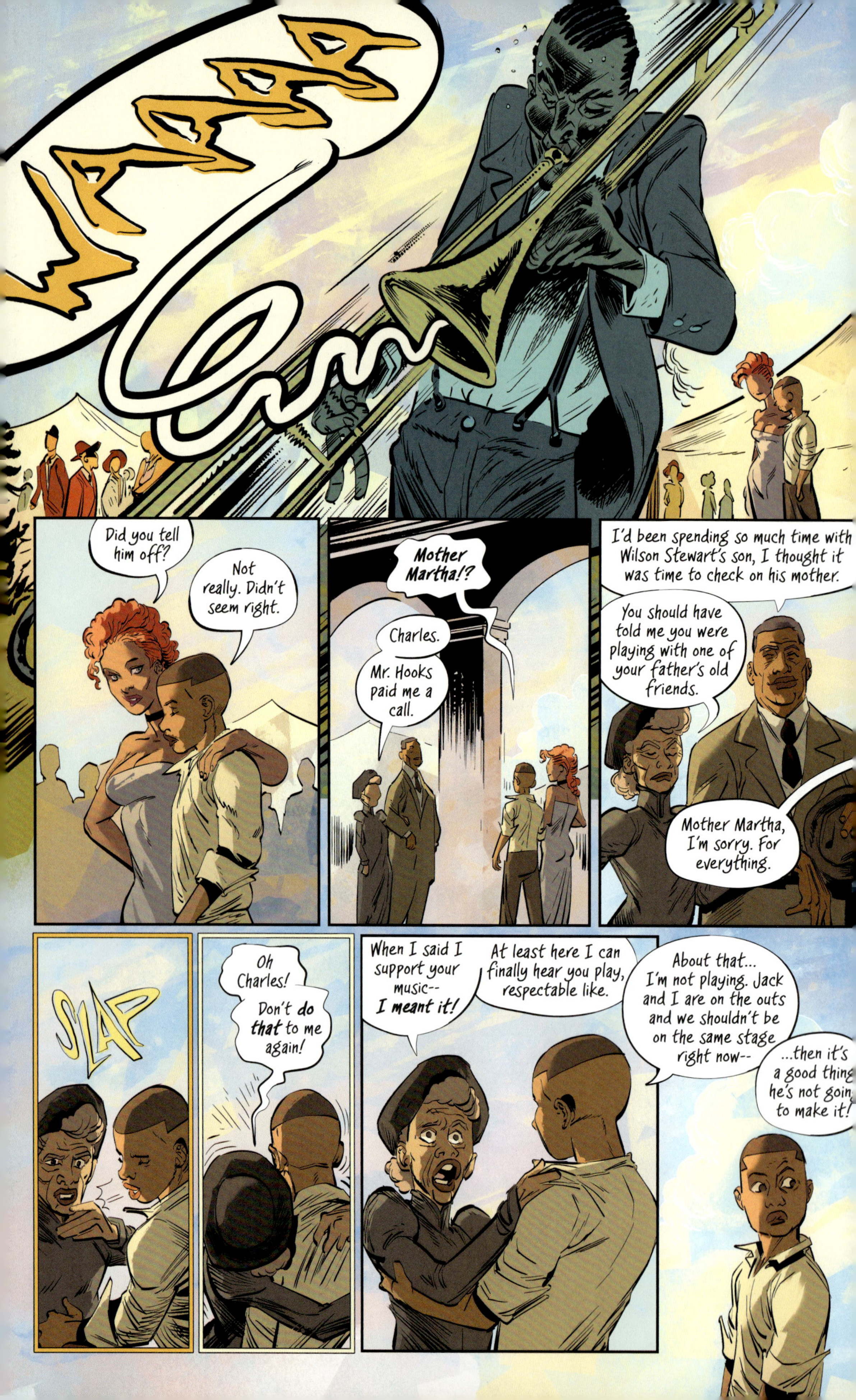
WAAAAAAMM
Did you tell him off?
Not really. Didn't seem right.
Mother Martha!?
Charles.
Mr. Hooks paid me a call.
I'd been spending so much time with Wilson Stewart's son, I thought it was time to check on his mother.
You should have told me you were playing with one of your father's old friends.
Mother Martha, I'm sorry. For everything.
SLAP
Oh Charles!
Don't do that to me again!
When I said I support your music-- I meant it!
At least here I can finally hear you play, respectable like.
About that... I'm not playing. Jack and I are on the outs and we shouldn't be on the same stage right now--
...then it's a good thing he's not goin to make it!

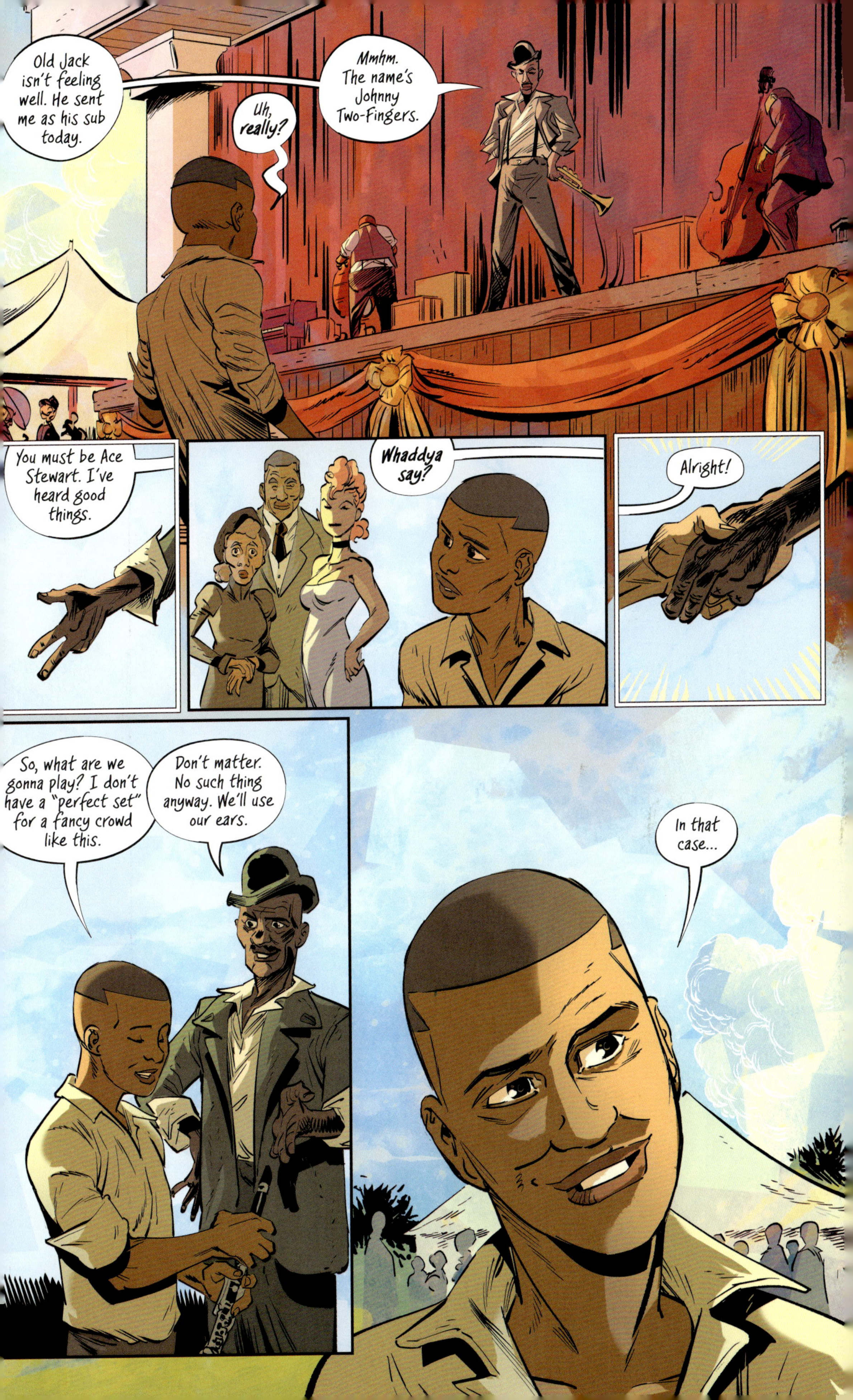
Old Jack isn't feeling well. He sent me as his sub today.
Uh, really?
Mmhm. The name's Johnny Two-Fingers.
You must be Ace Stewart. I've heard good things.
Whaddya say?
Alright!
So, what are we gonna play? I don't have a "perfect set" for a fancy crowd like this.
Don't matter. No such thing anyway. We'll use our ears.
In that case...

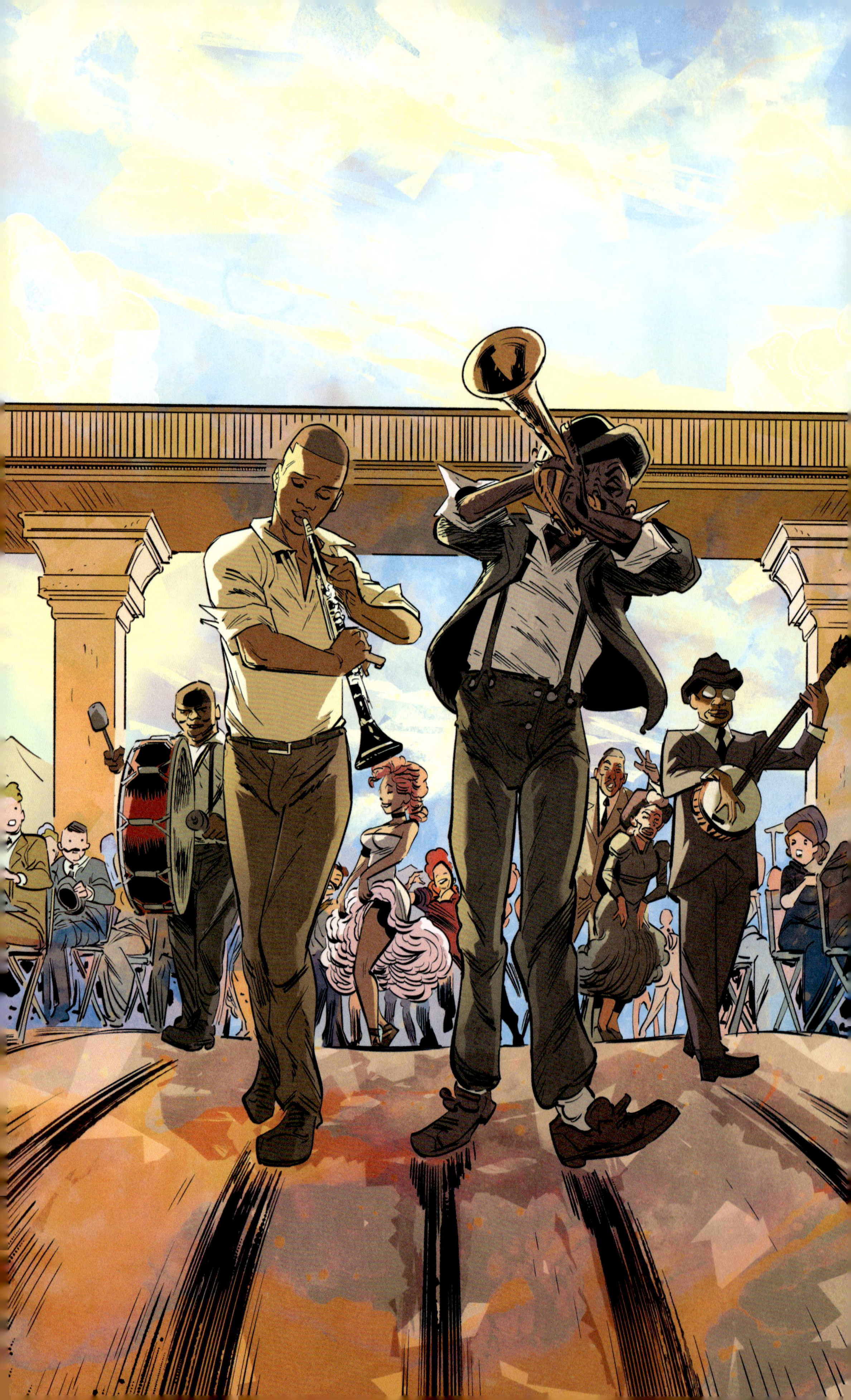

2.
SORRY, BUT I CAN'T TAKE YOU

CHICAGO
1928

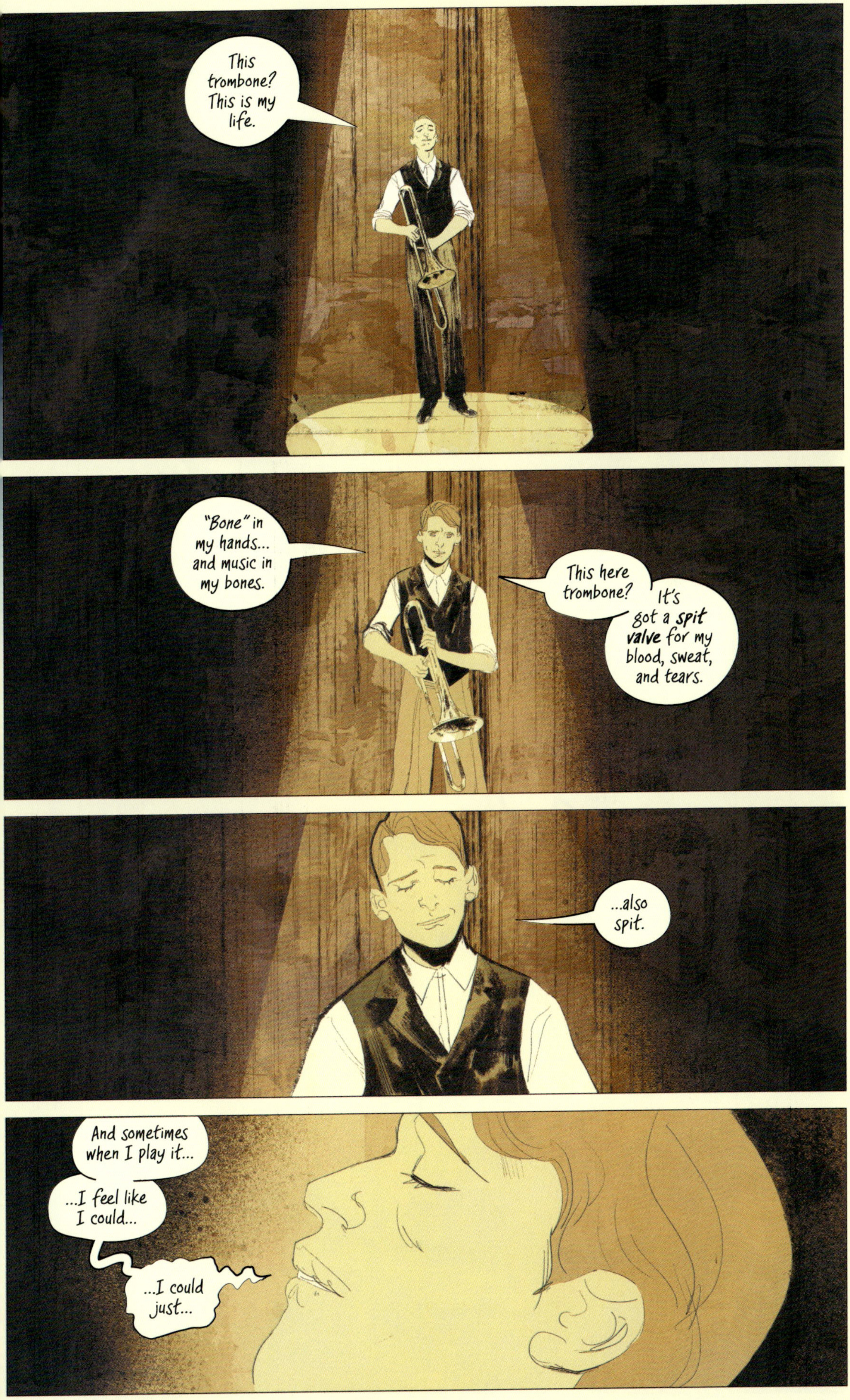
This trombone? This is my life.
"Bone" in my hands... and music in my bones.
This here trombone?
It's got a **spit valve** for my blood, sweat, and tears.
...also spit.
And sometimes when I play it...
...I feel like I could...
...I could just...

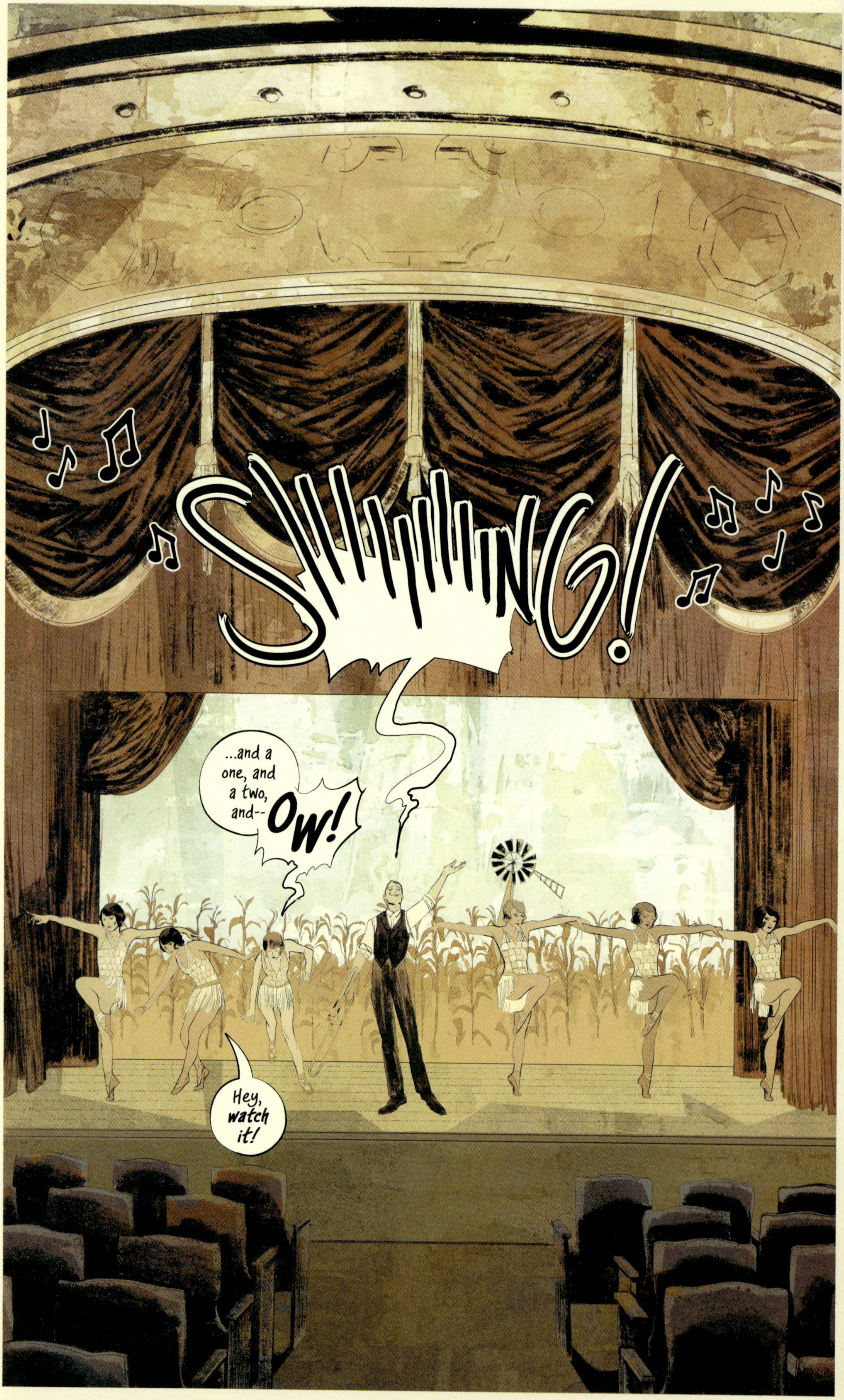
SHHHHING!
...and a one, and a two, and--
OW!
Hey, watch it!

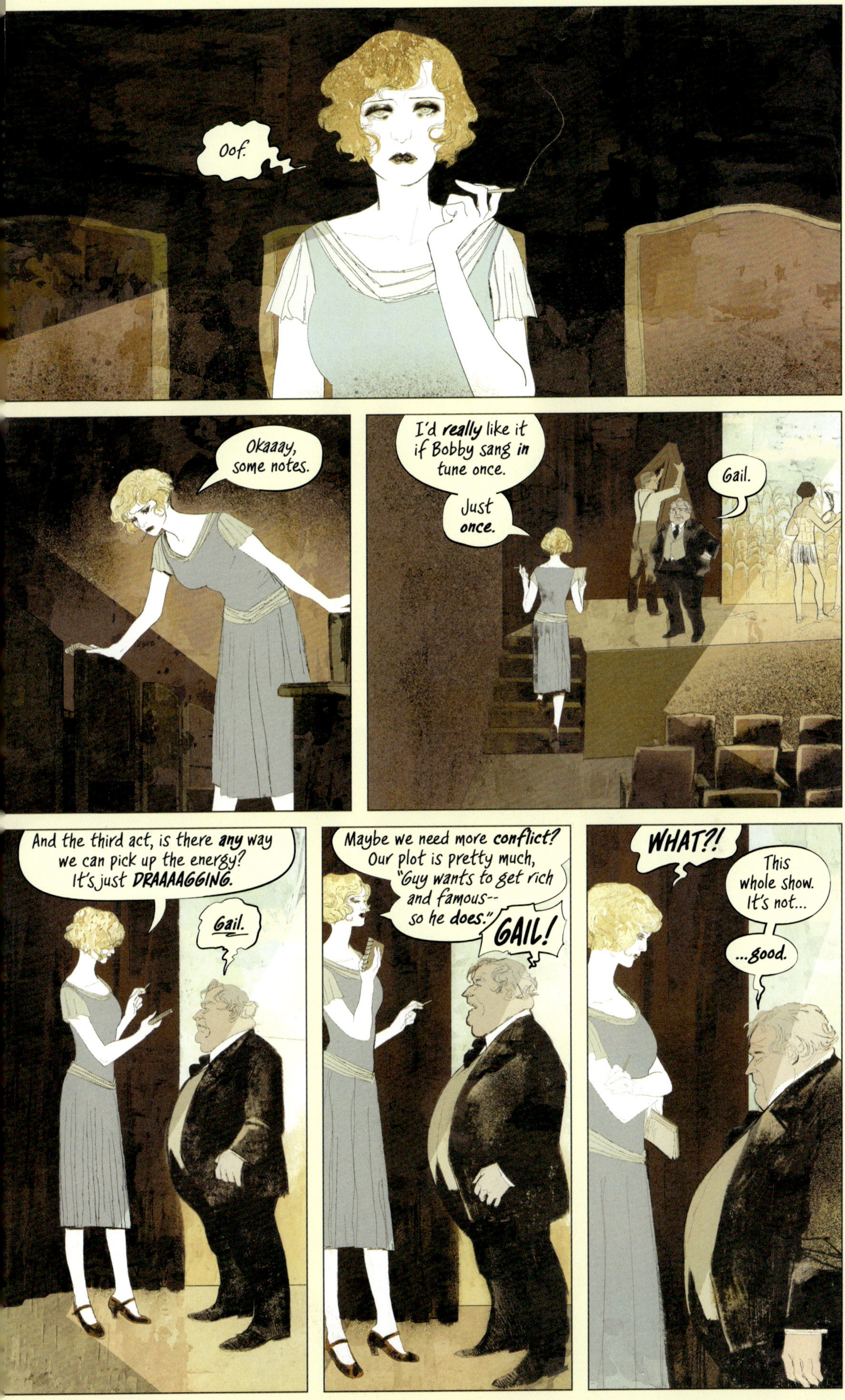
Oof.
Okaaay, some notes.
I'd **really** like it if Bobby sang **in** tune once.
Just **once.**
Gail.
And the third act, is there **any** way we can pick up the energy? It's just **DRAAAAGGING.**
Gail.
Maybe we need more **conflict?** Our plot is pretty much, "Guy wants to get rich and famous-- so he **does.**"
GAIL!
WHAT?!
This whole show. It's not...
...good.

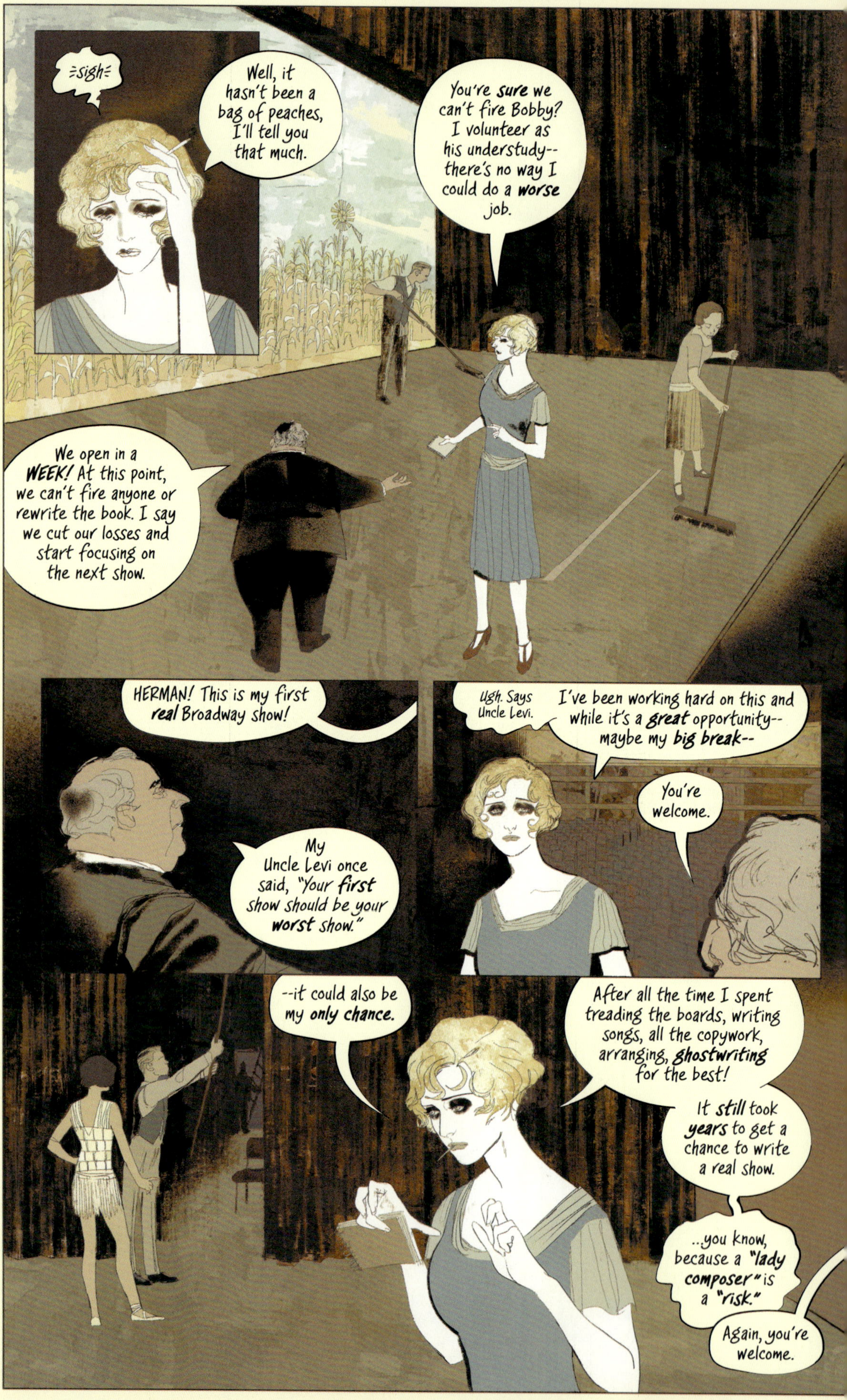

=sigh=
Well, it hasn't been a bag of peaches, I'll tell you that much.
You're sure we can't fire Bobby? I volunteer as his understudy--there's no way I could do a worse job.
We open in a WEEK! At this point, we can't fire anyone or rewrite the book. I say we cut our losses and start focusing on the next show.
HERMAN! This is my first real Broadway show!
My Uncle Levi once said, "Your first show should be your worst show."
Ugh. Says Uncle Levi.
I've been working hard on this and while it's a great opportunity--maybe my big break--
You're welcome.
--it could also be my only chance.
After all the time I spent treading the boards, writing songs, all the copywork, arranging, ghostwriting for the best!
It still took years to get a chance to write a real show.
...you know, because a "lady composer" is a "risk."
Again, you're welcome.

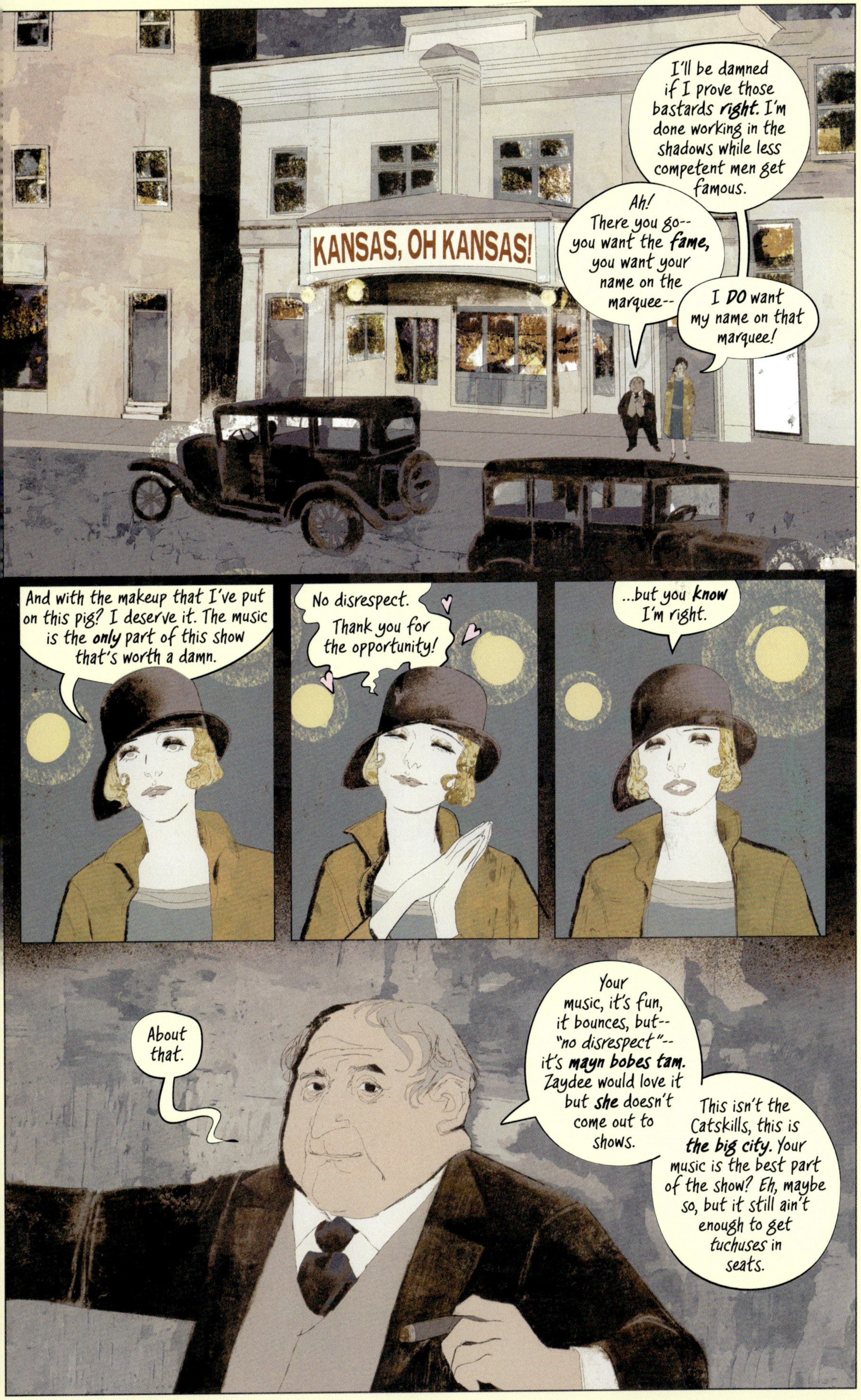
KANSAS, OH KANSAS!
I'll be damned if I prove those bastards right. I'm done working in the shadows while less competent men get famous.
Ah! There you go--you want the fame, you want your name on the marquee--
I DO want my name on that marquee!
And with the makeup that I've put on this pig? I deserve it. The music is the only part of this show that's worth a damn.
No disrespect. Thank you for the opportunity!
...but you know I'm right.
About that.
Your music, it's fun, it bounces, but--"no disrespect"--it's mayn bobes tam. Zaydee would love it but she doesn't come out to shows.
This isn't the Catskills, this is the big city. Your music is the best part of the show? Eh, maybe so, but it still ain't enough to get tuchuses in seats.

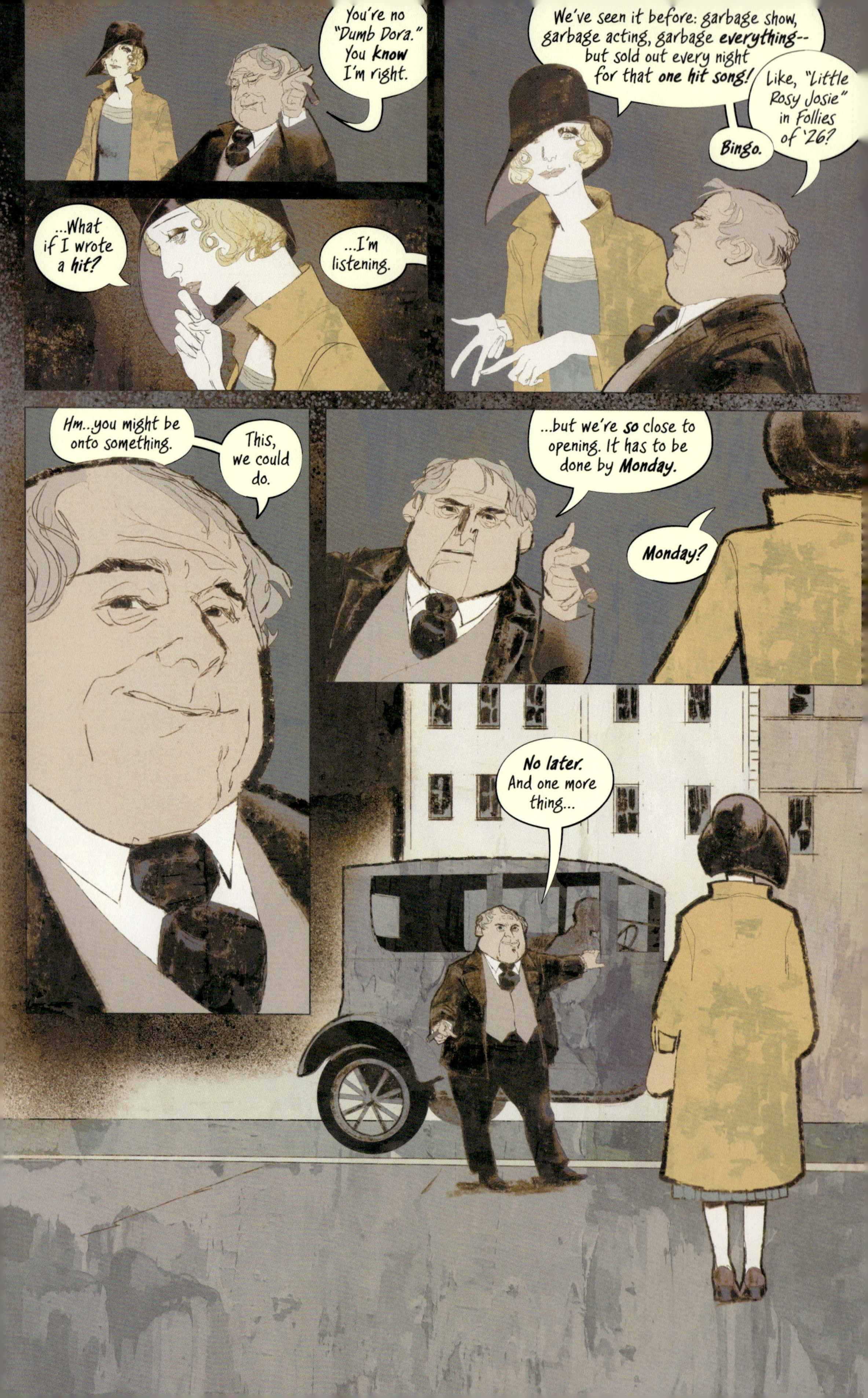
You're no "Dumb Dora." You know I'm right.
...What if I wrote a hit?
...I'm listening.
We've seen it before: garbage show, garbage acting, garbage everything--but sold out every night for that one hit song!
Like, "Little Rosy Josie" in Follies of '26?
Bingo.
Hm...you might be onto something.
This, we could do.
...but we're so close to opening. It has to be done by Monday.
Monday?
No later. And one more thing...

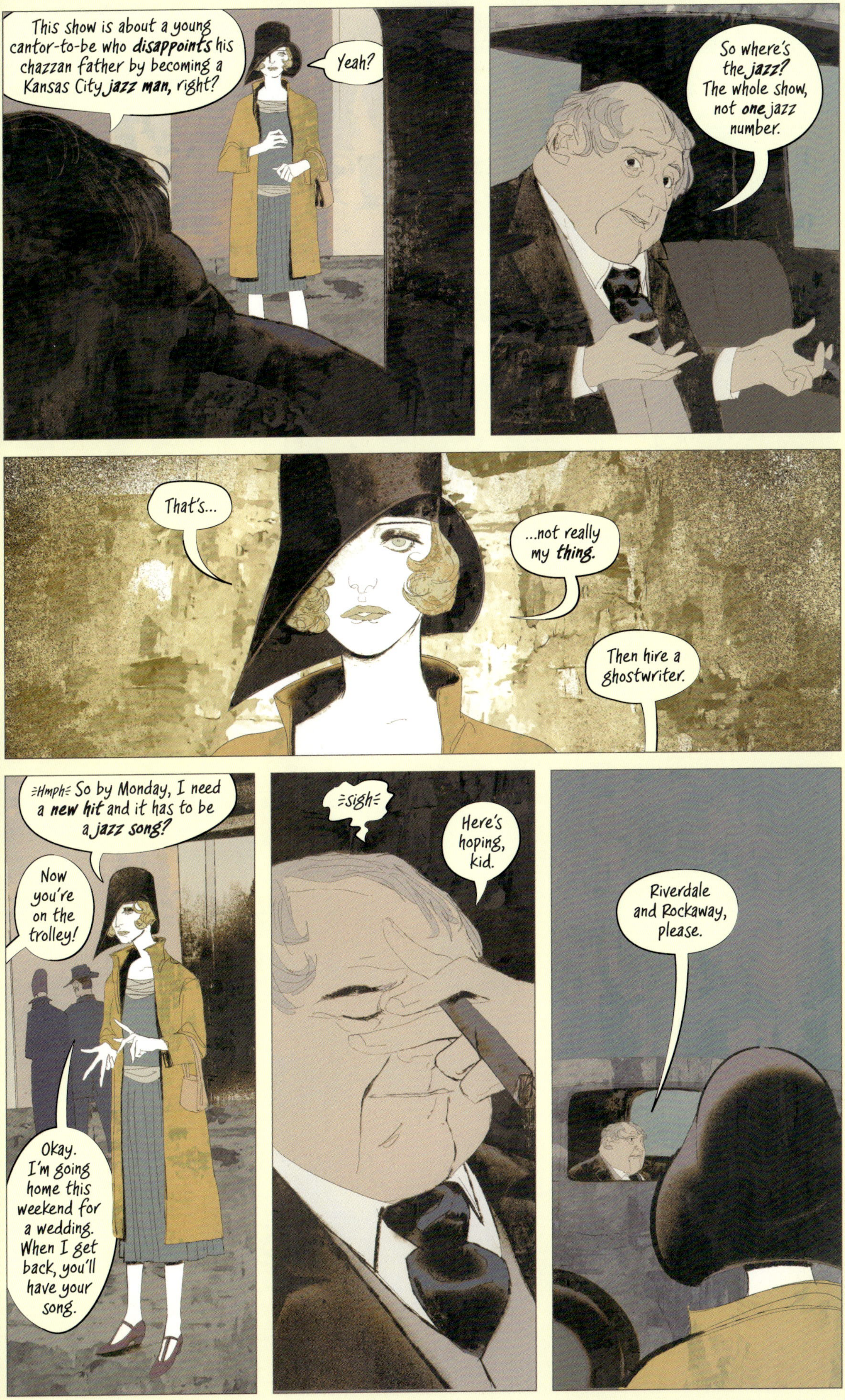
This show is about a young cantor-to-be who **disappoints** his chazzan father by becoming a Kansas City **jazz man,** right?
Yeah?
So where's the **jazz?** The whole show, not **one** jazz number.
That's...
...not really my **thing.**
Then hire a ghostwriter.
Hmph So by Monday, I need a **new hit** and it has to be a **jazz song?**
Now you're on the trolley!
Okay. I'm going home this weekend for a wedding. When I get back, you'll have your song.
sigh
Here's hoping, kid.
Riverdale and Rockaway, please.

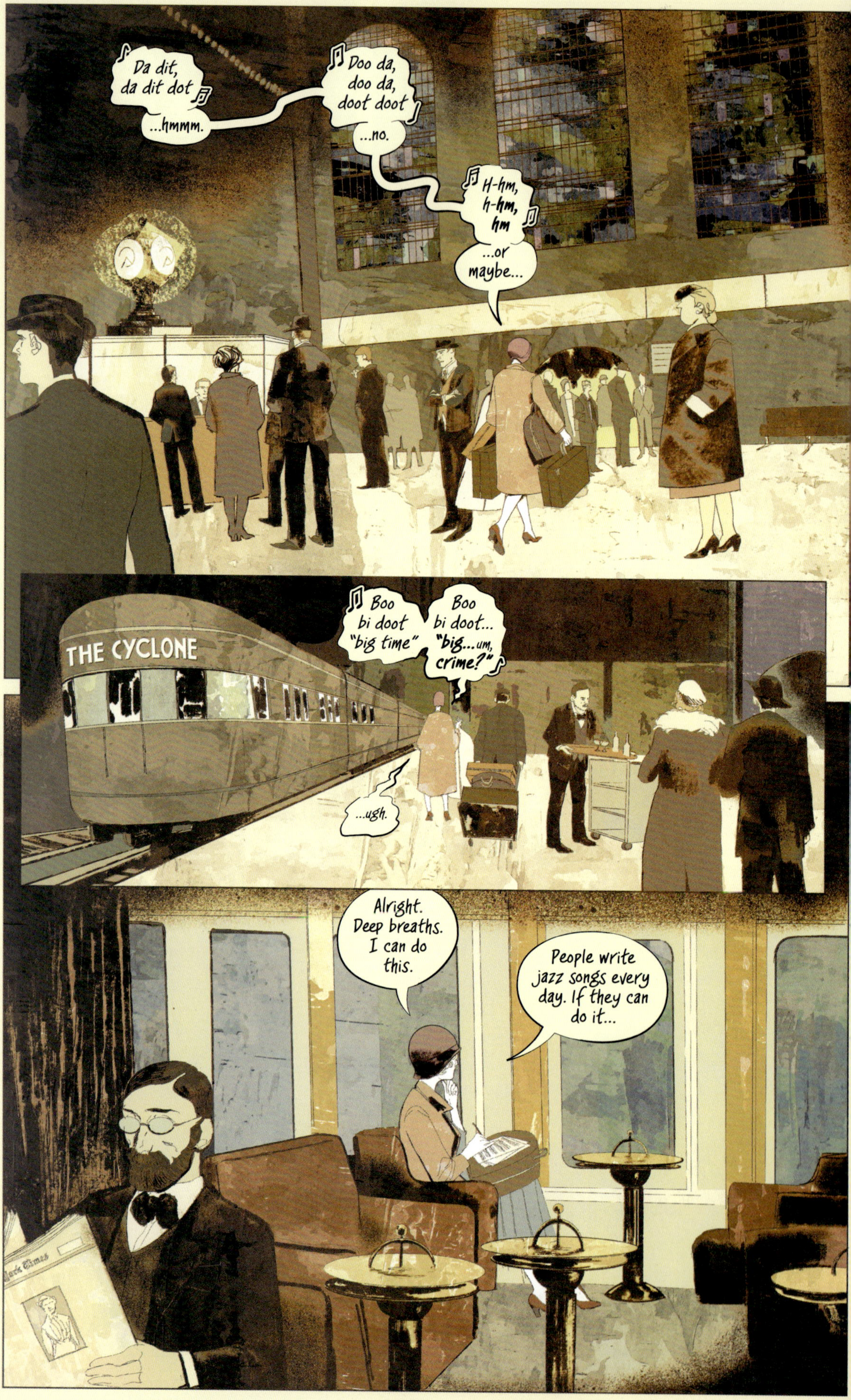

Da dit, da dit dot
...hmmm.
Doo da, doo da, doot doot
...no.
H-hm, h-hm, hm
...or maybe...
THE CYCLONE
Boo bi doot "big time"
Boo bi doot... "big...um, crime?"
...ugh.
Alright. Deep breaths. I can do this.
People write jazz songs every day. If they can do it...

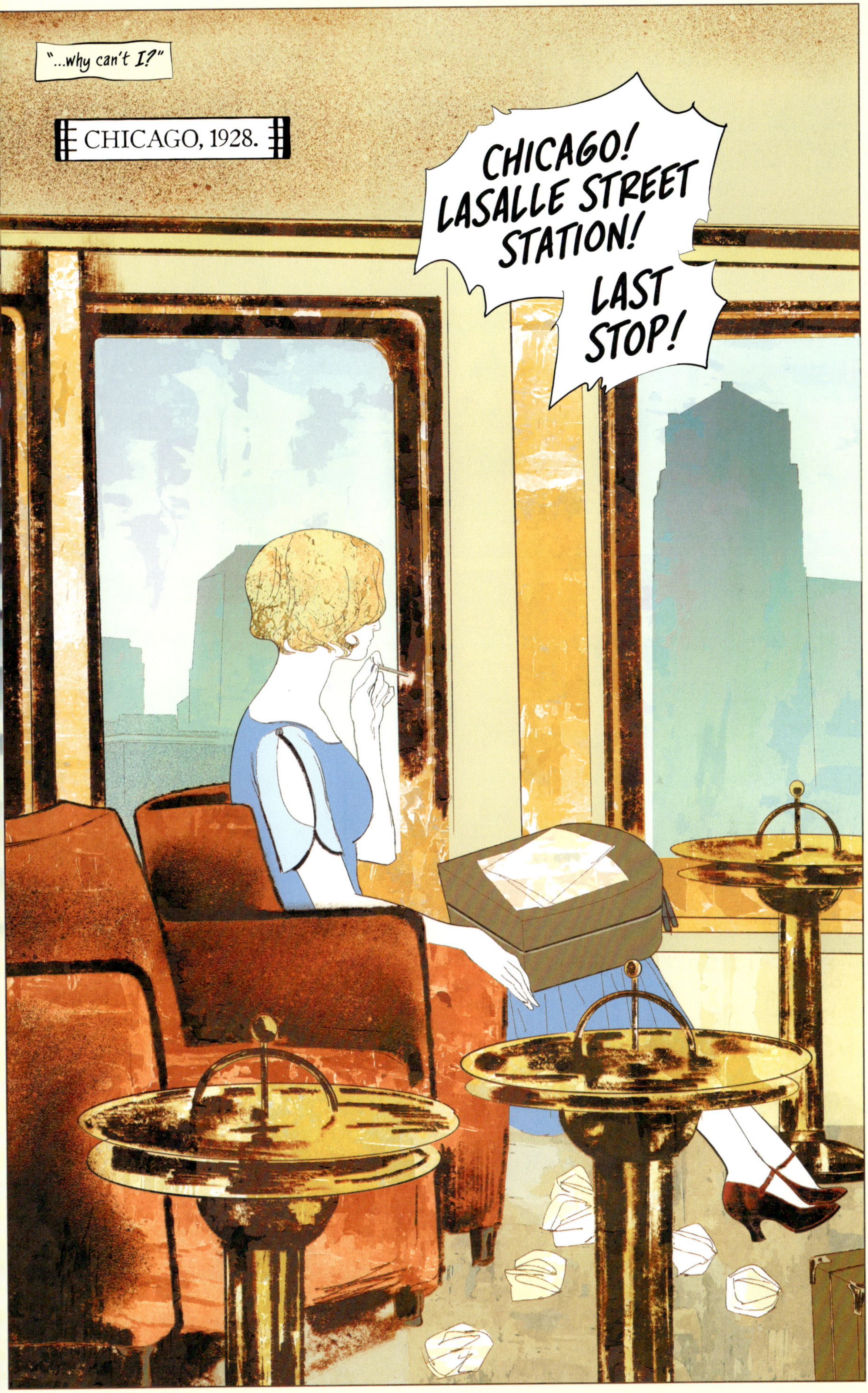
"...why can't I?"
CHICAGO, 1928.
CHICAGO! LASALLE STREET STATION!
LAST STOP!

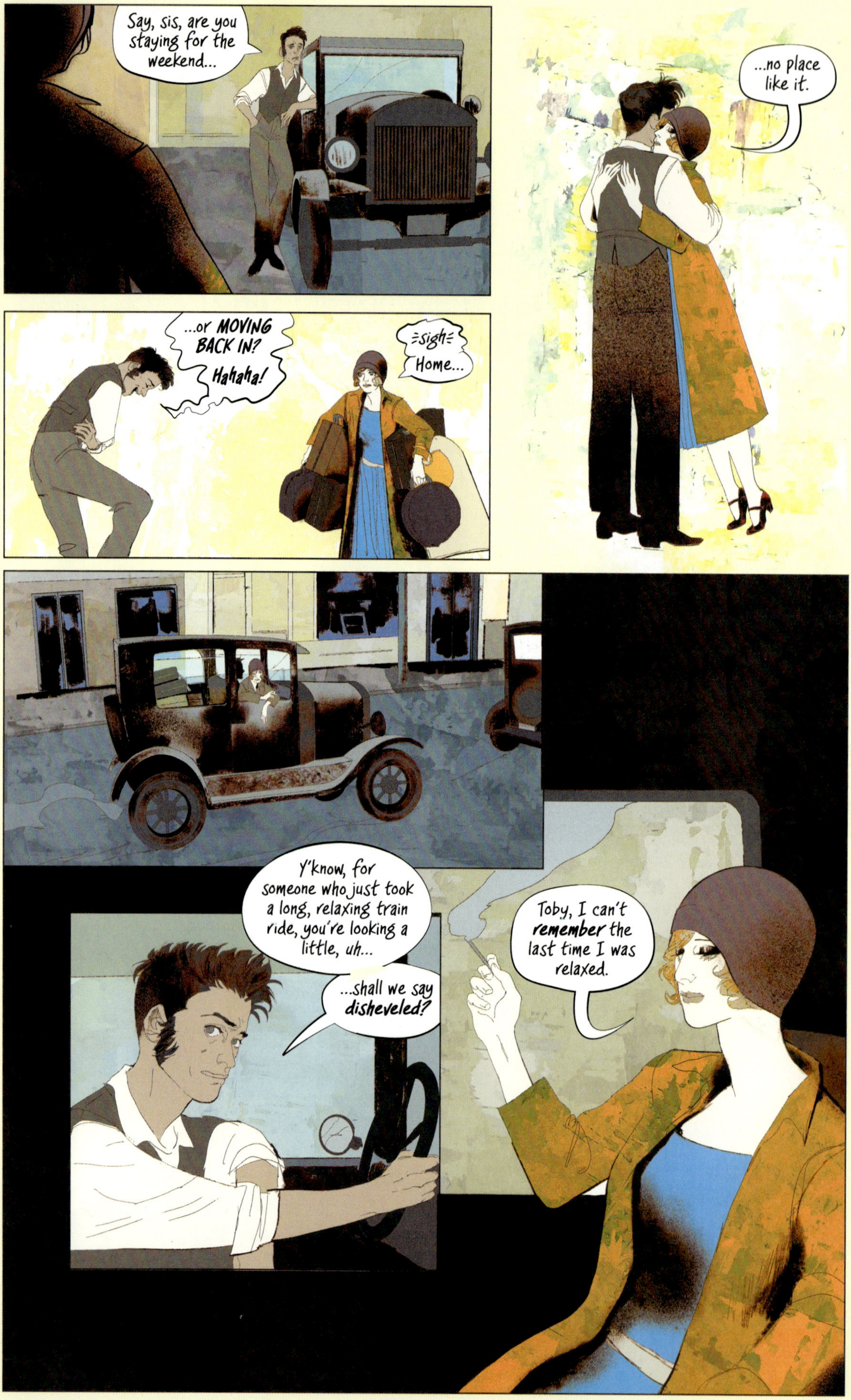
Say, sis, are you staying for the weekend...
...no place like it.
...or MOVING BACK IN?
Hahaha!
=sigh=
Home...
Y'know, for someone who just took a long, relaxing train ride, you're looking a little, uh...
...shall we say disheveled?
Toby, I can't remember the last time I was relaxed.

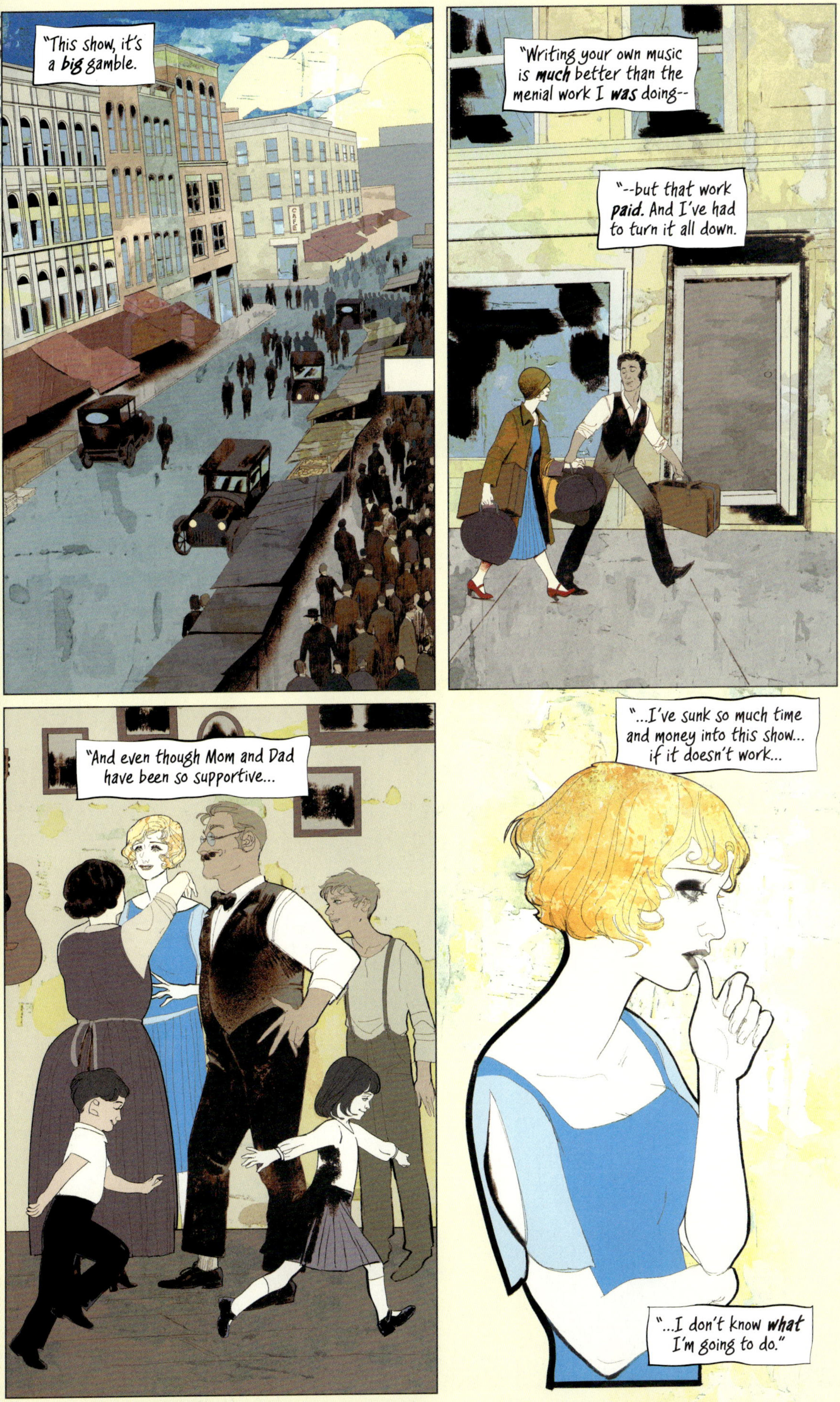
"This show, it's a **big** gamble.
"Writing your own music is **much** better than the menial work I **was** doing--
"--but that work **paid**. And I've had to turn it all down.
"And even though Mom and Dad have been so supportive...
"...I've sunk so much time and money into this show... if it doesn't work...
"...I don't know **what** I'm going to do."

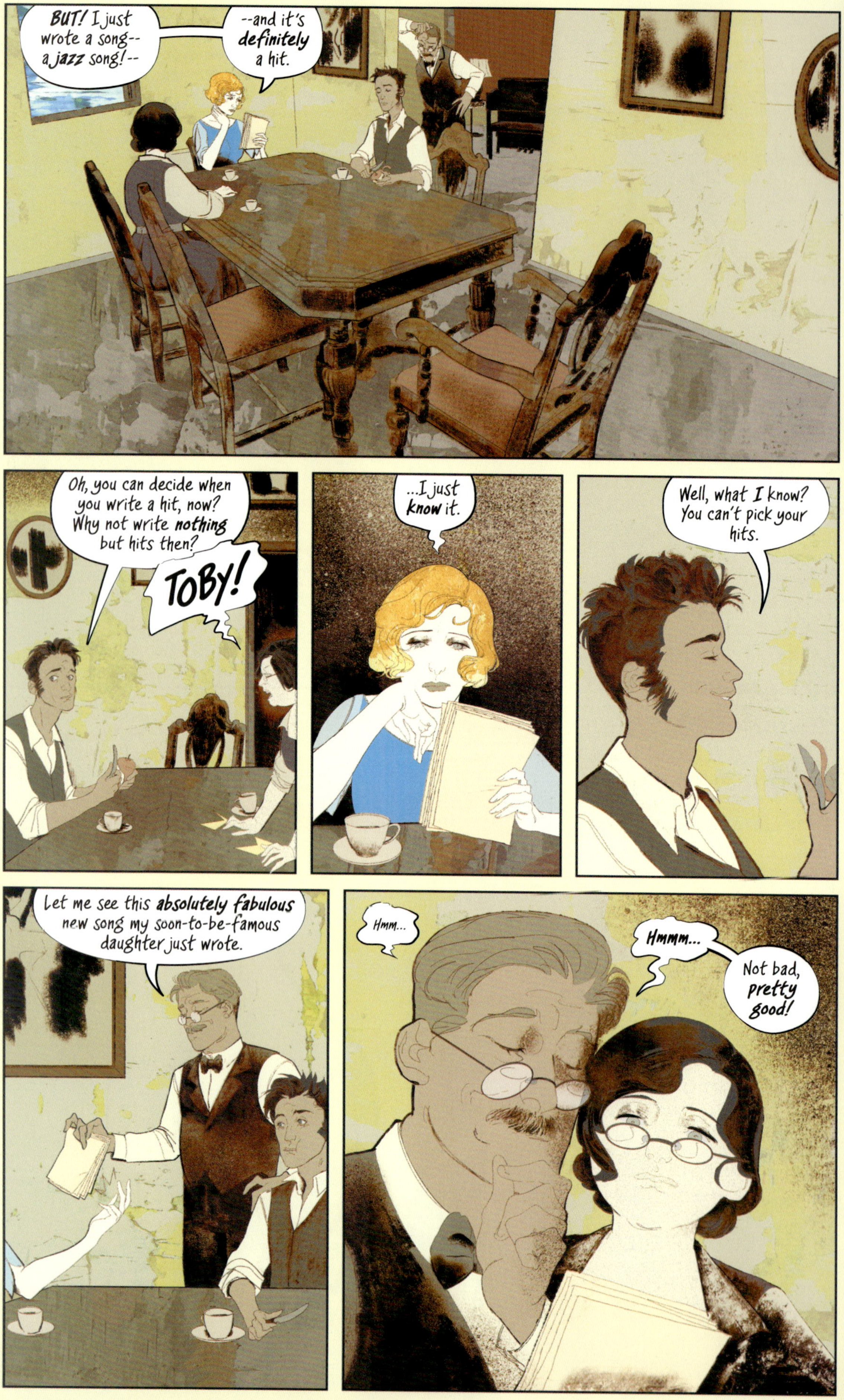
BUT! I just wrote a song-- a jazz song!--
--and it's definitely a hit.
Oh, you can decide when you write a hit, now? Why not write nothing but hits then?
TOBY!
...I just know it.
Well, what I know? You can't pick your hits.
Let me see this absolutely fabulous new song my soon-to-be-famous daughter just wrote.
Hmm...
Hmmm...
Not bad, pretty good!

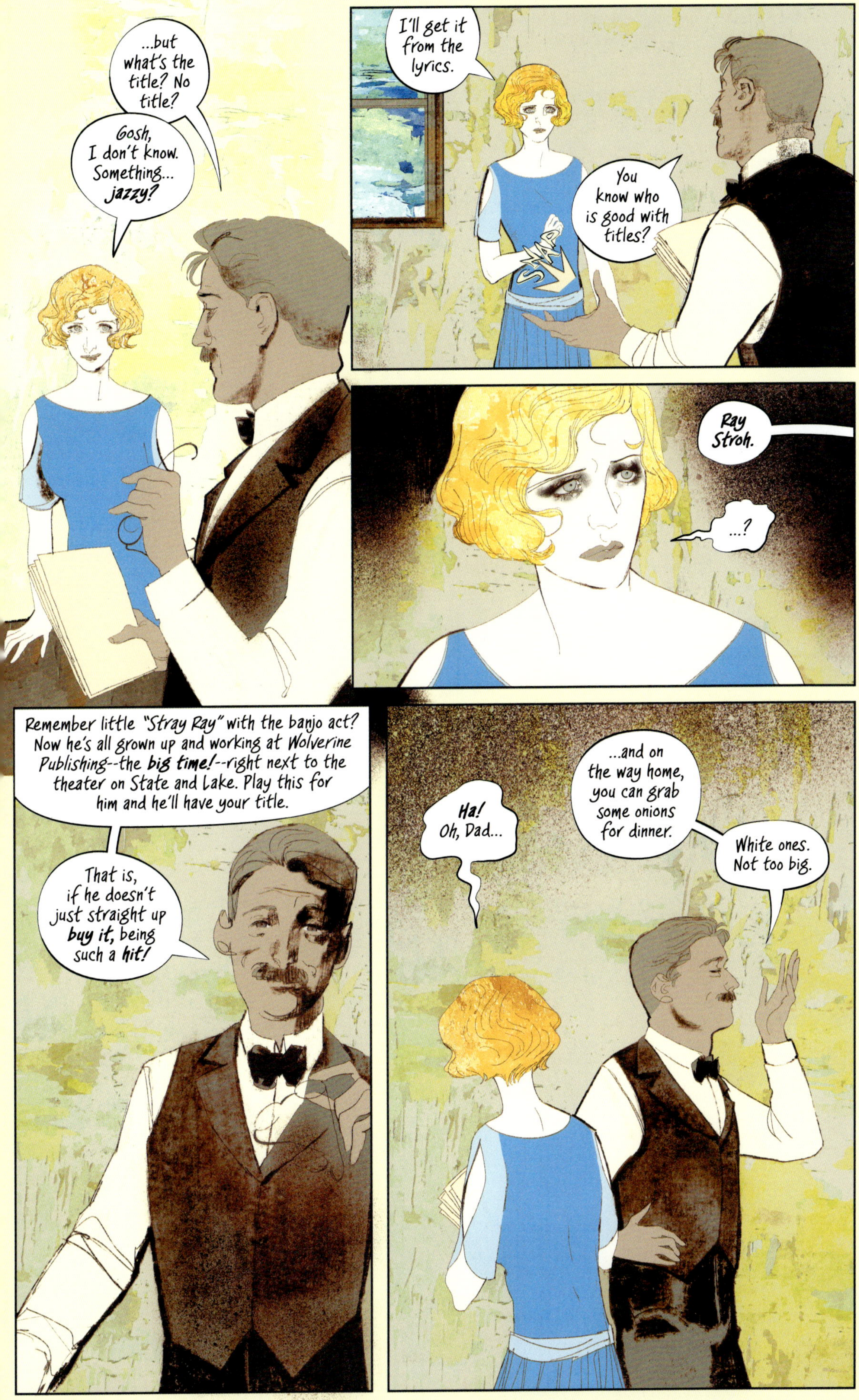
...but what's the title? No title?
Gosh, I don't know. Something... *jazzy?*
I'll get it from the lyrics.
You know who is good with titles?
Ray Stroh.
...?
Remember little "Stray Ray" with the banjo act? Now he's all grown up and working at Wolverine Publishing--the *big time!*--right next to the theater on State and Lake. Play this for him and he'll have your title.
That is, if he doesn't just straight up *buy it,* being such a *hit!*
...and on the way home, you can grab some onions for dinner.
Ha! Oh, Dad...
White ones. Not too big.

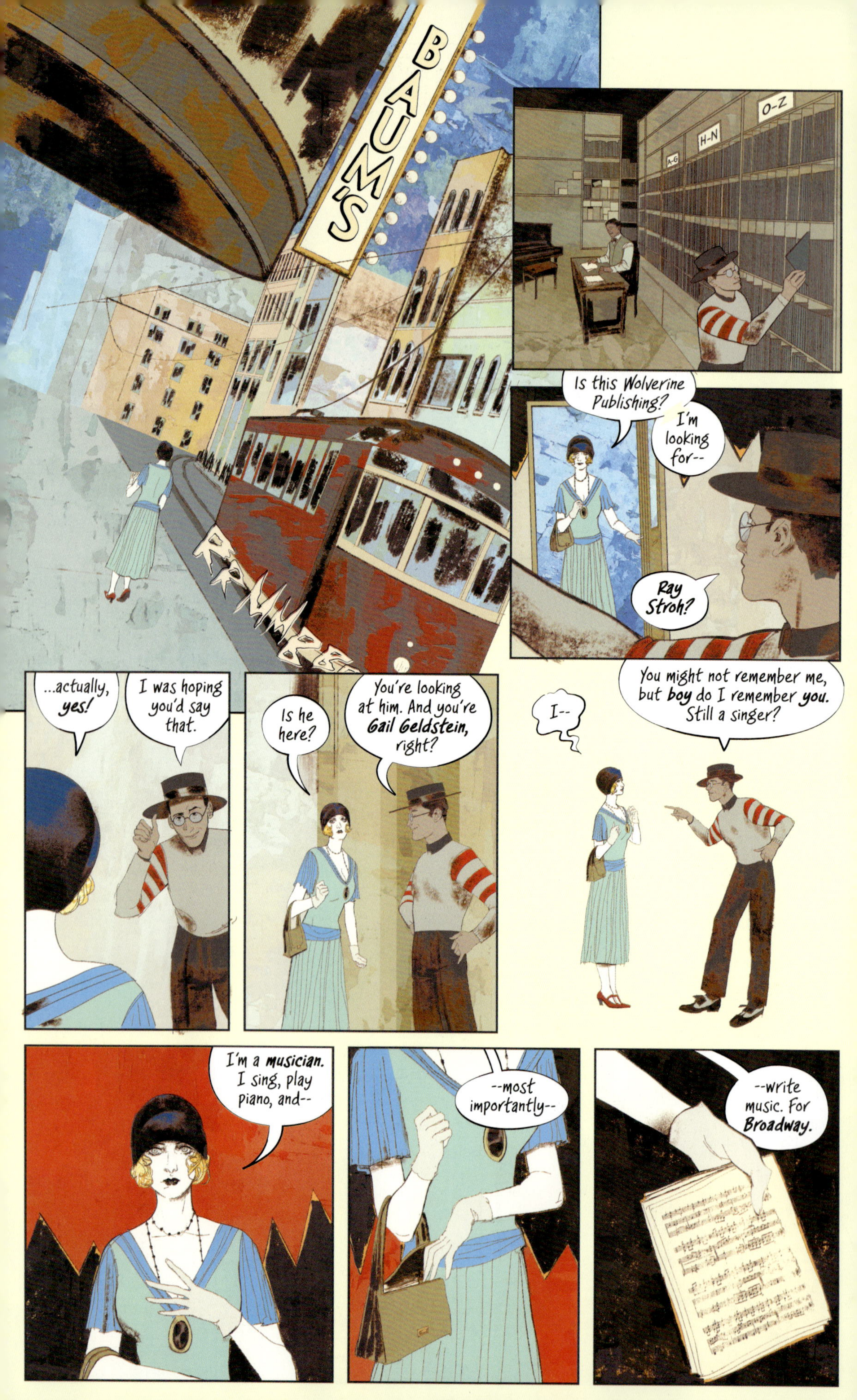
BAUM'S
O-Z
H-N
A-G
Is this Wolverine Publishing?
I'm looking for--
Ray Stroh?
...actually, yes!
I was hoping you'd say that.
Is he here?
You're looking at him. And you're Gail Geldstein, right?
I--
You might not remember me, but boy do I remember you. Still a singer?
I'm a musician. I sing, play piano, and--
--most importantly--
--write music. For Broadway.

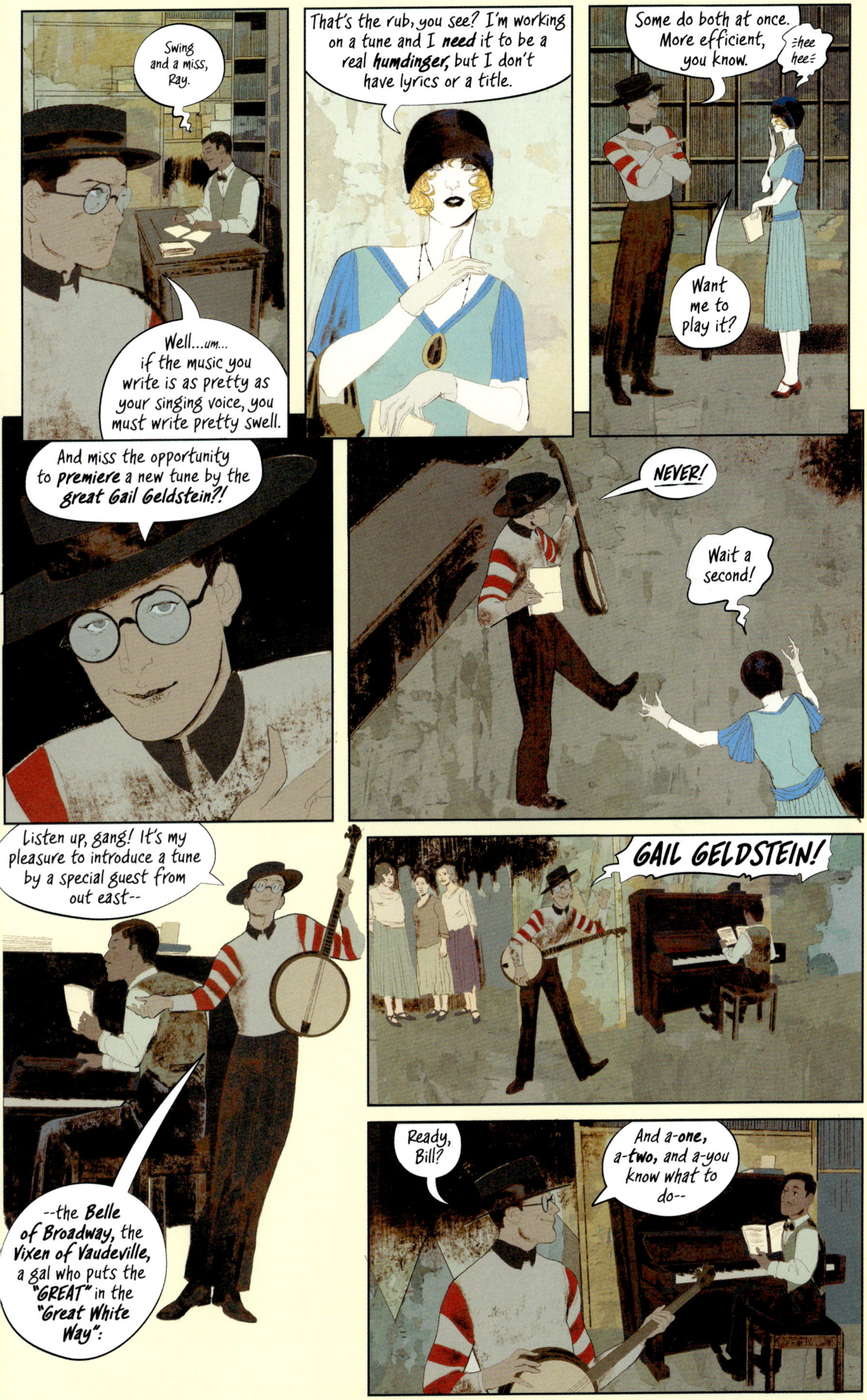
Swing and a miss, Ray.
Well...um... if the music you write is as pretty as your singing voice, you must write pretty swell.
That's the rub, you see? I'm working on a tune and I **need** it to be a real **humdinger,** but I don't have lyrics or a title.
Some do both at once. More efficient, you know.
hee hee
Want me to play it?
And miss the opportunity to **premiere** a new tune by the **great Gail Geldstein?!**
NEVER!
Wait a second!
Listen up, gang! It's my pleasure to introduce a tune by a special guest from out east--
--the **Belle of Broadway,** the **Vixen of Vaudeville,** a gal who puts the **"GREAT"** in the **"Great White Way":**
GAIL GELDSTEIN!
Ready, Bill?
And a-**one,** a-**two,** and a-you know what to do--

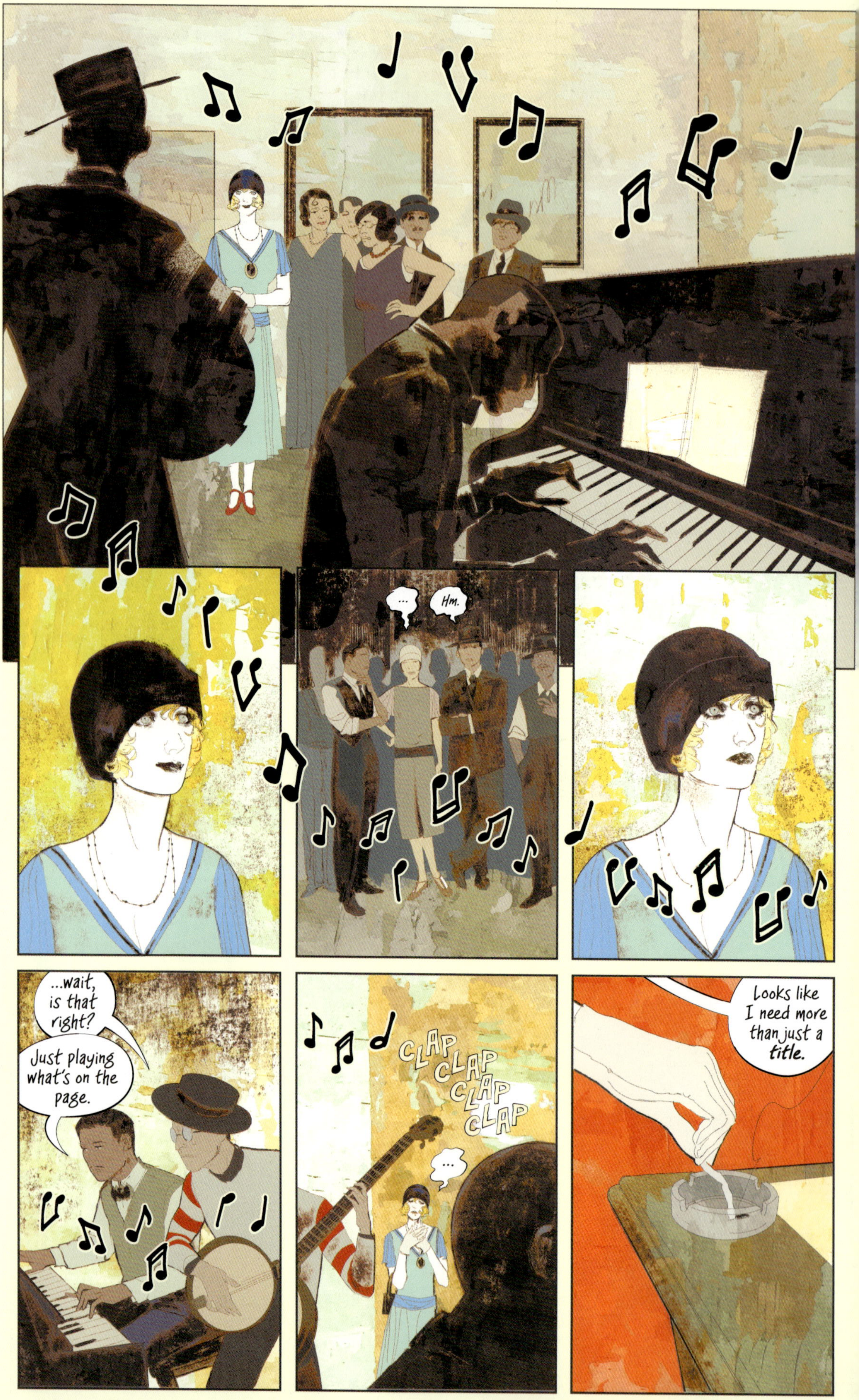
...
Hm.
...wait, is that right?
Just playing what's on the page.
CLAP CLAP CLAP CLAP
...
Looks like I need more than just a *title.*

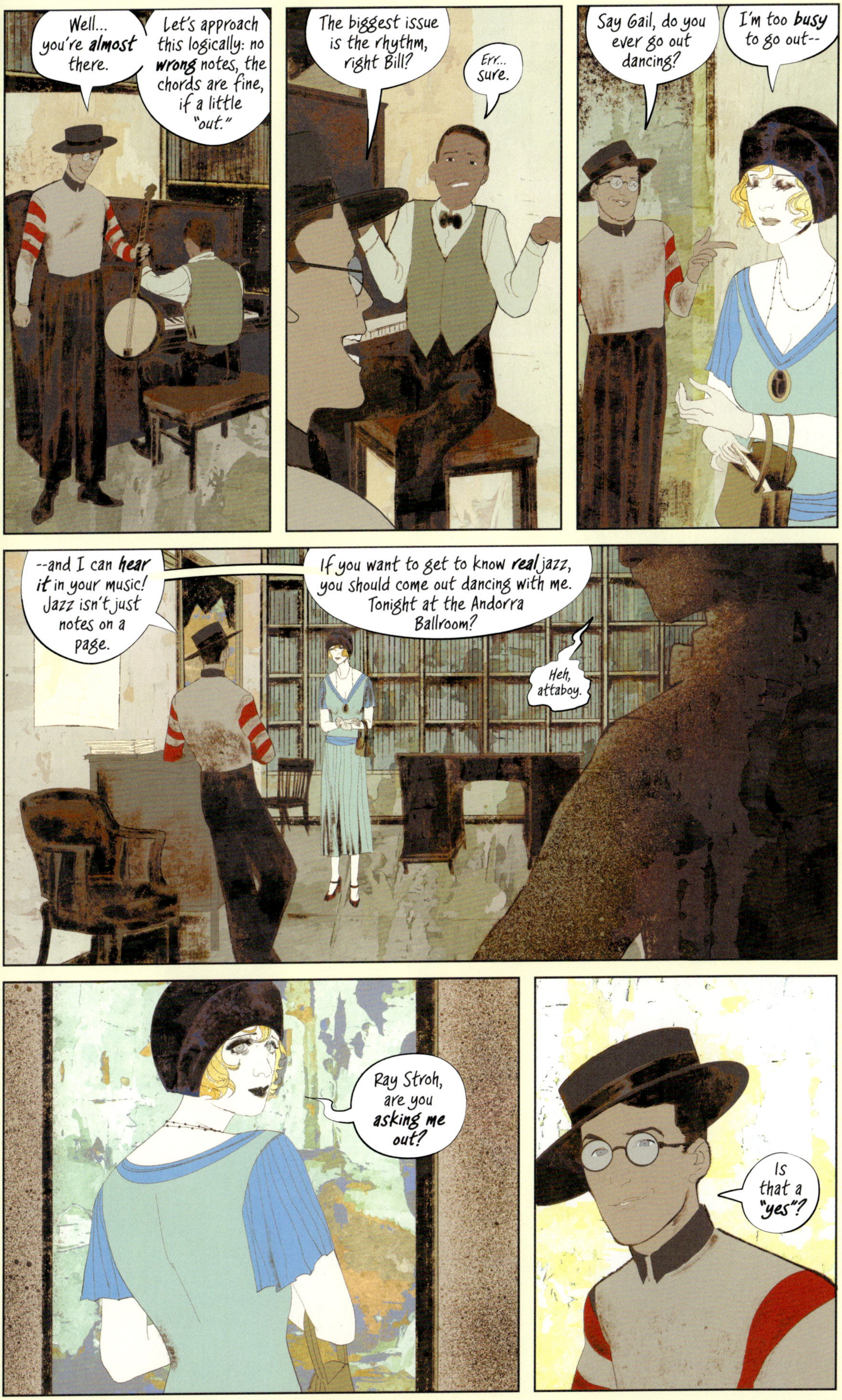
Well... you're **almost** there.
Let's approach this logically: no **wrong** notes, the chords are fine, if a little "out."
The biggest issue is the rhythm, right Bill?
Err... sure.
Say Gail, do you ever go out dancing?
I'm too **busy** to go out--
--and I can **hear it** in your music! Jazz isn't just notes on a page.
If you want to get to know **real** jazz, you should come out dancing with me. Tonight at the Andorra Ballroom?
Heh, attaboy.
Ray Stroh, are you **asking me out?**
Is that a **"yes"**?

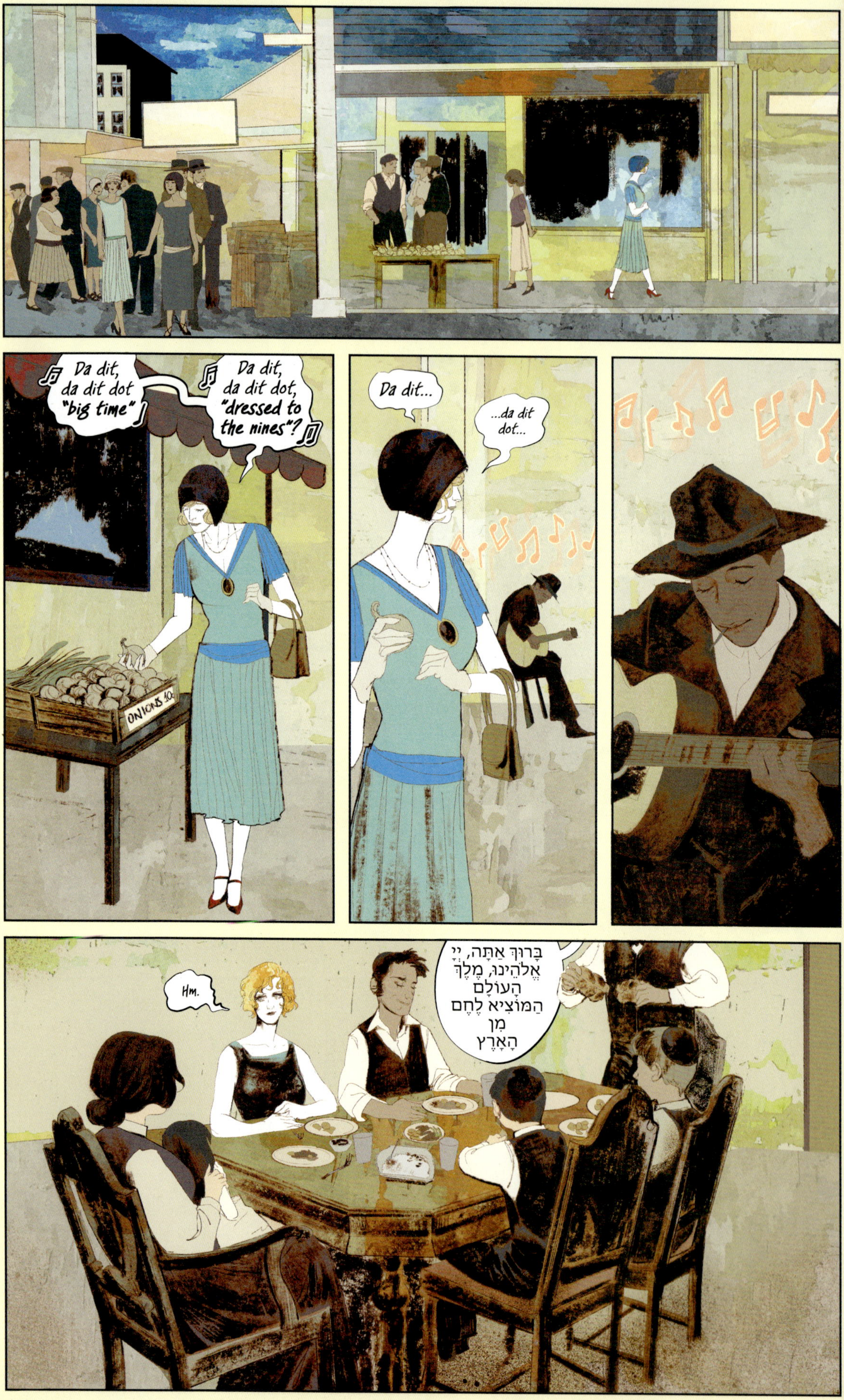
Da dit, da dit dot "big time"
Da dit, da dit dot, "dressed to the nines"?
ONIONS 10
Da dit...
...da dit dot...
Hm.
בָּרוּךְ אַתָּה, יְיָ אֱלֹהֵינוּ, מֶלֶךְ הָעוֹלָם הַמּוֹצִיא לֶחֶם מִן הָאָרֶץ

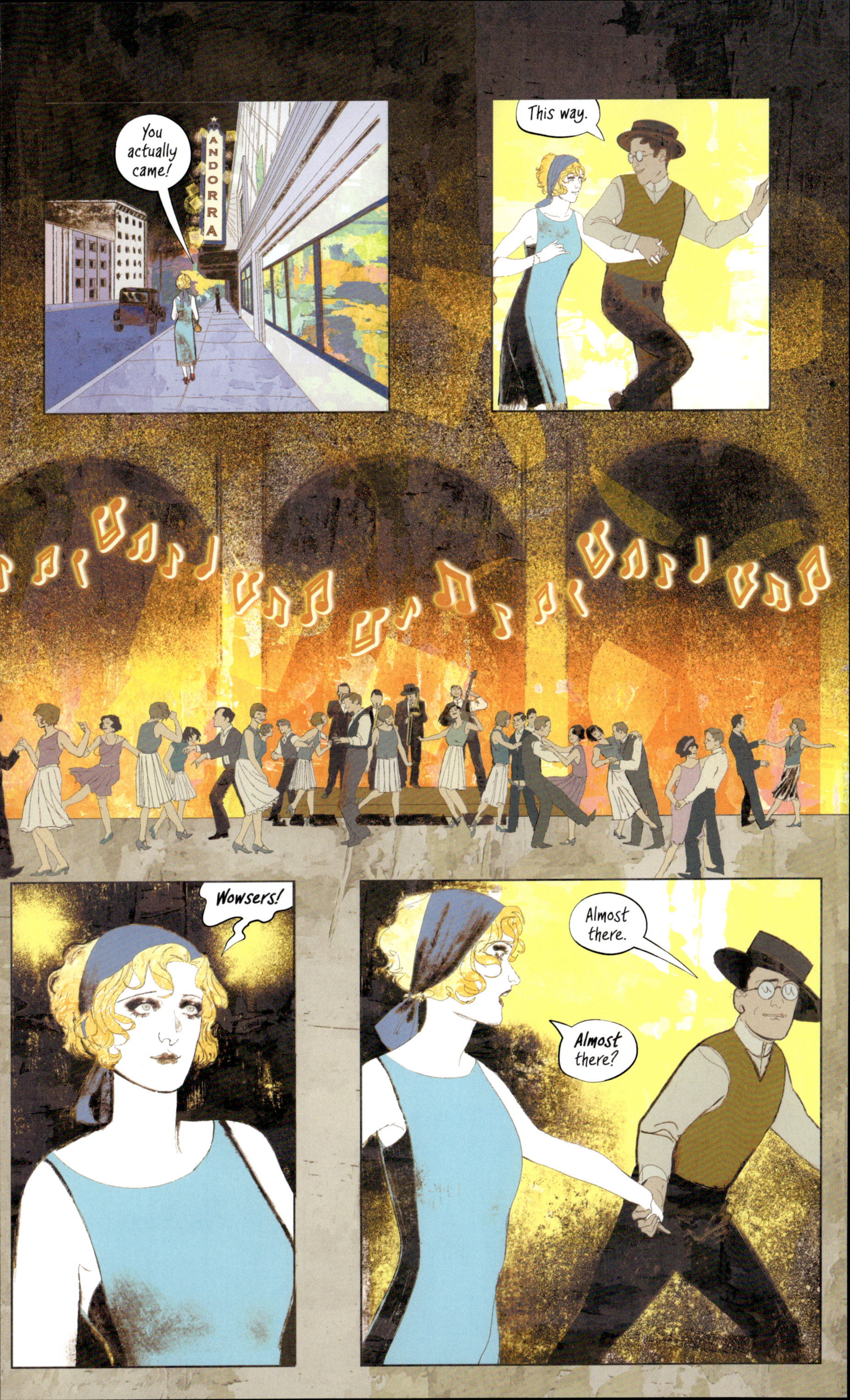
ANDORRA
You actually came!
This way.
Wowsers!
Almost there.
Almost there?

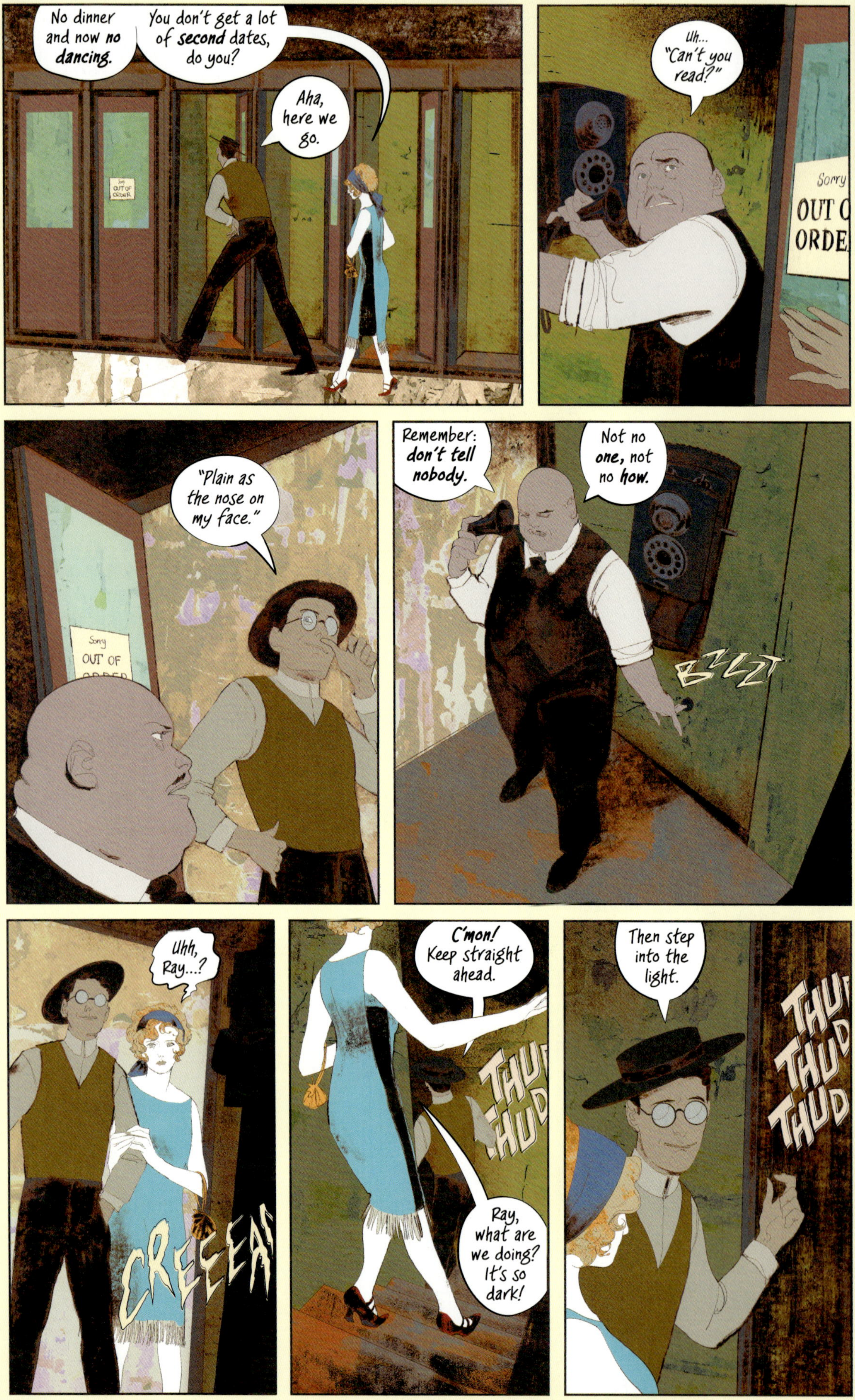
No dinner and now **no dancing.**
You don't get a lot of **second** dates, do you?
Aha, here we go.
Sorry OUT OF ORDER
Uh... "Can't you read?"
Sorry OUT O ORDE
"Plain as the nose on my face."
Sorry OUT OF ORDER
Remember: **don't tell nobody.**
Not no **one,** not no **how.**
BZZZT
Uhh, Ray...?
CREEEA
C'mon! Keep straight ahead.
THUD THUD
Ray, what are we doing? It's so dark!
Then step into the light.
THUD THUD THUD

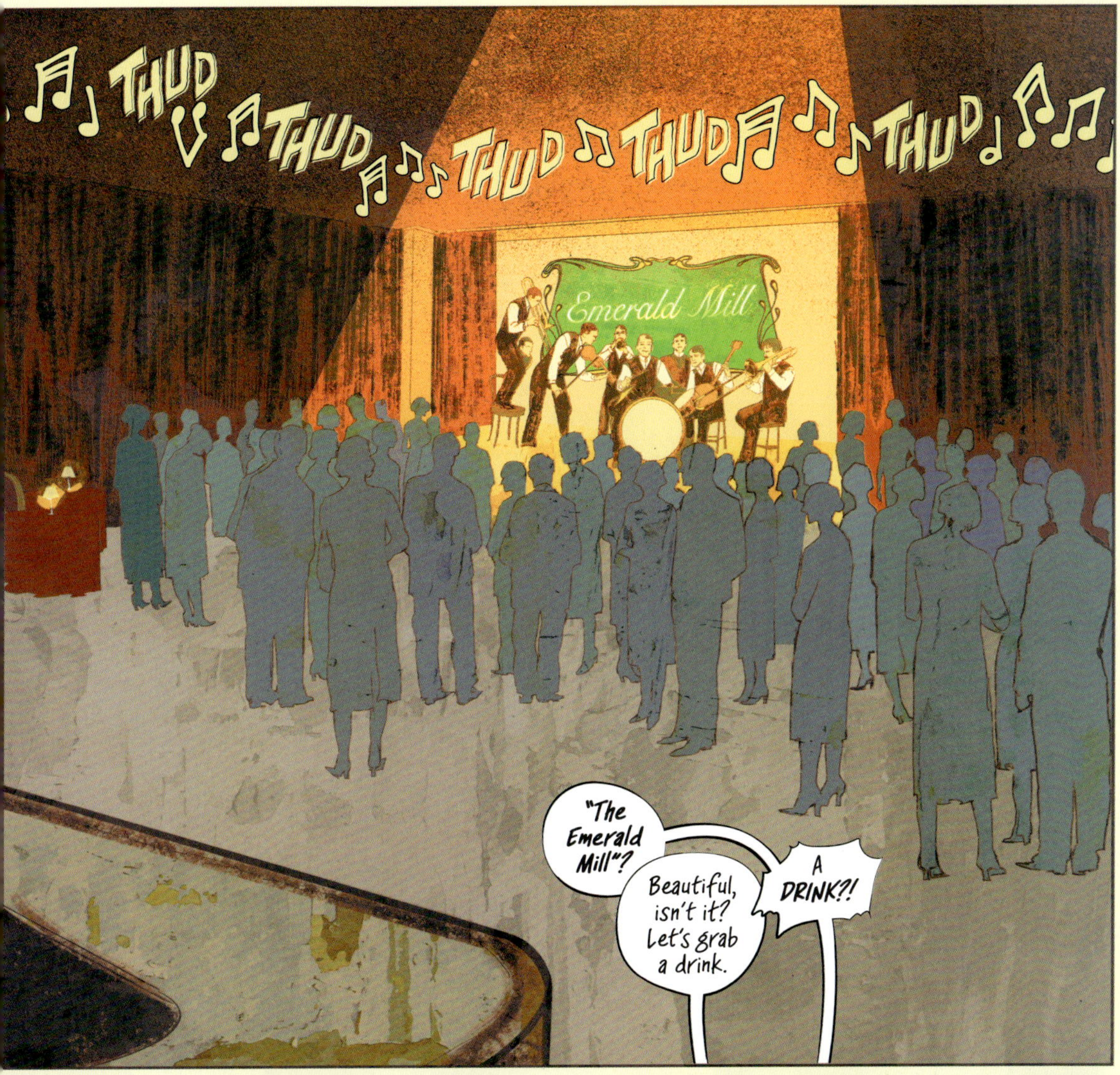
THUD THUD THUD THUD THUD
Emerald Mill
"The Emerald Mill"?
Beautiful, isn't it? Let's grab a drink.
A DRINK?!

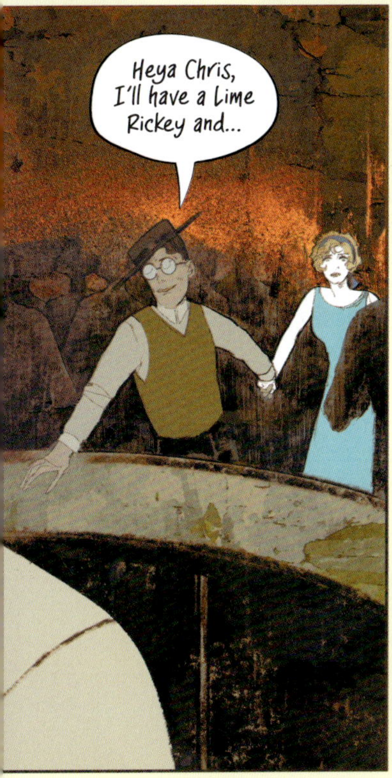
Heya Chris, I'll have a Lime Rickey and...

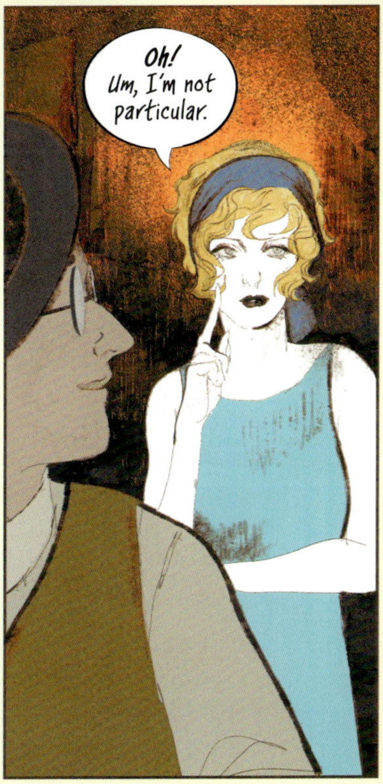
Oh! Um, I'm not particular.

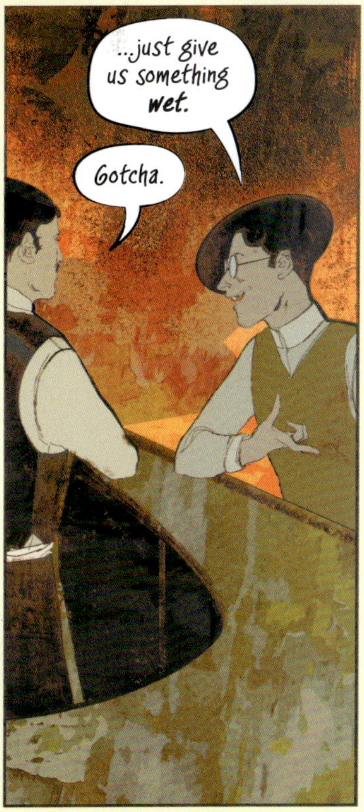
...just give us something wet.
Gotcha.

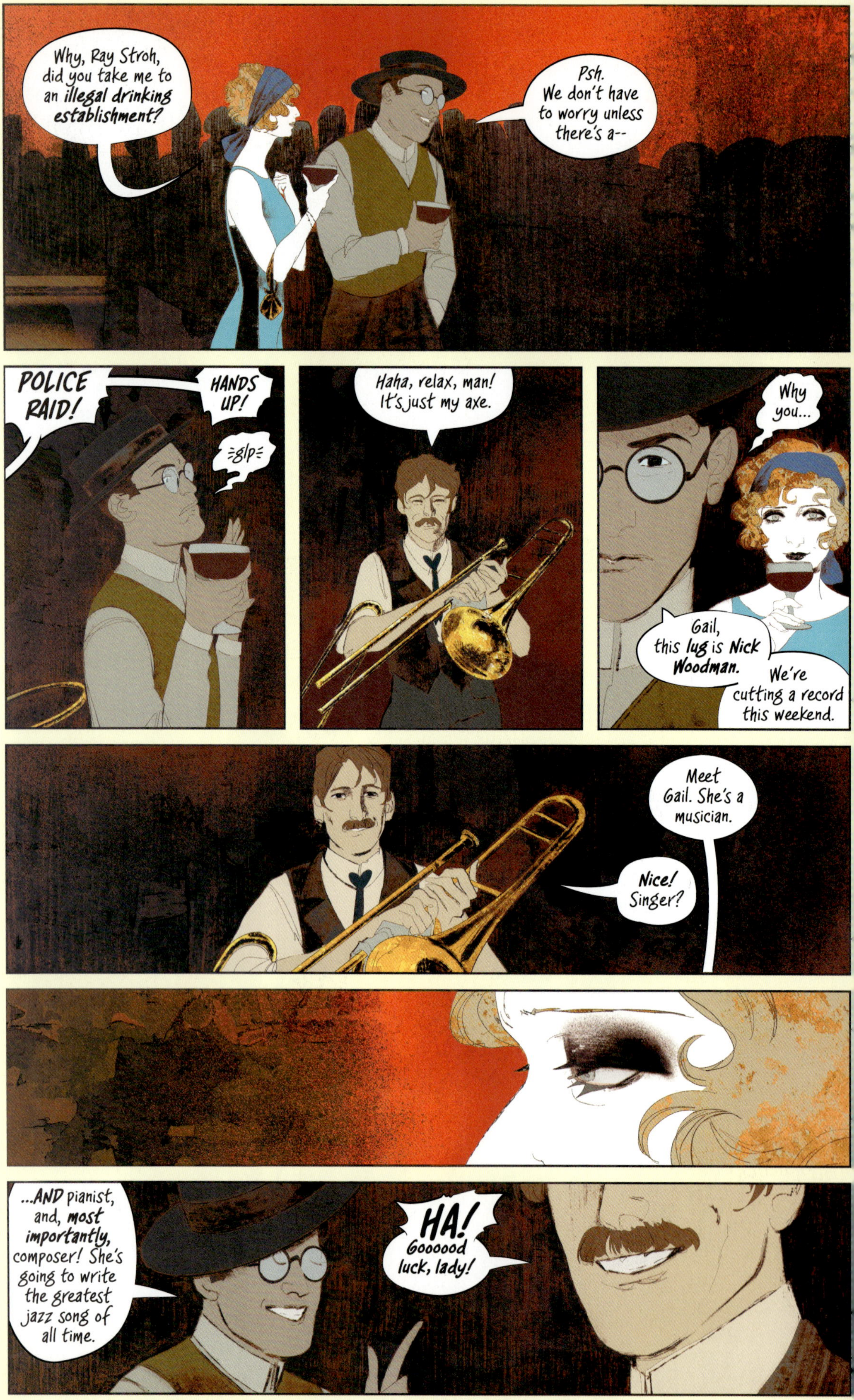
Why, Ray Stroh, did you take me to an illegal drinking establishment?
Psh. We don't have to worry unless there's a--
POLICE RAID!
HANDS UP!
glp
Haha, relax, man! It's just my axe.
Why you...
Gail, this lug is Nick Woodman.
We're cutting a record this weekend.
Meet Gail. She's a musician.
Nice! Singer?
...AND pianist, and, most importantly, composer! She's going to write the greatest jazz song of all time.
HA! Goooood luck, lady!

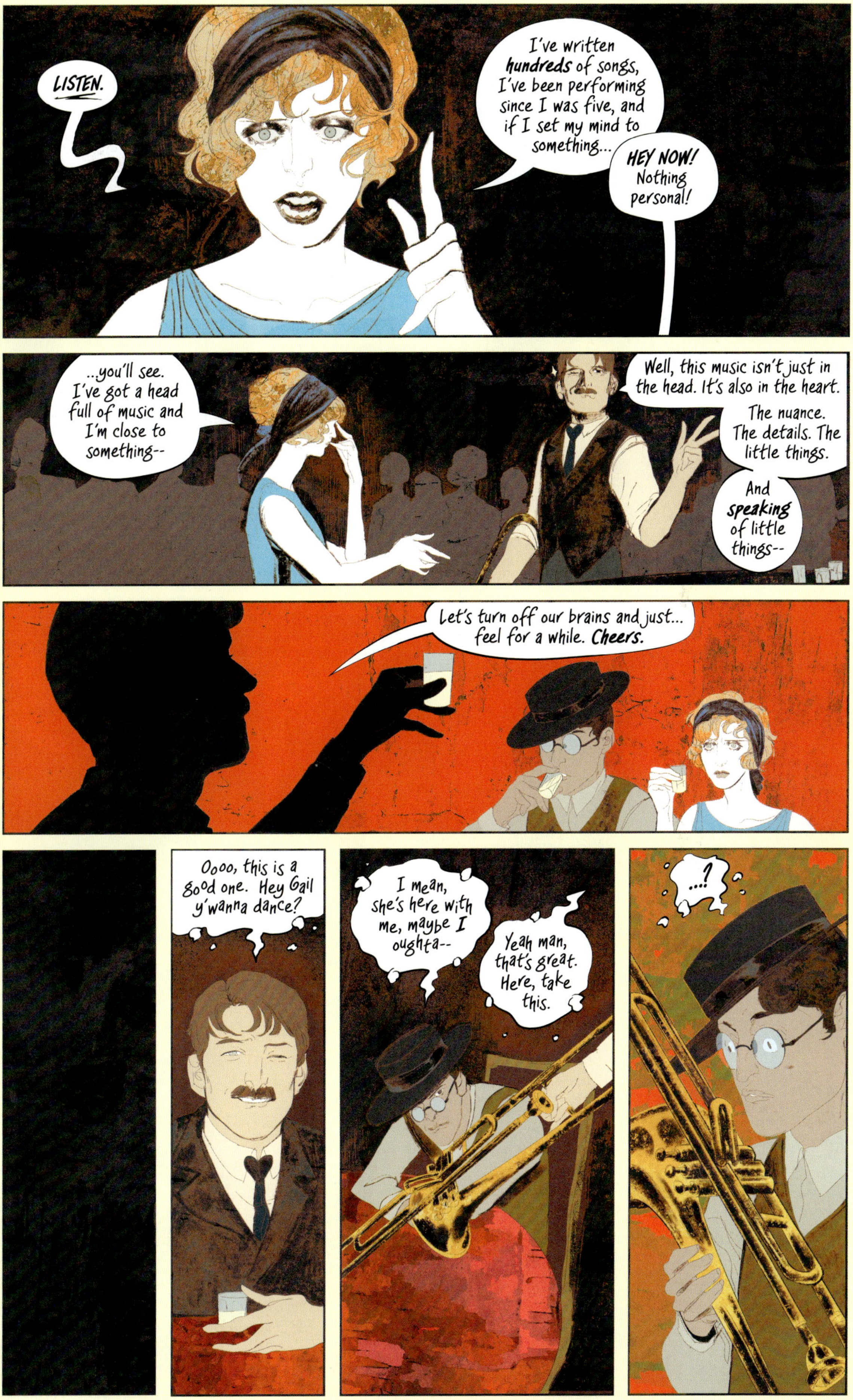

LISTEN.
I've written **hundreds** of songs, I've been performing since I was five, and if I set my mind to something...
HEY NOW! Nothing personal!
...you'll see. I've got a head full of music and I'm close to something--
Well, this music isn't just in the head. It's also in the heart.
The nuance. The details. The little things.
And **speaking** of little things--
Let's turn off our brains and just... feel for a while. **Cheers.**
Oooo, this is a good one. Hey Gail y'wanna dance?
I mean, she's here with me, maybe I oughta--
Yeah man, that's great. Here, take this.
...?

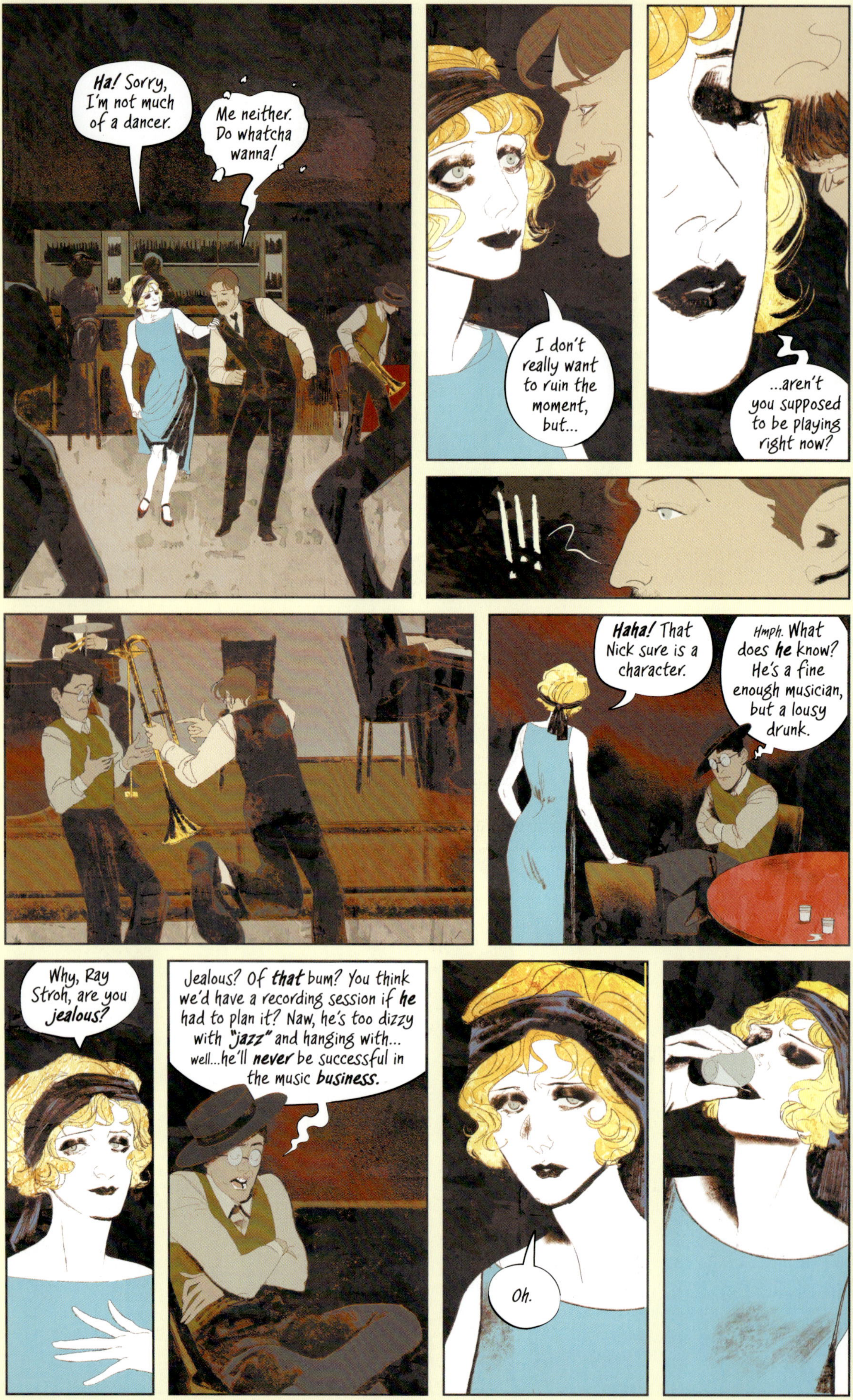
Ha! Sorry, I'm not much of a dancer.
Me neither. Do whatcha wanna!
I don't really want to ruin the moment, but...
...aren't you supposed to be playing right now?
!!!
Haha! That Nick sure is a character.
Hmph. What does he know? He's a fine enough musician, but a lousy drunk.
Why, Ray Stroh, are you jealous?
Jealous? Of that bum? You think we'd have a recording session if he had to plan it? Naw, he's too dizzy with "jazz" and hanging with... well...he'll never be successful in the music business.
Oh.

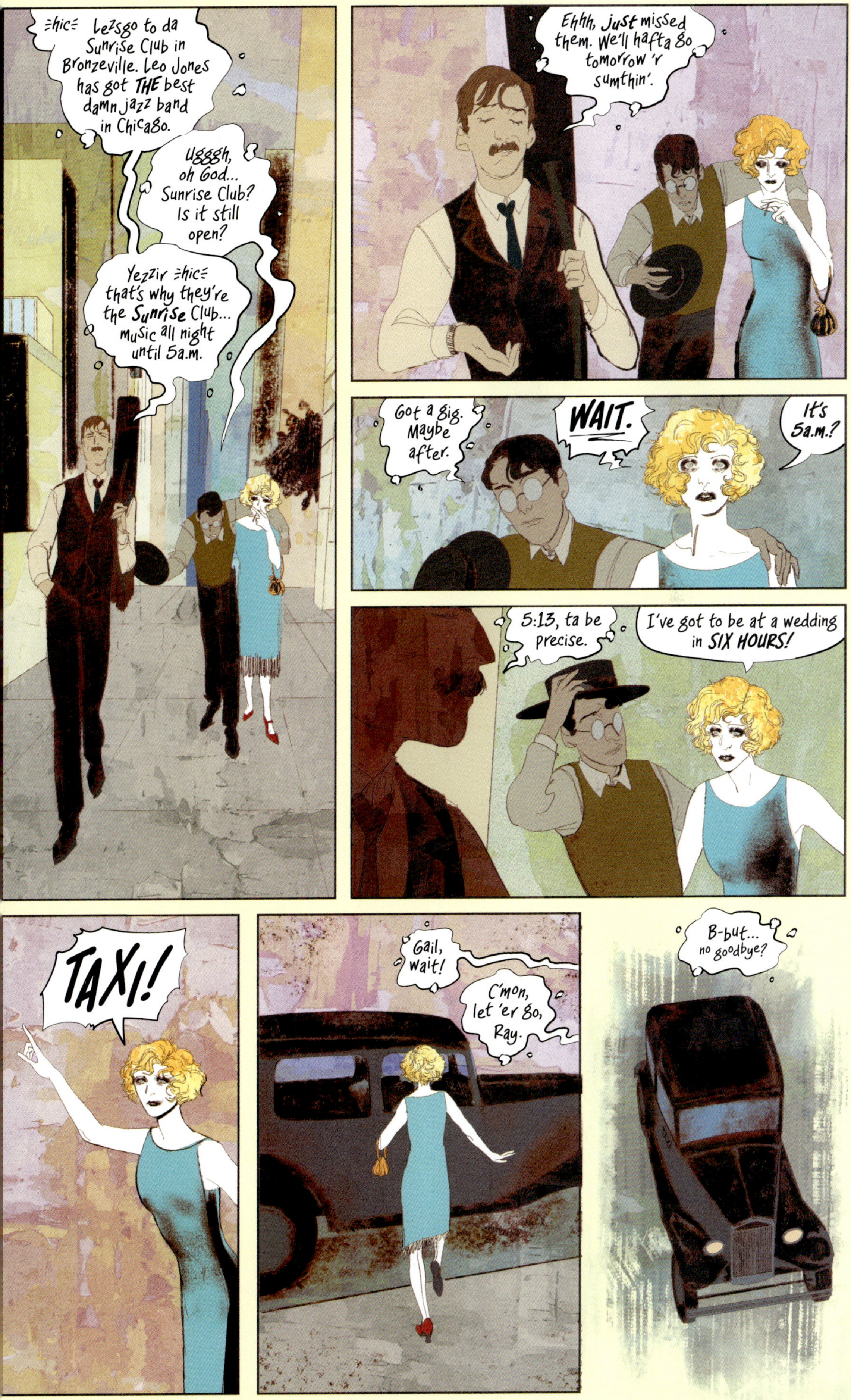

=hic= Lezsgo to da Sunrise Club in Bronzeville. Leo Jones has got THE best damn jazz band in Chicago.
Ugggh, oh God... Sunrise Club? Is it still open?
Yezzir =hic= that's why they're the Sunrise Club... music all night until 5a.m.
Ehhh, just missed them. We'll hafta go tomorrow 'r sumthin'.
Got a gig. Maybe after.
WAIT.
It's 5a.m.?
5:13, ta be precise.
I've got to be at a wedding in SIX HOURS!
TAXI!
Gail, wait!
C'mon, let 'er go, Ray.
B-but... no goodbye?

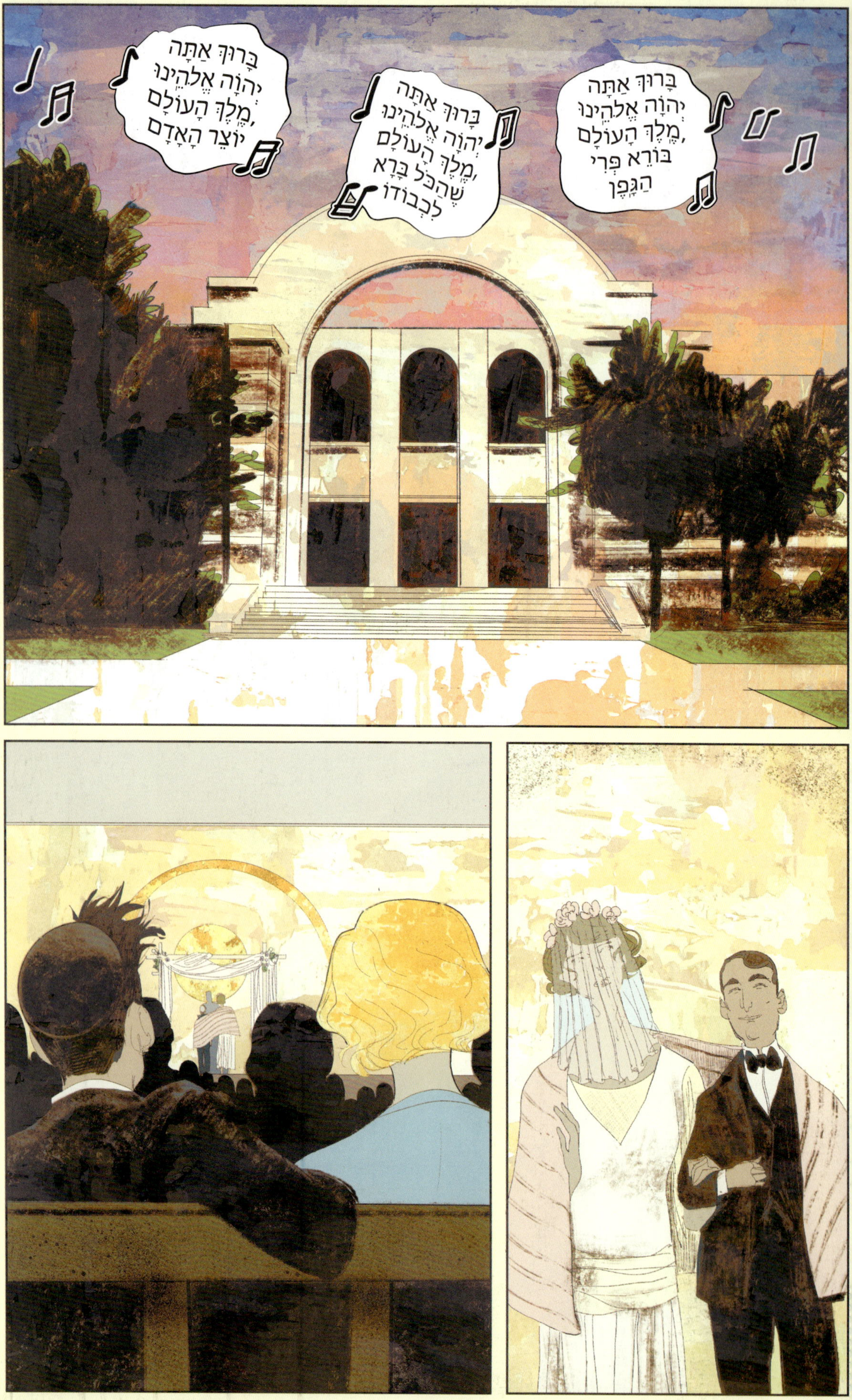
בָּרוּךְ אַתָּה יְהֹוָה אֱלֹהֵינוּ מֶלֶךְ הָעוֹלָם, בּוֹרֵא פְּרִי הַגָּפֶן
בָּרוּךְ אַתָּה יְהֹוָה אֱלֹהֵינוּ מֶלֶךְ הָעוֹלָם, שֶׁהַכֹּל בָּרָא לִכְבוֹדוֹ
בָּרוּךְ אַתָּה יְהֹוָה אֱלֹהֵינוּ מֶלֶךְ הָעוֹלָם, יוֹצֵר הָאָדָם

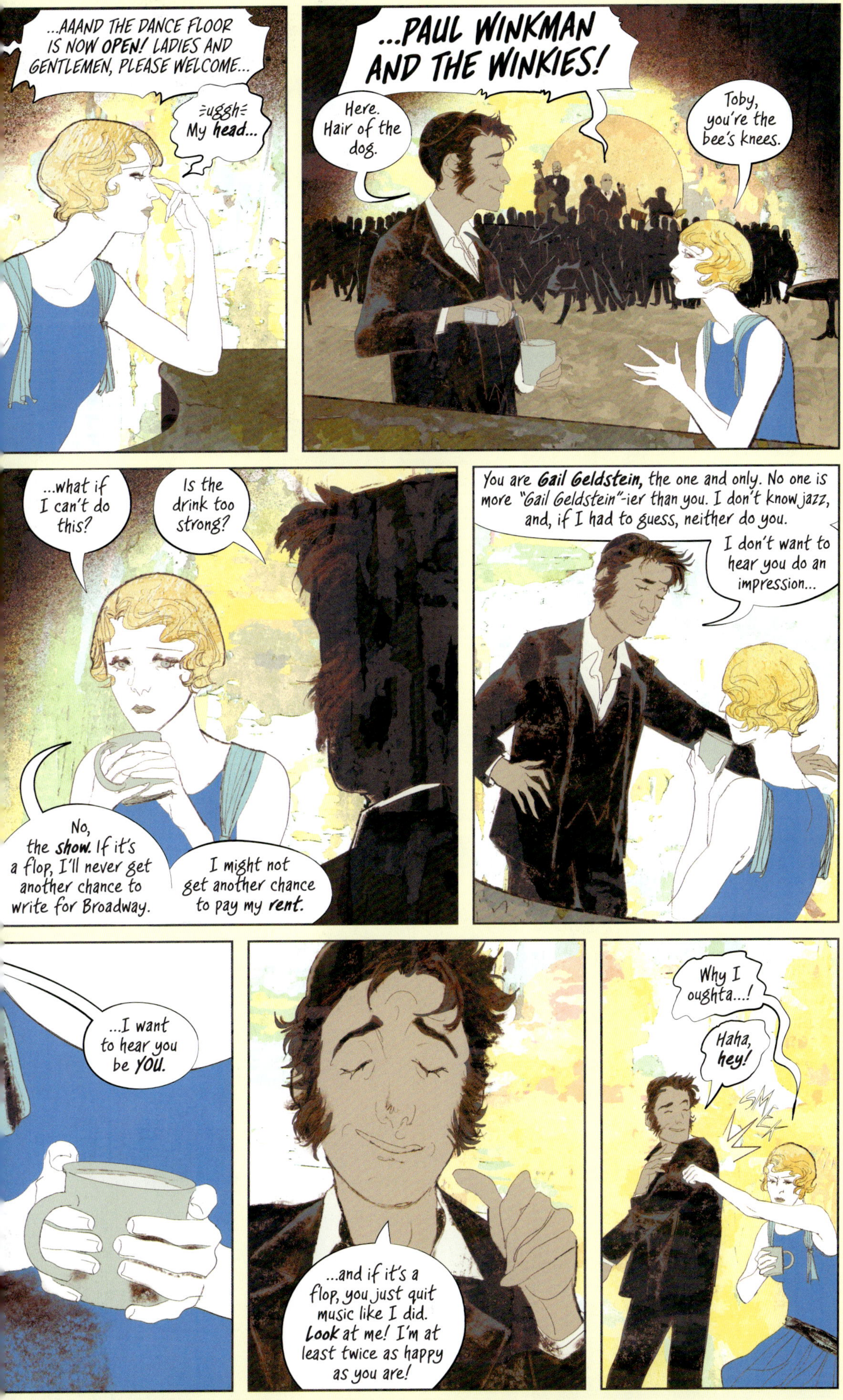
...AAAND THE DANCE FLOOR IS NOW OPEN! LADIES AND GENTLEMEN, PLEASE WELCOME...
ugghh My head...
...PAUL WINKMAN AND THE WINKIES!
Here. Hair of the dog.
Toby, you're the bee's knees.
...what if I can't do this?
Is the drink too strong?
No, the show. If it's a flop, I'll never get another chance to write for Broadway.
I might not get another chance to pay my rent.
You are Gail Geldstein, the one and only. No one is more "Gail Geldstein"-ier than you. I don't know jazz, and, if I had to guess, neither do you.
I don't want to hear you do an impression...
...I want to hear you be YOU.
...and if it's a flop, you just quit music like I did. Look at me! I'm at least twice as happy as you are!
Why I oughta...!
Haha, hey!
SMACK

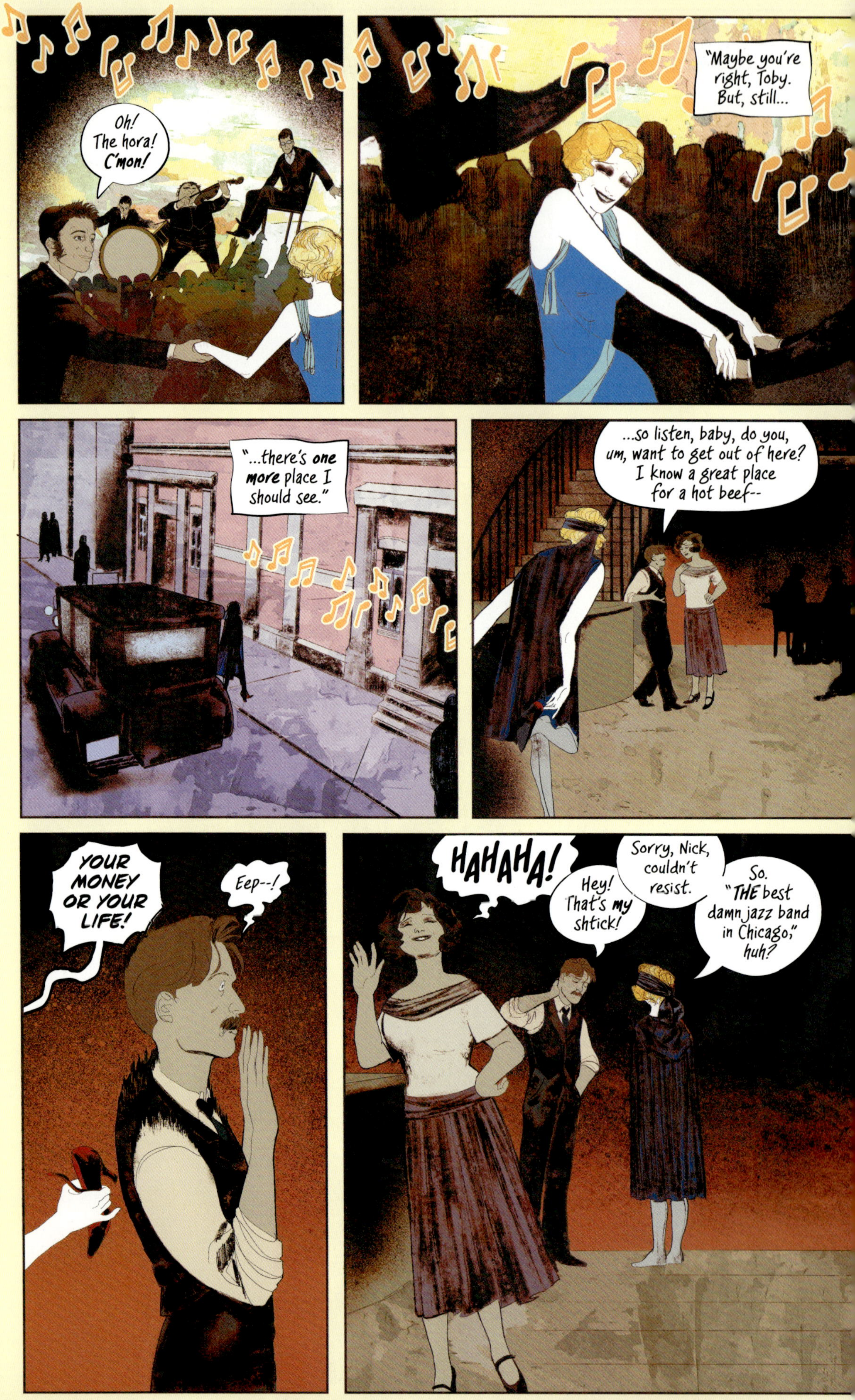
Oh! The hora! C'mon!
"Maybe you're right, Toby. But, still...
"...there's one more place I should see."
...so listen, baby, do you, um, want to get out of here? I know a great place for a hot beef--
YOUR MONEY OR YOUR LIFE!
Eep--!
HAHAHA!
Hey! That's my shtick!
Sorry, Nick, couldn't resist.
So. "THE best damn jazz band in Chicago," huh?

Oh yeah, the Sunrise has always had hot music, but these guys have got to be the most interesting combination in the whole city.

Tommy Johnson, that's the drummer, he came up from New Orleans in, when was it, '21? '2—

Whenever it was, he used to work in the Pullman factory during the day and then head up "The troll" to sit in with whatever band sounded hot. You do that enough

…the star of the show? Leonard "Leo". Also from… first time I saw him, my jaw dropped.

Now the bass player, he's a local yokel. Homer? I think he's named Homer. Anyway…

HEY! No goodbye?

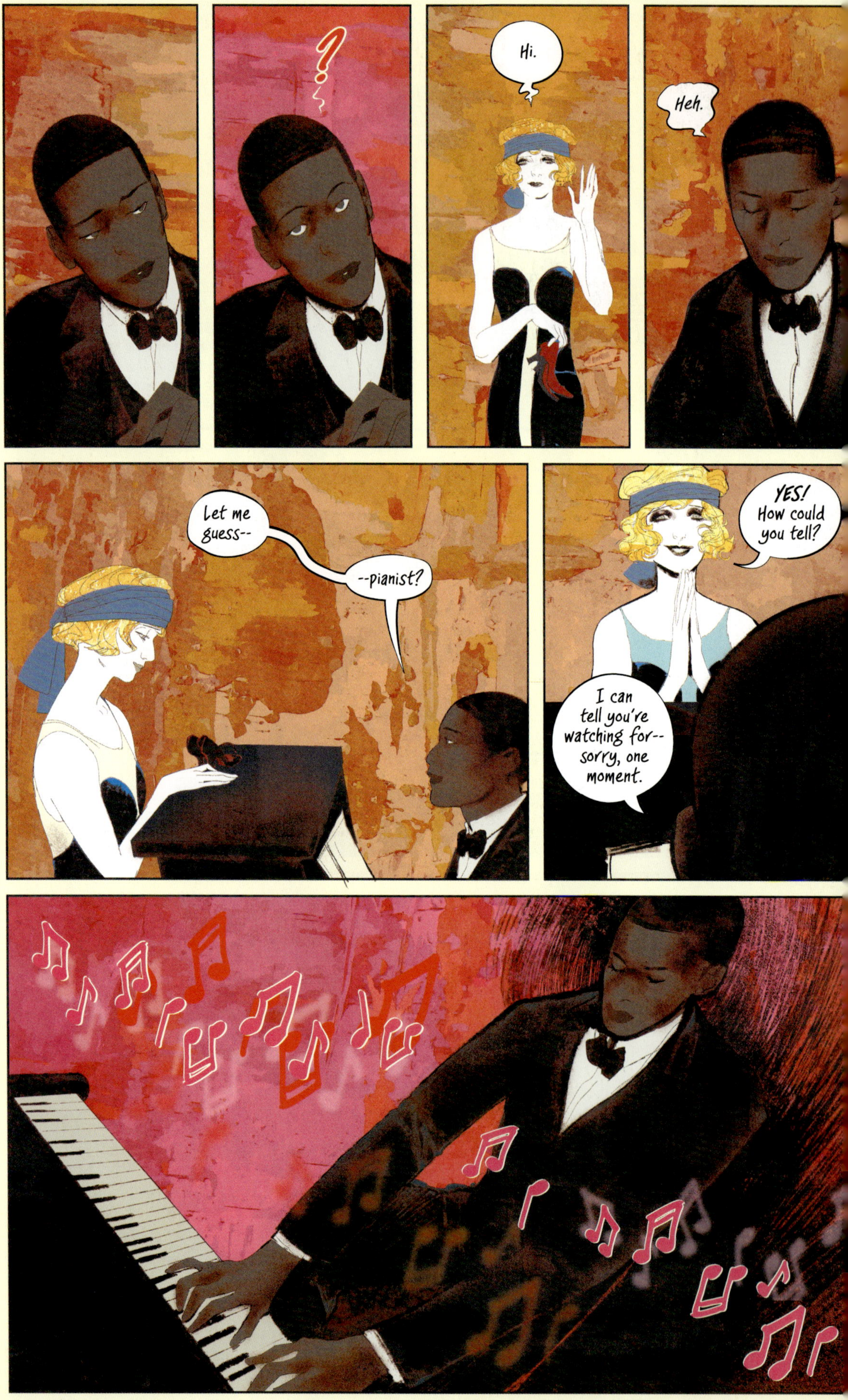
?
Hi.
Heh.
Let me guess--
--pianist?
YES! How could you tell?
I can tell you're watching for--sorry, one moment.

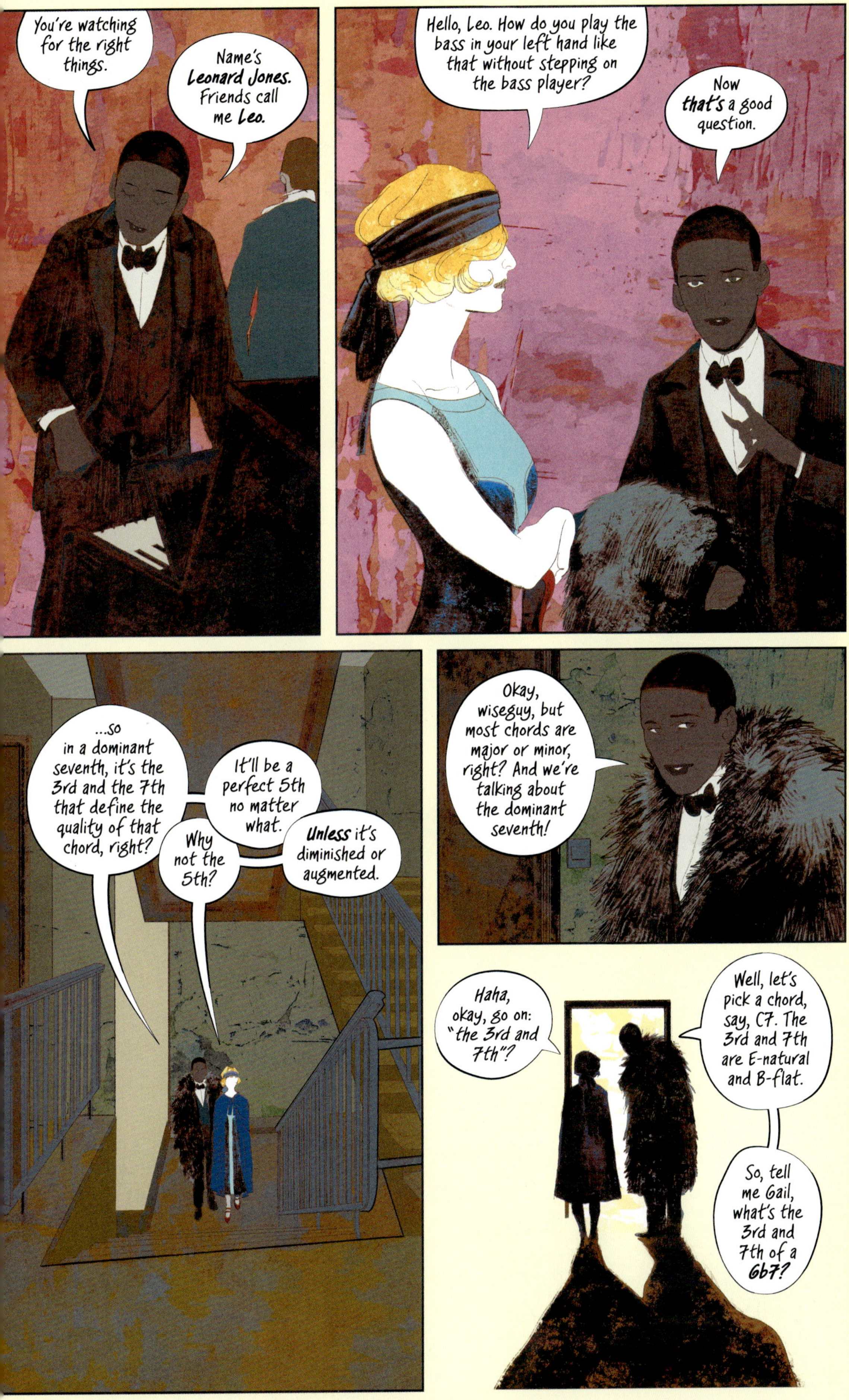
You're watching for the right things.
Name's **Leonard Jones.** Friends call me **Leo.**
Hello, Leo. How do you play the bass in your left hand like that without stepping on the bass player?
Now **that's** a good question.
...so in a dominant seventh, it's the 3rd and the 7th that define the quality of that chord, right?
It'll be a perfect 5th no matter what.
Why not the 5th?
Unless it's diminished or augmented.
Okay, wiseguy, but most chords are major or minor, right? And we're talking about the dominant seventh!
Haha, okay, go on: "the 3rd and 7th"?
Well, let's pick a chord, say, C7. The 3rd and 7th are E-natural and B-flat.
So, tell me Gail, what's the 3rd and 7th of a **Gb7?**

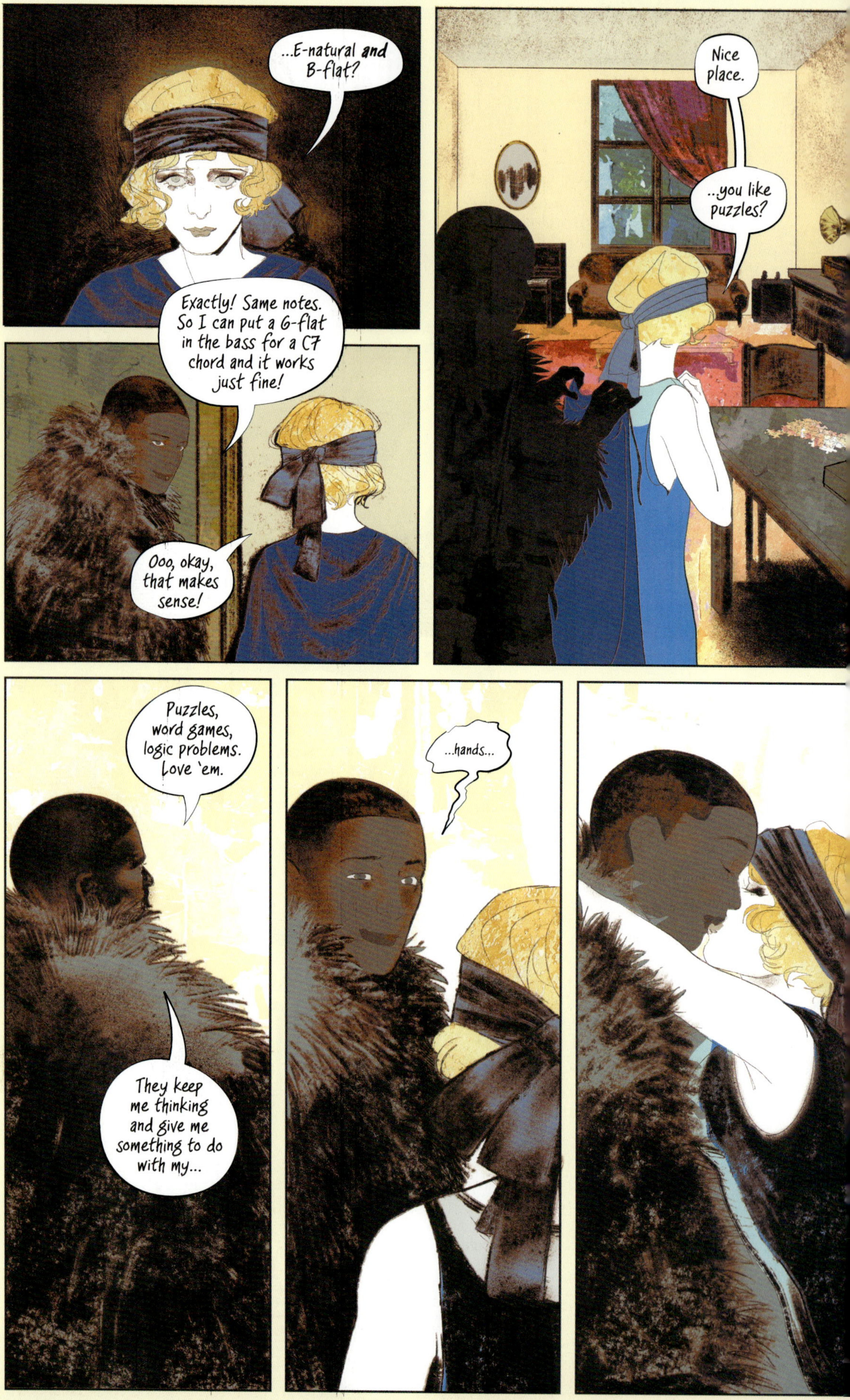
...E-natural and B-flat?
Exactly! Same notes. So I can put a G-flat in the bass for a C7 chord and it works just fine!
Ooo, okay, that makes sense!
Nice place.
...you like puzzles?
Puzzles, word games, logic problems. Love 'em.
They keep me thinking and give me something to do with my...
...hands...

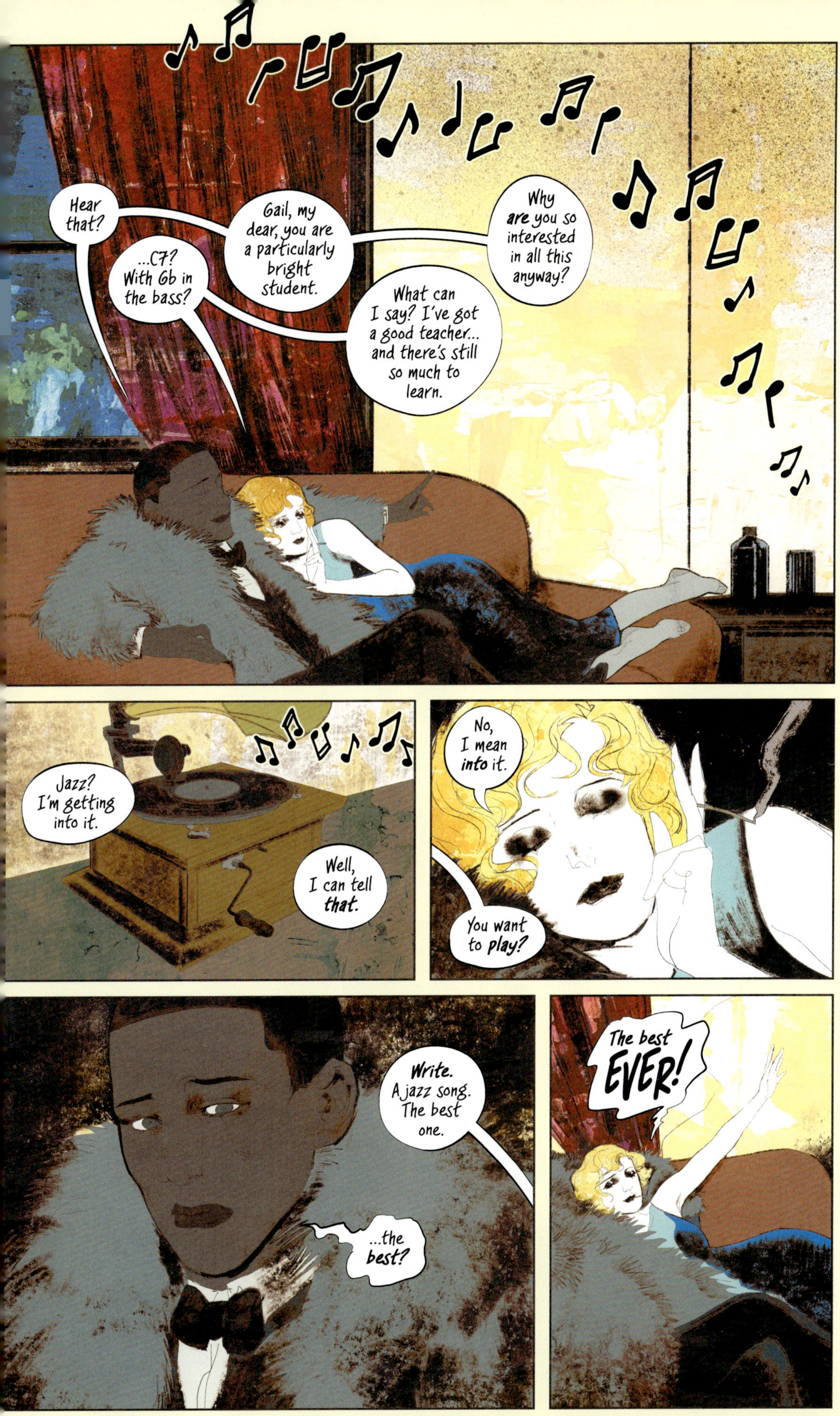
Hear that?
Gail, my dear, you are a particularly bright student.
Why **are** you so interested in all this anyway?
...C7? With Gb in the bass?
What can I say? I've got a good teacher... and there's still so much to learn.
Jazz? I'm getting into it.
Well, I can tell **that**.
No, I mean **into** it.
You want to **play?**
Write. A jazz song. The best one.
...the **best?**
The best **EVER!**

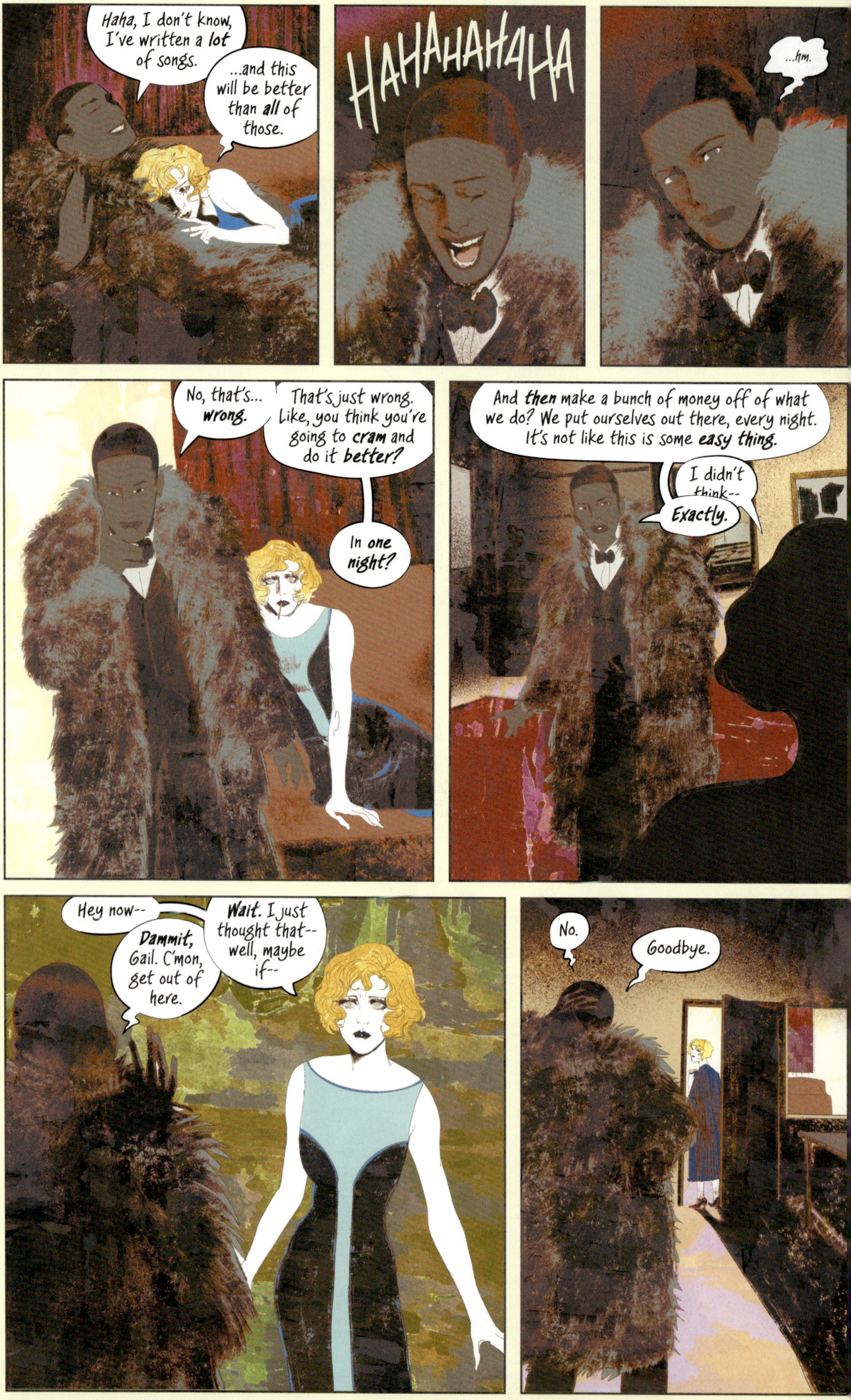
Haha, I don't know, I've written a lot of songs.
...and this will be better than all of those.
HAHAHAHAHA
...hm.
No, that's... wrong.
That's just wrong. Like, you think you're going to cram and do it better?
In one night?
And then make a bunch of money off of what we do? We put ourselves out there, every night. It's not like this is some easy thing.
I didn't think--
Exactly.
Hey now--
Dammit, Gail. C'mon, get out of here.
Wait. I just thought that--well, maybe if--
No.
Goodbye.

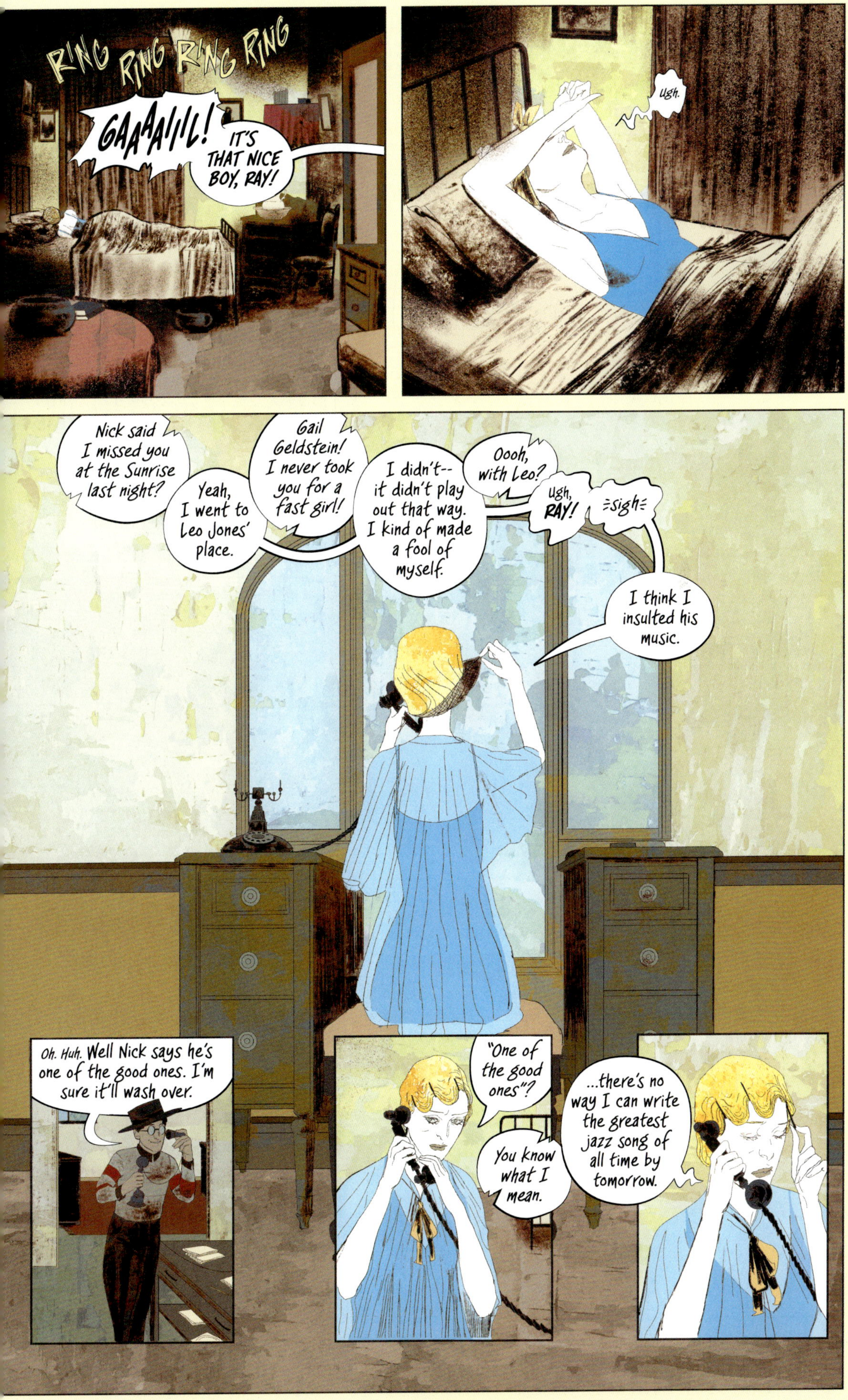
RING RING RING RING
GAAAAIL!
IT'S THAT NICE BOY, RAY!
Ugh.
Nick said I missed you at the Sunrise last night?
Yeah, I went to Leo Jones' place.
Gail Geldstein! I never took you for a fast girl!
I didn't-- it didn't play out that way. I kind of made a fool of myself.
Oooh, with Leo?
Ugh, RAY!
sigh
I think I insulted his music.
Oh. Huh. Well Nick says he's one of the good ones. I'm sure it'll wash over.
"One of the good ones"?
You know what I mean.
...there's no way I can write the greatest jazz song of all time by tomorrow.

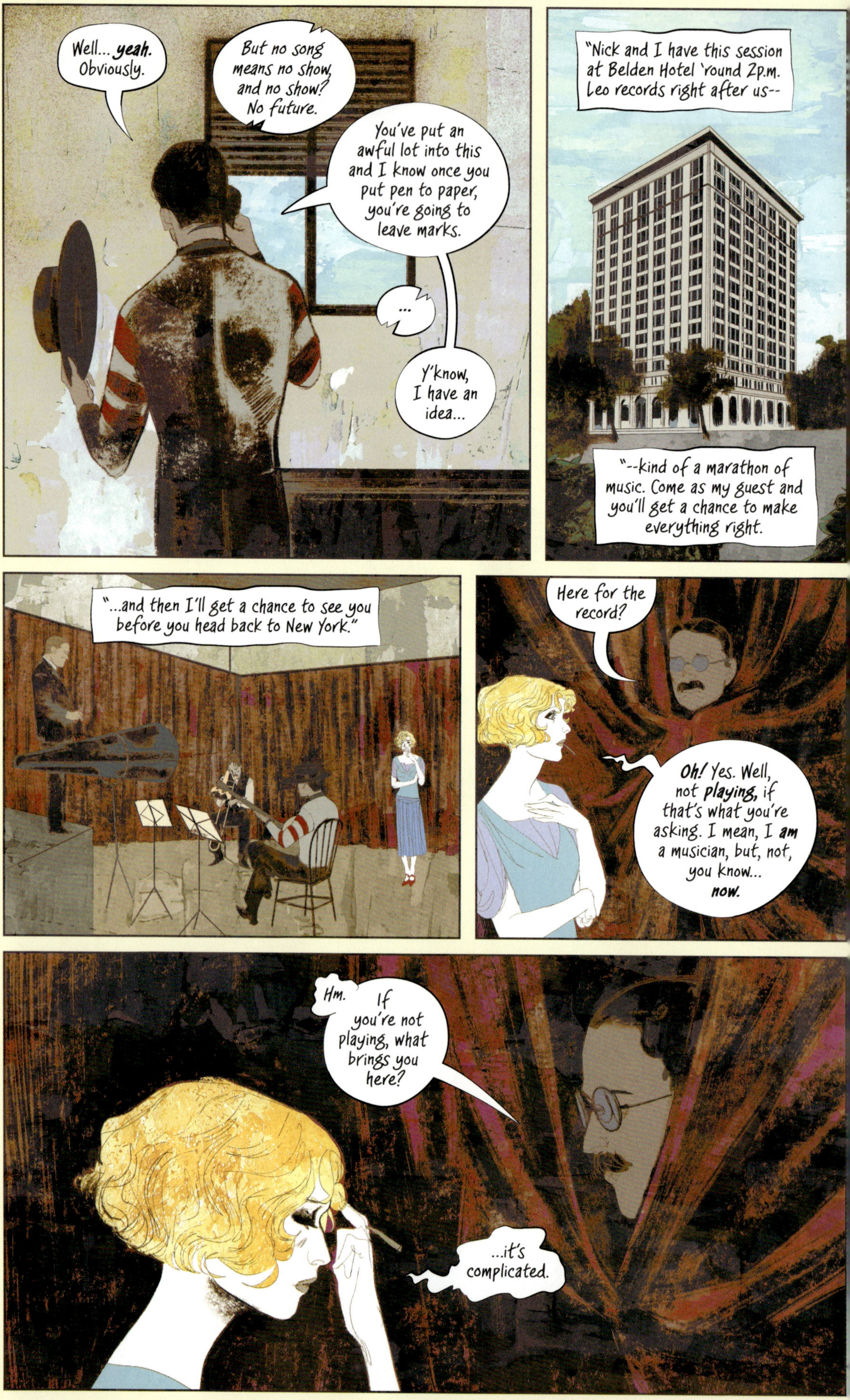
Well... yeah. Obviously.
But no song means no show, and no show? No future.
You've put an awful lot into this and I know once you put pen to paper, you're going to leave marks.
...
Y'know, I have an idea...
"Nick and I have this session at Belden Hotel 'round 2p.m. Leo records right after us--
"--kind of a marathon of music. Come as my guest and you'll get a chance to make everything right.
"...and then I'll get a chance to see you before you head back to New York."
Here for the record?
Oh! Yes. Well, not playing, if that's what you're asking. I mean, I am a musician, but, not, you know... now.
Hm.
If you're not playing, what brings you here?
...it's complicated.

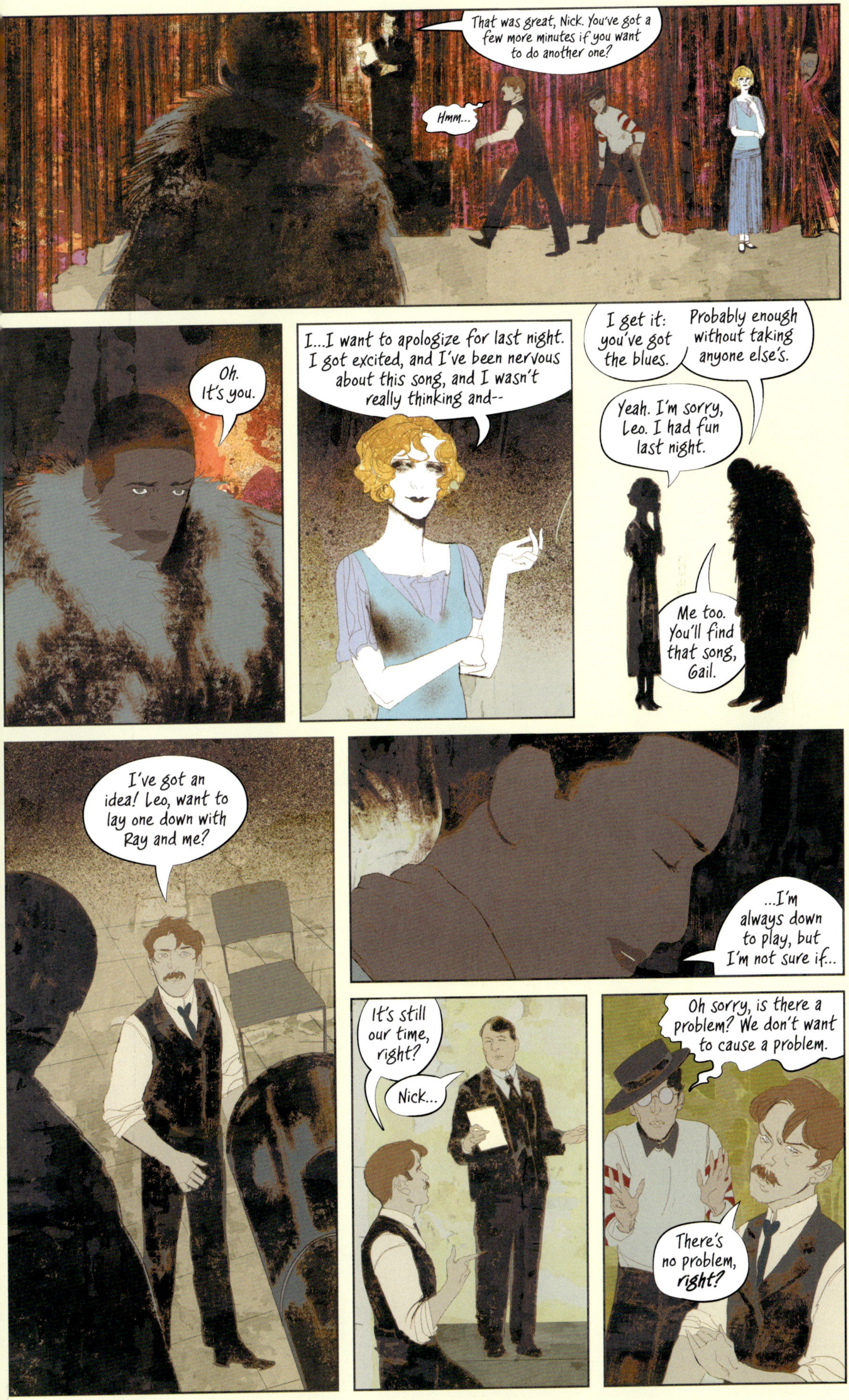
That was great, Nick. You've got a few more minutes if you want to do another one?
Hmm...
Oh. It's you.
I...I want to apologize for last night. I got excited, and I've been nervous about this song, and I wasn't really thinking and--
I get it: you've got the blues.
Probably enough without taking anyone else's.
Yeah. I'm sorry, Leo. I had fun last night.
Me too. You'll find that song, Gail.
I've got an idea! Leo, want to lay one down with Ray and me?
...I'm always down to play, but I'm not sure if...
It's still our time, right?
Nick...
Oh sorry, is there a problem? We don't want to cause a problem.
There's no problem, *right?*

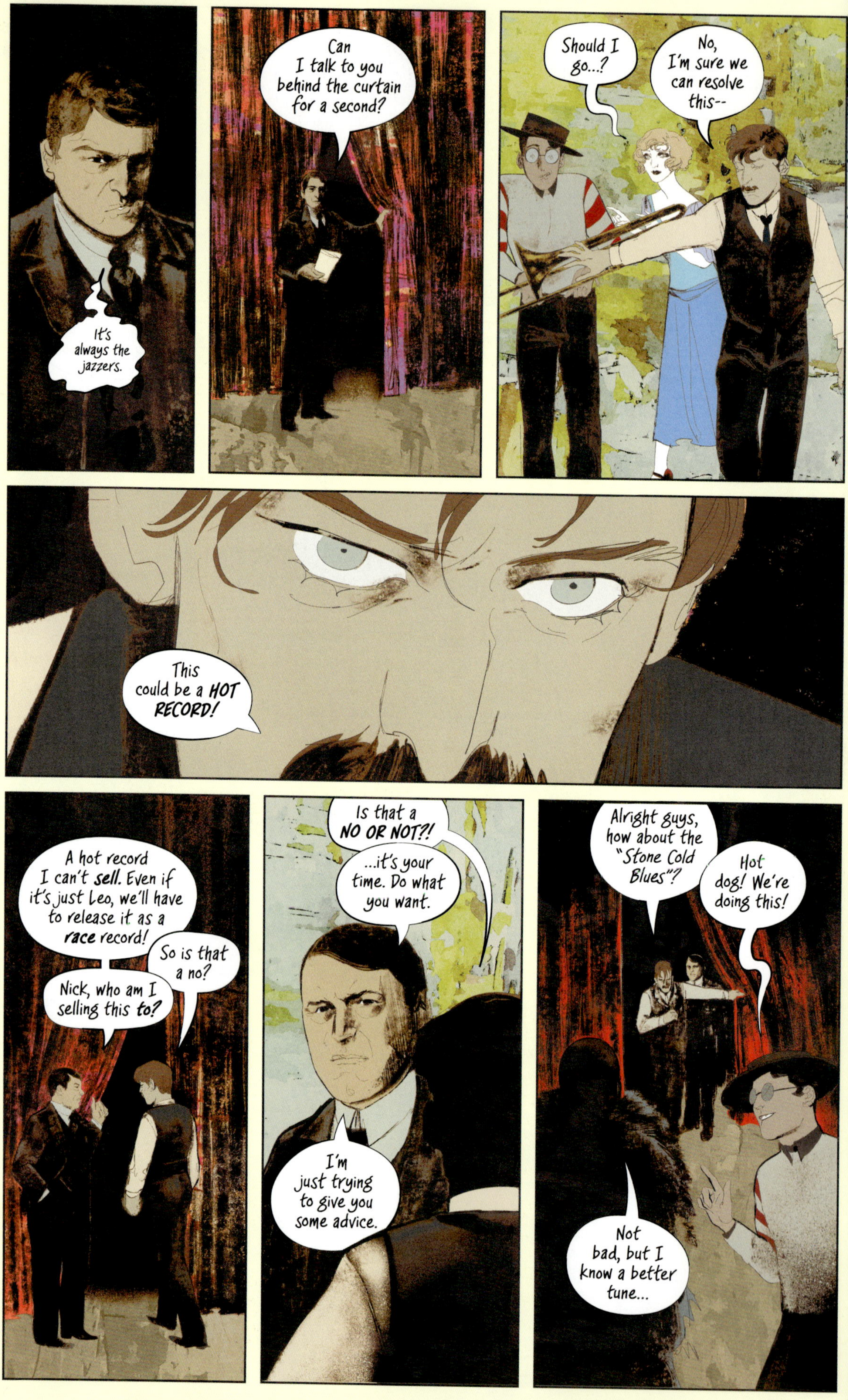
It's always the jazzers.
Can I talk to you behind the curtain for a second?
Should I go...?
No, I'm sure we can resolve this--
This could be a **HOT RECORD!**
A hot record I can't **sell.** Even if it's just Leo, we'll have to release it as a **race** record!
Nick, who am I selling this **to?**
So is that a no?
Is that a **NO OR NOT?!**
...it's your time. Do what you want.
I'm just trying to give you some advice.
Alright guys, how about the "Stone Cold Blues"?
Hot dog! We're doing this!
Not bad, but I know a better tune...

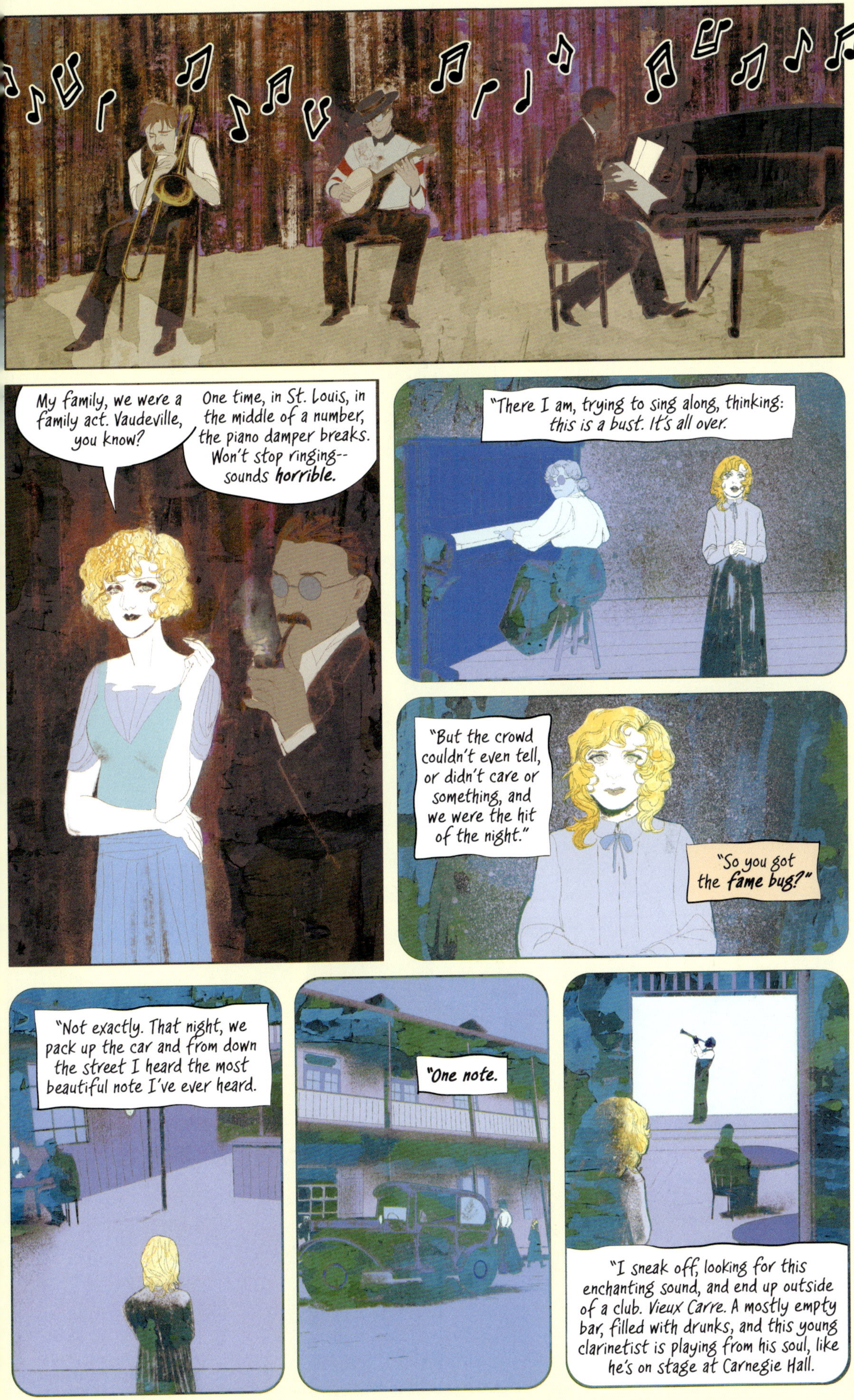
My family, we were a family act. Vaudeville, you know?
One time, in St. Louis, in the middle of a number, the piano damper breaks. Won't stop ringing-- sounds **horrible.**
"There I am, trying to sing along, thinking: *this is a bust. It's all over.*
"But the crowd couldn't even tell, or didn't care or something, and we were the hit of the night."
"So you got the **fame bug?**"
"Not exactly. That night, we pack up the car and from down the street I heard the most beautiful note I've ever heard.
"One note.
"I sneak off, looking for this enchanting sound, and end up outside of a club. *Vieux Carre.* A mostly empty bar, filled with drunks, and this young clarinetist is playing from his soul, like he's on stage at Carnegie Hall.

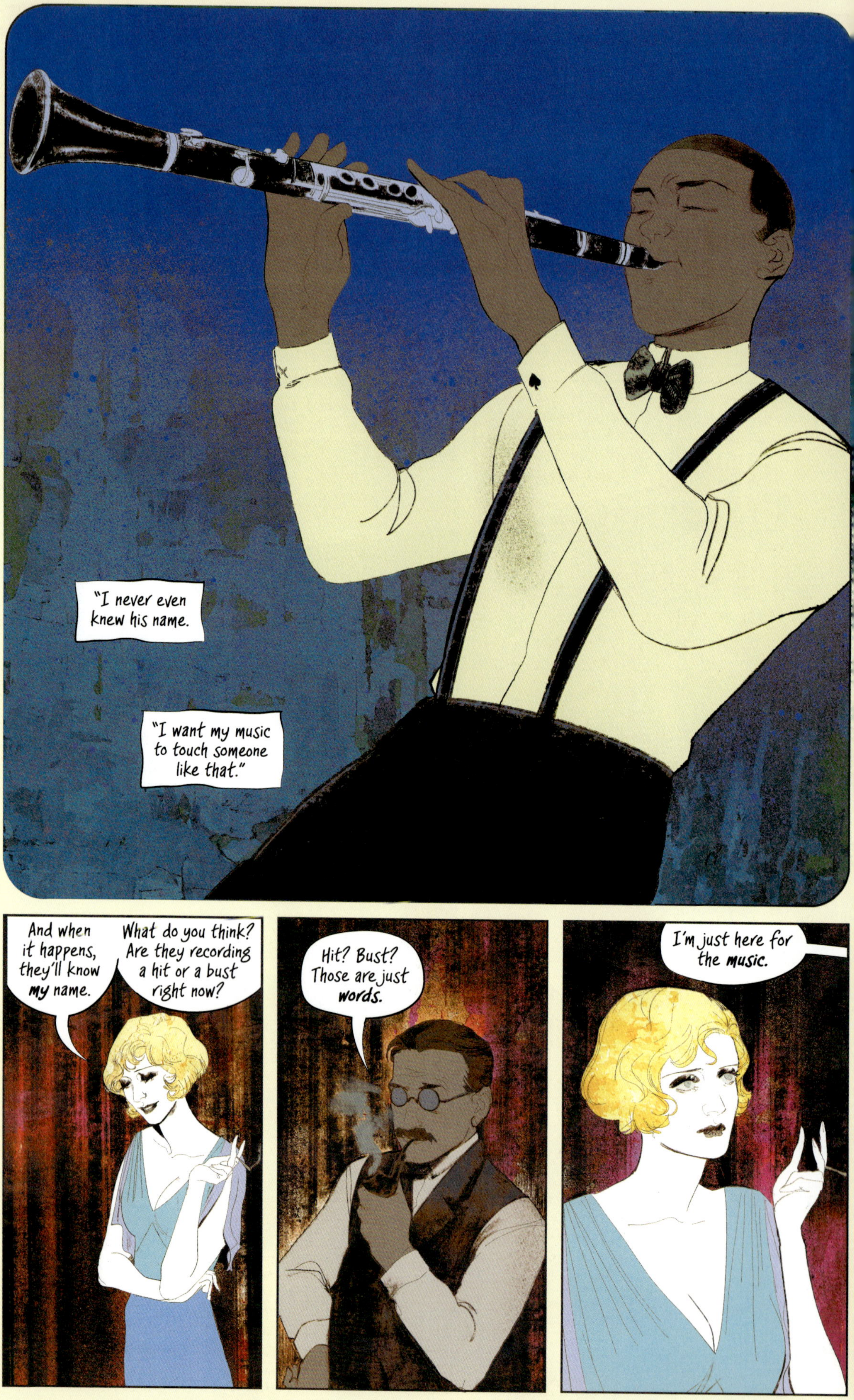
"I never even knew his name.
"I want my music to touch someone like that."
And when it happens, they'll know **my** name.
What do you think? Are they recording a hit or a bust right now?
Hit? Bust? Those are just **words.**
I'm just here for the **music.**

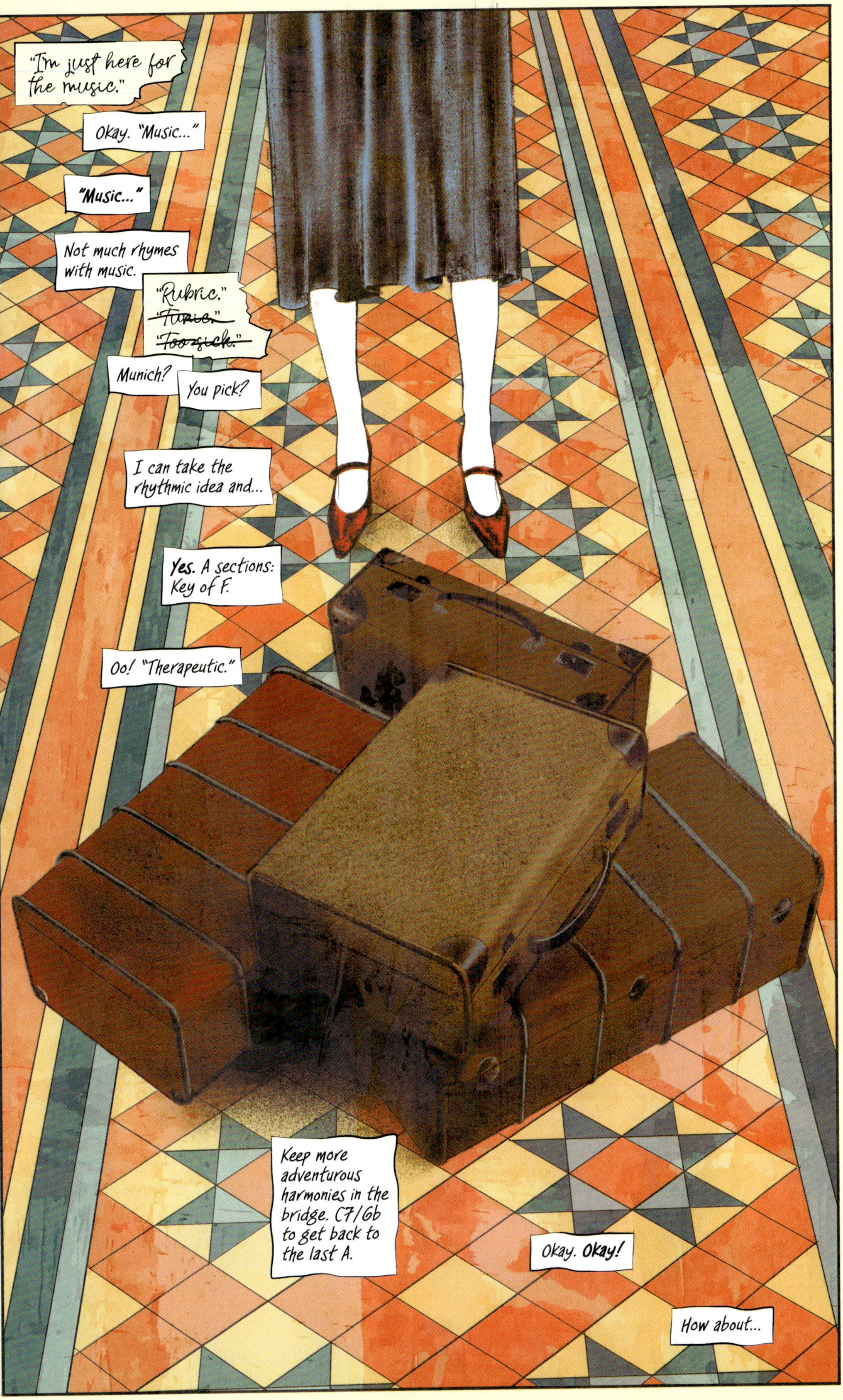

"I'm just here for the music."
Okay. "Music..."
"Music..."
Not much rhymes with music.
"Rubric."
~~"Furic."~~
~~"Foozsick."~~
Munich?
You pick?
I can take the rhythmic idea and...
Yes. A sections: Key of F.
Oo! "Therapeutic."
Keep more adventurous harmonies in the bridge. C7/Gb to get back to the last A.
Okay. **Okay!**
How about...

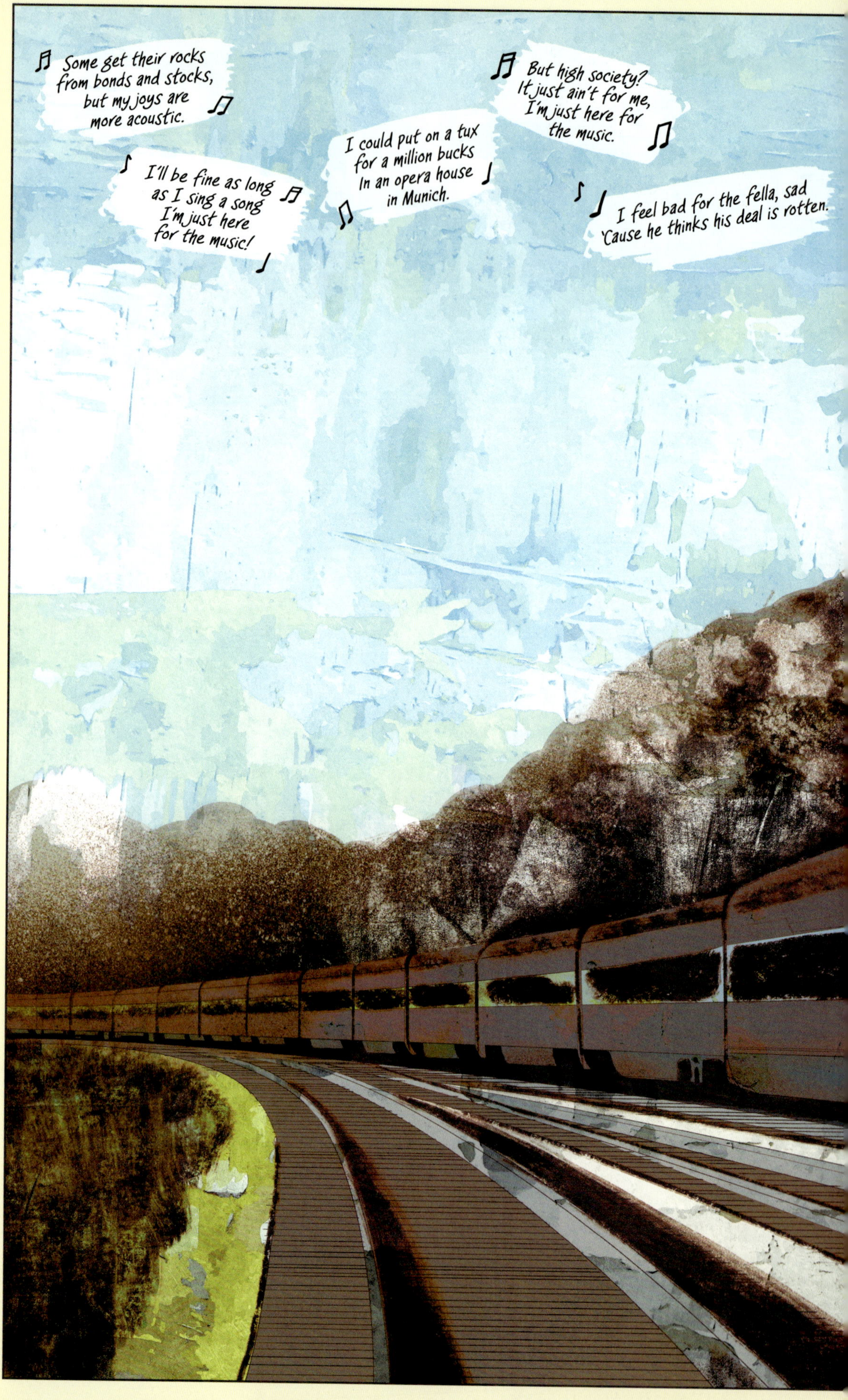
Some get their rocks from bonds and stocks, but my joys are more acoustic.
I'll be fine as long as I sing a song I'm just here for the music!
I could put on a tux for a million bucks In an opera house in Munich.
But high society? It just ain't for me, I'm just here for the music.
I feel bad for the fella, sad 'Cause he thinks his deal is rotten.

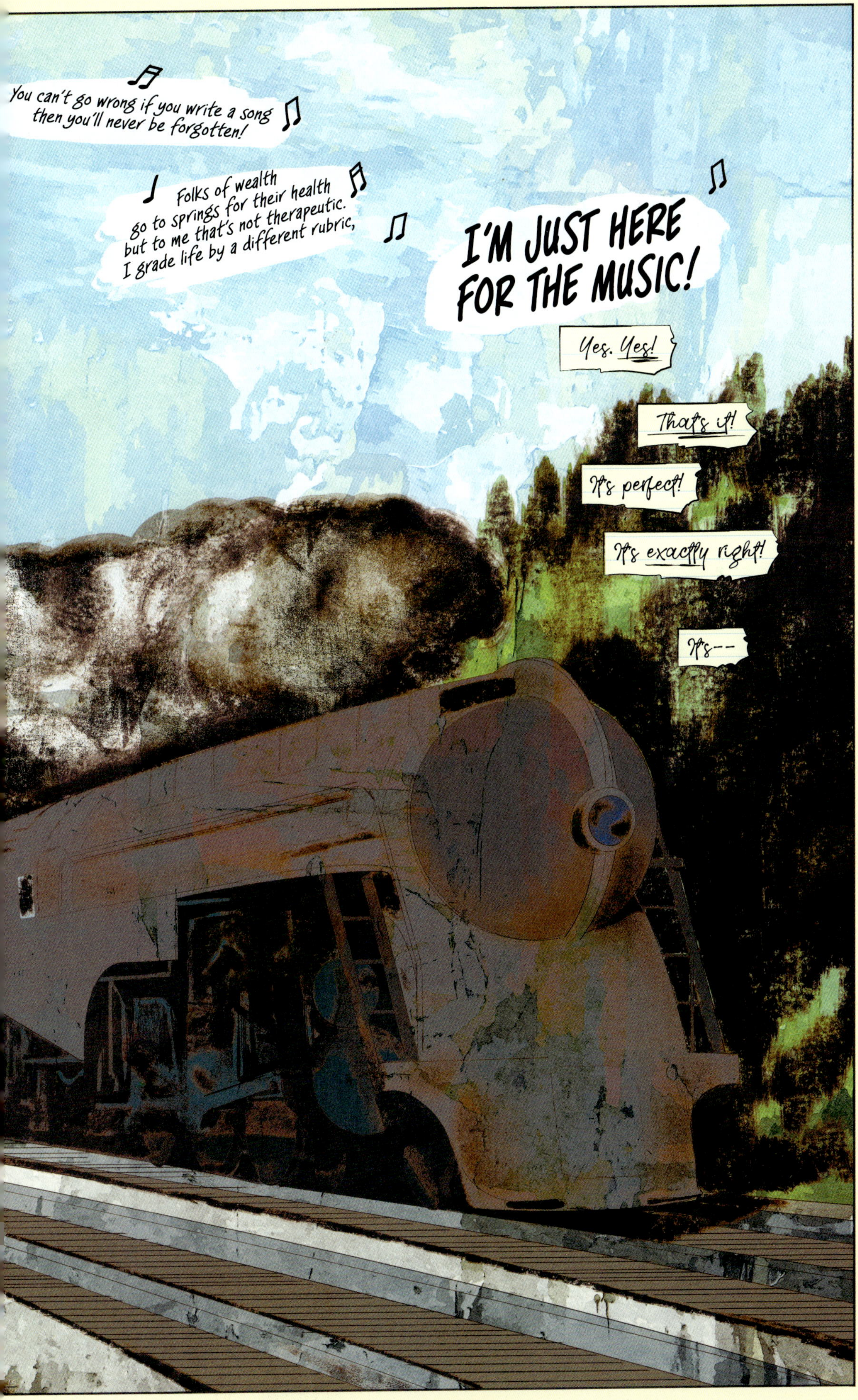
You can't go wrong if you write a song then you'll never be forgotten!
Folks of wealth go to springs for their health but to me that's not therapeutic. I grade life by a different rubric,
I'M JUST HERE FOR THE MUSIC!
Yes. Yes!
That's it!
It's perfect!
It's exactly right!
It's--

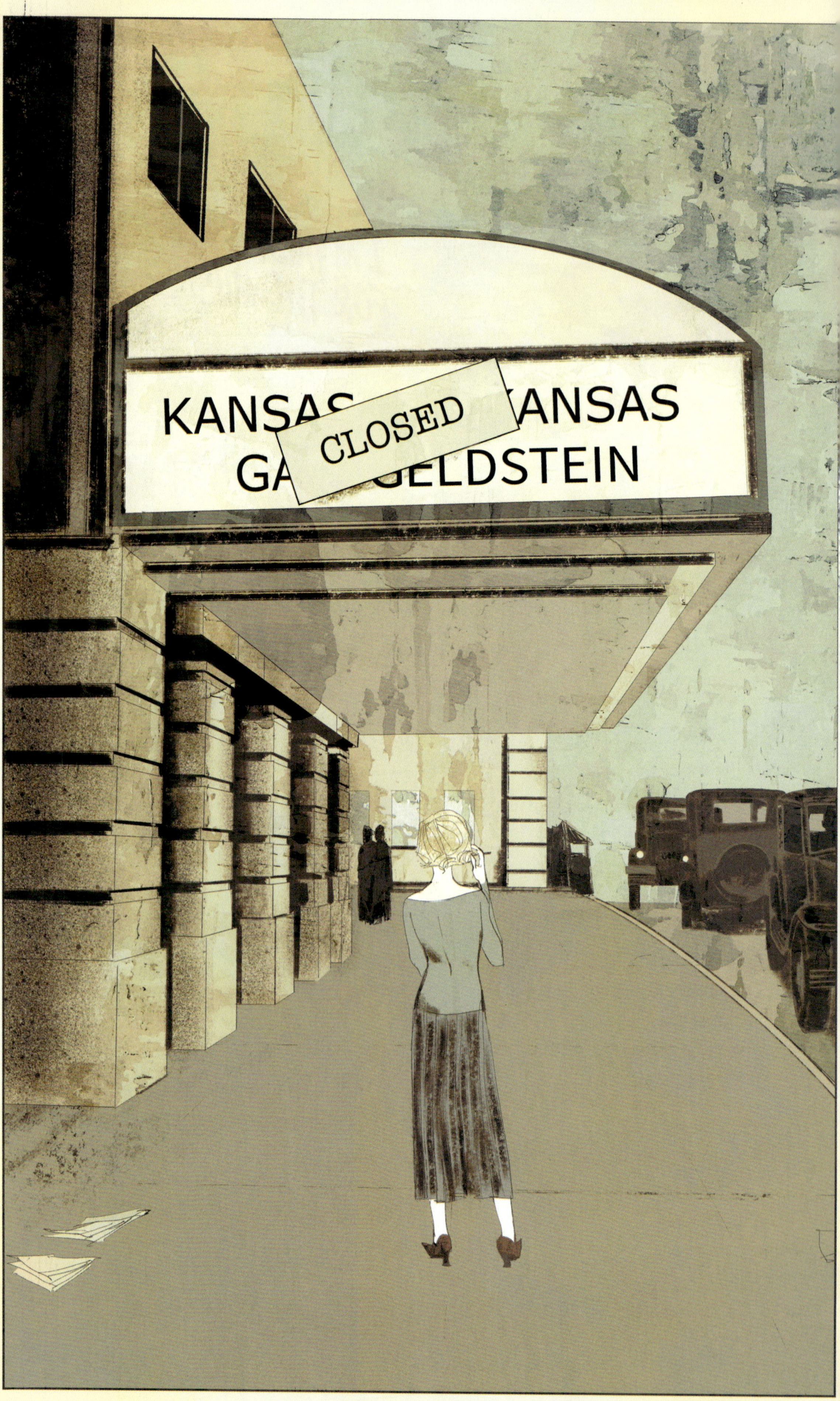
KANSAS
CLOSED
ANSAS
GA
GELDSTEIN

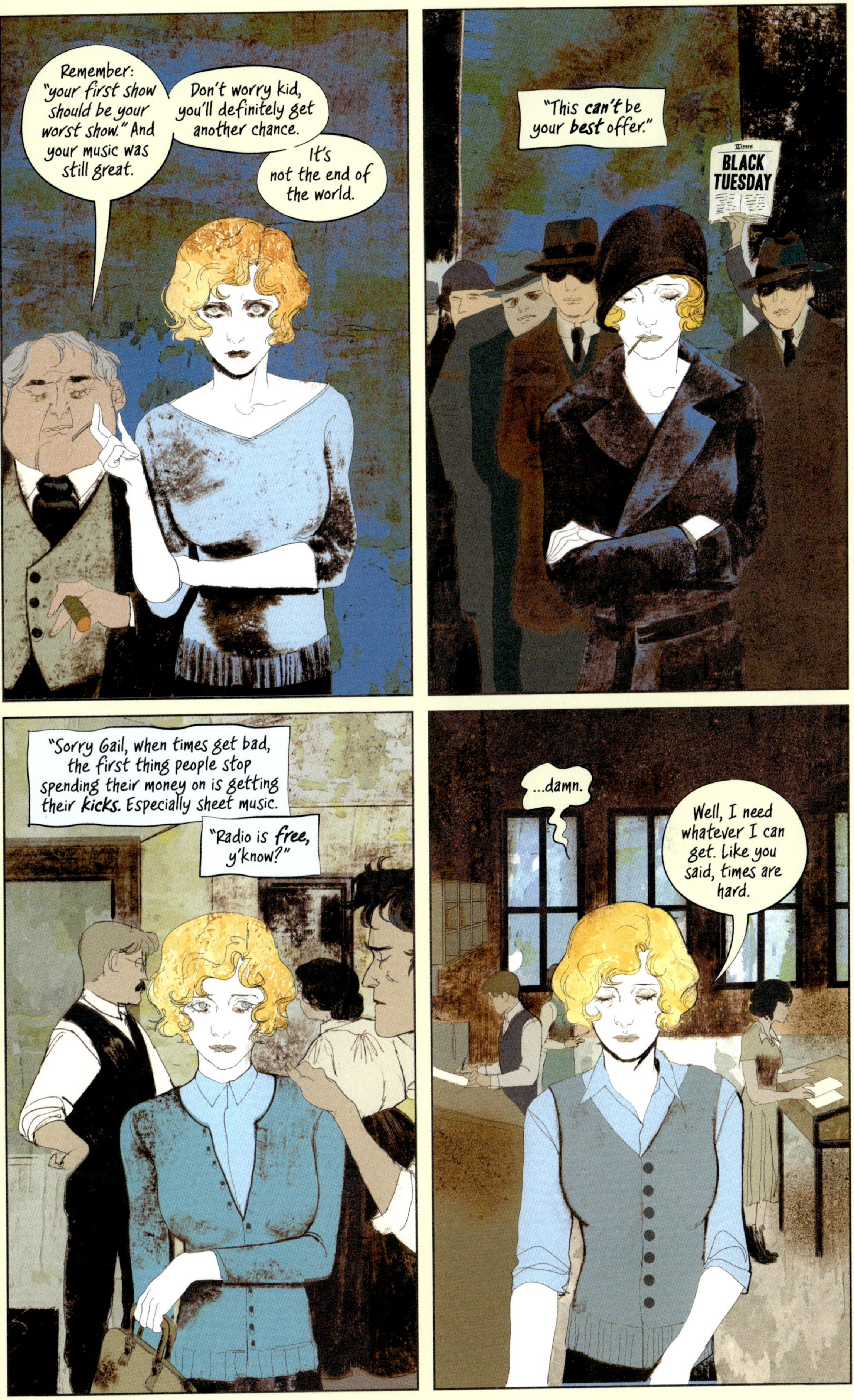
Remember: "your first show should be your worst show." And your music was still great.
Don't worry kid, you'll definitely get another chance.
It's not the end of the world.
"This can't be your best offer."
Times
BLACK TUESDAY
"Sorry Gail, when times get bad, the first thing people stop spending their money on is getting their kicks. Especially sheet music.
"Radio is free, y'know?"
...damn.
Well, I need whatever I can get. Like you said, times are hard.

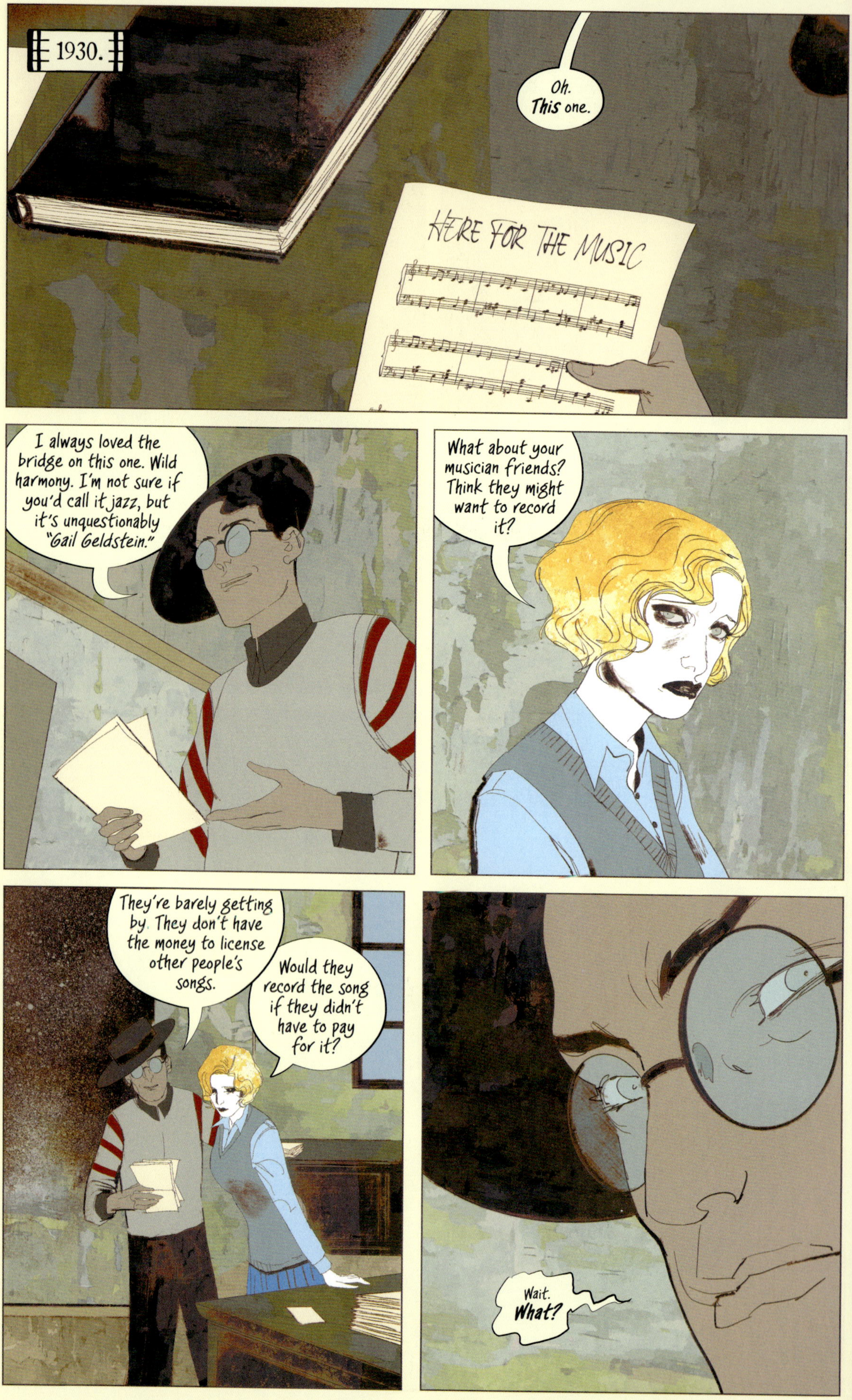
1930.
Oh. This one.
HERE FOR THE MUSIC
I always loved the bridge on this one. Wild harmony. I'm not sure if you'd call it jazz, but it's unquestionably "Gail Geldstein."
What about your musician friends? Think they might want to record it?
They're barely getting by. They don't have the money to license other people's songs.
Would they record the song if they didn't have to pay for it?
Wait. What?

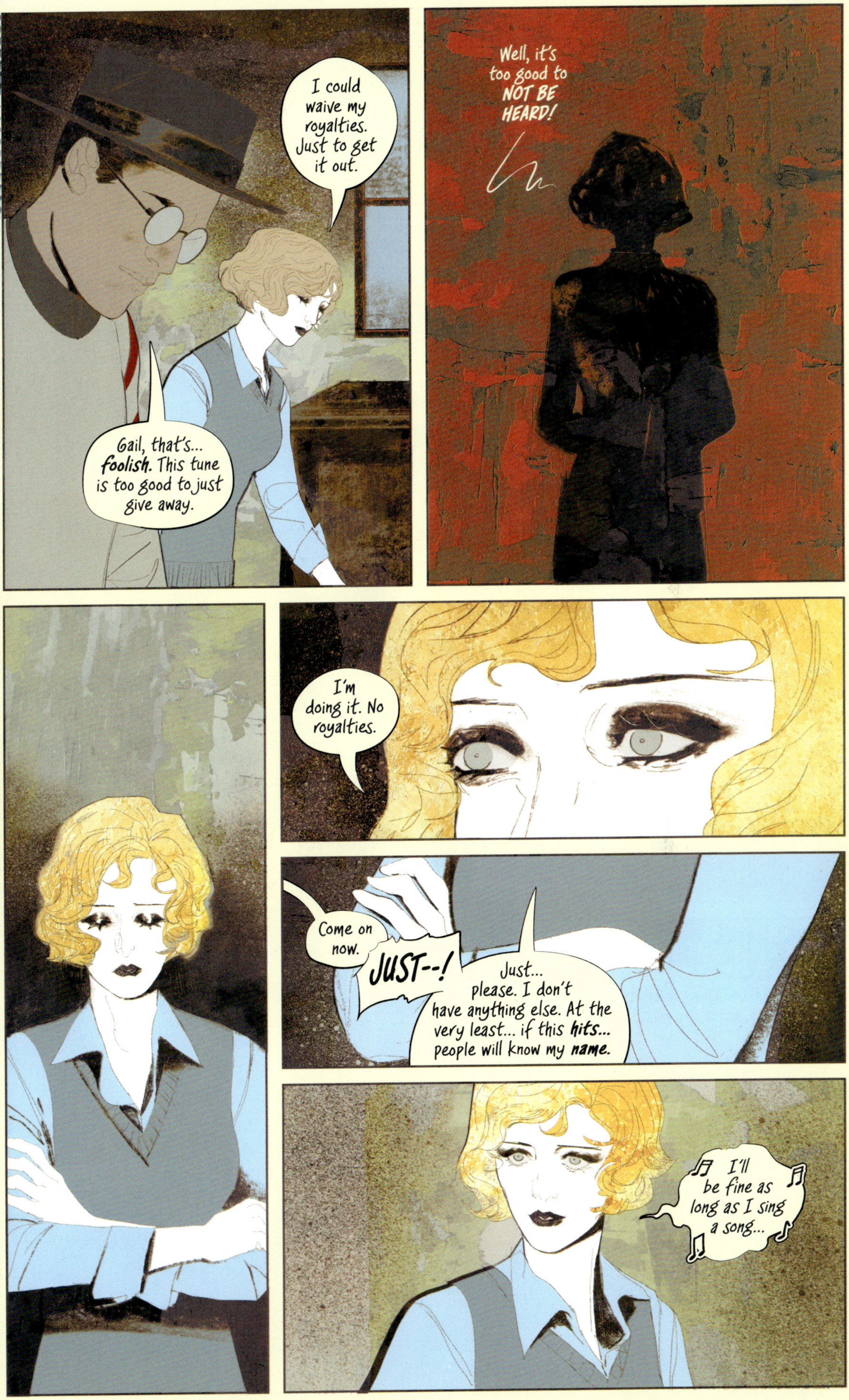
I could waive my royalties. Just to get it out.
Gail, that's... **foolish.** This tune is too good to just give away.
Well, it's too good to **NOT BE HEARD!**
I'm doing it. No royalties.
Come on now.
JUST--!
Just... please. I don't have anything else. At the very least... if this **hits...** people will know my **name.**
I'll be fine as long as I sing a song...

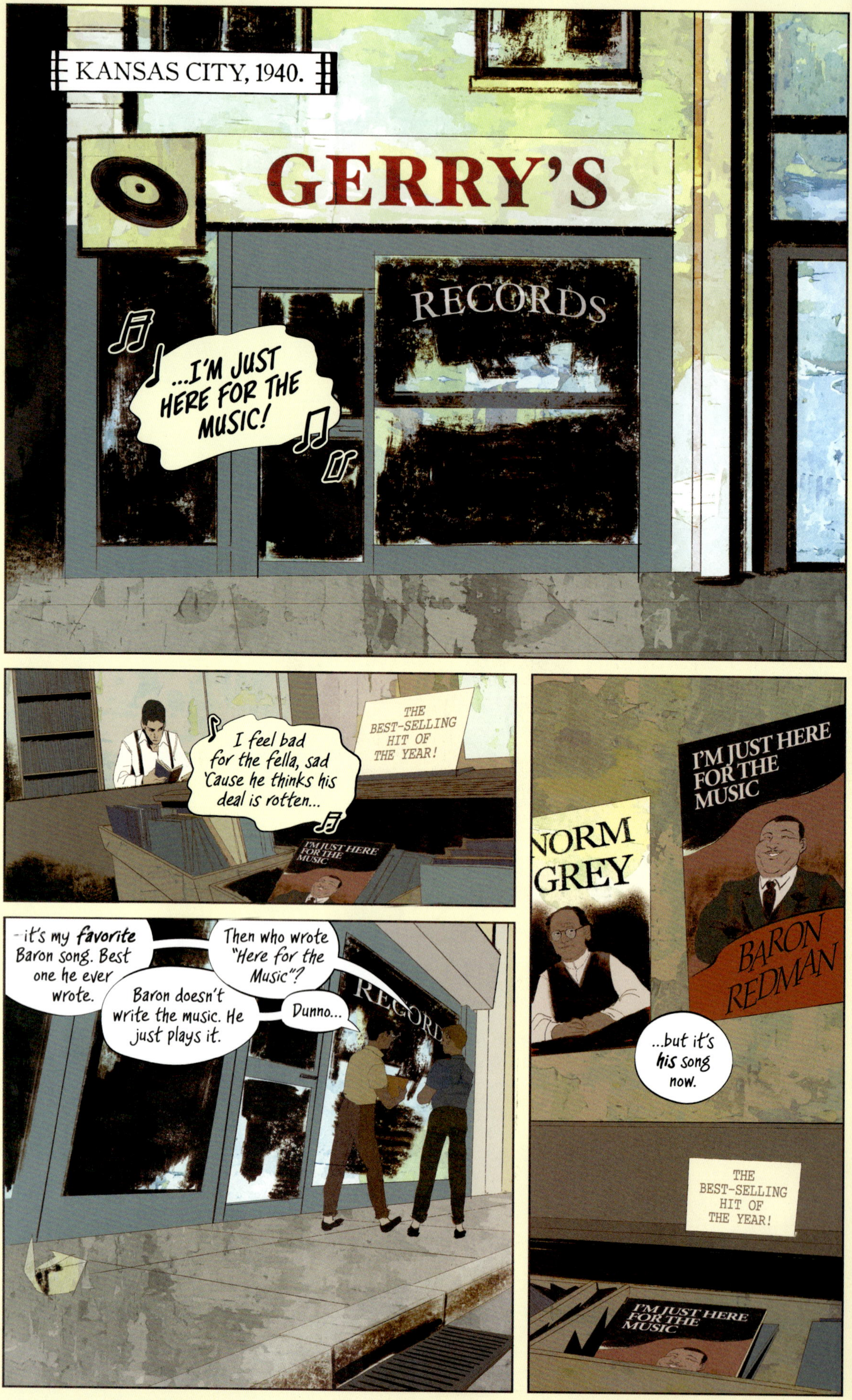
KANSAS CITY, 1940.
GERRY'S
RECORDS
...I'M JUST HERE FOR THE MUSIC!
I feel bad for the fella, sad 'Cause he thinks his deal is rotten...
THE BEST-SELLING HIT OF THE YEAR!
I'M JUST HERE FOR THE MUSIC
I'M JUST HERE FOR THE MUSIC
NORM GREY
BARON REDMAN
–it's my **favorite** Baron song. Best one he ever wrote.
Then who wrote "Here for the Music"?
Baron doesn't write the music. He just plays it.
Dunno...
RECORD
...but it's **his** song now.
THE BEST-SELLING HIT OF THE YEAR!
I'M JUST HERE FOR THE MUSIC

3.
K.C. BLUES

KANSAS CITY
1940

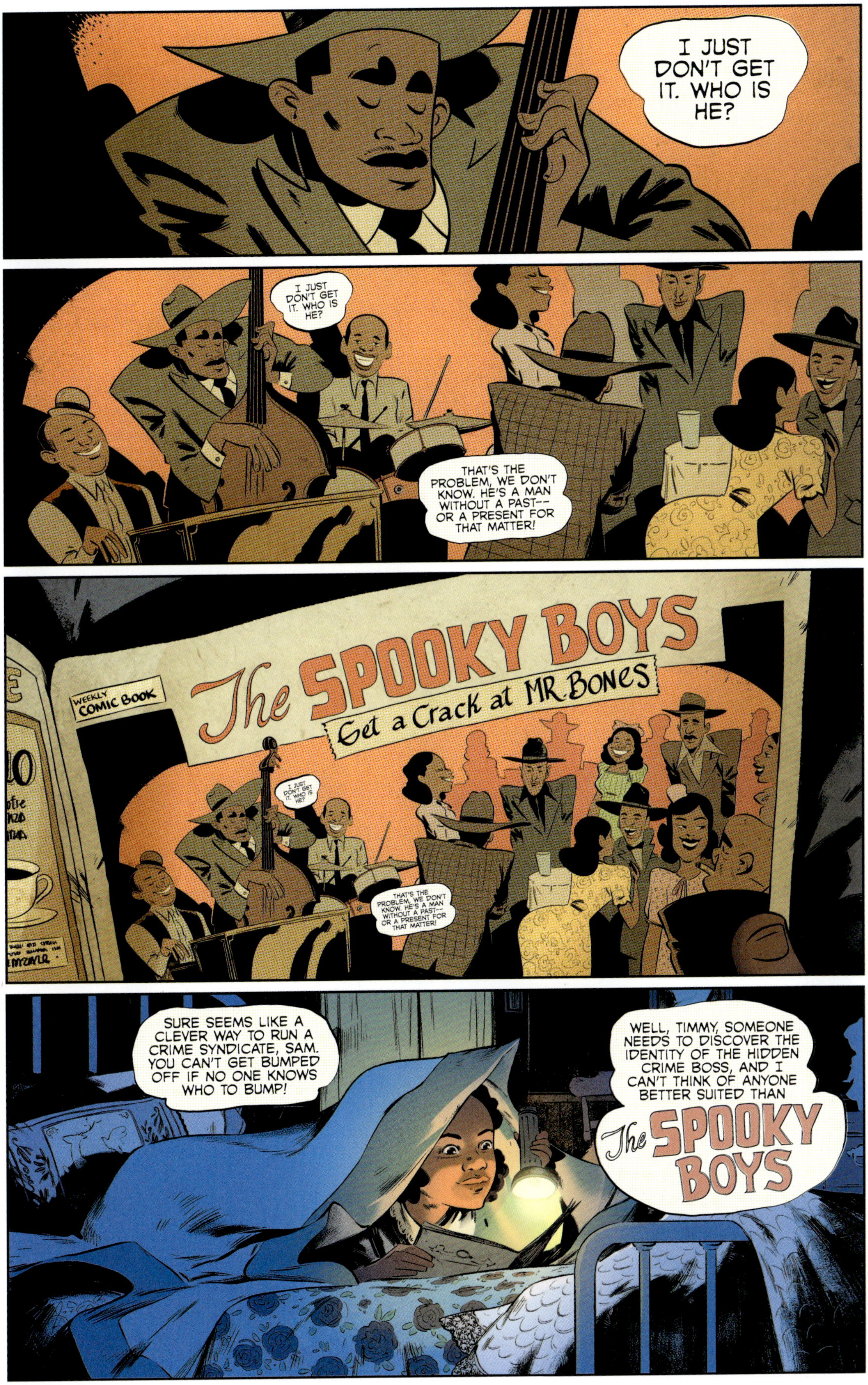
I JUST DON'T GET IT. WHO IS HE?
I JUST DON'T GET IT. WHO IS HE?
THAT'S THE PROBLEM, WE DON'T KNOW. HE'S A MAN WITHOUT A PAST-- OR A PRESENT FOR THAT MATTER!
WEEKLY COMIC BOOK
The SPOOKY BOYS
Get a Crack at MR Bones
I JUST DON'T GET IT. WHO IS HE?
THAT'S THE PROBLEM, WE DON'T KNOW. HE'S A MAN WITHOUT A PAST-- OR A PRESENT FOR THAT MATTER!
SURE SEEMS LIKE A CLEVER WAY TO RUN A CRIME SYNDICATE, SAM. YOU CAN'T GET BUMPED OFF IF NO ONE KNOWS WHO TO BUMP!
WELL, TIMMY, SOMEONE NEEDS TO DISCOVER THE IDENTITY OF THE HIDDEN CRIME BOSS, AND I CAN'T THINK OF ANYONE BETTER SUITED THAN
The SPOOKY BOYS

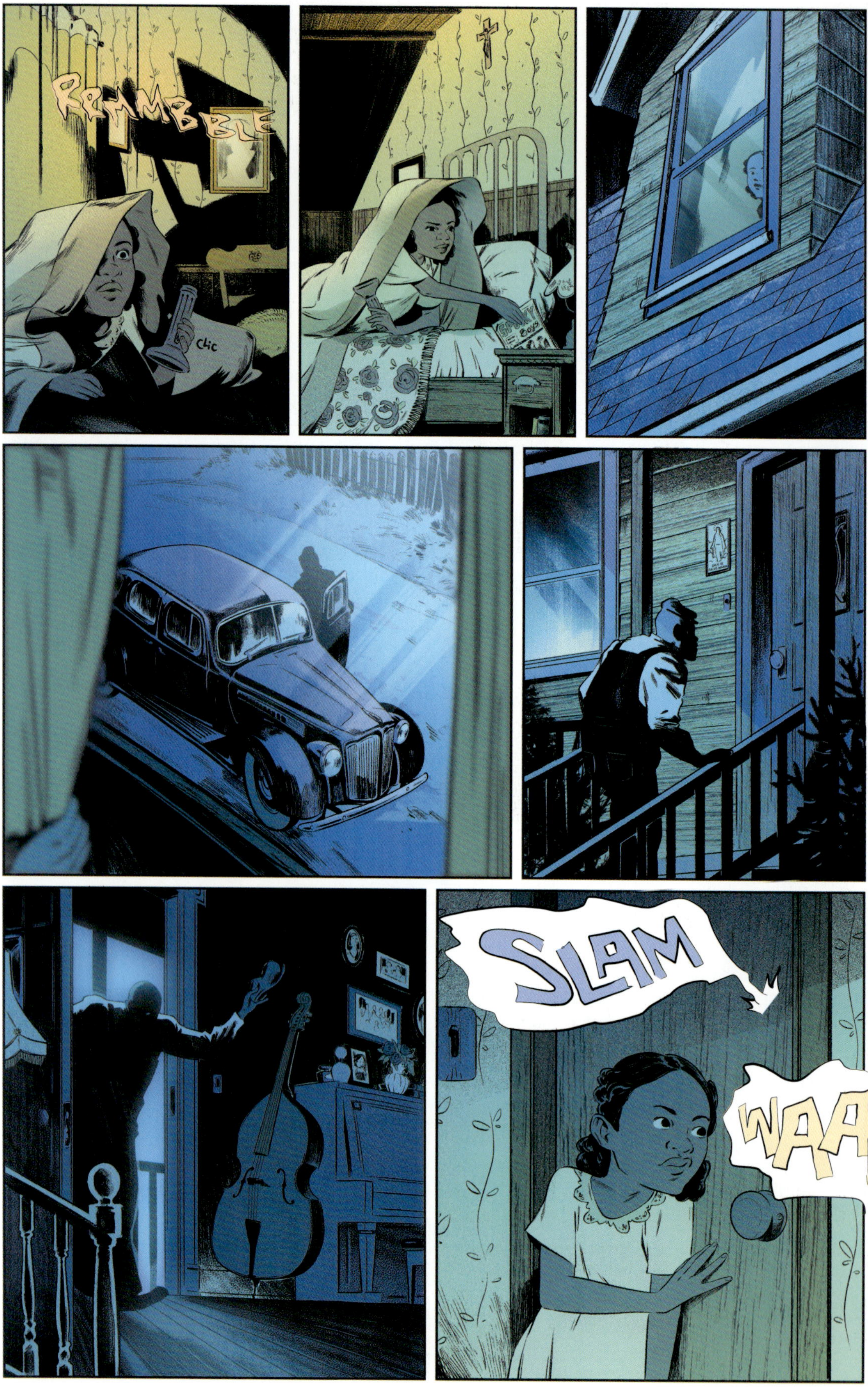
RRMMBBLE
CLIC
SLAM
WAA

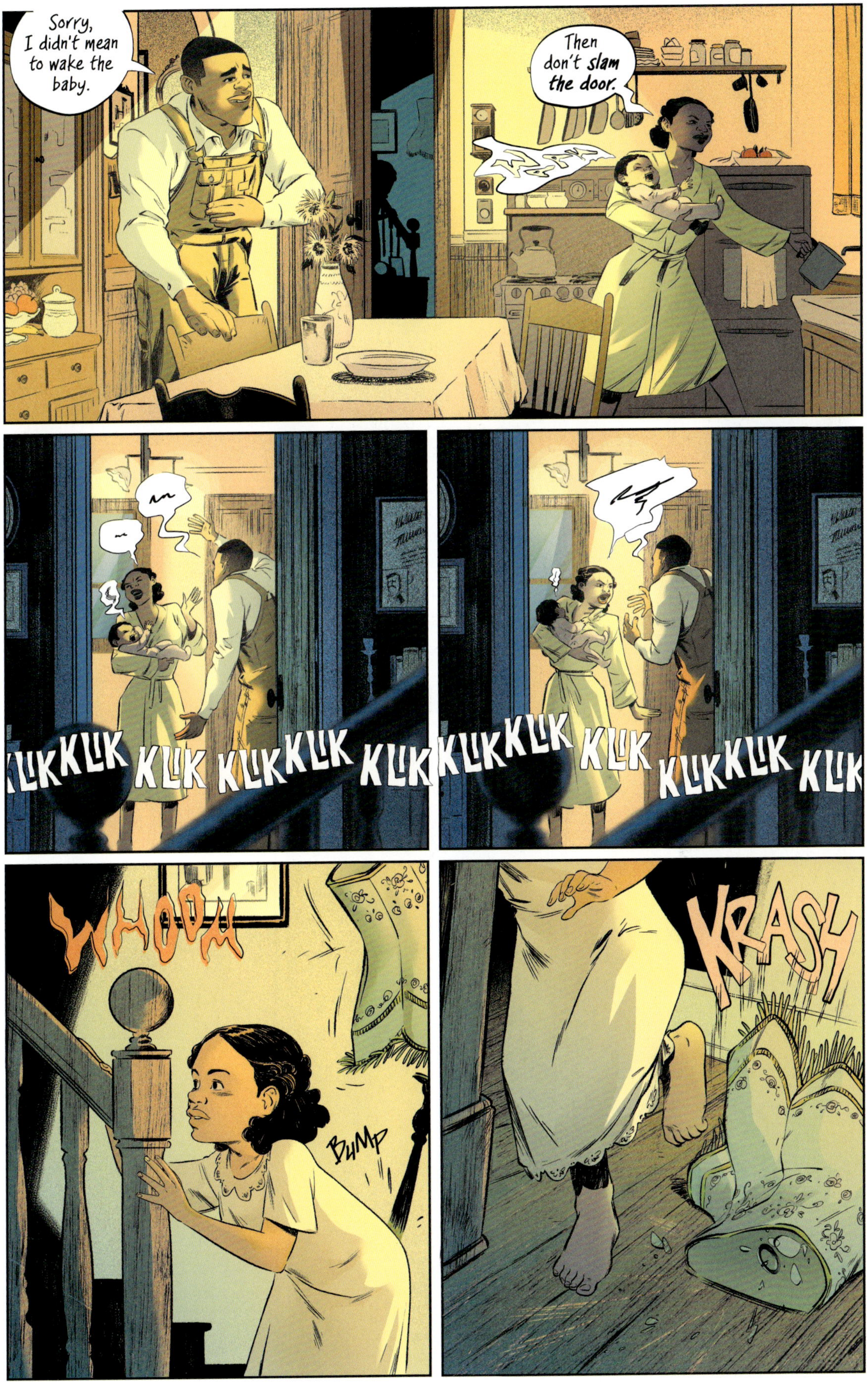
Sorry, I didn't mean to wake the baby.
Then don't **slam the door.**
KLIKKLIK KLIK KLIKKLIK KLIK
KLIKKLIK KLIK KLIKKLIK KLIK
WHOOM
BUMP
KRASH

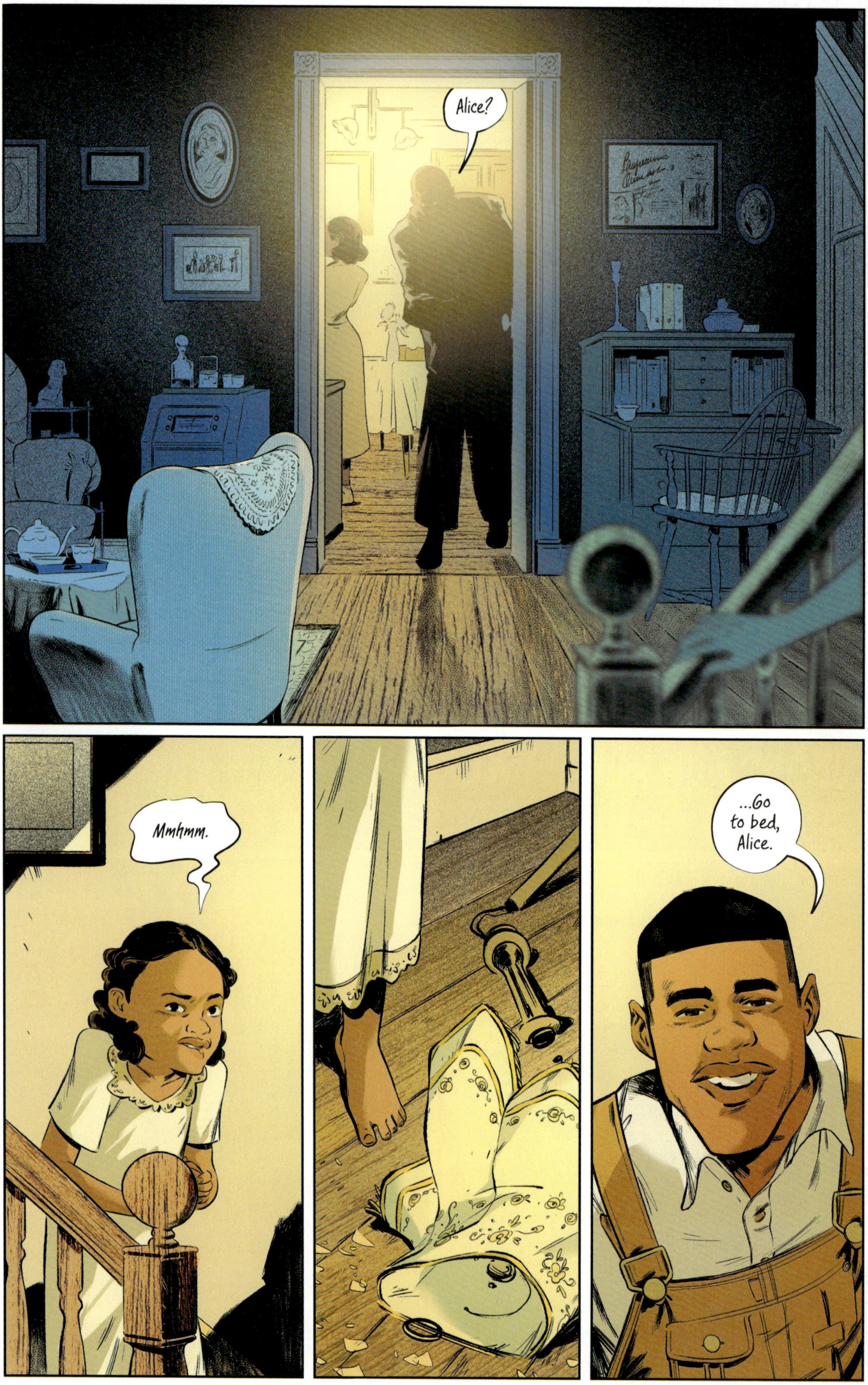
Alice?
Mmhmm.
...Go to bed, Alice.

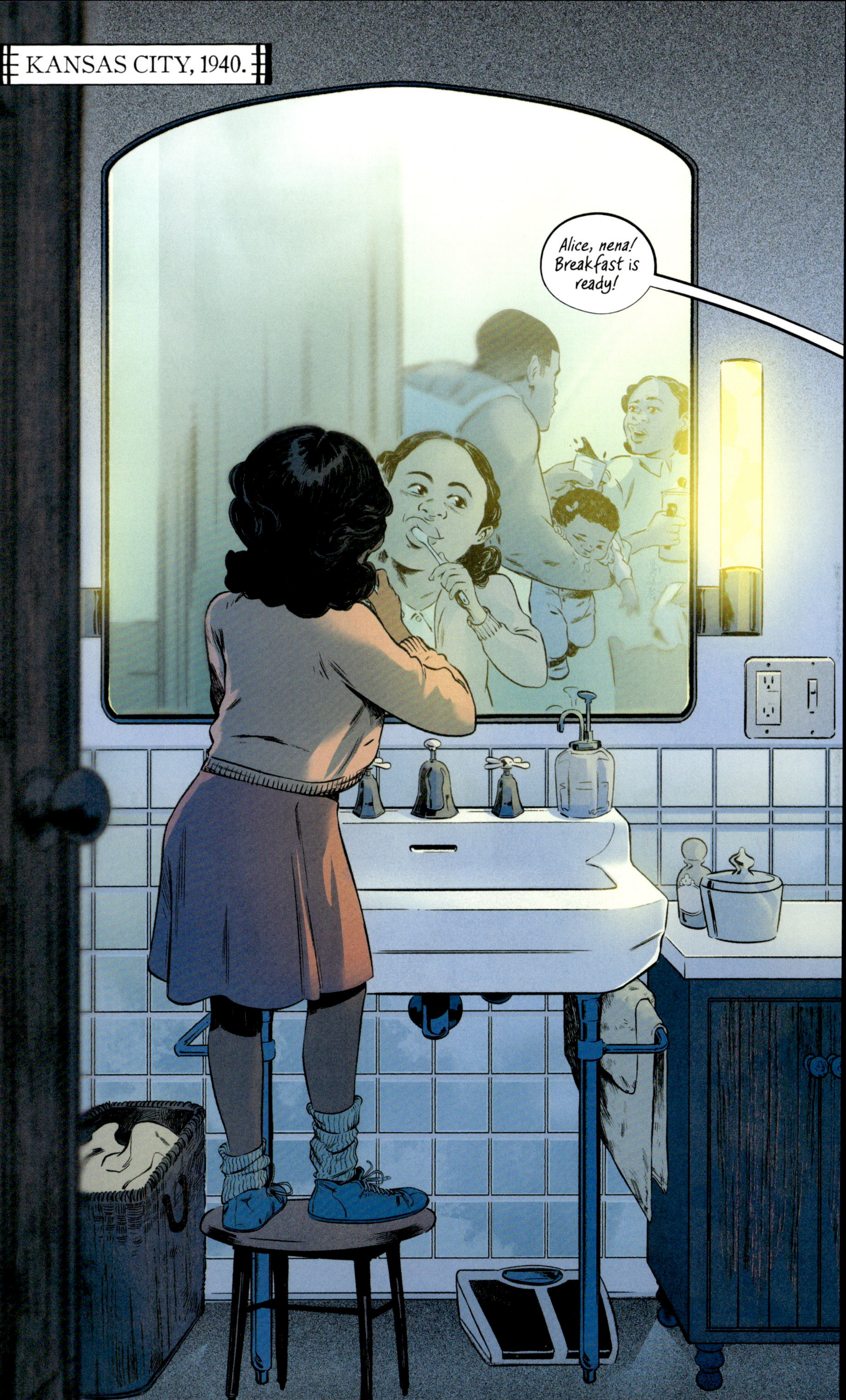
KANSAS CITY, 1940.
Alice, nena! Breakfast is ready!

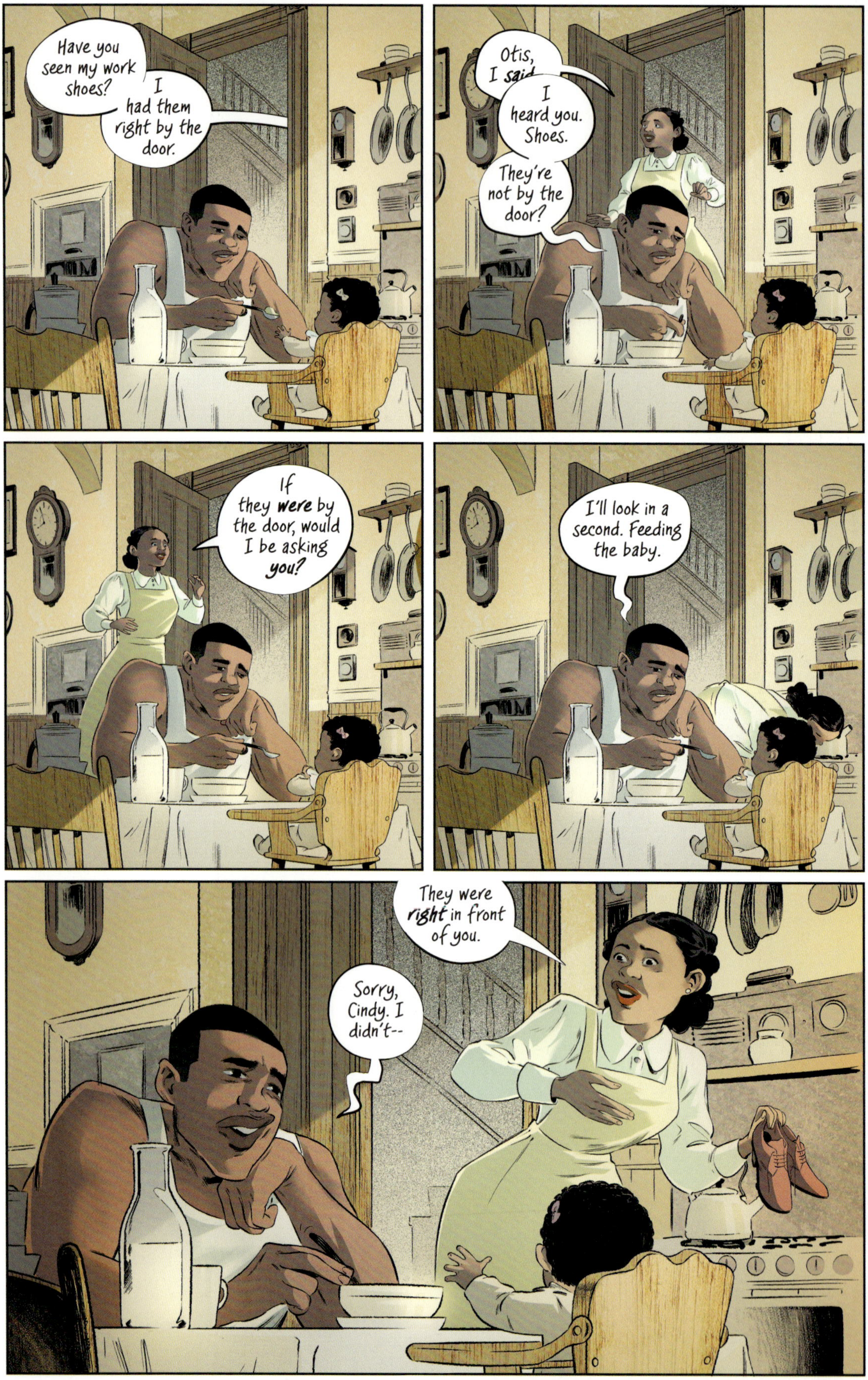
Have you seen my work shoes?
I had them right by the door.
Otis, I sai
I heard you. Shoes.
They're not by the door?
If they **were** by the door, would I be asking **you?**
I'll look in a second. Feeding the baby.
They were **right** in front of you.
Sorry, Cindy. I didn't--

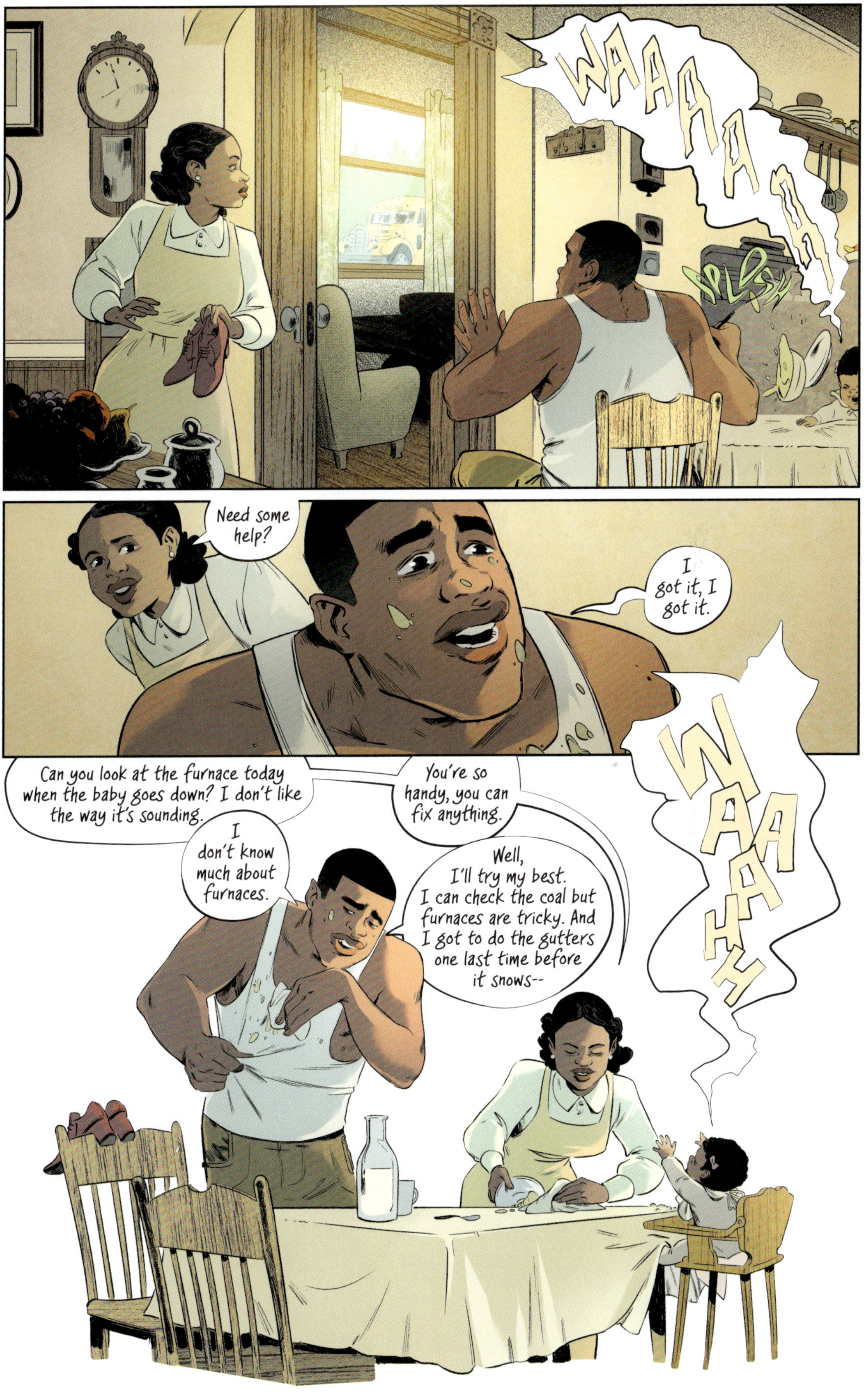
WAAAAAAH
SPLOOSH
Need some help?
I got it, I got it.
WAAAAHH
Can you look at the furnace today when the baby goes down? I don't like the way it's sounding.
I don't know much about furnaces.
You're so handy, you can fix anything.
Well, I'll try my best. I can check the coal but furnaces are tricky. And I got to do the gutters one last time before it snows--

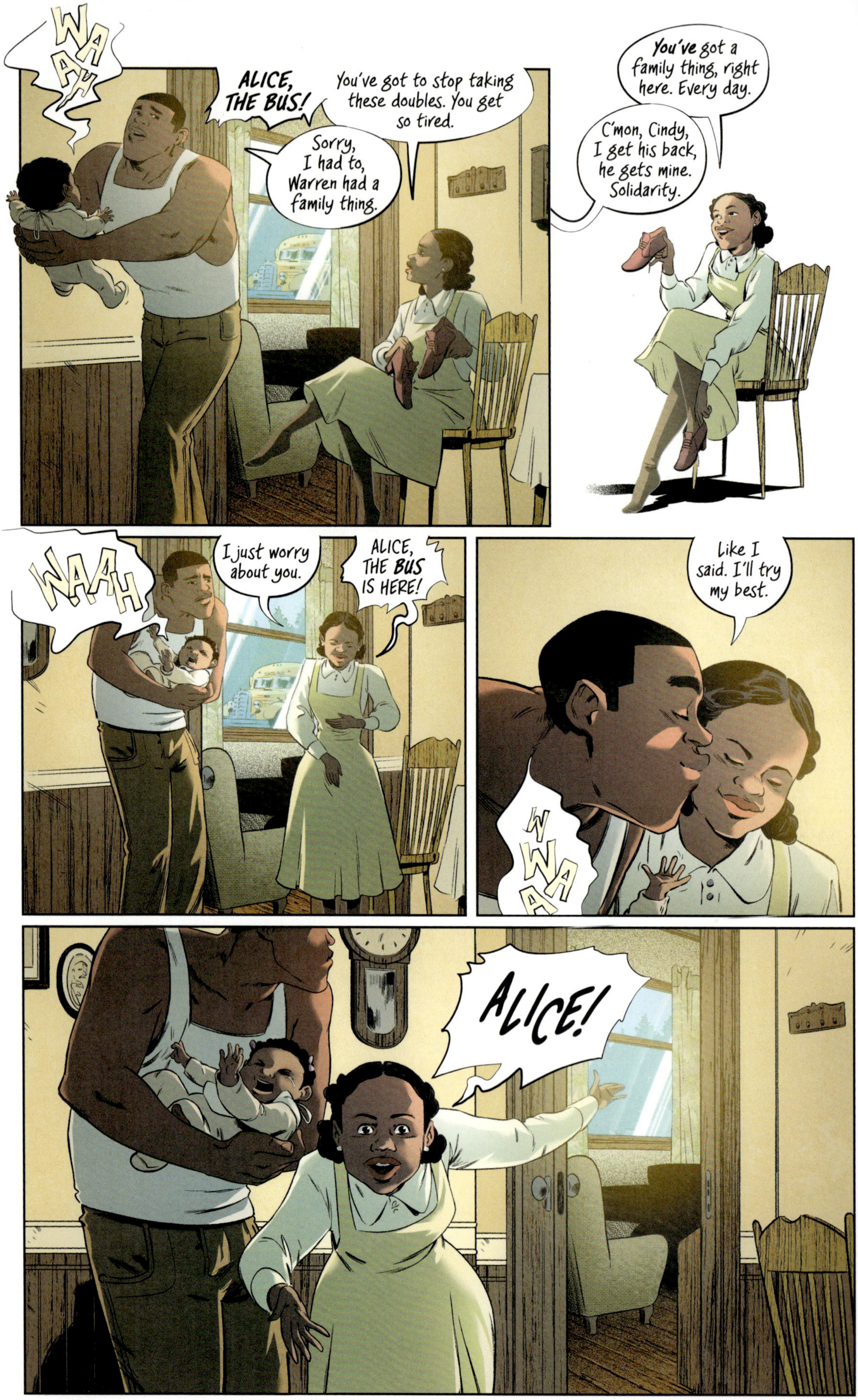
WAAH
ALICE, THE BUS!
You've got to stop taking these doubles. You get so tired.
Sorry, I had to, Warren had a family thing.
You've got a family thing, right here. Every day.
C'mon, Cindy, I get his back, he gets mine. Solidarity.
WAAAH
I just worry about you.
ALICE, THE BUS IS HERE!
Like I said. I'll try my best.
WWAA
ALICE!

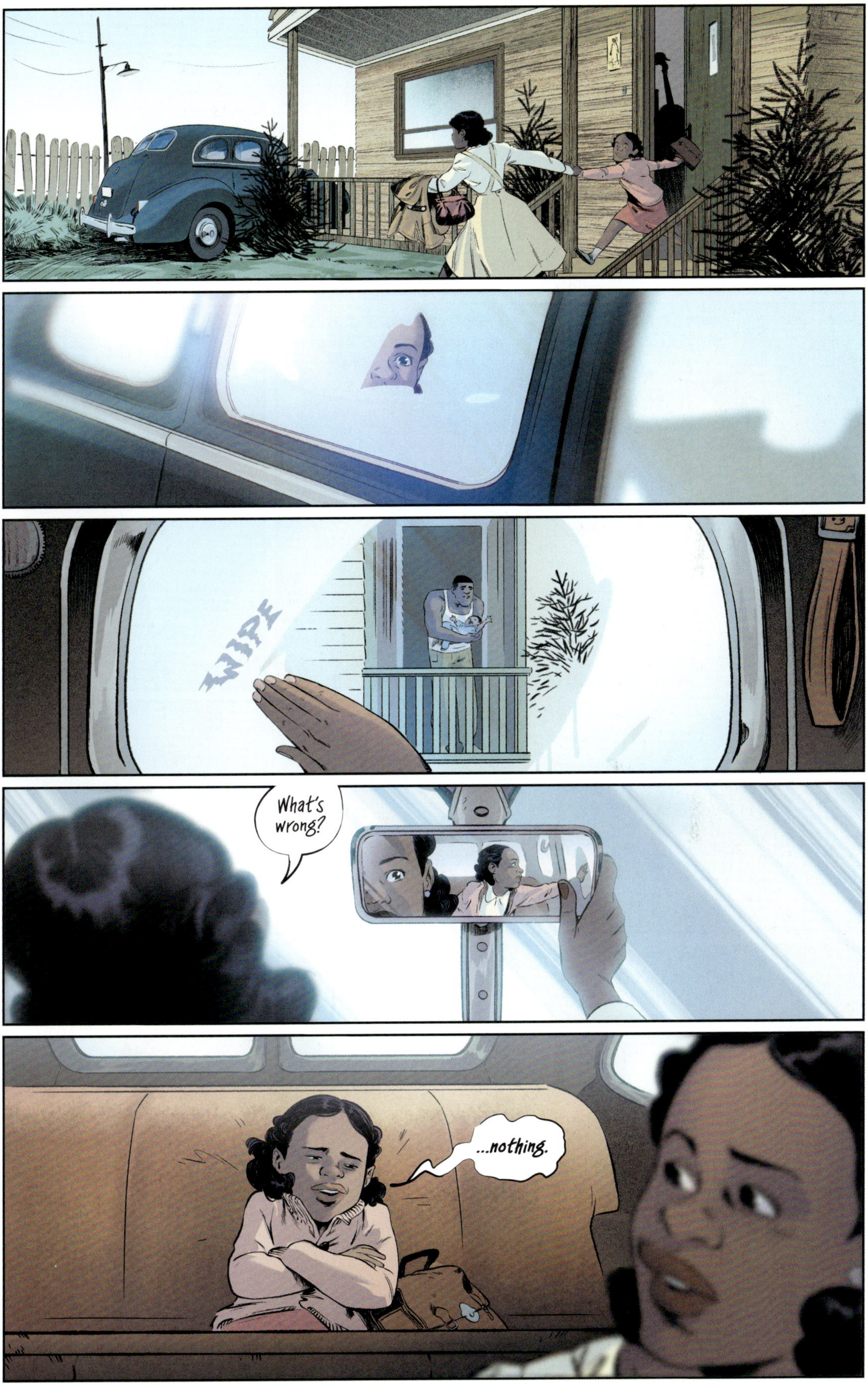
WIPE
What's wrong?
...nothing.

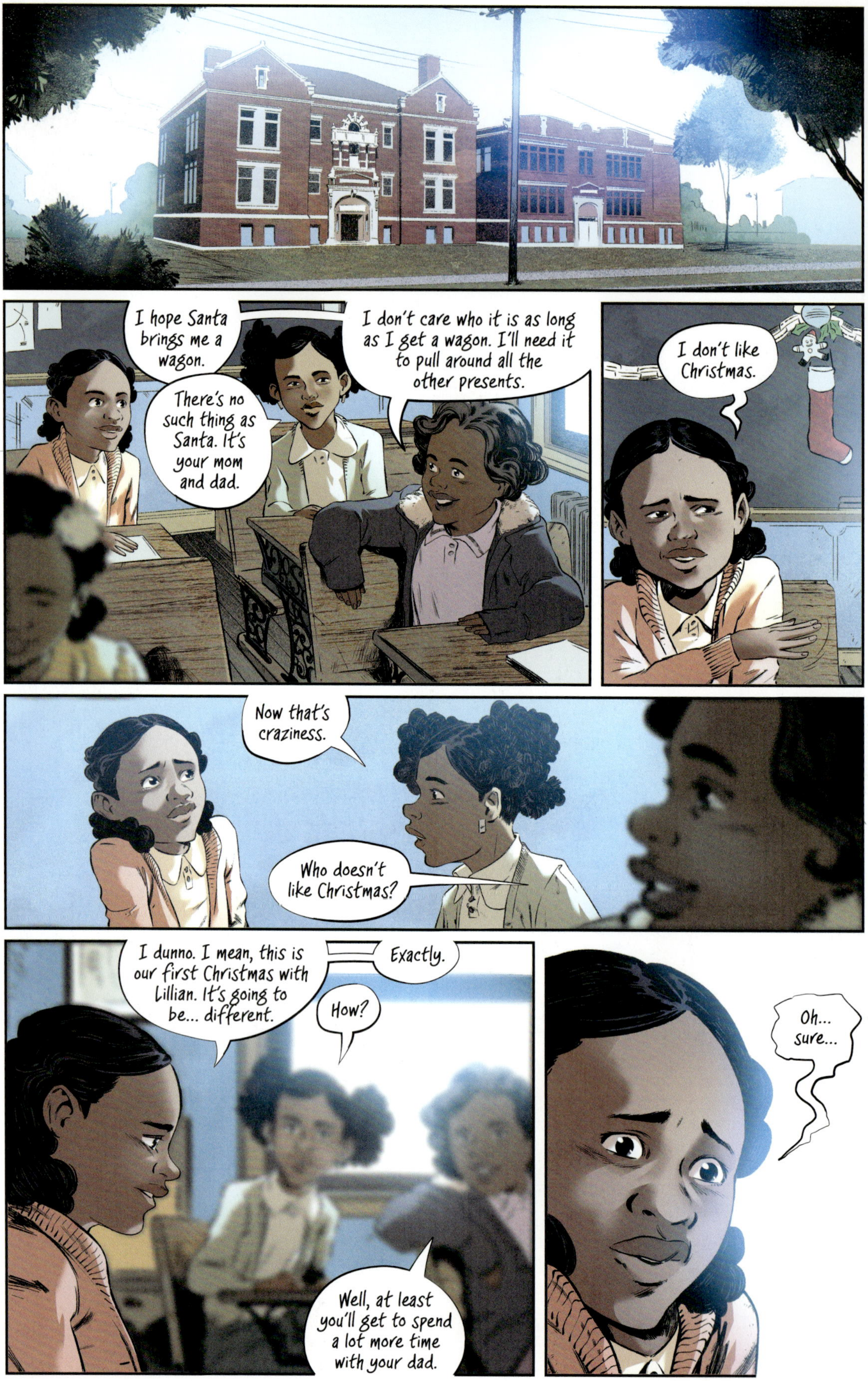
I hope Santa brings me a wagon.
There's no such thing as Santa. It's your mom and dad.
I don't care who it is as long as I get a wagon. I'll need it to pull around all the other presents.
I don't like Christmas.
Now that's craziness.
Who doesn't like Christmas?
I dunno. I mean, this is our first Christmas with Lillian. It's going to be... different.
Exactly.
How?
Well, at least you'll get to spend a lot more time with your dad.
Oh... sure...

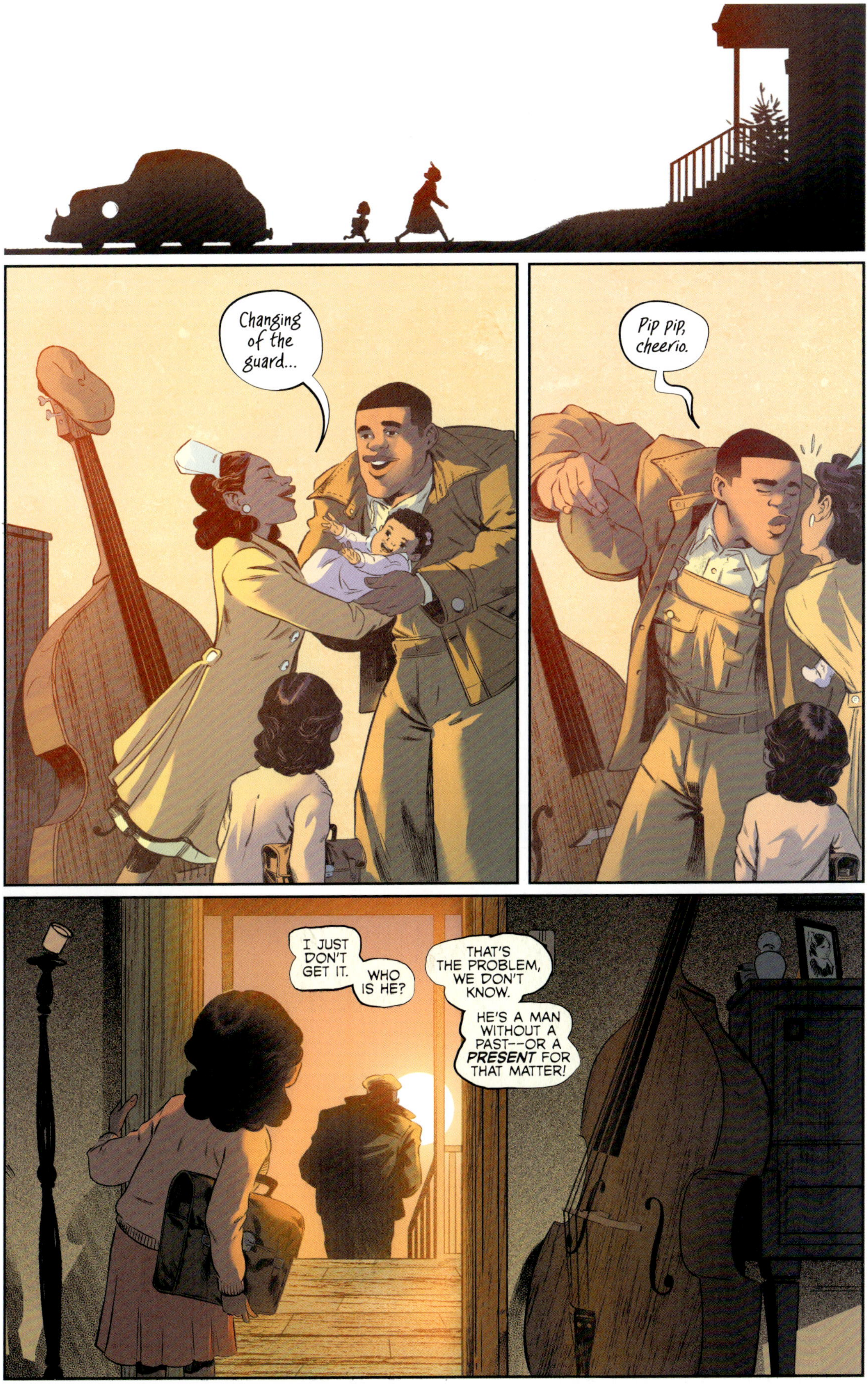
Changing of the guard...
Pip pip, cheerio.
I JUST DON'T GET IT.
WHO IS HE?
THAT'S THE PROBLEM, WE DON'T KNOW.
HE'S A MAN WITHOUT A PAST--OR A *PRESENT* FOR THAT MATTER!

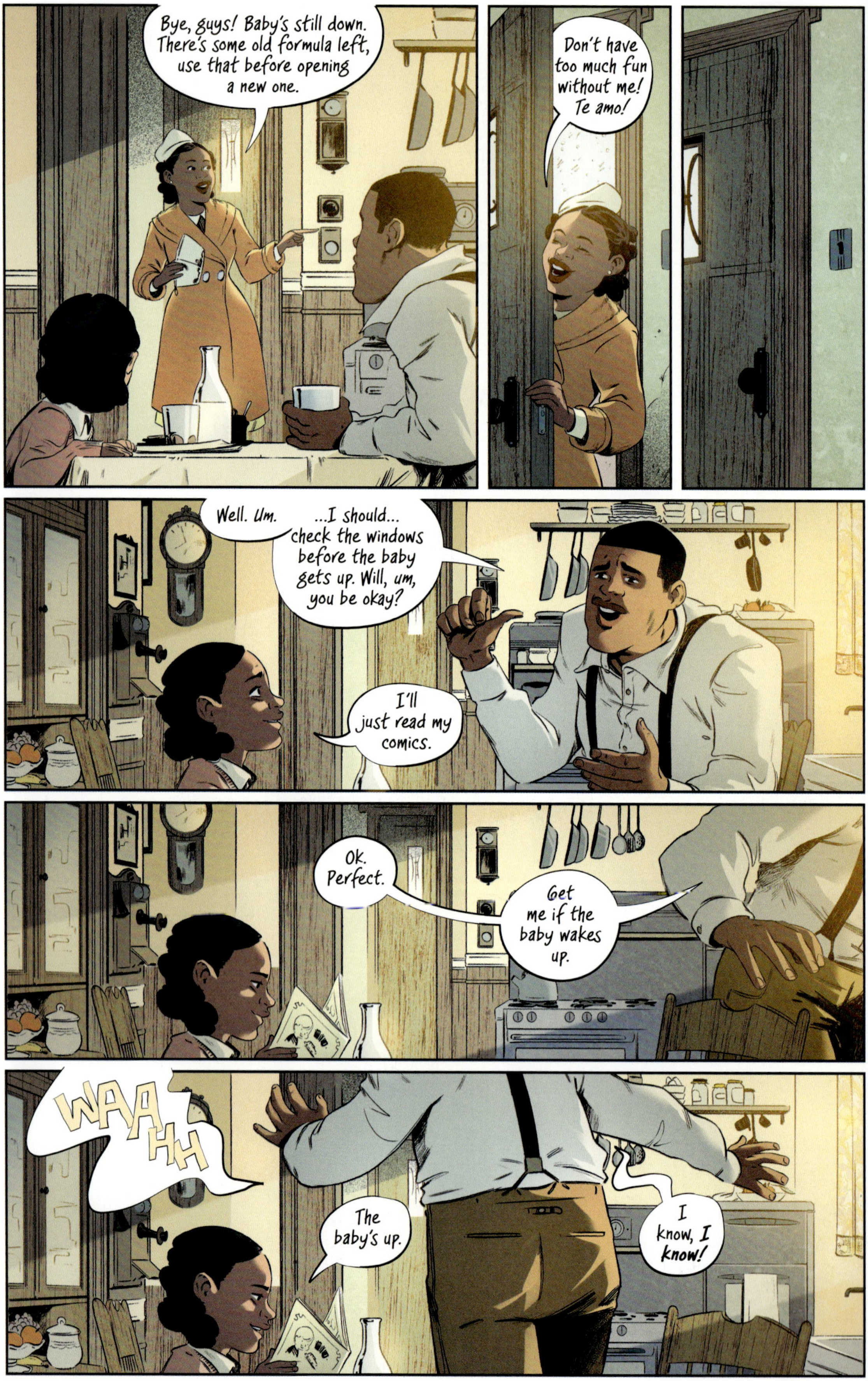
Bye, guys! Baby's still down. There's some old formula left, use that before opening a new one.
Don't have too much fun without me! Te amo!
Well. Um.
...I should... check the windows before the baby gets up. Will, um, you be okay?
I'll just read my comics.
Ok. Perfect.
Get me if the baby wakes up.
WAAHH
The baby's up.
I know, I know!

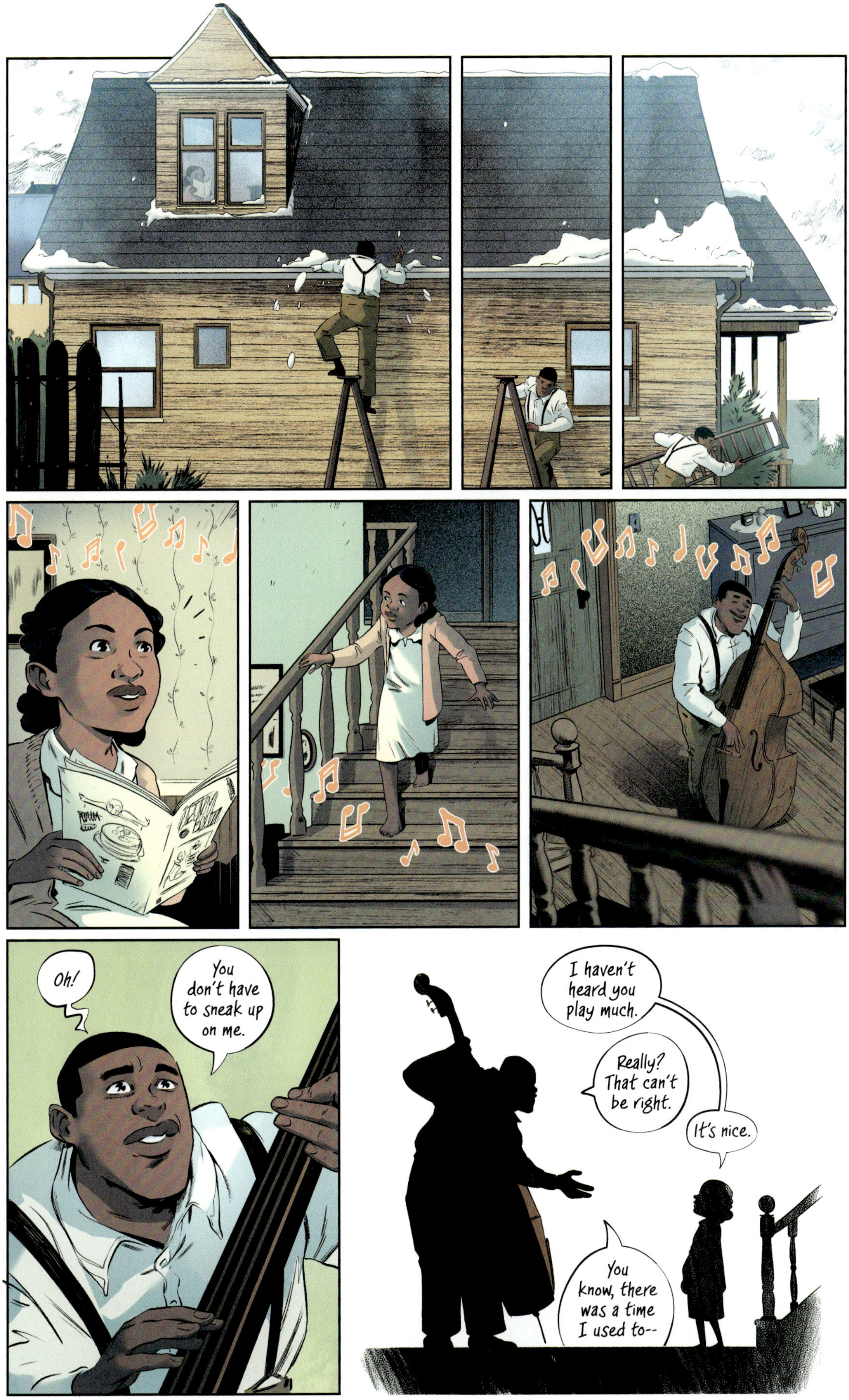
Oh!
You don't have to sneak up on me.
I haven't heard you play much.
Really? That can't be right.
It's nice.
You know, there was a time I used to--

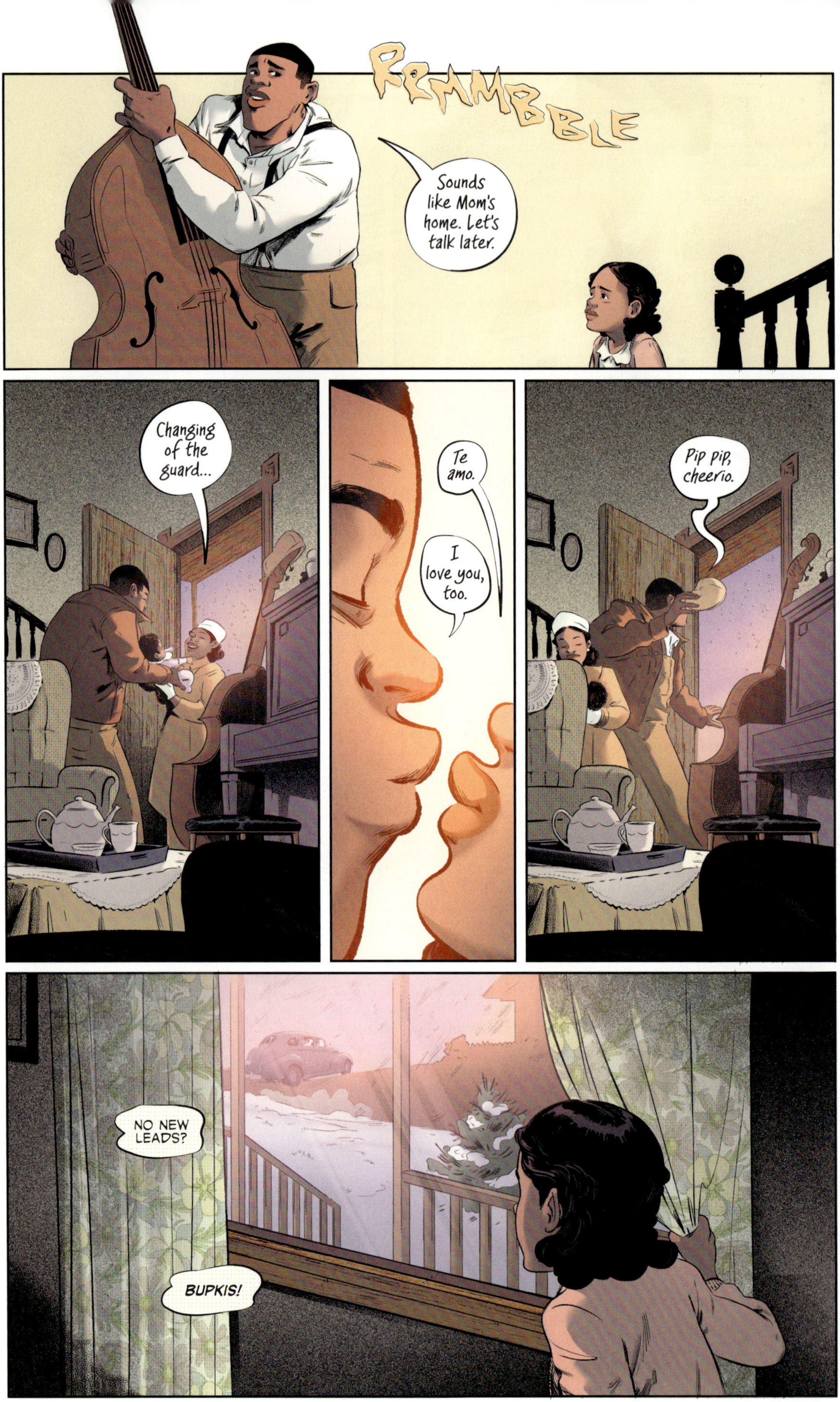
RRMMBBLE
Sounds like Mom's home. Let's talk later.
Changing of the guard...
Te amo.
I love you, too.
Pip pip, cheerio.
NO NEW LEADS?
BUPKIS!

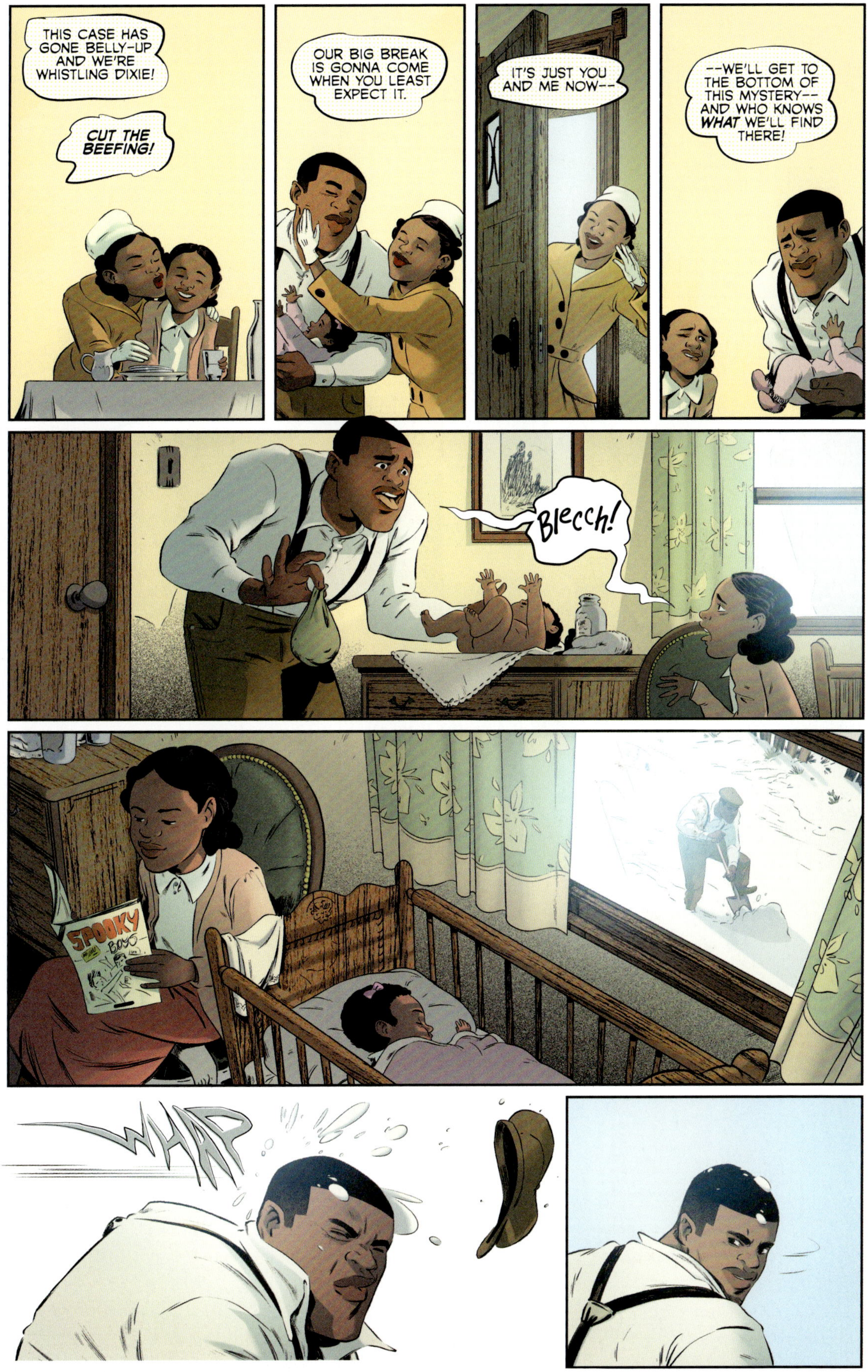
THIS CASE HAS GONE BELLY-UP AND WE'RE WHISTLING DIXIE!
CUT THE BEEFING!
OUR BIG BREAK IS GONNA COME WHEN YOU LEAST EXPECT IT.
IT'S JUST YOU AND ME NOW--
--WE'LL GET TO THE BOTTOM OF THIS MYSTERY--AND WHO KNOWS WHAT WE'LL FIND THERE!
Blecch!
SPOOKY BOYS
WHAP

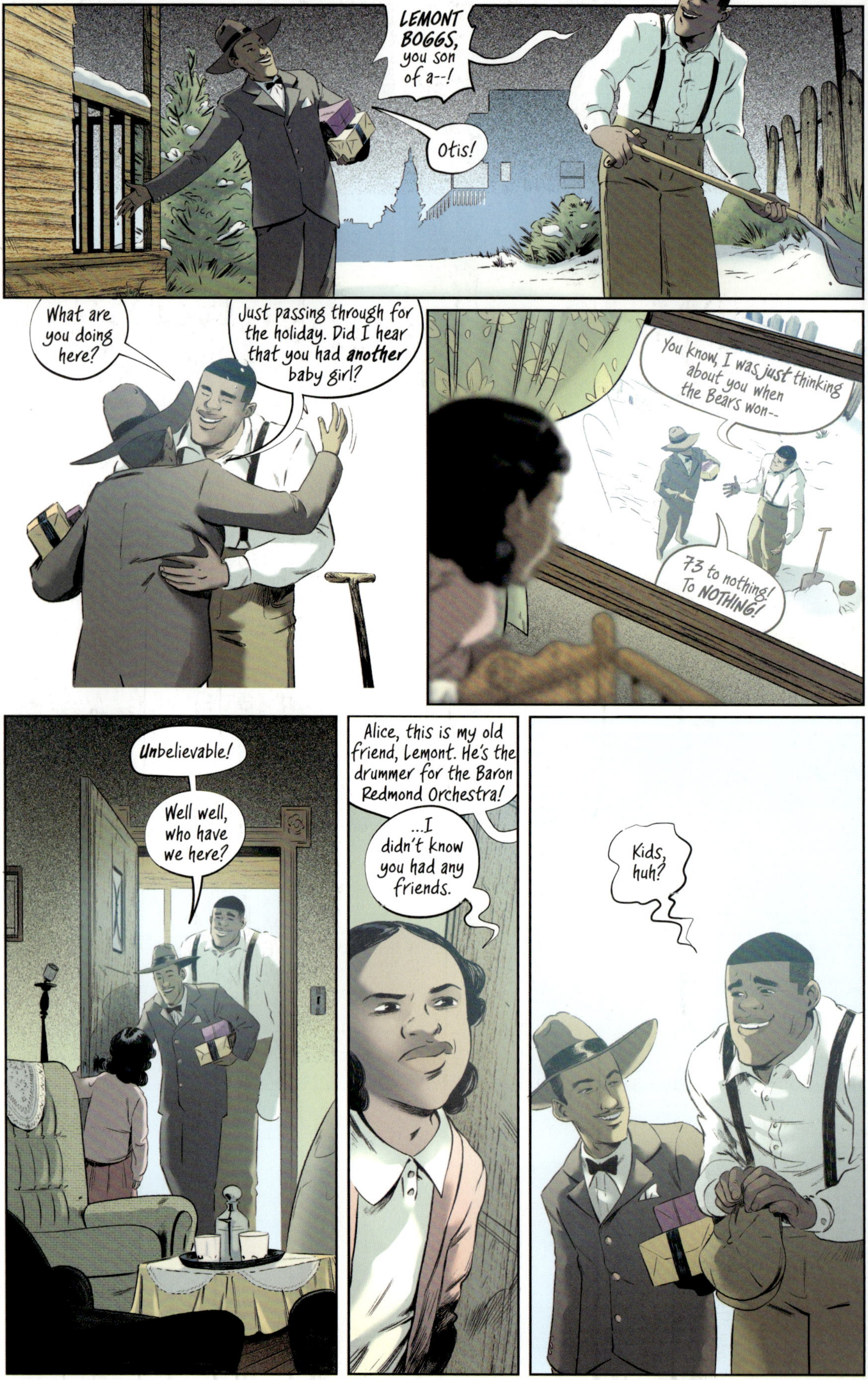
LEMONT BOGGS, you son of a--!
Otis!
What are you doing here?
Just passing through for the holiday. Did I hear that you had **another** baby girl?
You know, I was **just** thinking about you when the Bears won--
73 to nothing! To **NOTHING!**
Unbelievable!
Well well, who have we here?
Alice, this is my old friend, Lemont. He's the drummer for the Baron Redmond Orchestra!
...I didn't know you had any friends.
Kids, huh?

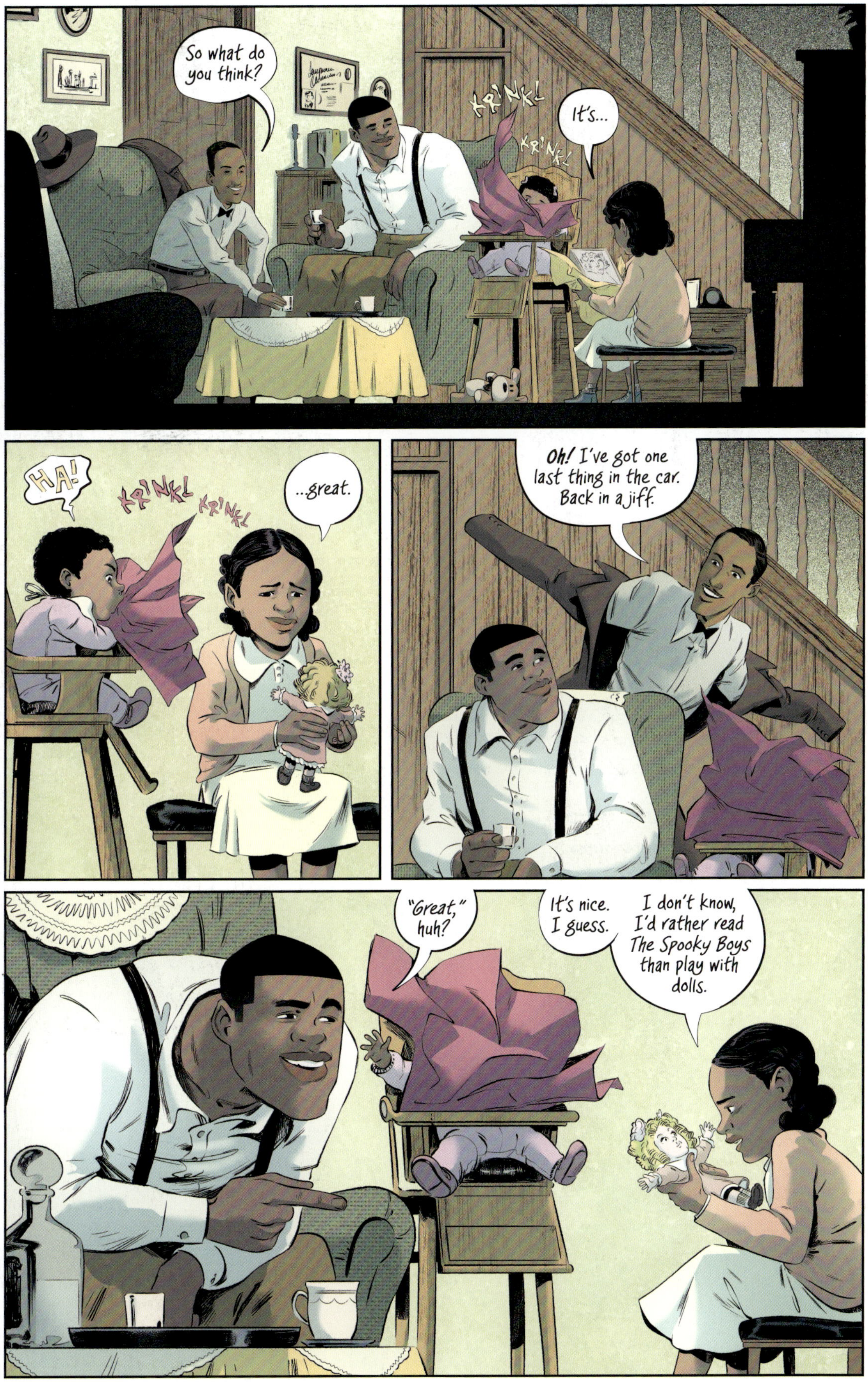
So what do you think?
KRINKL
KRINKL
It's...
HA!
KRINKL KRINKL
...great.
Oh! I've got one last thing in the car. Back in a jiff.
"Great," huh?
It's nice. I guess.
I don't know, I'd rather read The Spooky Boys than play with dolls.

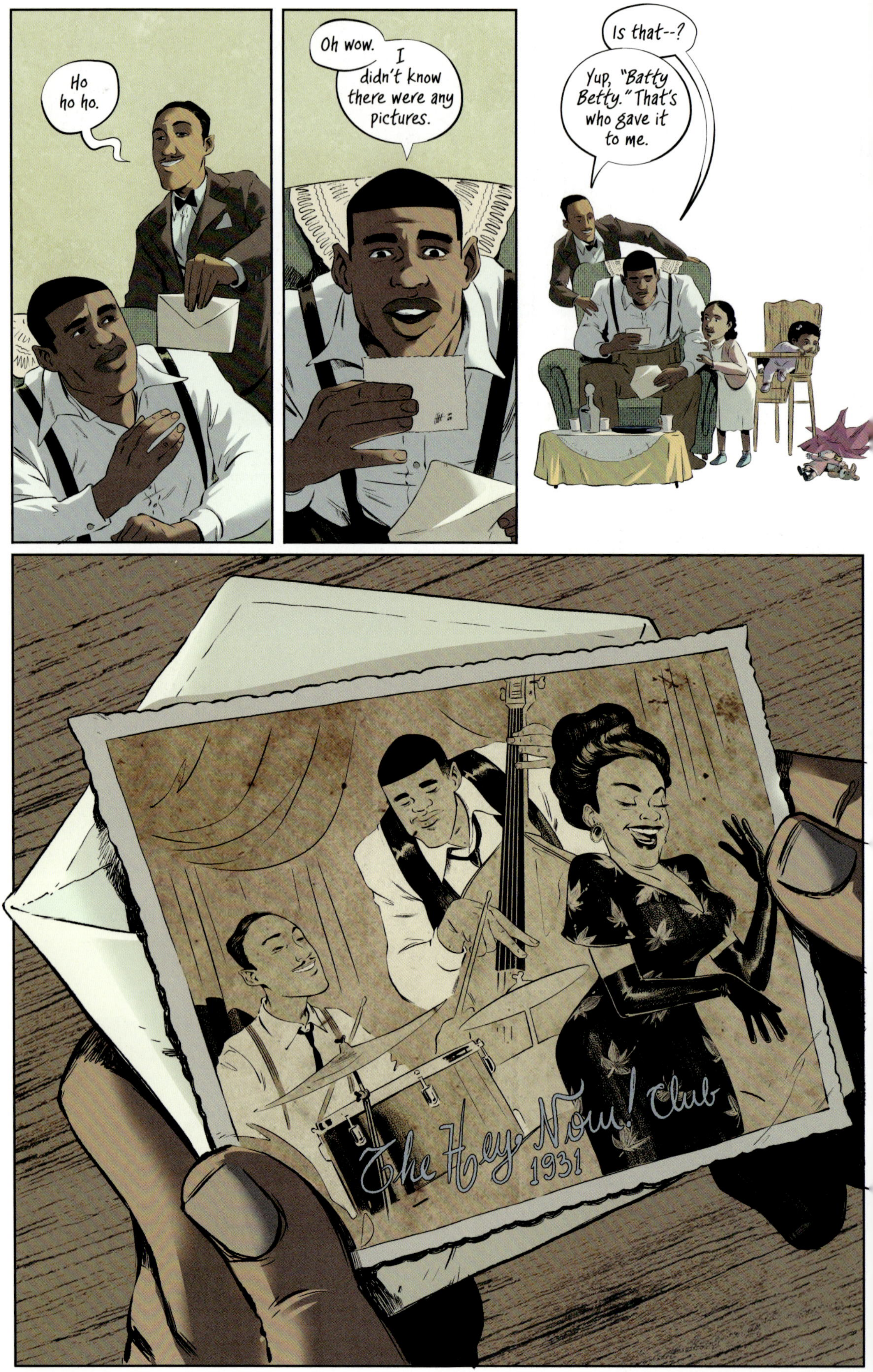
Ho ho ho.
Oh wow.
I didn't know there were any pictures.
Is that--?
Yup, "Batty Betty." That's who gave it to me.
The Hey Now! Club
1931

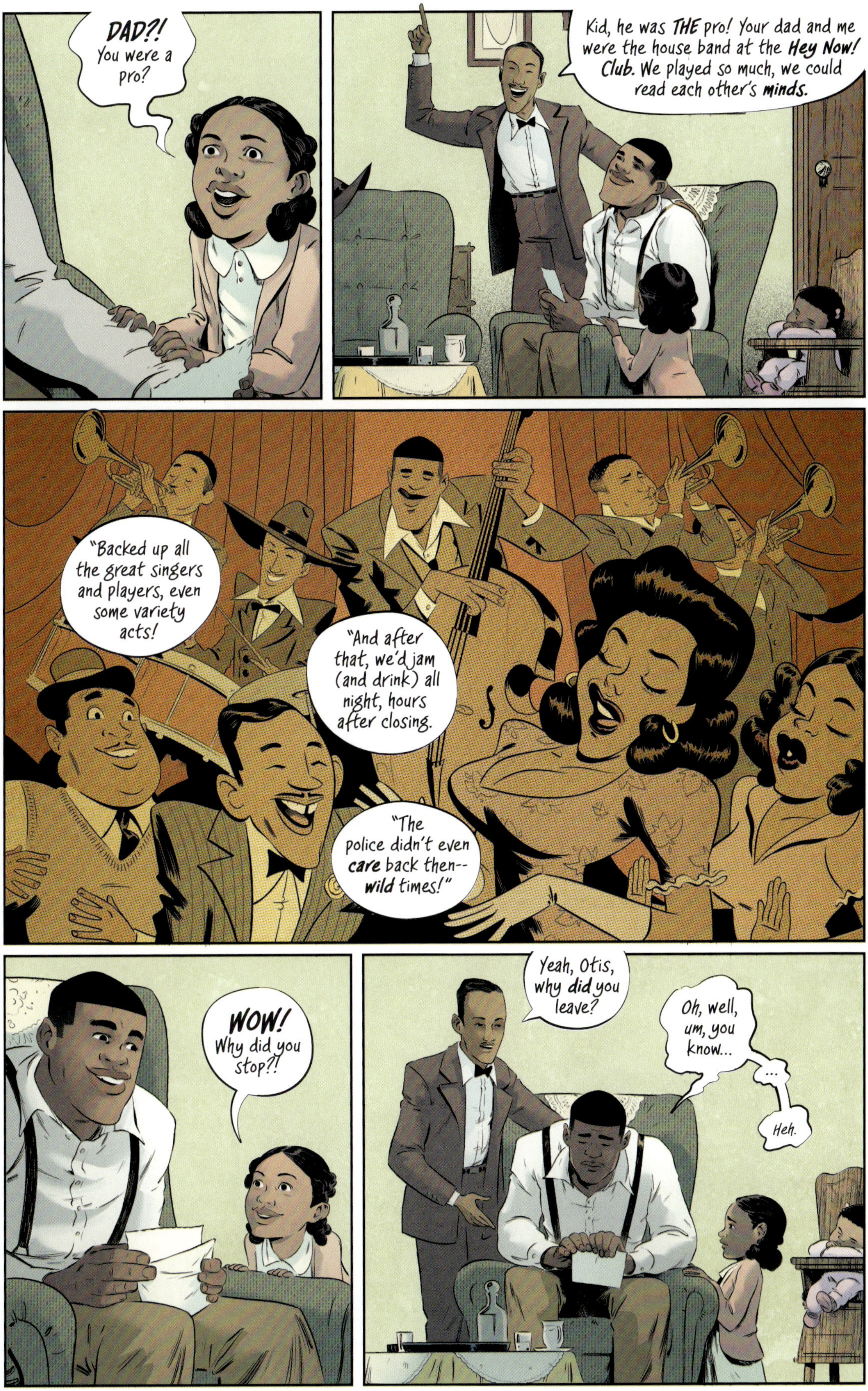
DAD?! You were a pro?
Kid, he was THE pro! Your dad and me were the house band at the Hey Now! Club. We played so much, we could read each other's minds.
"Backed up all the great singers and players, even some variety acts!
"And after that, we'd jam (and drink) all night, hours after closing.
"The police didn't even care back then-- wild times!"
WOW! Why did you stop?!
Yeah, Otis, why did you leave?
Oh, well, um, you know...
...
Heh.

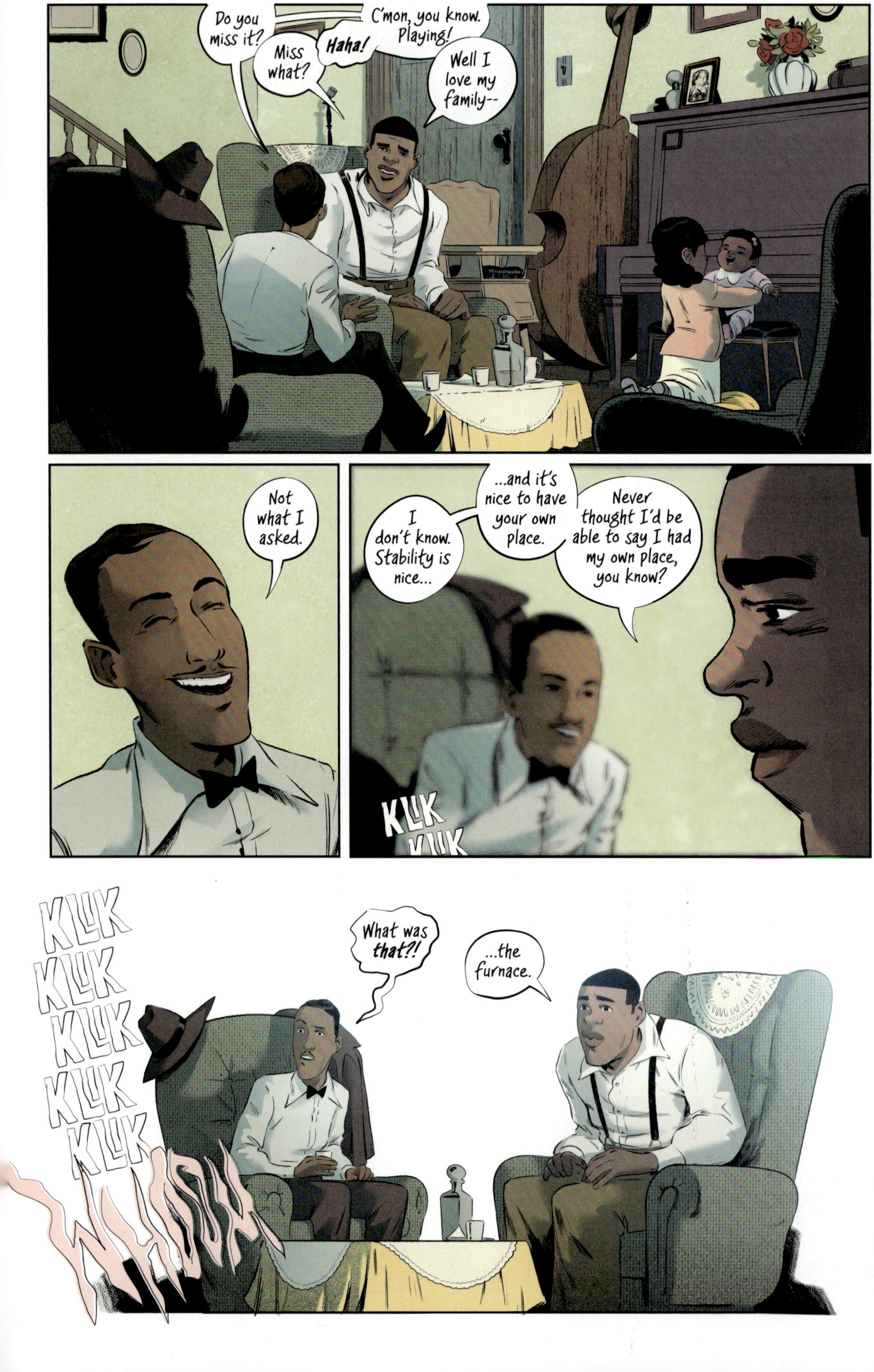
Do you miss it?
Miss what?
Haha!
C'mon, you know. Playing!
Well I love my family--
Not what I asked.
I don't know. Stability is nice...
...and it's nice to have your own place.
Never thought I'd be able to say I had my own place, you know?
KLIK
KLIK KLIK KLIK KLIK KLIK
What was that?!
...the furnace.

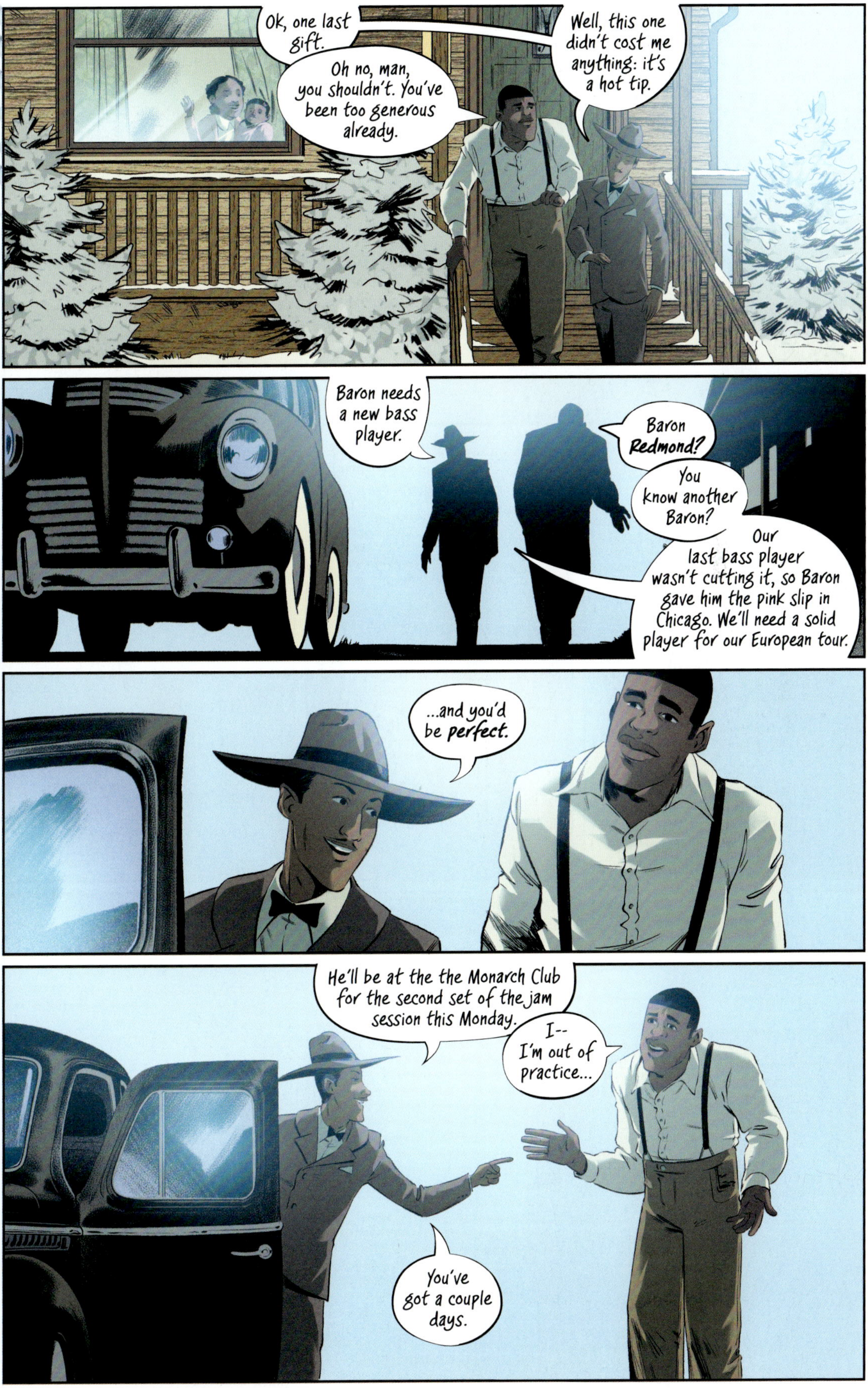
Ok, one last gift.
Well, this one didn't cost me anything: it's a hot tip.
Oh no, man, you shouldn't. You've been too generous already.
Baron needs a new bass player.
Baron **Redmond?**
You know another Baron?
Our last bass player wasn't cutting it, so Baron gave him the pink slip in Chicago. We'll need a solid player for our European tour.
...and you'd be ***perfect.***
He'll be at the the Monarch Club for the second set of the jam session this Monday.
I-- I'm out of practice...
You've got a couple days.

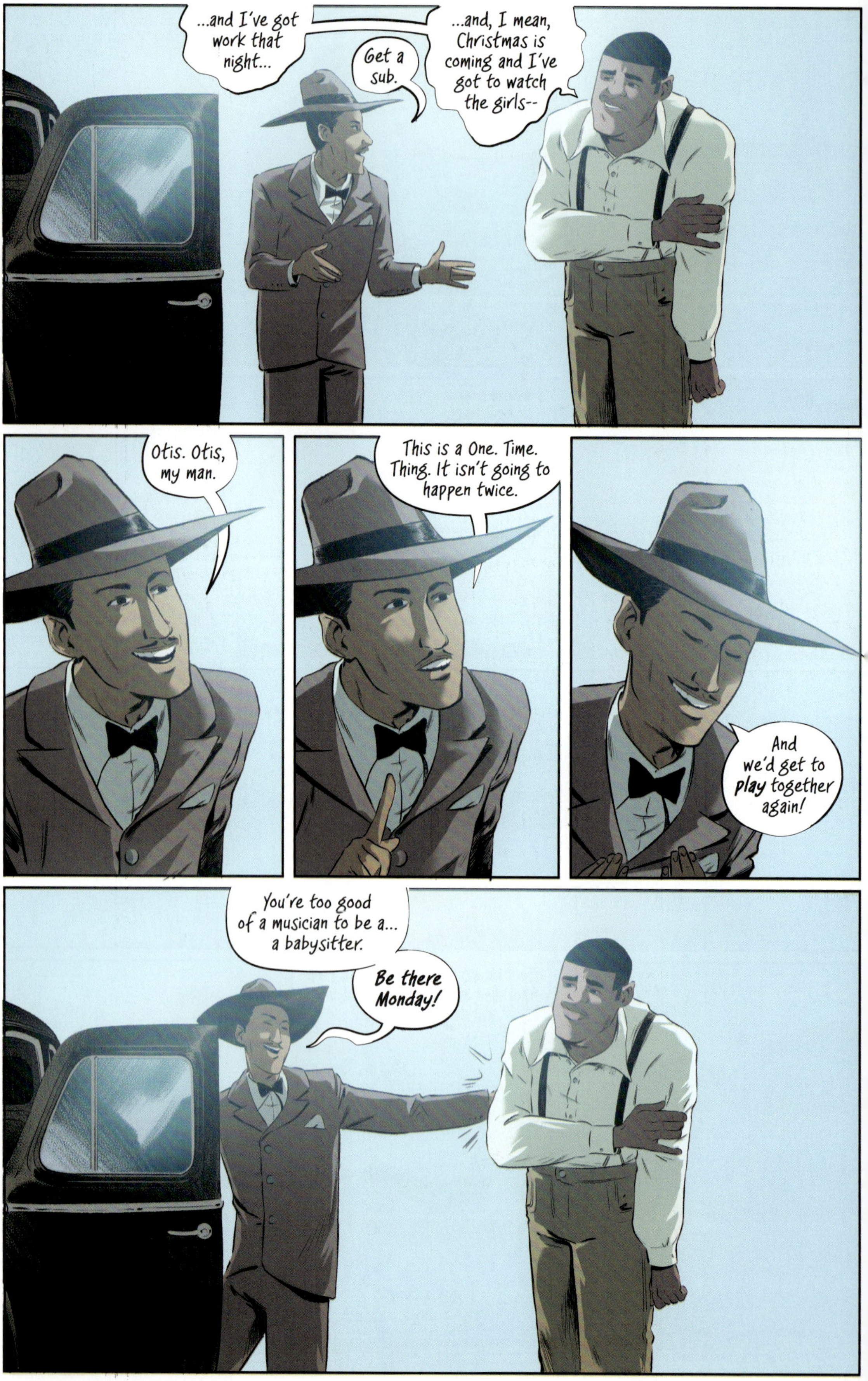
...and I've got work that night...
Get a sub.
...and, I mean, Christmas is coming and I've got to watch the girls--
Otis. Otis, my man.
This is a One. Time. Thing. It isn't going to happen twice.
And we'd get to play together again!
You're too good of a musician to be a... a babysitter.
Be there Monday!

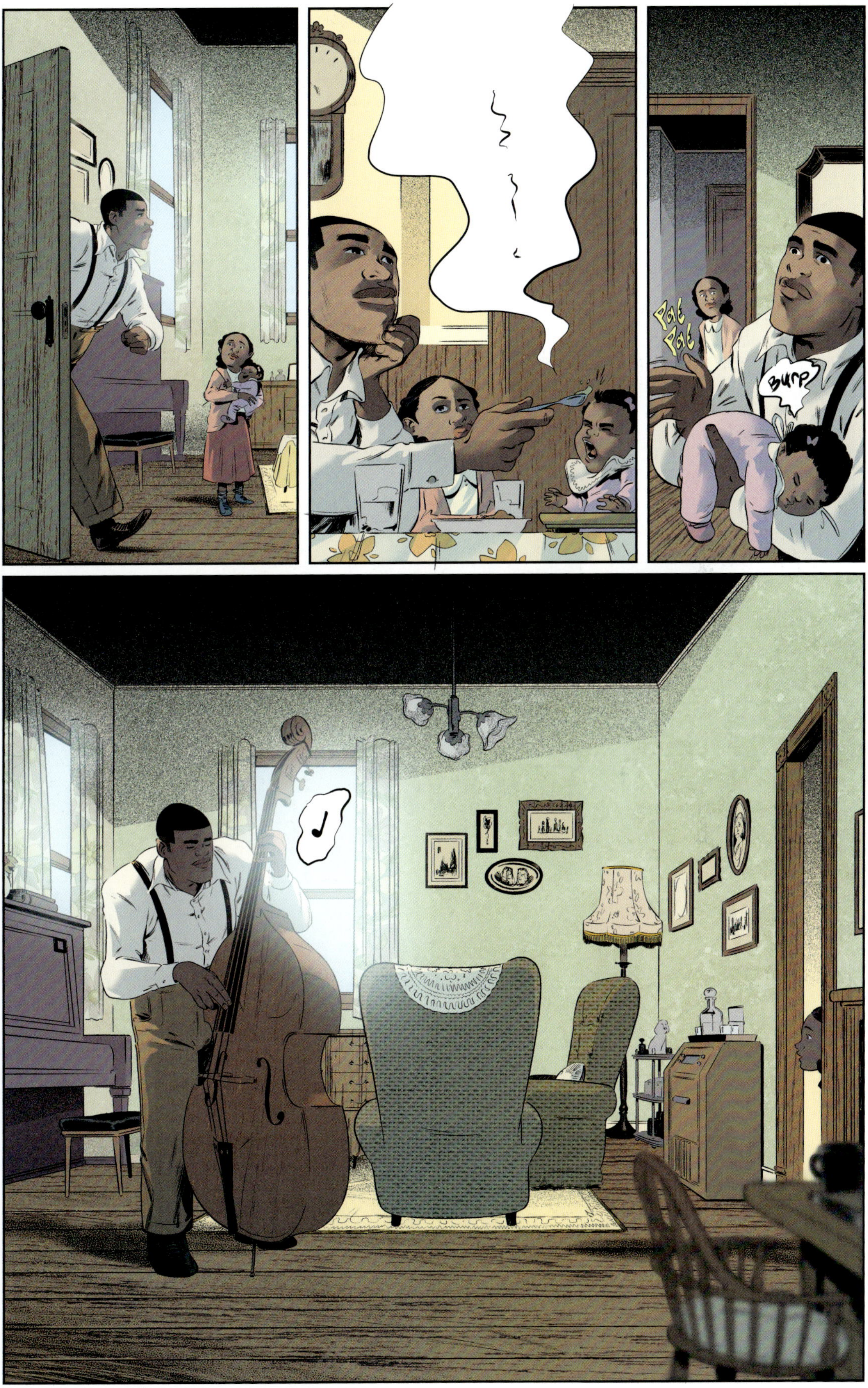
Pat Pat
Burp

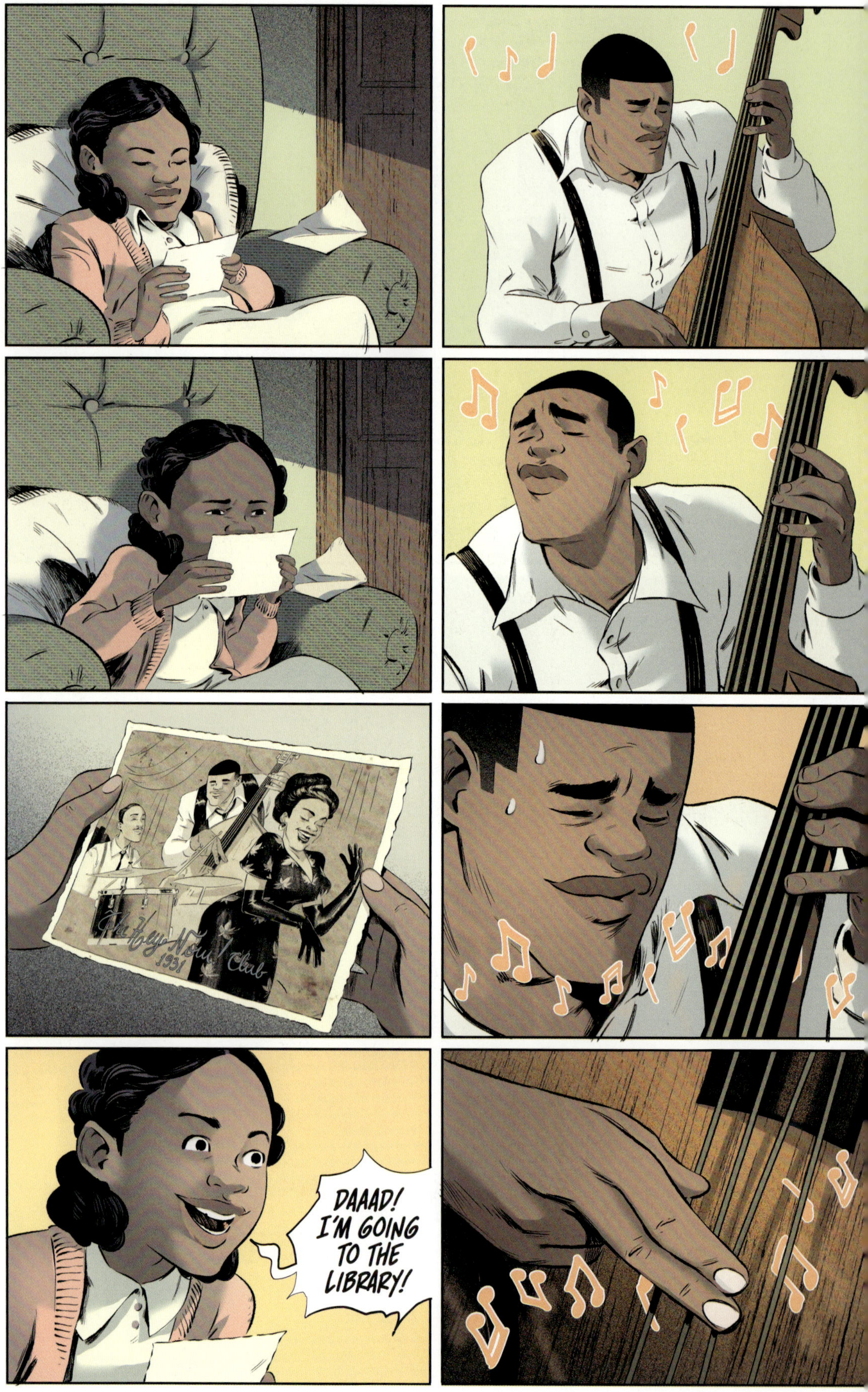
The Hey Now! Club
1931
DAAAD! I'M GOING TO THE LIBRARY!

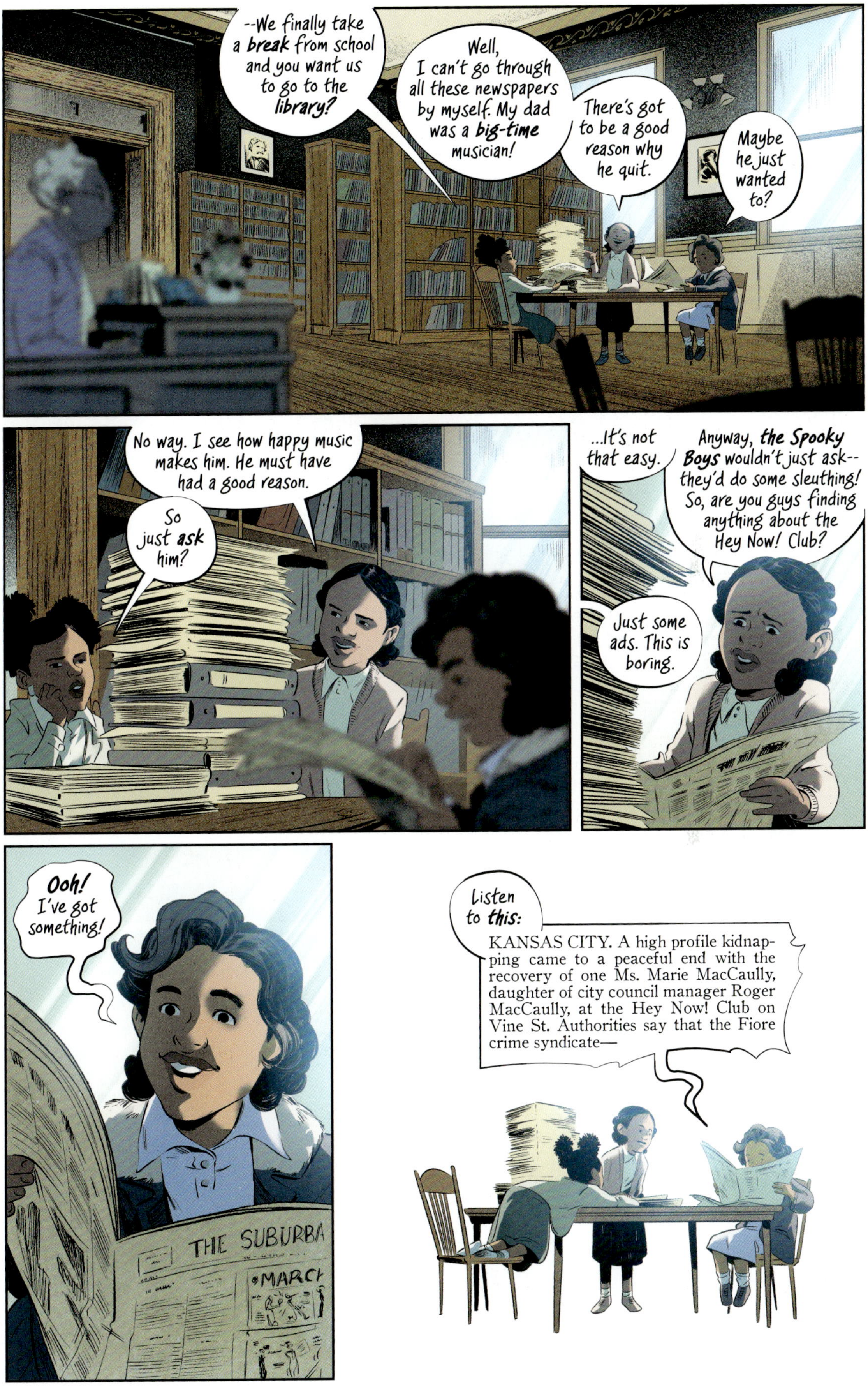
--We finally take a break from school and you want us to go to the library?
Well, I can't go through all these newspapers by myself. My dad was a big-time musician!
There's got to be a good reason why he quit.
Maybe he just wanted to?
No way. I see how happy music makes him. He must have had a good reason.
So just ask him?
...It's not that easy.
Anyway, the Spooky Boys wouldn't just ask--they'd do some sleuthing! So, are you guys finding anything about the Hey Now! Club?
Just some ads. This is boring.
Ooh! I've got something!
THE SUBURBA
MARC
Listen to this:
KANSAS CITY. A high profile kidnapping came to a peaceful end with the recovery of one Ms. Marie MacCaully, daughter of city council manager Roger MacCaully, at the Hey Now! Club on Vine St. Authorities say that the Fiore crime syndicate—

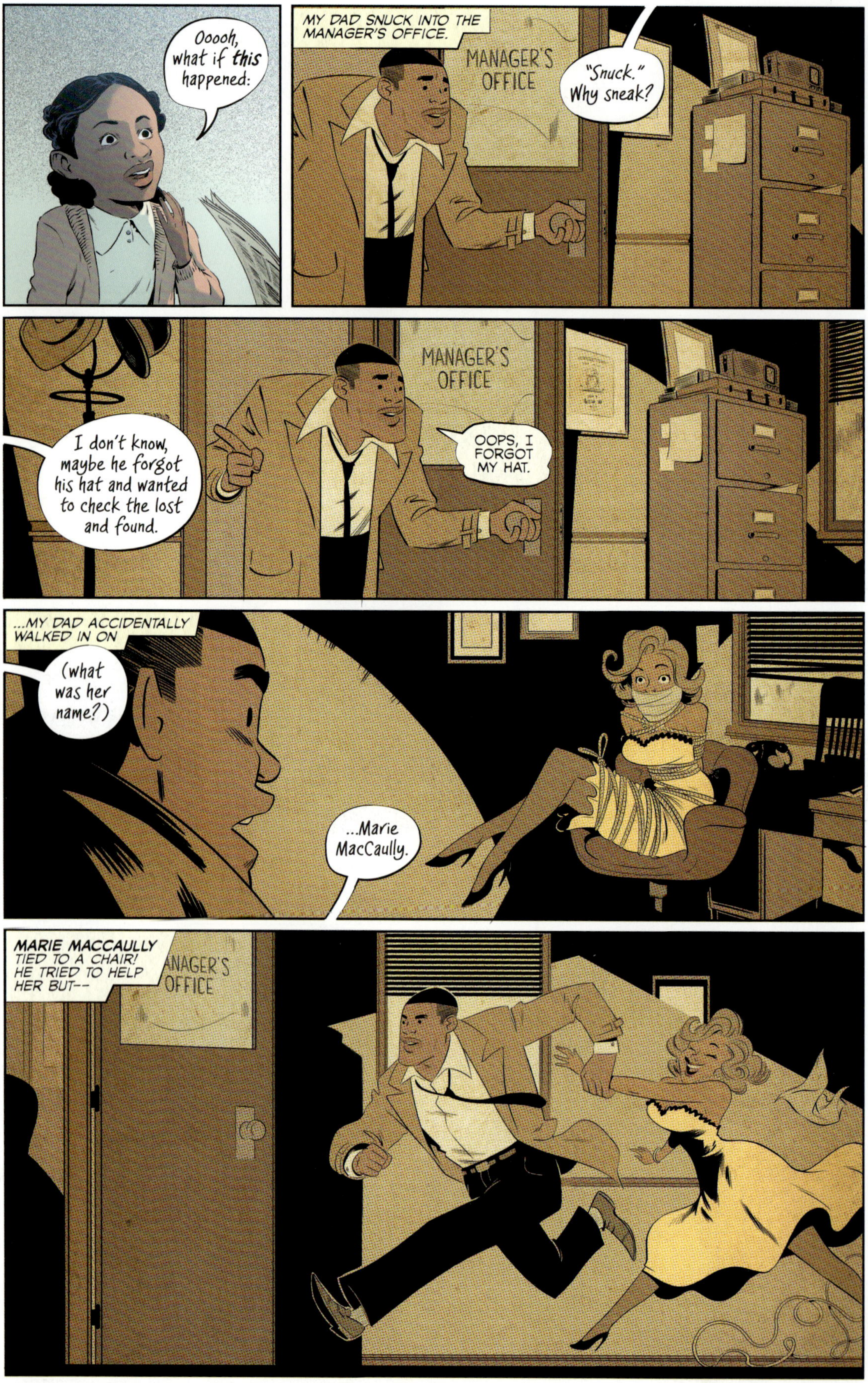
Ooooh, what if this happened:
MY DAD SNUCK INTO THE MANAGER'S OFFICE.
MANAGER'S OFFICE
"Snuck." Why sneak?
MANAGER'S OFFICE
I don't know, maybe he forgot his hat and wanted to check the lost and found.
OOPS, I FORGOT MY HAT.
...MY DAD ACCIDENTALLY WALKED IN ON
(what was her name?)
...Marie MacCaully.
MARIE MACCAULLY TIED TO A CHAIR! HE TRIED TO HELP HER BUT--
ANAGER'S OFFICE

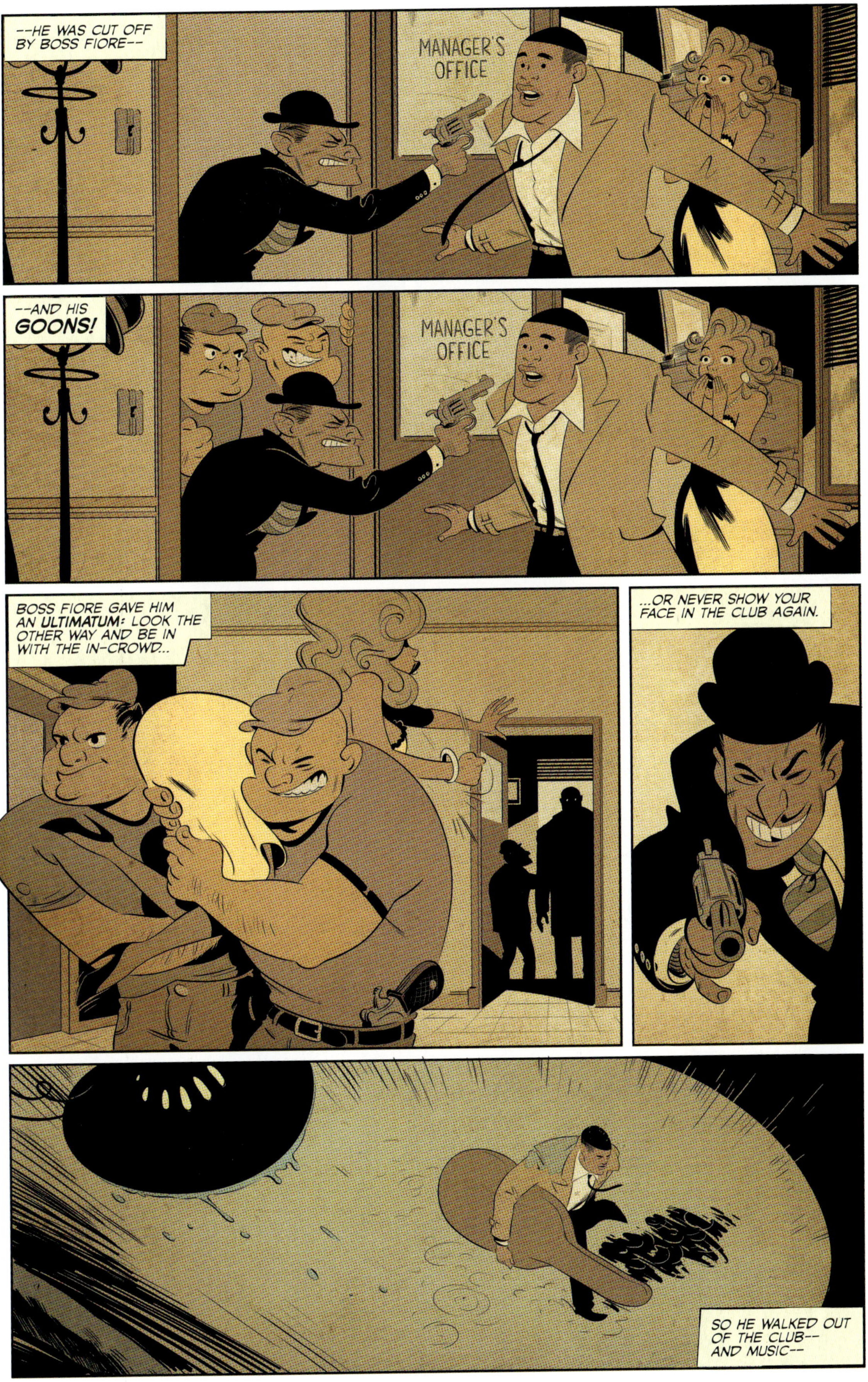
--HE WAS CUT OFF BY BOSS FIORE--
MANAGER'S OFFICE
--AND HIS GOONS!
MANAGER'S OFFICE
BOSS FIORE GAVE HIM AN ULTIMATUM: LOOK THE OTHER WAY AND BE IN WITH THE IN-CROWD...
...OR NEVER SHOW YOUR FACE IN THE CLUB AGAIN.
SO HE WALKED OUT OF THE CLUB-- AND MUSIC--

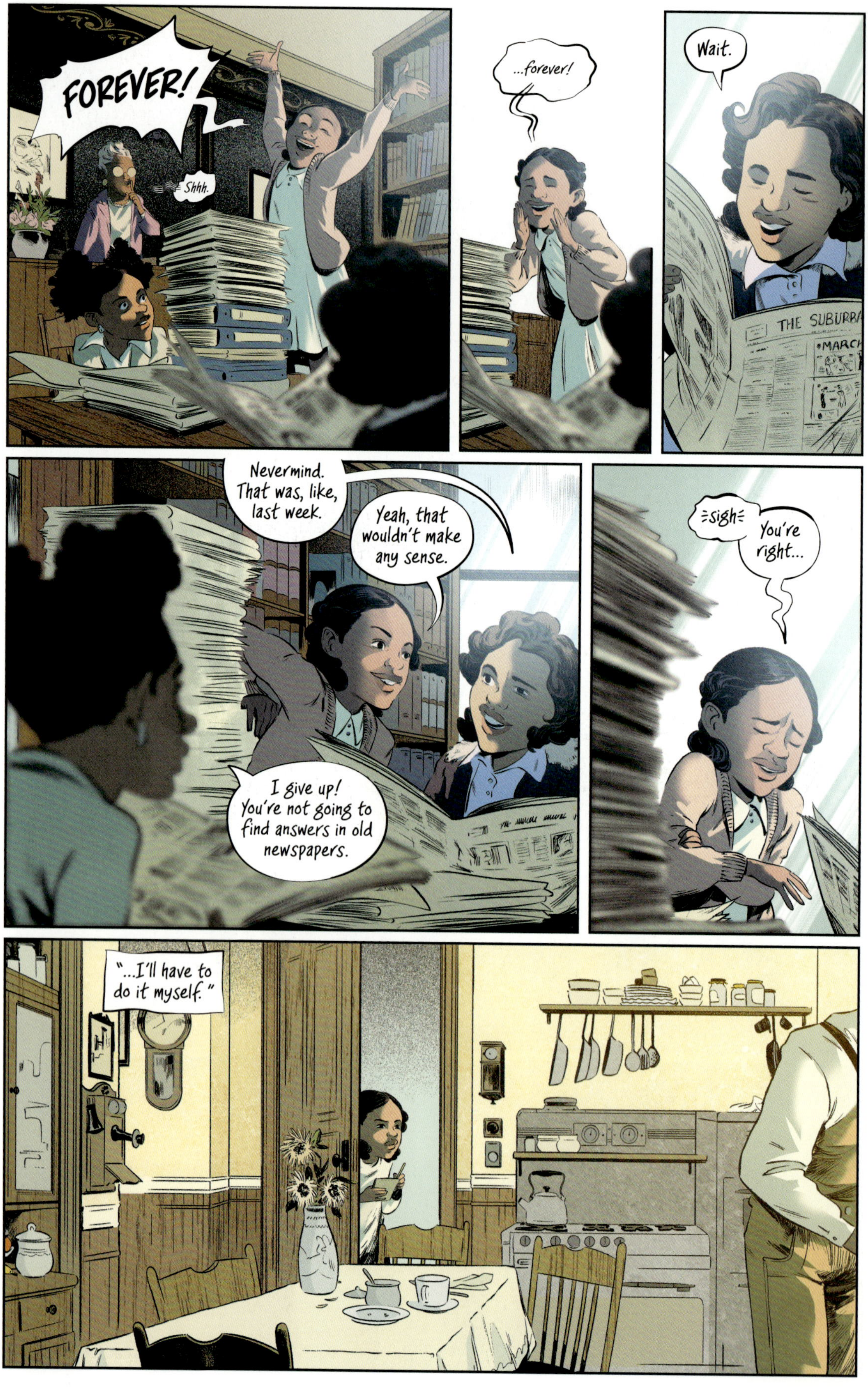
FOREVER!
Shhh.
...forever!
Wait.
THE SUBURBA
MARCH
Nevermind. That was, like, last week.
Yeah, that wouldn't make any sense.
I give up! You're not going to find answers in old newspapers.
sigh
You're right...
"...I'll have to do it myself."

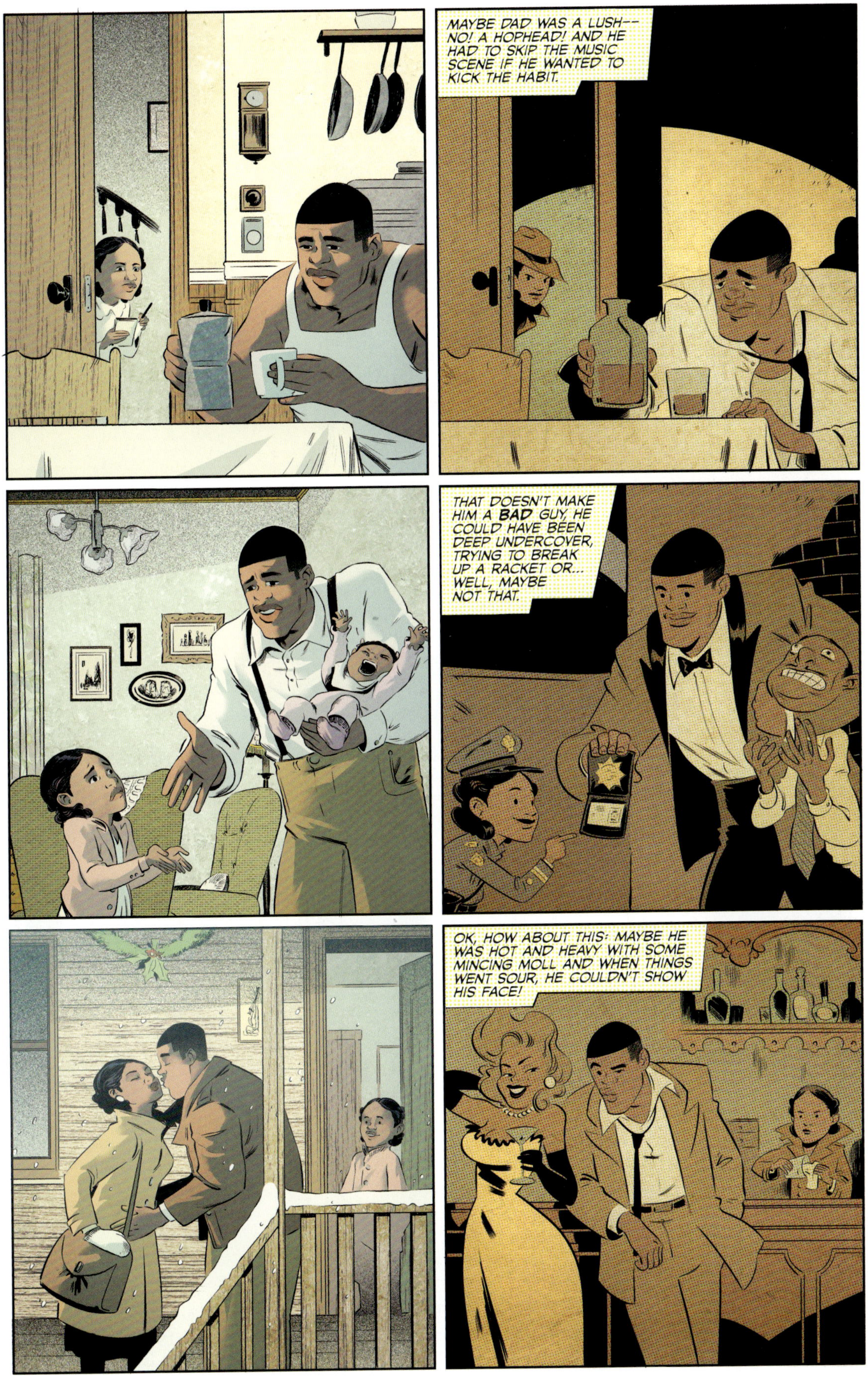
MAYBE DAD WAS A LUSH-- NO! A HOPHEAD! AND HE HAD TO SKIP THE MUSIC SCENE IF HE WANTED TO KICK THE HABIT.
THAT DOESN'T MAKE HIM A **BAD** GUY, HE COULD HAVE BEEN DEEP UNDERCOVER, TRYING TO BREAK UP A RACKET OR... WELL, MAYBE NOT THAT.
OK, HOW ABOUT THIS: MAYBE HE WAS HOT AND HEAVY WITH SOME MINCING MOLL AND WHEN THINGS WENT SOUR, HE COULDN'T SHOW HIS FACE!

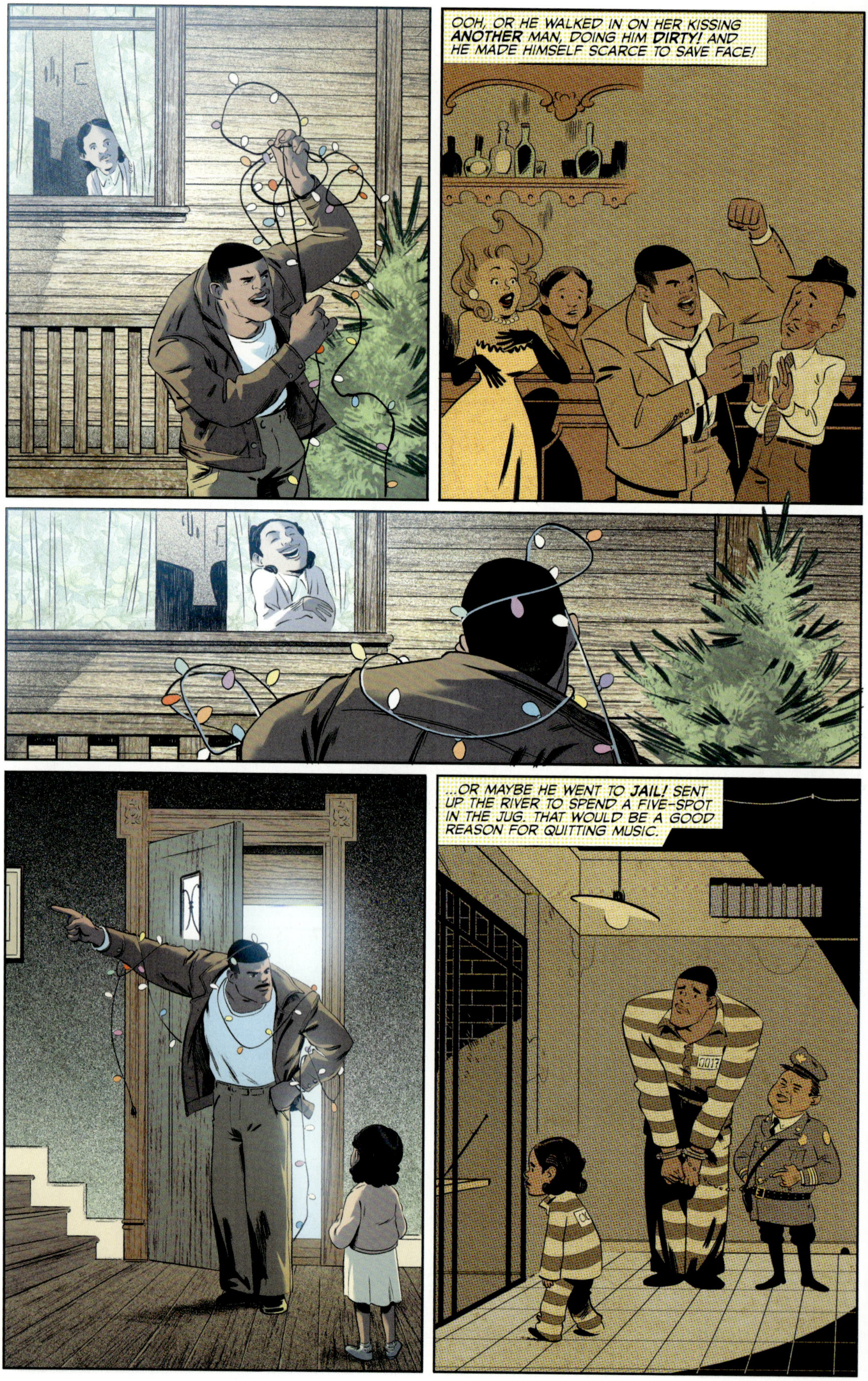
OOH, OR HE WALKED IN ON HER KISSING ANOTHER MAN, DOING HIM DIRTY! AND HE MADE HIMSELF SCARCE TO SAVE FACE!
...OR MAYBE HE WENT TO JAIL! SENT UP THE RIVER TO SPEND A FIVE-SPOT IN THE JUG. THAT WOULD BE A GOOD REASON FOR QUITTING MUSIC.

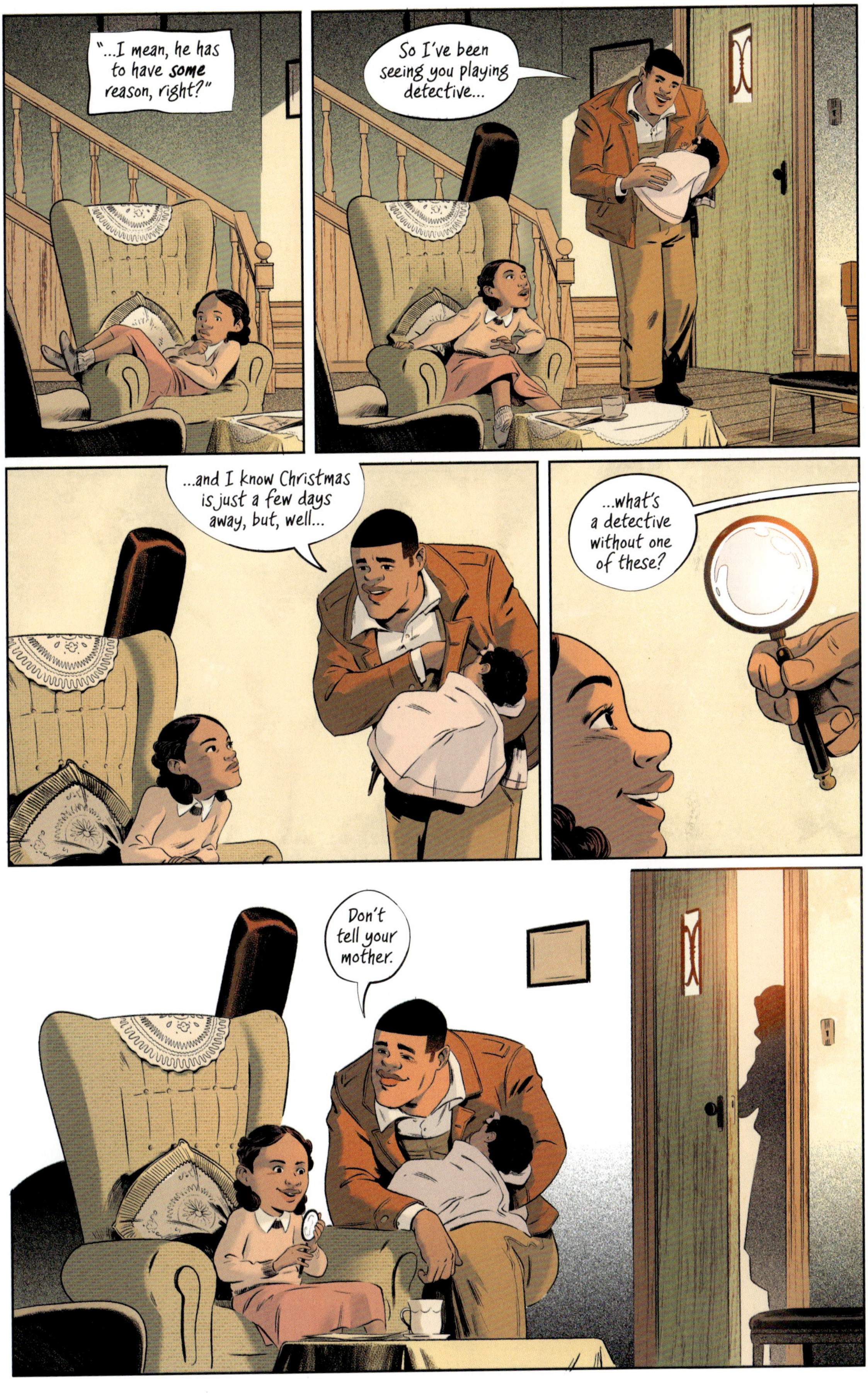
"...I mean, he has to have **some** reason, right?"
So I've been seeing you playing detective...
...and I know Christmas is just a few days away, but, well...
...what's a detective without one of these?
Don't tell your mother.

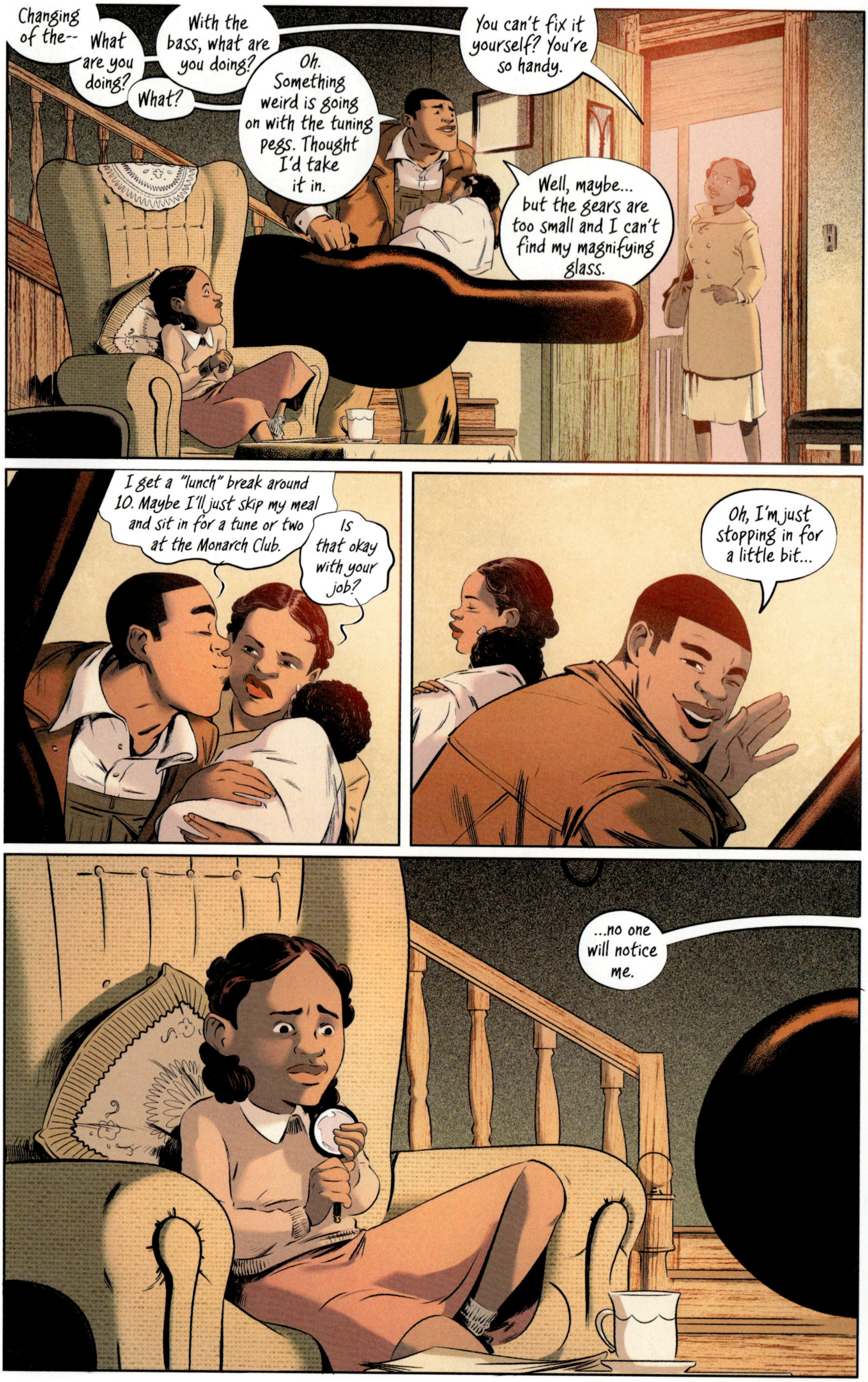
Changing of the--
What are you doing?
With the bass, what are you doing?
What?
Oh. Something weird is going on with the tuning pegs. Thought I'd take it in.
You can't fix it yourself? You're so handy.
Well, maybe... but the gears are too small and I can't find my magnifying glass.
I get a "lunch" break around 10. Maybe I'll just skip my meal and sit in for a tune or two at the Monarch Club.
Is that okay with your job?
Oh, I'm just stopping in for a little bit...
...no one will notice me.

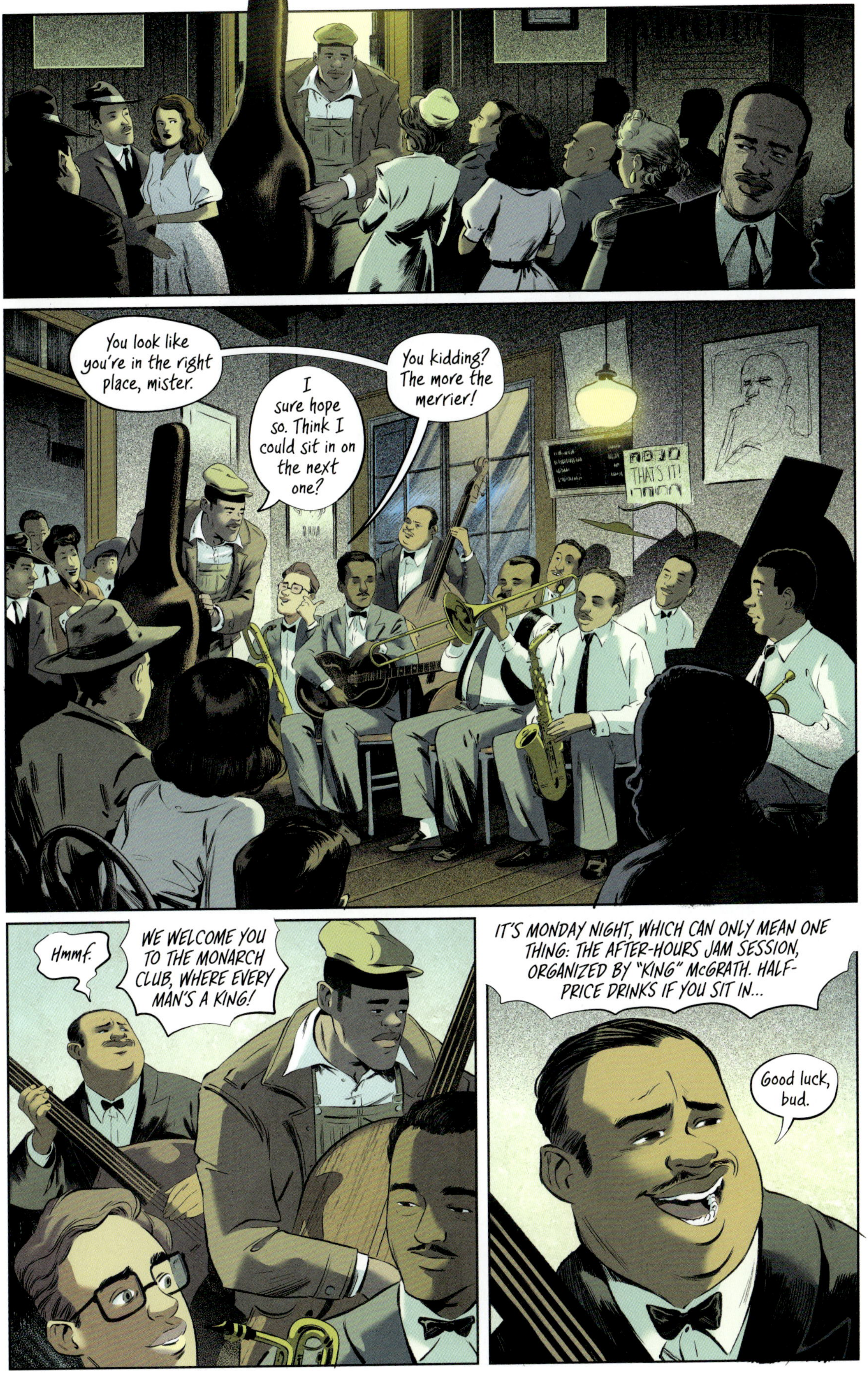
You look like you're in the right place, mister.
I sure hope so. Think I could sit in on the next one?
You kidding? The more the merrier!
THAT'S IT!
Hmmf.
WE WELCOME YOU TO THE MONARCH CLUB, WHERE EVERY MAN'S A KING!
IT'S MONDAY NIGHT, WHICH CAN ONLY MEAN ONE THING: THE AFTER-HOURS JAM SESSION, ORGANIZED BY "KING" McGRATH. HALF-PRICE DRINKS IF YOU SIT IN...
Good luck, bud.

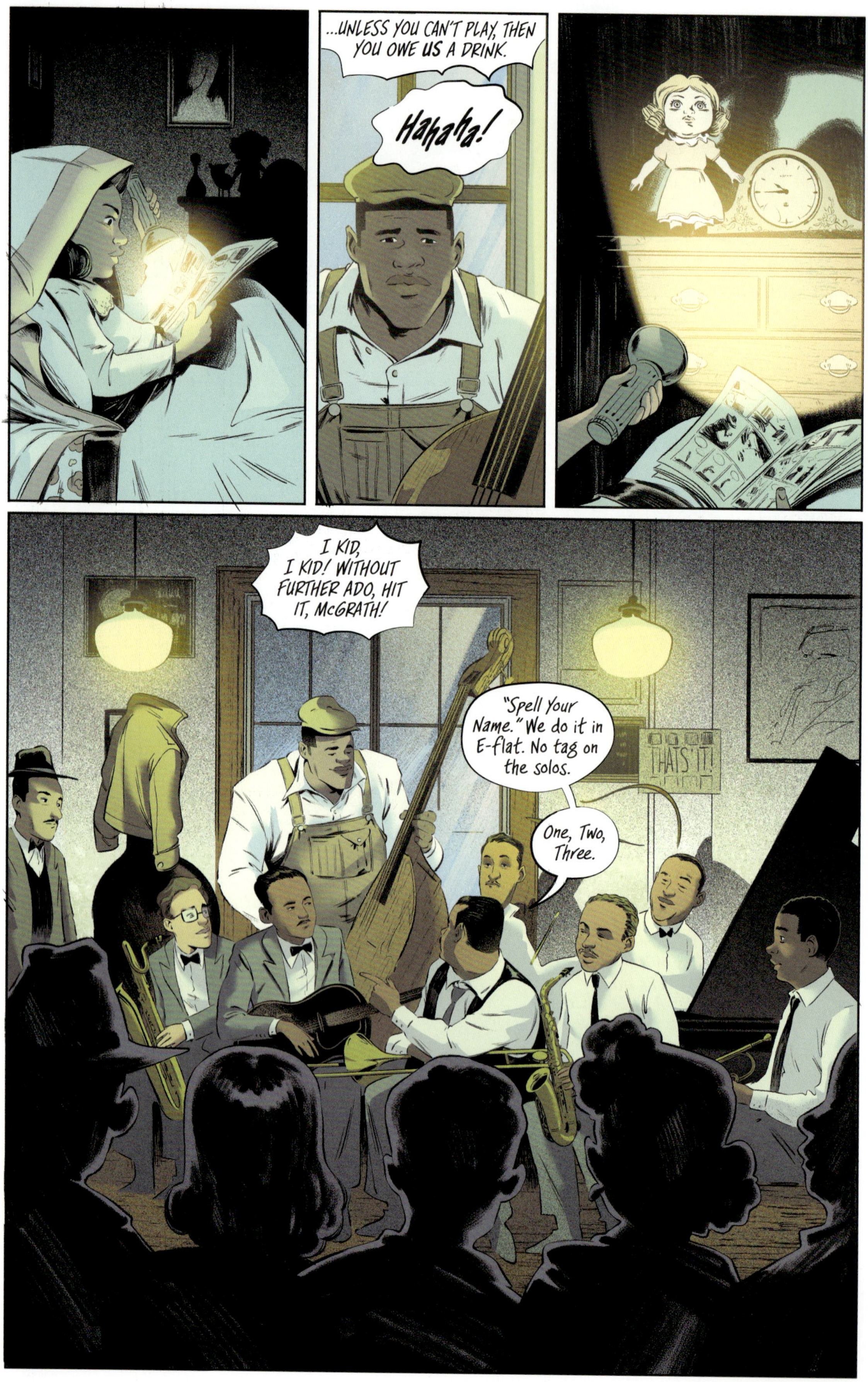
...UNLESS YOU CAN'T PLAY, THEN YOU OWE US A DRINK.
Hahaha!
I KID, I KID! WITHOUT FURTHER ADO, HIT IT, McGRATH!
"Spell Your Name." We do it in E-flat. No tag on the solos.
One, Two, Three.
THAT'S IT!

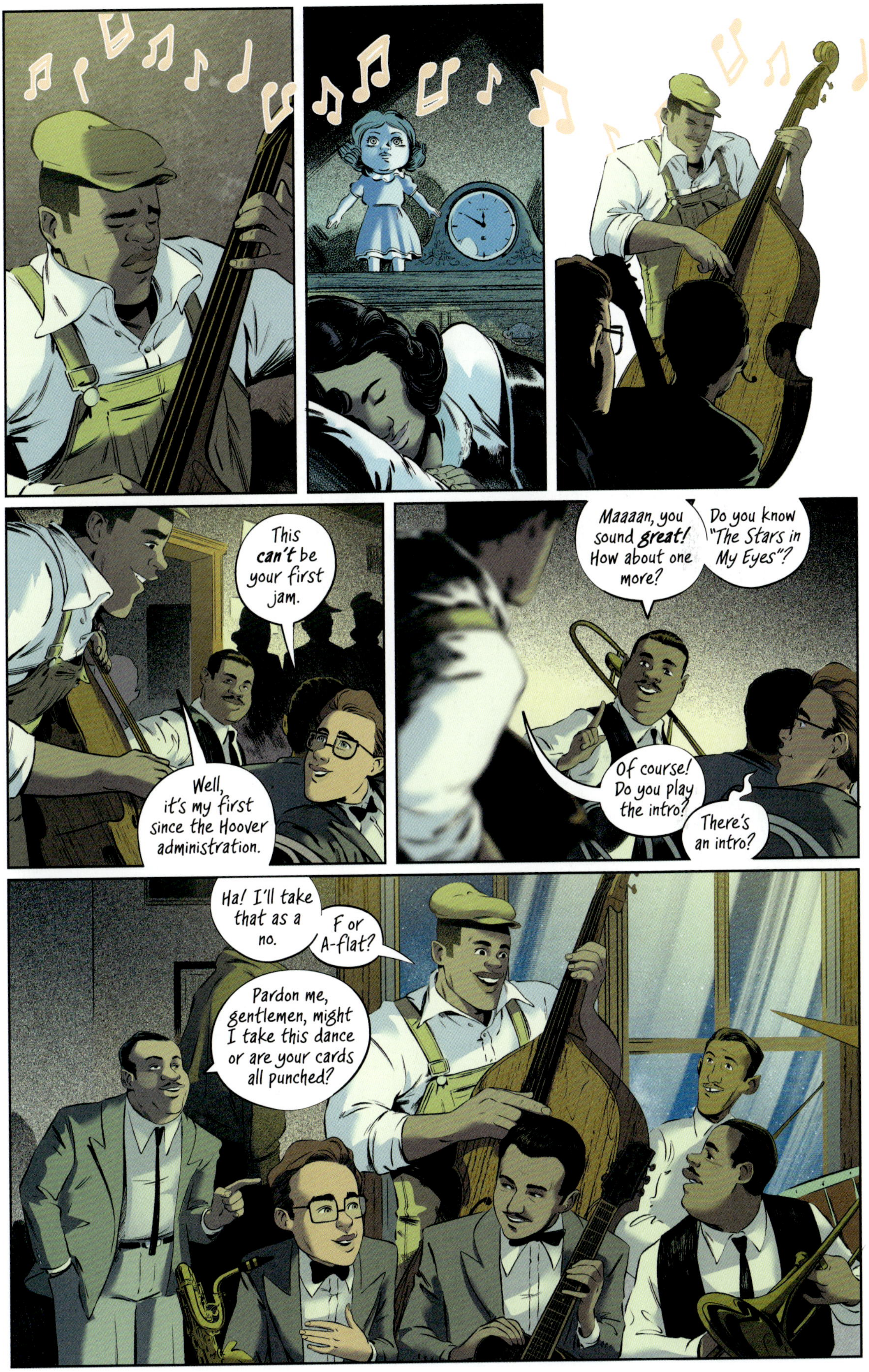
This can't be your first jam.
Well, it's my first since the Hoover administration.
Maaaan, you sound great! How about one more?
Do you know "The Stars in My Eyes"?
Of course! Do you play the intro?
There's an intro?
Ha! I'll take that as a no.
F or A-flat?
Pardon me, gentlemen, might I take this dance or are your cards all punched?

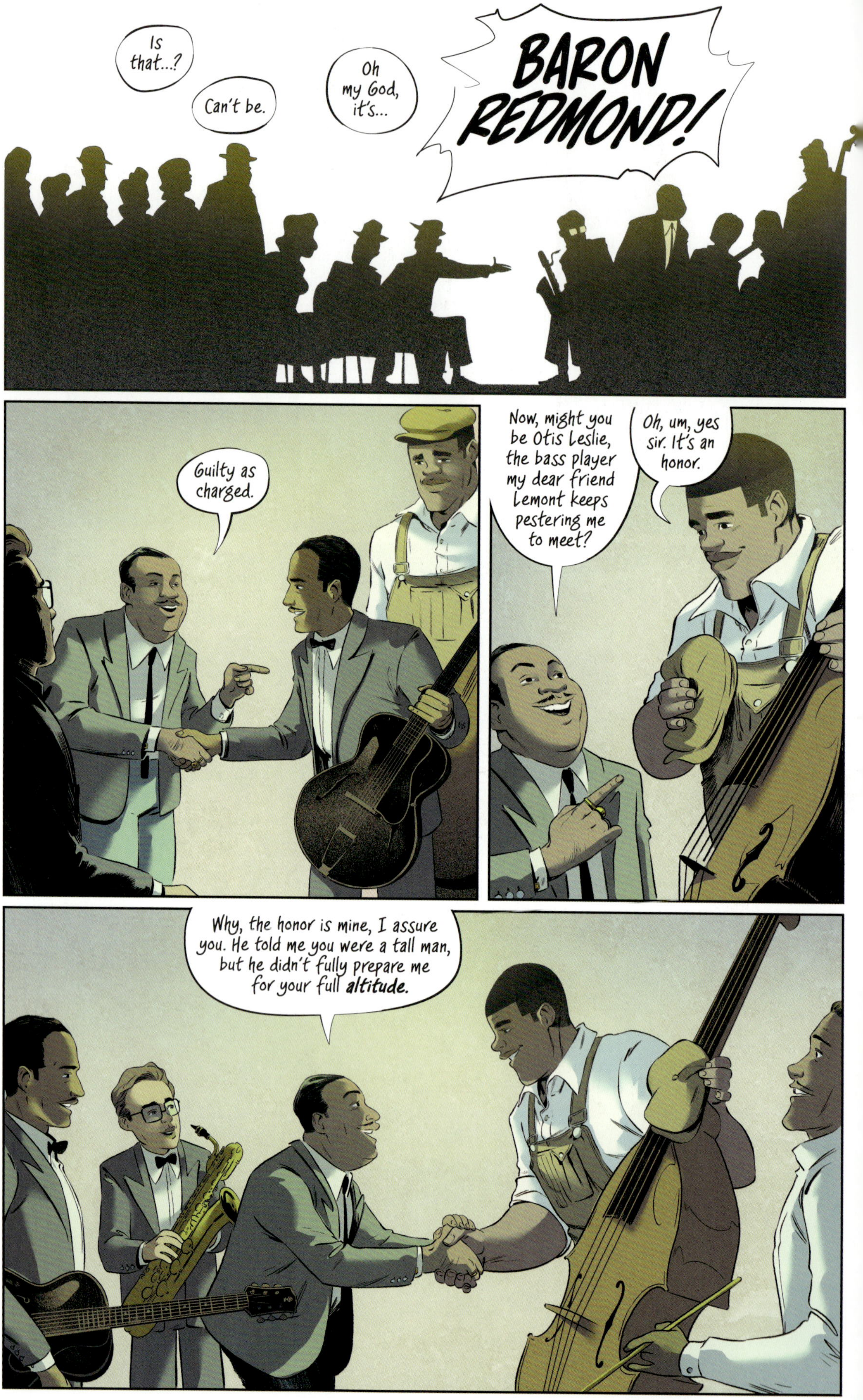
Is that...?
Can't be.
Oh my God, it's...
BARON REDMOND!
Guilty as charged.
Now, might you be Otis Leslie, the bass player my dear friend Lemont keeps pestering me to meet?
Oh, um, yes sir. It's an honor.
Why, the honor is mine, I assure you. He told me you were a tall man, but he didn't fully prepare me for your full **altitude**.

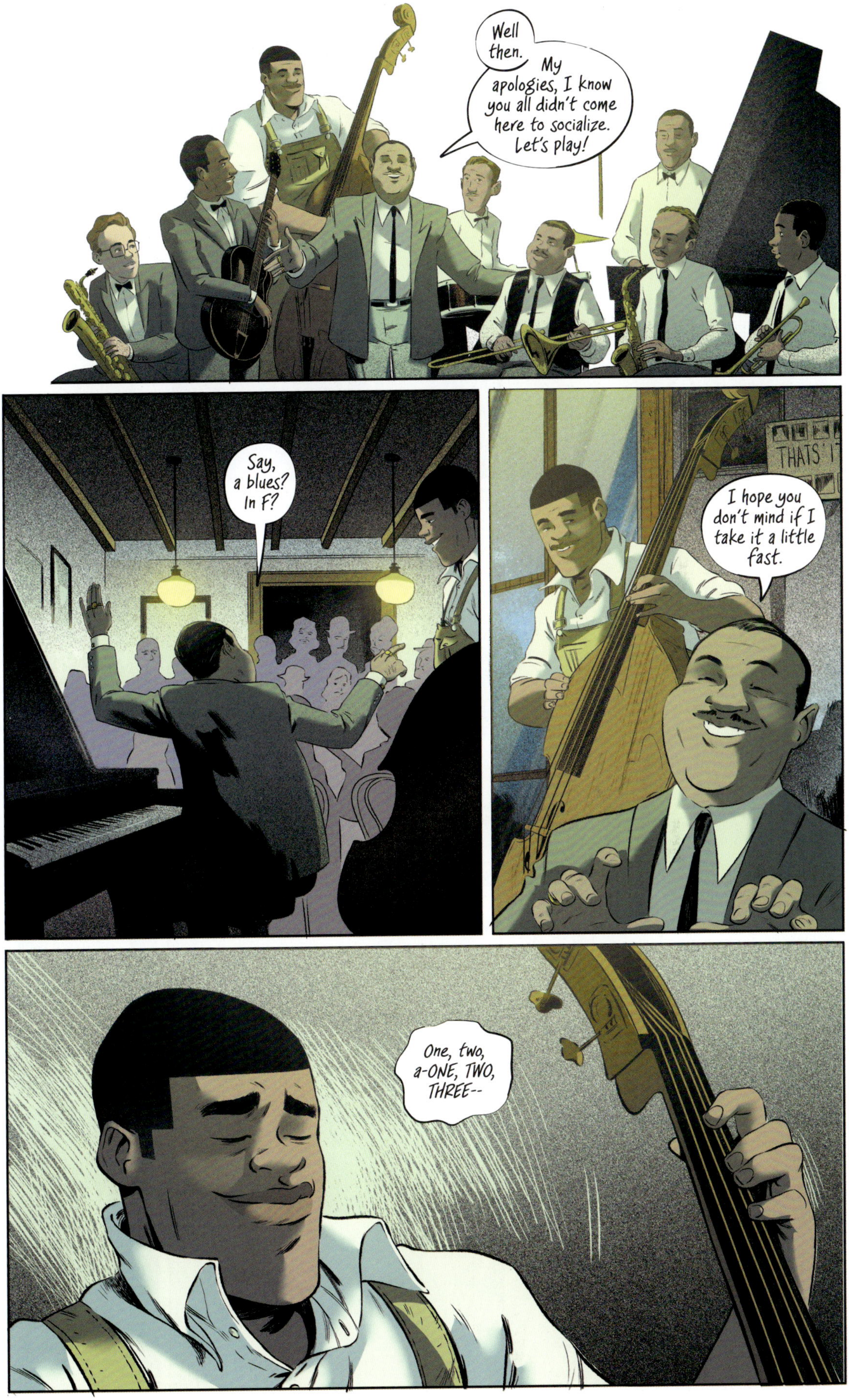
Well then.
My apologies, I know you all didn't come here to socialize. Let's play!
Say, a blues? In F?
THATS I
I hope you don't mind if I take it a little fast.
One, two, a-ONE, TWO, THREE--

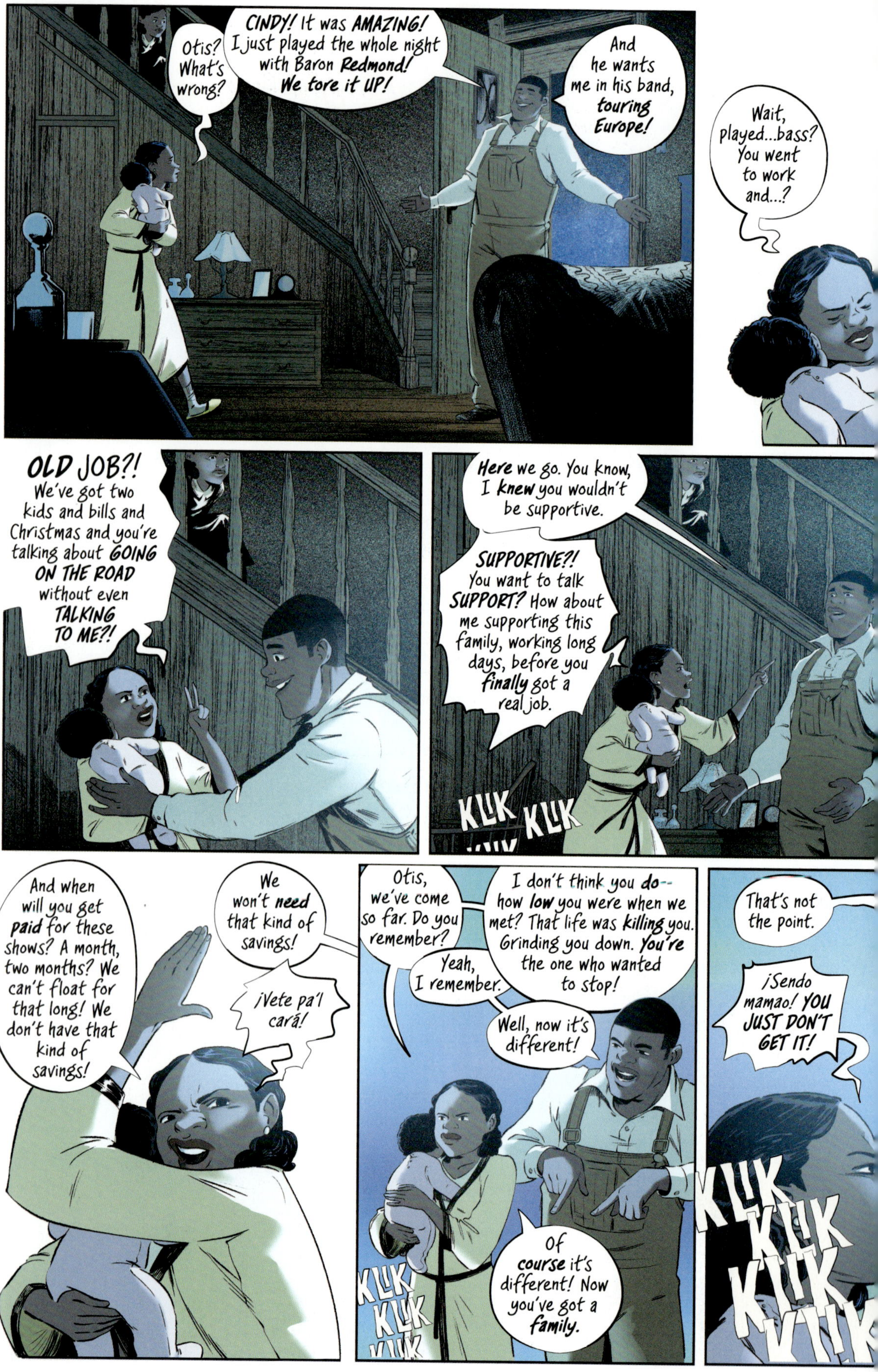
Otis? What's wrong?
CINDY! It was AMAZING! I just played the whole night with Baron Redmond! We tore it UP!
And he wants me in his band, touring Europe!
Wait, played...bass? You went to work and...?
OLD JOB?! We've got two kids and bills and Christmas and you're talking about GOING ON THE ROAD without even TALKING TO ME?!
Here we go. You know, I knew you wouldn't be supportive.
SUPPORTIVE?! You want to talk SUPPORT? How about me supporting this family, working long days, before you finally got a real job.
KLIK KLIK
And when will you get paid for these shows? A month, two months? We can't float for that long! We don't have that kind of savings!
We won't need that kind of savings!
¡Vete pa'l cará!
Otis, we've come so far. Do you remember?
Yeah, I remember.
I don't think you do--how low you were when we met? That life was killing you. Grinding you down. You're the one who wanted to stop!
Well, now it's different!
Of course it's different! Now you've got a family.
KLIK KLIK
That's not the point.
¡Sendo mamao! YOU JUST DON'T GET IT!
KLIK KLIK KLIK

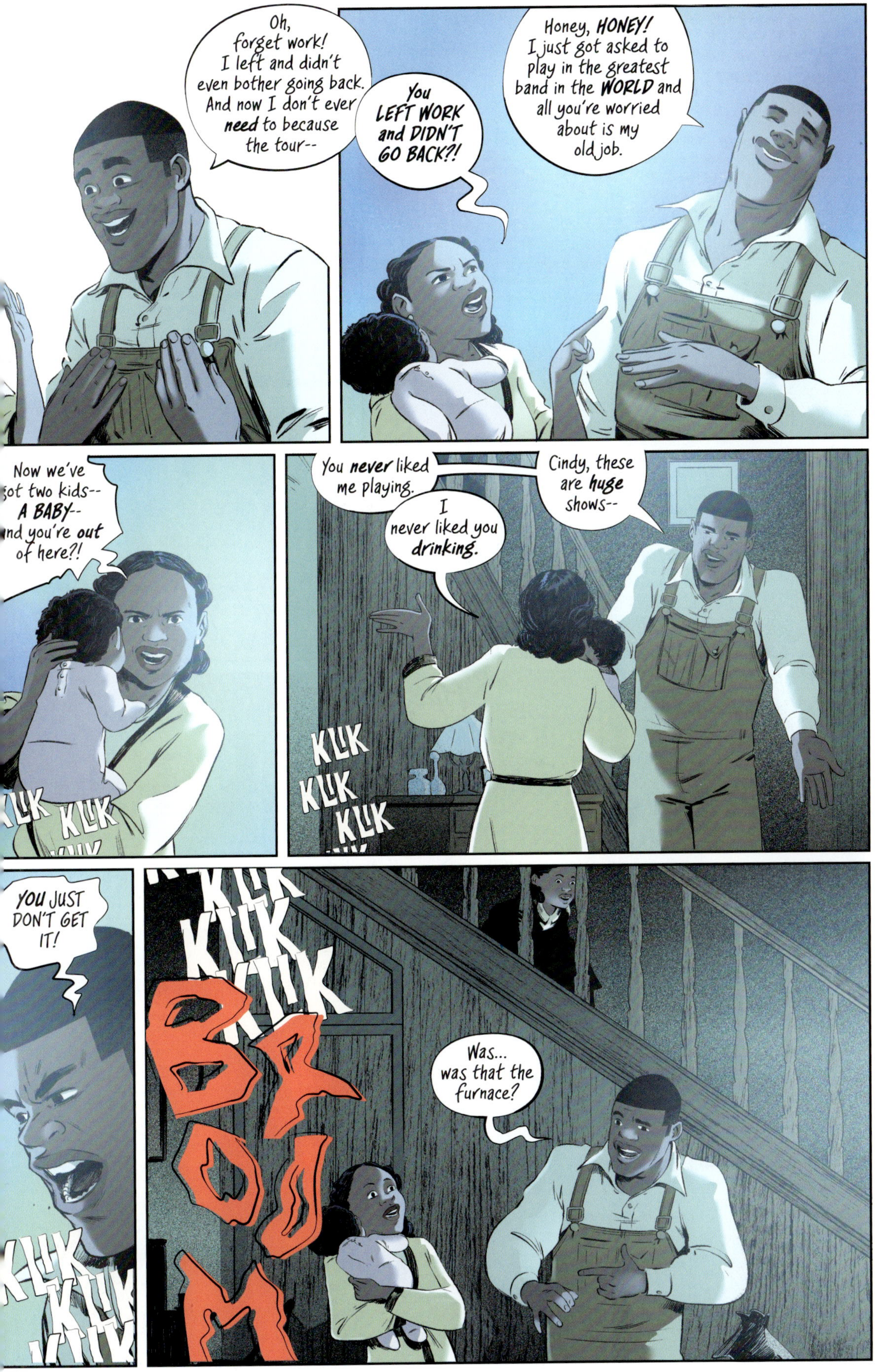

Oh, forget work! I left and didn't even bother going back. And now I don't ever **need** to because the tour--
You **LEFT WORK and DIDN'T GO BACK?!**
Honey, **HONEY!** I just got asked to play in the greatest band in the **WORLD** and all you're worried about is my old job.
Now we've got two kids-- **A BABY**-- and you're **out** of here?!
KLIK KLIK
You **never** liked me playing.
I never liked you **drinking.**
Cindy, these are **huge** shows--
KLIK KLIK KLIK
YOU JUST DON'T GET IT!
KLIK KLIK
KLIK KLIK
BROOM
Was... was that the furnace?

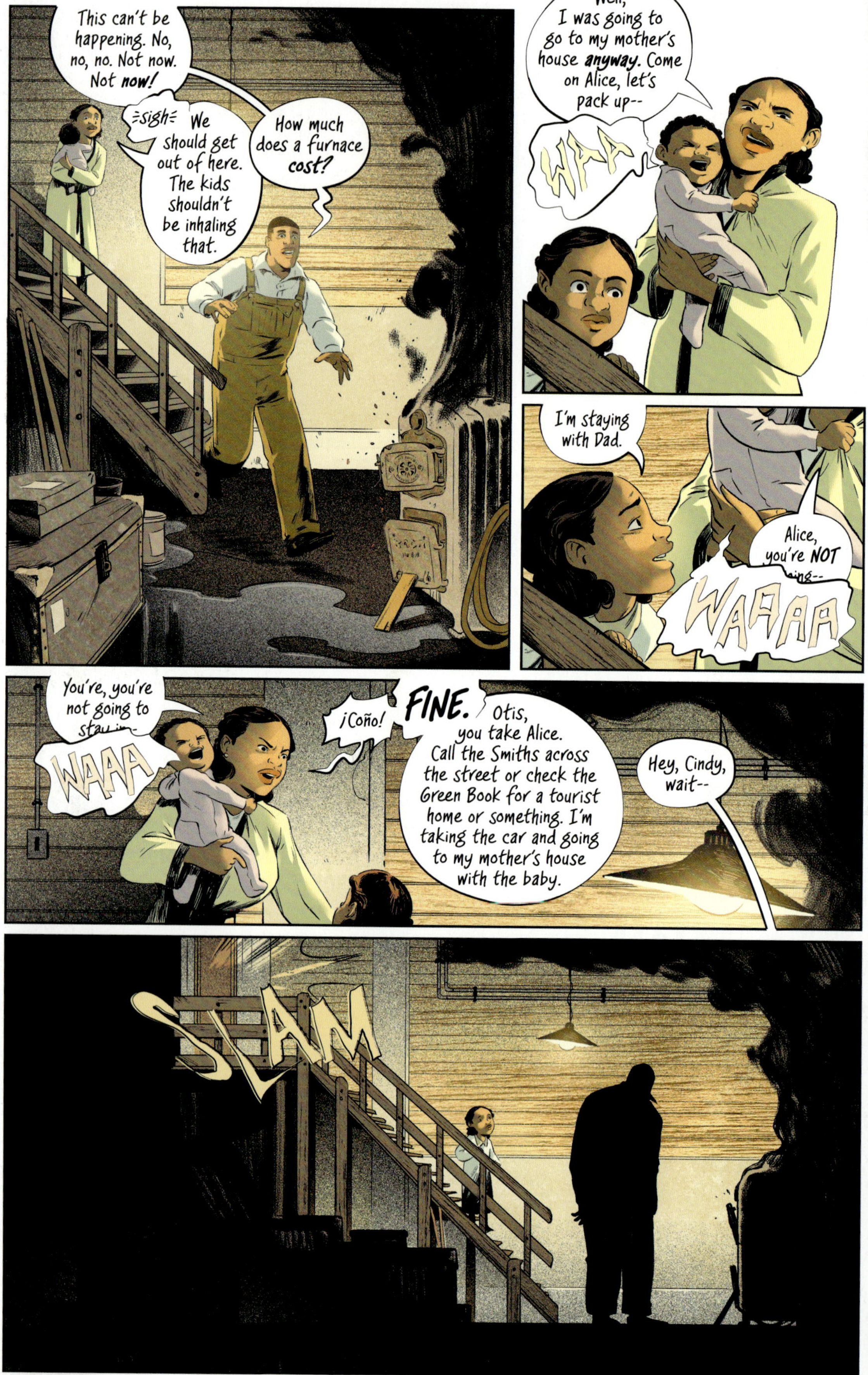
This can't be happening. No, no, no. Not now. Not **now!**
=sigh= We should get out of here. The kids shouldn't be inhaling that.
How much does a furnace **cost?**
Well, I was going to go to my mother's house **anyway.** Come on Alice, let's pack up--
WAA
I'm staying with Dad.
Alice, you're **NOT**
WAAAA
You're, you're not going to
WAAA
¡Coño!
FINE.
Otis, you take Alice. Call the Smiths across the street or check the Green Book for a tourist home or something. I'm taking the car and going to my mother's house with the baby.
Hey, Cindy, wait--
SLAM

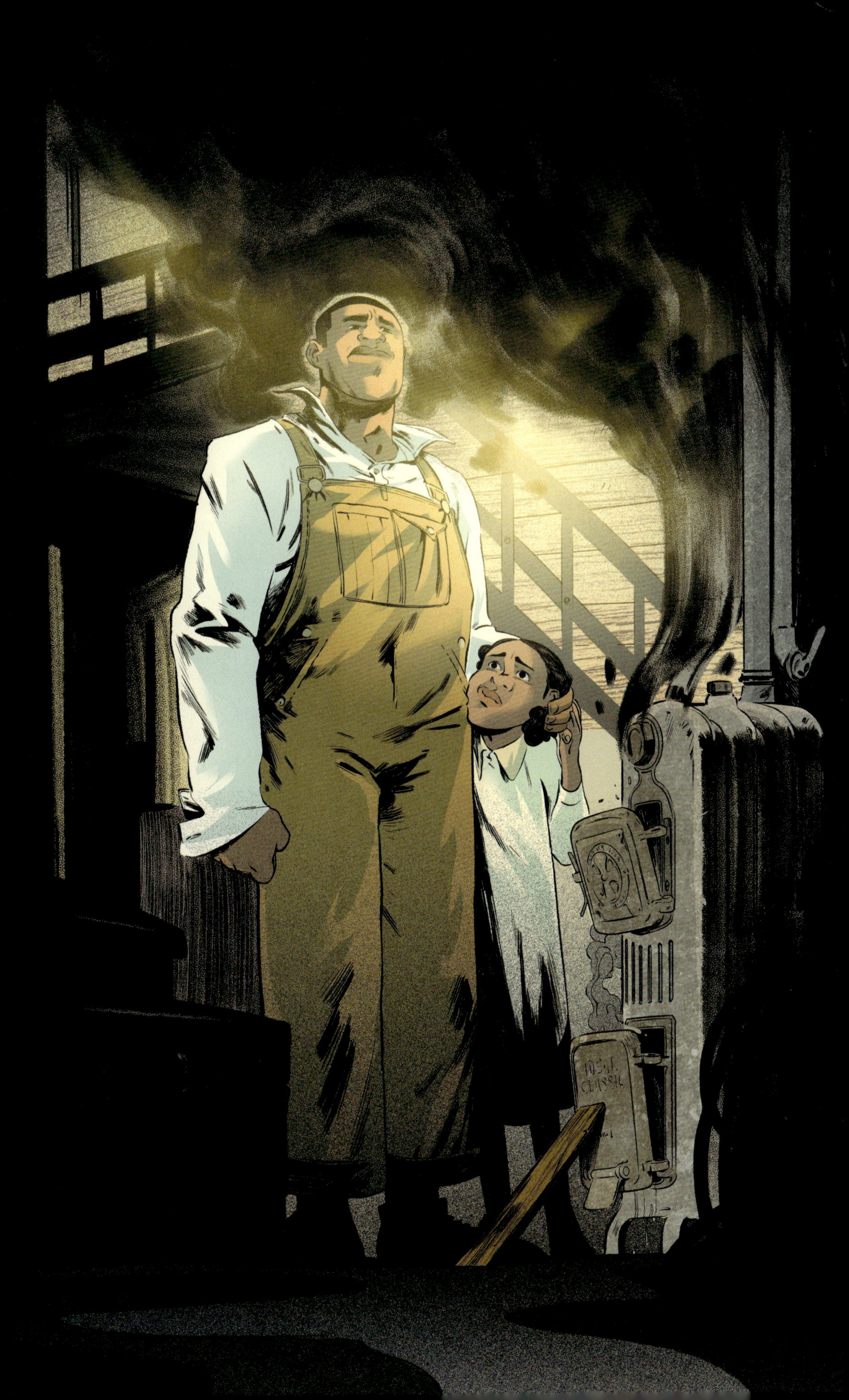
IDEAL
CLASSIC

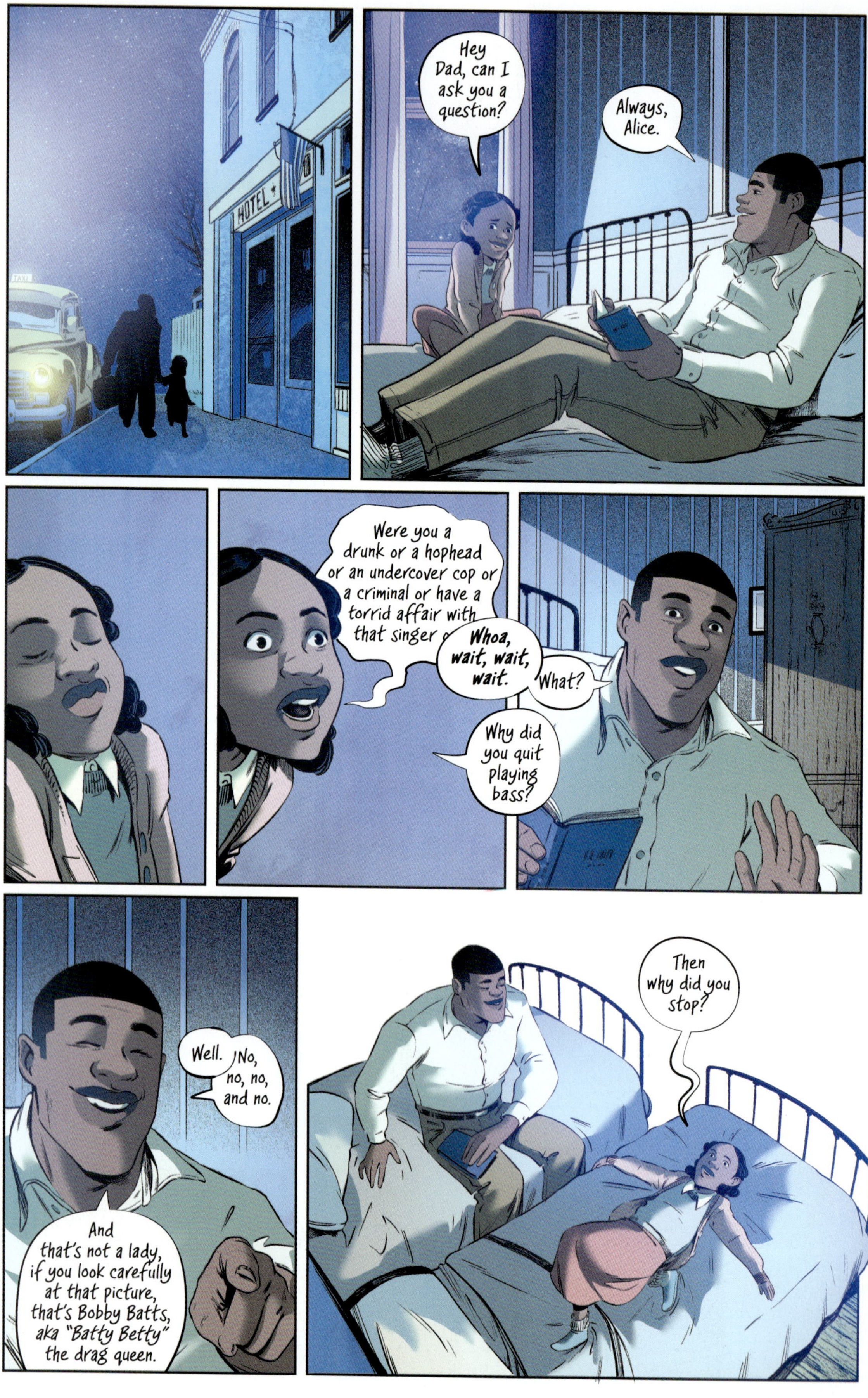
HOTEL
Hey Dad, can I ask you a question?
Always, Alice.
Were you a drunk or a hophead or an undercover cop or a criminal or have a torrid affair with that singer o
Whoa, wait, wait, wait.
What?
Why did you quit playing bass?
Well.
No, no, no, and no.
And that's not a lady, if you look carefully at that picture, that's Bobby Batts, aka "Batty Betty" the drag queen.
Then why did you stop?

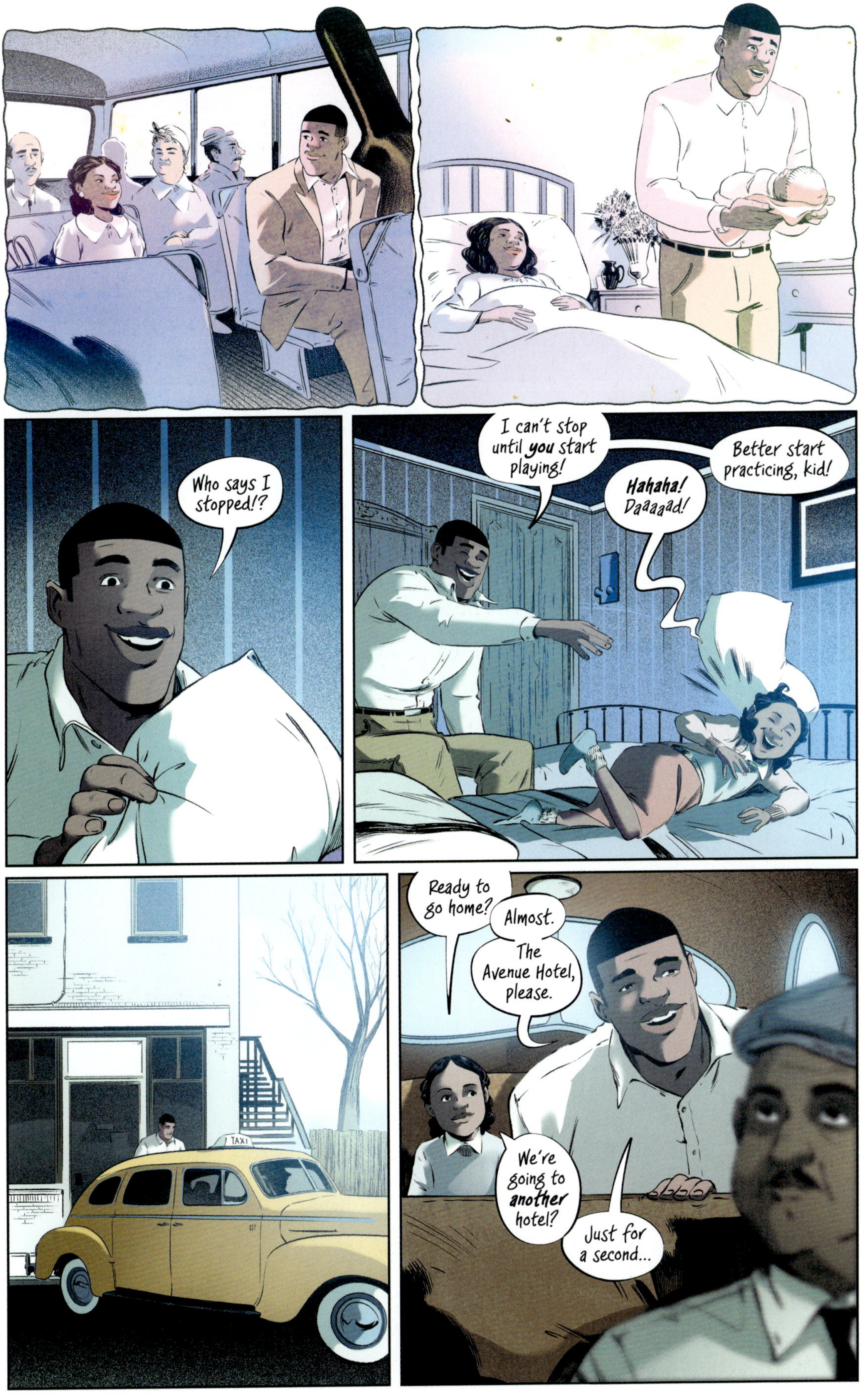

Who says I stopped!?
I can't stop until you start playing!
Hahaha! Daaaaad!
Better start practicing, kid!
TAXI
Ready to go home?
Almost.
The Avenue Hotel, please.
We're going to another hotel?
Just for a second...

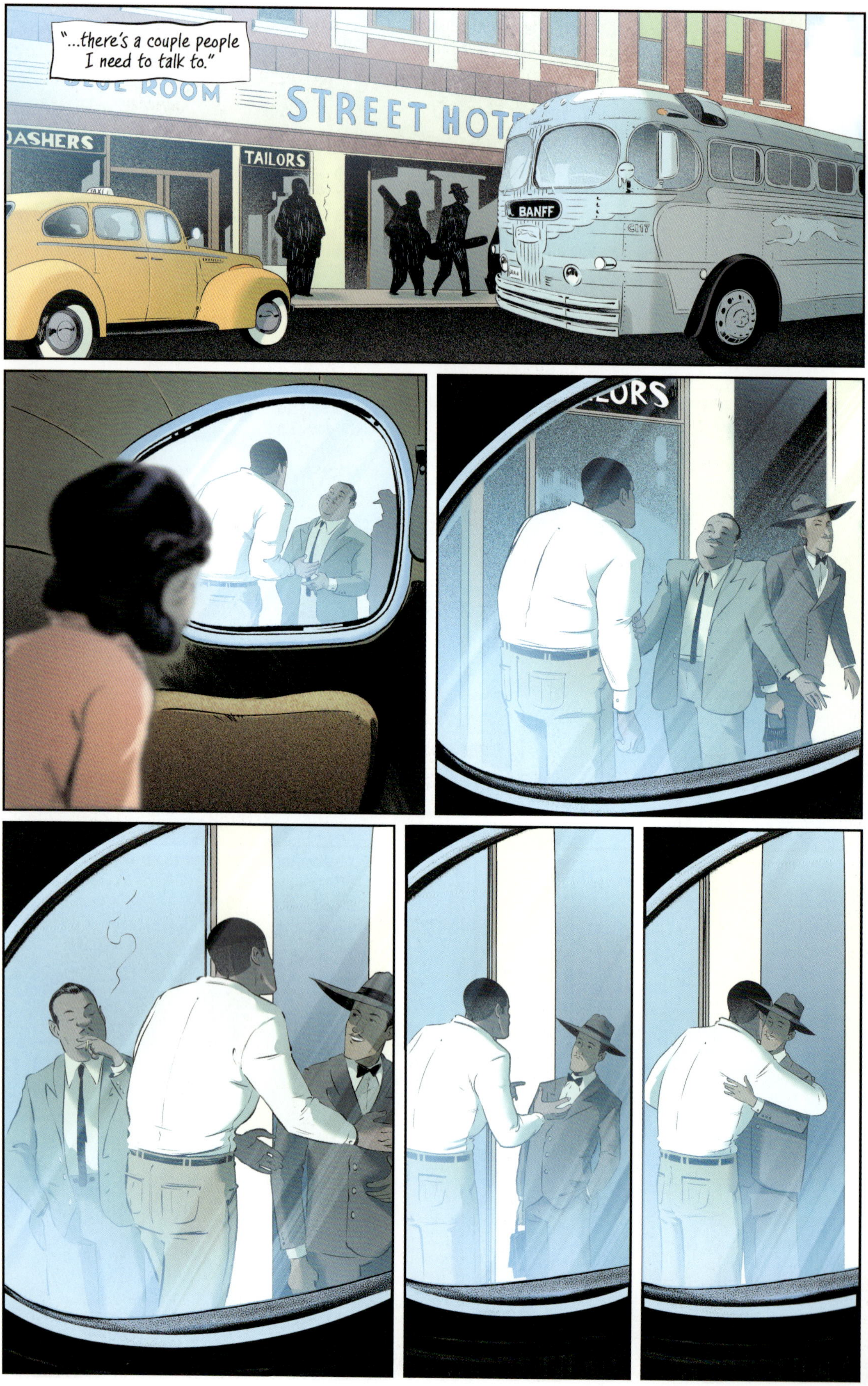
"...there's a couple people I need to talk to."
BLUE ROOM
STREET HOT
DASHERS
TAILORS
TAXI
BANFF
LORS

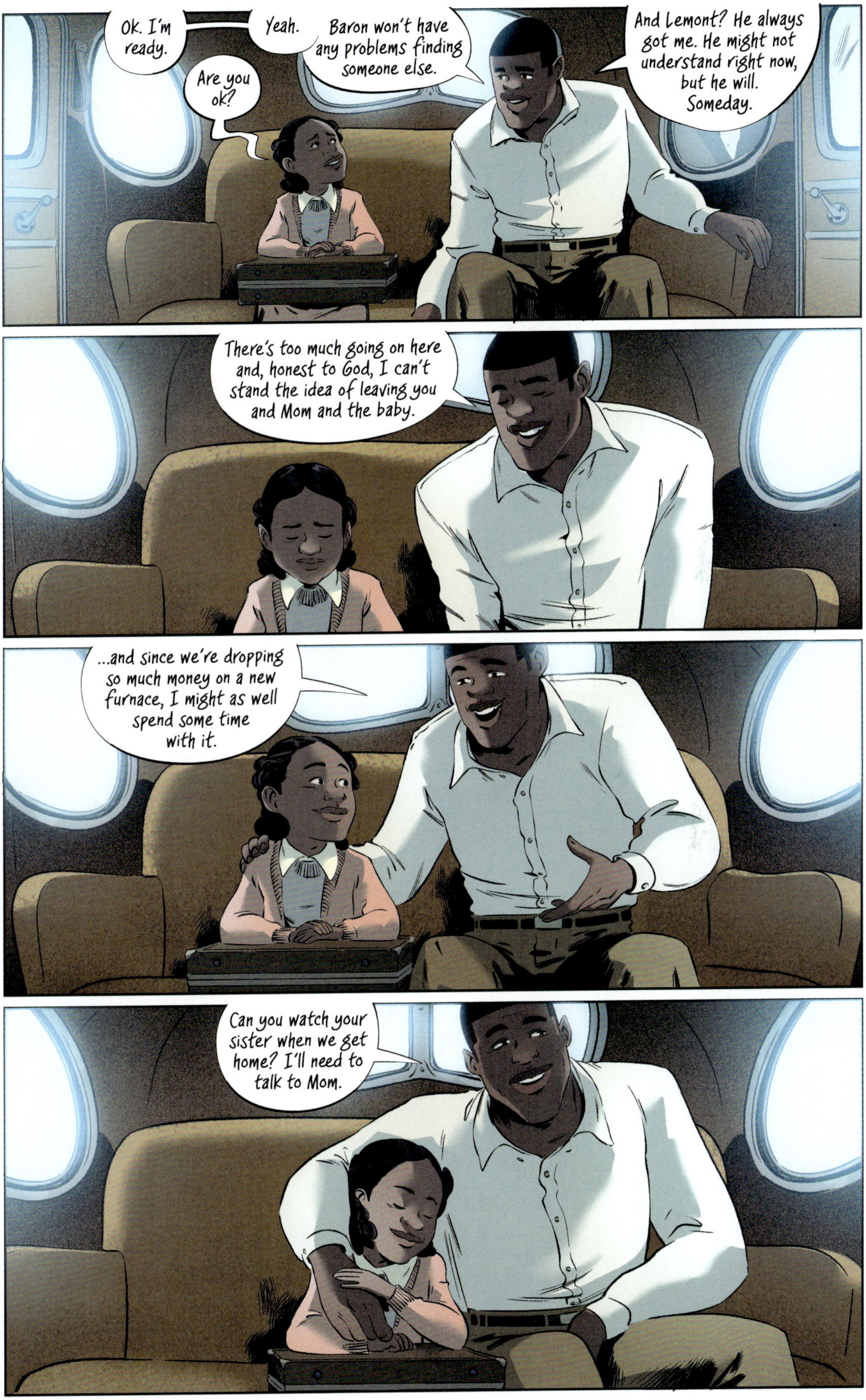
Ok. I'm ready.
Yeah.
Are you ok?
Baron won't have any problems finding someone else.
And Lemont? He always got me. He might not understand right now, but he will. Someday.
There's too much going on here and, honest to God, I can't stand the idea of leaving you and Mom and the baby.
...and since we're dropping so much money on a new furnace, I might as well spend some time with it.
Can you watch your sister when we get home? I'll need to talk to Mom.

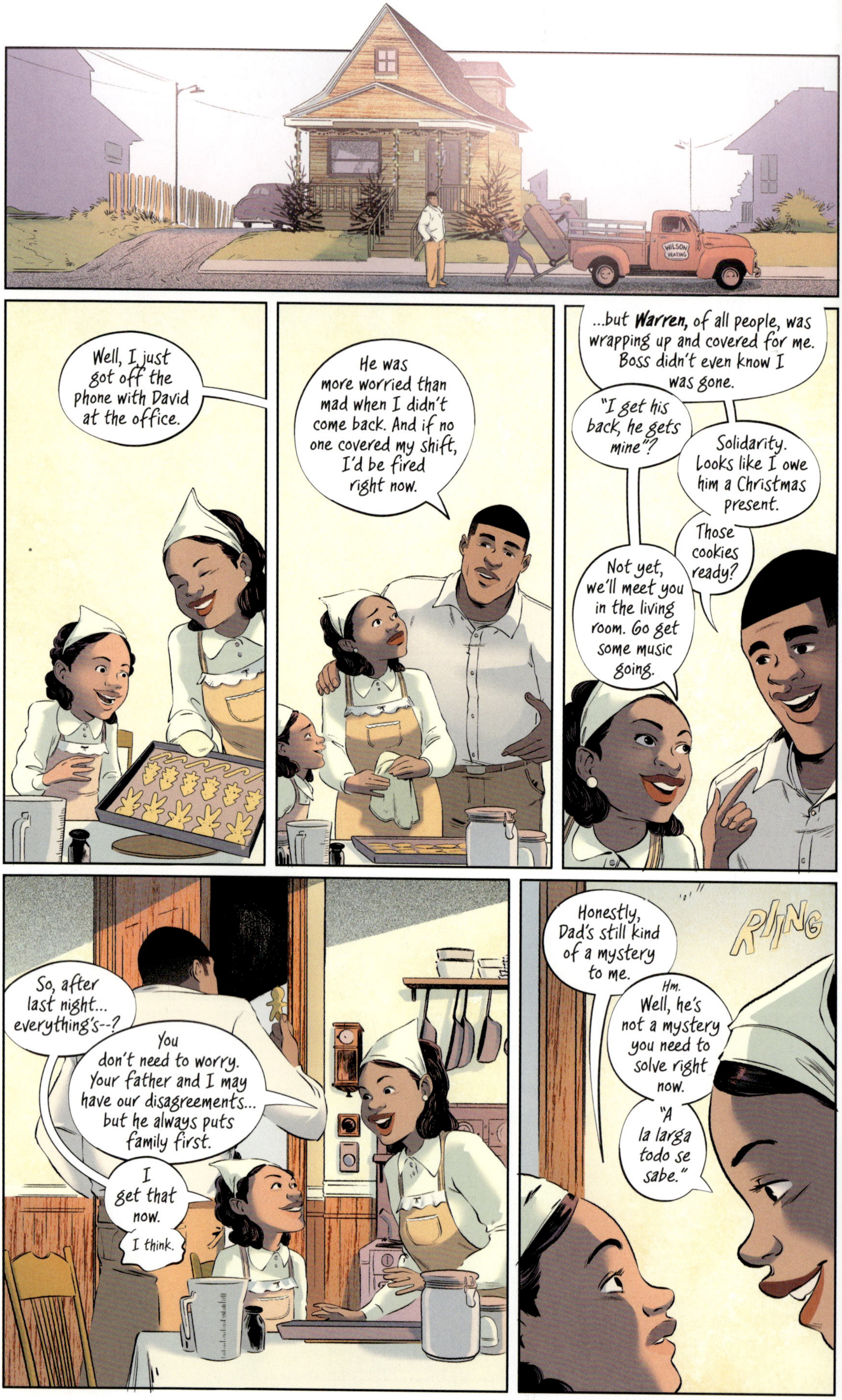
WILSON HEATING
Well, I just got off the phone with David at the office.
He was more worried than mad when I didn't come back. And if no one covered my shift, I'd be fired right now.
...but Warren, of all people, was wrapping up and covered for me. Boss didn't even know I was gone.
"I get his back, he gets mine"?
Solidarity. Looks like I owe him a Christmas present.
Those cookies ready?
Not yet, we'll meet you in the living room. Go get some music going.
So, after last night... everything's--?
You don't need to worry. Your father and I may have our disagreements... but he always puts family first.
I get that now.
I think.
Honestly, Dad's still kind of a mystery to me.
RIING
Hm.
Well, he's not a mystery you need to solve right now.
"A la larga todo se sabe."

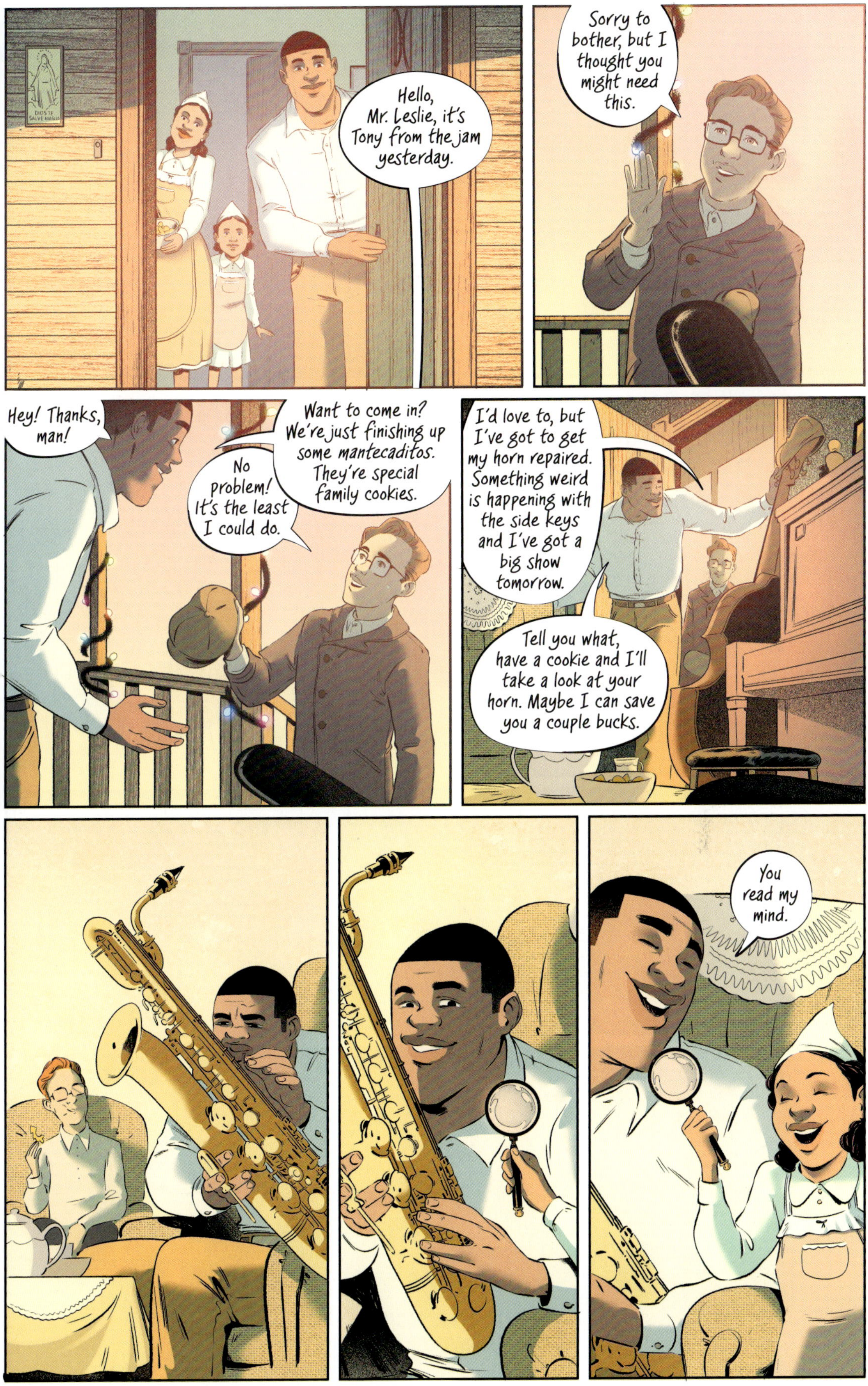
Hello, Mr. Leslie, it's Tony from the jam yesterday.
Sorry to bother, but I thought you might need this.
Hey! Thanks, man!
No problem! It's the least I could do.
Want to come in? We're just finishing up some mantecaditos. They're special family cookies.
I'd love to, but I've got to get my horn repaired. Something weird is happening with the side keys and I've got a big show tomorrow.
Tell you what, have a cookie and I'll take a look at your horn. Maybe I can save you a couple bucks.
You read my mind.

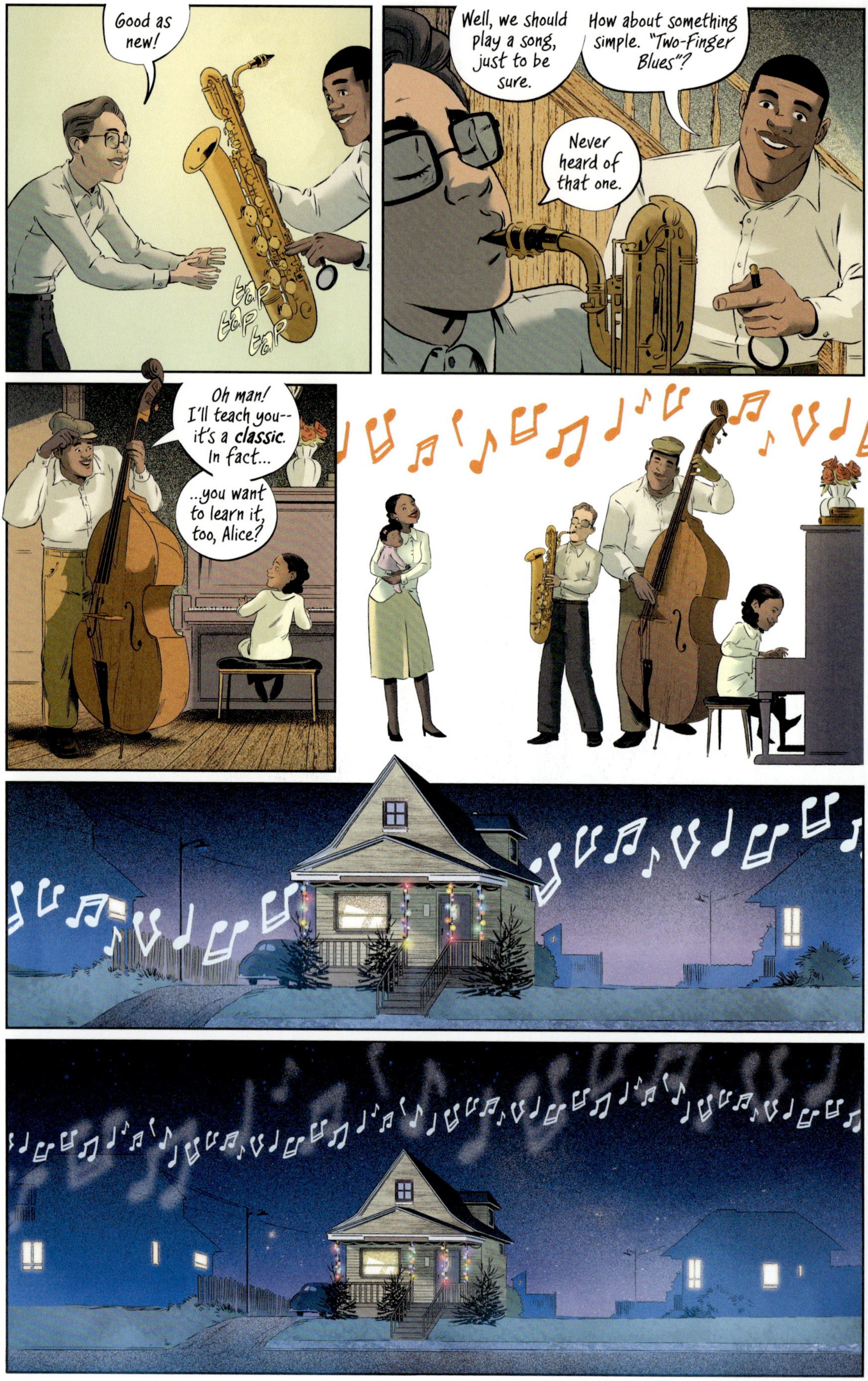
Good as new!
tap tap tap
Well, we should play a song, just to be sure.
How about something simple. "Two-Finger Blues"?
Never heard of that one.
Oh man! I'll teach you-- it's a classic. In fact...
...you want to learn it, too, Alice?

4.

BLUE NOTES

NEW YORK CITY
1956

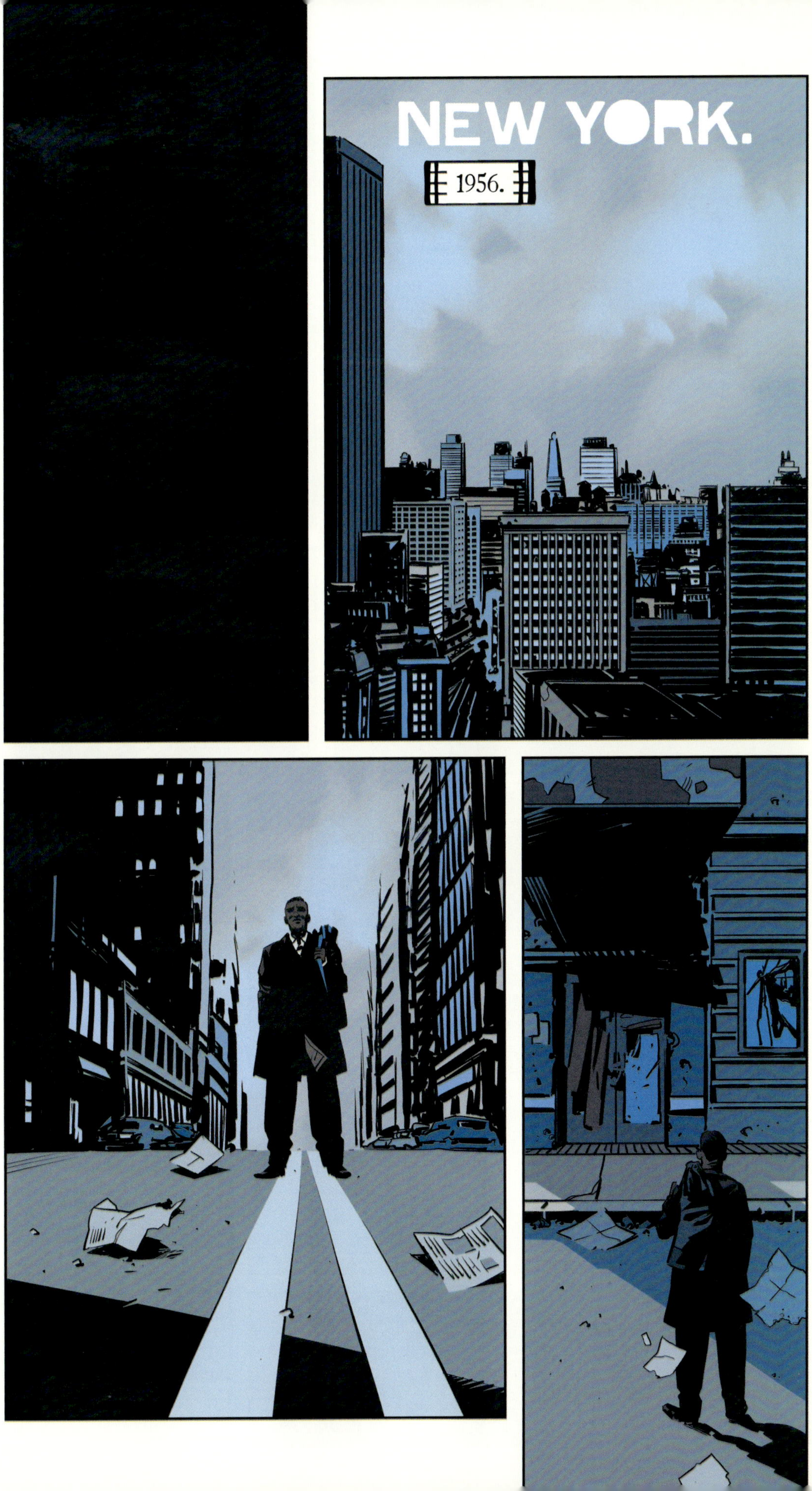
NEW YORK.
1956.

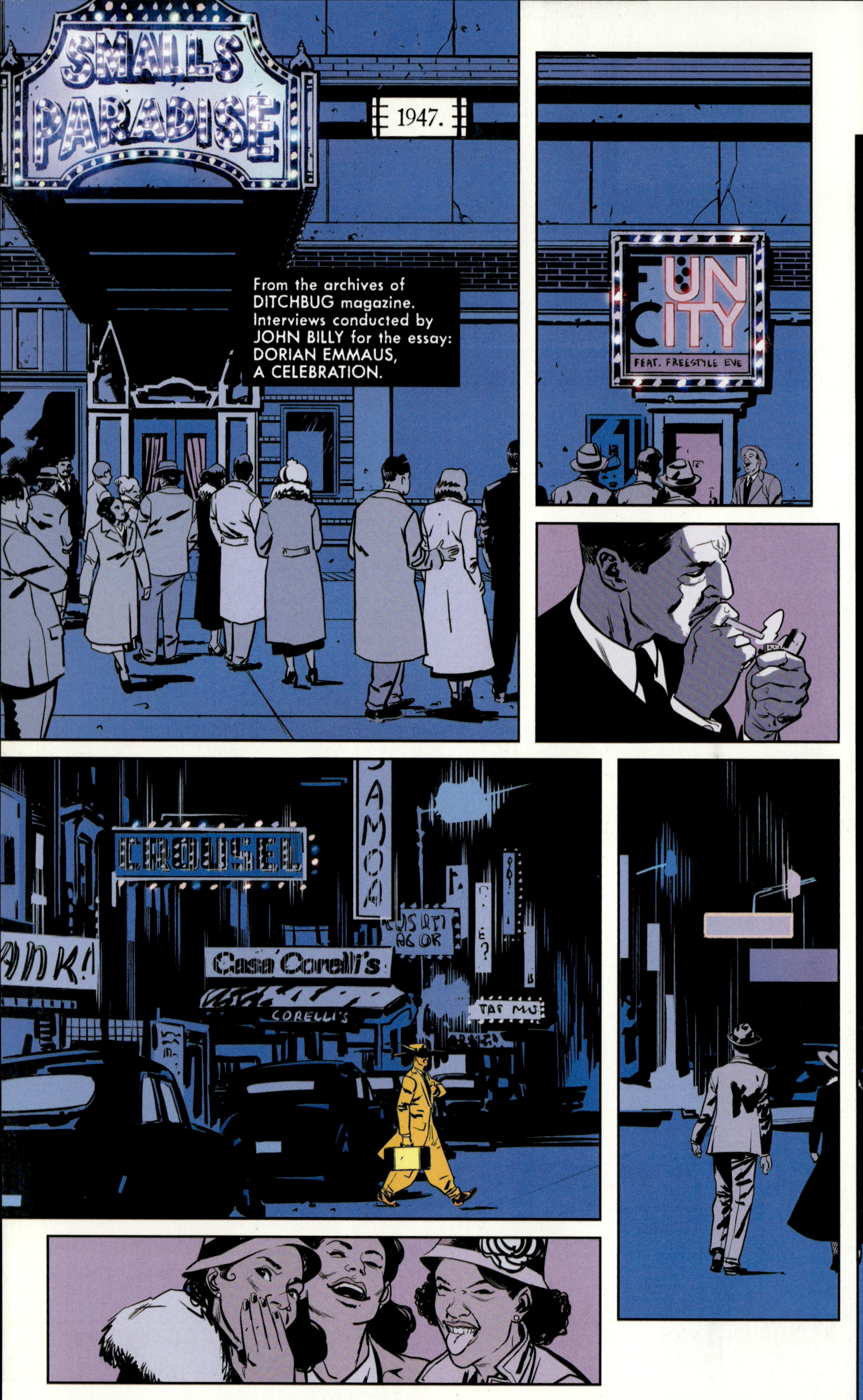
SMALLS PARADISE
1947.
From the archives of DITCHBUG magazine. Interviews conducted by JOHN BILLY for the essay: DORIAN EMMAUS, A CELEBRATION.
FUN CITY
FEAT. FREESTYLE EVE
SAMOA
Casa Corelli's
CORELLI'S

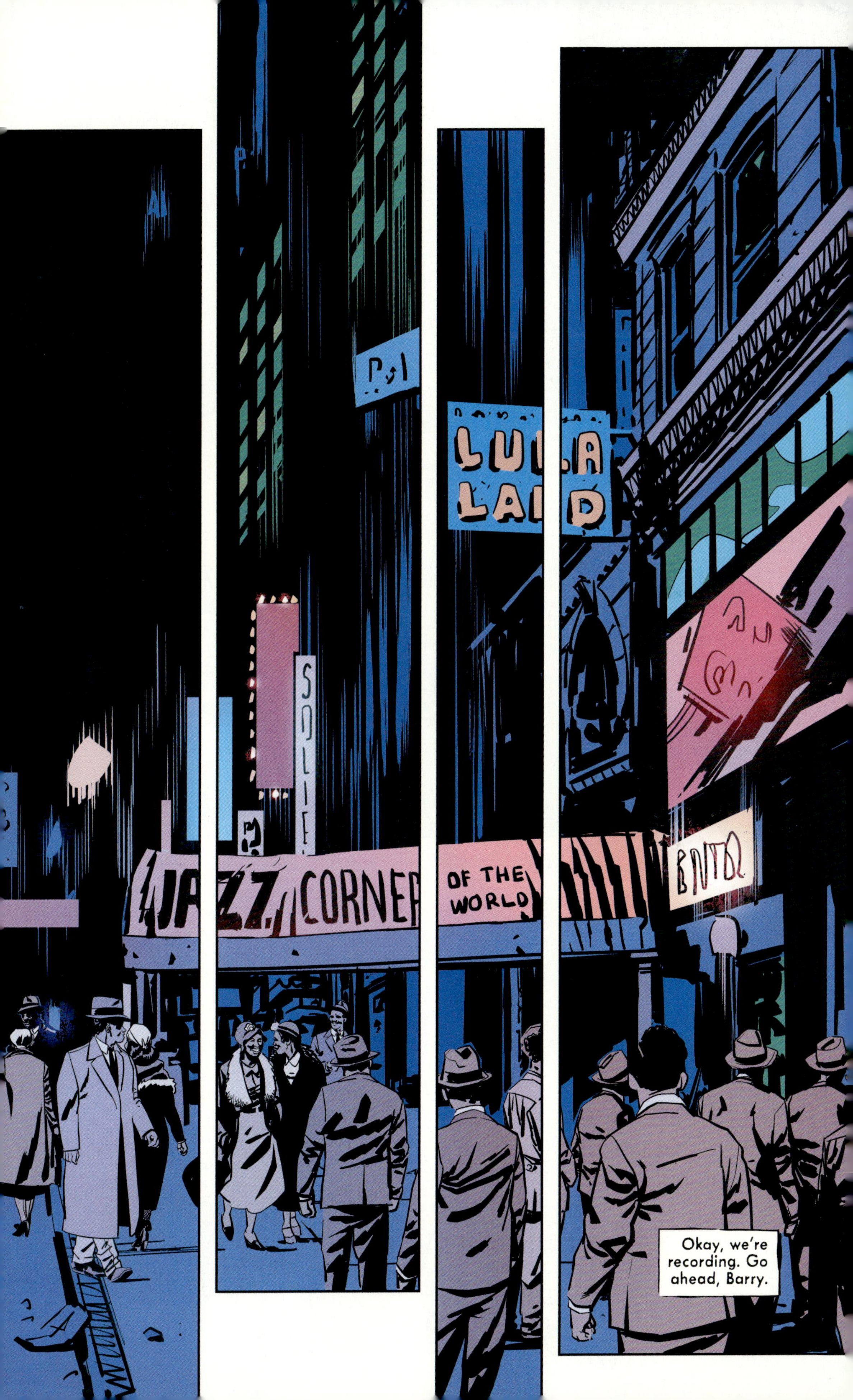
OF THE WORLD
Okay, we're recording. Go ahead, Barry.

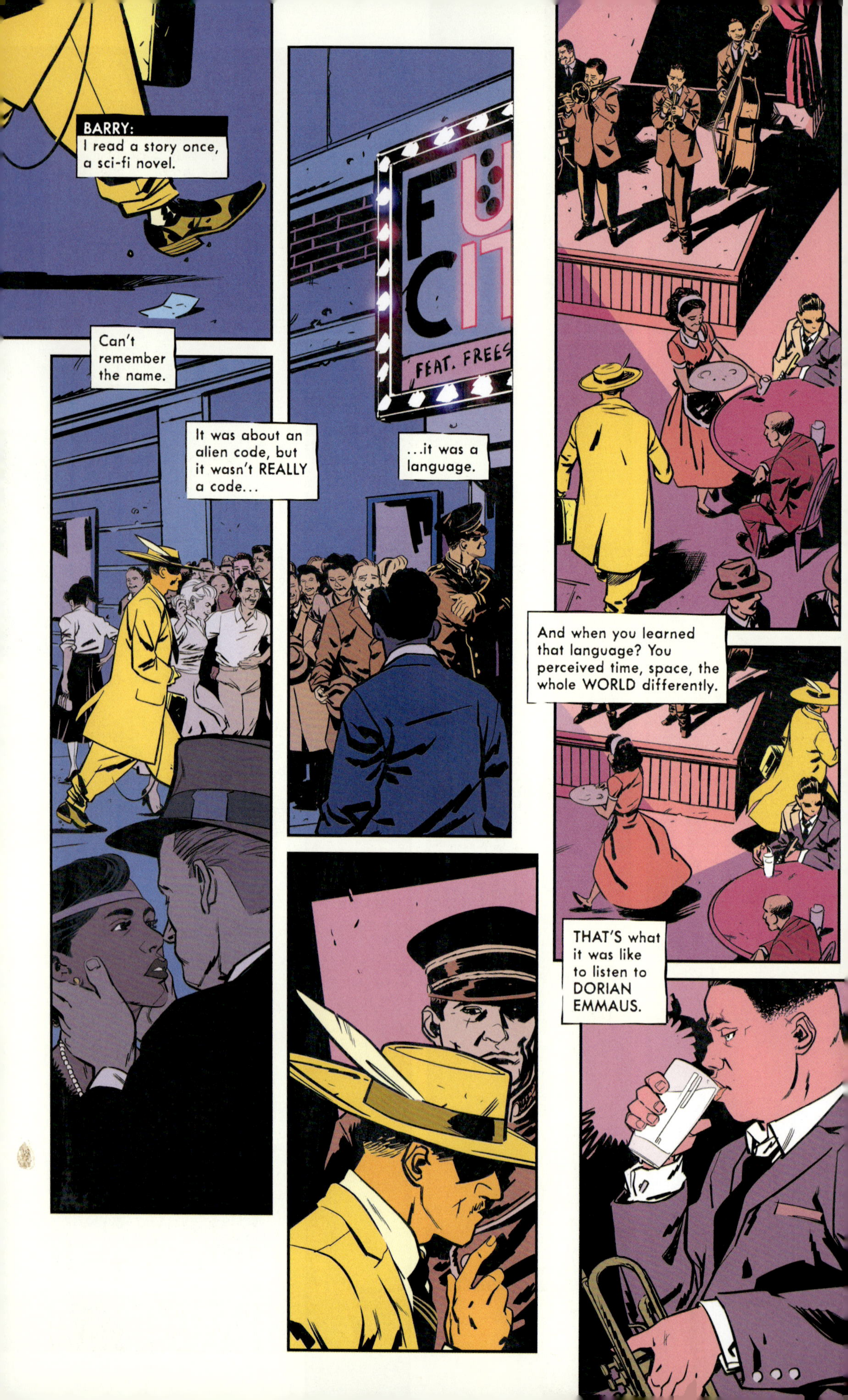
BARRY:
I read a story once, a sci-fi novel.
Can't remember the name.
It was about an alien code, but it wasn't REALLY a code...
...it was a language.
FEAT. FREE
And when you learned that language? You perceived time, space, the whole WORLD differently.
THAT'S what it was like to listen to DORIAN EMMAUS.

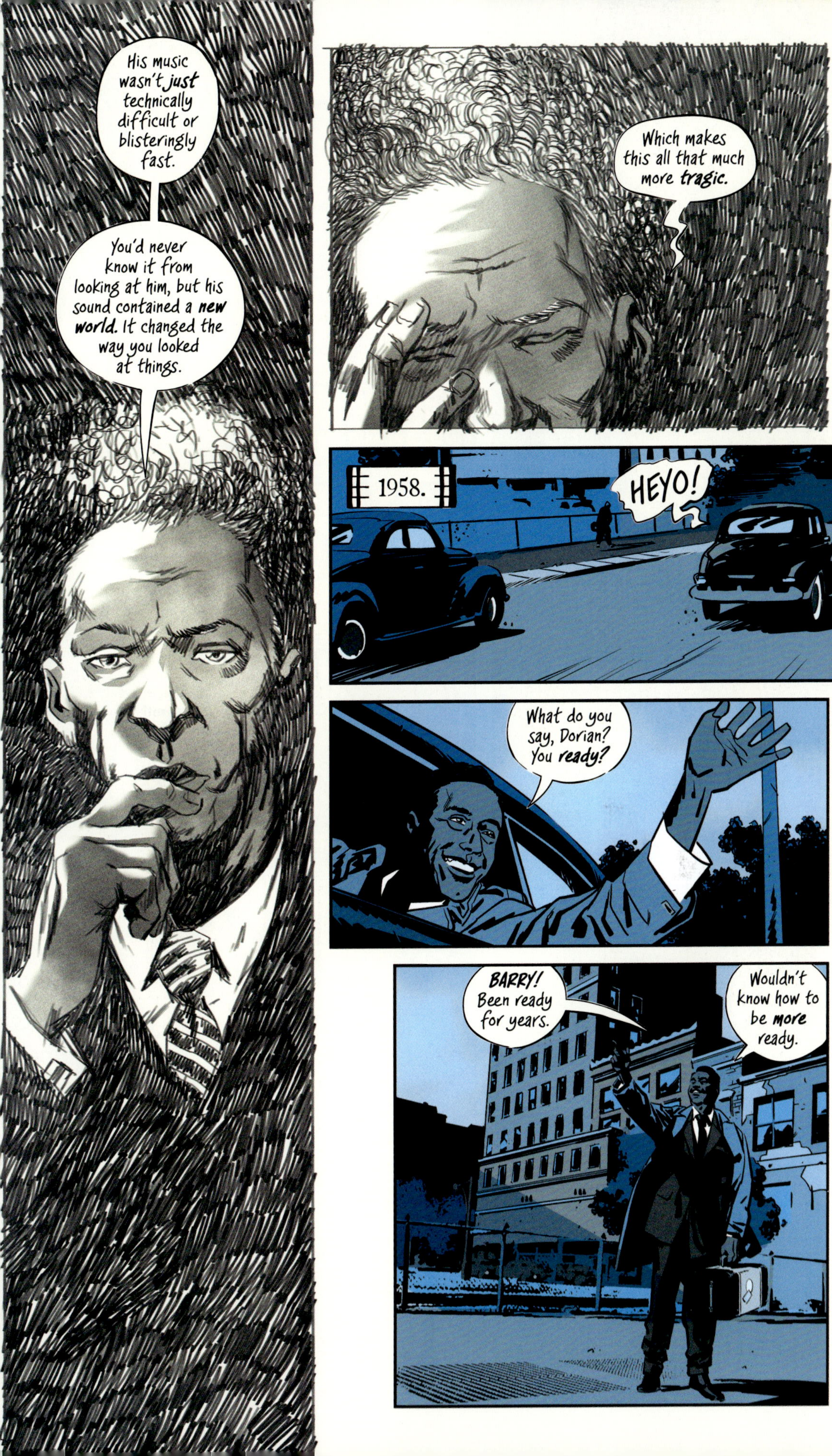
His music wasn't *just* technically difficult or blisteringly fast.
You'd never know it from looking at him, but his sound contained a ***new world.*** It changed the way you looked at things.
Which makes this all that much more ***tragic.***
1958.
HEYO!
What do you say, Dorian? You ***ready?***
BARRY! Been ready for years.
Wouldn't know how to be ***more*** ready.

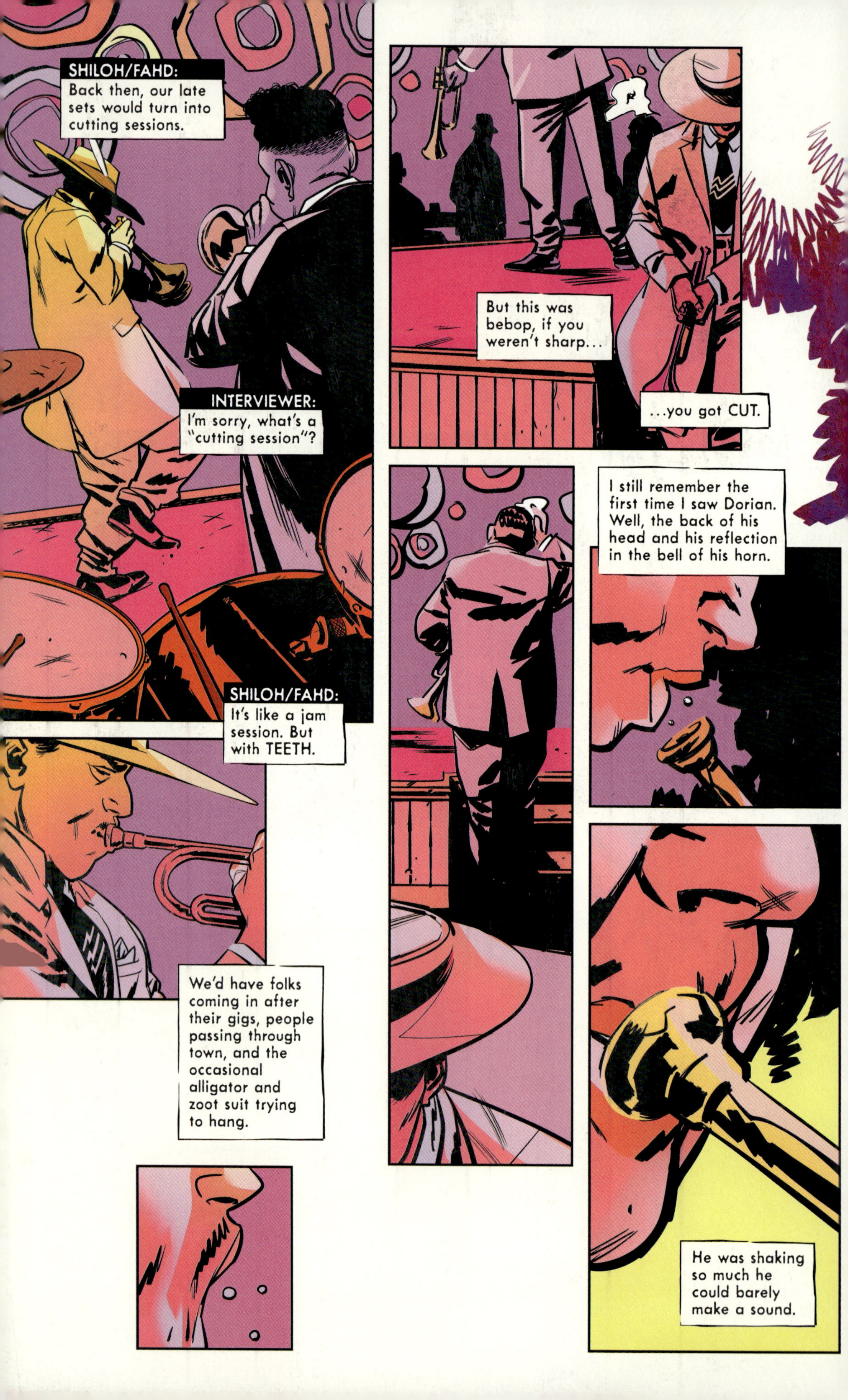
SHILOH/FAHD:
Back then, our late sets would turn into cutting sessions.
INTERVIEWER:
I'm sorry, what's a "cutting session"?
SHILOH/FAHD:
It's like a jam session. But with TEETH.
We'd have folks coming in after their gigs, people passing through town, and the occasional alligator and zoot suit trying to hang.
But this was bebop, if you weren't sharp...
...you got CUT.
I still remember the first time I saw Dorian. Well, the back of his head and his reflection in the bell of his horn.
He was shaking so much he could barely make a sound.

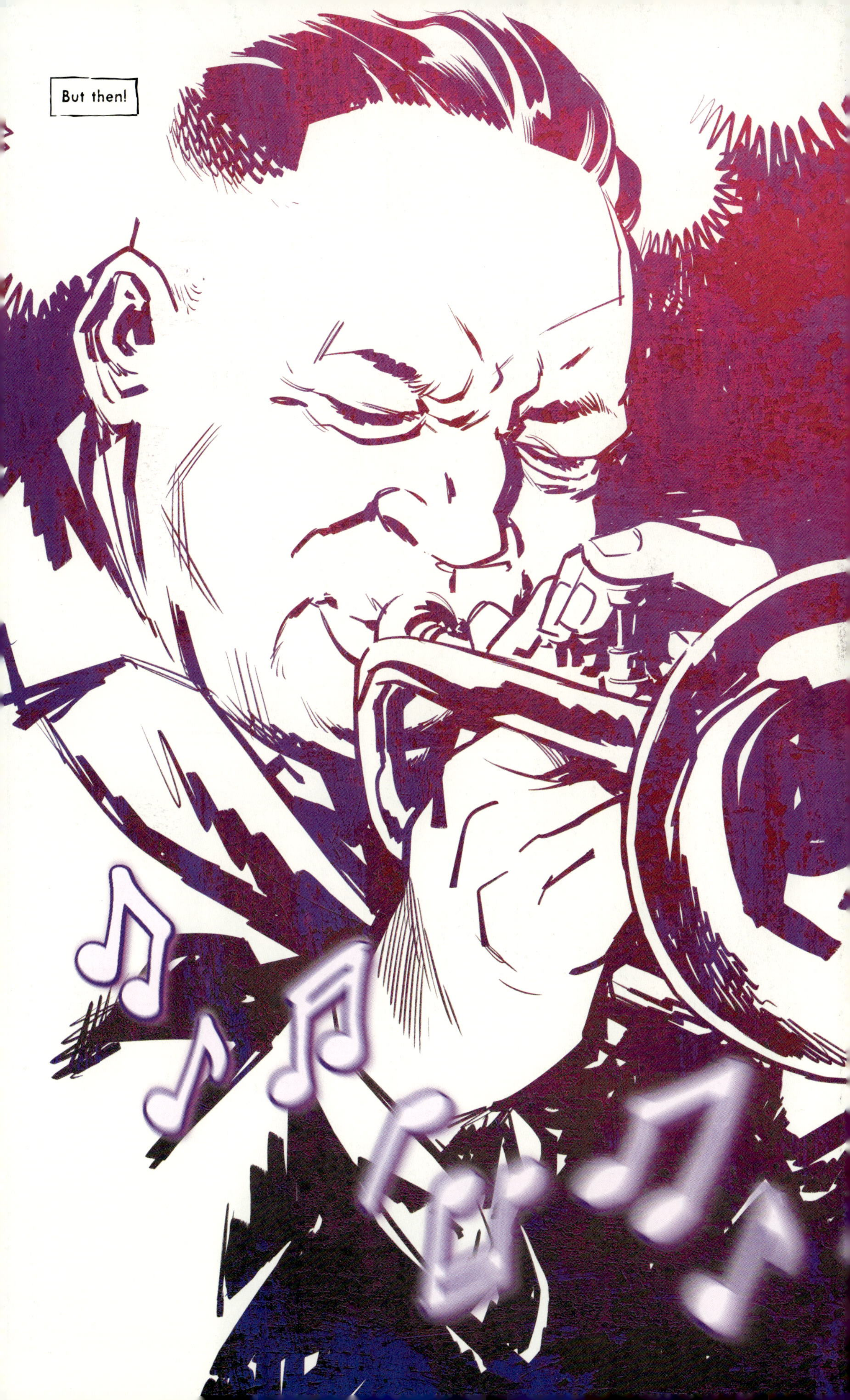
But then!

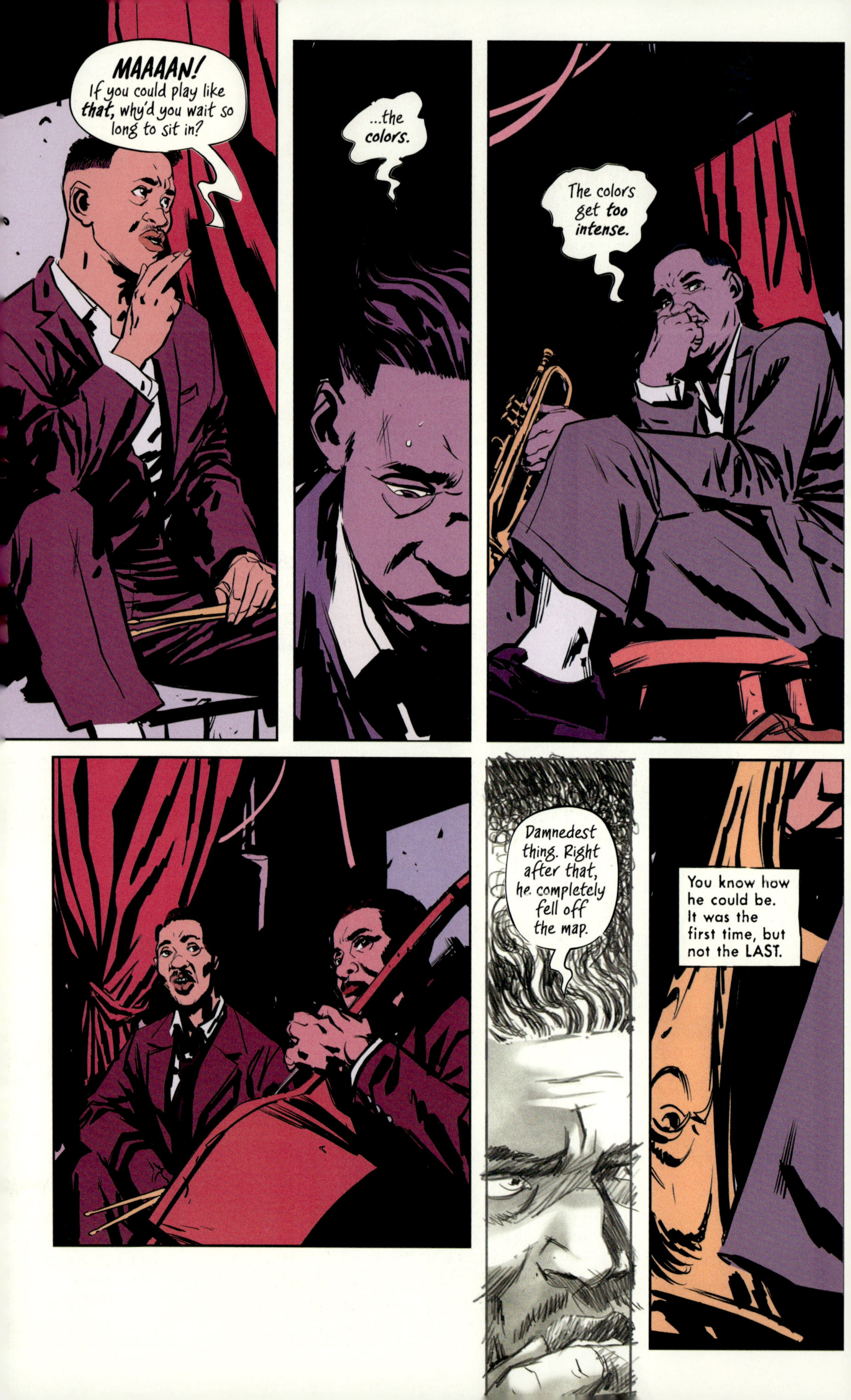
MAAAAN! If you could play like that, why'd you wait so long to sit in?
...the colors.
The colors get too intense.
Damnedest thing. Right after that, he completely fell off the map.
You know how he could be. It was the first time, but not the LAST.

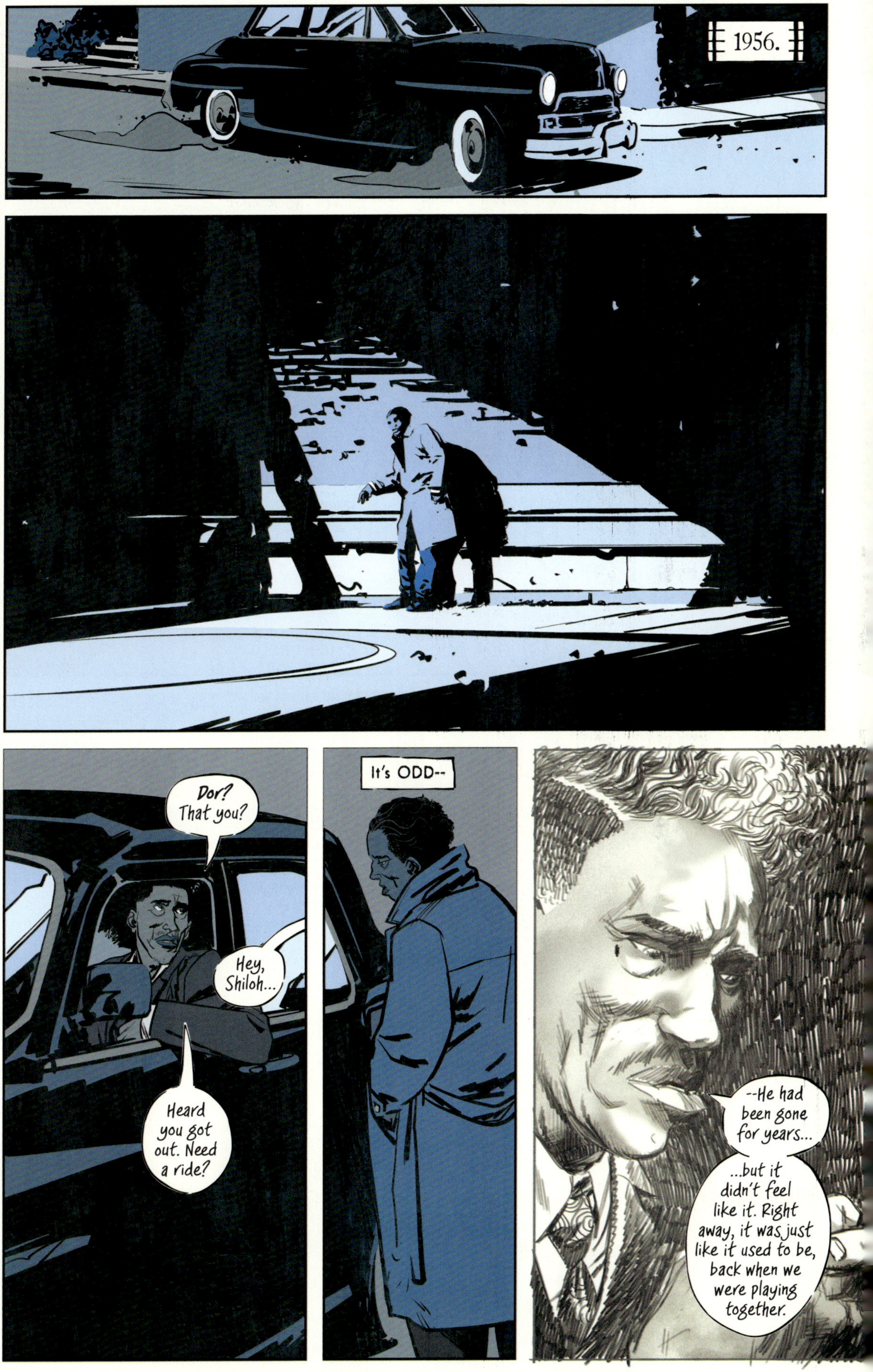
1956.
Dor? That you?
Hey, Shiloh...
Heard you got out. Need a ride?
It's ODD--
--He had been gone for years...
...but it didn't feel like it. Right away, it was just like it used to be, back when we were playing together.

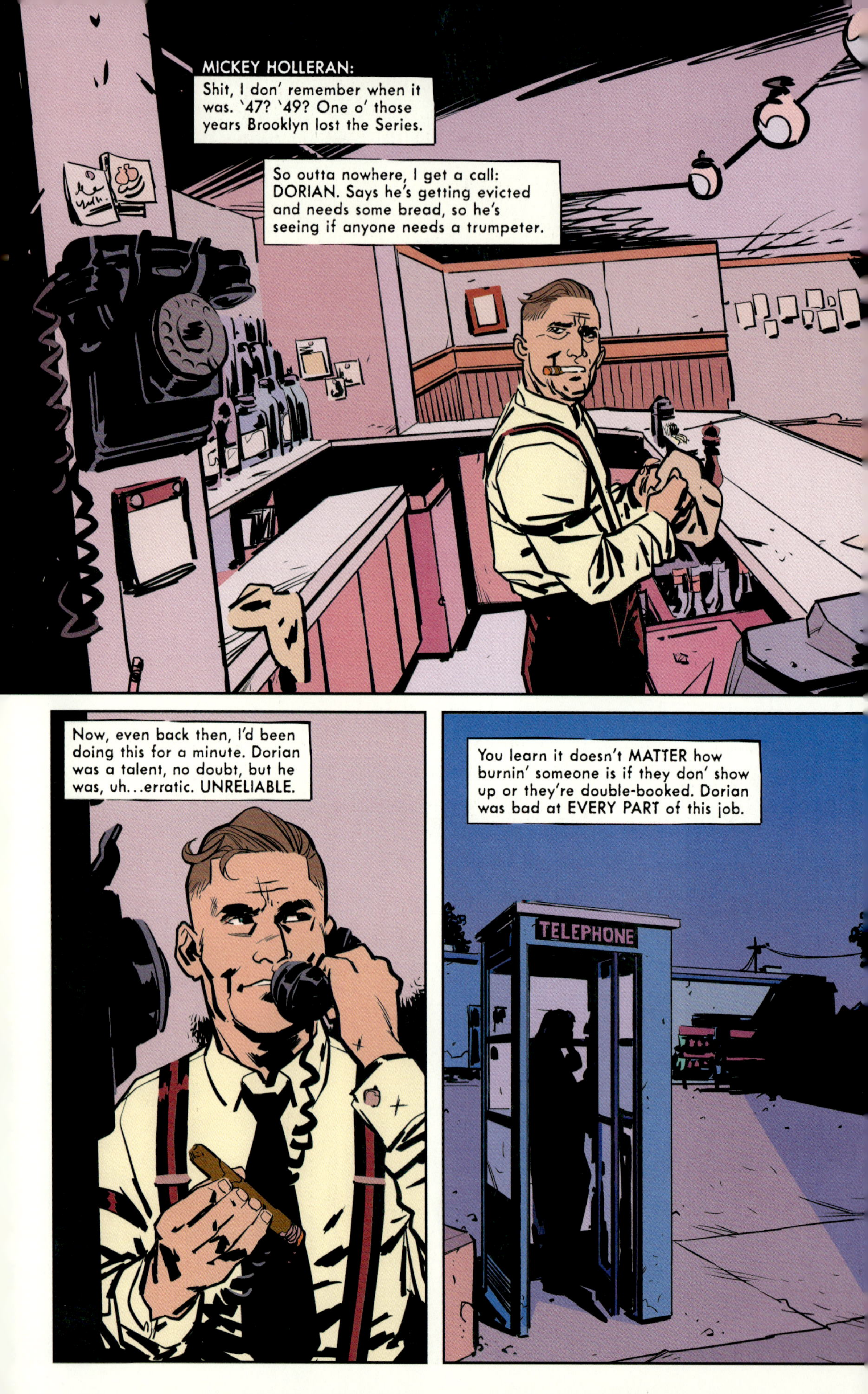
MICKEY HOLLERAN:
Shit, I don' remember when it was. `47? `49? One o' those years Brooklyn lost the Series.
So outta nowhere, I get a call: DORIAN. Says he's getting evicted and needs some bread, so he's seeing if anyone needs a trumpeter.
Now, even back then, I'd been doing this for a minute. Dorian was a talent, no doubt, but he was, uh...erratic. UNRELIABLE.
You learn it doesn't MATTER how burnin' someone is if they don' show up or they're double-booked. Dorian was bad at EVERY PART of this job.
TELEPHONE

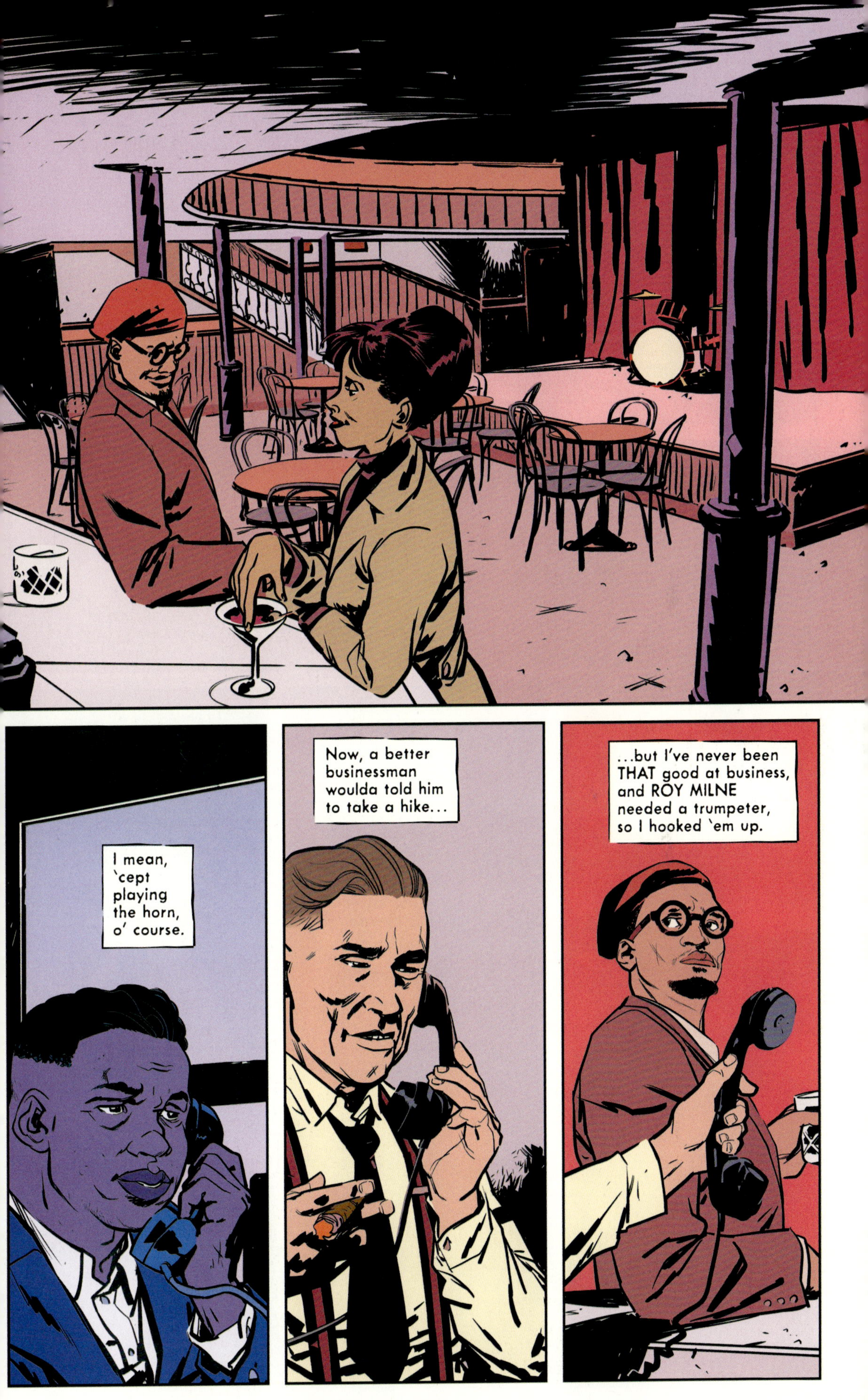
I mean, `cept playing the horn, o' course.
Now, a better businessman woulda told him to take a hike...
...but I've never been THAT good at business, and ROY MILNE needed a trumpeter, so I hooked `em up.

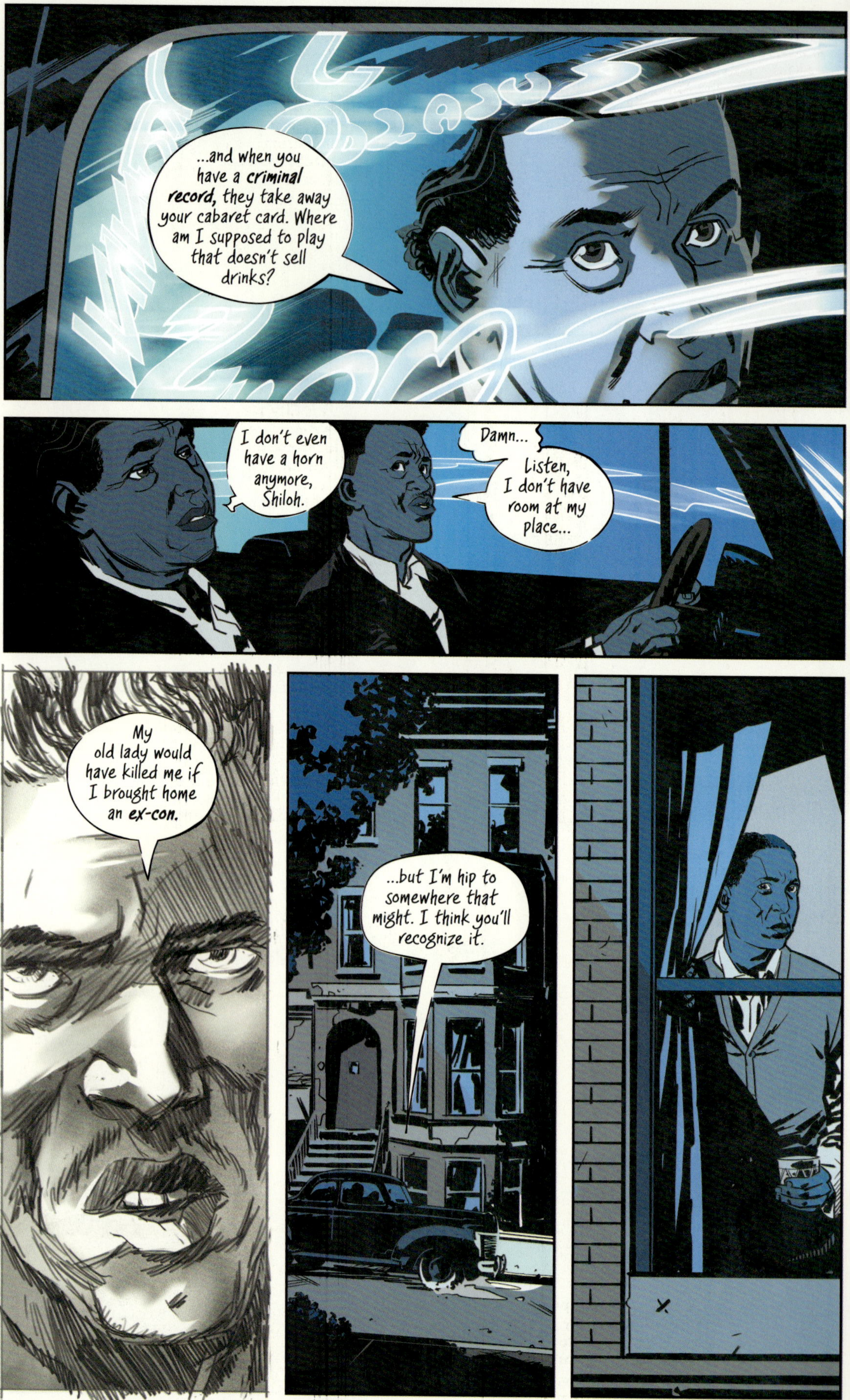
...and when you have a **criminal record,** they take away your cabaret card. Where am I supposed to play that doesn't sell drinks?
I don't even have a horn anymore, Shiloh.
Damn...
Listen, I don't have room at my place...
My old lady would have killed me if I brought home an **ex-con.**
...but I'm hip to somewhere that might. I think you'll recognize it.

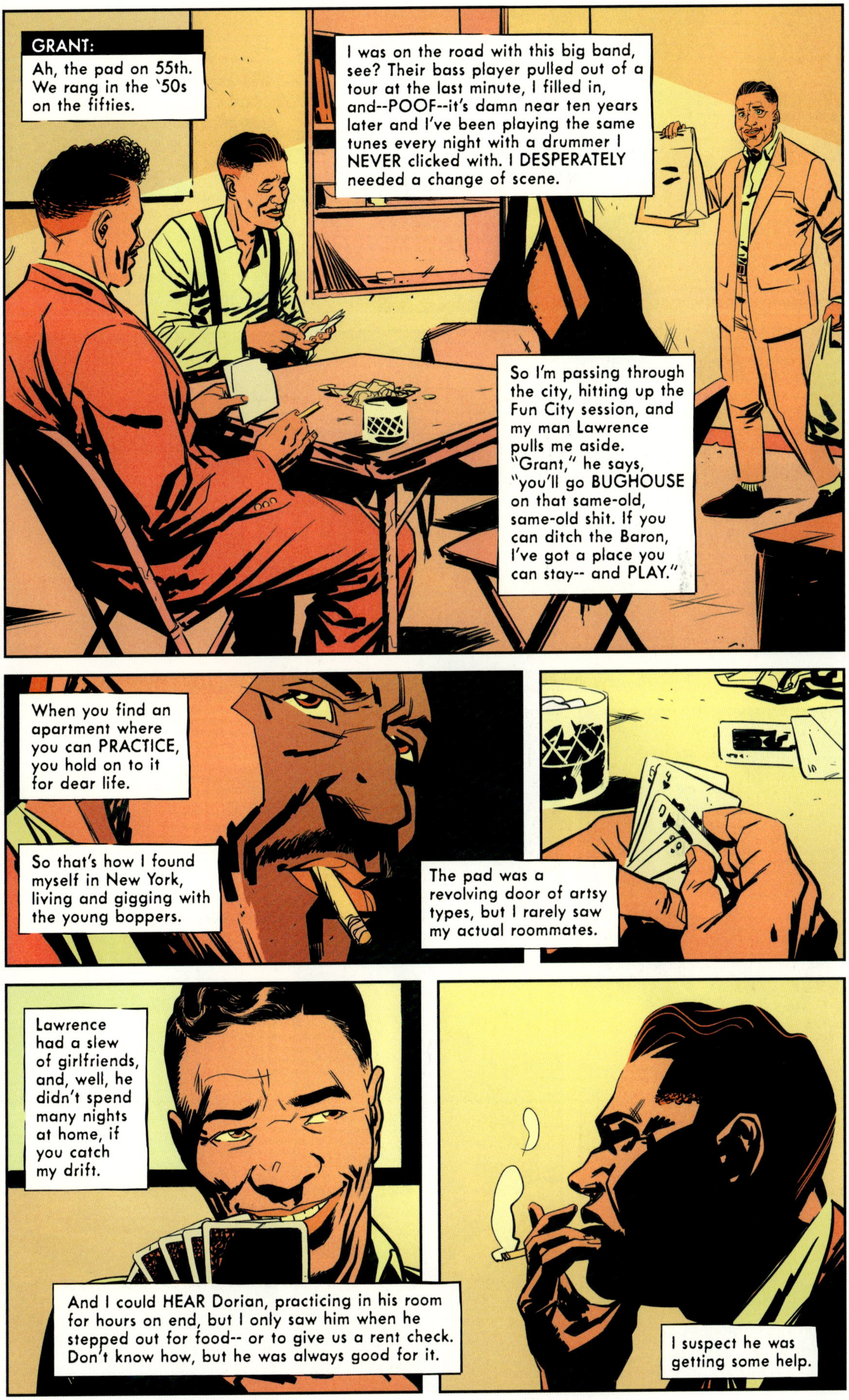
GRANT:
Ah, the pad on 55th. We rang in the '50s on the fifties.
I was on the road with this big band, see? Their bass player pulled out of a tour at the last minute, I filled in, and--POOF--it's damn near ten years later and I've been playing the same tunes every night with a drummer I NEVER clicked with. I DESPERATELY needed a change of scene.
So I'm passing through the city, hitting up the Fun City session, and my man Lawrence pulls me aside. "Grant," he says, "you'll go BUGHOUSE on that same-old, same-old shit. If you can ditch the Baron, I've got a place you can stay-- and PLAY."
When you find an apartment where you can PRACTICE, you hold on to it for dear life.
So that's how I found myself in New York, living and gigging with the young boppers.
The pad was a revolving door of artsy types, but I rarely saw my actual roommates.
Lawrence had a slew of girlfriends, and, well, he didn't spend many nights at home, if you catch my drift.
And I could HEAR Dorian, practicing in his room for hours on end, but I only saw him when he stepped out for food-- or to give us a rent check. Don't know how, but he was always good for it.
I suspect he was getting some help.

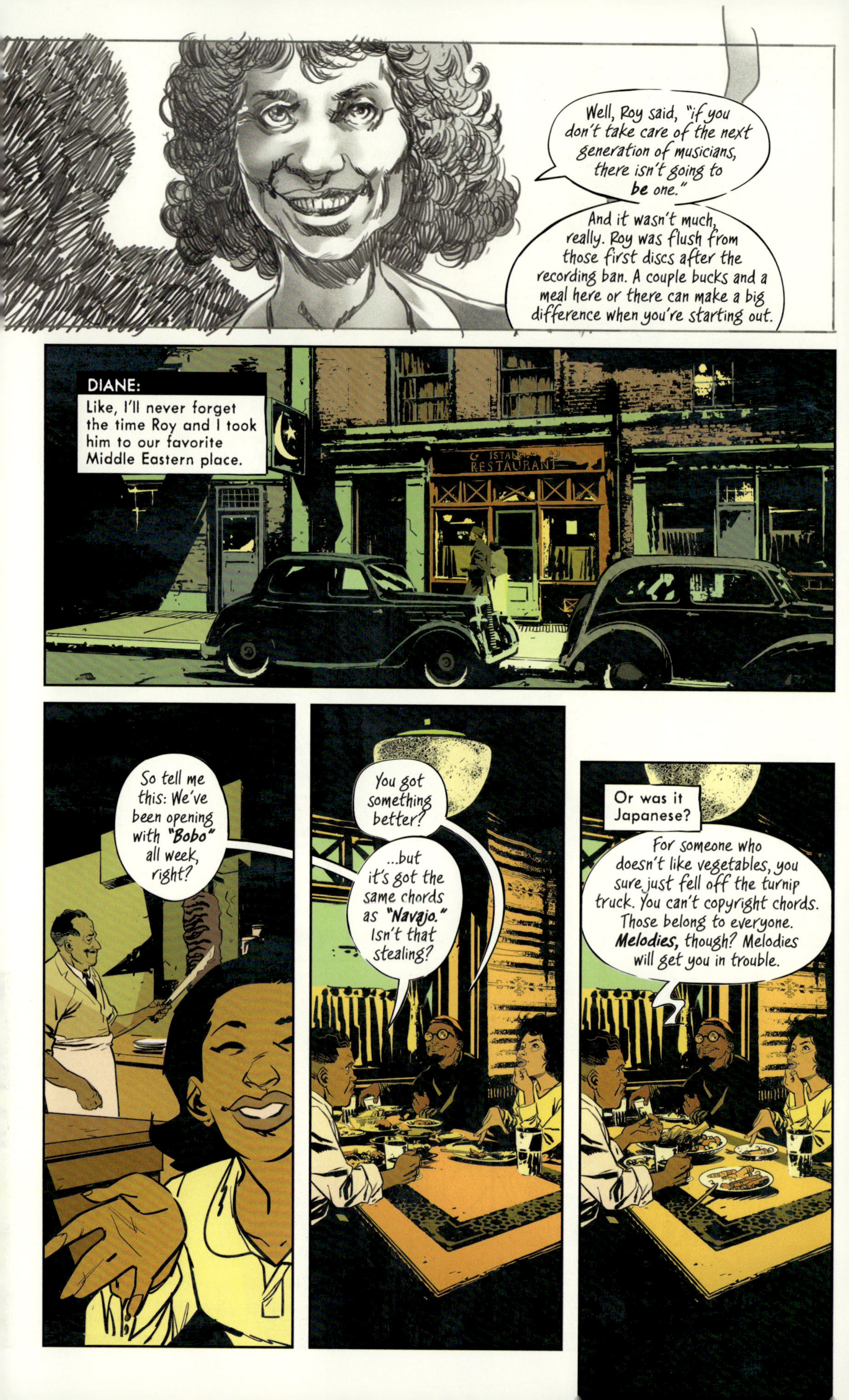
Well, Roy said, "if you don't take care of the next generation of musicians, there isn't going to be one."
And it wasn't much, really. Roy was flush from those first discs after the recording ban. A couple bucks and a meal here or there can make a big difference when you're starting out.
DIANE:
Like, I'll never forget the time Roy and I took him to our favorite Middle Eastern place.
RESTAURANT
So tell me this: We've been opening with "Bobo" all week, right?
...but it's got the same chords as "Navajo." Isn't that stealing?
You got something better?
Or was it Japanese?
For someone who doesn't like vegetables, you sure just fell off the turnip truck. You can't copyright chords. Those belong to everyone. Melodies, though? Melodies will get you in trouble.

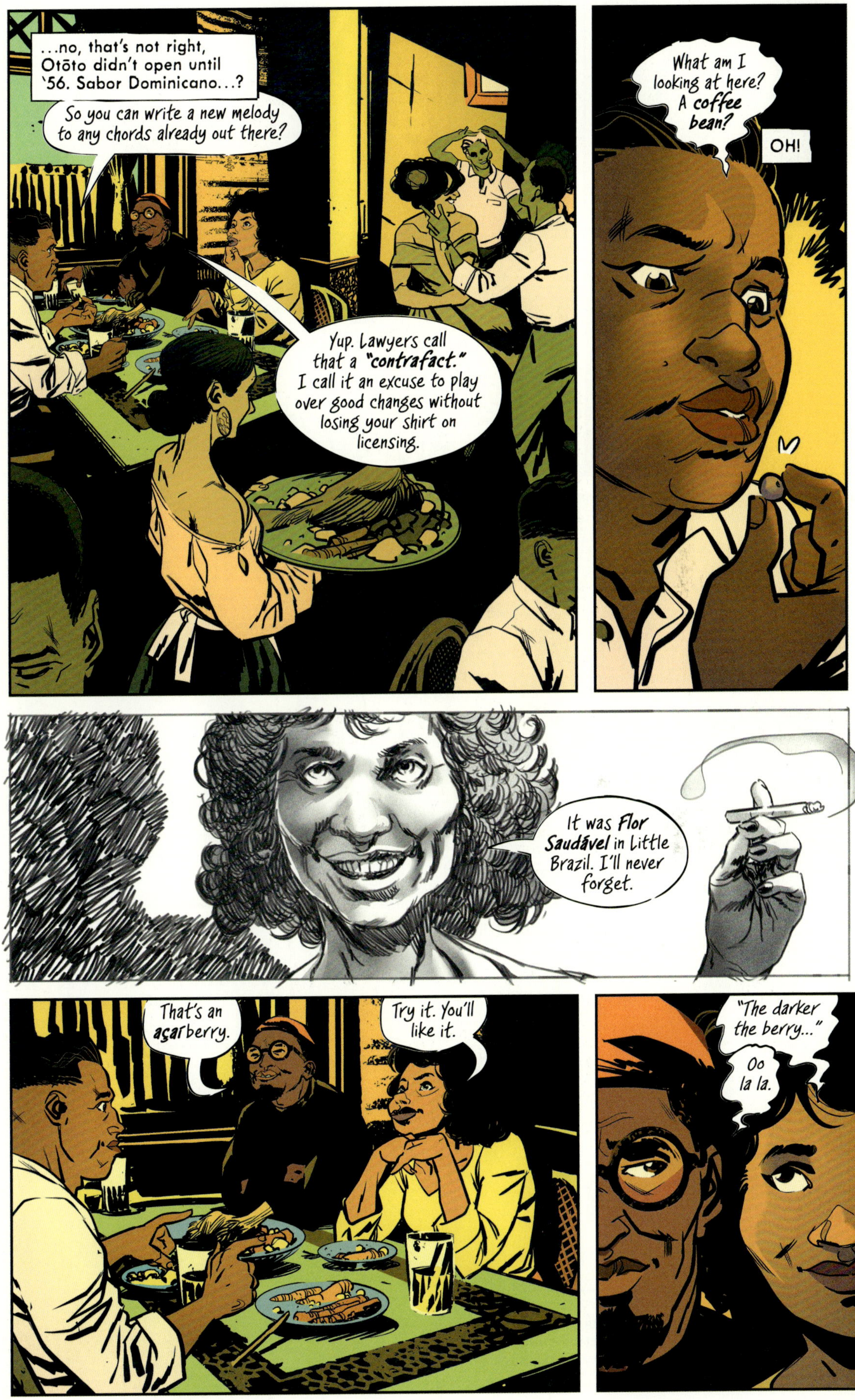
...no, that's not right, Otōto didn't open until '56. Sabor Dominicano...?
So you can write a new melody to any chords already out there?
Yup. Lawyers call that a "**contrafact.**" I call it an excuse to play over good changes without losing your shirt on licensing.
What am I looking at here? A **coffee bean?**
OH!
It was **Flor Saudável** in Little Brazil. I'll never forget.
That's an **açaí** berry.
Try it. You'll like it.
"The darker the berry..."
Oo la la.

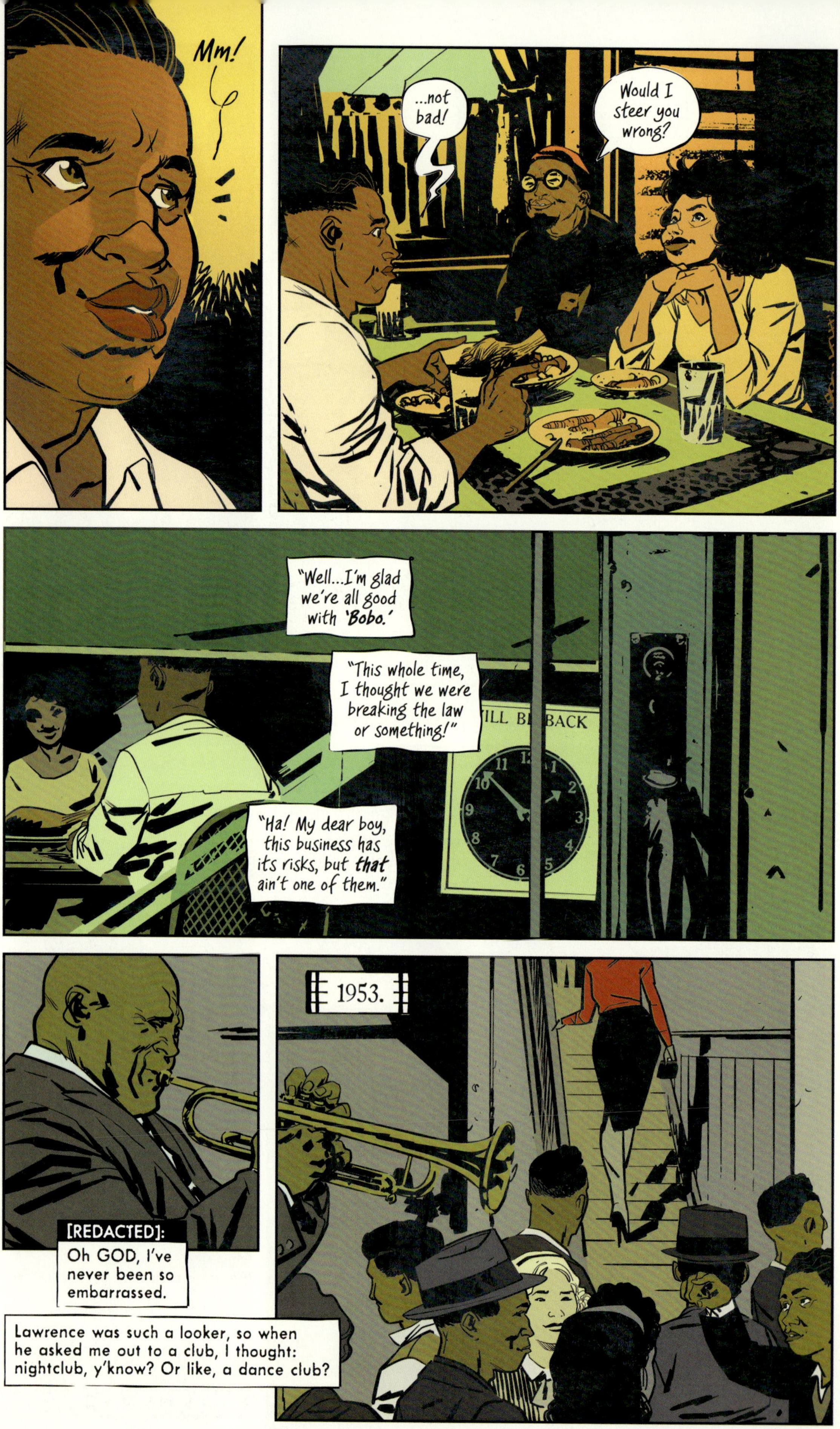
Mm!
...not bad!
Would I steer you wrong?
"Well...I'm glad we're all good with *'Bobo.'*
"This whole time, I thought we were breaking the law or something!"
"Ha! My dear boy, this business has its risks, but ***that*** ain't one of them."
1953.
[REDACTED]:
Oh GOD, I've never been so embarrassed.
Lawrence was such a looker, so when he asked me out to a club, I thought: nightclub, y'know? Or like, a dance club?

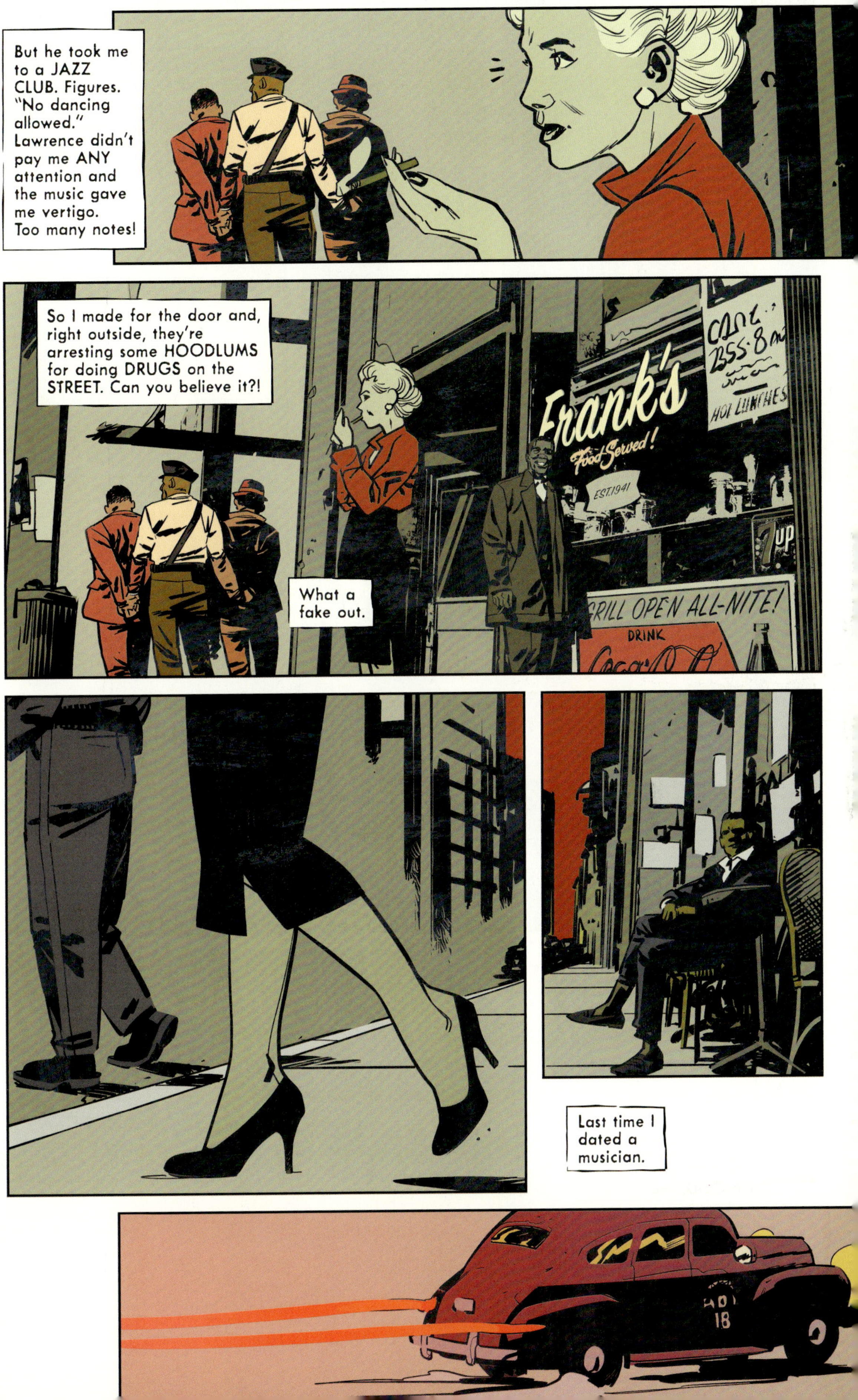
But he took me to a JAZZ CLUB. Figures. "No dancing allowed." Lawrence didn't pay me ANY attention and the music gave me vertigo. Too many notes!
So I made for the door and, right outside, they're arresting some HOODLUMS for doing DRUGS on the STREET. Can you believe it?!
Frank's
Food Served!
EST.1941
HOT LUNCHES
GRILL OPEN ALL-NITE!
DRINK
What a fake out.
Last time I dated a musician.

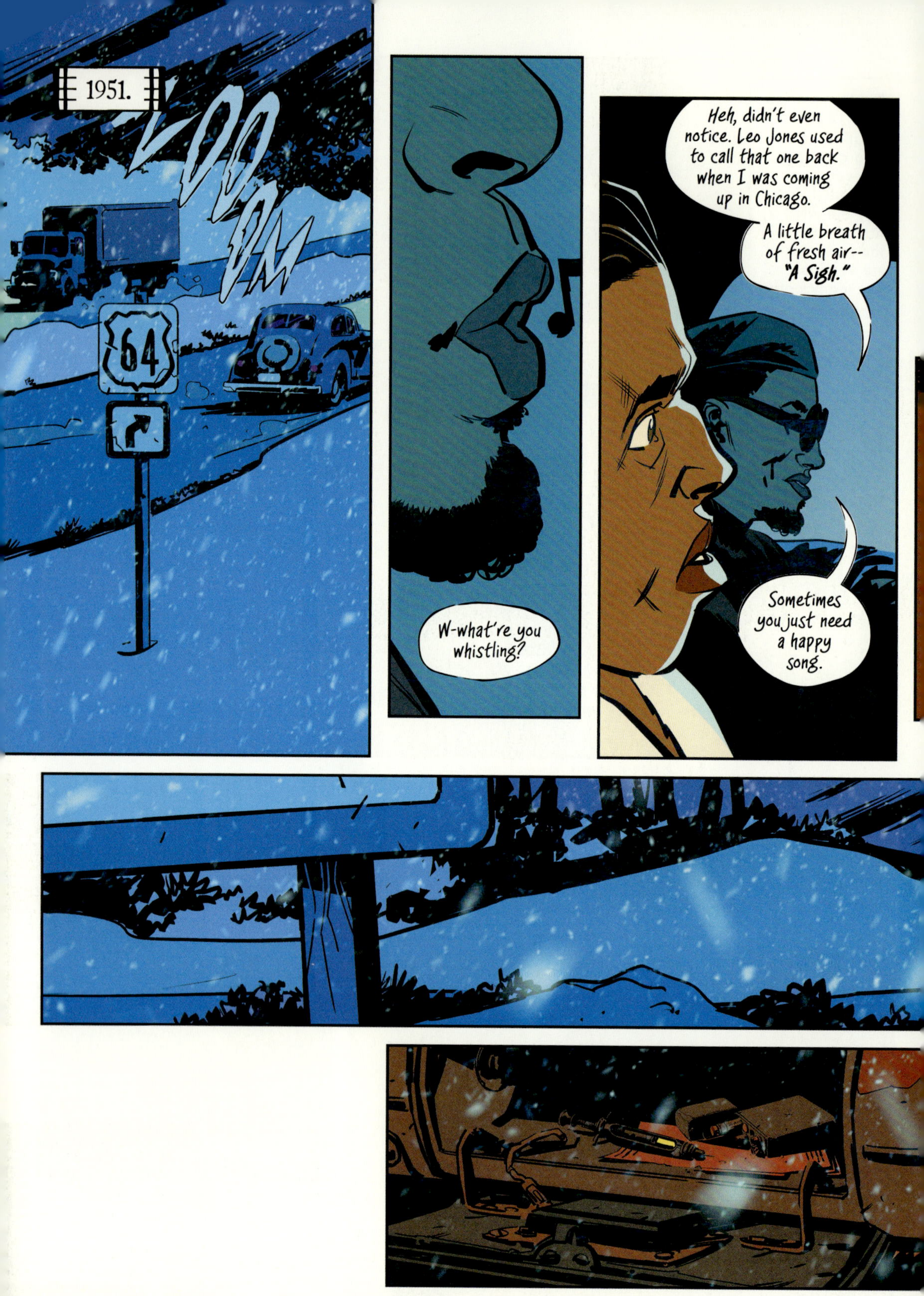
1951.
VOOOM
W-what're you whistling?
Heh, didn't even notice. Leo Jones used to call that one back when I was coming up in Chicago.
A little breath of fresh air--"A Sigh."
Sometimes you just need a happy song.

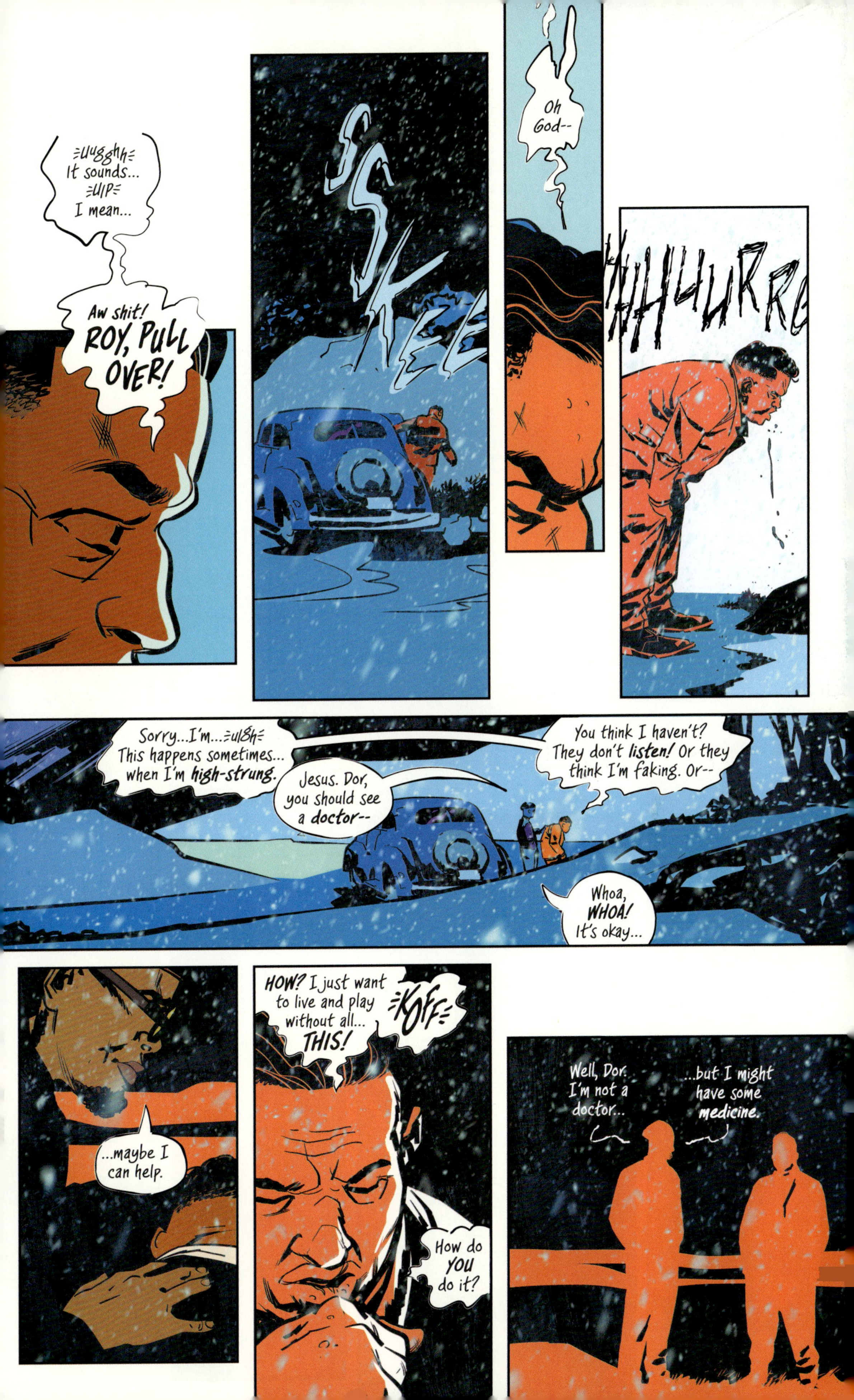

=Uuggh= It sounds... =UIP= I mean...
Aw shit! ROY, PULL OVER!
SSKEE
Oh God--
HHUURRG
Sorry...I'm...=ul8h= This happens sometimes... when I'm high-strung.
Jesus. Dor, you should see a doctor--
You think I haven't? They don't listen! Or they think I'm faking. Or--
Whoa, WHOA! It's okay...
...maybe I can help.
HOW? I just want to live and play without all... THIS!
KOFF
How do YOU do it?
Well, Dor. I'm not a doctor...
...but I might have some medicine.

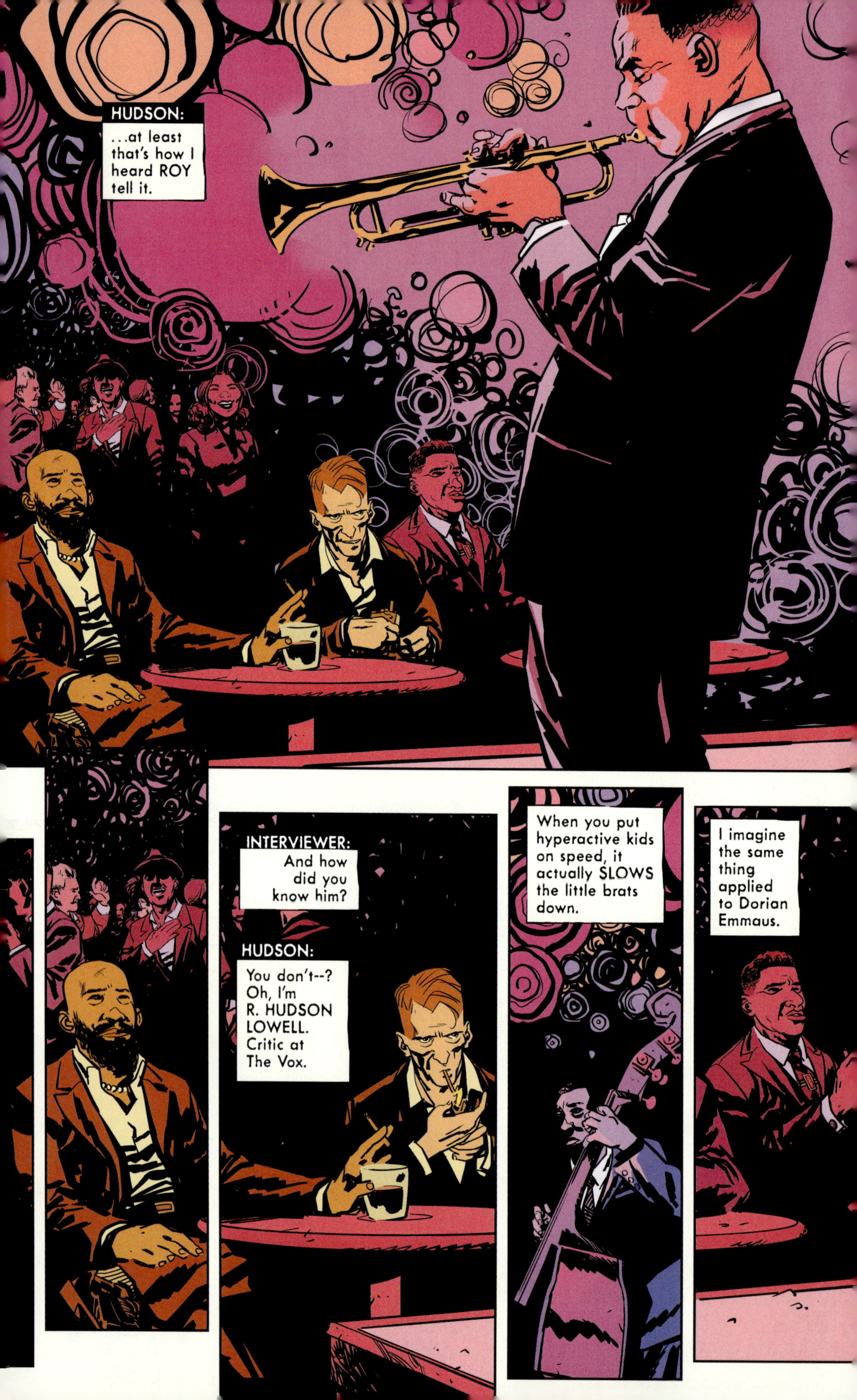
HUDSON:
...at least that's how I heard ROY tell it.
INTERVIEWER:
And how did you know him?
HUDSON:
You don't--? Oh, I'm R. HUDSON LOWELL. Critic at The Vox.
When you put hyperactive kids on speed, it actually SLOWS the little brats down.
I imagine the same thing applied to Dorian Emmaus.

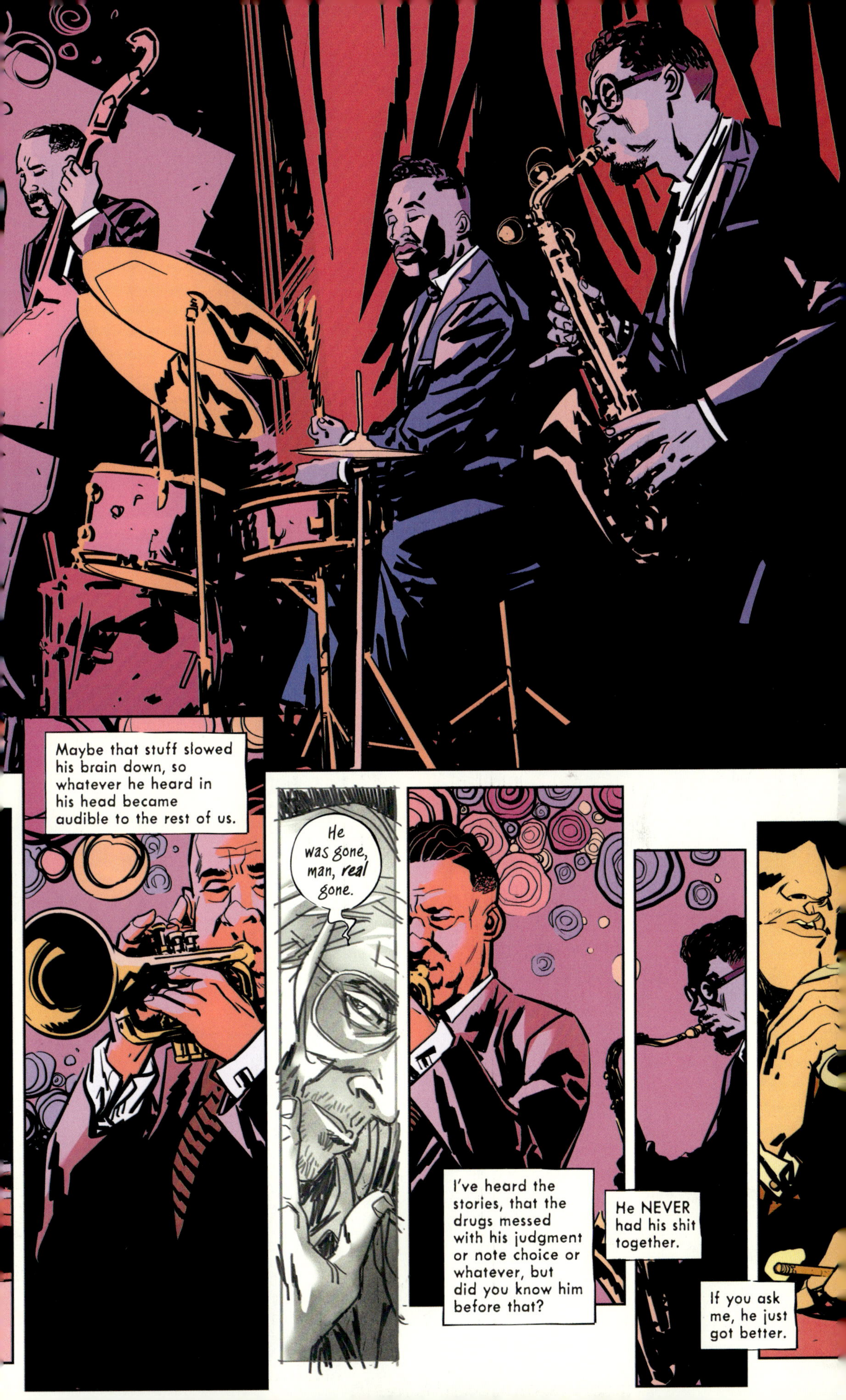
Maybe that stuff slowed his brain down, so whatever he heard in his head became audible to the rest of us.
He was gone, man, real gone.
I've heard the stories, that the drugs messed with his judgment or note choice or whatever, but did you know him before that?
He NEVER had his shit together.
If you ask me, he just got better.

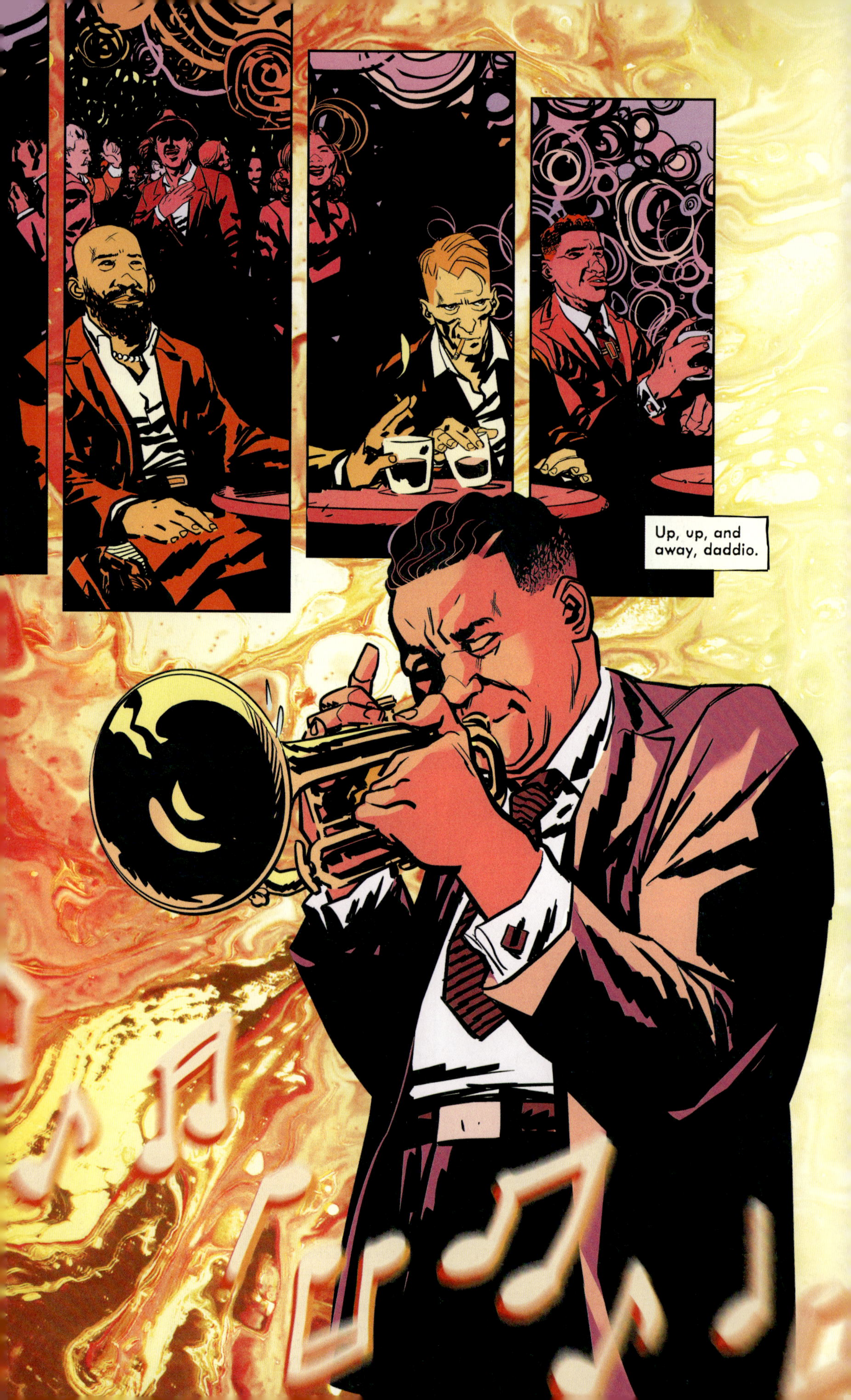
Up, up, and away, daddio.

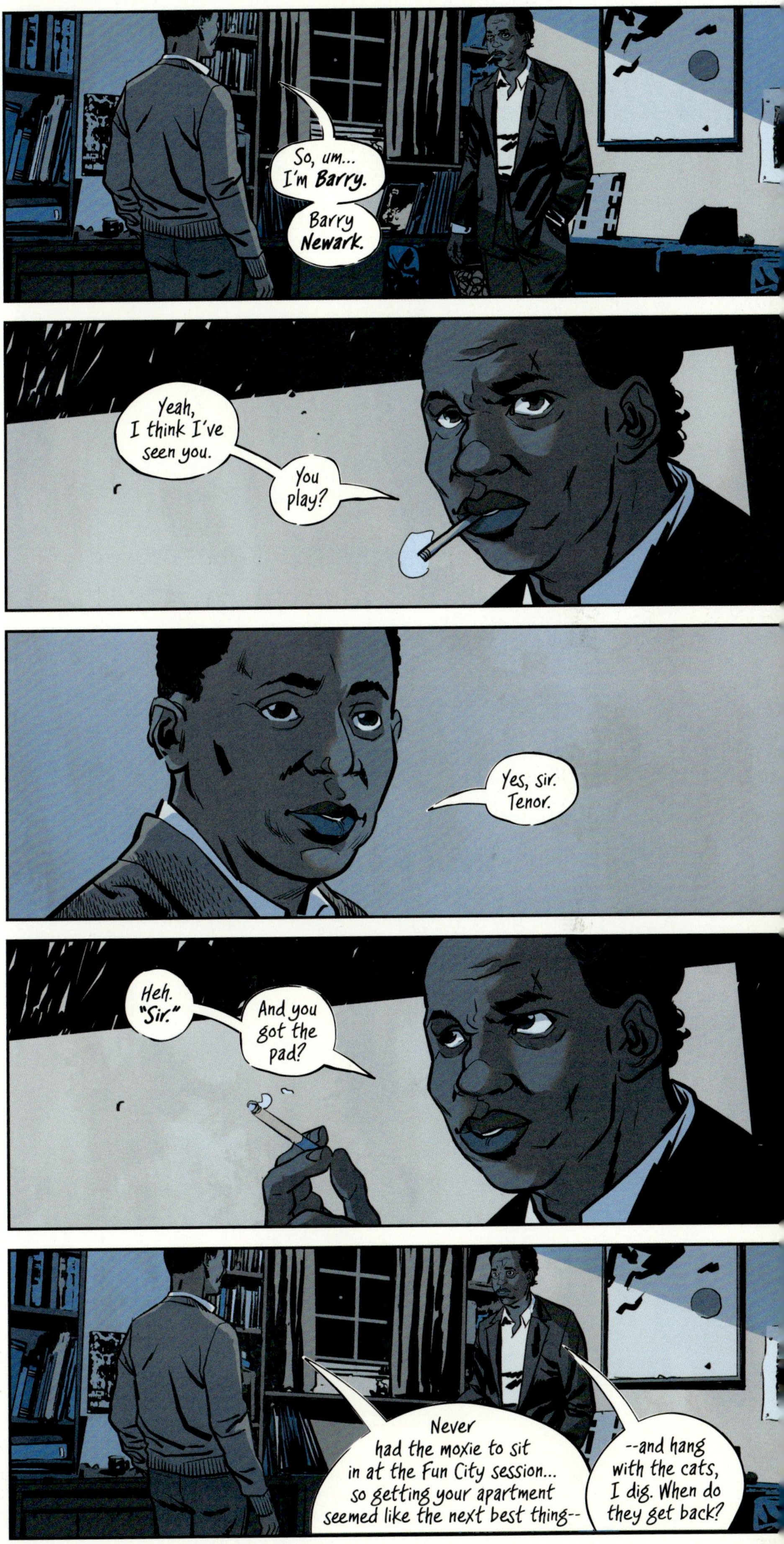

So, um... I'm Barry.
Barry Newark.
Yeah, I think I've seen you.
You play?
Yes, sir. Tenor.
Heh. "Sir."
And you got the pad?
Never had the moxie to sit in at the Fun City session... so getting your apartment seemed like the next best thing--
--and hang with the cats, I dig. When do they get back?

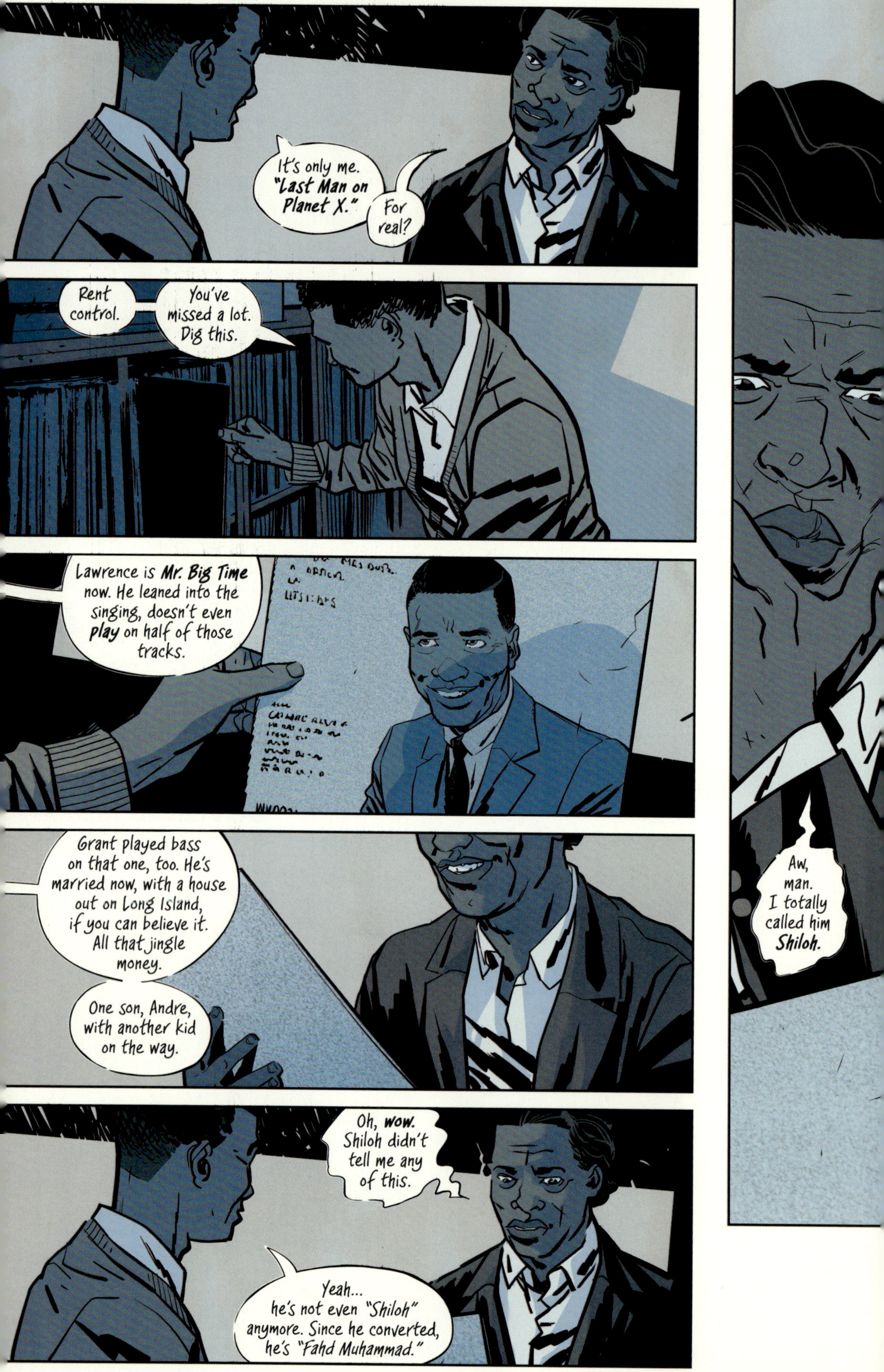

It's only me. "Last Man on Planet X."
For real?
Rent control.
You've missed a lot. Dig this.
Lawrence is Mr. Big Time now. He leaned into the singing, doesn't even play on half of those tracks.
Grant played bass on that one, too. He's married now, with a house out on Long Island, if you can believe it. All that jingle money.
One son, Andre, with another kid on the way.
Aw, man. I totally called him Shiloh.
Oh, wow. Shiloh didn't tell me any of this.
Yeah... he's not even "Shiloh" anymore. Since he converted, he's "Fahd Muhammad."

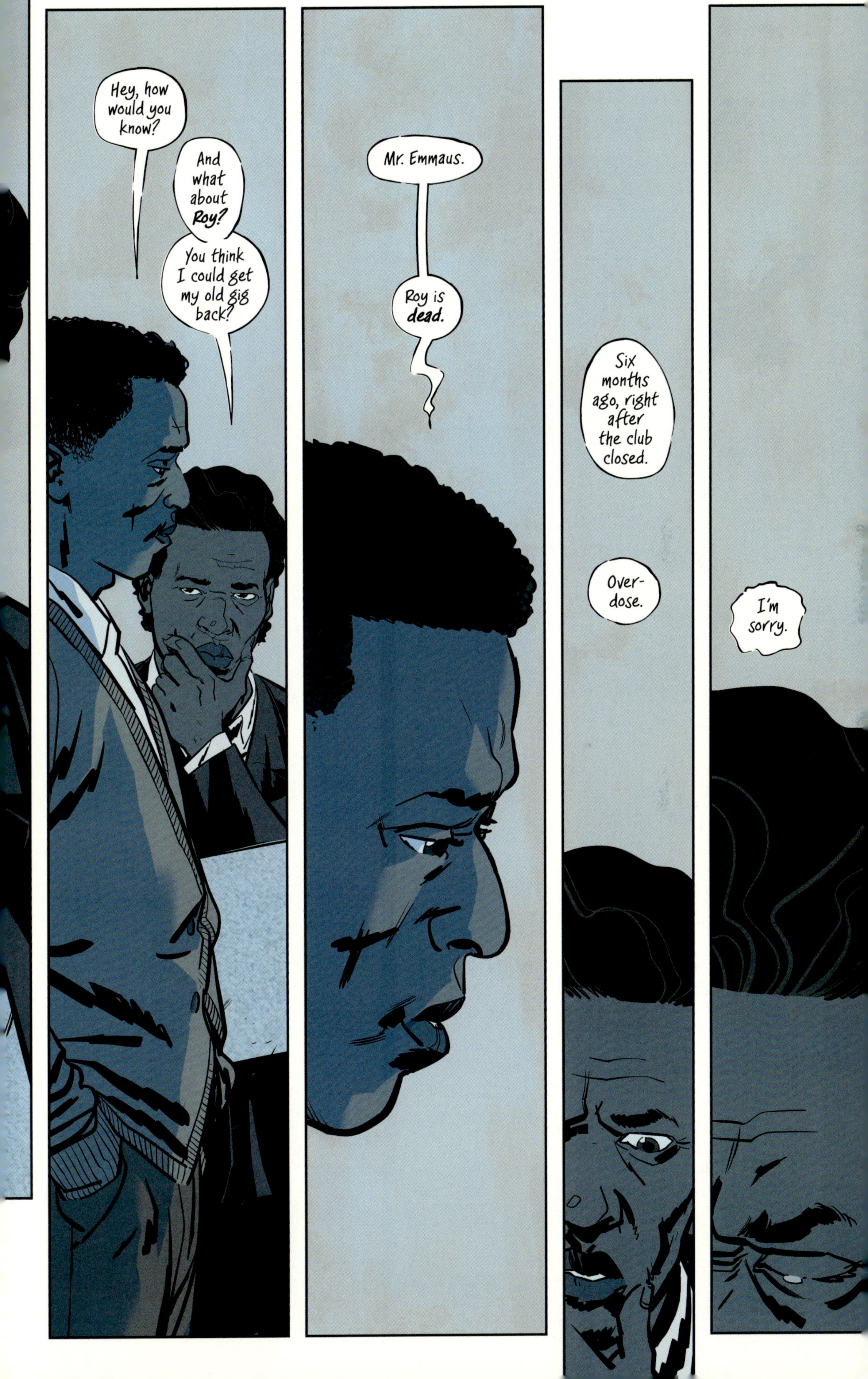
Hey, how would you know?
And what about Roy?
You think I could get my old gig back?
Mr. Emmaus.
Roy is dead.
Six months ago, right after the club closed.
Over-dose.
I'm sorry.

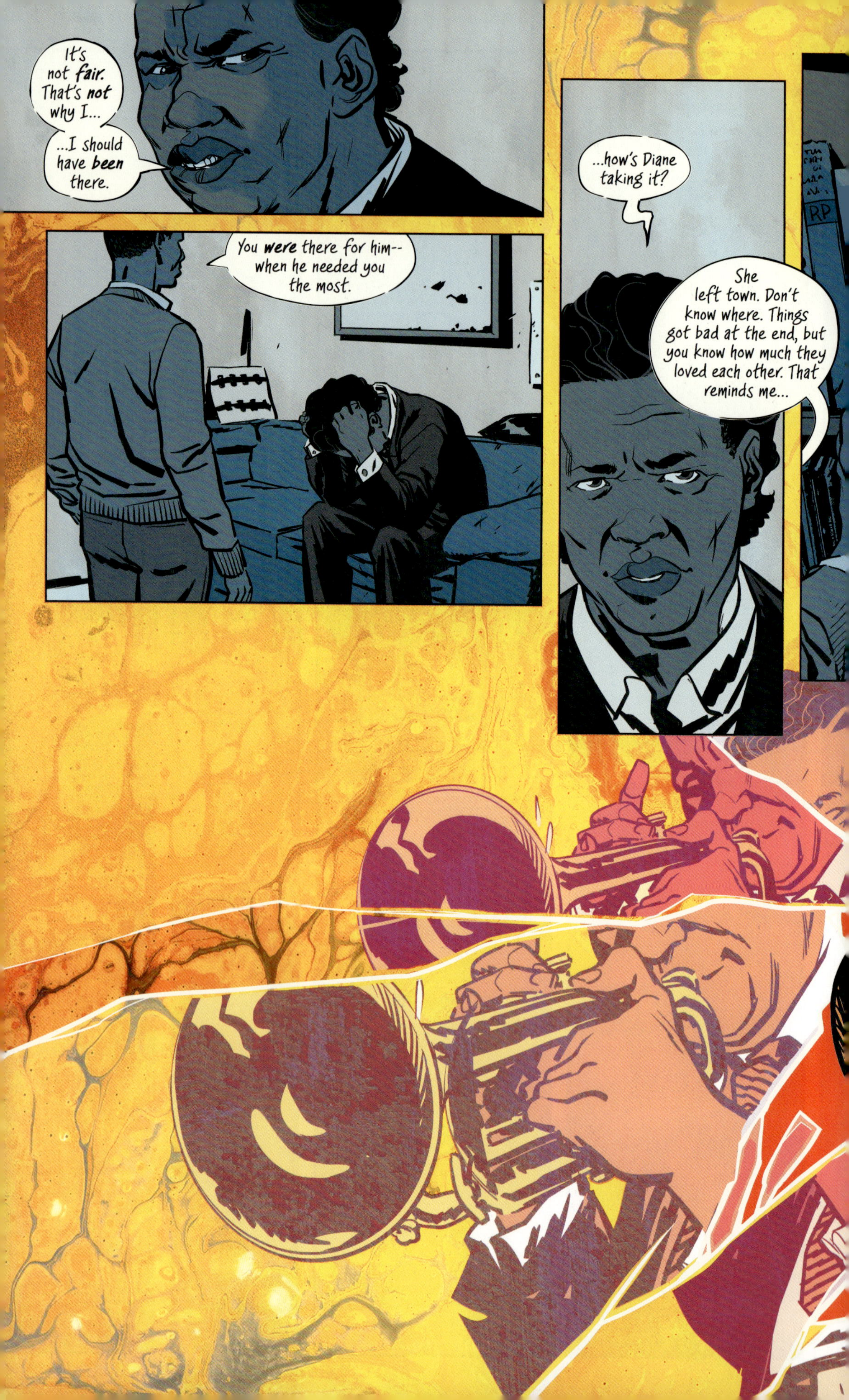
It's not fair. That's not why I...
...I should have been there.
You were there for him--when he needed you the most.
...how's Diane taking it?
She left town. Don't know where. Things got bad at the end, but you know how much they loved each other. That reminds me...

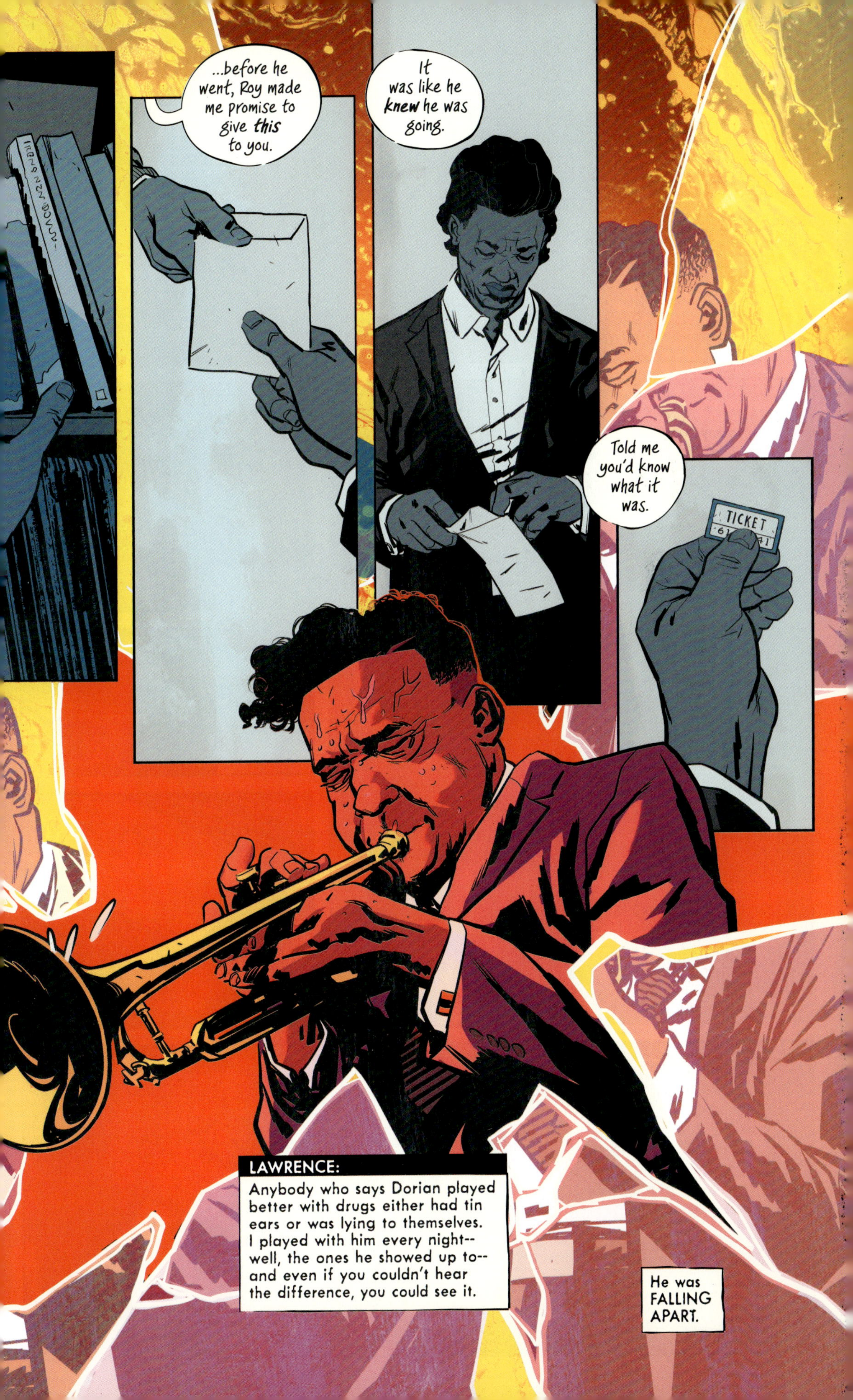
...before he went, Roy made me promise to give this to you.
It was like he knew he was going.
Told me you'd know what it was.
TICKET
LAWRENCE:
Anybody who says Dorian played better with drugs either had tin ears or was lying to themselves. I played with him every night--well, the ones he showed up to--and even if you couldn't hear the difference, you could see it.
He was FALLING APART.

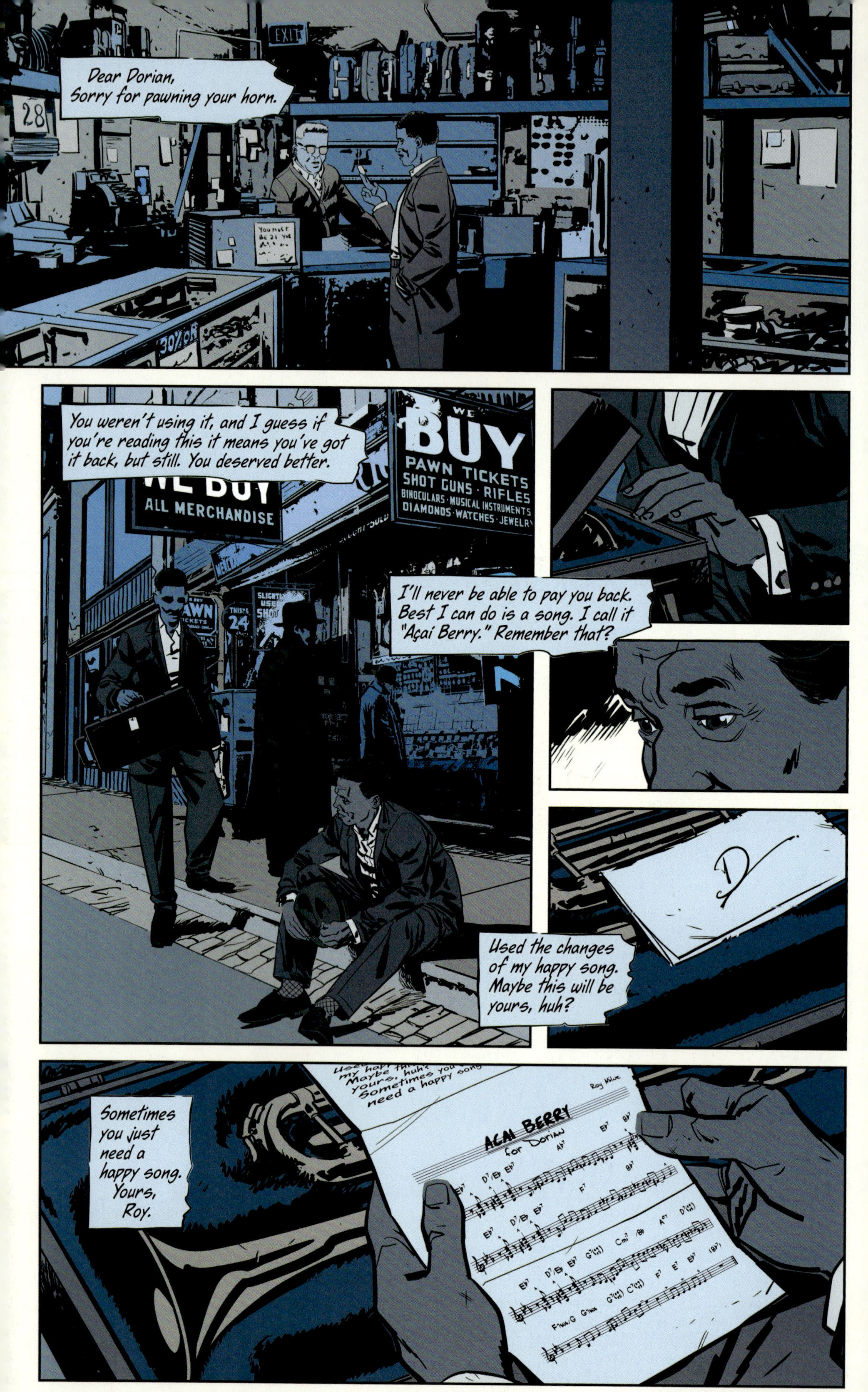
EXIT
28
Dear Dorian,
Sorry for pawning your horn.
30% off
You weren't using it, and I guess if you're reading this it means you've got it back, but still. You deserved better.
ALL MERCHANDISE
BUY
PAWN TICKETS
SHOT GUNS · RIFLES
BINOCULARS · MUSICAL INSTRUMENTS
DIAMONDS · WATCHES · JEWELRY
I'll never be able to pay you back. Best I can do is a song. I call it "Açai Berry." Remember that?
Used the changes of my happy song. Maybe this will be yours, huh?
Sometimes you just need a happy song. Yours, Roy.
ACAI BERRY
for Dorian

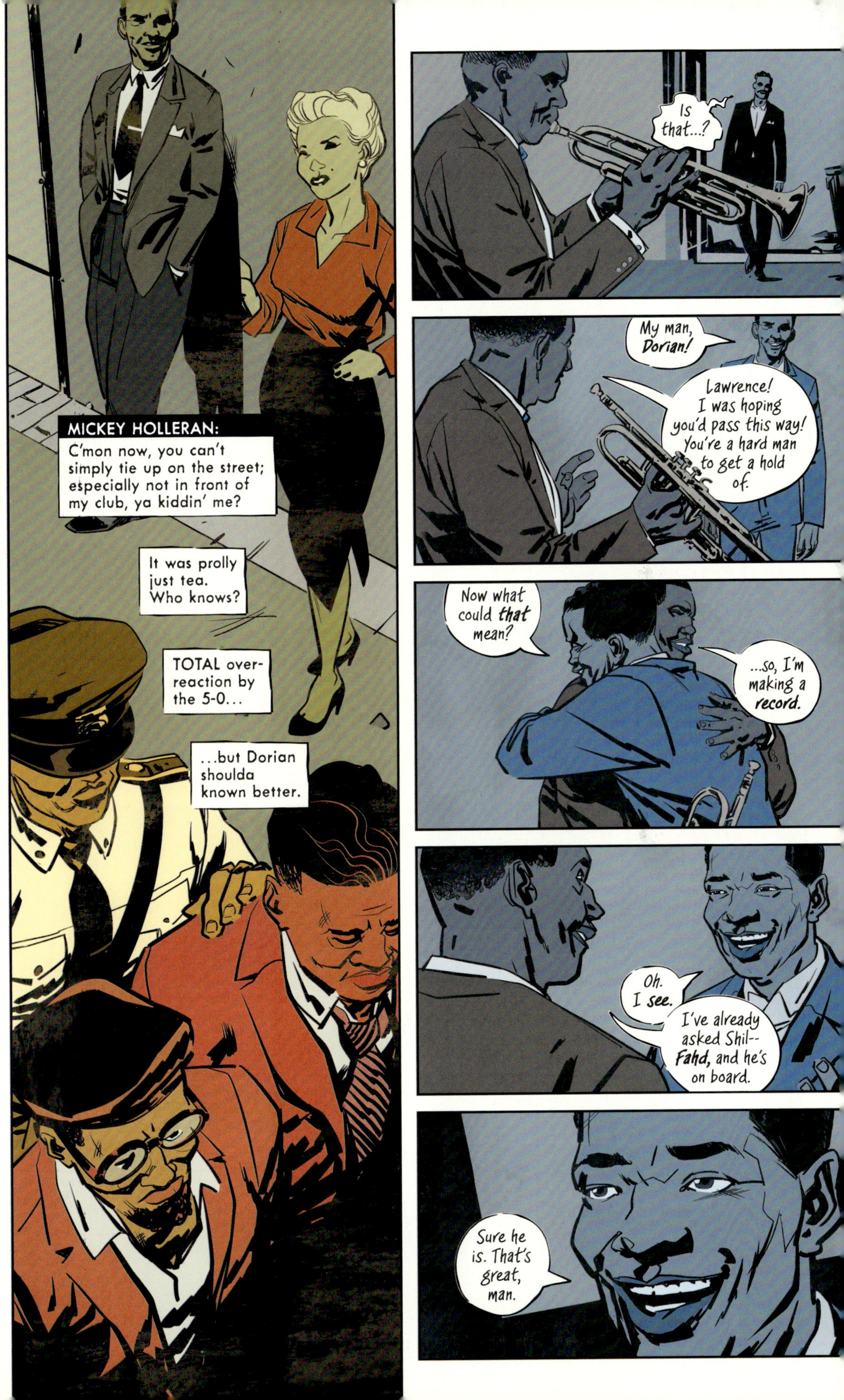
MICKEY HOLLERAN:
C'mon now, you can't simply tie up on the street; especially not in front of my club, ya kiddin' me?
It was prolly just tea. Who knows?
TOTAL over-reaction by the 5-0...
...but Dorian shoulda known better.
Is that...?
My man, Dorian!
Lawrence! I was hoping you'd pass this way! You're a hard man to get a hold of.
Now what could that mean?
...so, I'm making a record.
Oh. I see.
I've already asked Shil-- Fahd, and he's on board.
Sure he is. That's great, man.

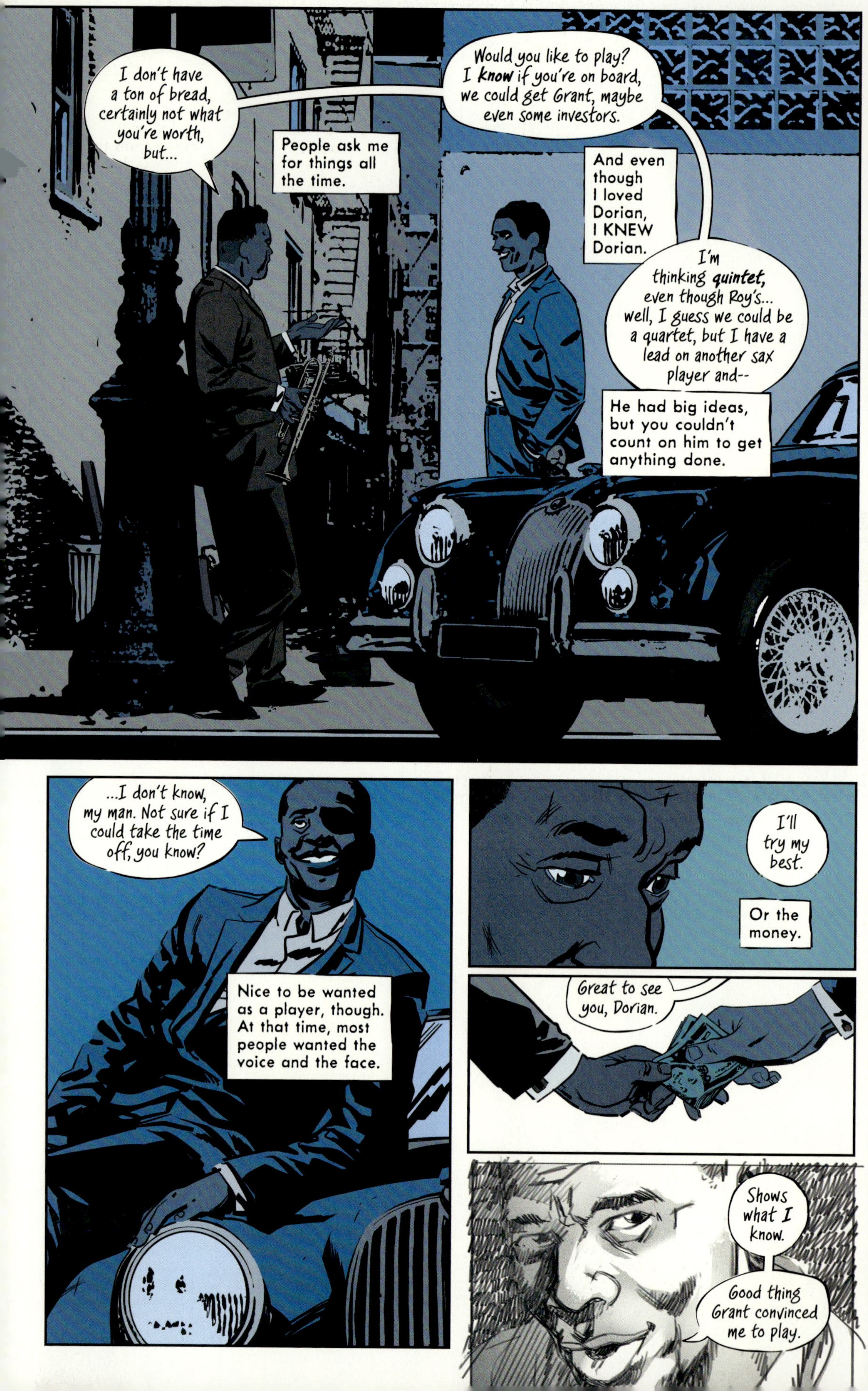
I don't have a ton of bread, certainly not what you're worth, but...
People ask me for things all the time.
Would you like to play? I **know** if you're on board, we could get Grant, maybe even some investors.
And even though I loved Dorian, I KNEW Dorian.
I'm thinking **quintet,** even though Roy's... well, I guess we could be a quartet, but I have a lead on another sax player and--
He had big ideas, but you couldn't count on him to get anything done.
...I don't know, my man. Not sure if I could take the time off, you know?
Nice to be wanted as a player, though. At that time, most people wanted the voice and the face.
I'll try my best.
Or the money.
Great to see you, Dorian.
Shows what **I** know.
Good thing Grant convinced me to play.

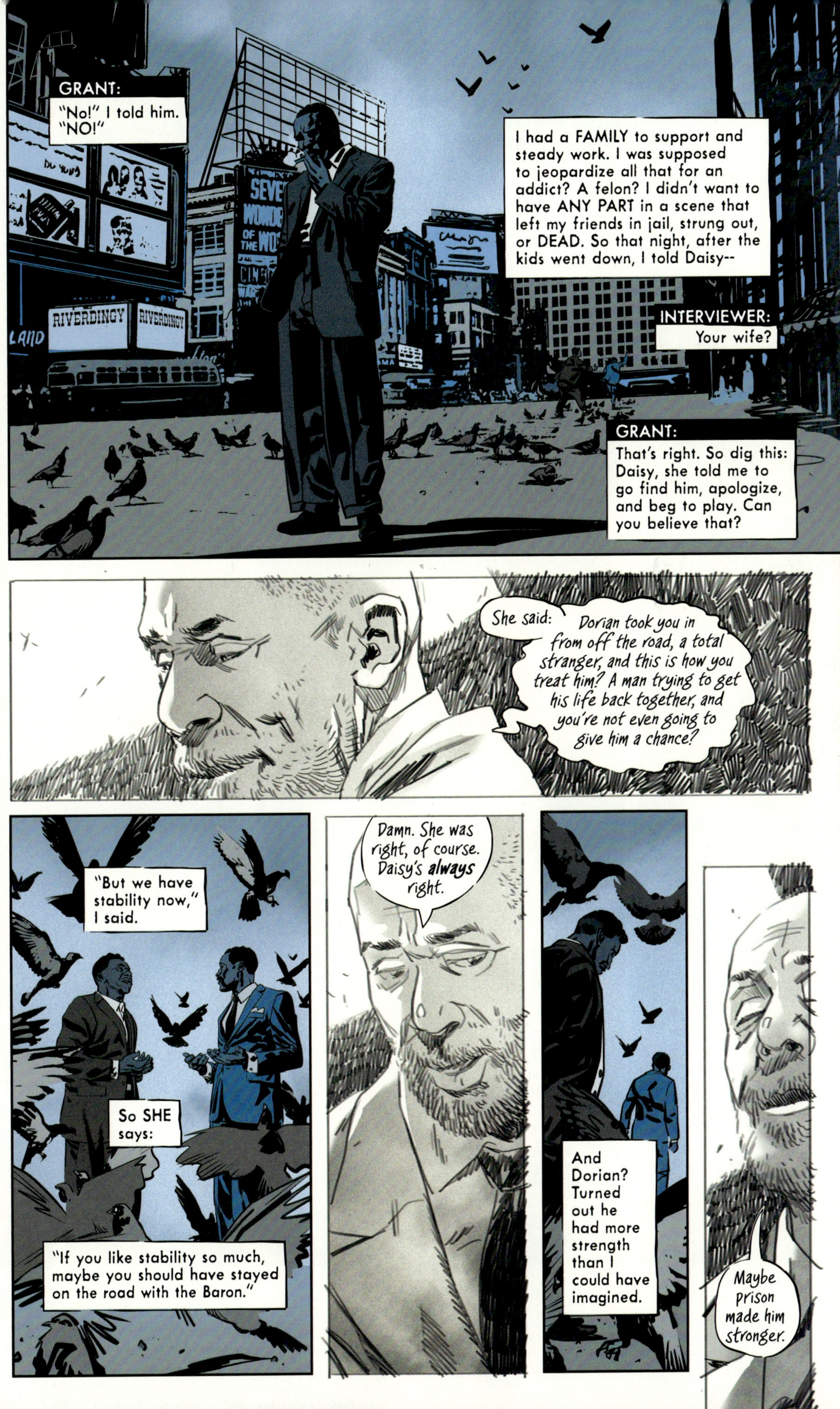
GRANT:
"No!" I told him. "NO!"
I had a FAMILY to support and steady work. I was supposed to jeopardize all that for an addict? A felon? I didn't want to have ANY PART in a scene that left my friends in jail, strung out, or DEAD. So that night, after the kids went down, I told Daisy--
INTERVIEWER:
Your wife?
GRANT:
That's right. So dig this: Daisy, she told me to go find him, apologize, and beg to play. Can you believe that?
She said:
Dorian took you in from off the road, a total stranger, and this is how you treat him? A man trying to get his life back together, and you're not even going to give him a chance?
"But we have stability now," I said.
So SHE says:
"If you like stability so much, maybe you should have stayed on the road with the Baron."
Damn. She was right, of course. Daisy's always right.
And Dorian? Turned out he had more strength than I could have imagined.
Maybe prison made him stronger.

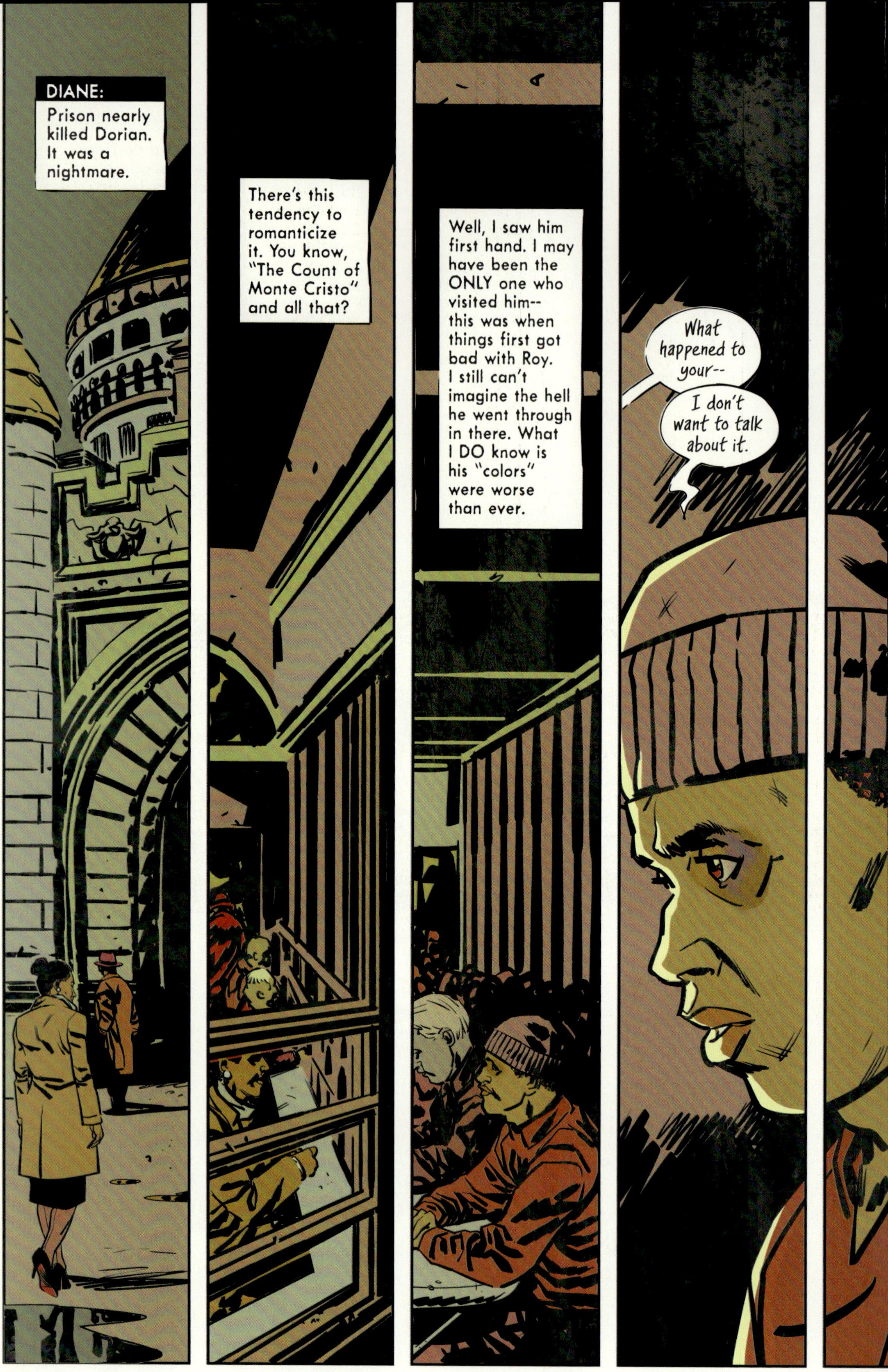
DIANE:
Prison nearly killed Dorian. It was a nightmare.
There's this tendency to romanticize it. You know, "The Count of Monte Cristo" and all that?
Well, I saw him first hand. I may have been the ONLY one who visited him-- this was when things first got bad with Roy. I still can't imagine the hell he went through in there. What I DO know is his "colors" were worse than ever.
What happened to your--
I don't want to talk about it.

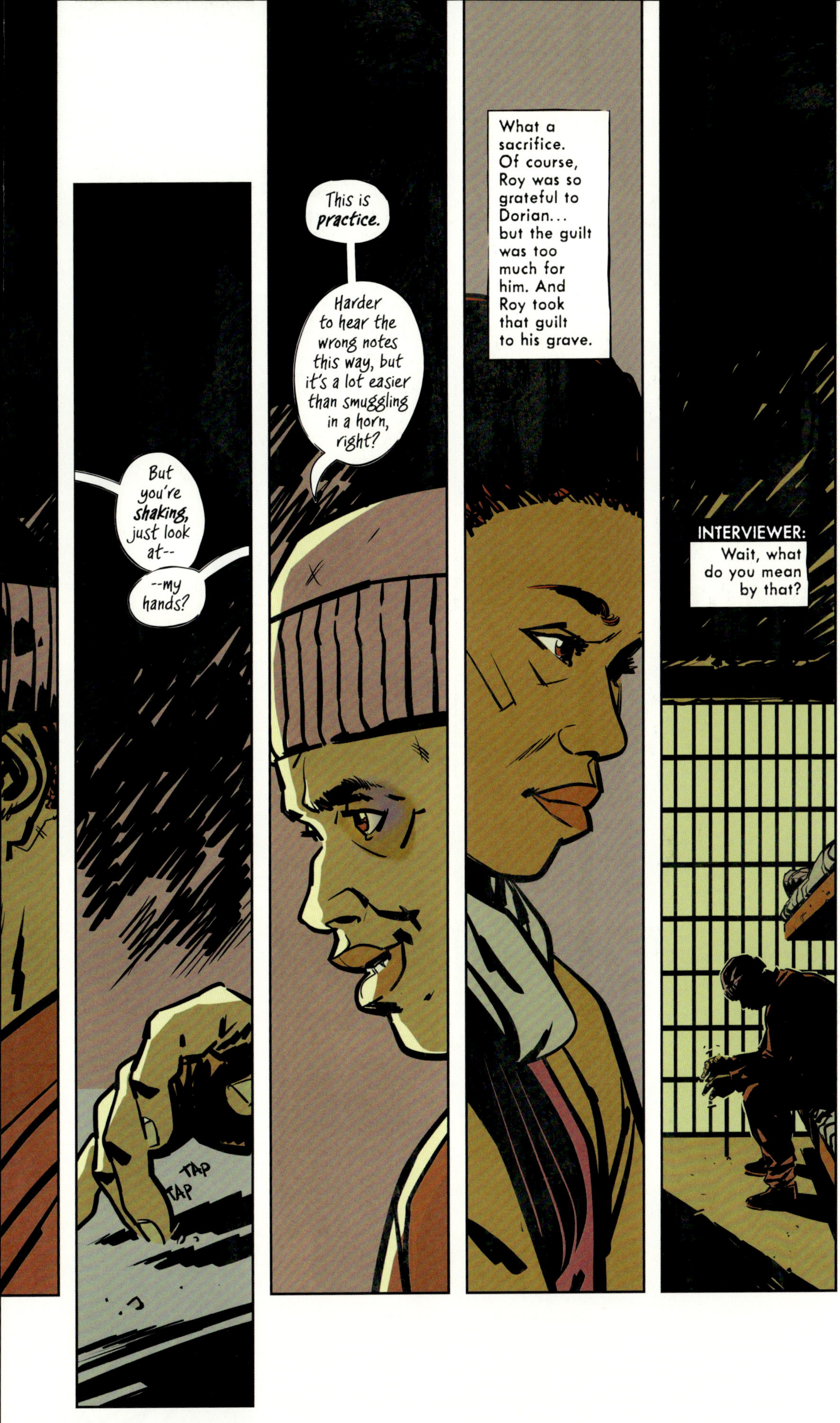
But you're *shaking*, just look at--
--my hands?
TAP TAP
This is *practice.*
Harder to hear the wrong notes this way, but it's a lot easier than smuggling in a horn, right?
What a sacrifice. Of course, Roy was so grateful to Dorian... but the guilt was too much for him. And Roy took that guilt to his grave.
INTERVIEWER:
Wait, what do you mean by that?

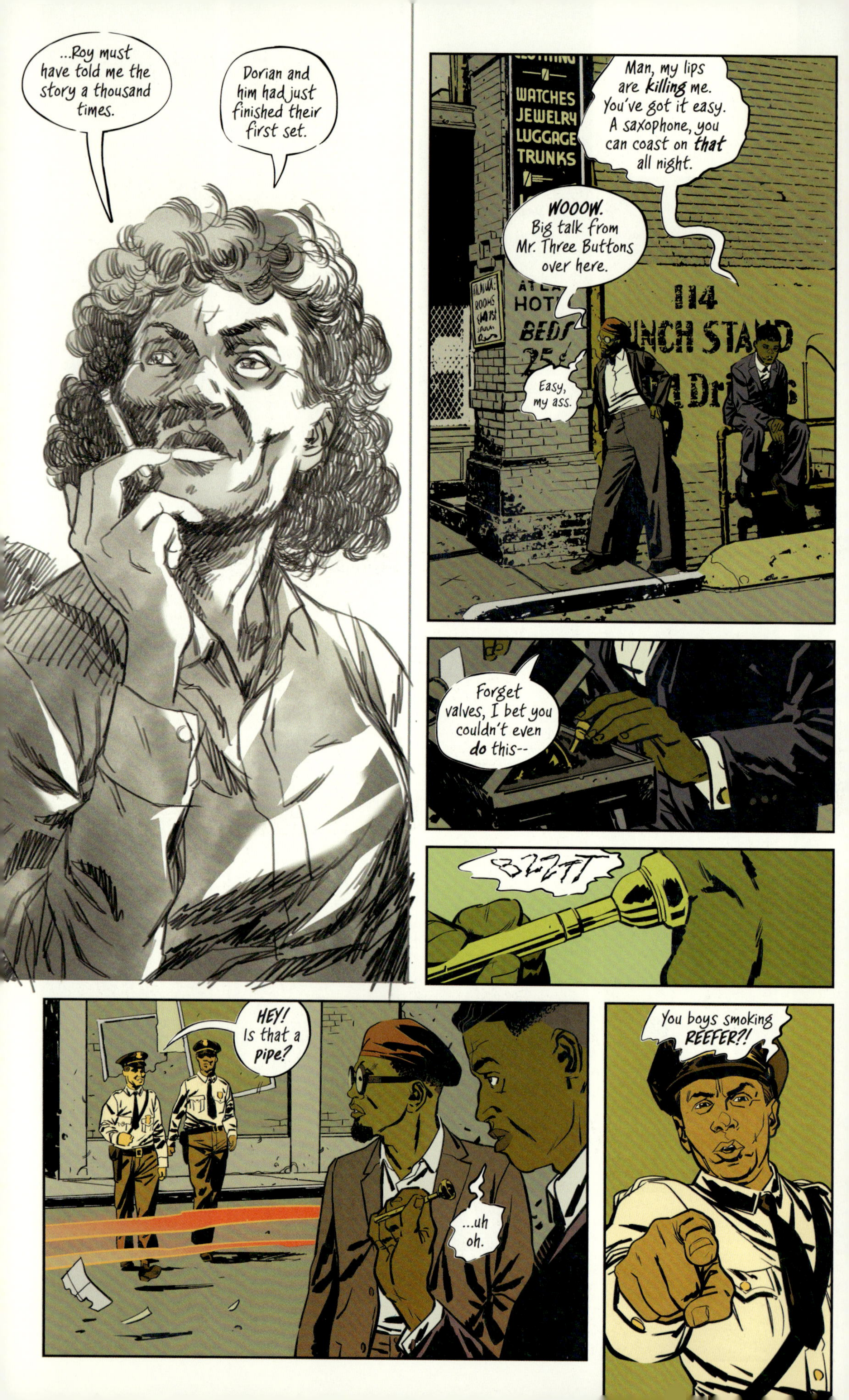

...Roy must have told me the story a thousand times.
Dorian and him had just finished their first set.
WATCHES JEWELRY LUGGAGE TRUNKS
Man, my lips are *killing* me. You've got it easy. A saxophone, you can coast on *that* all night.
WOOOW. Big talk from Mr. Three Buttons over here.
114
Easy, my ass.
Forget valves, I bet you couldn't even **do** this--
BZZZT
HEY! Is that a pipe?
...uh oh.
You boys smoking **REEFER?!**

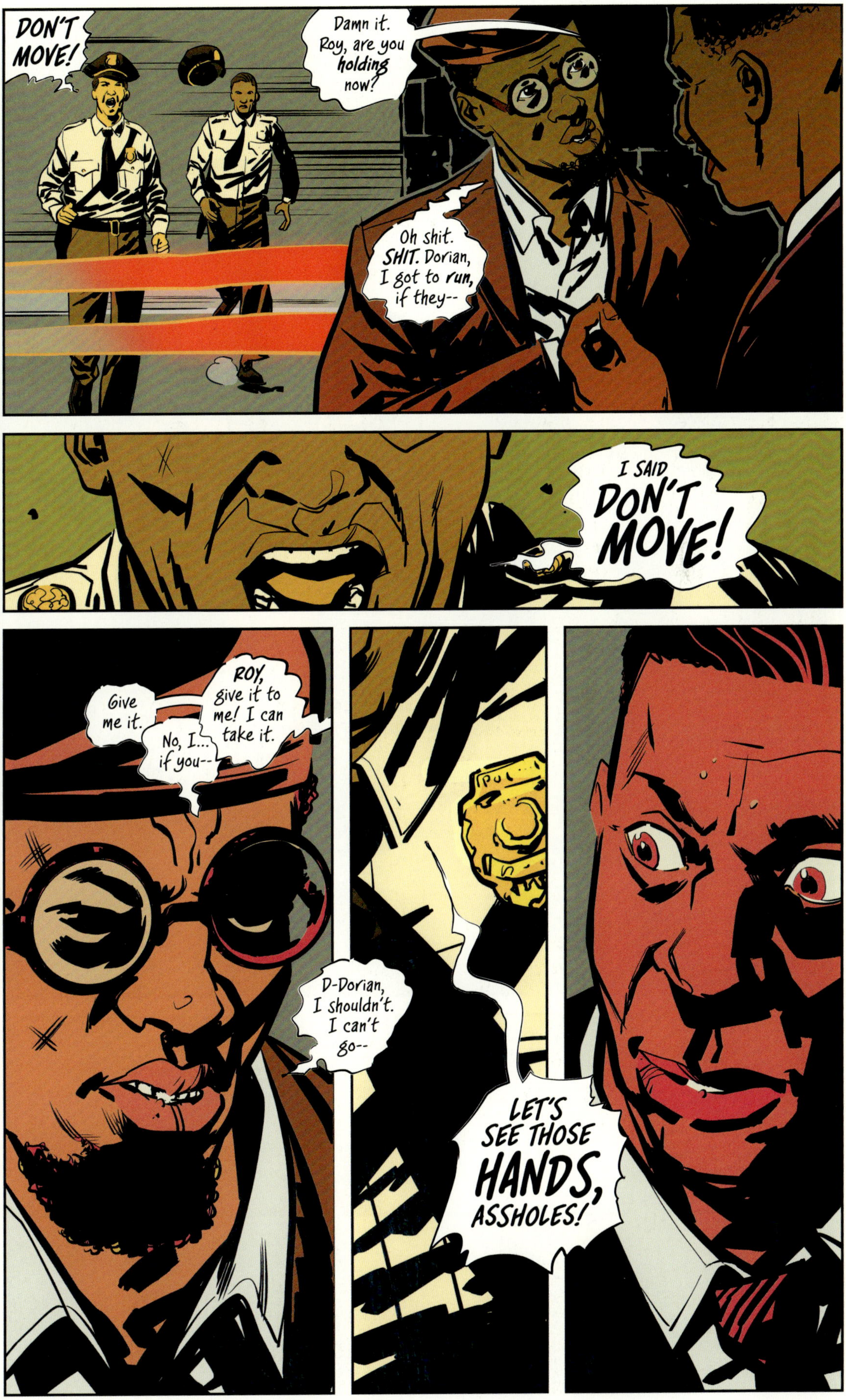
DON'T MOVE!
Damn it. Roy, are you holding now?
Oh shit. SHIT. Dorian, I got to run, if they--
I SAID DON'T MOVE!
Give me it.
ROY, give it to me! I can take it.
No, I... if you--
D-Dorian, I shouldn't. I can't go--
LET'S SEE THOSE HANDS, ASSHOLES!

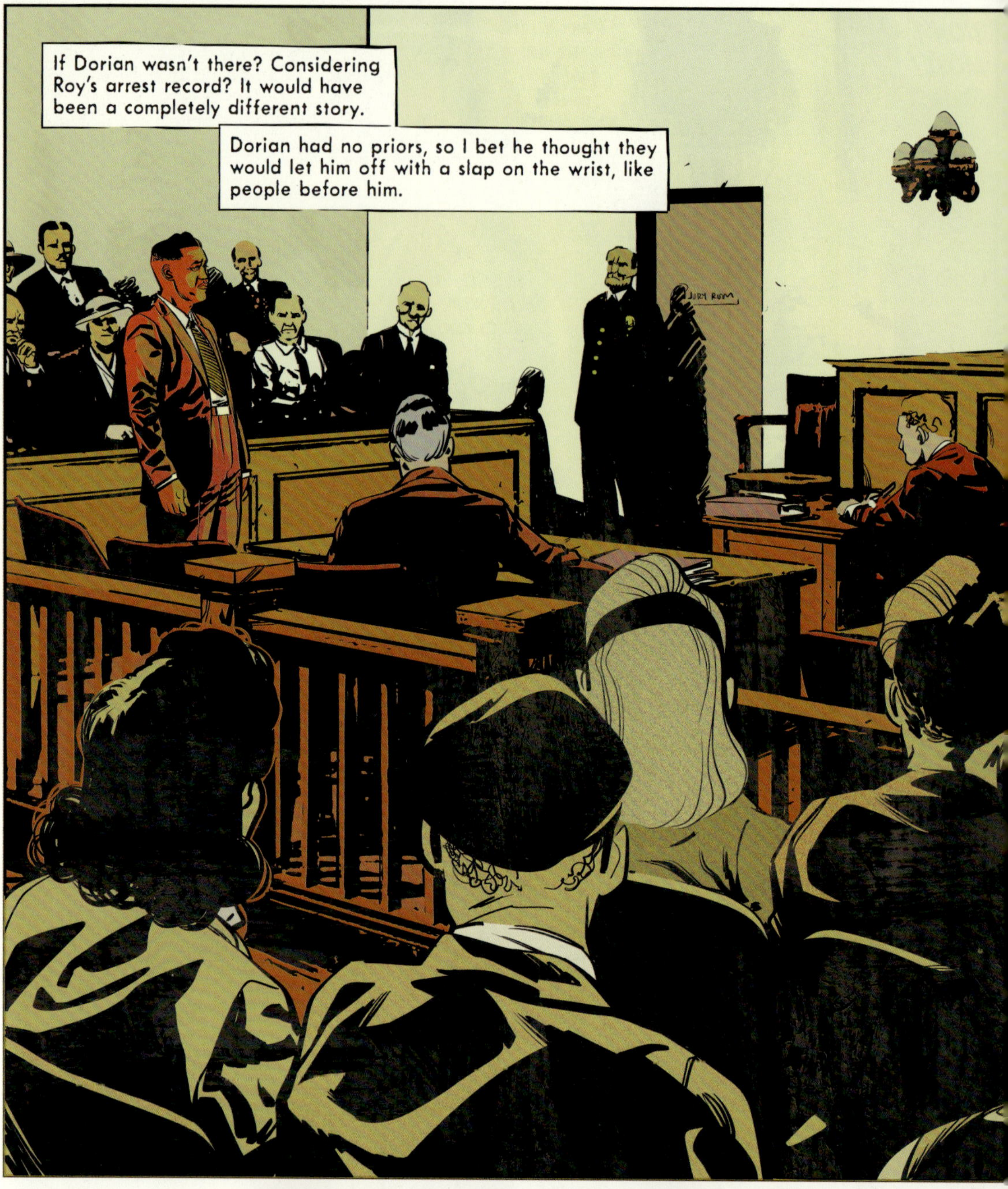
If Dorian wasn't there? Considering Roy's arrest record? It would have been a completely different story.
Dorian had no priors, so I bet he thought they would let him off with a slap on the wrist, like people before him.

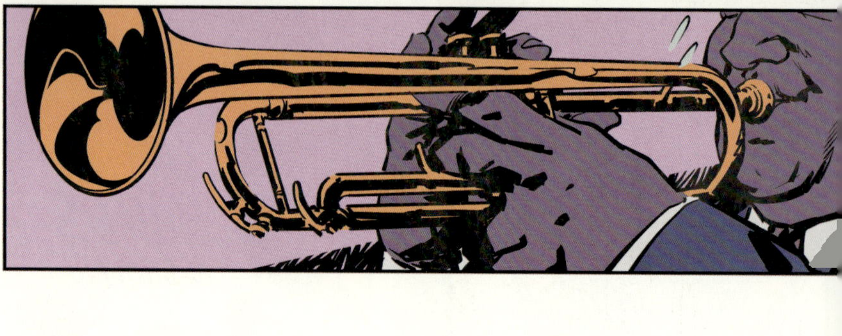

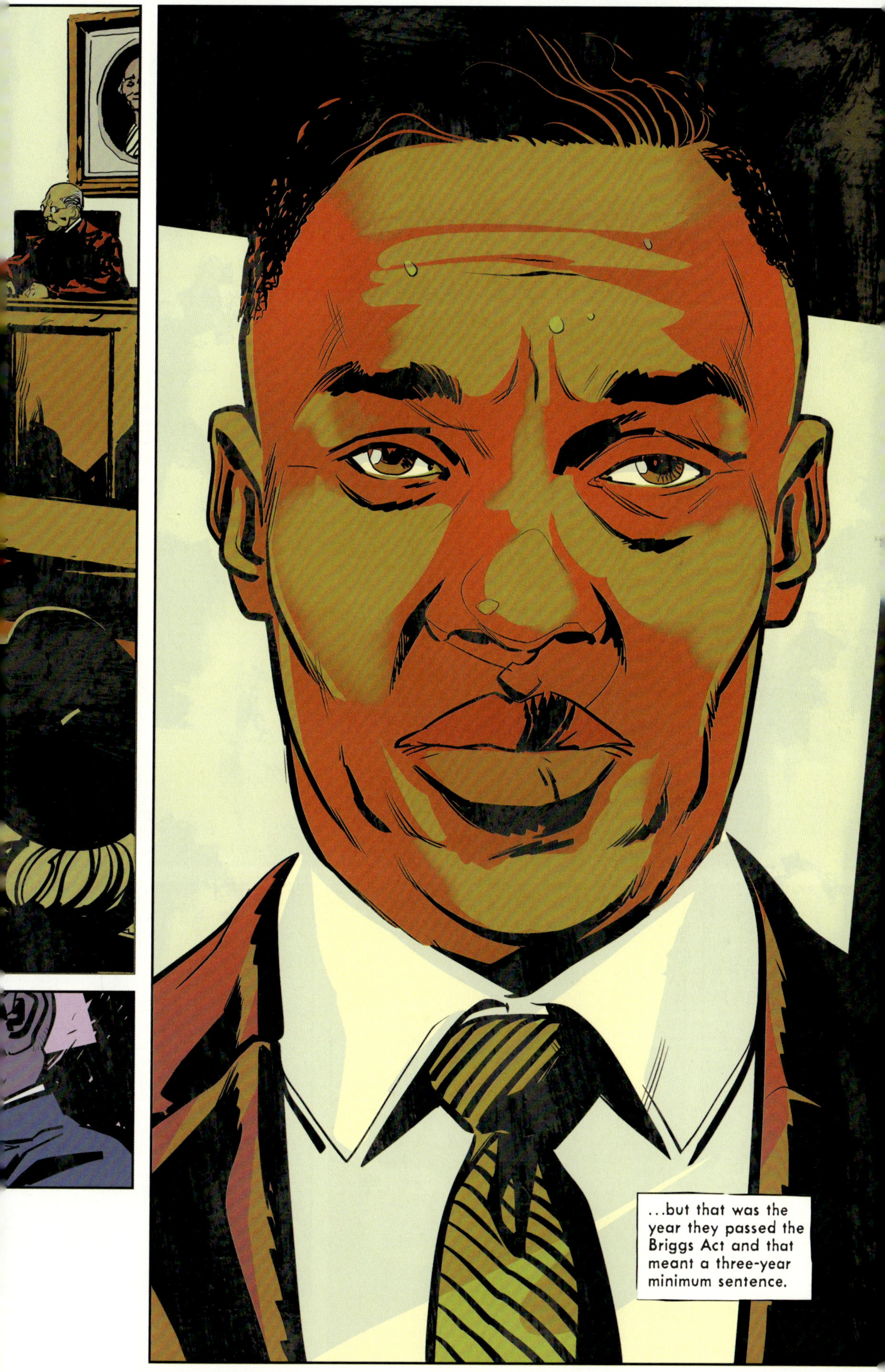
...but that was the year they passed the Briggs Act and that meant a three-year minimum sentence.

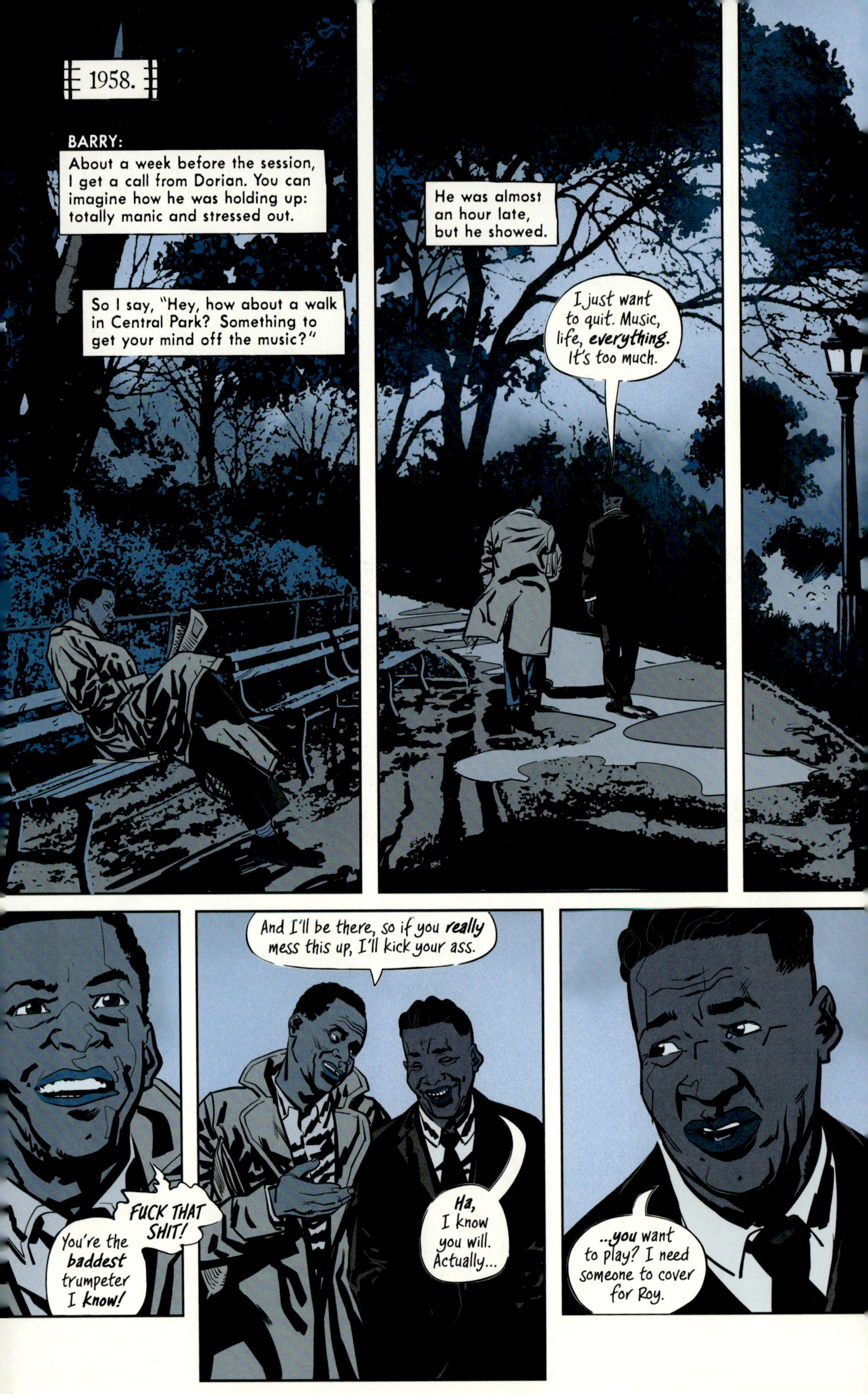
1958.
BARRY:
About a week before the session, I get a call from Dorian. You can imagine how he was holding up: totally manic and stressed out.
So I say, "Hey, how about a walk in Central Park? Something to get your mind off the music?"
He was almost an hour late, but he showed.
I just want to quit. Music, life, everything. It's too much.
FUCK THAT SHIT!
You're the baddest trumpeter I know!
And I'll be there, so if you really mess this up, I'll kick your ass.
Ha, I know you will. Actually...
...you want to play? I need someone to cover for Roy.

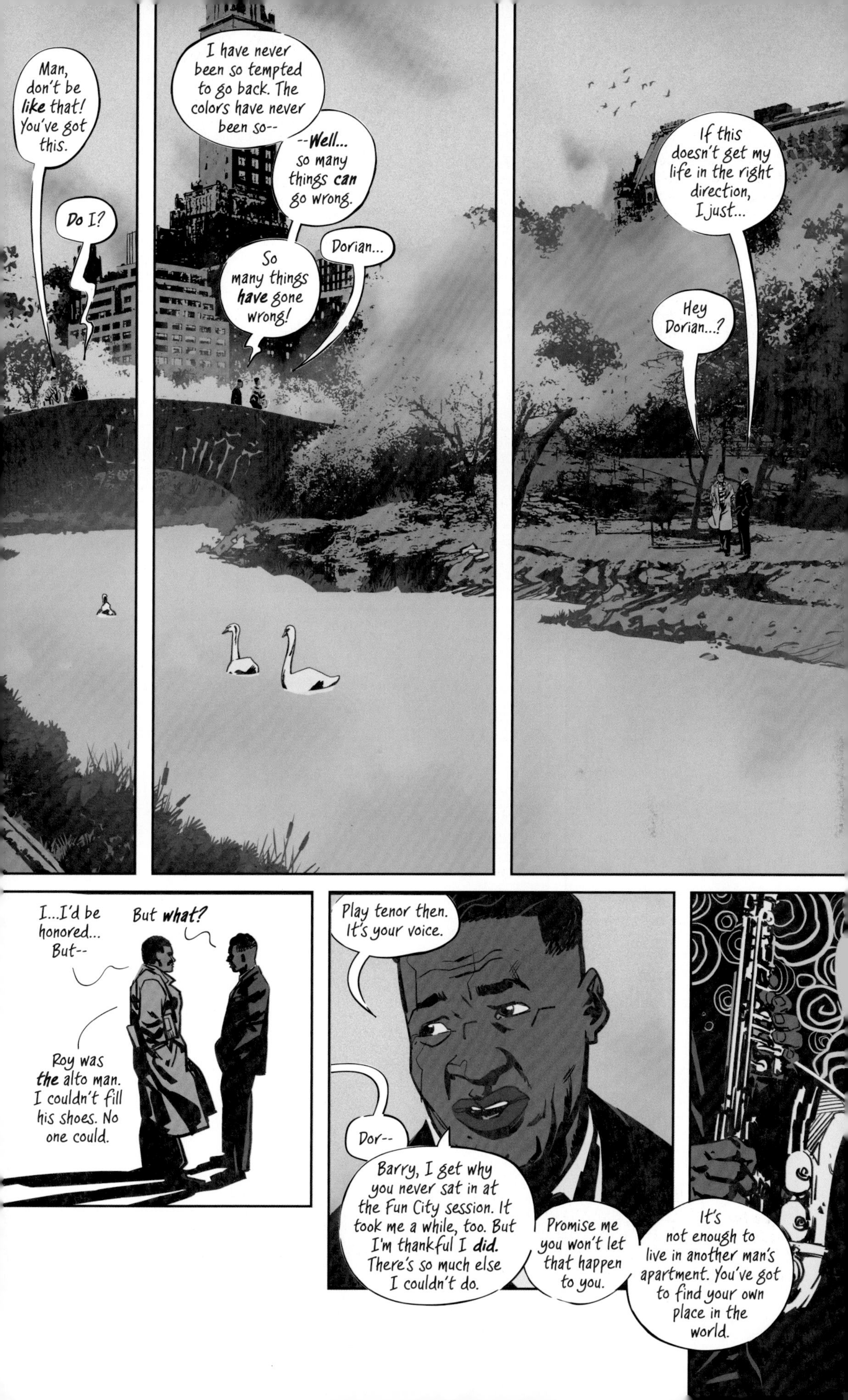
Man, don't be like that! You've got this.
Do I?
I have never been so tempted to go back. The colors have never been so--
--Well... so many things can go wrong.
So many things have gone wrong!
Dorian...
If this doesn't get my life in the right direction, I just...
Hey Dorian...?
I...I'd be honored... But--
But what?
Roy was the alto man. I couldn't fill his shoes. No one could.
Play tenor then. It's your voice.
Dor--
Barry, I get why you never sat in at the Fun City session. It took me a while, too. But I'm thankful I did. There's so much else I couldn't do.
Promise me you won't let that happen to you.
It's not enough to live in another man's apartment. You've got to find your own place in the world.

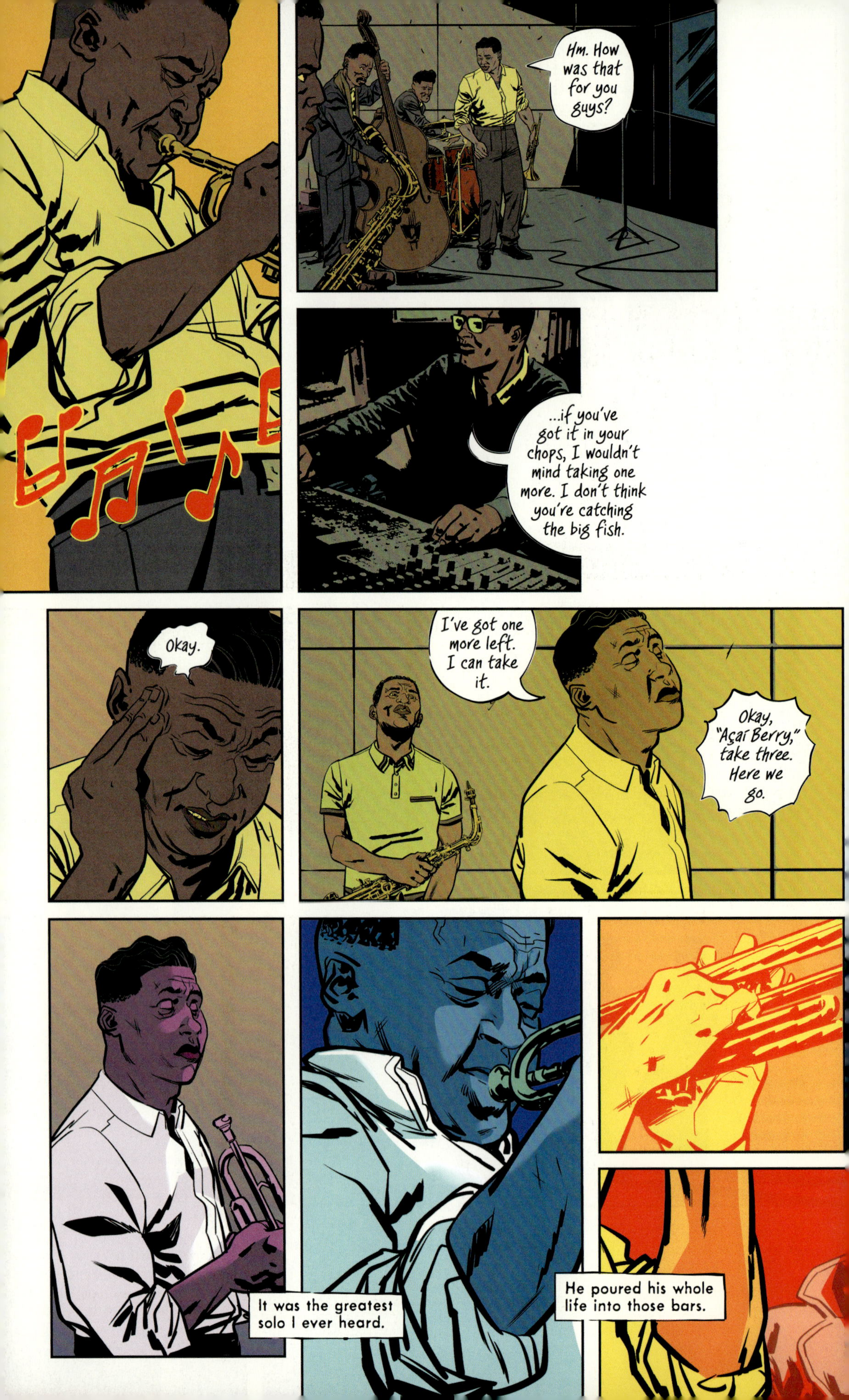
Hm. How was that for you guys?
...if you've got it in your chops, I wouldn't mind taking one more. I don't think you're catching the big fish.
Okay.
I've got one more left. I can take it.
Okay, "Açaí Berry," take three. Here we go.
It was the greatest solo I ever heard.
He poured his whole life into those bars.

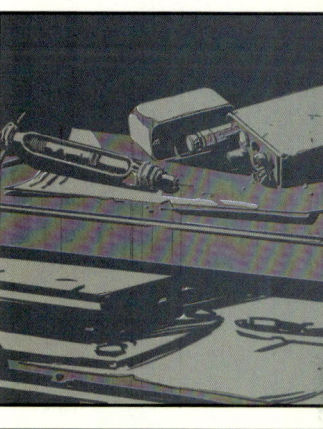

I get goosebumps thinking about it.

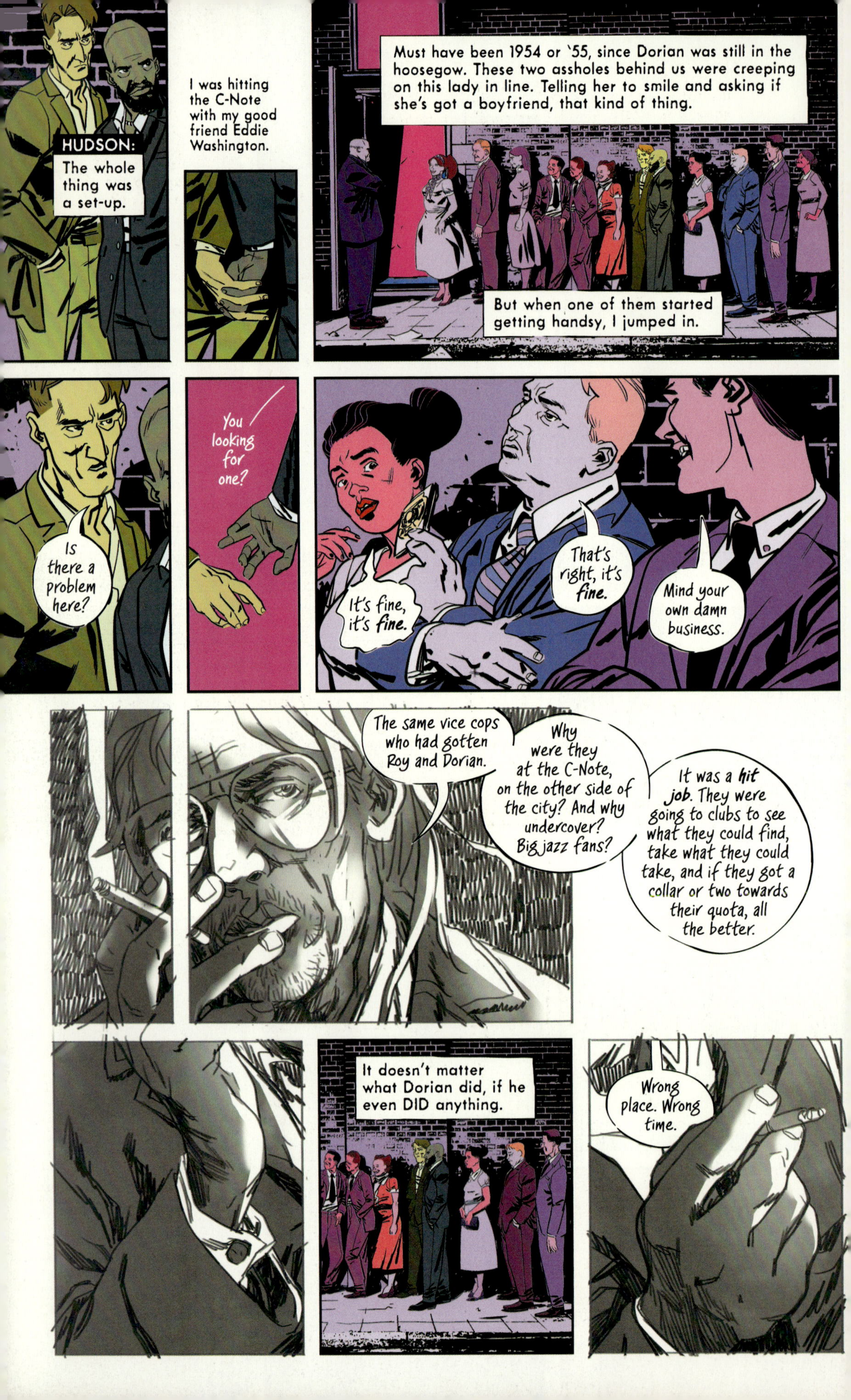
HUDSON:
The whole thing was a set-up.
I was hitting the C-Note with my good friend Eddie Washington.
Must have been 1954 or '55, since Dorian was still in the hoosegow. These two assholes behind us were creeping on this lady in line. Telling her to smile and asking if she's got a boyfriend, that kind of thing.
But when one of them started getting handsy, I jumped in.
Is there a problem here?
You looking for one?
It's fine, it's fine.
That's right, it's fine.
Mind your own damn business.
The same vice cops who had gotten Roy and Dorian.
Why were they at the C-Note, on the other side of the city? And why undercover? Big jazz fans?
It was a hit job. They were going to clubs to see what they could find, take what they could take, and if they got a collar or two towards their quota, all the better.
It doesn't matter what Dorian did, if he even DID anything.
Wrong place. Wrong time.

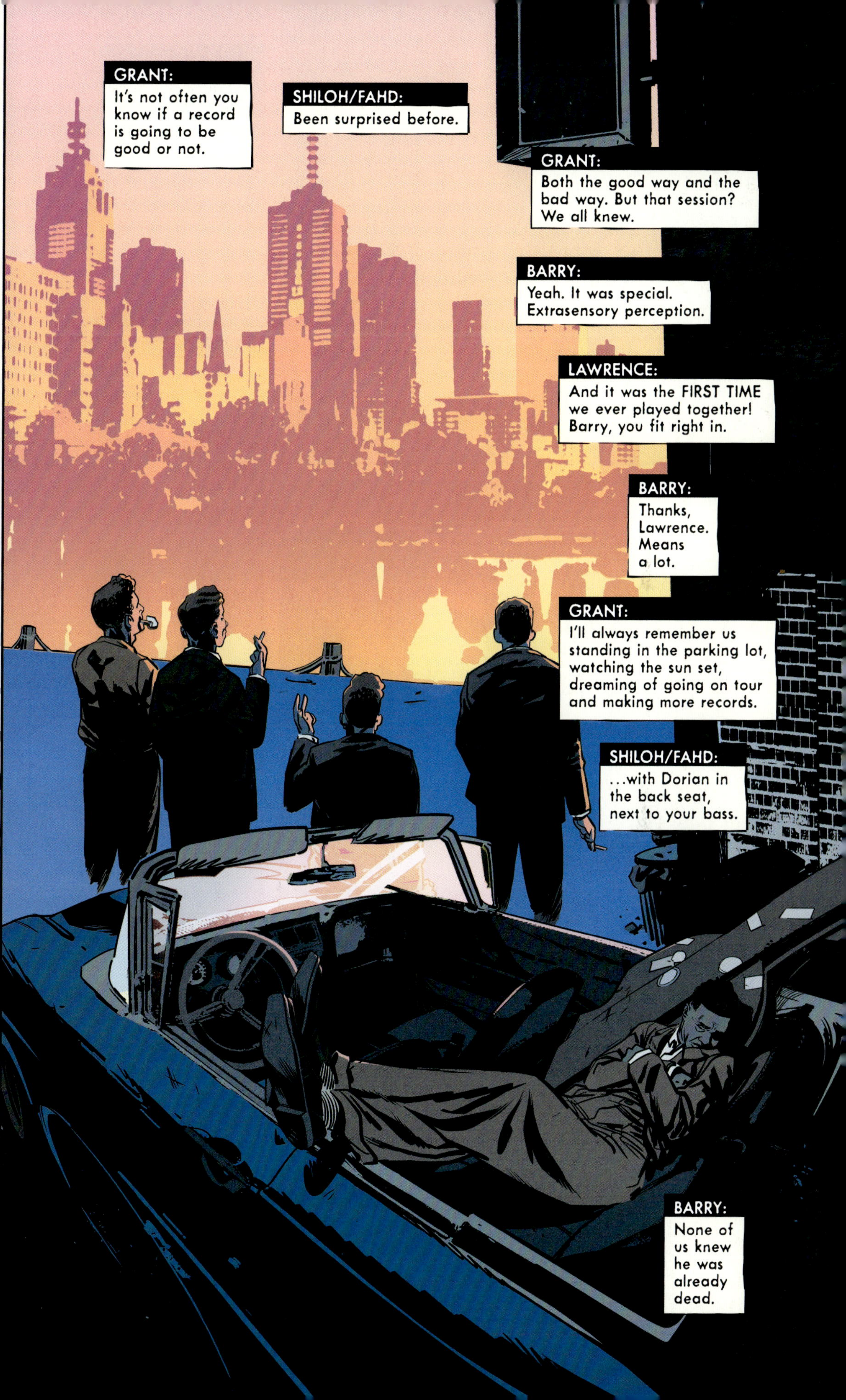
GRANT:
It's not often you know if a record is going to be good or not.
SHILOH/FAHD:
Been surprised before.
GRANT:
Both the good way and the bad way. But that session? We all knew.
BARRY:
Yeah. It was special. Extrasensory perception.
LAWRENCE:
And it was the FIRST TIME we ever played together! Barry, you fit right in.
BARRY:
Thanks, Lawrence. Means a lot.
GRANT:
I'll always remember us standing in the parking lot, watching the sun set, dreaming of going on tour and making more records.
SHILOH/FAHD:
...with Dorian in the back seat, next to your bass.
BARRY:
None of us knew he was already dead.

A benign intracranial tumor. **Largest** I've ever seen. Symptoms include tremors, nausea, erratic behavior, and synesthesia.
Sorry, what's "synesthesia"?
Oh, it's when your senses get flipped around. Tasting colors or seeing sounds.
So, did the drugs make him play better?
Doubtful. They may have made his life a little less painful in some ways... but a **lot** more painful in plenty of others.
With a tumor that big, it's a miracle he made it in life as far as he did.

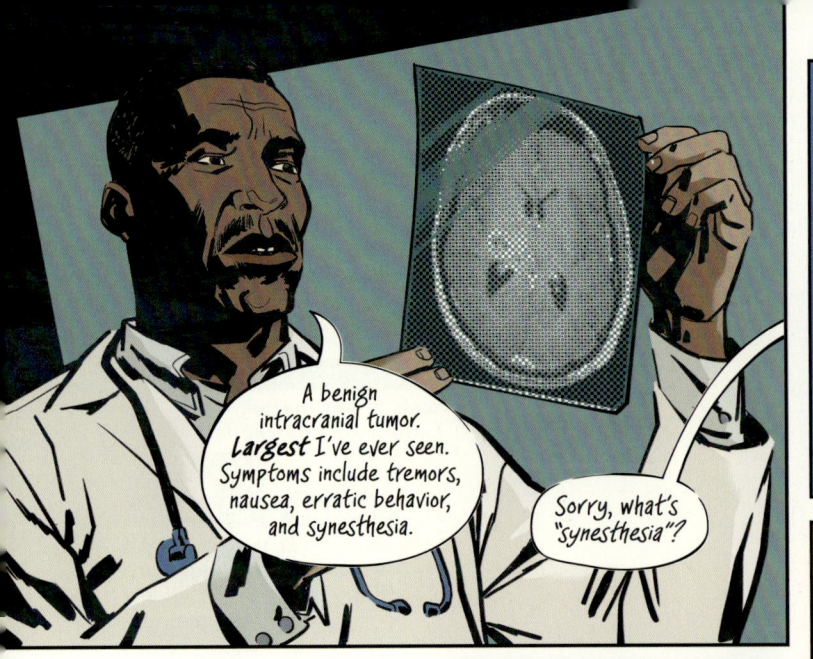

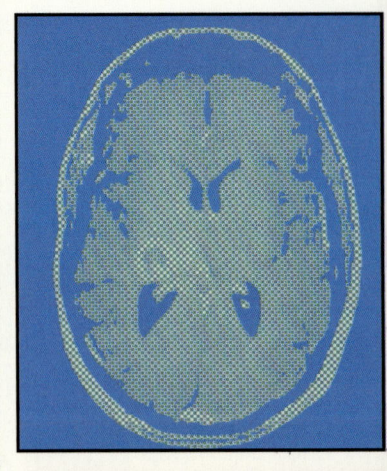

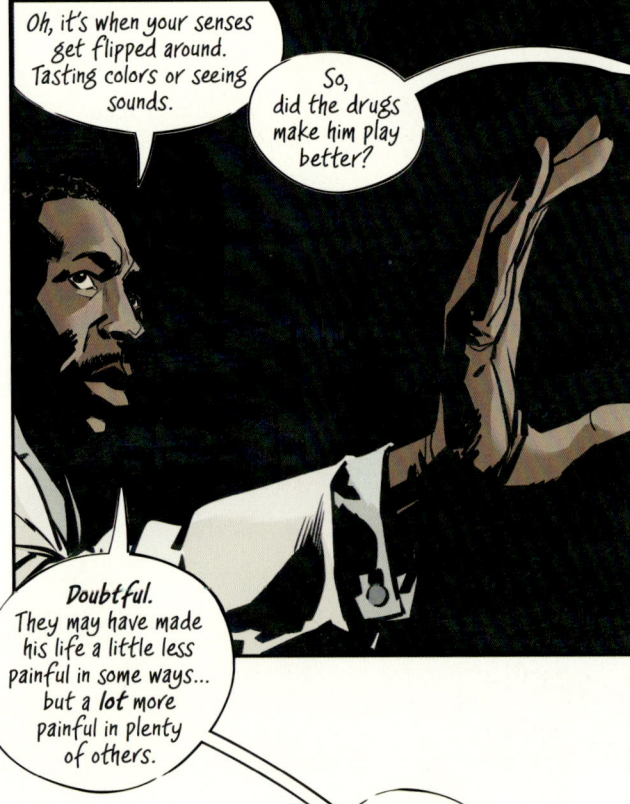

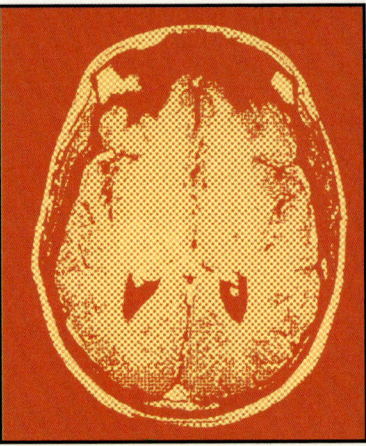

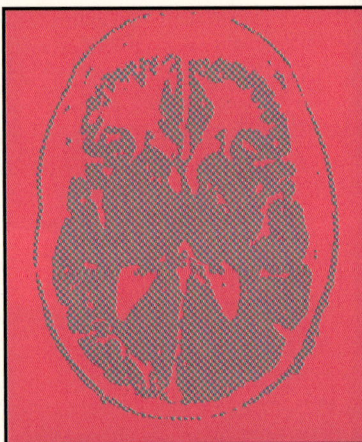

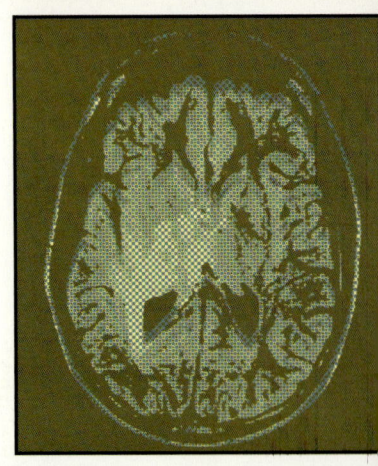

DIANE: This was the only letter we ever got from Dorian.

Dear Roy and Diane,

I hope this letter finds you well. I wish I could say things are good here. It's all very overwhelming. But how could I give up, knowing I have to make up for all the lunches we've missed?

The library here is sparse, but I found a little book on meditation that has been helpful. Thought you two would appreciate that.

I'm going to leave here a new man and make you both proud.

Miss you both terribly.

Love,
Dorian

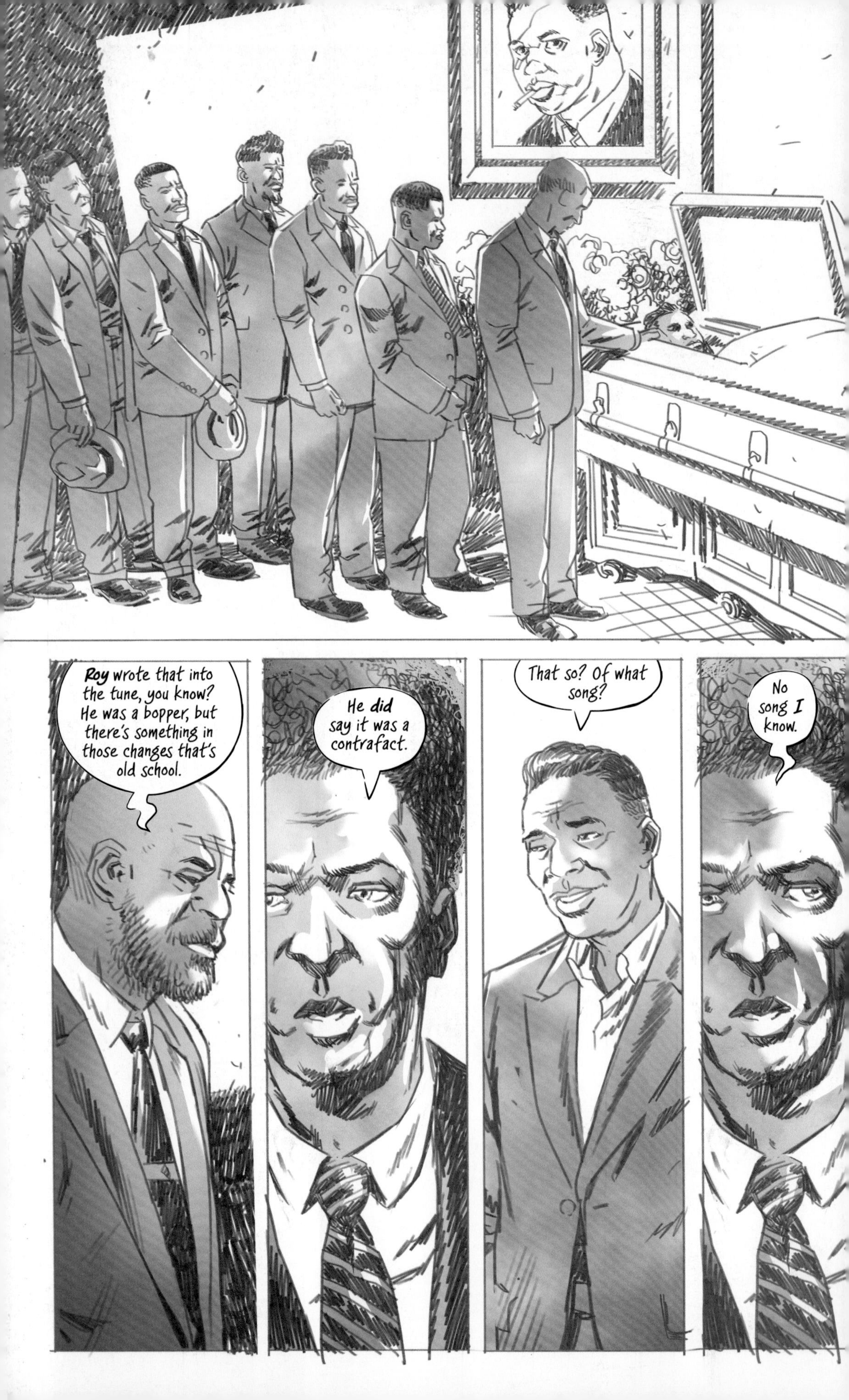
Roy wrote that into the tune, you know? He was a bopper, but there's something in those changes that's old school.
He did say it was a contrafact.
That so? Of what song?
No song I know.

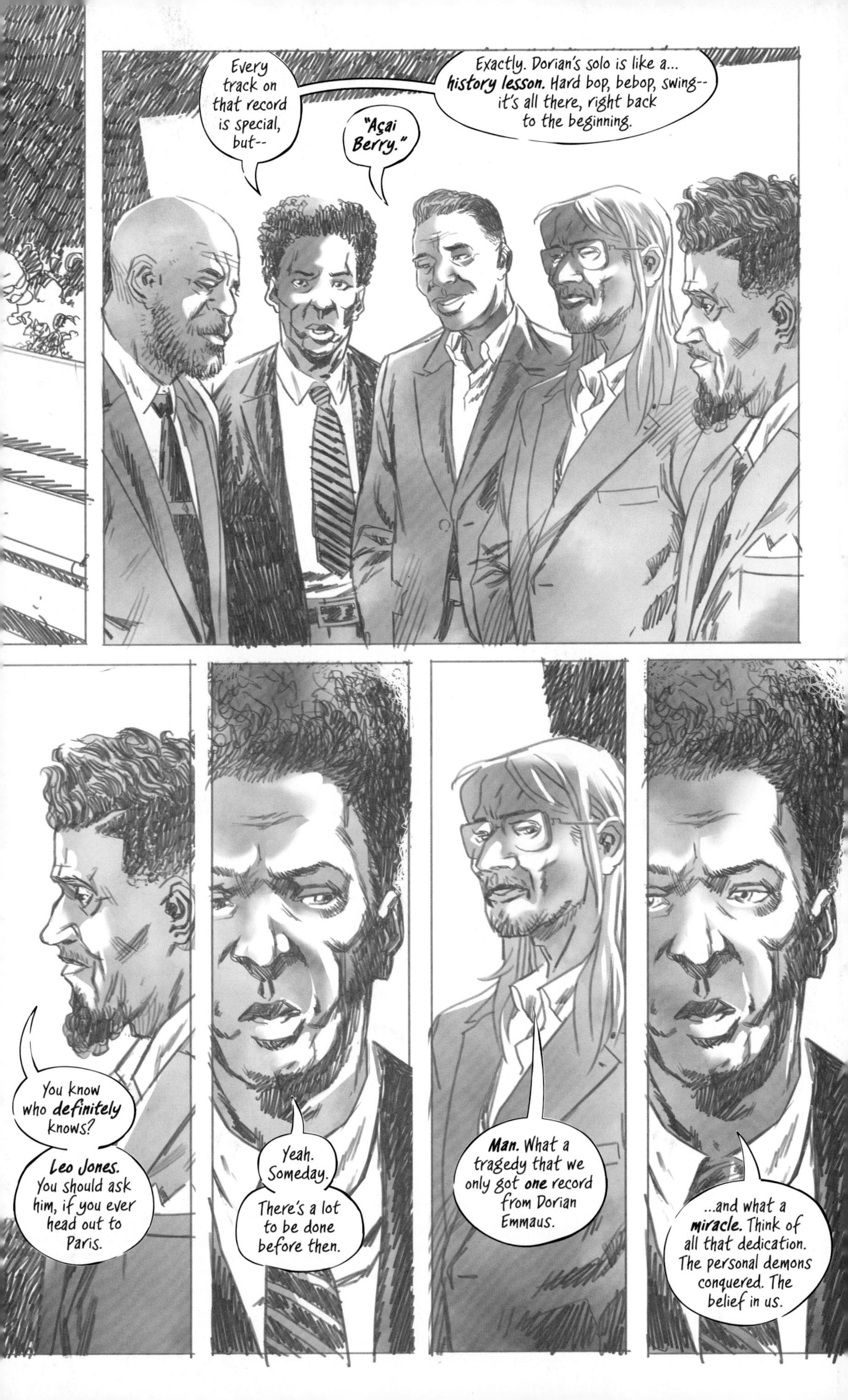
Every track on that record is special, but--
"Açai Berry."
Exactly. Dorian's solo is like a... **history lesson.** Hard bop, bebop, swing-- it's all there, right back to the beginning.
You know who **definitely** knows?
Leo Jones. You should ask him, if you ever head out to Paris.
Yeah. Someday.
There's a lot to be done before then.
Man. What a tragedy that we only got **one** record from Dorian Emmaus.
...and what a **miracle.** Think of all that dedication. The personal demons conquered. The belief in us.

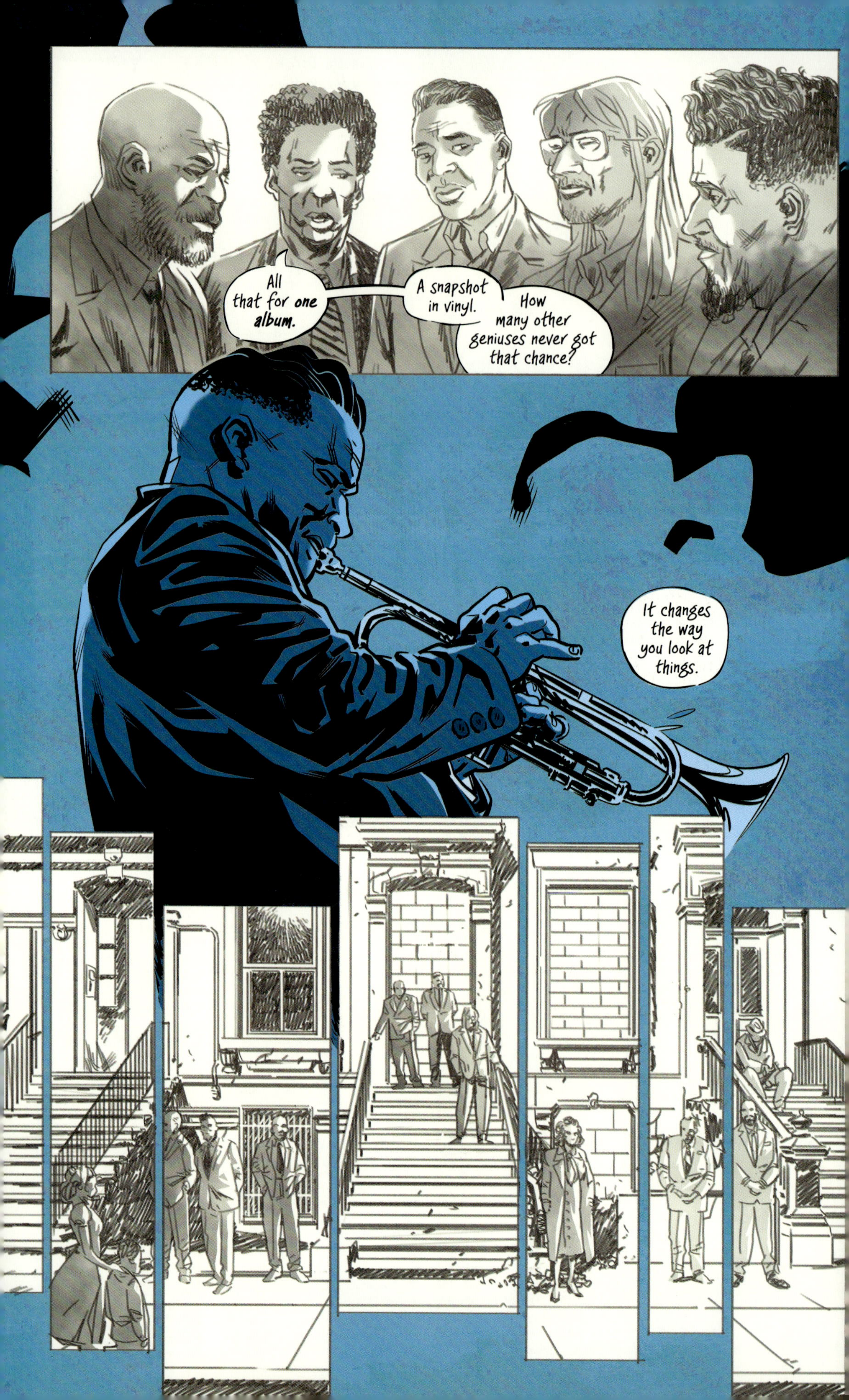
All that for one album.
A snapshot in vinyl.
How many other geniuses never got that chance?
It changes the way you look at things.

5.
SEEKING//
SECRETS

LOS ANGELES
1968

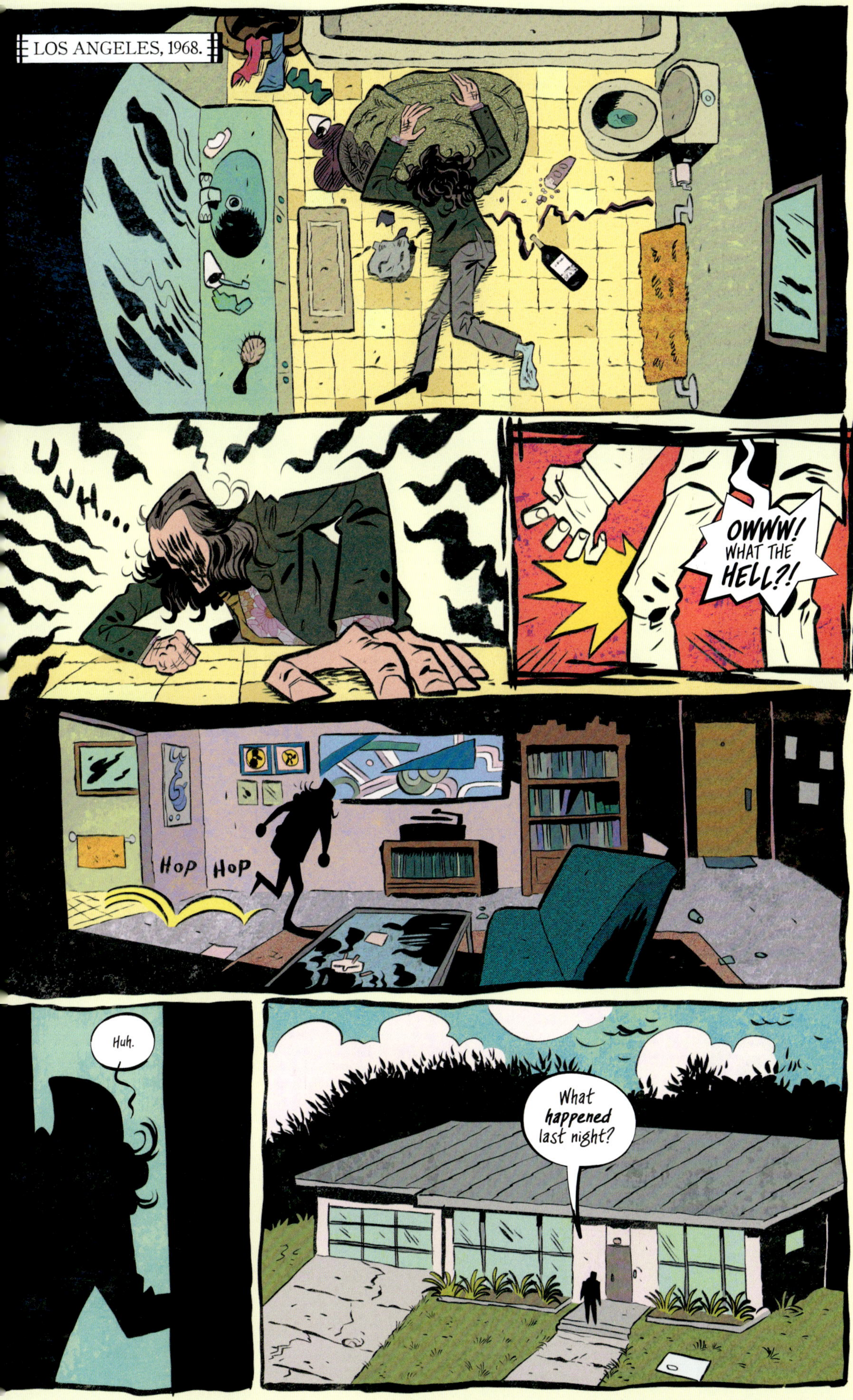
LOS ANGELES, 1968.
UNH...
OWWW! WHAT THE HELL?!
HOP HOP
Huh.
What happened last night?

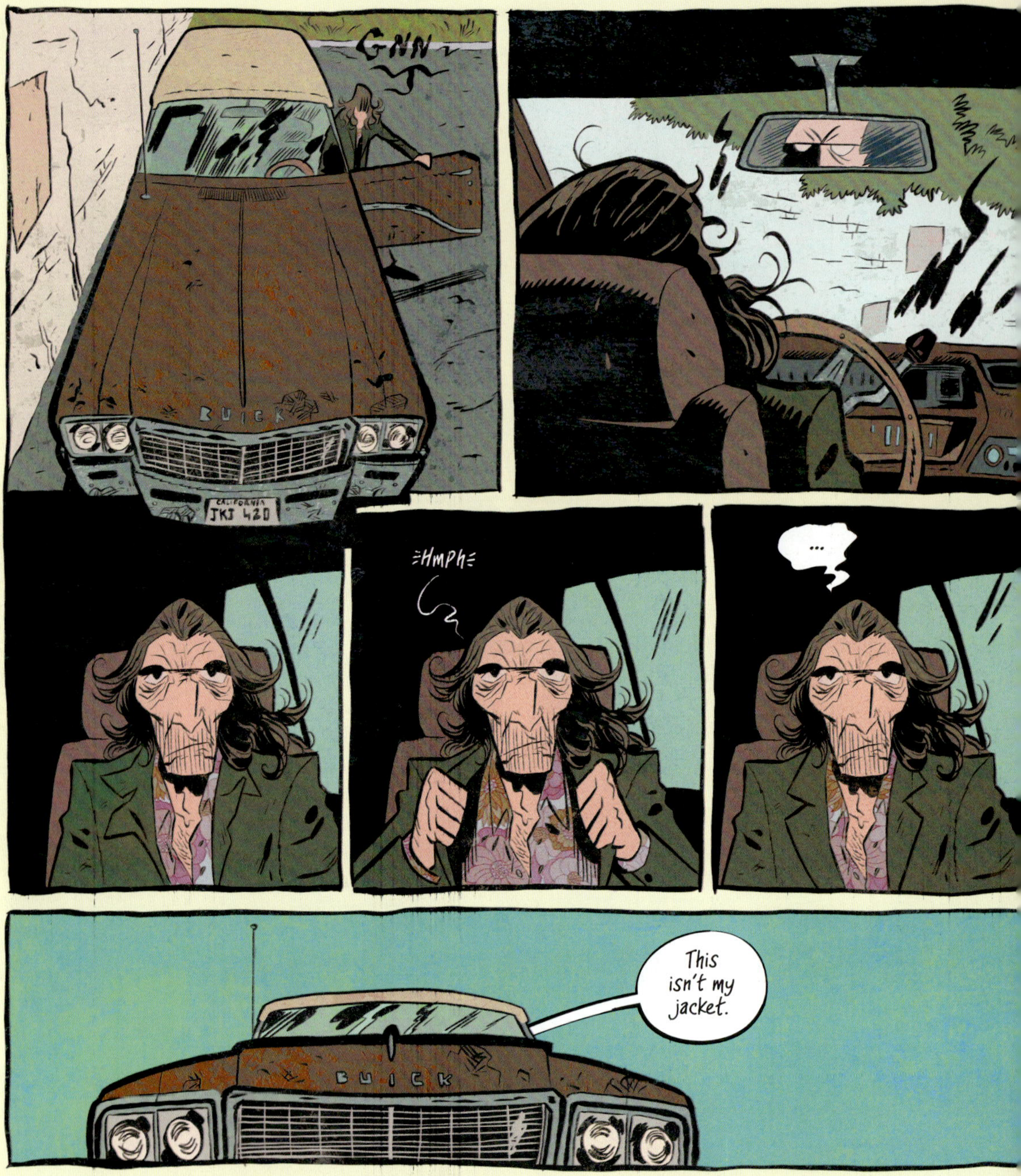
GNN
HMPH
...
This isn't my jacket.

8 SEEKING//SECRETS

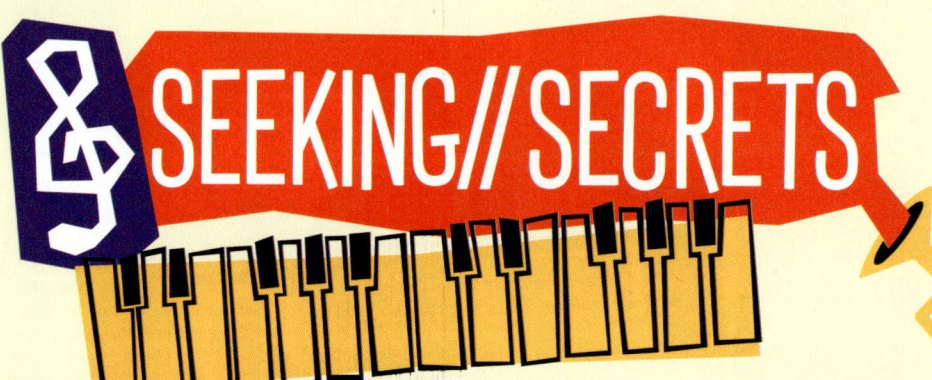

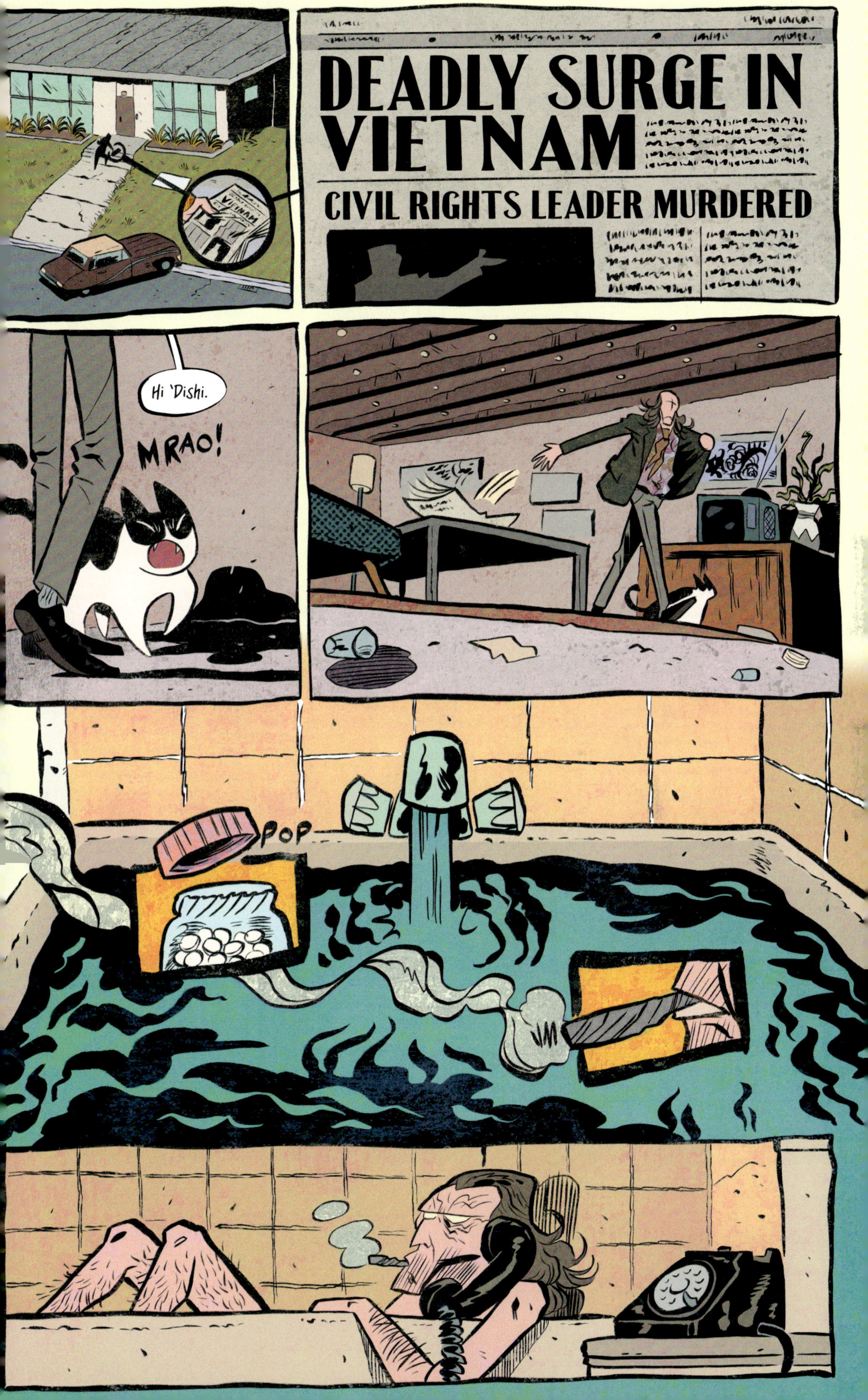
DEADLY SURGE IN VIETNAM
CIVIL RIGHTS LEADER MURDERED
Hi 'Dishi.
MRAO!
POP

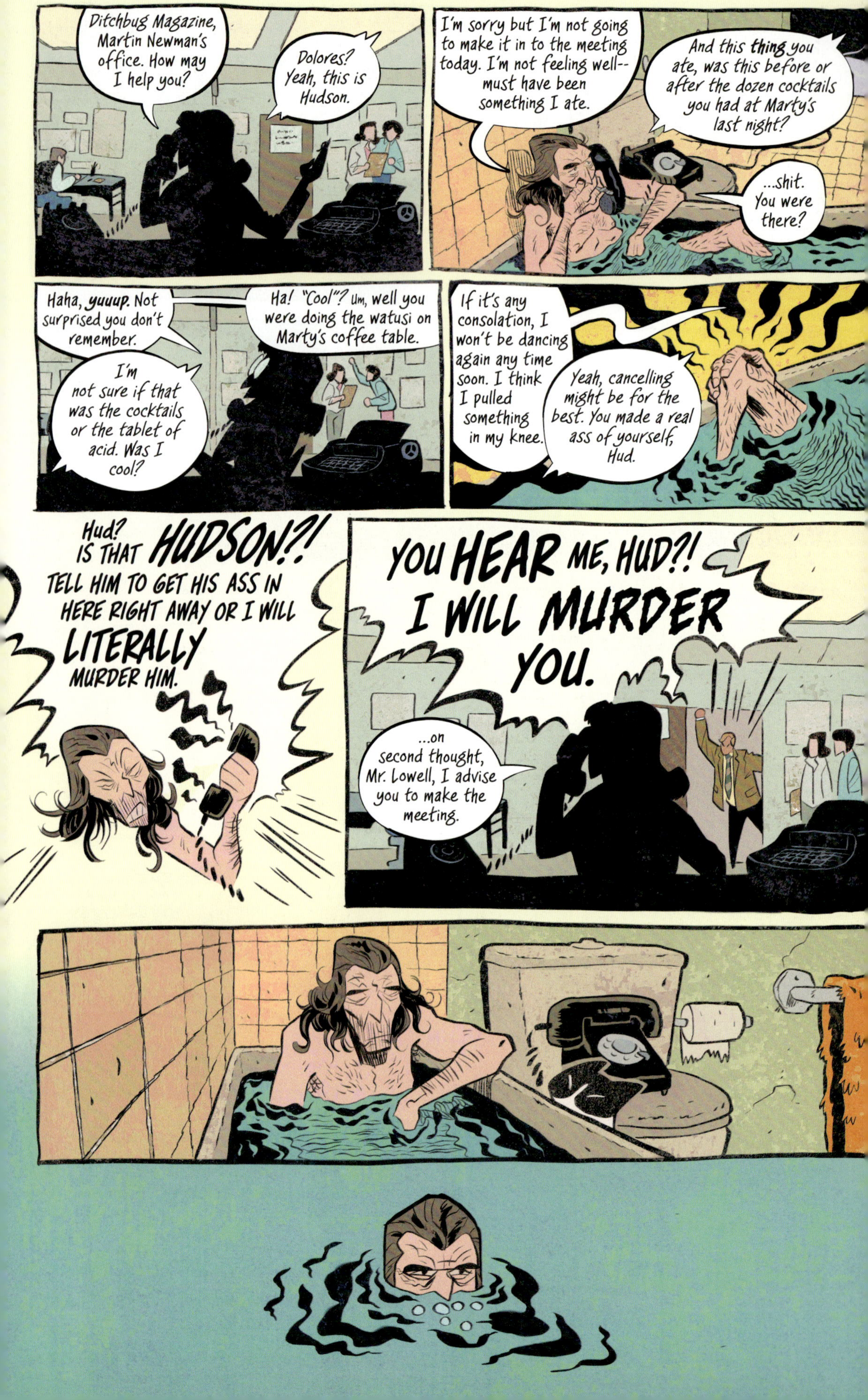
Ditchbug Magazine, Martin Newman's office. How may I help you?
Dolores? Yeah, this is Hudson.
I'm sorry but I'm not going to make it in to the meeting today. I'm not feeling well--must have been something I ate.
And this thing you ate, was this before or after the dozen cocktails you had at Marty's last night?
...shit. You were there?
Haha, yuuup. Not surprised you don't remember.
I'm not sure if that was the cocktails or the tablet of acid. Was I cool?
Ha! "Cool"? Um, well you were doing the watusi on Marty's coffee table.
If it's any consolation, I won't be dancing again any time soon. I think I pulled something in my knee.
Yeah, cancelling might be for the best. You made a real ass of yourself, Hud.
Hud? IS THAT HUDSON?! TELL HIM TO GET HIS ASS IN HERE RIGHT AWAY OR I WILL LITERALLY MURDER HIM.
YOU HEAR ME, HUD?! I WILL MURDER YOU.
...on second thought, Mr. Lowell, I advise you to make the meeting.

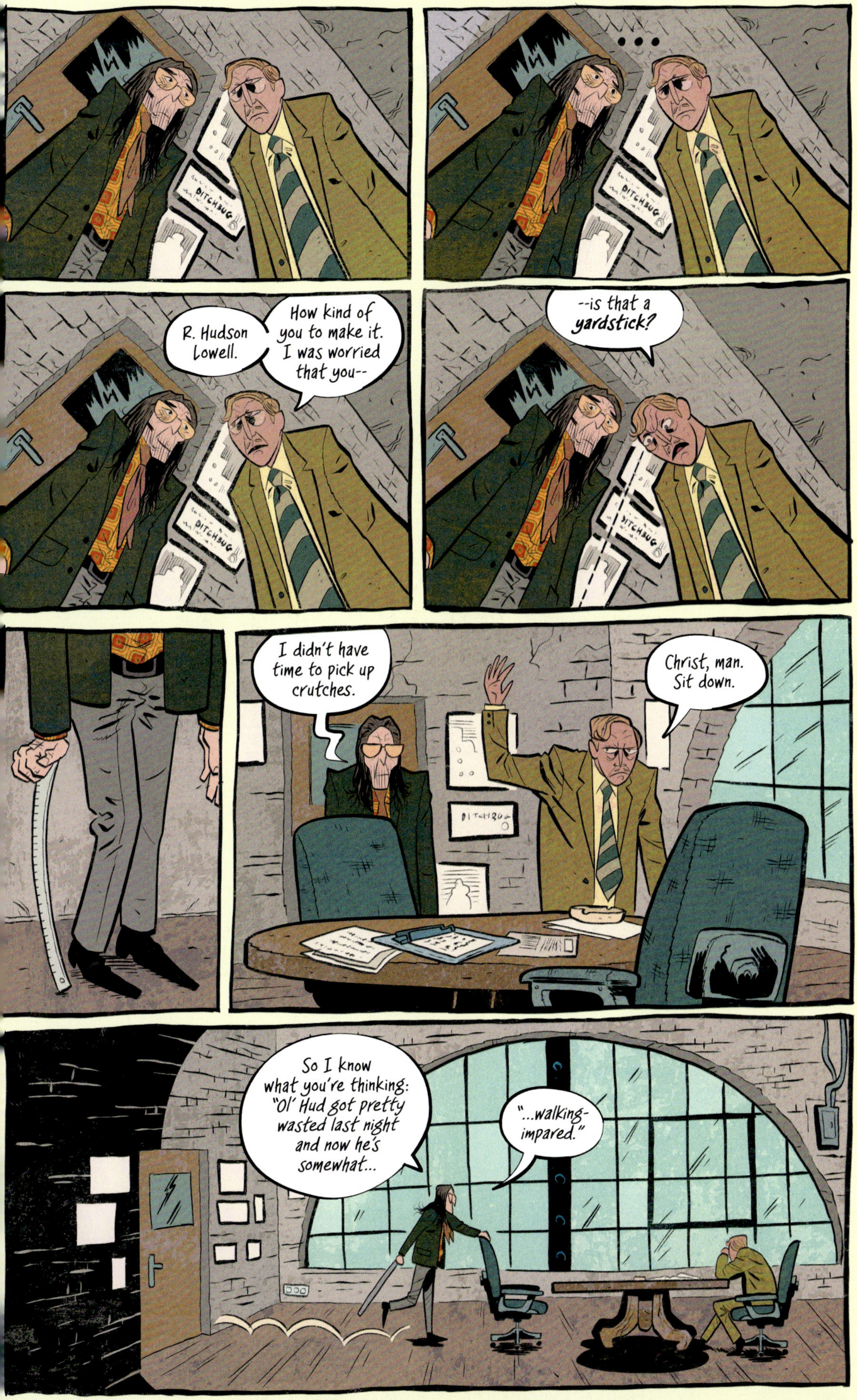
DITCHBUG
...
R. Hudson Lowell.
How kind of you to make it. I was worried that you--
--is that a *yardstick?*
I didn't have time to pick up crutches.
Christ, man. Sit down.
So I know what you're thinking: "Ol' Hud got pretty wasted last night and now he's somewhat...
"...walking-impared."

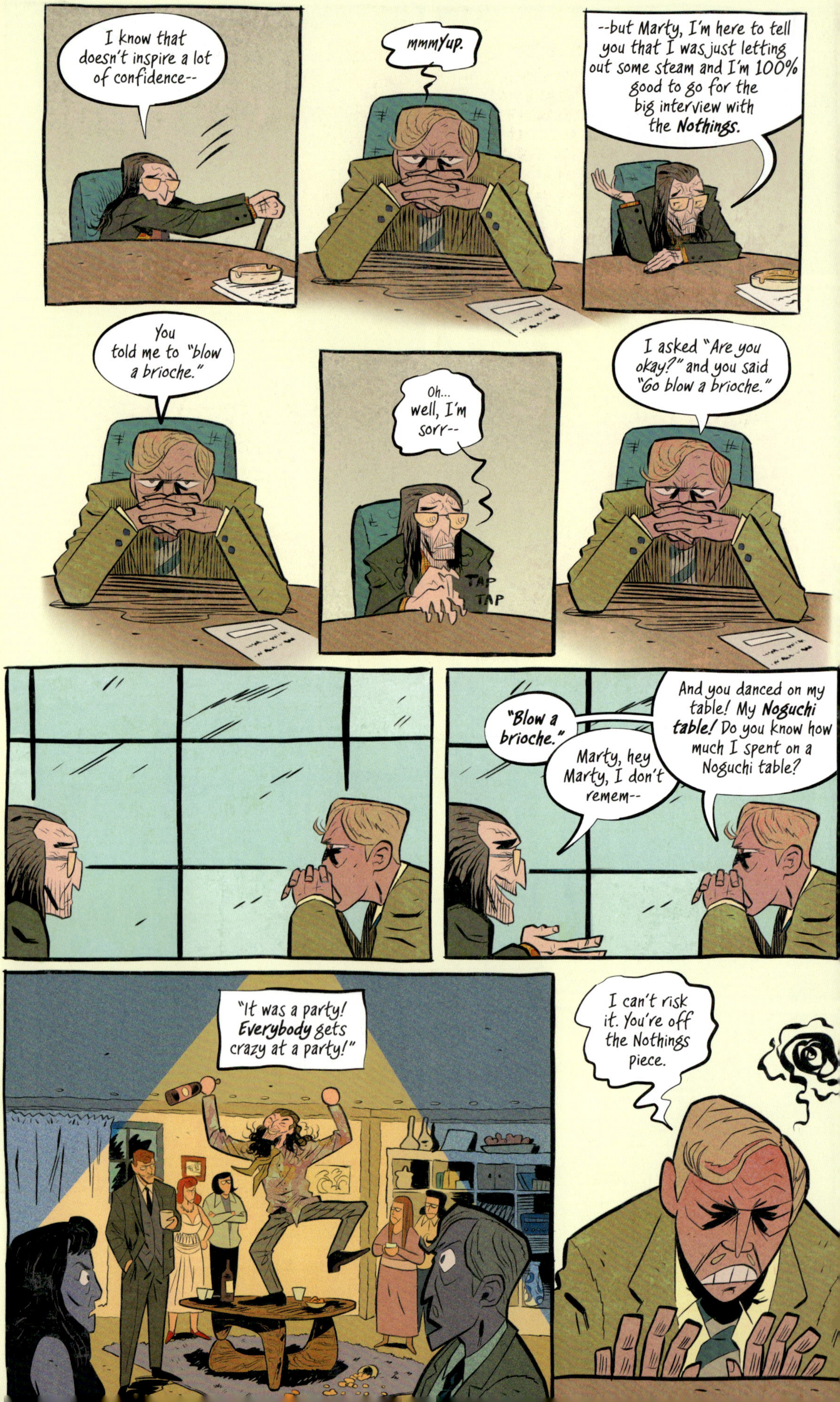
I know that doesn't inspire a lot of confidence--
mmmYup.
--but Marty, I'm here to tell you that I was just letting out some steam and I'm 100% good to go for the big interview with the **Nothings.**
You told me to "blow a brioche."
Oh... well, I'm sorr--
TAP TAP
I asked "Are you okay?" and you said "Go blow a brioche."
"Blow a brioche."
Marty, hey Marty, I don't remem--
And you danced on my table! My **Noguchi table!** Do you know how much I spent on a Noguchi table?
"It was a party! **Everybody** gets crazy at a party!"
I can't risk it. You're off the Nothings piece.

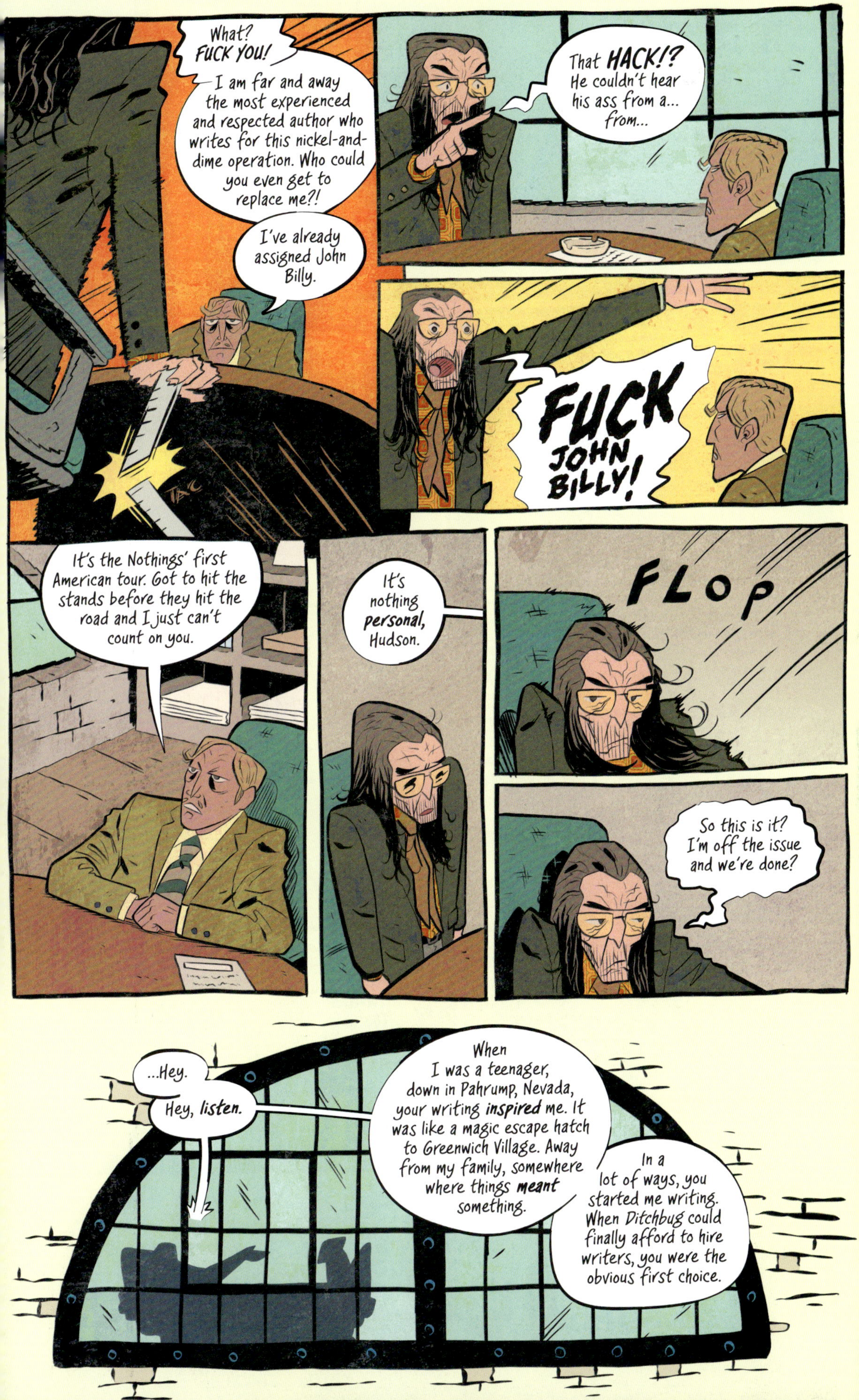
What? FUCK YOU!
I am far and away the most experienced and respected author who writes for this nickel-and-dime operation. Who could you even get to replace me?!
I've already assigned John Billy.
TAC
That HACK!? He couldn't hear his ass from a... from...
FUCK JOHN BILLY!
It's the Nothings' first American tour. Got to hit the stands before they hit the road and I just can't count on you.
It's nothing personal, Hudson.
FLOP
So this is it? I'm off the issue and we're done?
...Hey.
Hey, listen.
When I was a teenager, down in Pahrump, Nevada, your writing inspired me. It was like a magic escape hatch to Greenwich Village. Away from my family, somewhere where things meant something.
In a lot of ways, you started me writing. When Ditchbug could finally afford to hire writers, you were the obvious first choice.

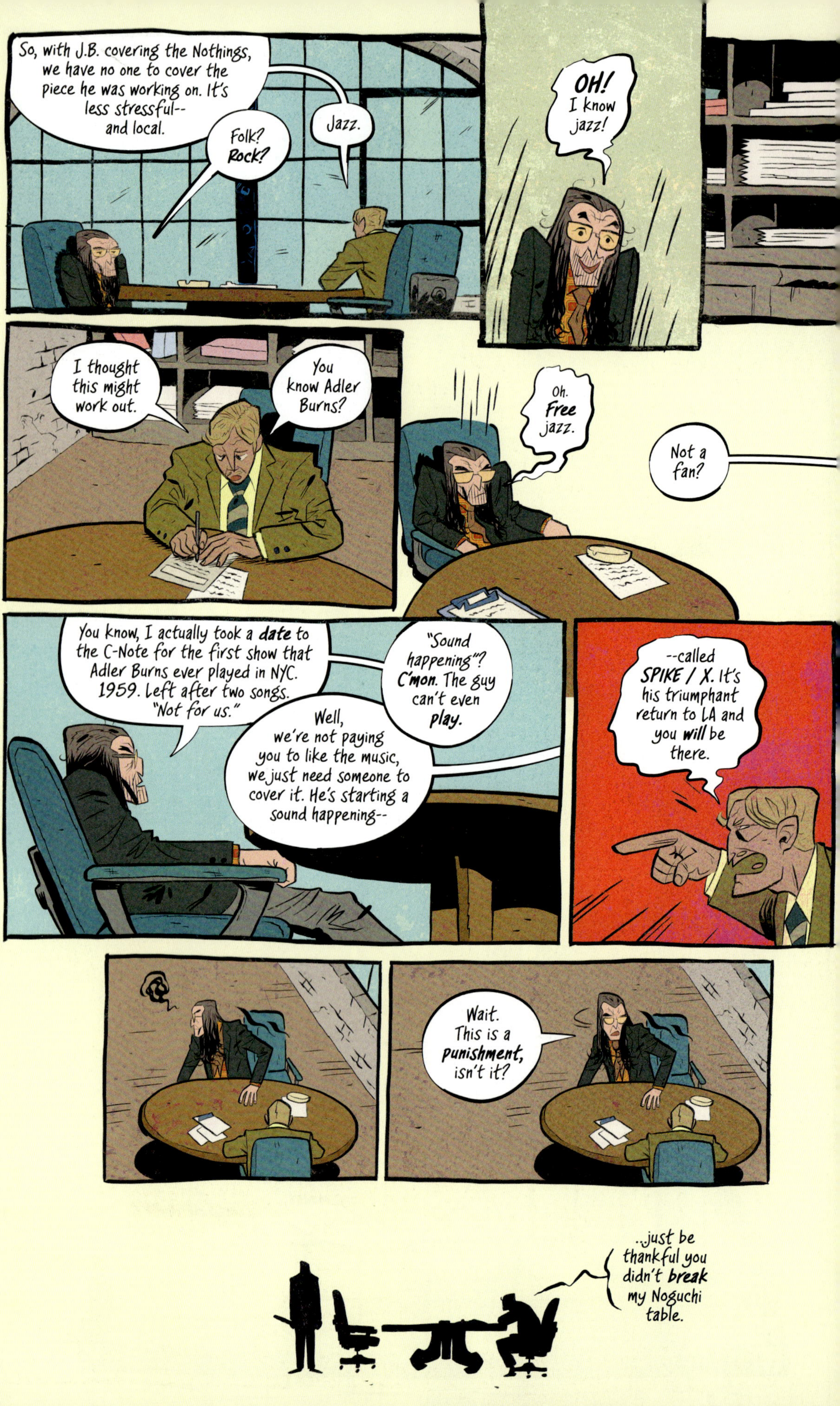

So, with J.B. covering the Nothings, we have no one to cover the piece he was working on. It's less stressful-- and local.
Folk? **Rock?**
Jazz.
OH! I know jazz!
I thought this might work out.
You know Adler Burns?
Oh. **Free** jazz.
Not a fan?
You know, I actually took a **date** to the C-Note for the first show that Adler Burns ever played in NYC. 1959. Left after two songs. "Not for us."
Well, we're not paying you to like the music, we just need someone to cover it. He's starting a sound happening--
"Sound happening"? **C'mon.** The guy can't even **play.**
--called **SPIKE / X.** It's his triumphant return to LA and you **will** be there.
Wait. This is a **punishment,** isn't it?
..just be thankful you didn't **break** my Noguchi table.

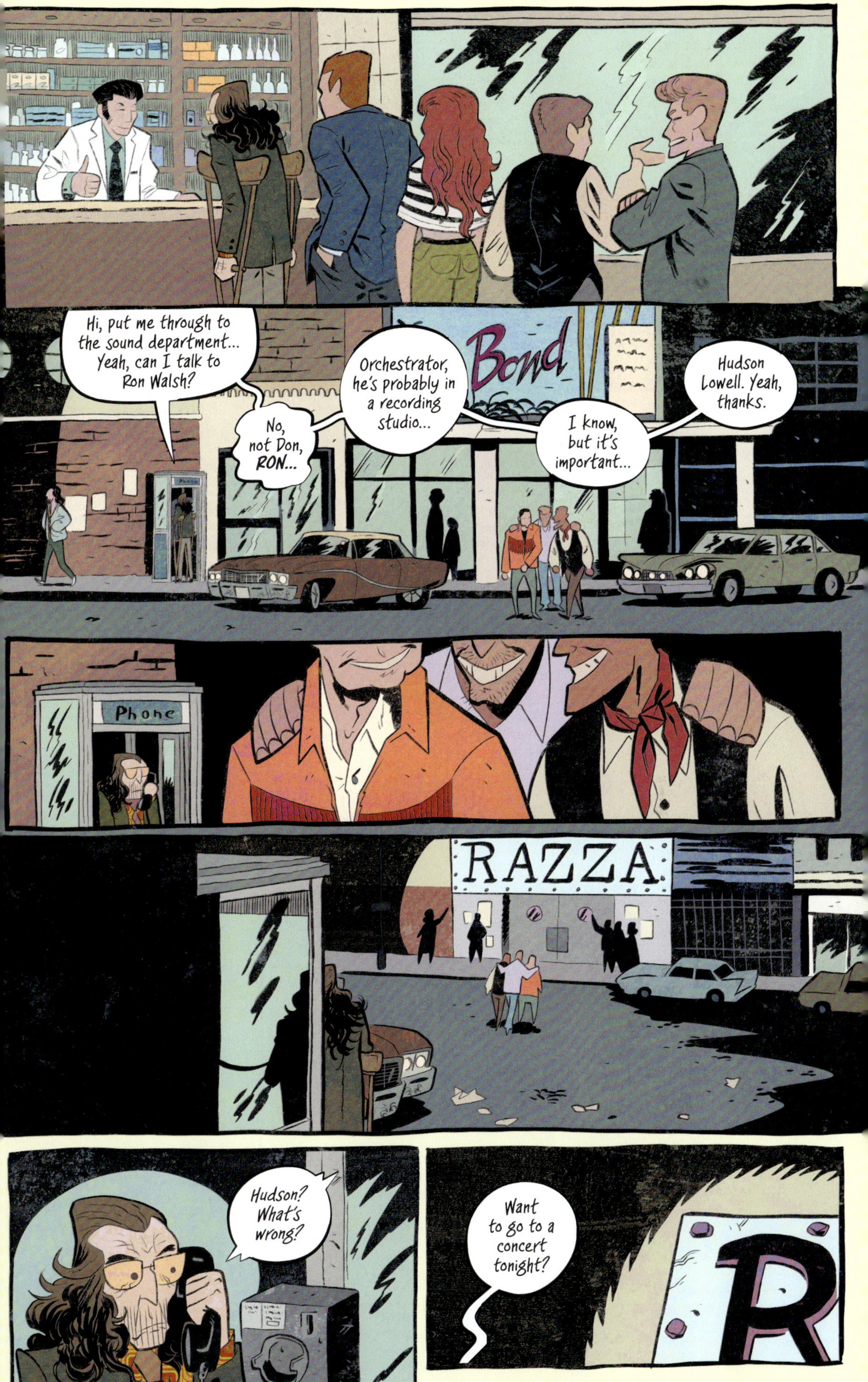

Hi, put me through to the sound department... Yeah, can I talk to Ron Walsh?
No, not Don, RON...
Orchestrator, he's probably in a recording studio...
I know, but it's important...
Hudson Lowell. Yeah, thanks.
Bond
Phone
RAZZA
Hudson? What's wrong?
Want to go to a concert tonight?
R

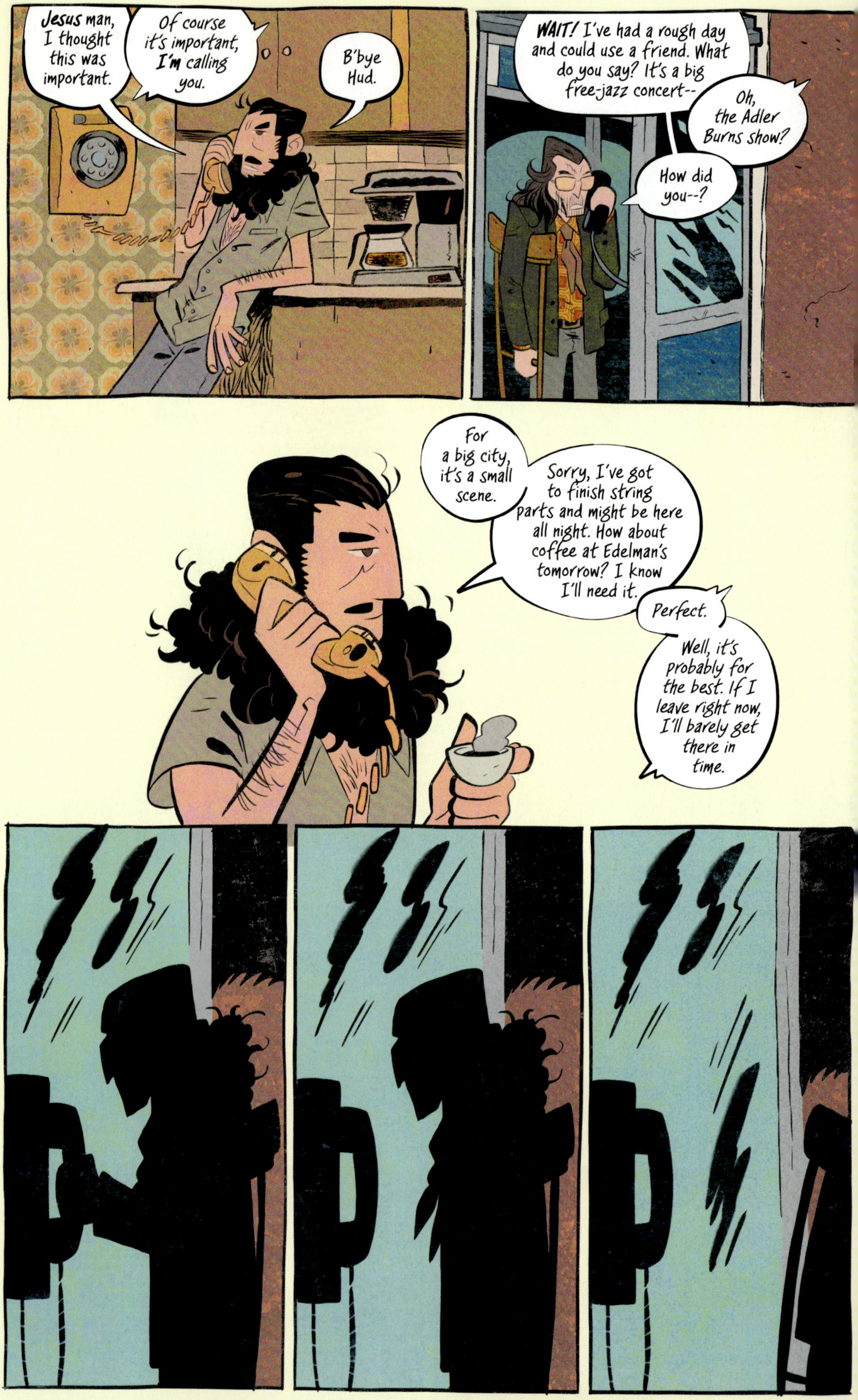
Jesus man, I thought this was important.
Of course it's important, I'm calling you.
B'bye Hud.
WAIT! I've had a rough day and could use a friend. What do you say? It's a big free-jazz concert--
Oh, the Adler Burns show?
How did you--?
For a big city, it's a small scene.
Sorry, I've got to finish string parts and might be here all night. How about coffee at Edelman's tomorrow? I know I'll need it.
Perfect.
Well, it's probably for the best. If I leave right now, I'll barely get there in time.

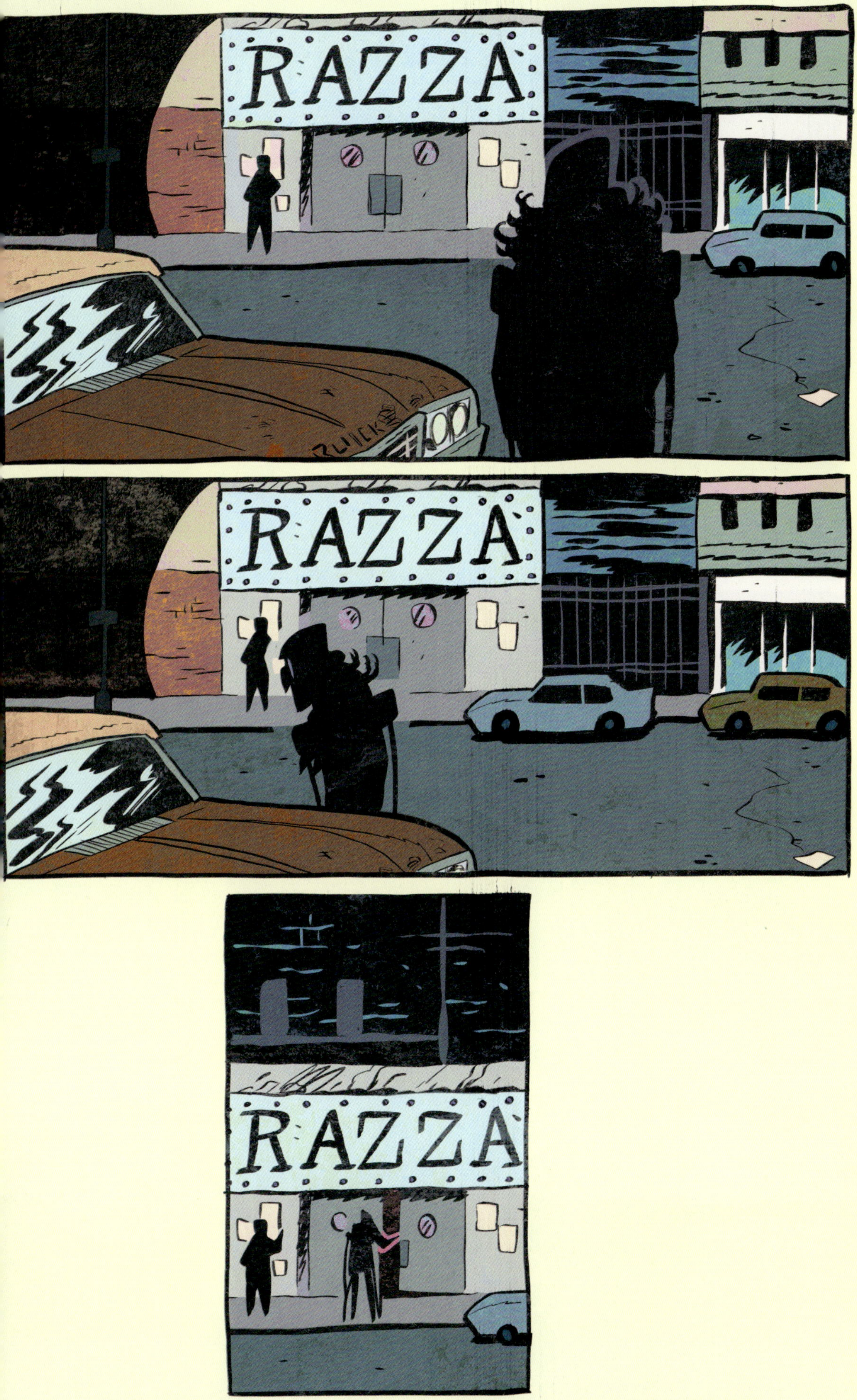
RAZZA
RAZZA
RAZZA

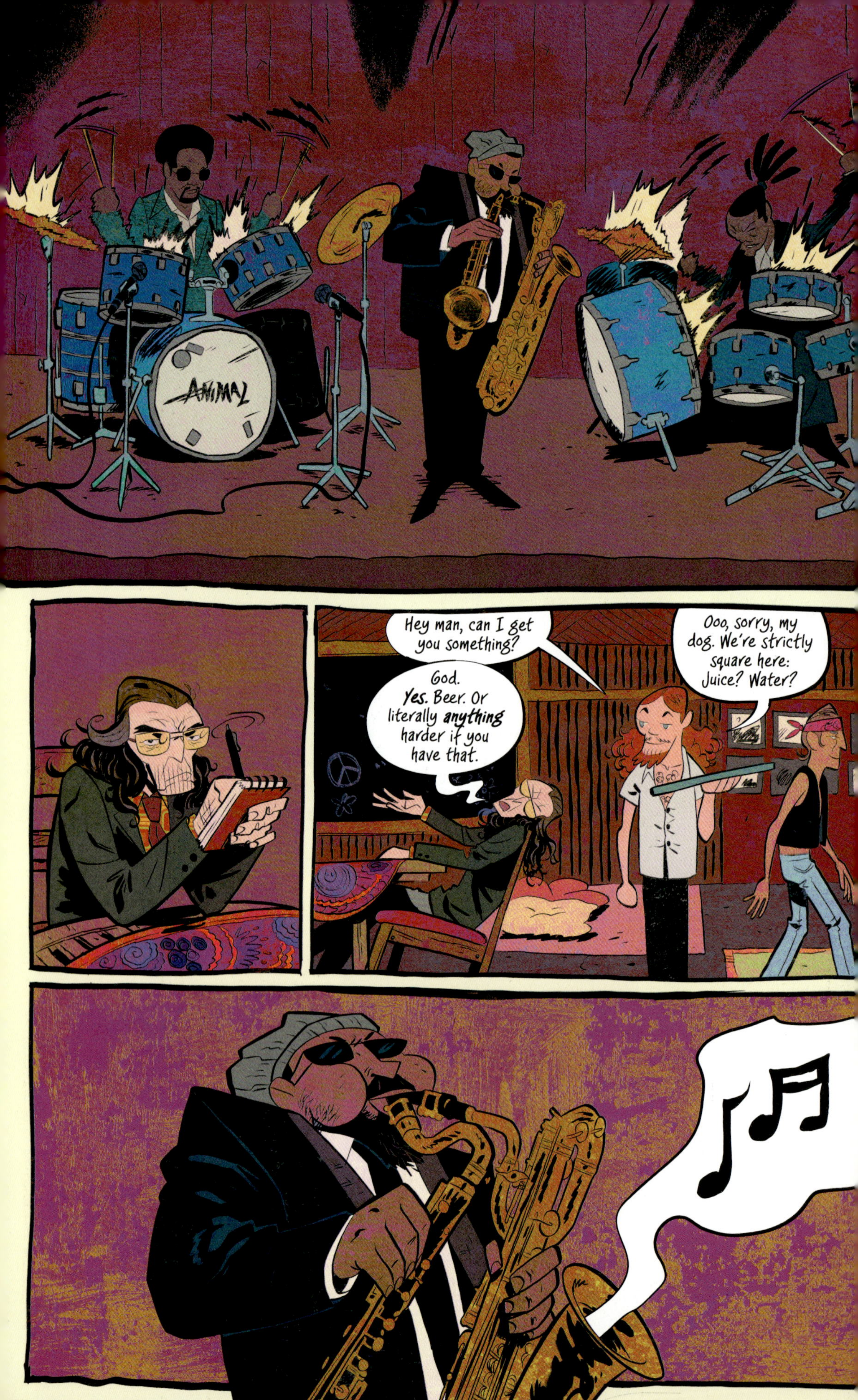
ANIMAL
Hey man, can I get you something?
God. *Yes.* Beer. Or literally ***anything*** harder if you have that.
Ooo, sorry, my dog. We're strictly square here: Juice? Water?

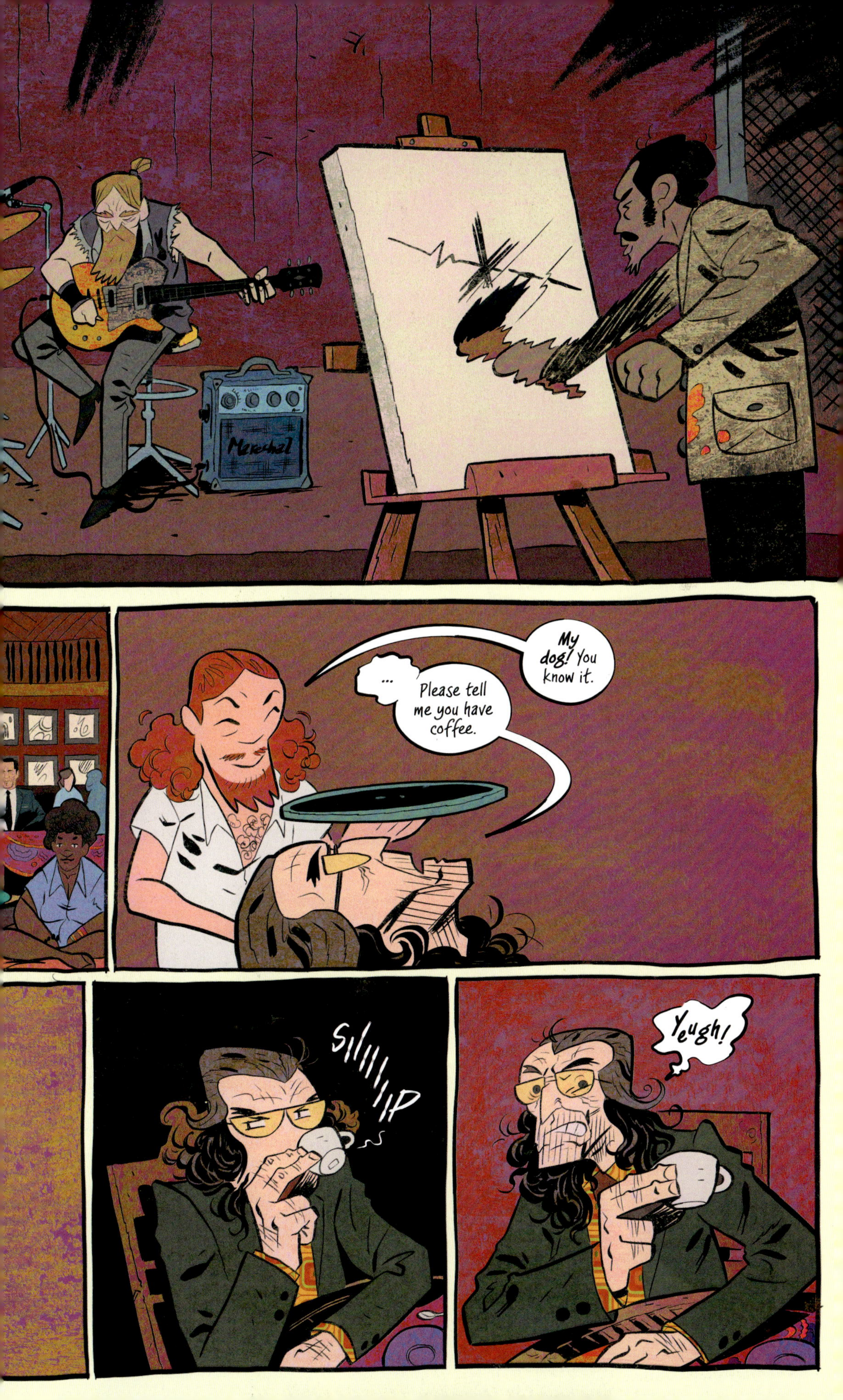
Marechal
...
Please tell me you have coffee.
My dog! You know it.
SIIIIIIP
Yeugh!

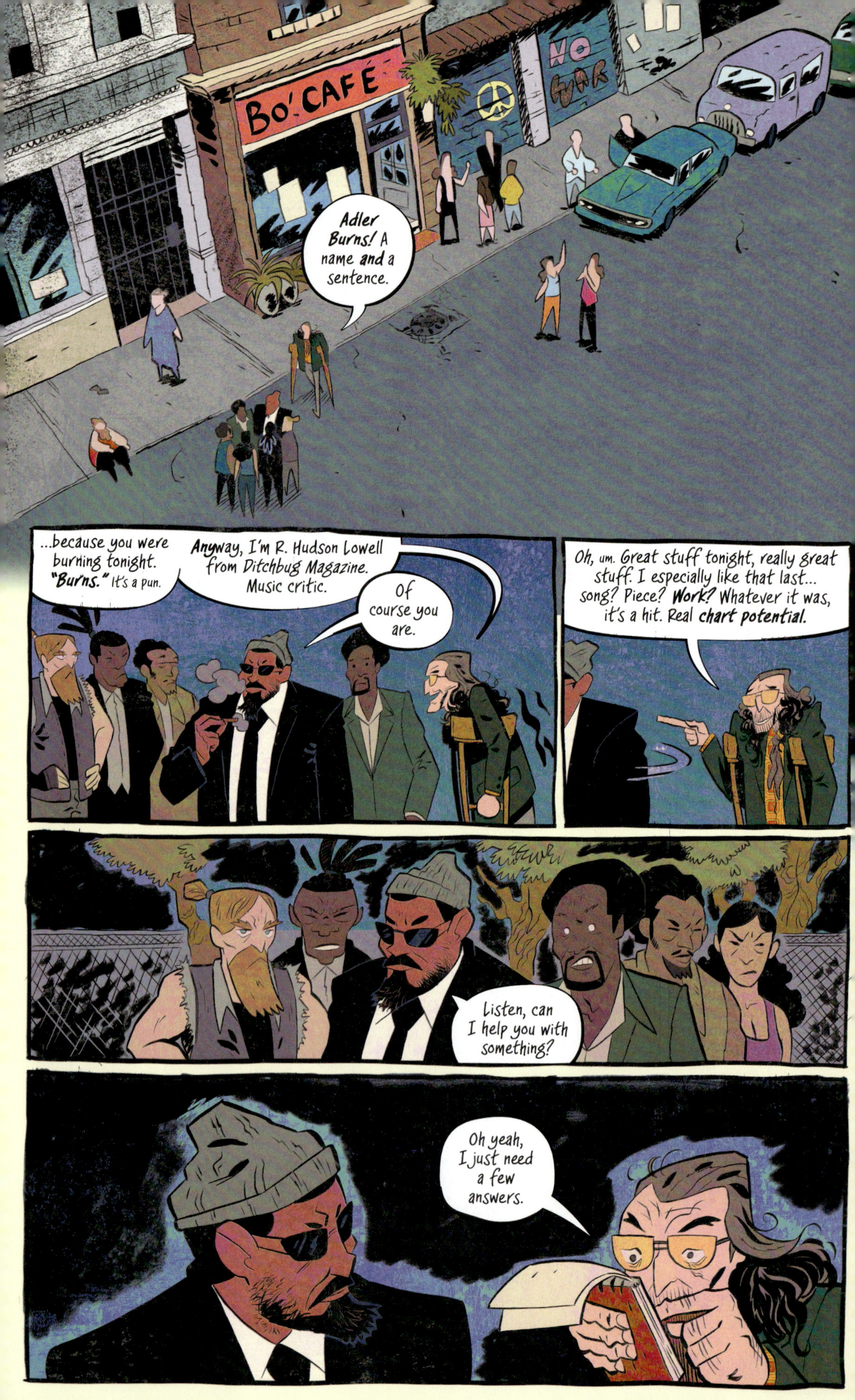
BO' CAFÉ
NO WAR
Adler Burns! A name and a sentence.
...because you were burning tonight. "Burns." It's a pun.
Anyway, I'm R. Hudson Lowell from Ditchbug Magazine. Music critic.
Of course you are.
Oh, um. Great stuff tonight, really great stuff. I especially like that last... song? Piece? Work? Whatever it was, it's a hit. Real chart potential.
Listen, can I help you with something?
Oh yeah, I just need a few answers.

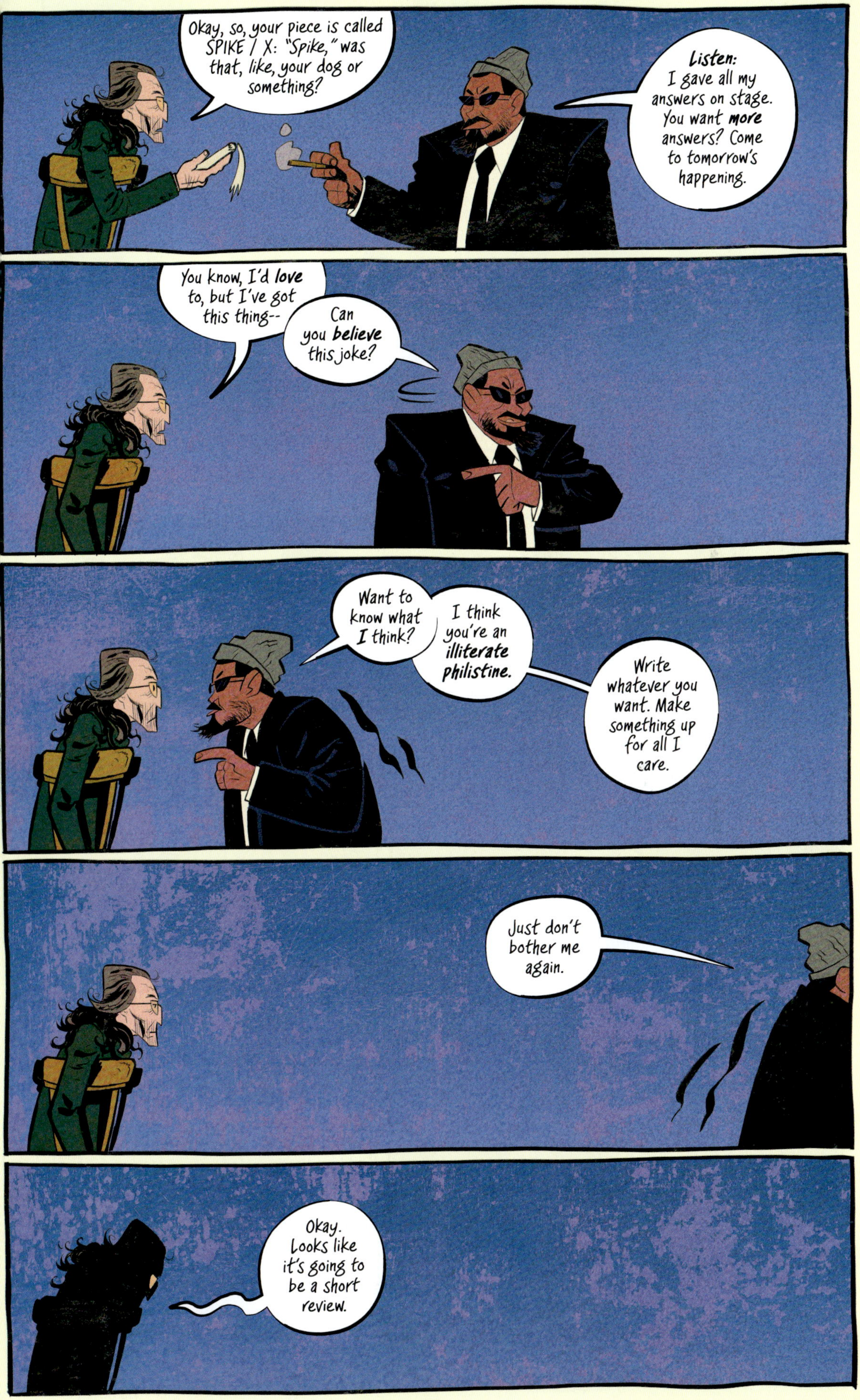

Okay, so, your piece is called SPIKE / X: "Spike," was that, like, your dog or something?
Listen: I gave all my answers on stage. You want **more** answers? Come to tomorrow's happening.
You know, I'd **love** to, but I've got this thing--
Can you **believe** this joke?
Want to know what **I** think?
I think you're an ***illiterate philistine.***
Write whatever you want. Make something up for all I care.
Just don't bother me again.
Okay. Looks like it's going to be a short review.

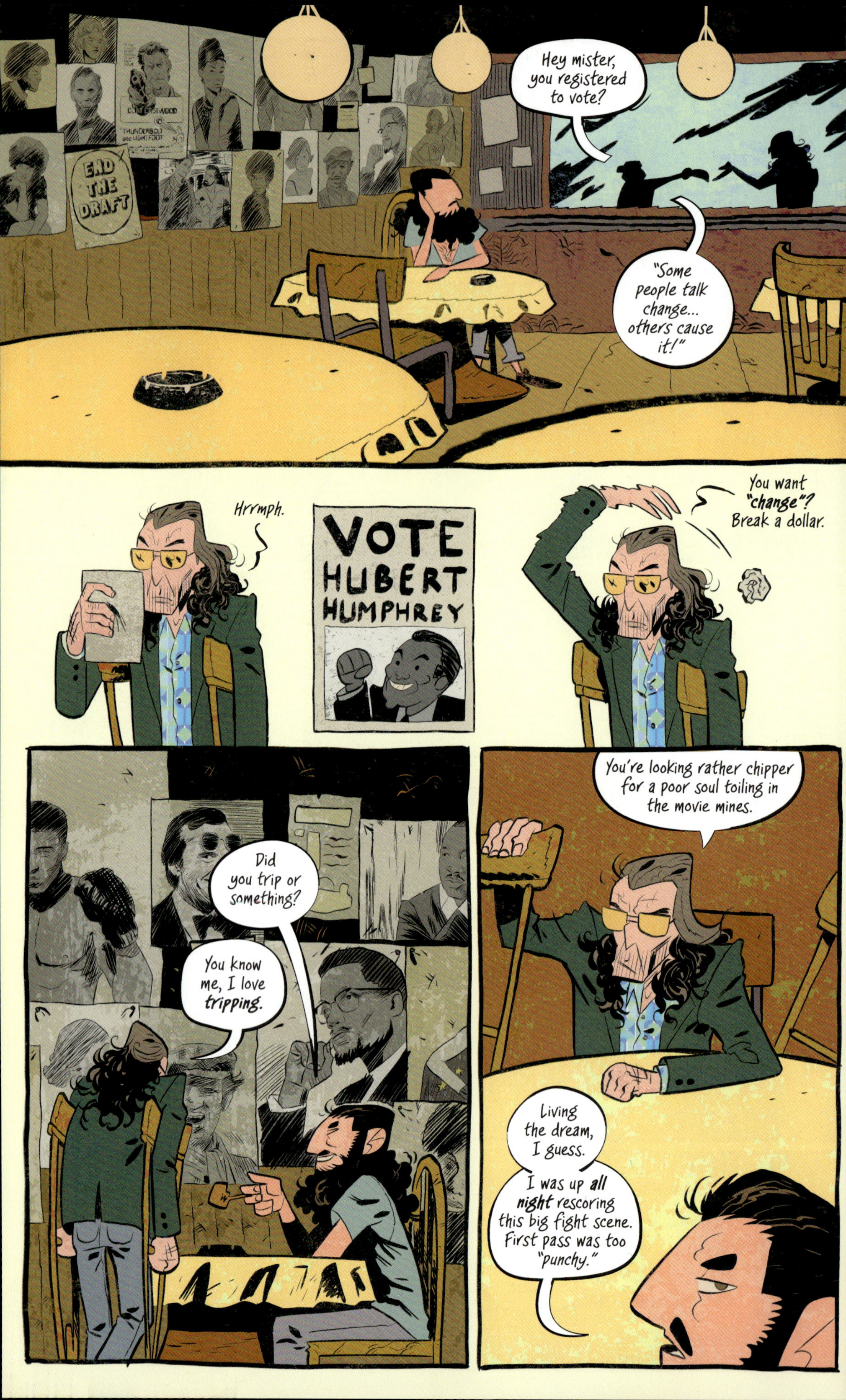
END THE DRAFT
Hey mister, you registered to vote?
"Some people talk change... others cause it!"
Hrrmph.
VOTE HUBERT HUMPHREY
You want "change"? Break a dollar.
Did you trip or something?
You know me, I love tripping.
You're looking rather chipper for a poor soul toiling in the movie mines.
Living the dream, I guess.
I was up all night rescoring this big fight scene. First pass was too "punchy."

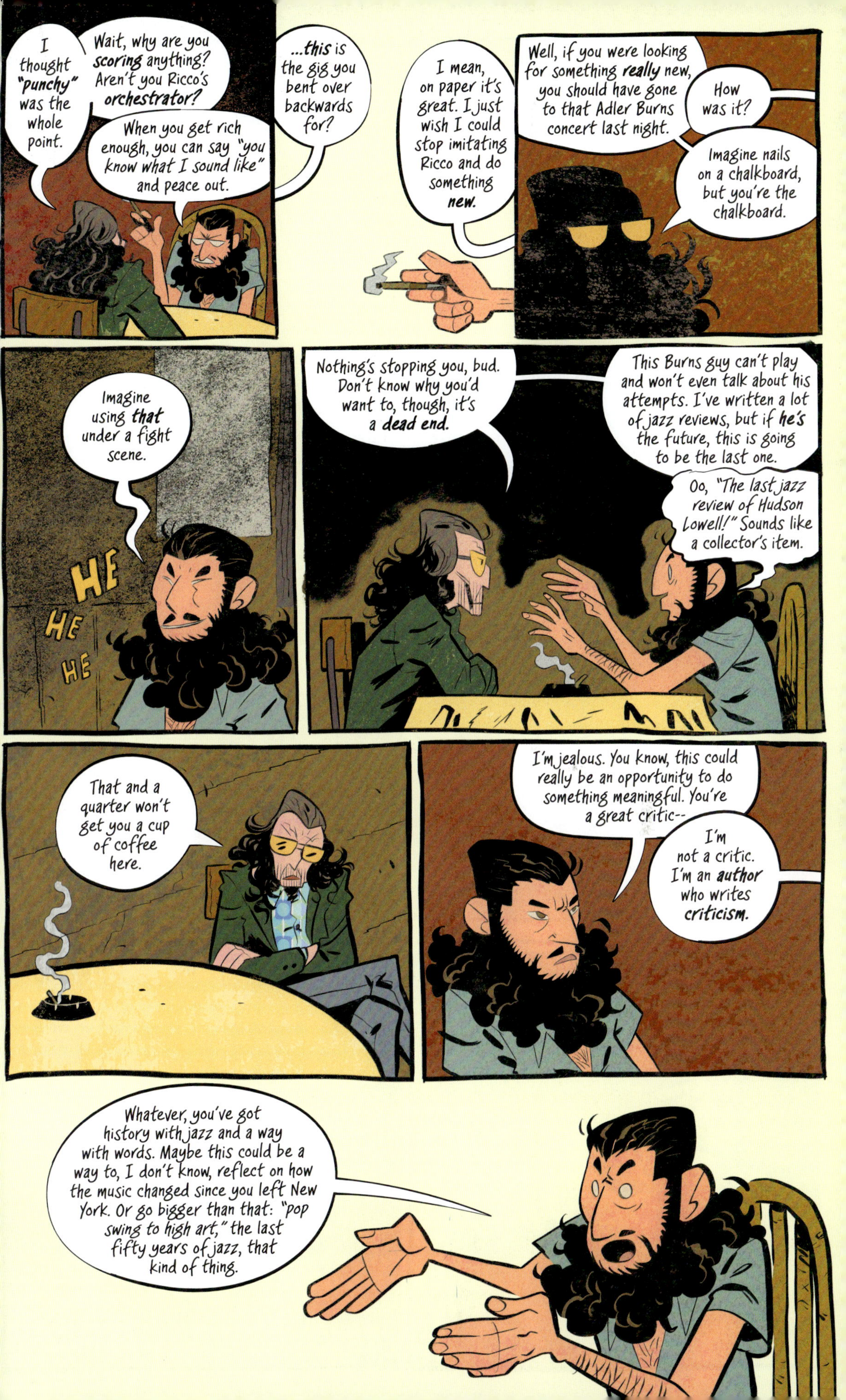
I thought "punchy" was the whole point.
Wait, why are you scoring anything? Aren't you Ricco's orchestrator?
When you get rich enough, you can say "you know what I sound like" and peace out.
...this is the gig you bent over backwards for?
I mean, on paper it's great. I just wish I could stop imitating Ricco and do something new.
Well, if you were looking for something really new, you should have gone to that Adler Burns concert last night.
How was it?
Imagine nails on a chalkboard, but you're the chalkboard.
Imagine using that under a fight scene.
HE HE HE
Nothing's stopping you, bud. Don't know why you'd want to, though, it's a dead end.
This Burns guy can't play and won't even talk about his attempts. I've written a lot of jazz reviews, but if he's the future, this is going to be the last one.
Oo, "The last jazz review of Hudson Lowell!" Sounds like a collector's item.
That and a quarter won't get you a cup of coffee here.
I'm jealous. You know, this could really be an opportunity to do something meaningful. You're a great critic--
I'm not a critic. I'm an author who writes criticism.
Whatever, you've got history with jazz and a way with words. Maybe this could be a way to, I don't know, reflect on how the music changed since you left New York. Or go bigger than that: "pop swing to high art," the last fifty years of jazz, that kind of thing.

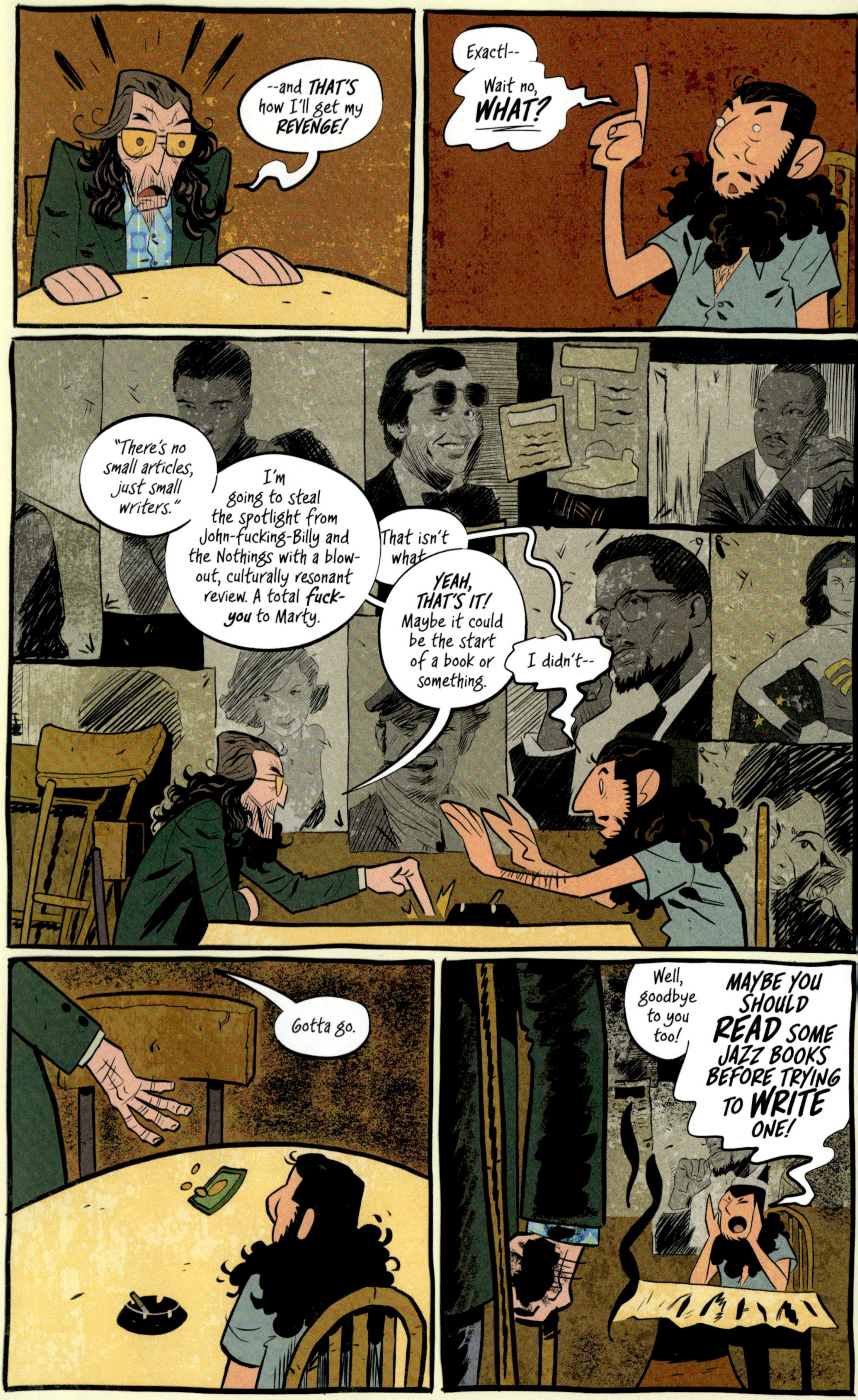
--and THAT'S how I'll get my REVENGE!
Exactl--
Wait no, WHAT?
"There's no small articles, just small writers."
I'm going to steal the spotlight from John-fucking-Billy and the Nothings with a blow-out, culturally resonant review. A total fuck-you to Marty.
That isn't what
YEAH, THAT'S IT! Maybe it could be the start of a book or something.
I didn't--
Gotta go.
Well, goodbye to you too!
MAYBE YOU SHOULD READ SOME JAZZ BOOKS BEFORE TRYING TO WRITE ONE!

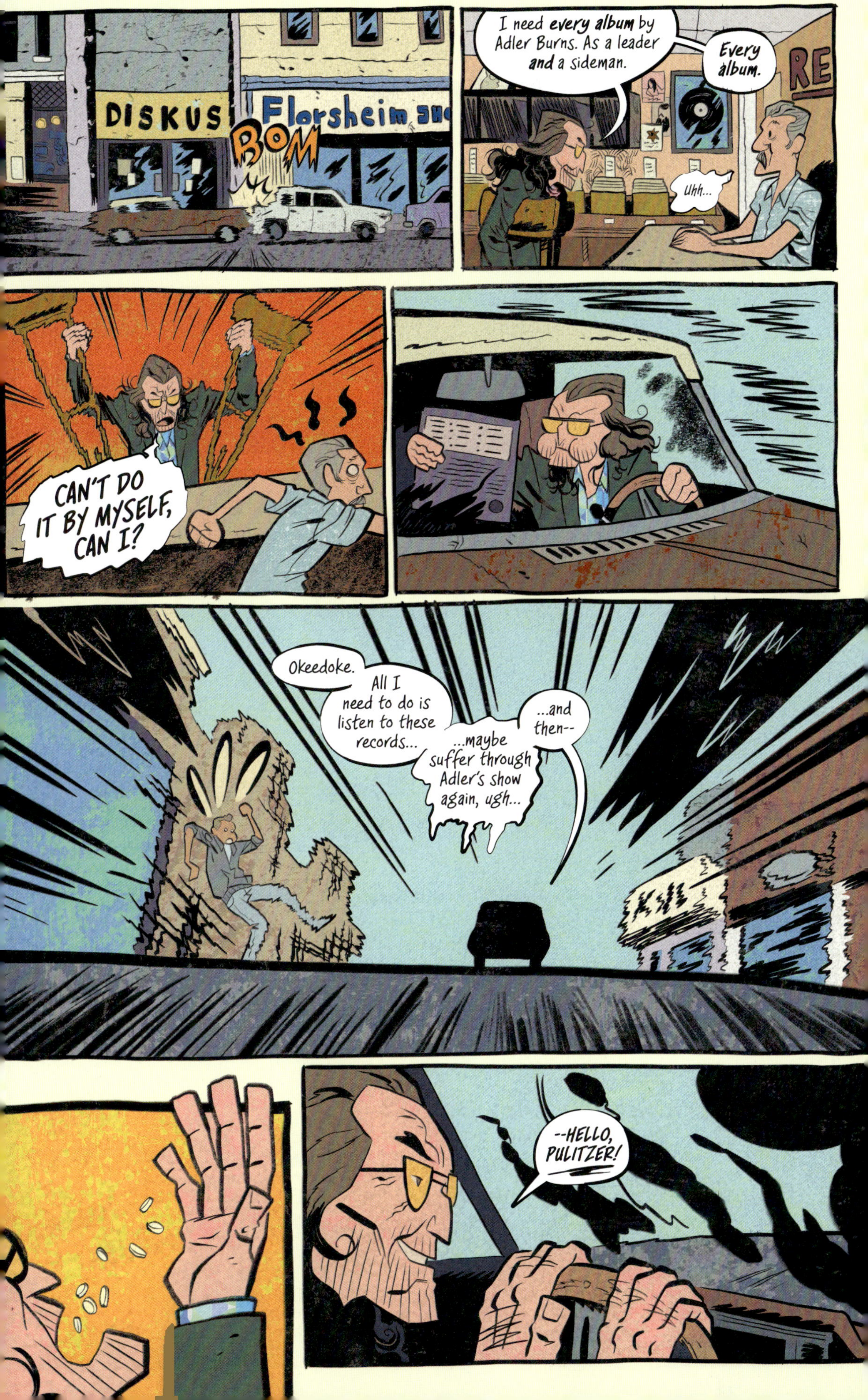
DISKUS
Florsheim
BOM
I need every album by Adler Burns. As a leader and a sideman.
Every album.
Uhh...
RE
CAN'T DO IT BY MYSELF, CAN I?
Okeedoke.
All I need to do is listen to these records...
...maybe suffer through Adler's show again, ugh...
...and then--
--HELLO, PULITZER!

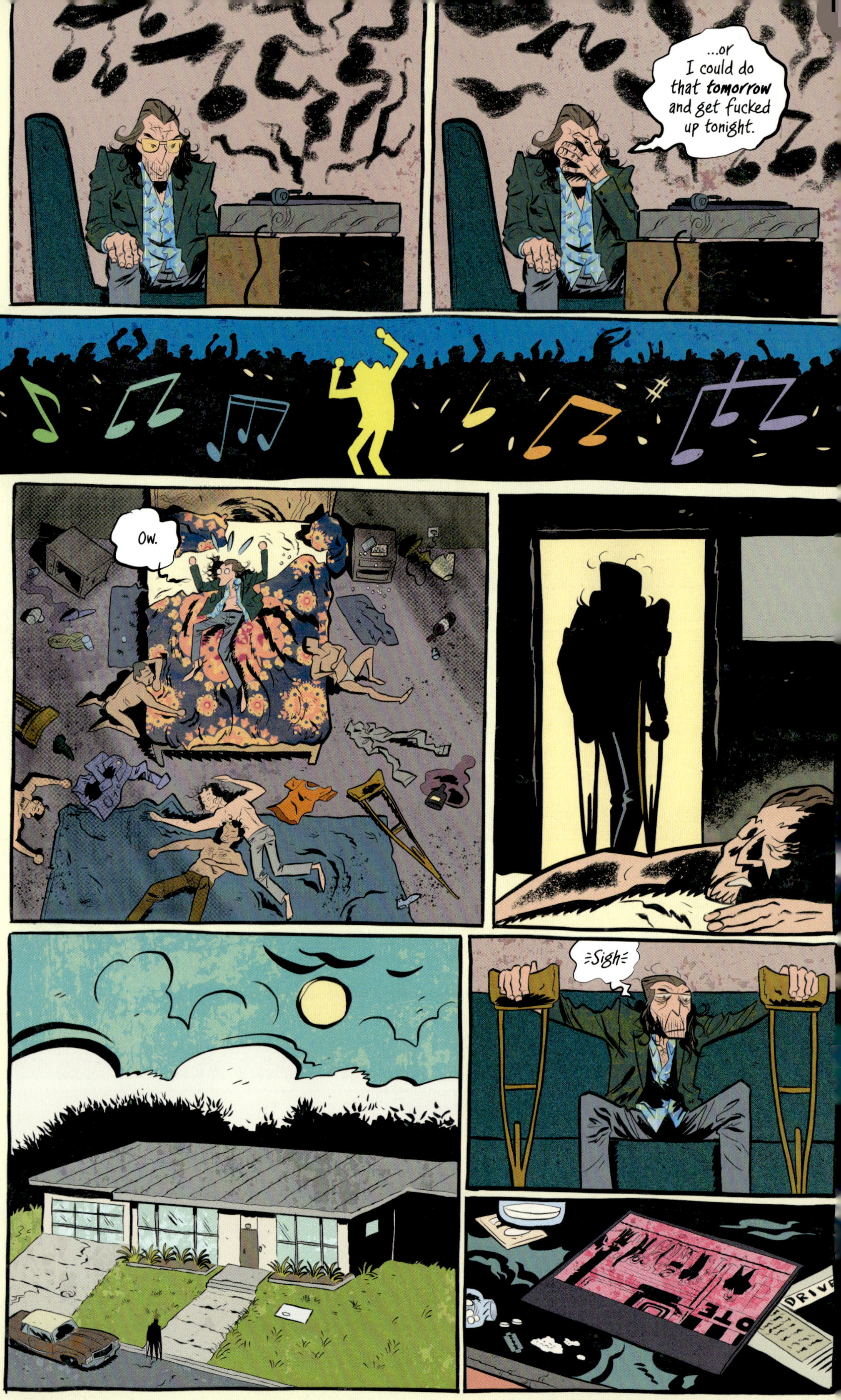
...or I could do that **tomorrow** and get fucked up tonight.
Ow.
Sigh
DRIVE

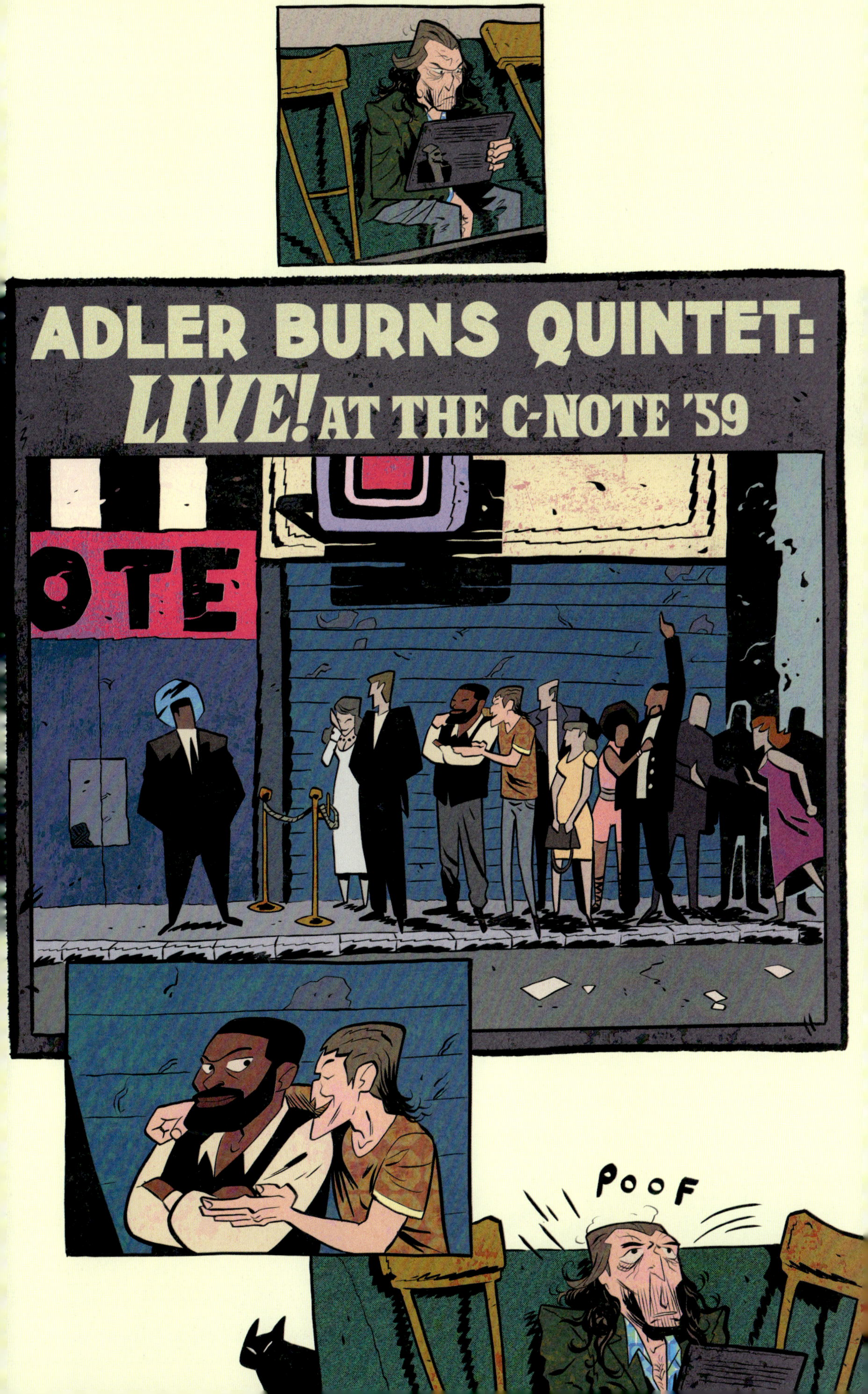
ADLER BURNS QUINTET:
LIVE! AT THE C-NOTE '59
OTE
POOF

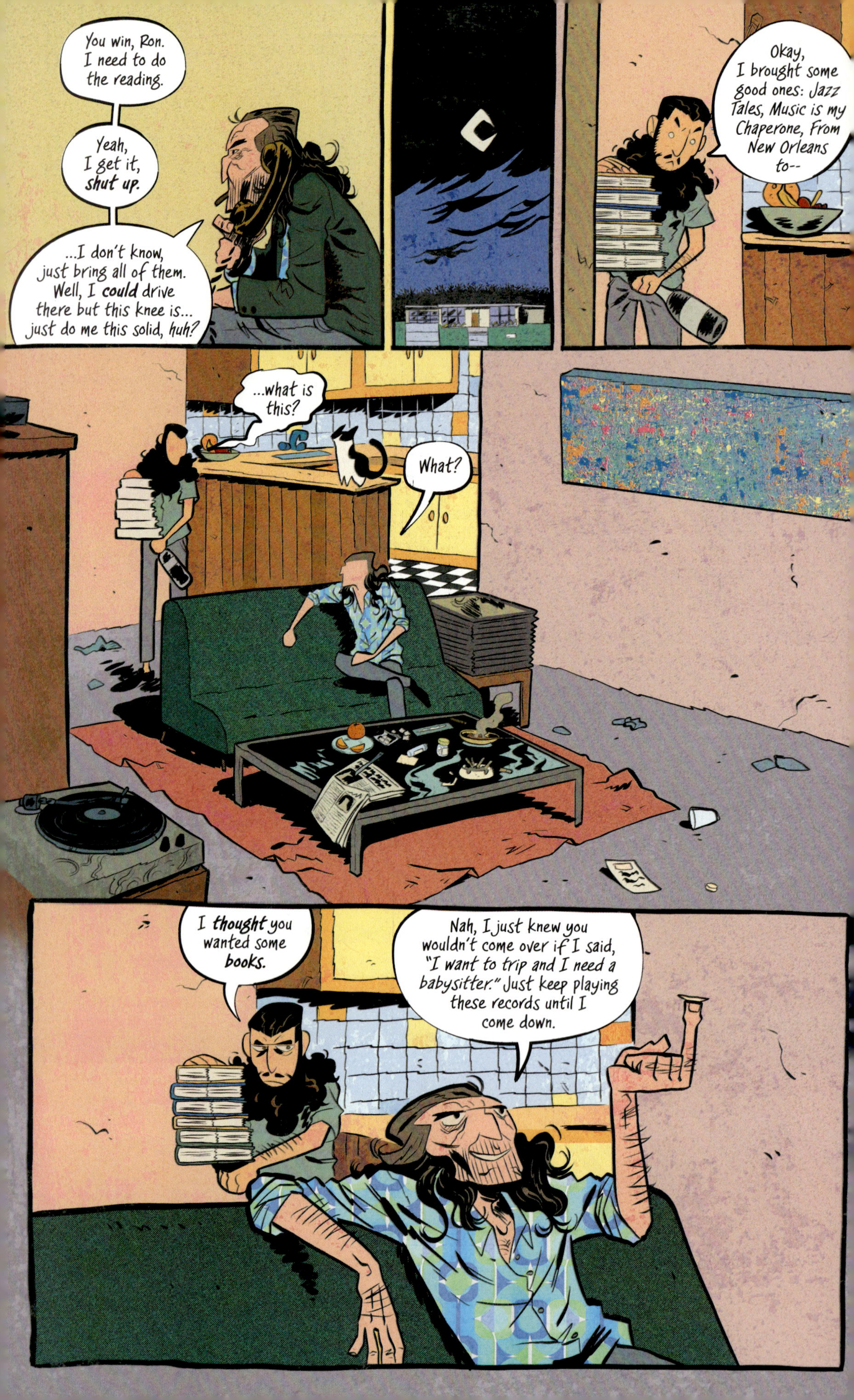
You win, Ron. I need to do the reading.
Yeah, I get it, **shut up.**
...I don't know, just bring all of them. Well, I **could** drive there but this knee is... just do me this solid, huh?
Okay, I brought some good ones: Jazz Tales, Music is my Chaperone, From New Orleans to--
...what is this?
What?
I **thought** you wanted some **books.**
Nah, I just knew you wouldn't come over if I said, "I want to trip and I need a babysitter." Just keep playing these records until I come down.

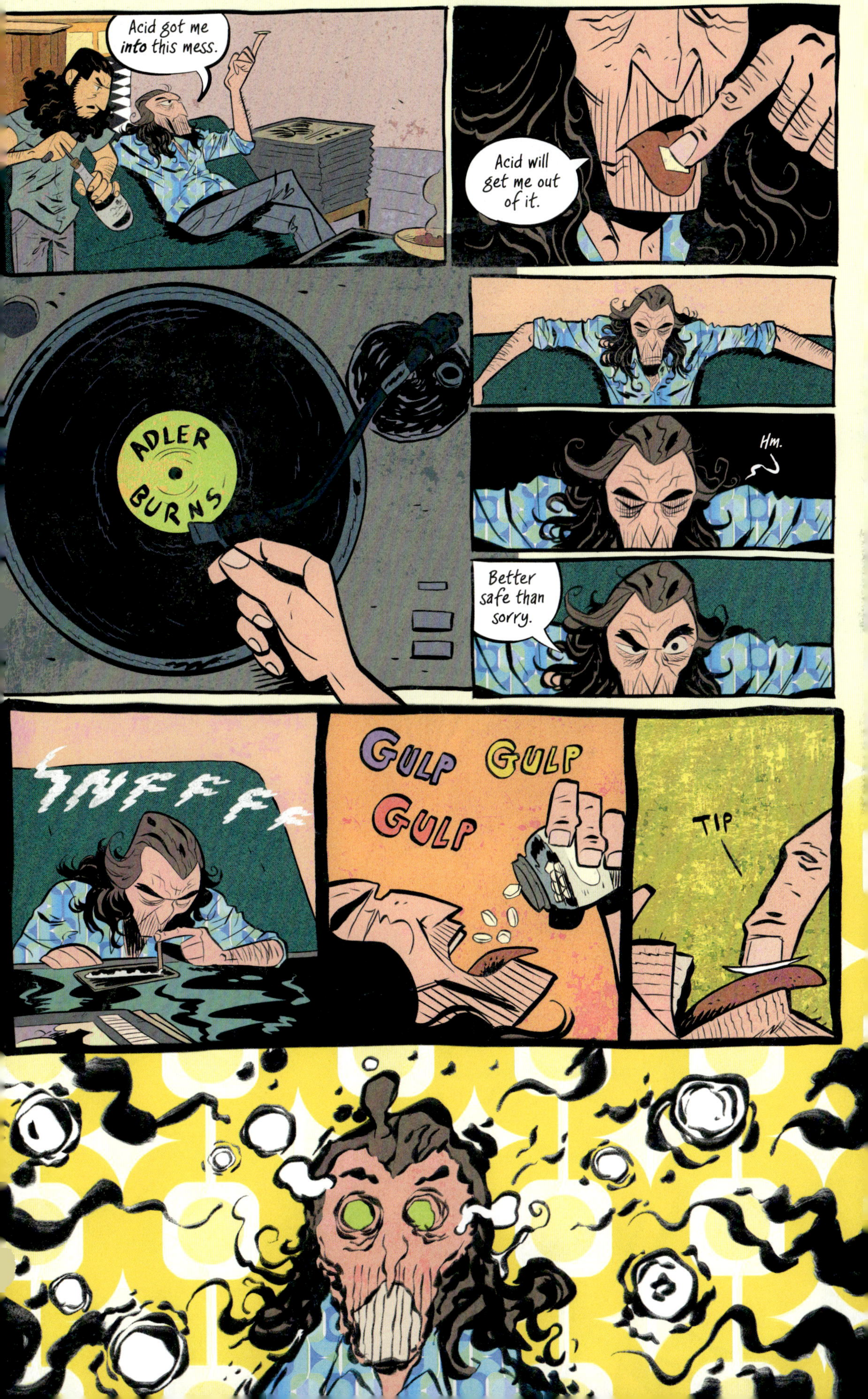

Acid got me *into* this mess.
Acid will get me out of it.
ADLER BURNS
Hm.
Better safe than sorry.
SNFFFF
GULP GULP
GULP
TIP

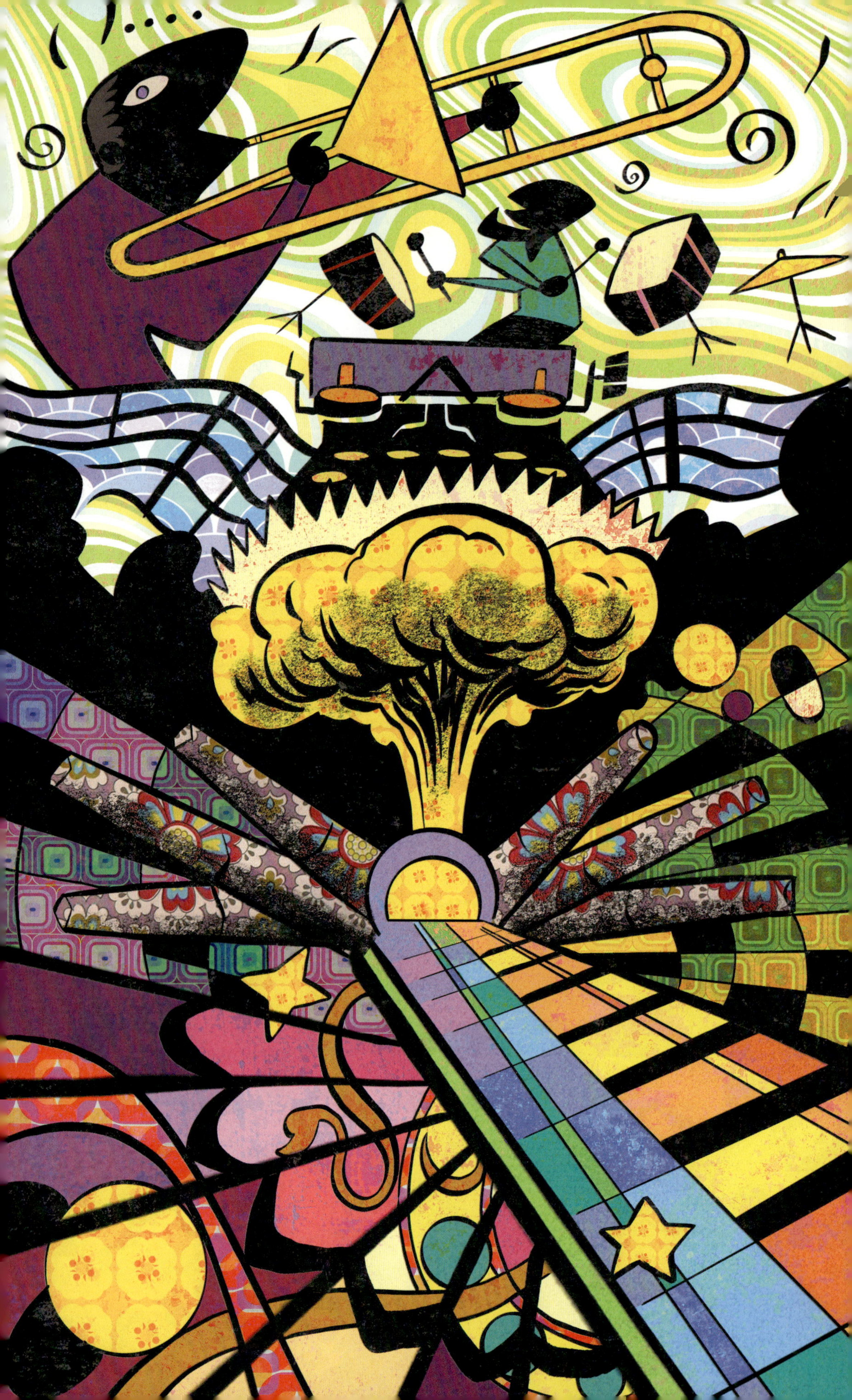

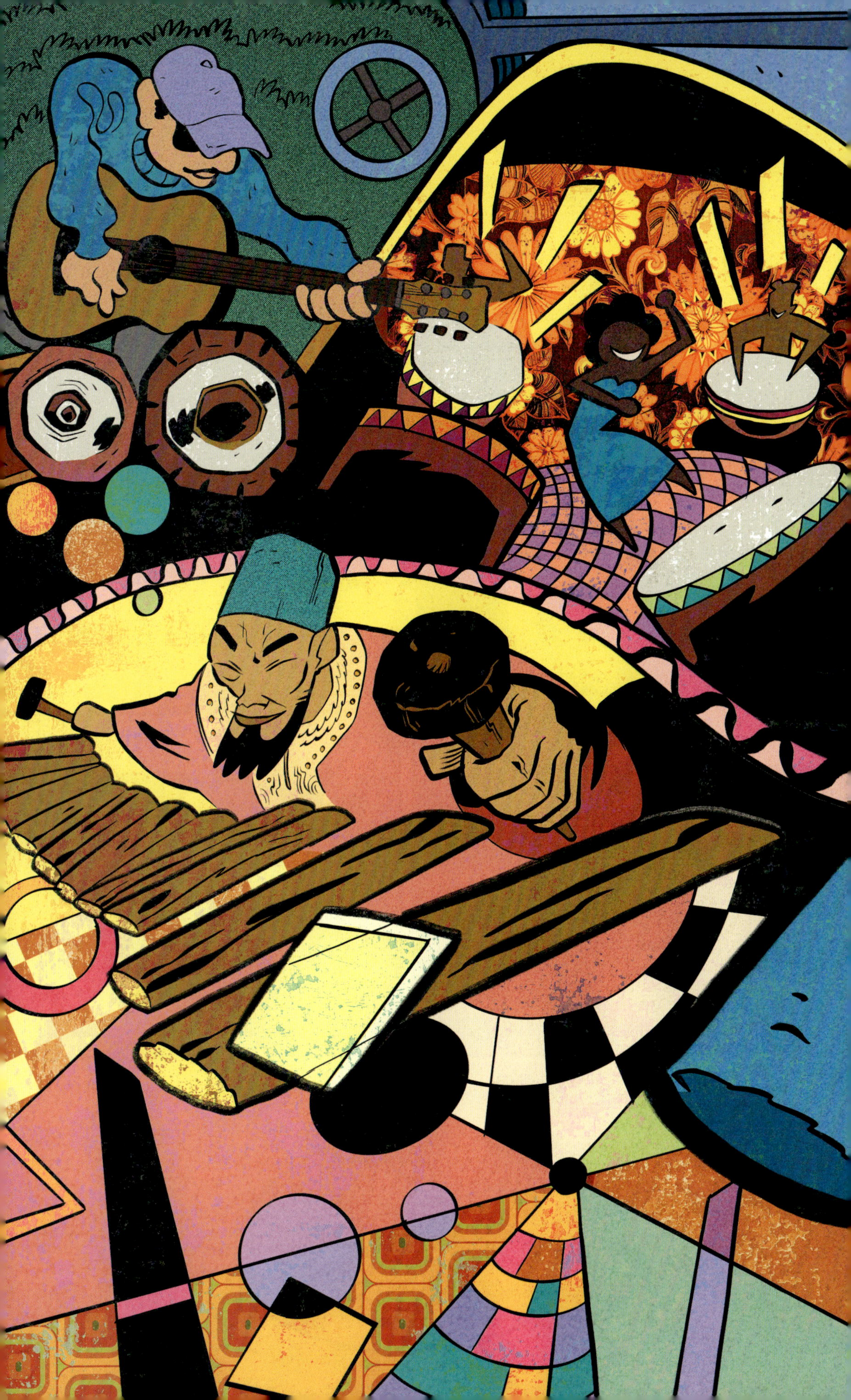

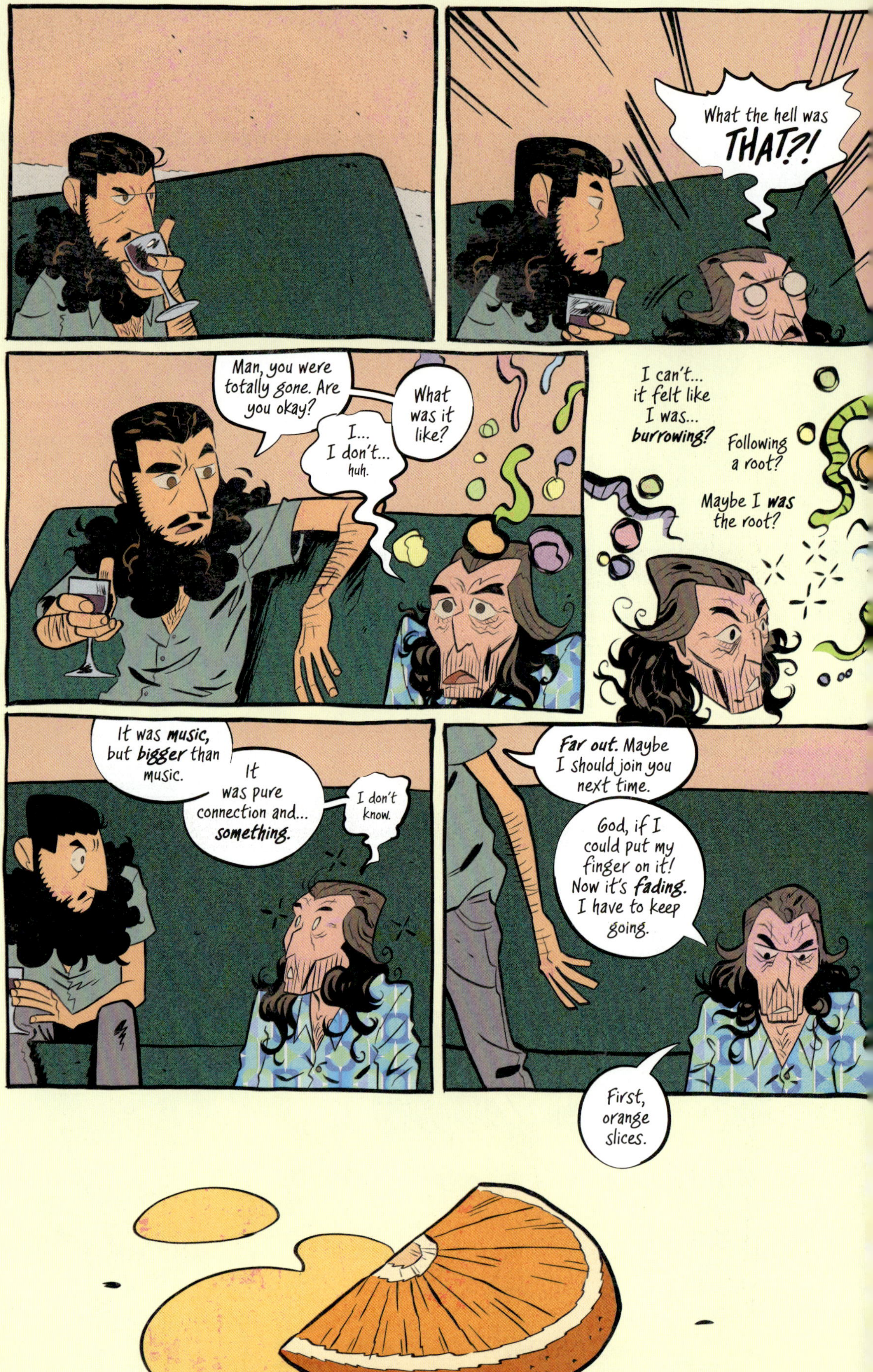
What the hell was THAT?!
Man, you were totally gone. Are you okay?
What was it like?
I... I don't... huh.
I can't... it felt like I was... burrowing?
Following a root?
Maybe I was the root?
It was music, but bigger than music.
It was pure connection and... something.
I don't know.
Far out. Maybe I should join you next time.
God, if I could put my finger on it! Now it's fading. I have to keep going.
First, orange slices.

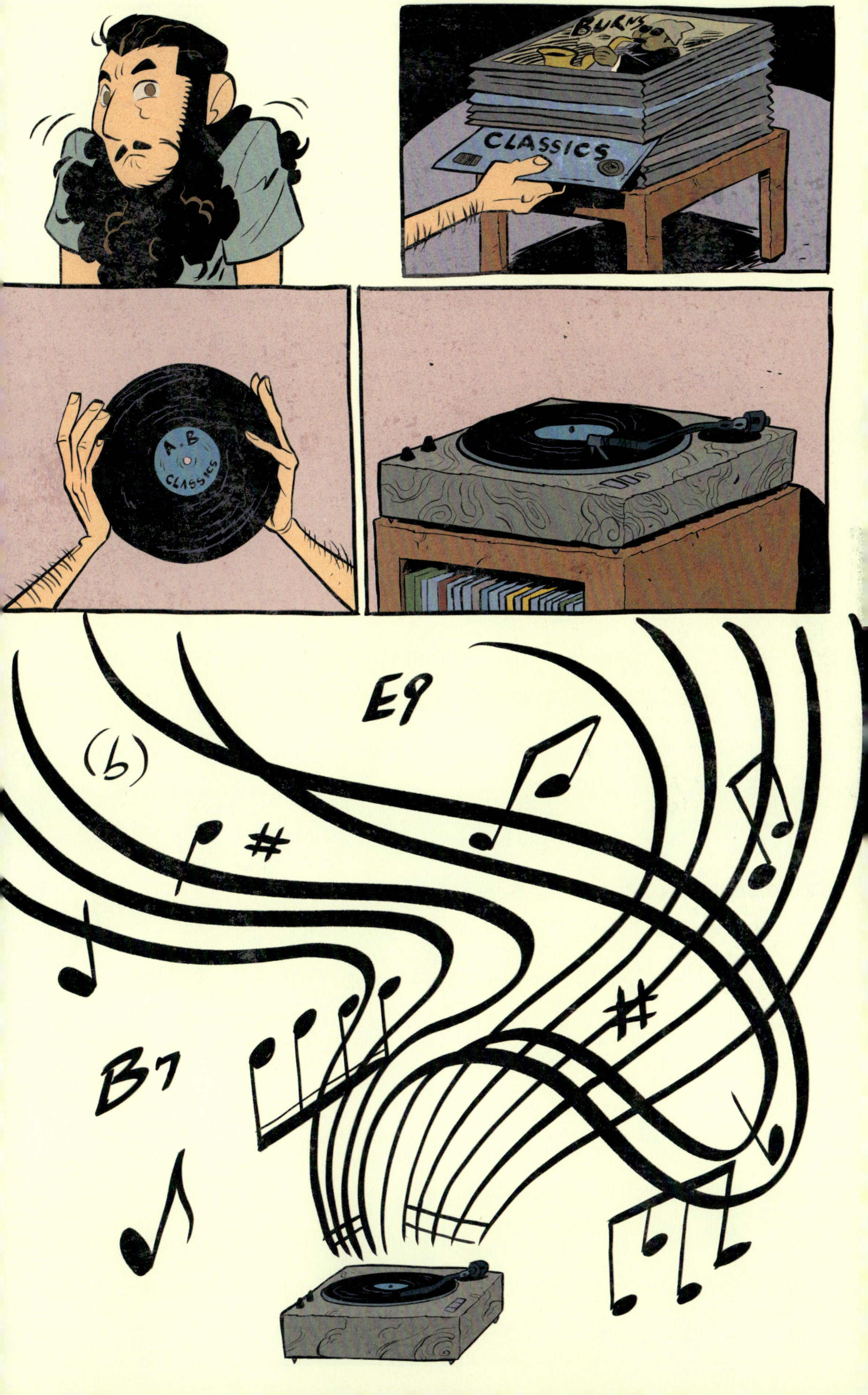
BURNS
CLASSICS
A.B
CLASSICS
E9
(b)
#
#
B7

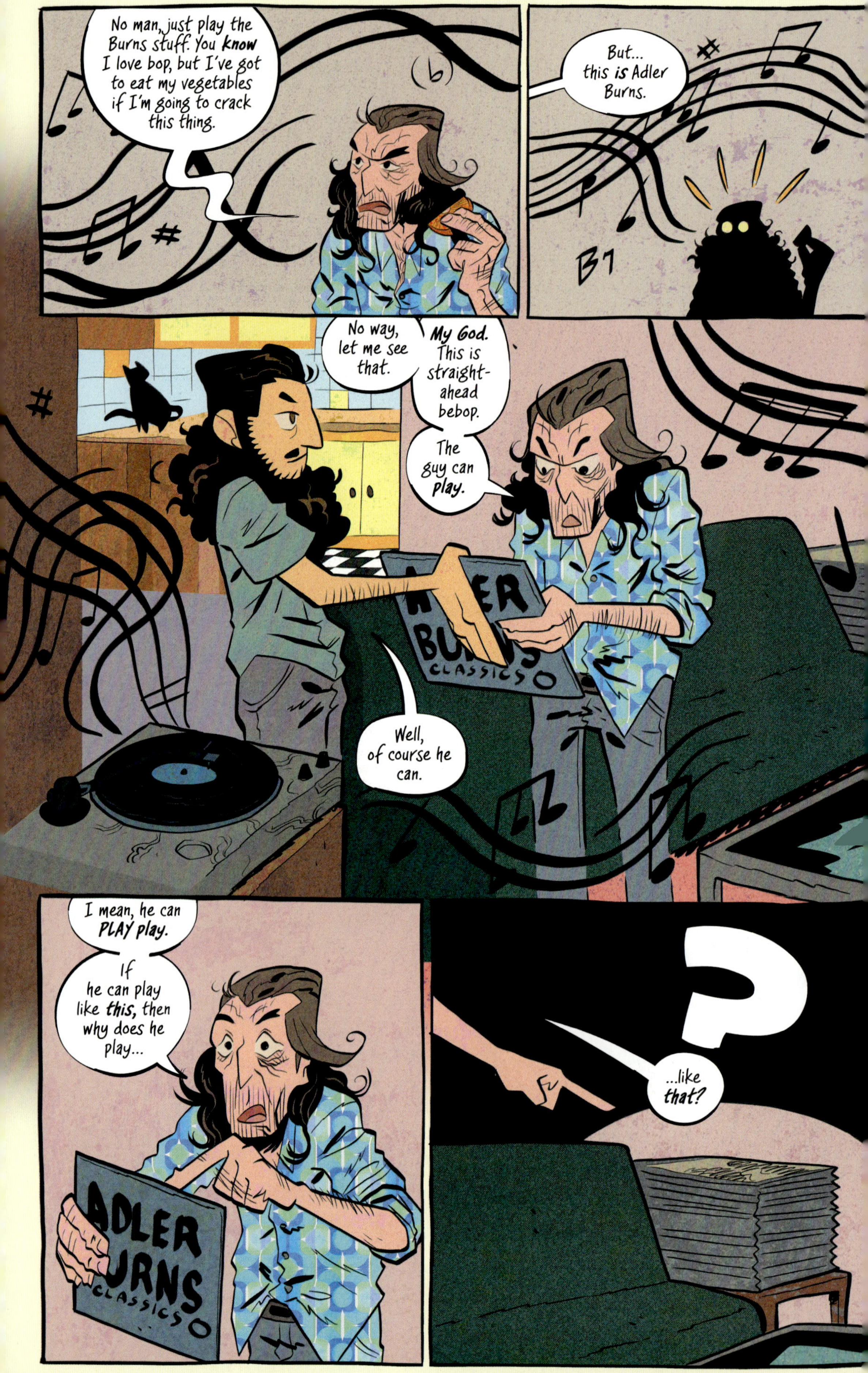
No man, just play the Burns stuff. You **know** I love bop, but I've got to eat my vegetables if I'm going to crack this thing.
But... this **is** Adler Burns.
B7
No way, let me see that.
My God. This is straight-ahead bebop.
The guy can **play.**
ADLER BURNS CLASSICS
Well, of course he can.
I mean, he can **PLAY play.**
If he can play like **this,** then why does he play...
ADLER BURNS CLASSICS
...like **that?**

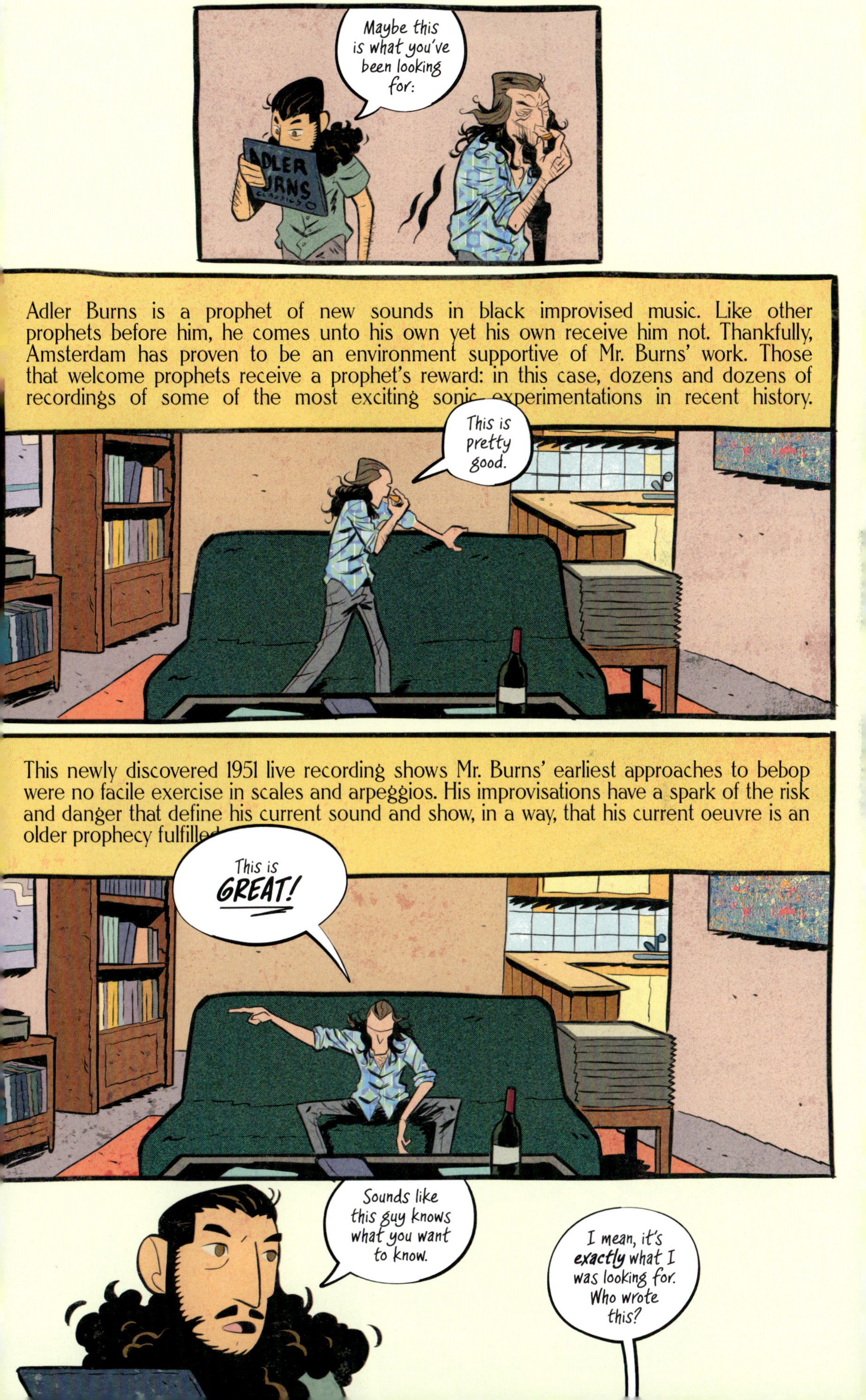
Maybe this is what you've been looking for:
ADLER BURNS
Adler Burns is a prophet of new sounds in black improvised music. Like other prophets before him, he comes unto his own yet his own receive him not. Thankfully, Amsterdam has proven to be an environment supportive of Mr. Burns' work. Those that welcome prophets receive a prophet's reward: in this case, dozens and dozens of recordings of some of the most exciting sonic experimentations in recent history.
This is pretty good.
This newly discovered 1951 live recording shows Mr. Burns' earliest approaches to bebop were no facile exercise in scales and arpeggios. His improvisations have a spark of the risk and danger that define his current sound and show, in a way, that his current oeuvre is an older prophecy fulfilled.
This is GREAT!
Sounds like this guy knows what you want to know.
I mean, it's exactly what I was looking for. Who wrote this?

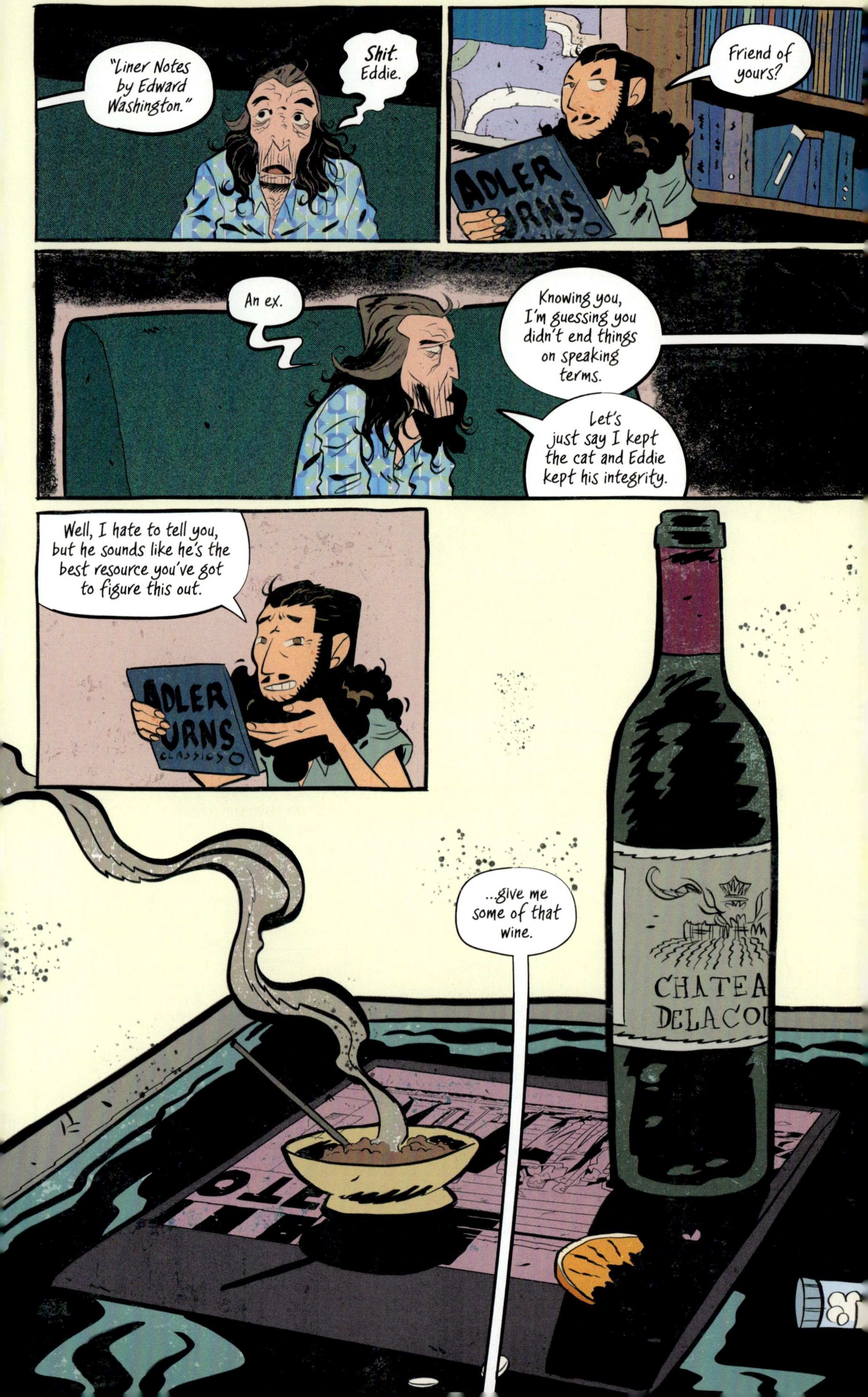
"Liner Notes by Edward Washington."
Shit. Eddie.
Friend of yours?
ADLER URNS
An ex.
Knowing you, I'm guessing you didn't end things on speaking terms.
Let's just say I kept the cat and Eddie kept his integrity.
Well, I hate to tell you, but he sounds like he's the best resource you've got to figure this out.
ADLER URNS CLASSICS
...give me some of that wine.
CHATEA DELACOU

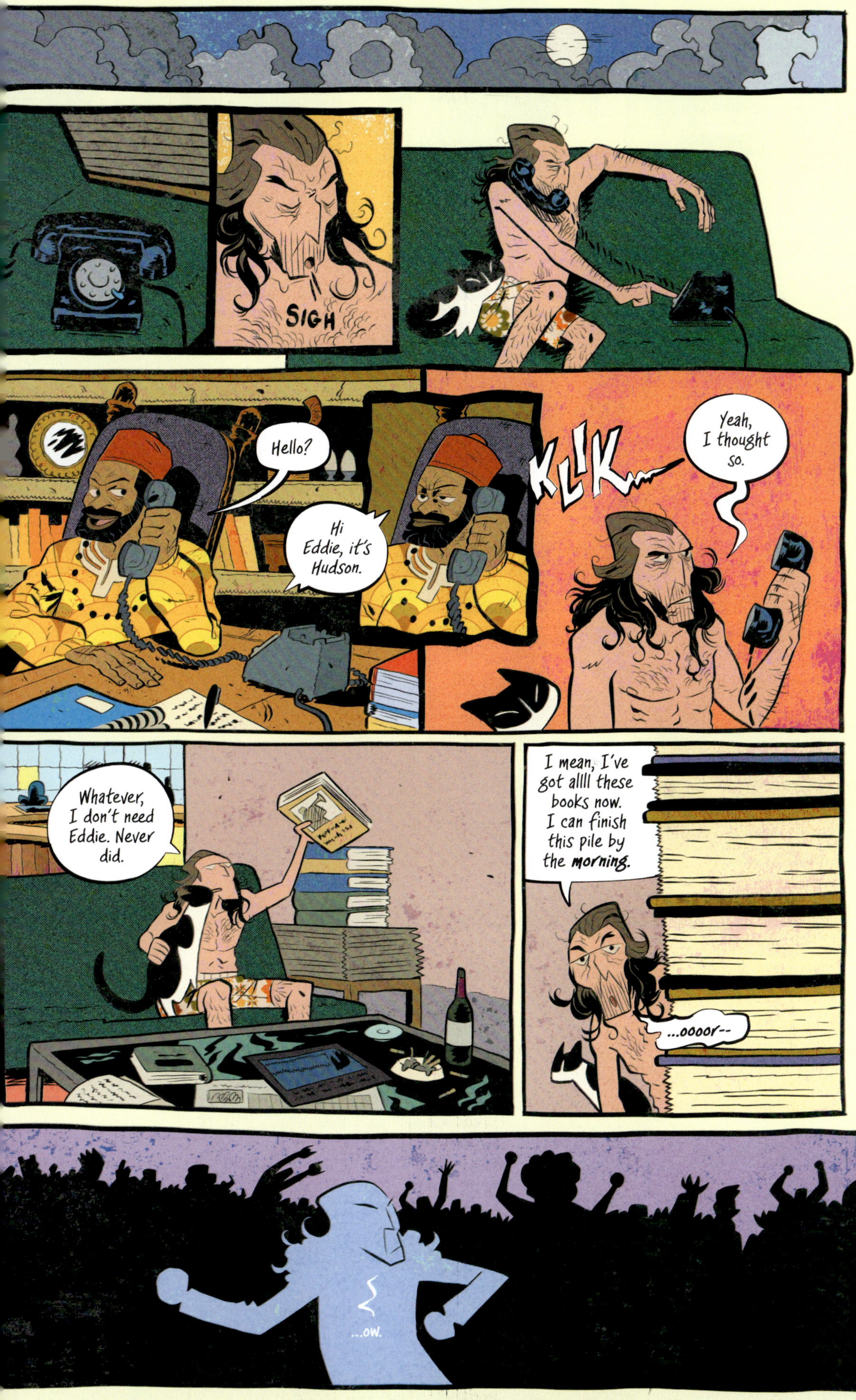
SIGH
Hello?
Hi Eddie, it's Hudson.
KLIK
Yeah, I thought so.
Whatever, I don't need Eddie. Never did.
I mean, I've got allll these books now. I can finish this pile by the **morning.**
...ooor--
...ow.

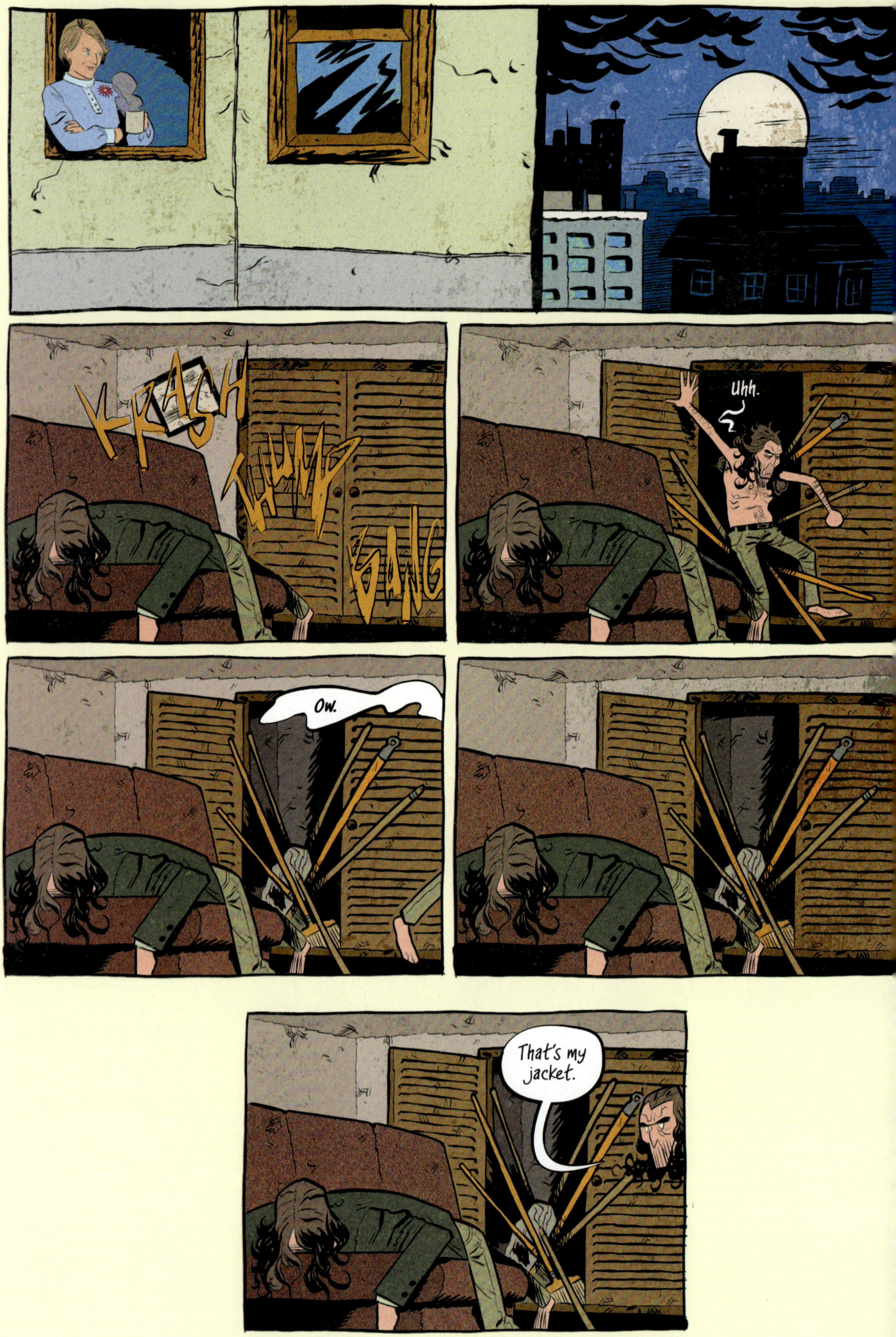
KRASH
THUMP
SPANG
Uhh.
Ow.
That's my jacket.

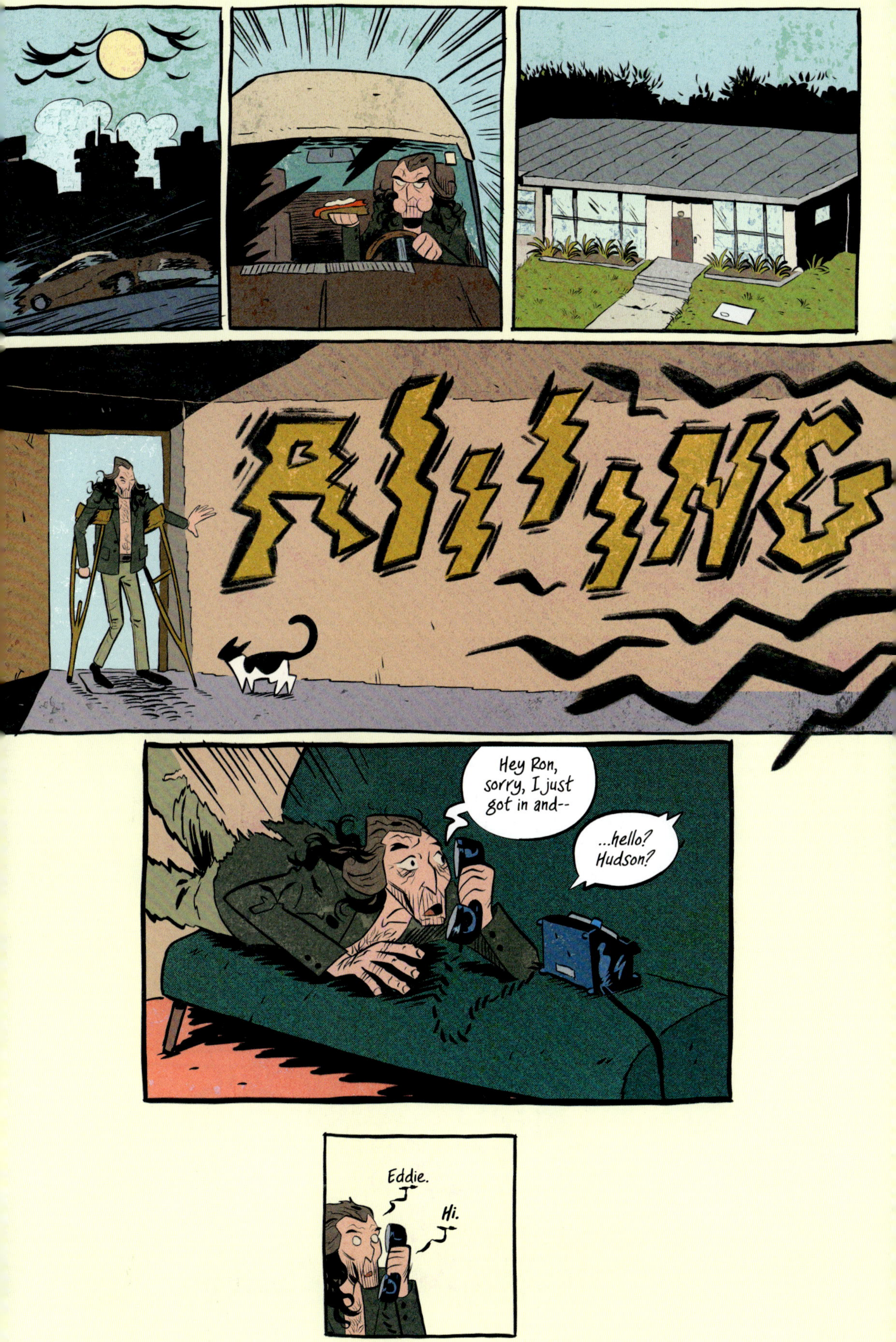
RIIIING
Hey Ron, sorry, I just got in and--
...hello? Hudson?
Eddie.
Hi.

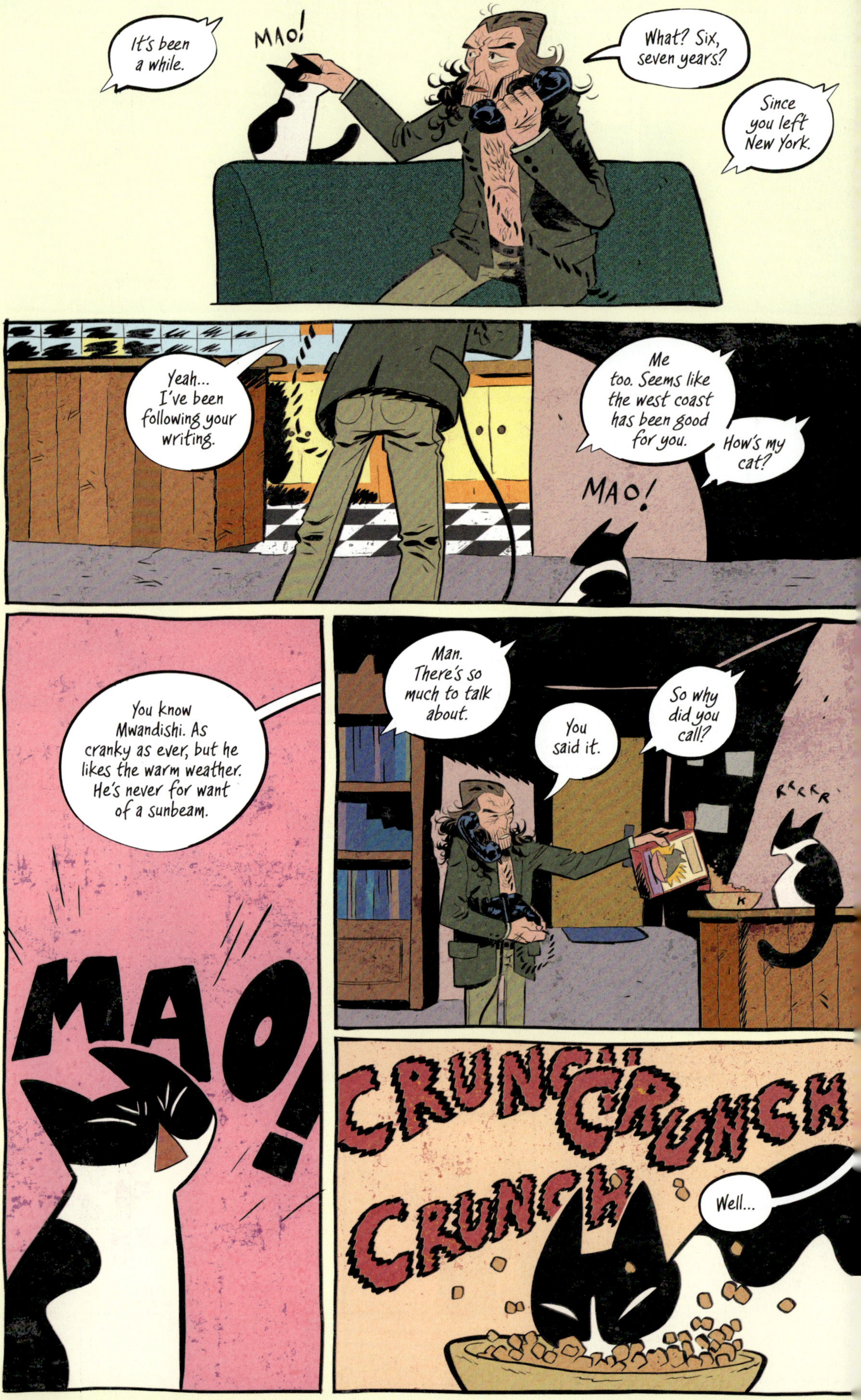
It's been a while.
MAO!
What? Six, seven years?
Since you left New York.
Yeah... I've been following your writing.
Me too. Seems like the west coast has been good for you.
How's my cat?
MAO!
You know Mwandishi. As cranky as ever, but he likes the warm weather. He's never for want of a sunbeam.
MAO!
Man. There's so much to talk about.
You said it.
So why did you call?
RRRRR
CRUNCH CRUNCH
CRUNCH
Well...

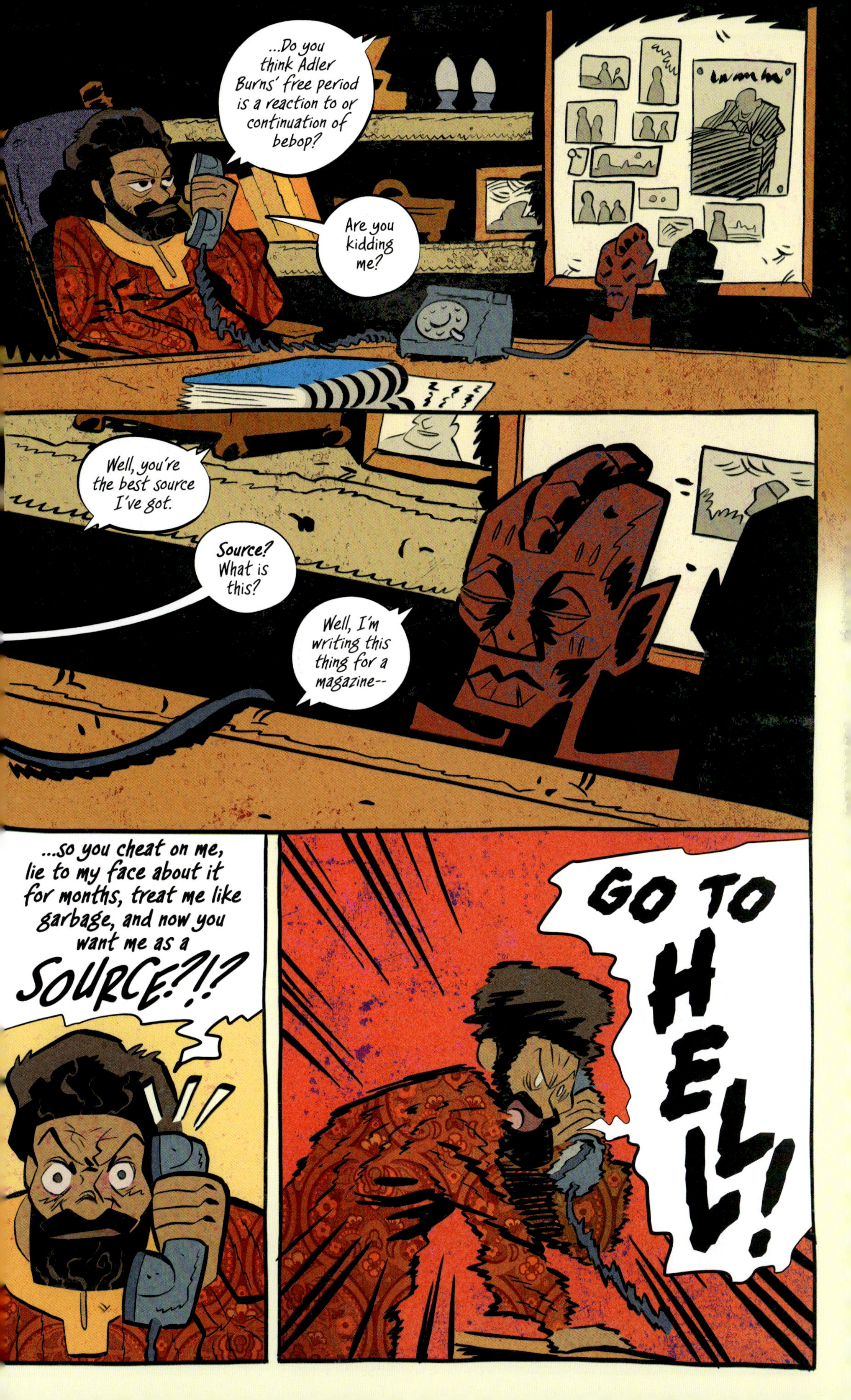
...Do you think Adler Burns' free period is a reaction to or continuation of bebop?
Are you kidding me?
Well, you're the best source I've got.
Source? What is this?
Well, I'm writing this thing for a magazine--
...so you cheat on me, lie to my face about it for months, treat me like garbage, and now you want me as a SOURCE?!?
GO TO HELL!

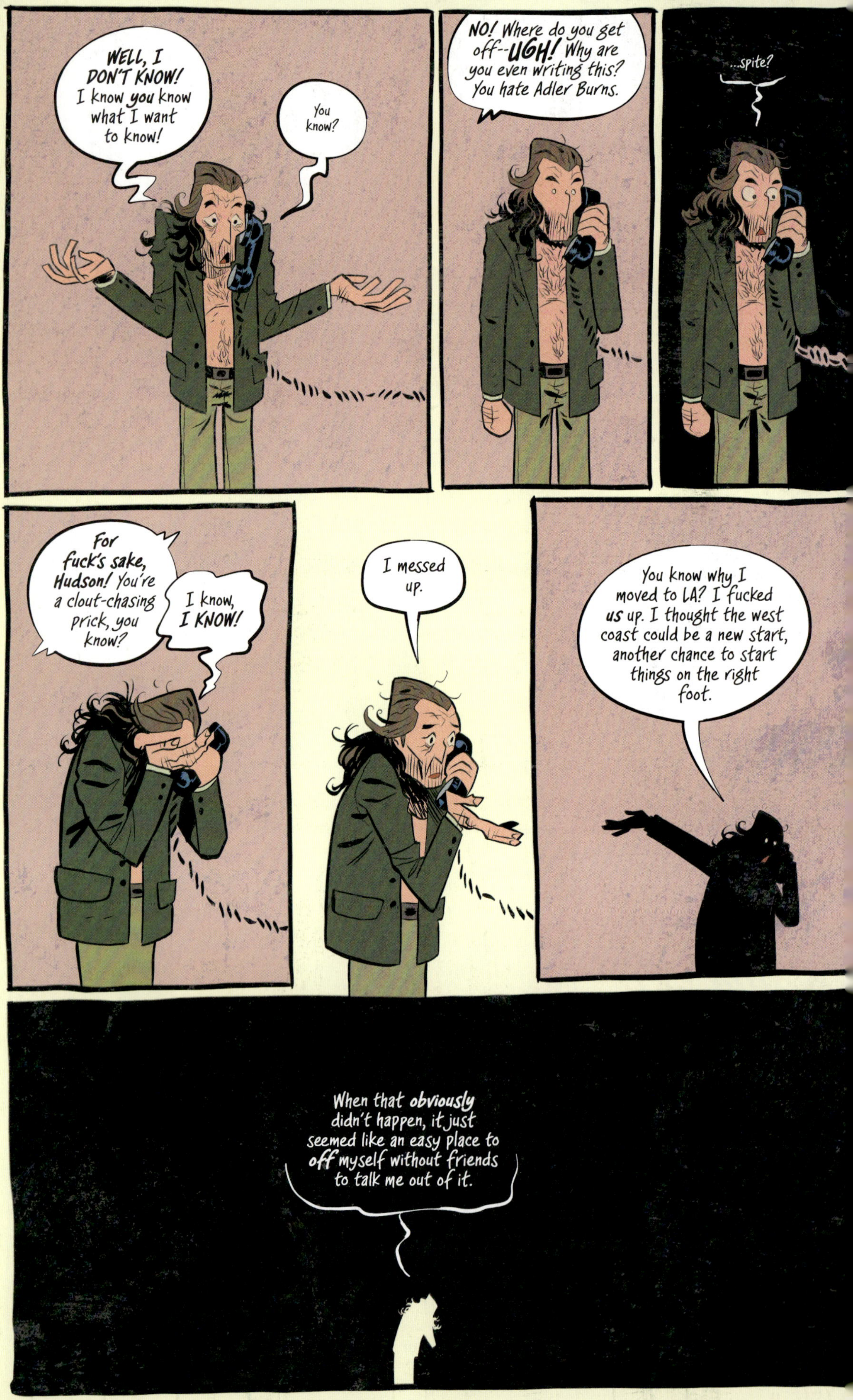
WELL, I DON'T KNOW! I know you know what I want to know!
You know?
NO! Where do you get off--UGH! Why are you even writing this? You hate Adler Burns.
...spite?
For fuck's sake, Hudson! You're a clout-chasing prick, you know?
I know, I KNOW!
I messed up.
You know why I moved to LA? I fucked us up. I thought the west coast could be a new start, another chance to start things on the right foot.
When that obviously didn't happen, it just seemed like an easy place to off myself without friends to talk me out of it.

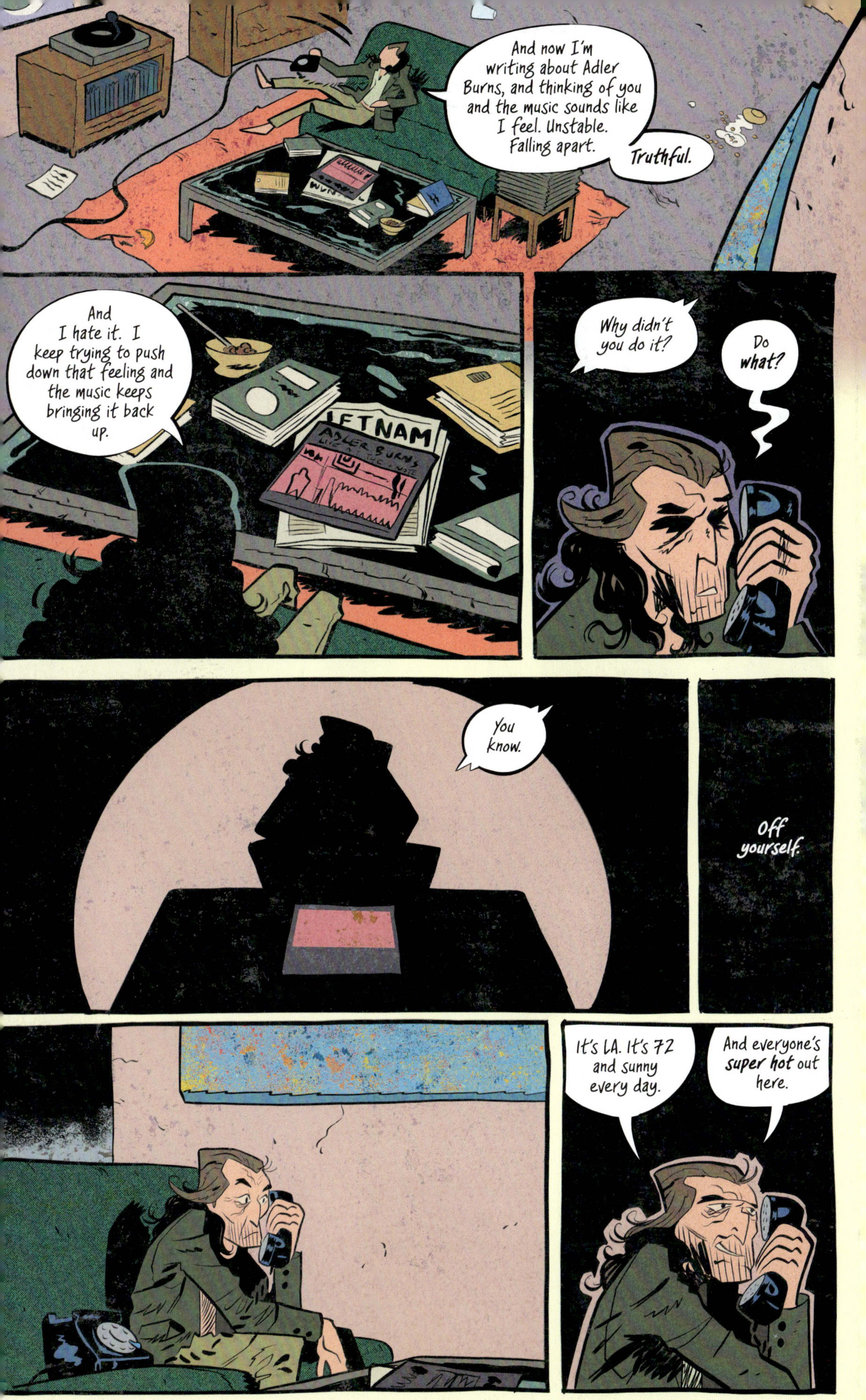
And now I'm writing about Adler Burns, and thinking of you and the music sounds like I feel. Unstable. Falling apart.
Truthful.
And I hate it. I keep trying to push down that feeling and the music keeps bringing it back up.
LETNAM
ADLER BURNS
Why didn't you do it?
Do what?
You know.
Off yourself.
It's LA. It's 72 and sunny every day.
And everyone's super hot out here.

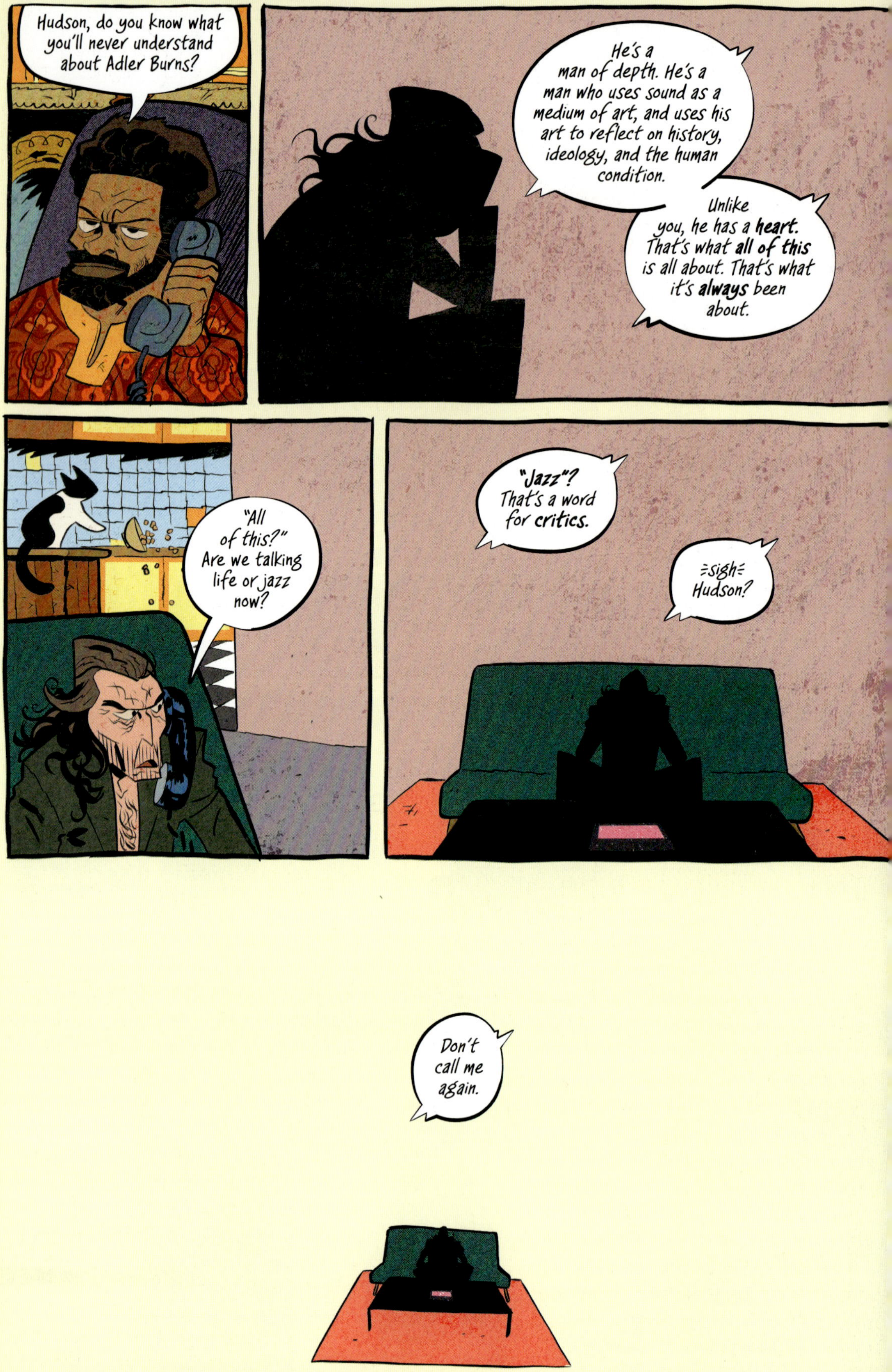
Hudson, do you know what you'll never understand about Adler Burns?
He's a man of depth. He's a man who uses sound as a medium of art, and uses his art to reflect on history, ideology, and the human condition.
Unlike you, he has a **heart**. That's what **all of this** is all about. That's what it's **always** been about.
"All of this?" Are we talking life or jazz now?
"Jazz"? That's a word for **critics**.
=sigh= Hudson?
Don't call me again.

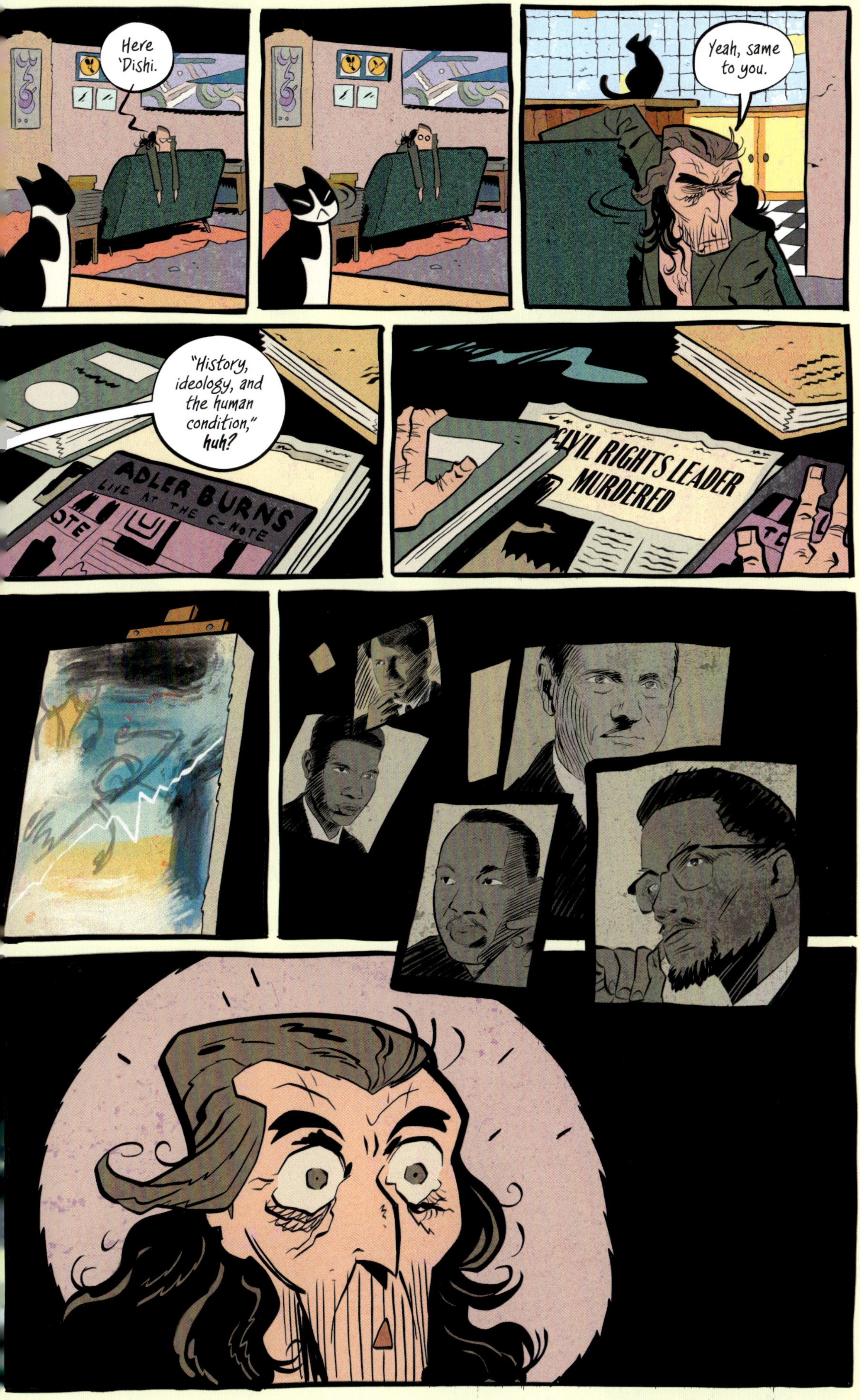
Here 'Dishi.
Yeah, same to you.
"History, ideology, and the human condition," huh?
ADLER BURNS
LIVE AT THE C-NOTE
CIVIL RIGHTS LEADER MURDERED

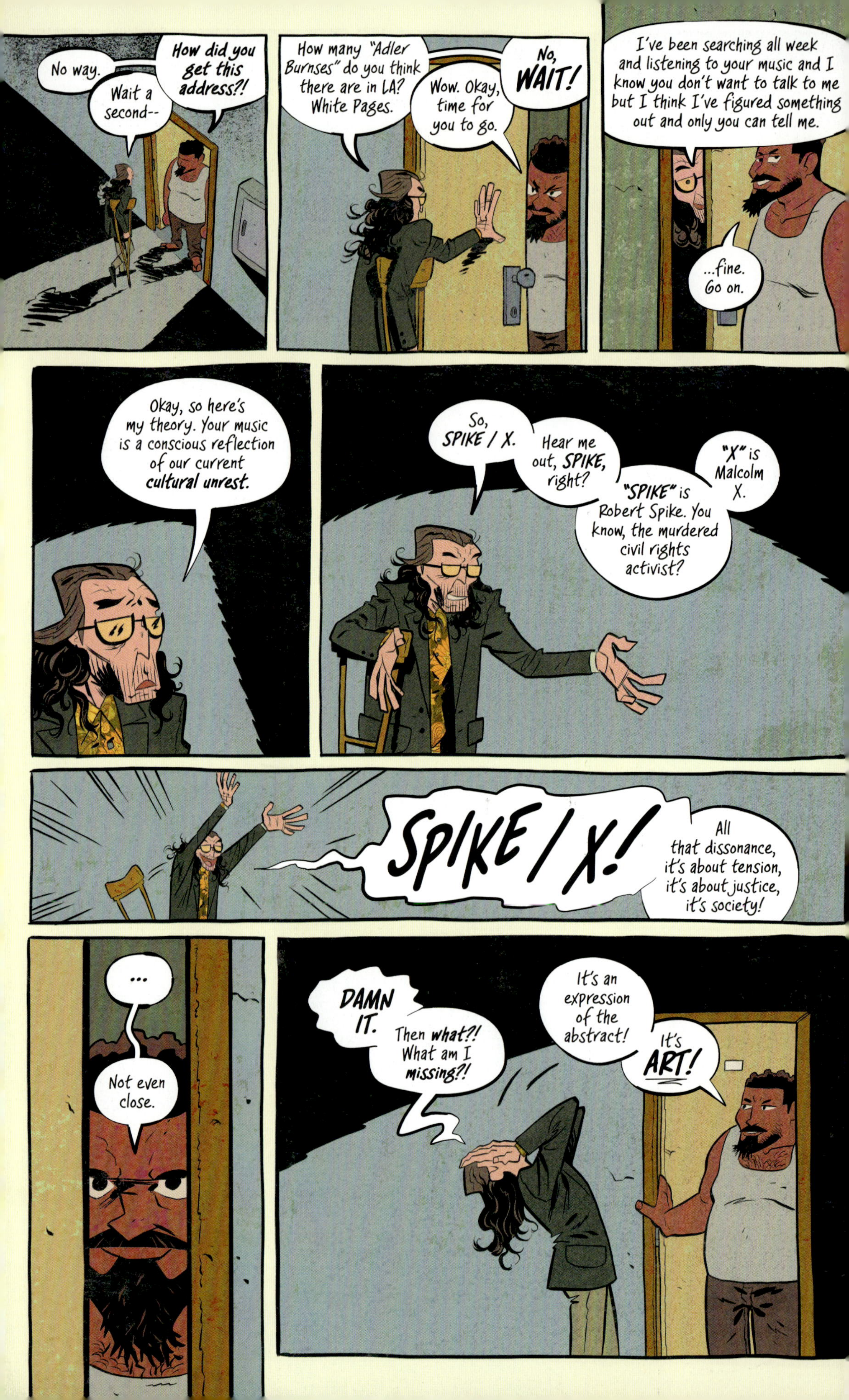
No way.
Wait a second--
How did you get this address?!
How many "Adler Burnses" do you think there are in LA? White Pages.
Wow. Okay, time for you to go.
No, WAIT!
I've been searching all week and listening to your music and I know you don't want to talk to me but I think I've figured something out and only you can tell me.
...fine. Go on.
Okay, so here's my theory. Your music is a conscious reflection of our current cultural unrest.
So, SPIKE / X.
Hear me out, SPIKE, right?
"SPIKE" is Robert Spike. You know, the murdered civil rights activist?
"X" is Malcolm X.
SPIKE / X!
All that dissonance, it's about tension, it's about justice, it's society!
...
Not even close.
DAMN IT.
Then what?! What am I missing?!
It's an expression of the abstract!
It's ART!

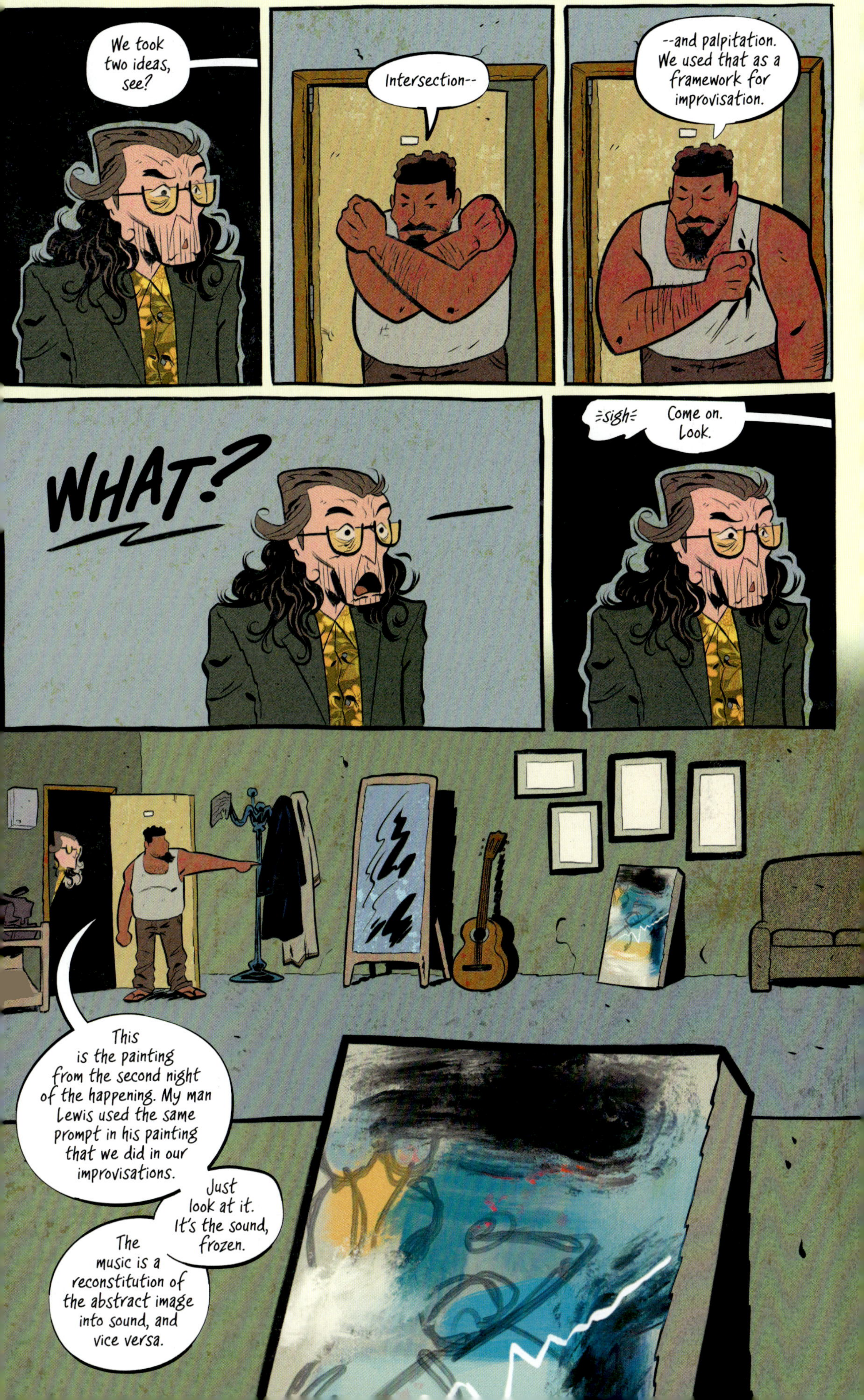

We took two ideas, see?
Intersection--
--and palpitation. We used that as a framework for improvisation.
WHAT?
=sigh= Come on. Look.
This is the painting from the second night of the happening. My man Lewis used the same prompt in his painting that we did in our improvisations.
Just look at it. It's the sound, frozen.
The music is a reconstitution of the abstract image into sound, and vice versa.

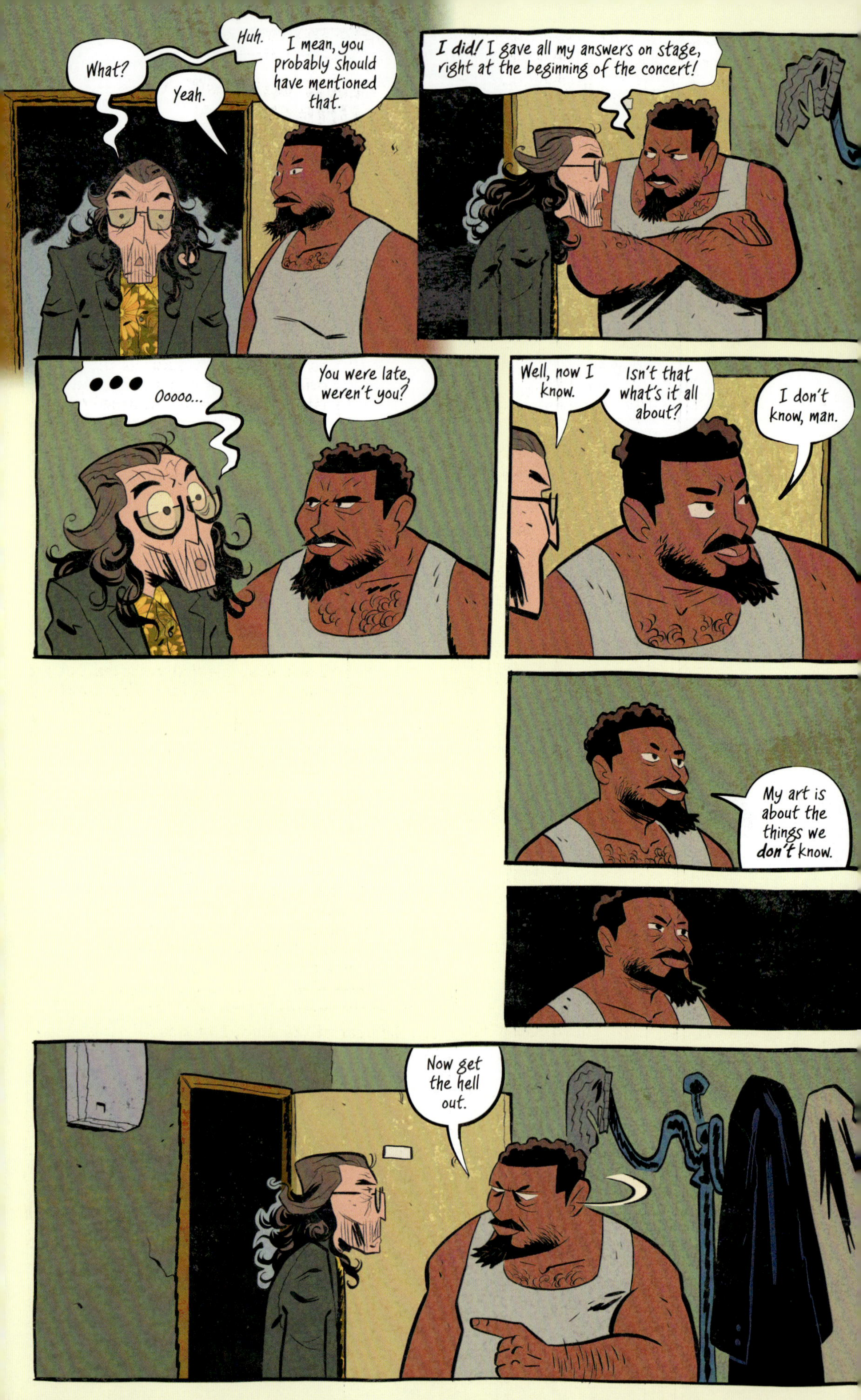
What?
Huh.
Yeah.
I mean, you probably should have mentioned that.
I did! I gave all my answers on stage, right at the beginning of the concert!
... Ooooo...
You were late, weren't you?
Well, now I know.
Isn't that what's it all about?
I don't know, man.
My art is about the things we don't know.
Now get the hell out.

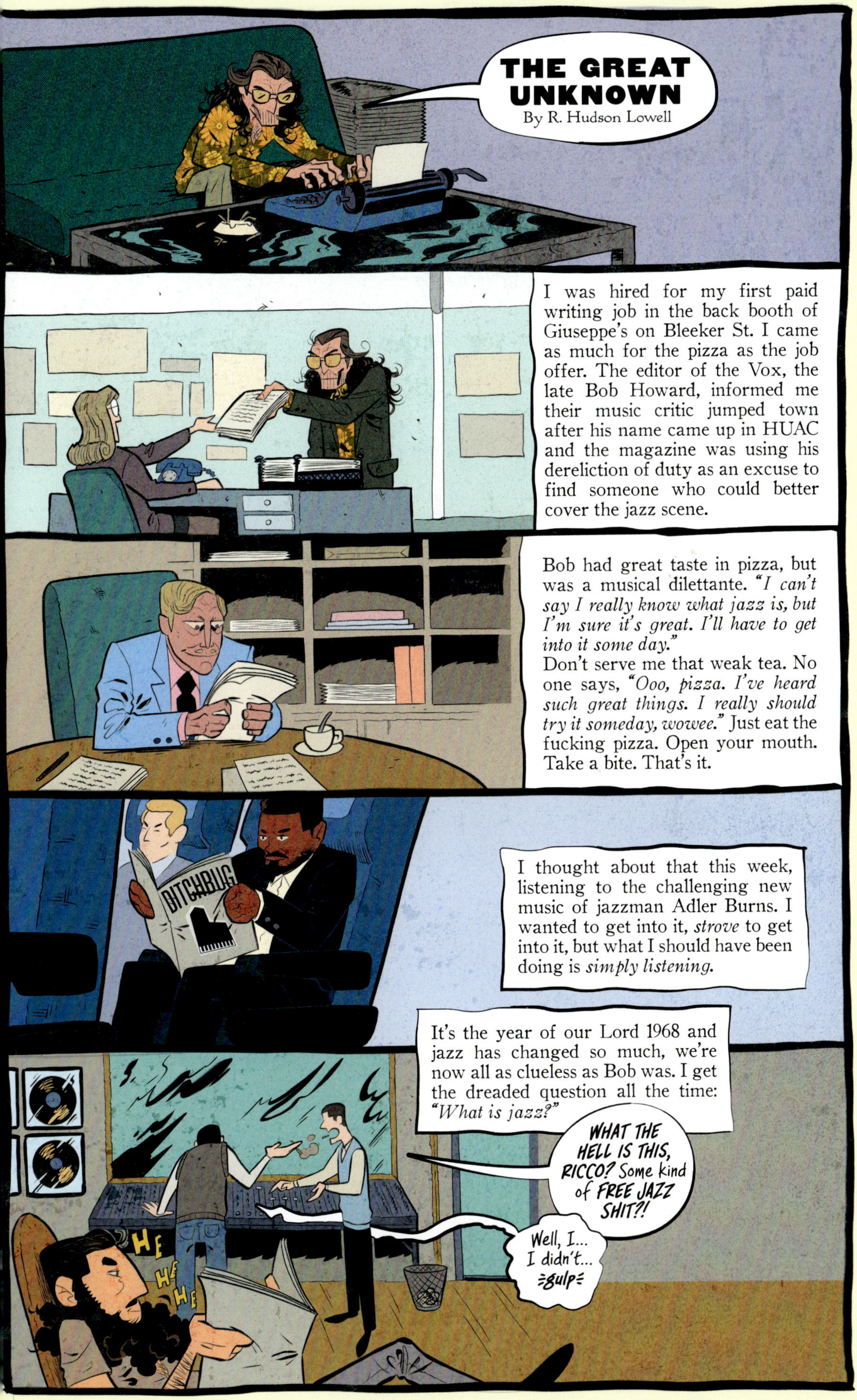

THE GREAT UNKNOWN
By R. Hudson Lowell
I was hired for my first paid writing job in the back booth of Giuseppe's on Bleeker St. I came as much for the pizza as the job offer. The editor of the Vox, the late Bob Howard, informed me their music critic jumped town after his name came up in HUAC and the magazine was using his dereliction of duty as an excuse to find someone who could better cover the jazz scene.
Bob had great taste in pizza, but was a musical dilettante. *"I can't say I really know what jazz is, but I'm sure it's great. I'll have to get into it some day."*
Don't serve me that weak tea. No one says, *"Ooo, pizza. I've heard such great things. I really should try it someday, wowee."* Just eat the fucking pizza. Open your mouth. Take a bite. That's it.
BITCHBUG
I thought about that this week, listening to the challenging new music of jazzman Adler Burns. I wanted to get into it, *strove* to get into it, but what I should have been doing is *simply listening.*
It's the year of our Lord 1968 and jazz has changed so much, we're now all as clueless as Bob was. I get the dreaded question all the time: *"What is jazz?"*
WHAT THE HELL IS THIS, RICCO? Some kind of FREE JAZZ SHIT?!
Well, I... I didn't... ≈gulp≈
HE HE HE

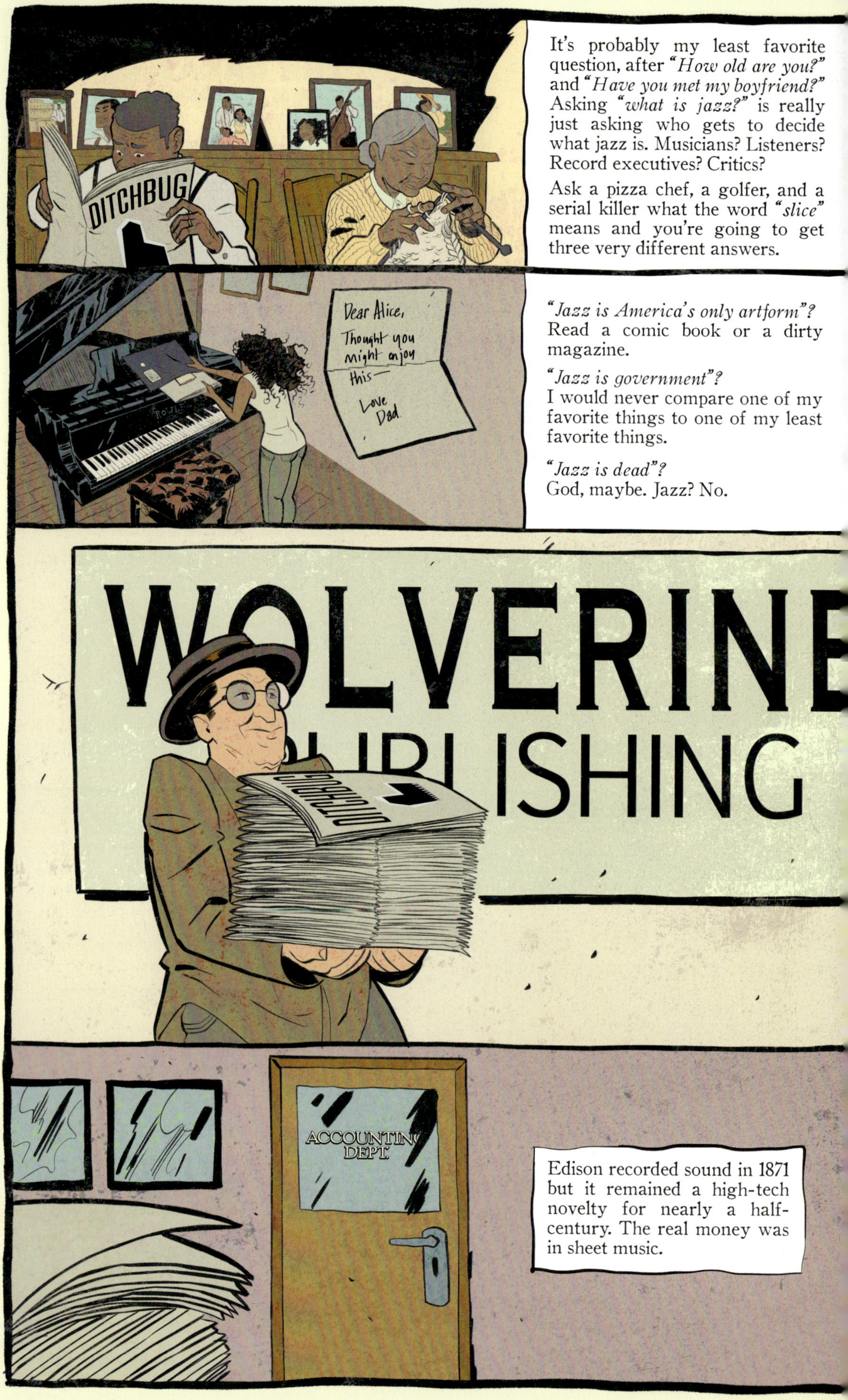

It's probably my least favorite question, after *"How old are you?"* and *"Have you met my boyfriend?"* Asking *"what is jazz?"* is really just asking who gets to decide what jazz is. Musicians? Listeners? Record executives? Critics?
Ask a pizza chef, a golfer, and a serial killer what the word *"slice"* means and you're going to get three very different answers.
DITCHBUG
"Jazz is America's only artform"? Read a comic book or a dirty magazine.
"Jazz is government"? I would never compare one of my favorite things to one of my least favorite things.
"Jazz is dead"? God, maybe. Jazz? No.
Dear Alice,
Thought you might enjoy this—
Love Dad
WOLVERINE
Edison recorded sound in 1871 but it remained a high-tech novelty for nearly a half-century. The real money was in sheet music.

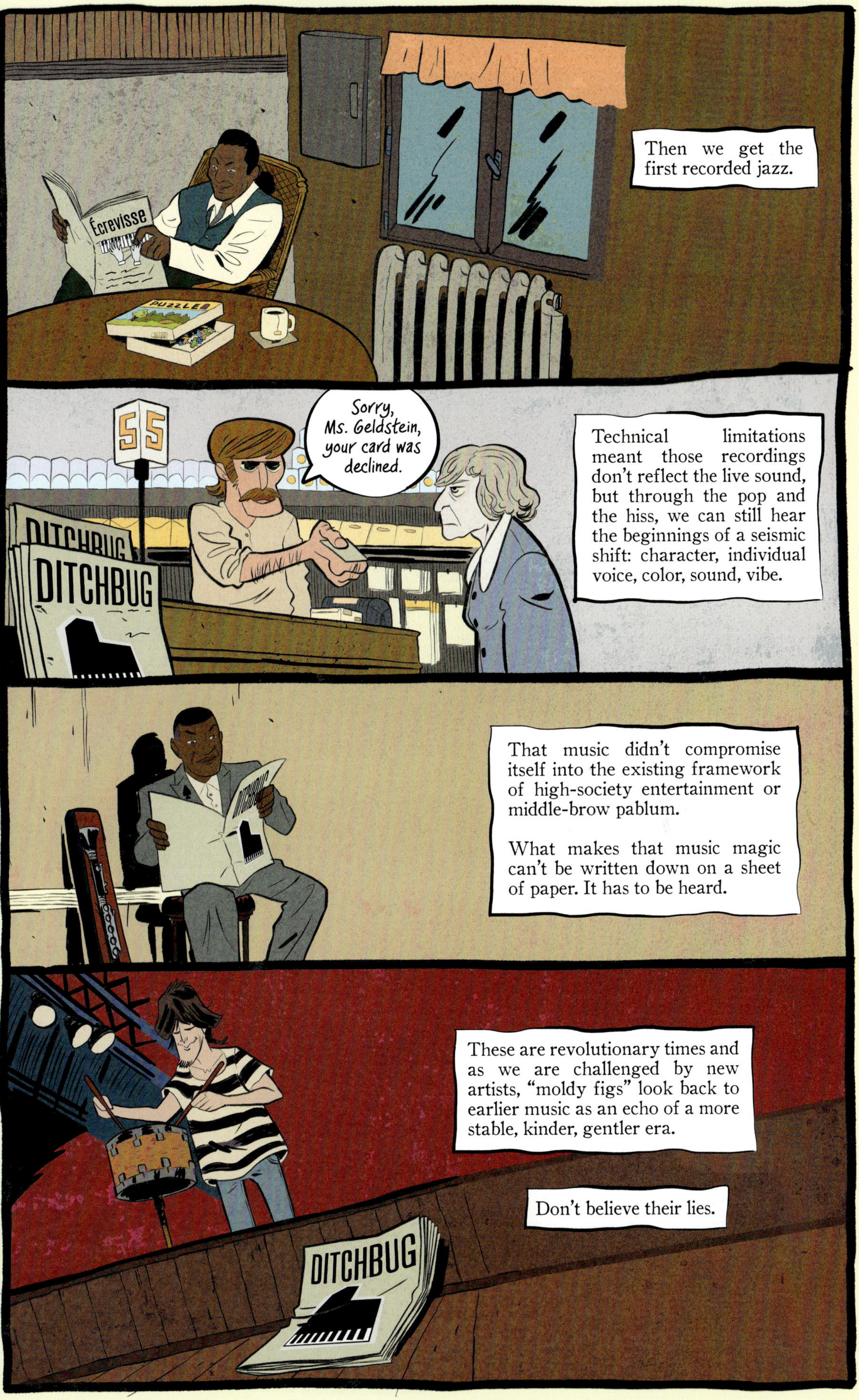

Écrevisse
PUZZLE
Then we get the first recorded jazz.
55
DITCHBUG
DITCHBUG
Sorry, Ms. Geldstein, your card was declined.
Technical limitations meant those recordings don't reflect the live sound, but through the pop and the hiss, we can still hear the beginnings of a seismic shift: character, individual voice, color, sound, vibe.
That music didn't compromise itself into the existing framework of high-society entertainment or middle-brow pablum.
What makes that music magic can't be written down on a sheet of paper. It has to be heard.
These are revolutionary times and as we are challenged by new artists, "moldy figs" look back to earlier music as an echo of a more stable, kinder, gentler era.
Don't believe their lies.
DITCHBUG

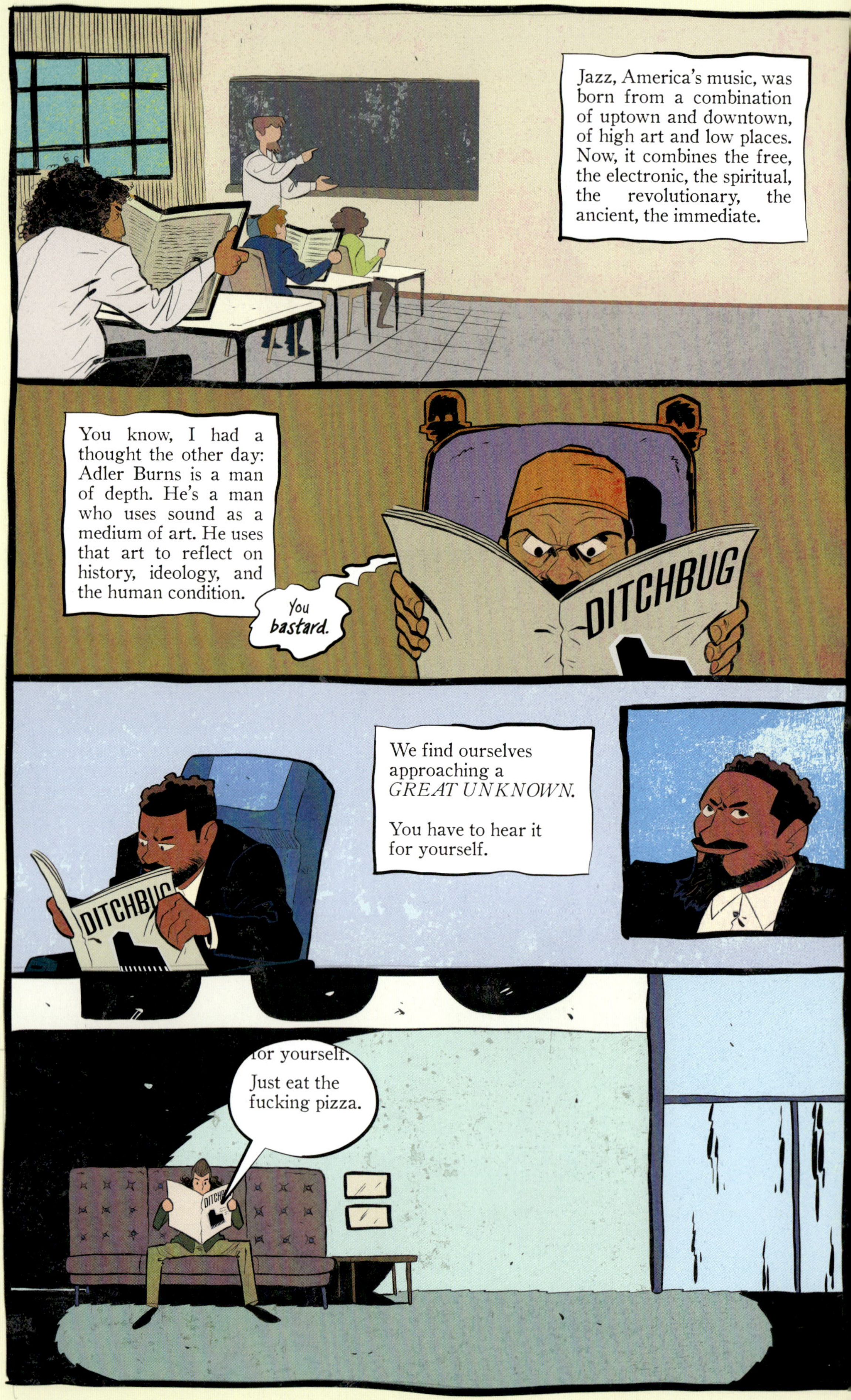
Jazz, America's music, was born from a combination of uptown and downtown, of high art and low places. Now, it combines the free, the electronic, the spiritual, the revolutionary, the ancient, the immediate.
You know, I had a thought the other day: Adler Burns is a man of depth. He's a man who uses sound as a medium of art. He uses that art to reflect on history, ideology, and the human condition.
You bastard.
DITCHBUG
We find ourselves approaching a *GREAT UNKNOWN.*
You have to hear it for yourself.
for yourself.
Just eat the fucking pizza.

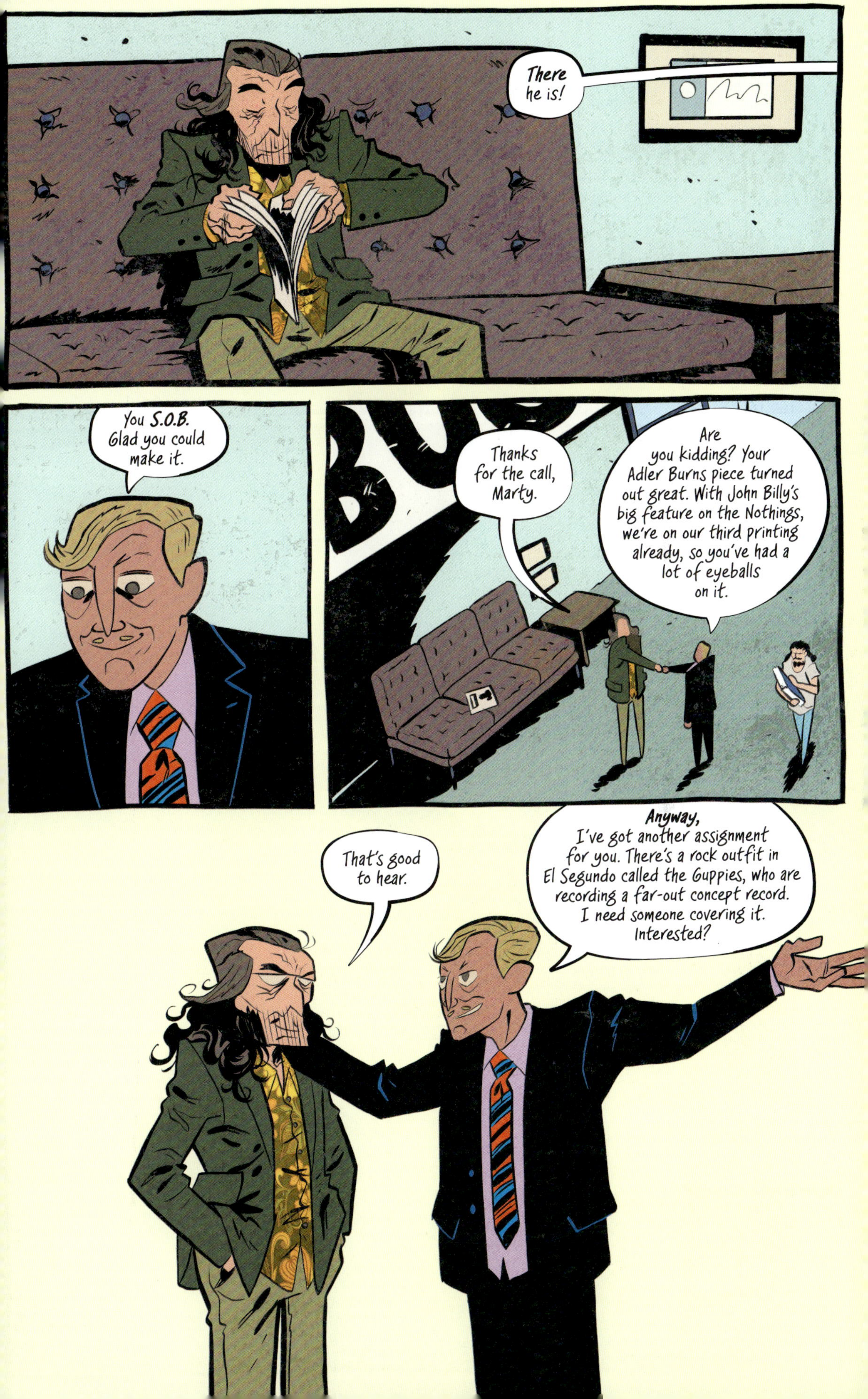
There he is!
You S.O.B. Glad you could make it.
Thanks for the call, Marty.
Are you kidding? Your Adler Burns piece turned out great. With John Billy's big feature on the Nothings, we're on our third printing already, so you've had a lot of eyeballs on it.
That's good to hear.
Anyway, I've got another assignment for you. There's a rock outfit in El Segundo called the Guppies, who are recording a far-out concept record. I need someone covering it. Interested?

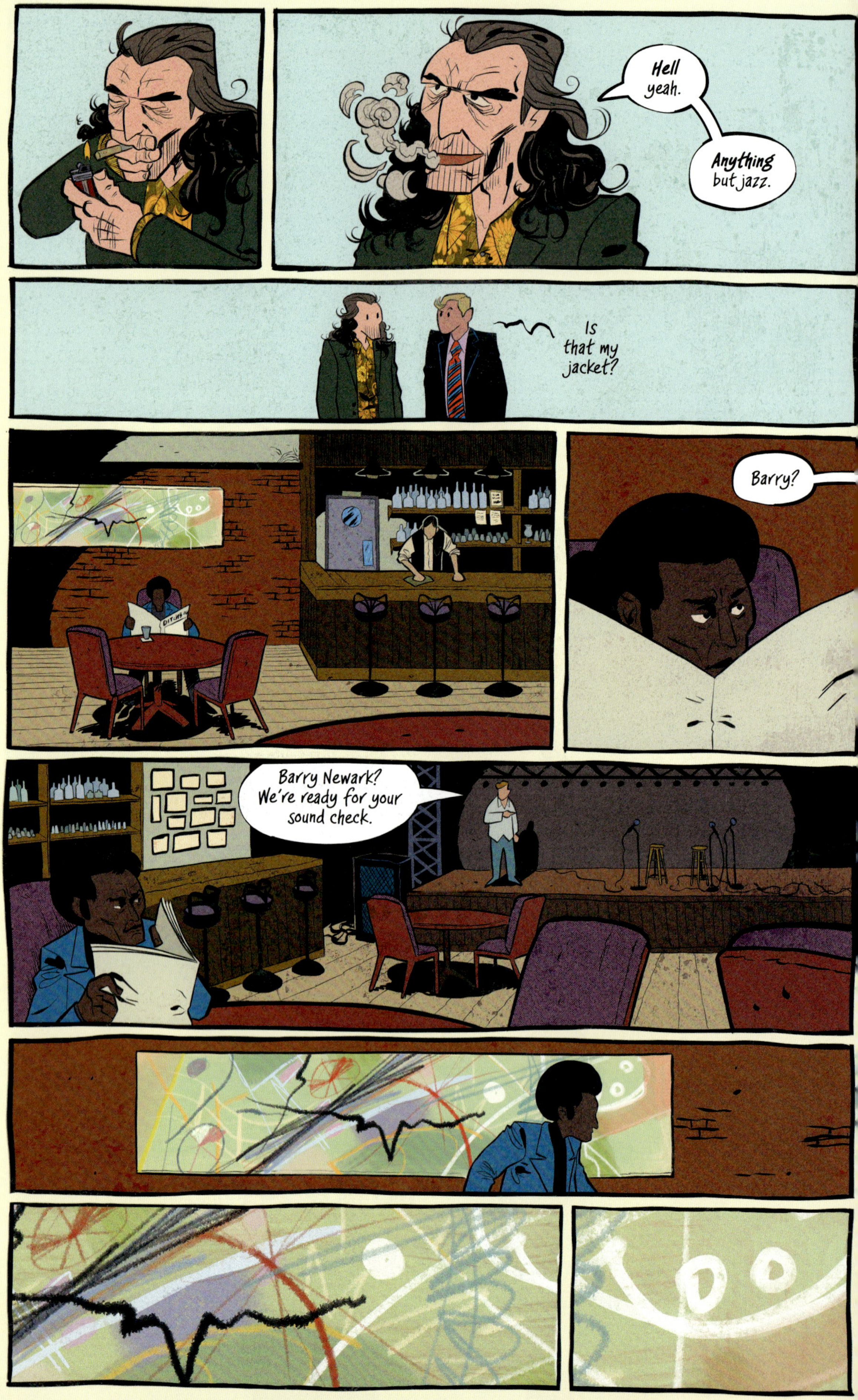
Hell yeah.
Anything but jazz.
Is that my jacket?
Barry?
Barry Newark? We're ready for your sound check.

6.
THE GREAT UNKNOWN

WORLDWIDE
1977

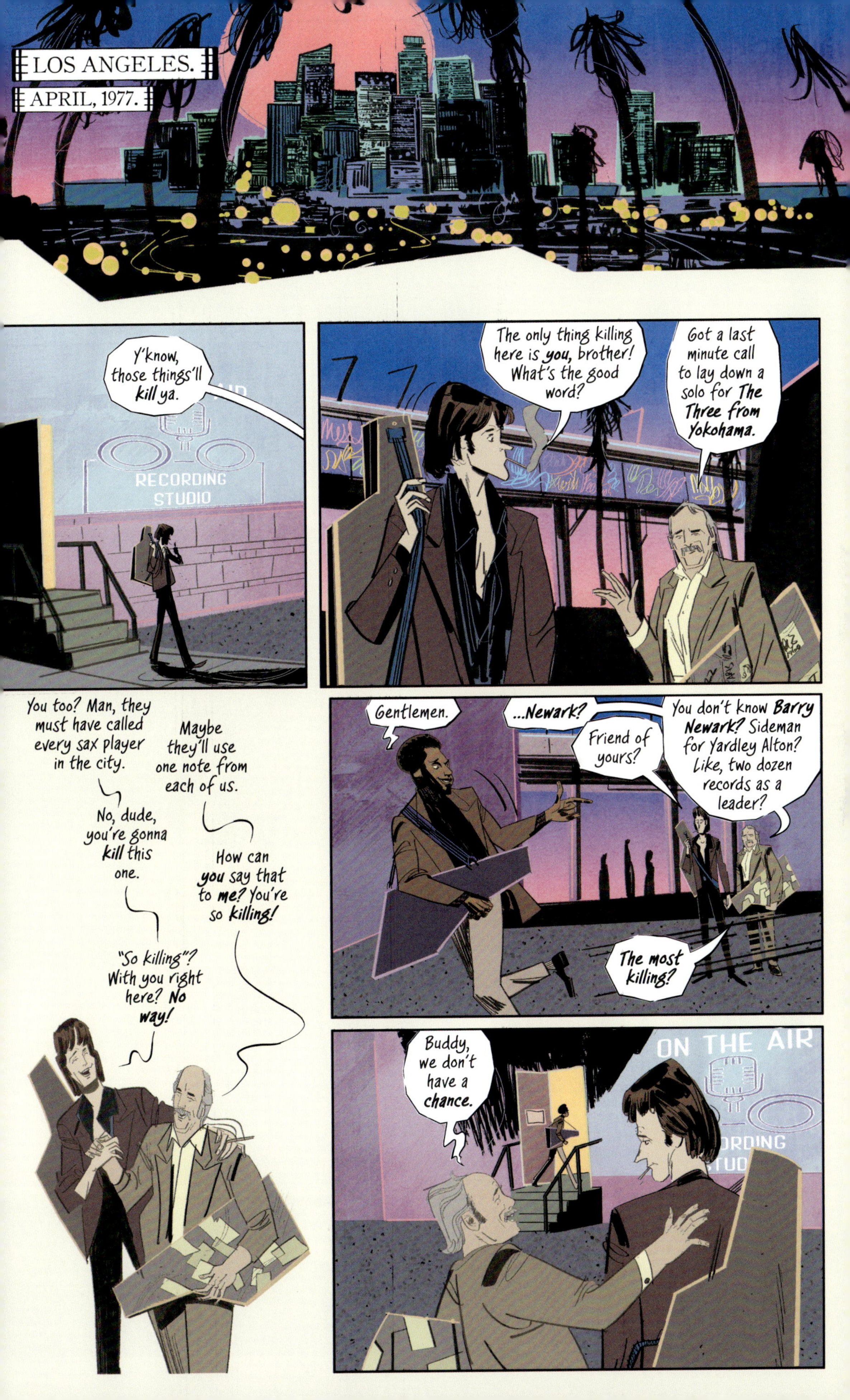
LOS ANGELES.
APRIL, 1977.
Y'know, those things'll kill ya.
RECORDING STUDIO
The only thing killing here is you, brother! What's the good word?
Got a last minute call to lay down a solo for The Three from Yokohama.
You too? Man, they must have called every sax player in the city.
Maybe they'll use one note from each of us.
No, dude, you're gonna kill this one.
How can you say that to me? You're so killing!
"So killing"? With you right here? No way!
Gentlemen.
...Newark?
Friend of yours?
You don't know Barry Newark? Sideman for Yardley Alton? Like, two dozen records as a leader?
The most killing?
ON THE AIR
Buddy, we don't have a chance.

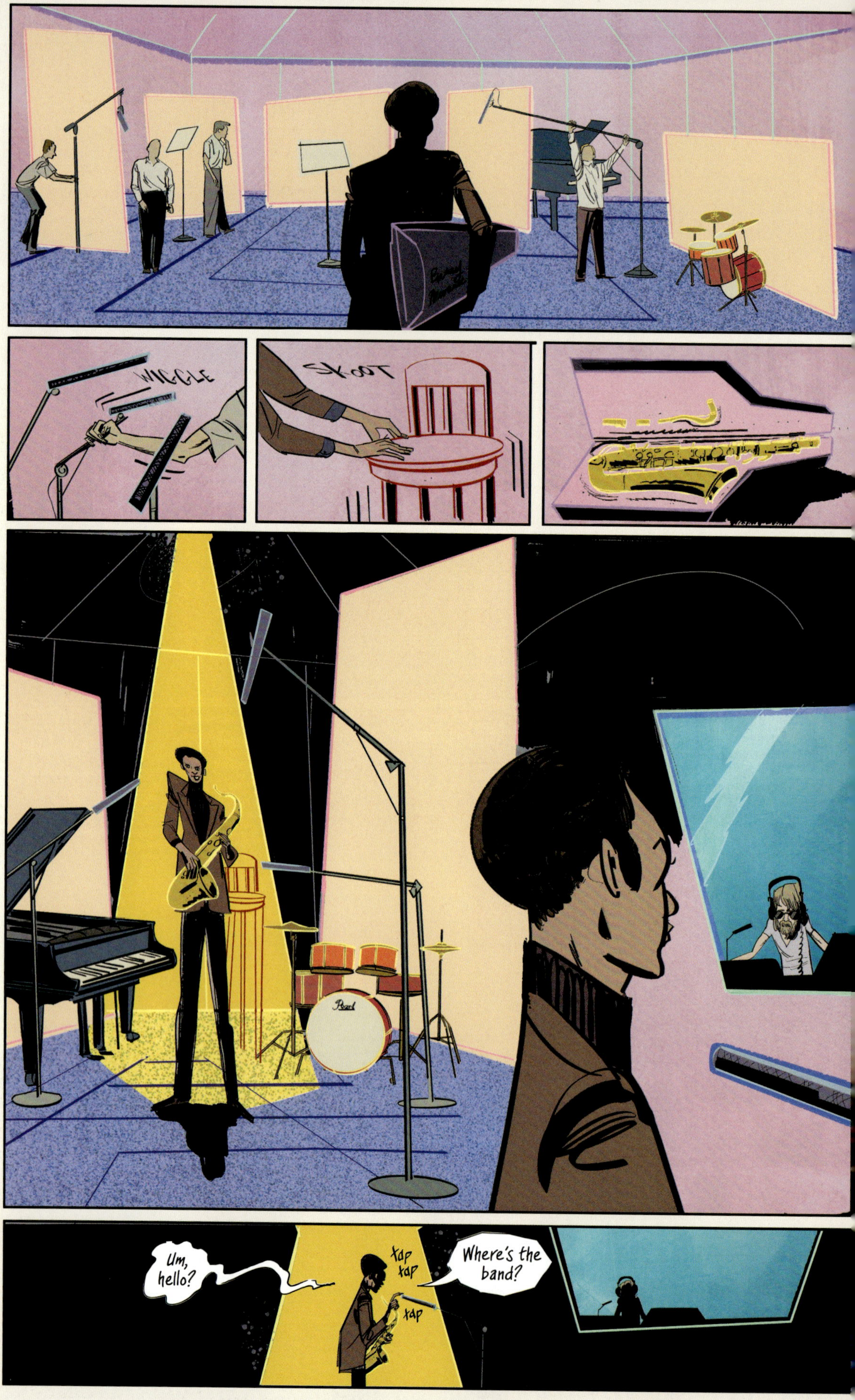
WIGGLE
SKOOT
Um, hello?
tap tap
tap
Where's the band?

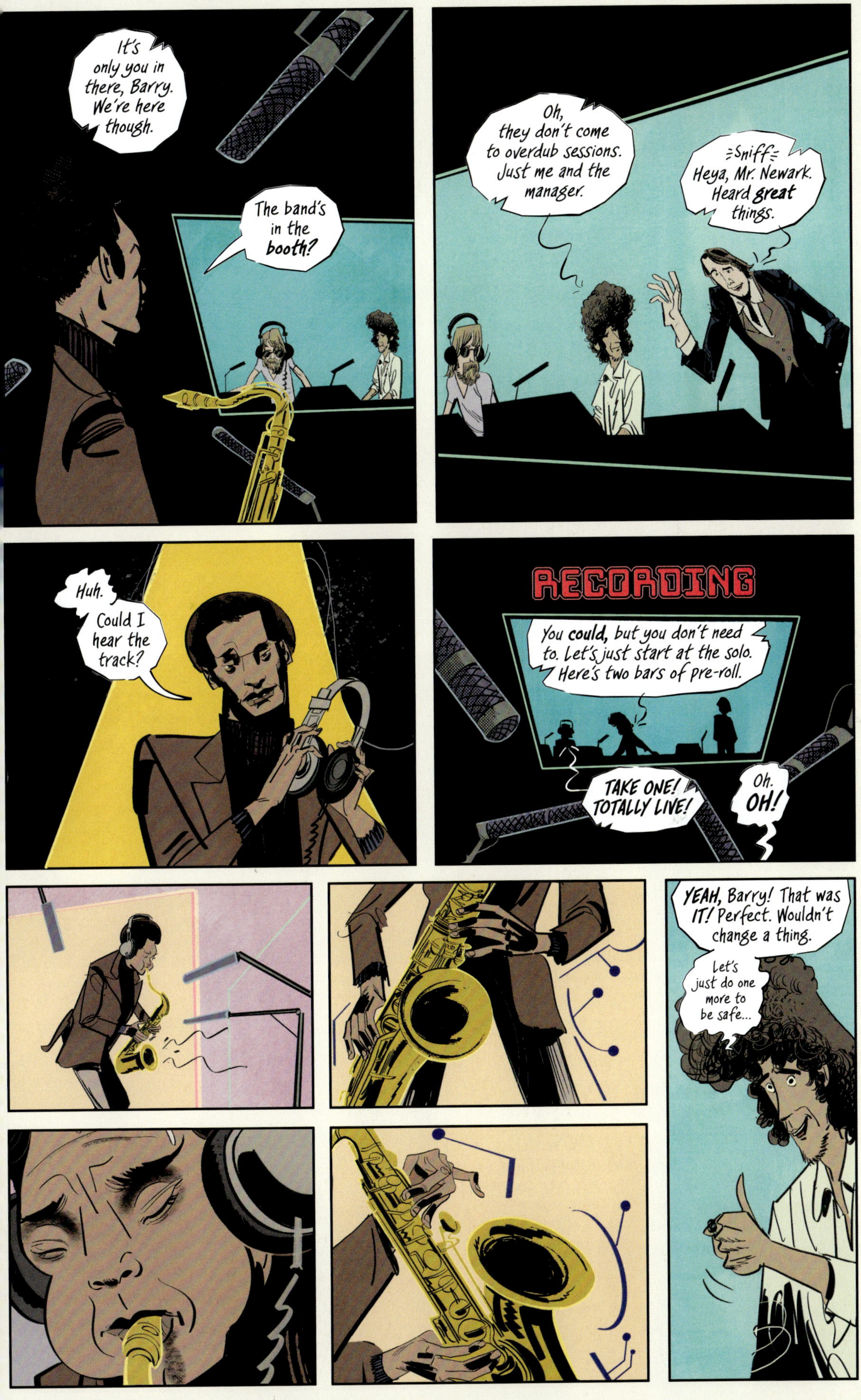
It's only you in there, Barry. We're here though.
The band's in the booth?
Oh, they don't come to overdub sessions. Just me and the manager.
Sniff
Heya, Mr. Newark. Heard great things.
Huh.
Could I hear the track?
RECORDING
You could, but you don't need to. Let's just start at the solo. Here's two bars of pre-roll.
TAKE ONE! TOTALLY LIVE!
Oh. OH!
YEAH, Barry! That was IT! Perfect. Wouldn't change a thing.
Let's just do one more to be safe...

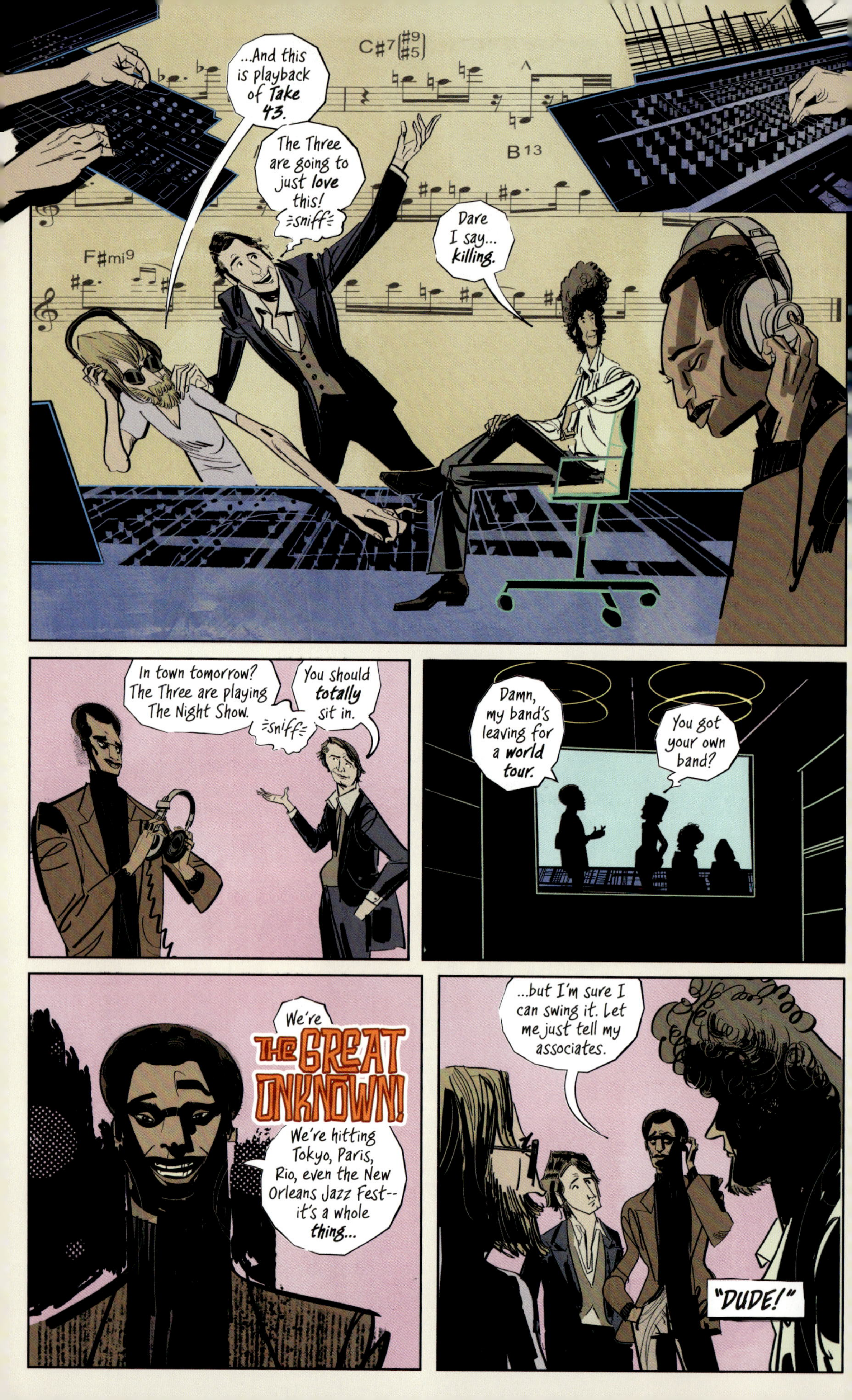

...And this is playback of Take 43.
The Three are going to just love this!
=sniff=
C#7(#9 #5)
B13
F#mi9
Dare I say... killing.
In town tomorrow? The Three are playing The Night Show.
=sniff=
You should totally sit in.
Damn, my band's leaving for a world tour.
You got your own band?
We're
THE GREAT UNKNOWN!
We're hitting Tokyo, Paris, Rio, even the New Orleans Jazz Fest--it's a whole thing...
...but I'm sure I can swing it. Let me just tell my associates.
"DUDE!"

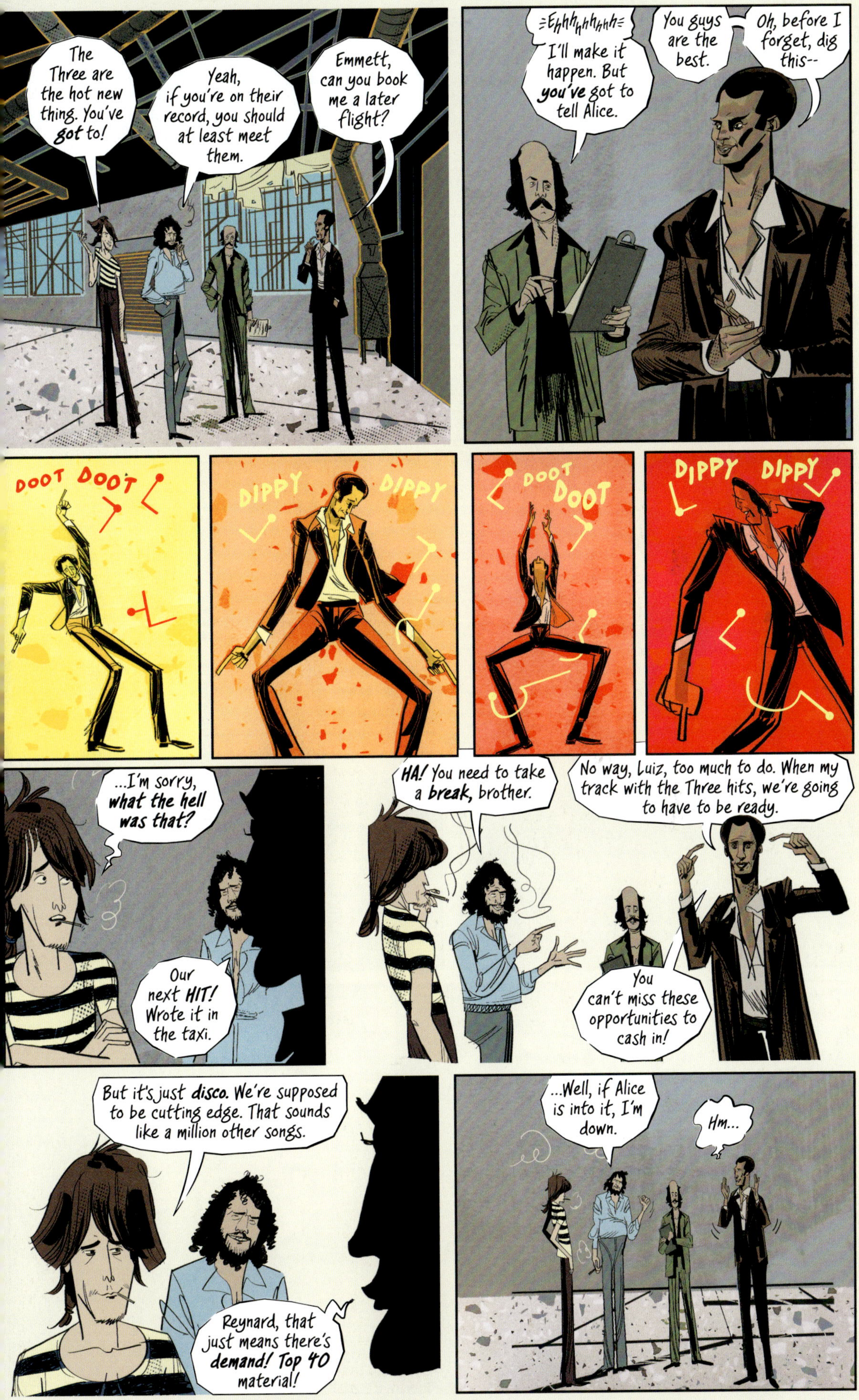

The Three are the hot new thing. You've **got** to!
Yeah, if you're on their record, you should at least meet them.
Emmett, can you book me a later flight?
=Ehhhhhhhh=
I'll make it happen. But **you've** got to tell Alice.
You guys are the best.
Oh, before I forget, dig this--
DOOT DOOT
DIPPY DIPPY
DOOT DOOT
DIPPY DIPPY
...I'm sorry, **what the hell was that?**
Our next **HIT!** Wrote it in the taxi.
HA! You need to take a **break**, brother.
No way, Luiz, too much to do. When my track with the Three hits, we're going to have to be ready.
You can't miss these opportunities to cash in!
But it's just **disco.** We're supposed to be cutting edge. That sounds like a million other songs.
Reynard, that just means there's **demand! Top 40** material!
...Well, if Alice is into it, I'm down.
Hm...

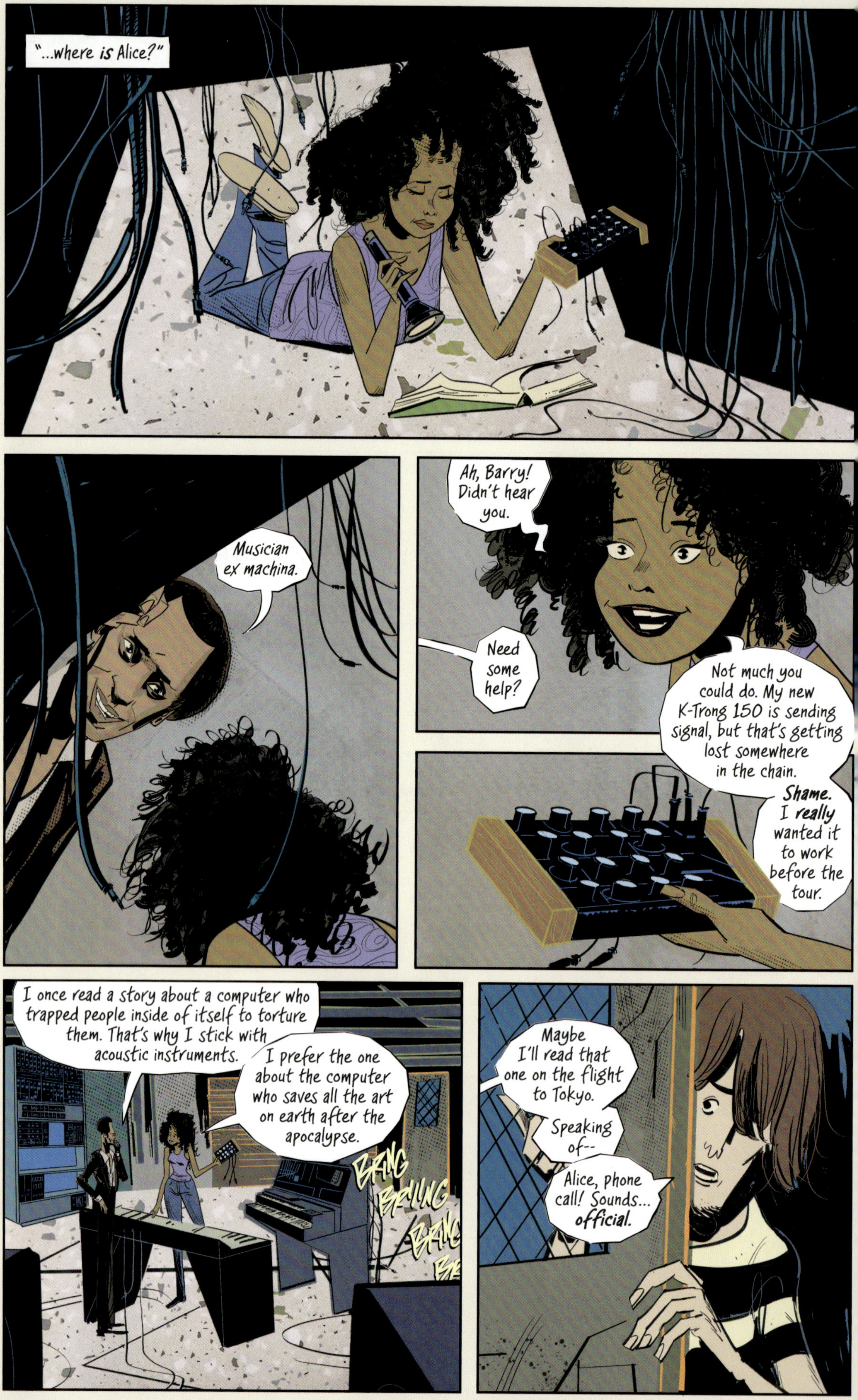
"...where is Alice?"
Musician ex machina.
Ah, Barry! Didn't hear you.
Need some help?
Not much you could do. My new K-Trong 150 is sending signal, but that's getting lost somewhere in the chain.
Shame. I really wanted it to work before the tour.
I once read a story about a computer who trapped people inside of itself to torture them. That's why I stick with acoustic instruments.
I prefer the one about the computer who saves all the art on earth after the apocalypse.
BRING BRING BRING
Maybe I'll read that one on the flight to Tokyo.
Speaking of--
Alice, phone call! Sounds... official.

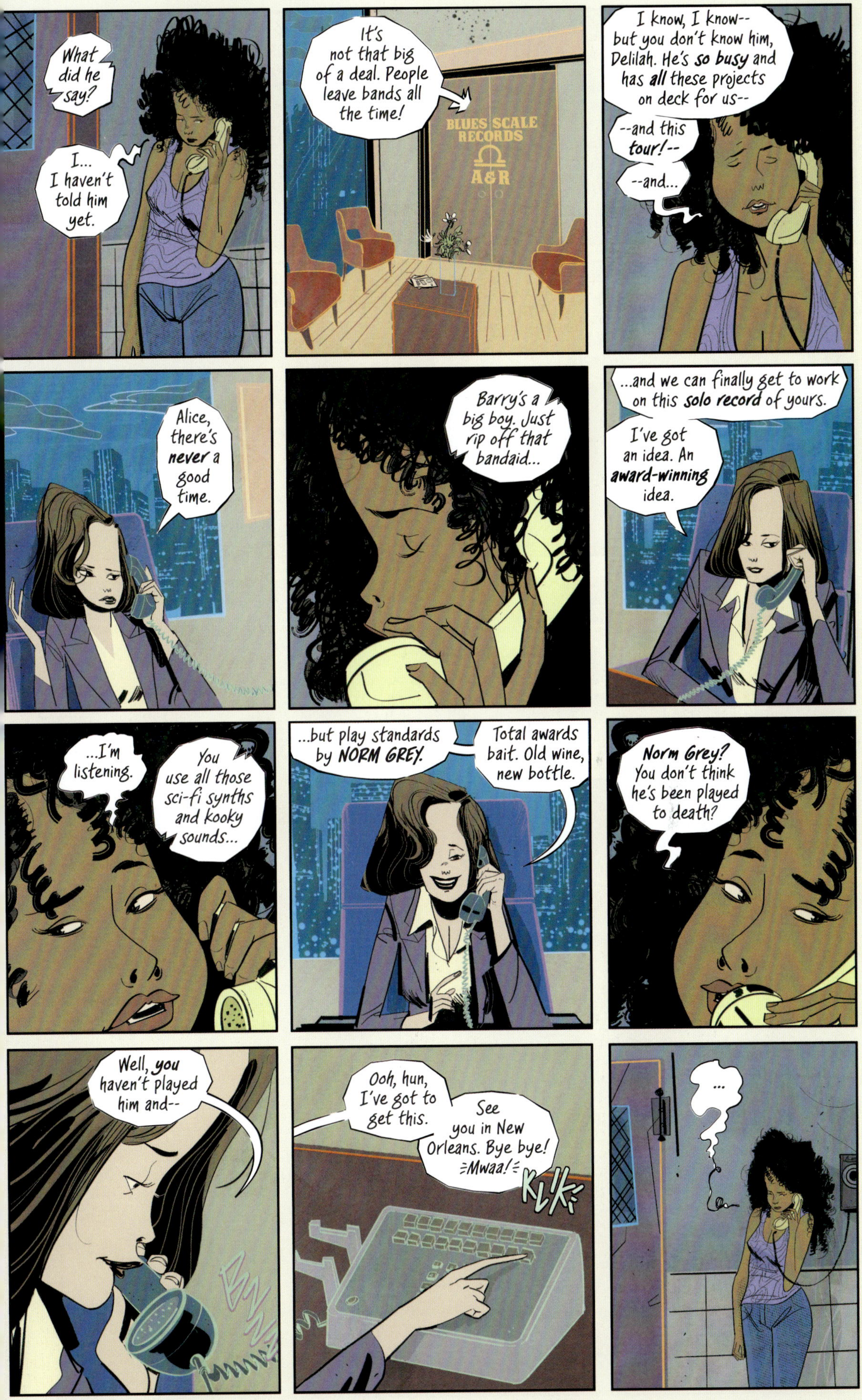
What did he say?
I... I haven't told him yet.
It's not that big of a deal. People leave bands all the time!
BLUES SCALE RECORDS
A&R
I know, I know-- but you don't know him, Delilah. He's **so busy** and has **all** these projects on deck for us--
--and this **tour!**--
--and...
Alice, there's **never** a good time.
Barry's a big boy. Just rip off that bandaid...
...and we can finally get to work on this **solo record** of yours.
I've got an idea. An **award-winning** idea.
...I'm listening.
You use all those sci-fi synths and kooky sounds...
...but play standards by **NORM GREY.**
Total awards bait. Old wine, new bottle.
Norm Grey? You don't think he's been played to death?
Well, **you** haven't played him and--
Ooh, hun, I've got to get this.
See you in New Orleans. Bye bye! Mwaa!
KLIK
...

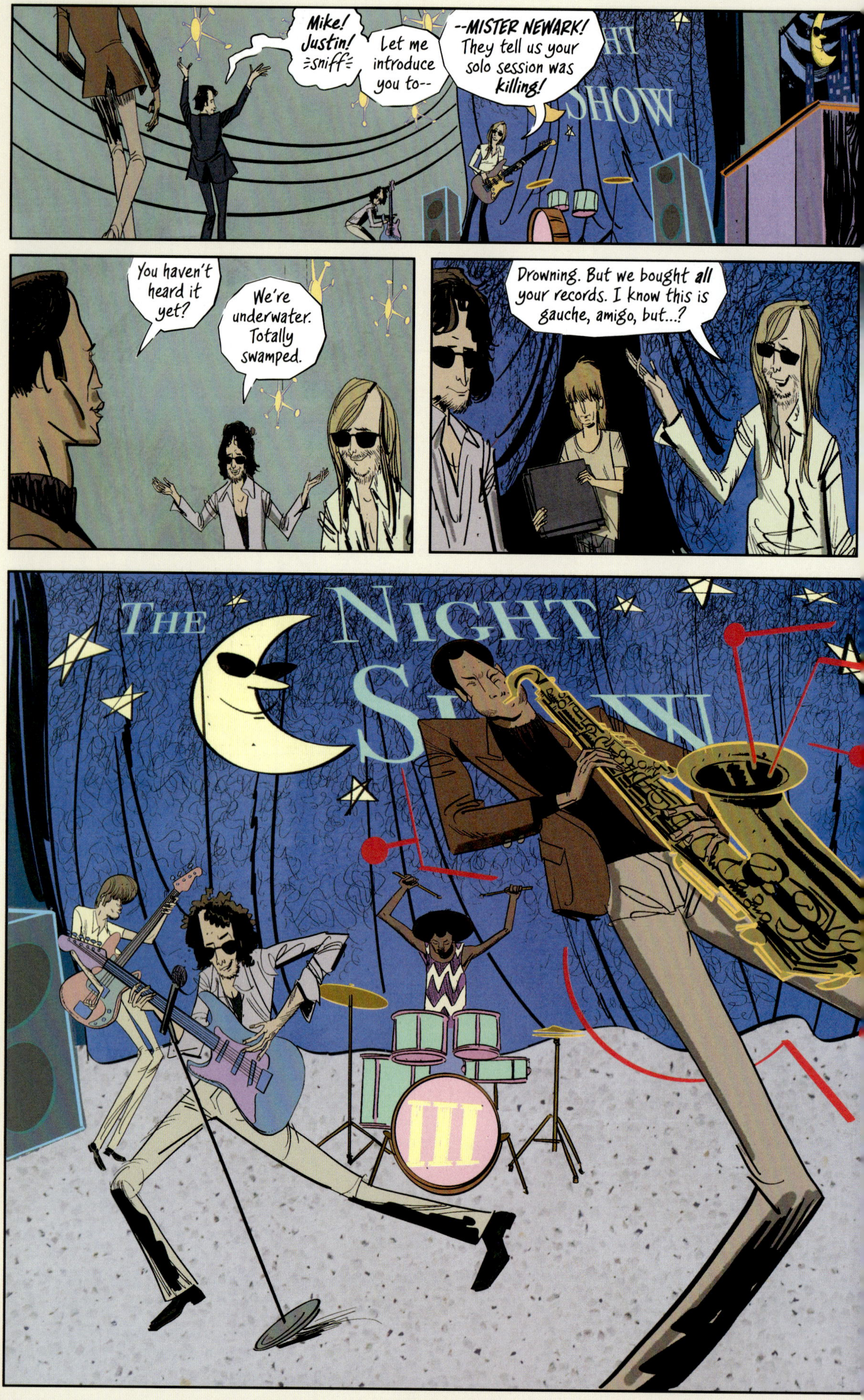
Mike! Justin! sniff
Let me introduce you to--
--MISTER NEWARK! They tell us your solo session was killing!
You haven't heard it yet?
We're underwater. Totally swamped.
Drowning. But we bought all your records. I know this is gauche, amigo, but...?
THE NIGHT SHOW
III

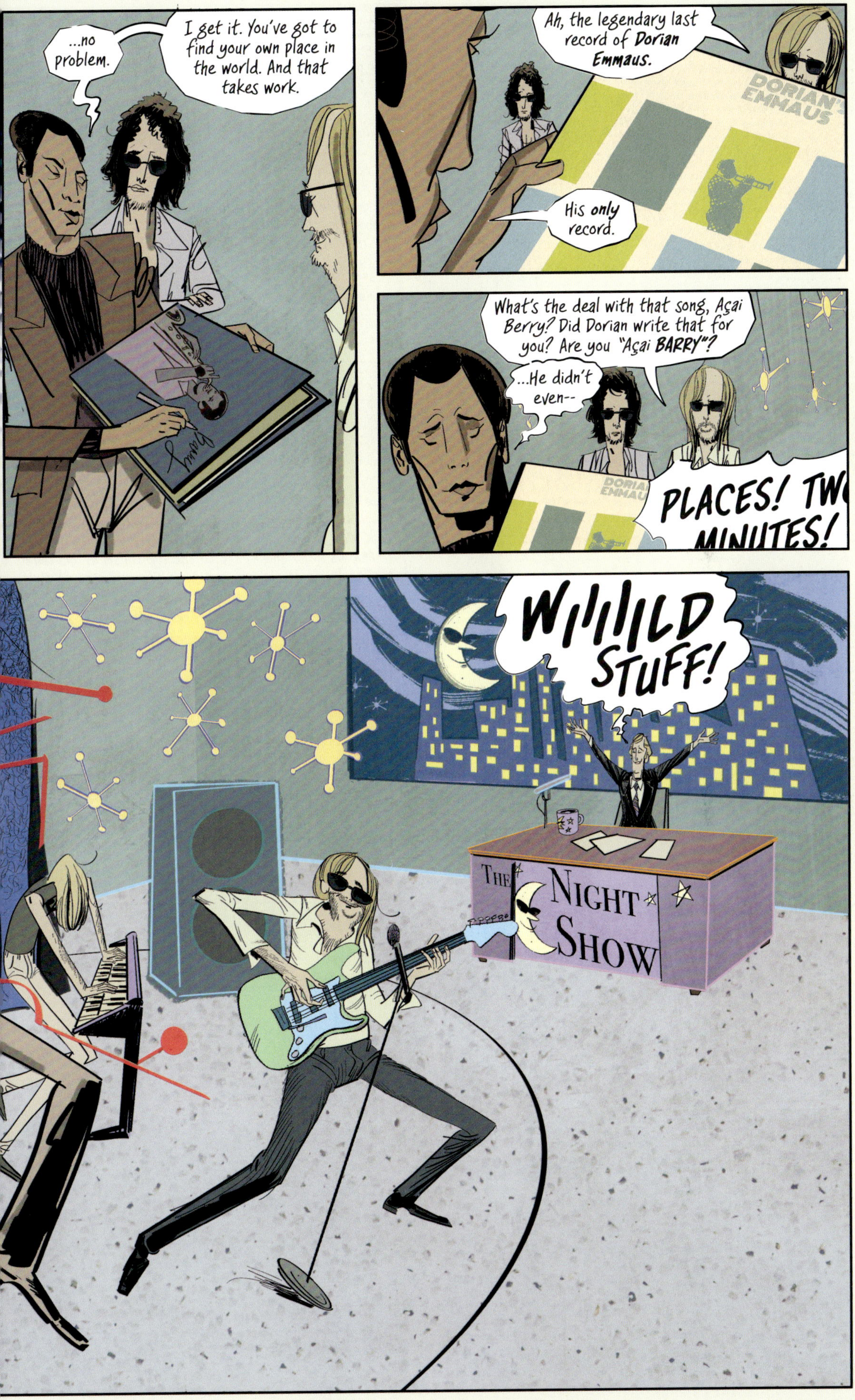
...no problem.
I get it. You've got to find your own place in the world. And that takes work.
Ah, the legendary last record of Dorian Emmaus.
DORIAN EMMAUS
His only record.
What's the deal with that song, Açai Berry? Did Dorian write that for you? Are you "Açai BARRY"?
...He didn't even--
DORIAN EMMAUS
PLACES! TWO MINUTES!
WIIIILD STUFF!
THE NIGHT SHOW

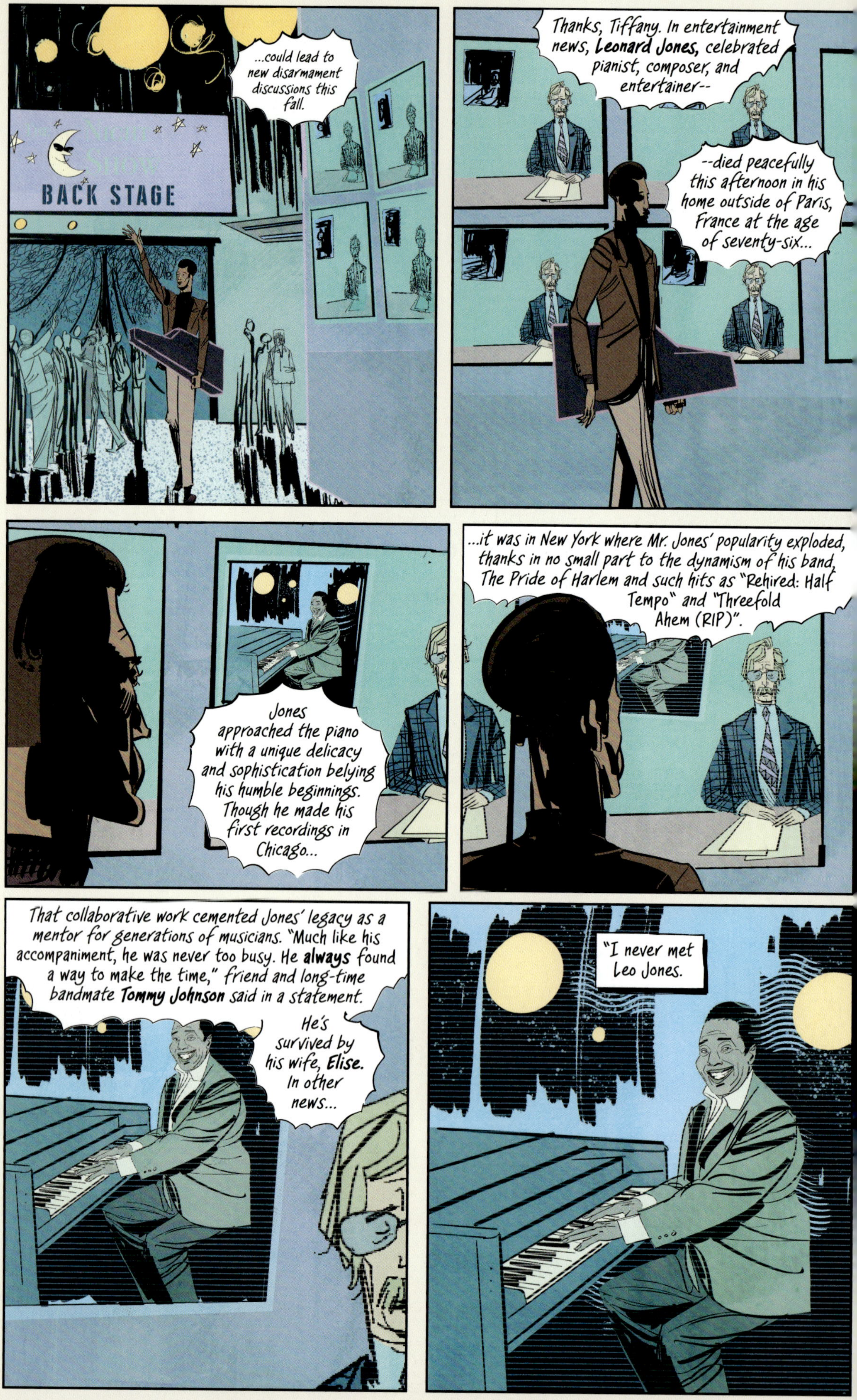
...could lead to new disarmament discussions this fall.
BACK STAGE
Thanks, Tiffany. In entertainment news, Leonard Jones, celebrated pianist, composer, and entertainer--
--died peacefully this afternoon in his home outside of Paris, France at the age of seventy-six...
Jones approached the piano with a unique delicacy and sophistication belying his humble beginnings. Though he made his first recordings in Chicago...
...it was in New York where Mr. Jones' popularity exploded, thanks in no small part to the dynamism of his band, The Pride of Harlem and such hits as "Rehired: Half Tempo" and "Threefold Ahem (RIP)".
That collaborative work cemented Jones' legacy as a mentor for generations of musicians. "Much like his accompaniment, he was never too busy. He always found a way to make the time," friend and long-time bandmate Tommy Johnson said in a statement.
He's survived by his wife, Elise. In other news...
"I never met Leo Jones.

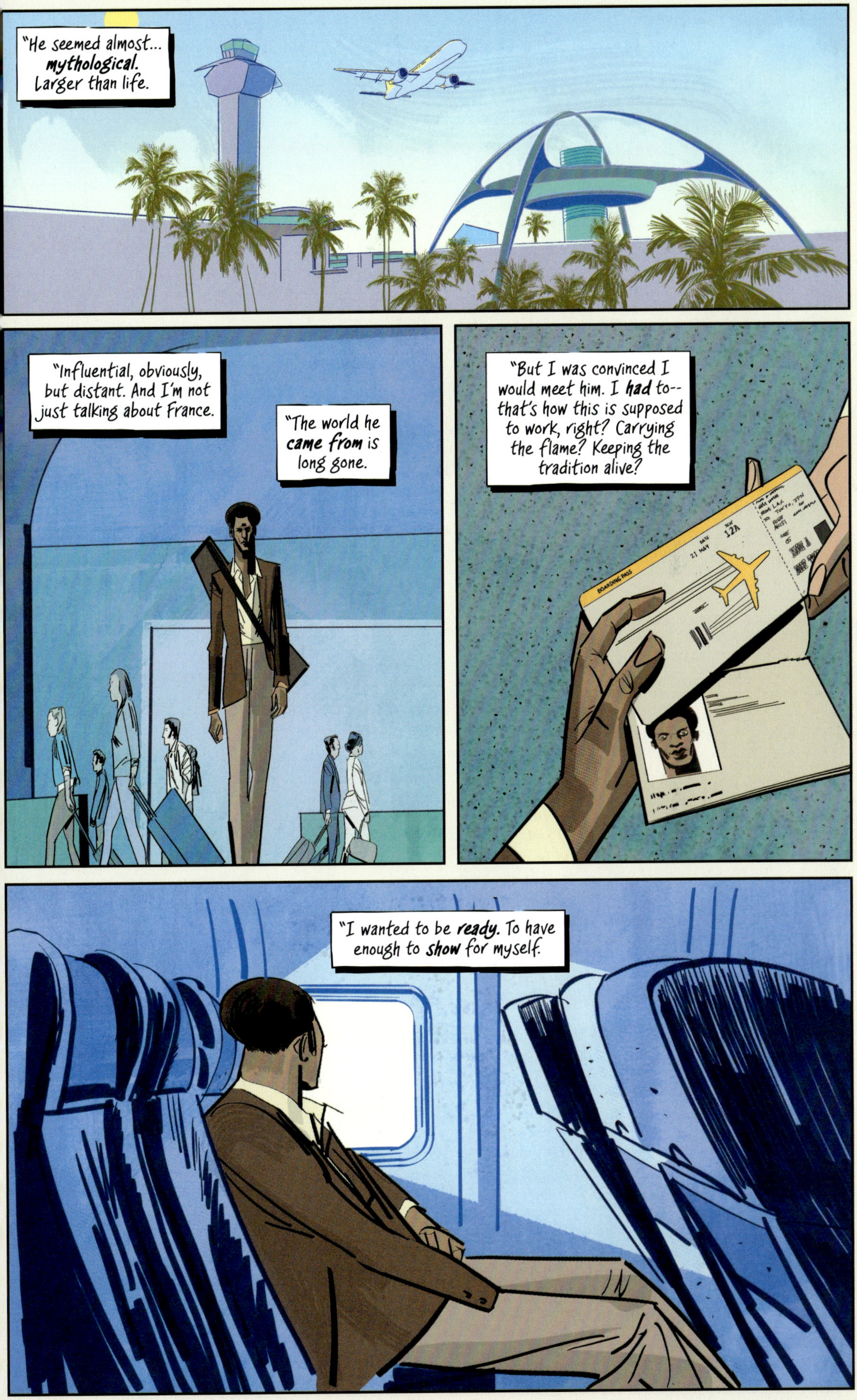
"He seemed almost... **mythological.** Larger than life.
"Influential, obviously, but distant. And I'm not just talking about France.
"The world he **came from** is long gone.
"But I was convinced I would meet him. I **had** to--that's how this is supposed to work, right? Carrying the flame? Keeping the tradition alive?
"I wanted to be **ready.** To have enough to **show** for myself.

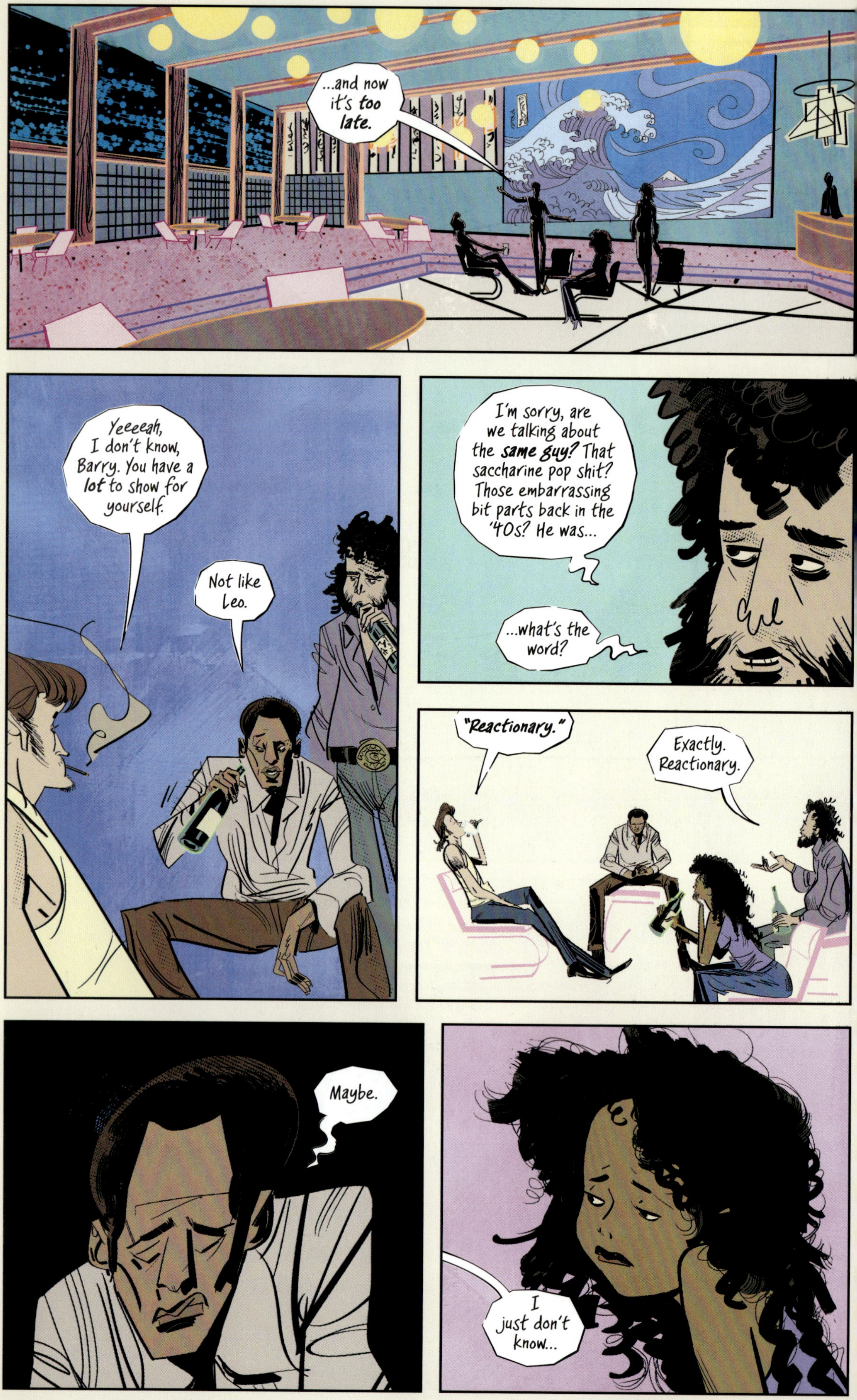
...and now it's too late.
Yeeeeah, I don't know, Barry. You have a lot to show for yourself.
Not like Leo.
I'm sorry, are we talking about the same guy? That saccharine pop shit? Those embarrassing bit parts back in the '40s? He was...
...what's the word?
"Reactionary."
Exactly. Reactionary.
Maybe.
I just don't know...

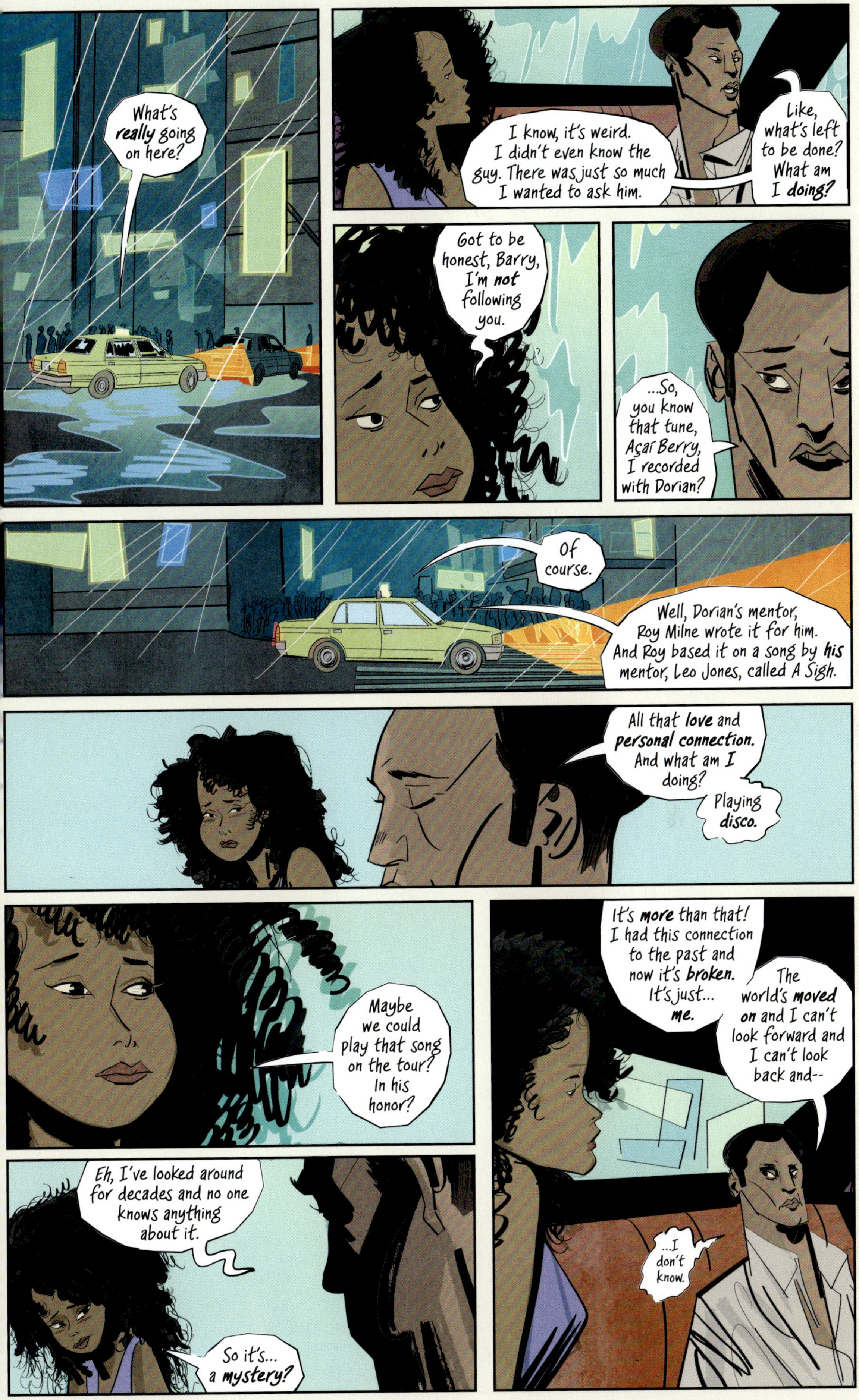
What's *really* going on here?
I know, it's weird. I didn't even know the guy. There was just so much I wanted to ask him.
Like, what's left to be done? What am I *doing?*
Got to be honest, Barry, I'm *not* following you.
...So, you know that tune, Açaí Berry, I recorded with Dorian?
Of course.
Well, Dorian's mentor, Roy Milne wrote it for him. And Roy based it on a song by *his* mentor, Leo Jones, called A Sigh.
All that *love* and *personal connection.* And what am I doing?
Playing *disco.*
Maybe we could play that song on the tour? In his honor?
Eh, I've looked around for decades and no one knows anything about it.
So it's... a *mystery?*
It's *more* than that! I had this connection to the past and now it's *broken.* It's just... *me.*
The world's *moved on* and I can't look forward and I can't look back and--
...I don't know.

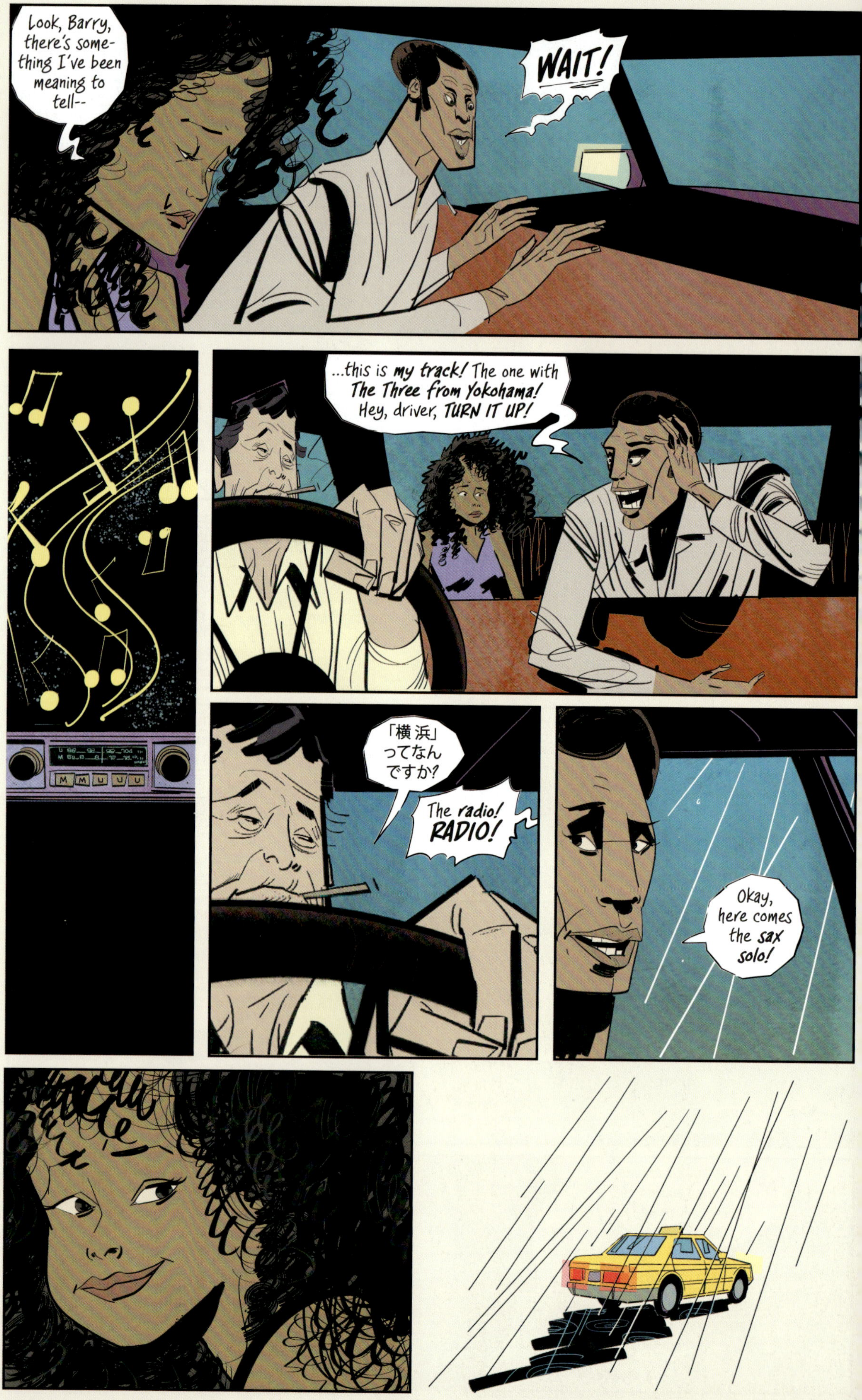
Look, Barry, there's something I've been meaning to tell--
WAIT!
...this is my track! The one with The Three from Yokohama! Hey, driver, TURN IT UP!
「横浜」ってなんですか?
The radio! RADIO!
Okay, here comes the sax solo!

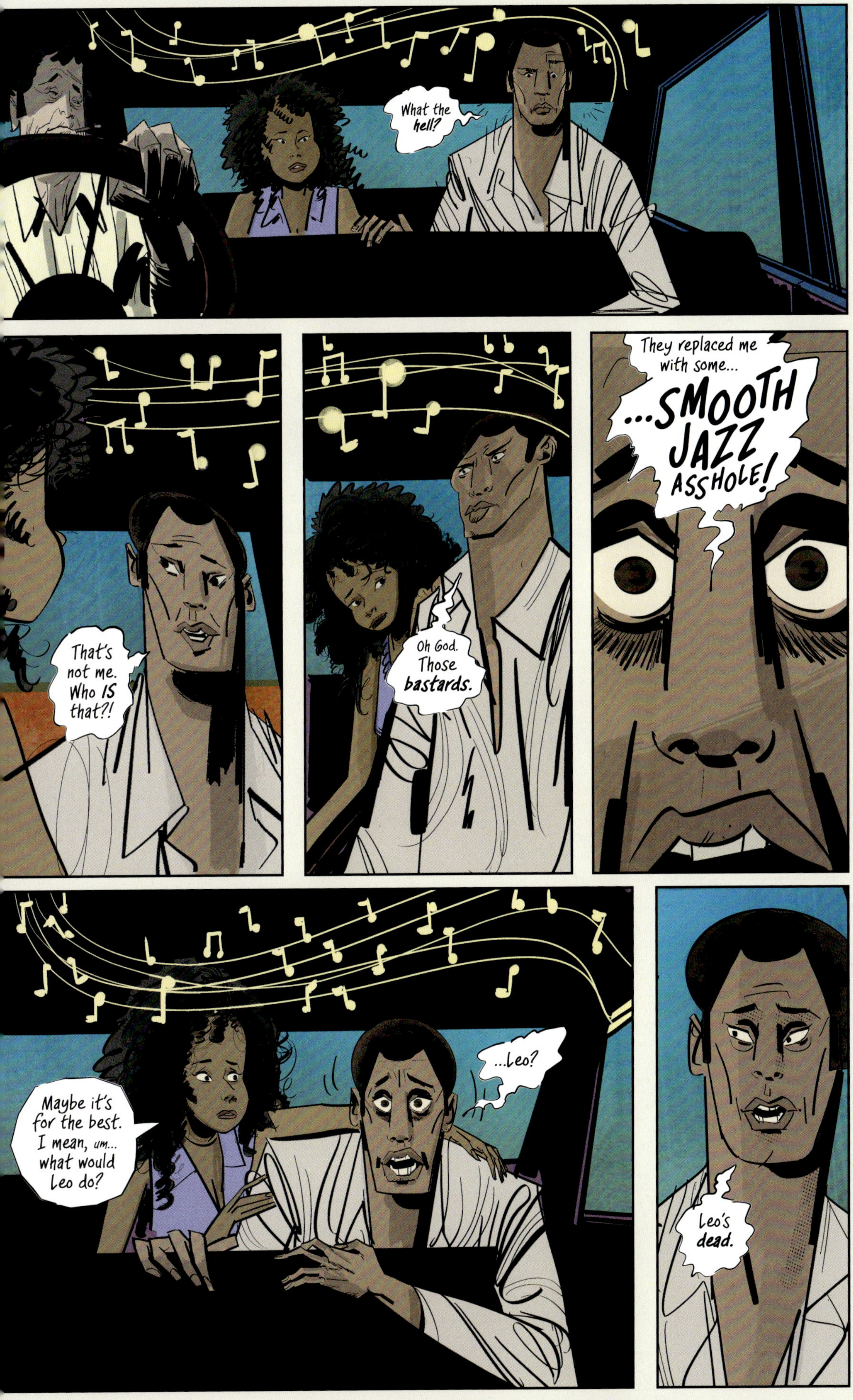
What the hell?
That's not me. Who IS that?!
Oh God. Those bastards.
They replaced me with some...
...SMOOTH JAZZ ASSHOLE!
Maybe it's for the best. I mean, um... what would Leo do?
...Leo?
Leo's dead.

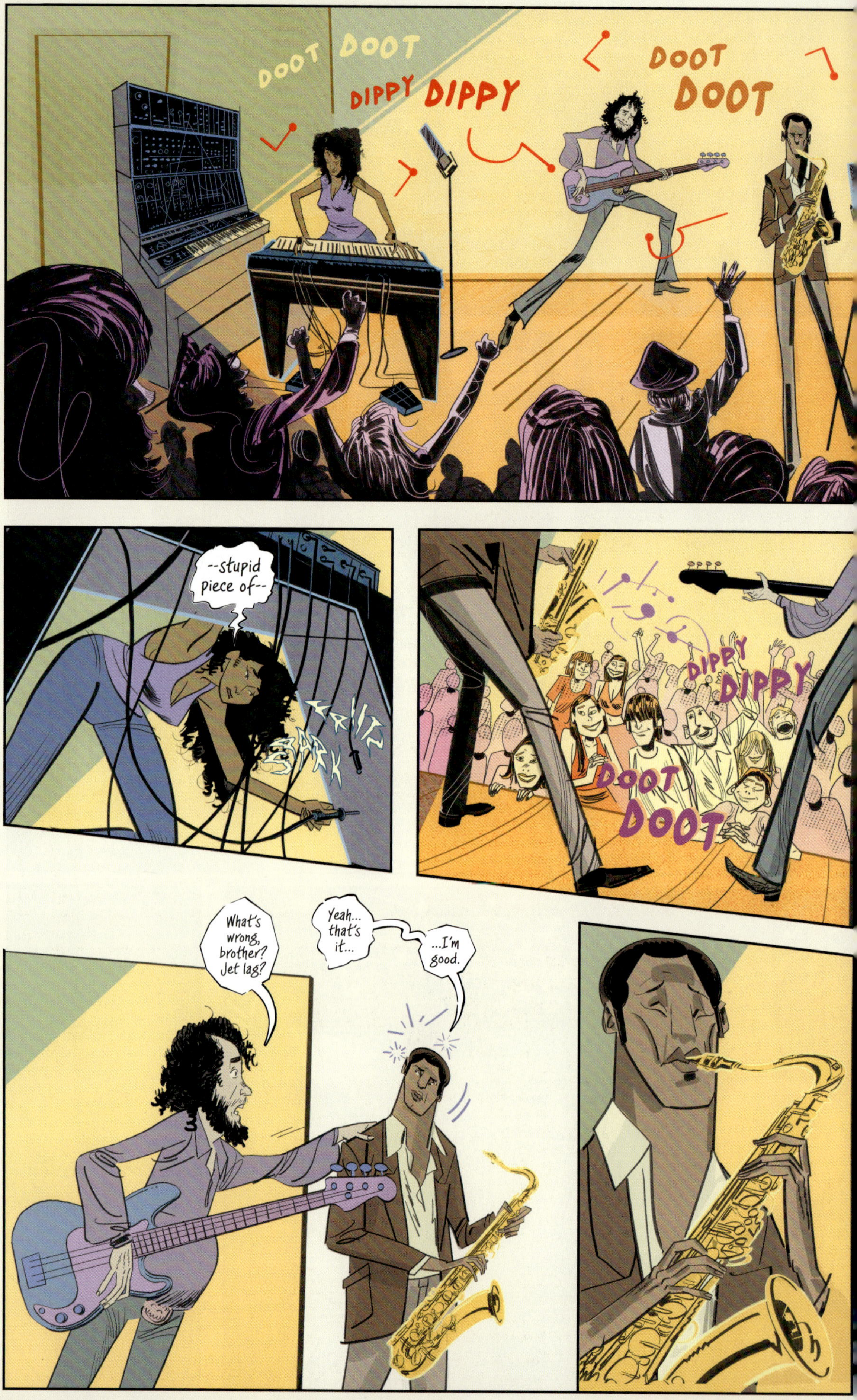
DOOT DOOT
DIPPY DIPPY
DOOT DOOT
--stupid piece of--
DIPPY DIPPY
DOOT DOOT
What's wrong, brother? Jet lag?
Yeah... that's it...
...I'm good.

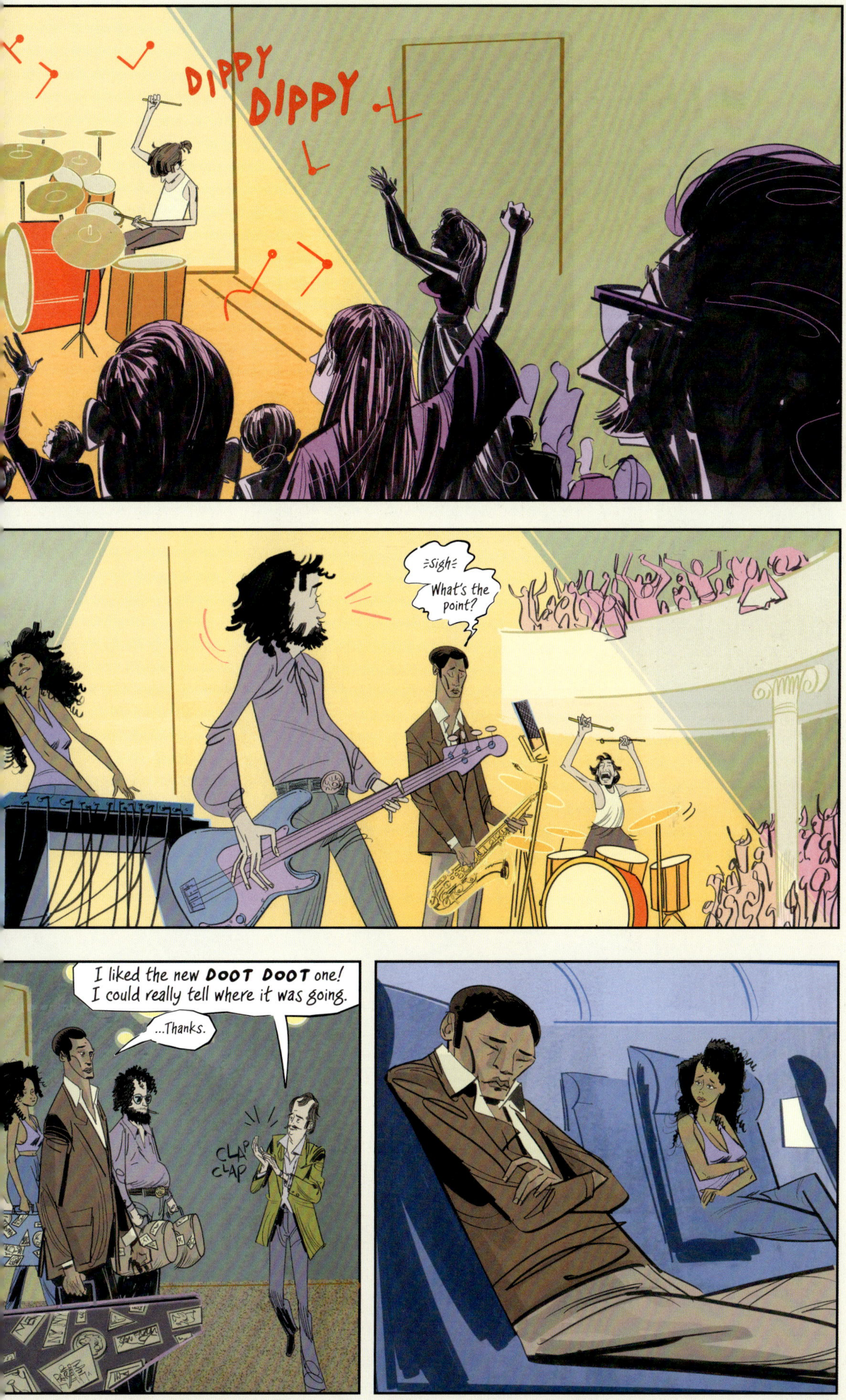
DIPPY
DIPPY
=Sigh=
What's the point?
I liked the new DOOT DOOT one! I could really tell where it was going.
...Thanks.
CLAP CLAP

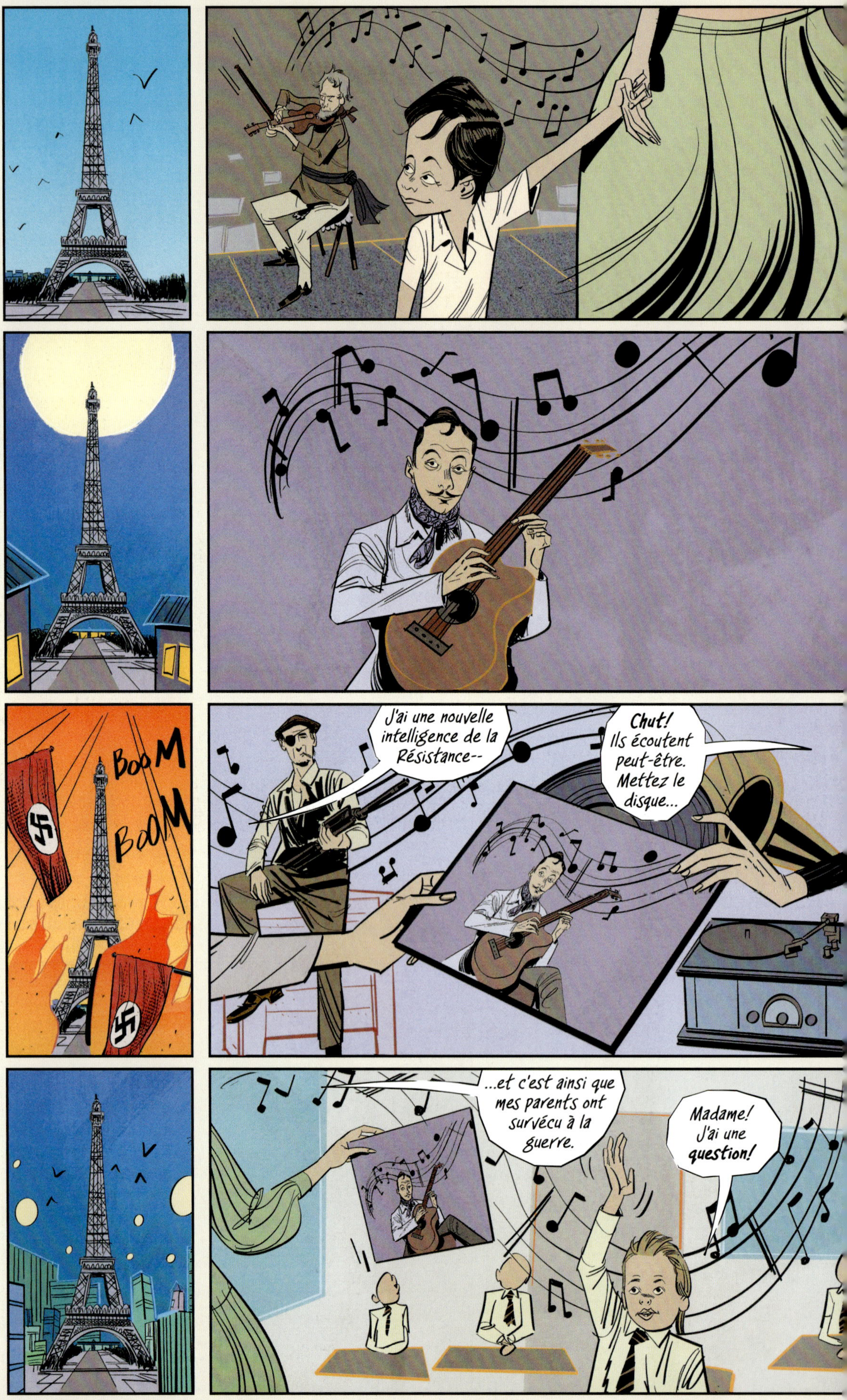
BOOM
BOOM
J'ai une nouvelle intelligence de la Résistance--
Chut! Ils écoutent peut-être. Mettez le disque...
...et c'est ainsi que mes parents ont survécu à la guerre.
Madame! J'ai une question!

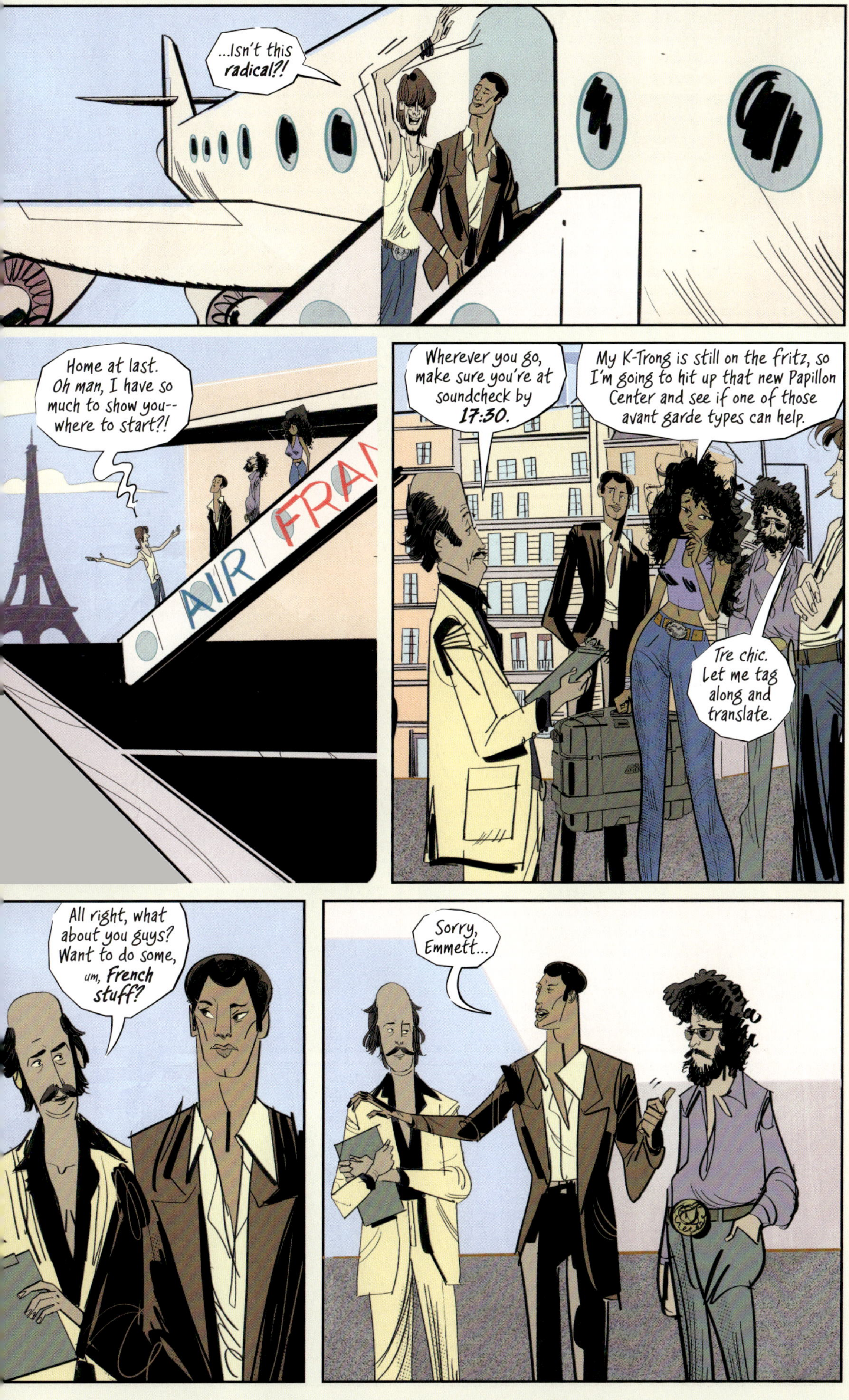
...Isn't this radical?!
Home at last. Oh man, I have so much to show you--where to start?!
AIR FRAN
Wherever you go, make sure you're at soundcheck by 17:30.
My K-Trong is still on the fritz, so I'm going to hit up that new Papillon Center and see if one of those avant garde types can help.
Tre chic. Let me tag along and translate.
All right, what about you guys? Want to do some, um, French stuff?
Sorry, Emmett...

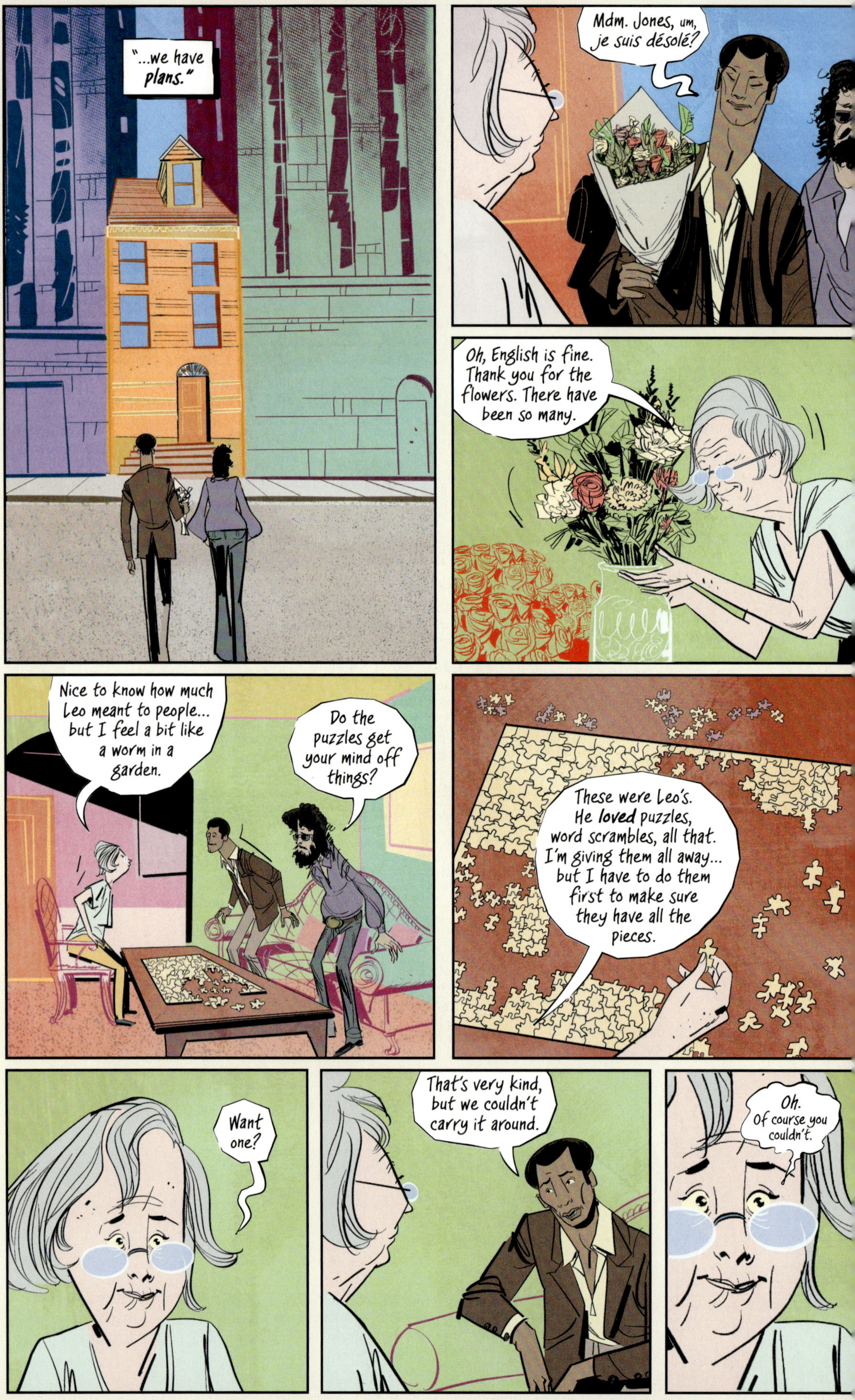
"...we have *plans.*"
Mdm. Jones, um, je suis désolé?
Oh, English is fine. Thank you for the flowers. There have been so many.
Nice to know how much Leo meant to people... but I feel a bit like a worm in a garden.
Do the puzzles get your mind off things?
These were Leo's. He *loved* puzzles, word scrambles, all that. I'm giving them all away... but I have to do them first to make sure they have all the pieces.
Want one?
That's very kind, but we couldn't carry it around.
Oh. Of course you couldn't.

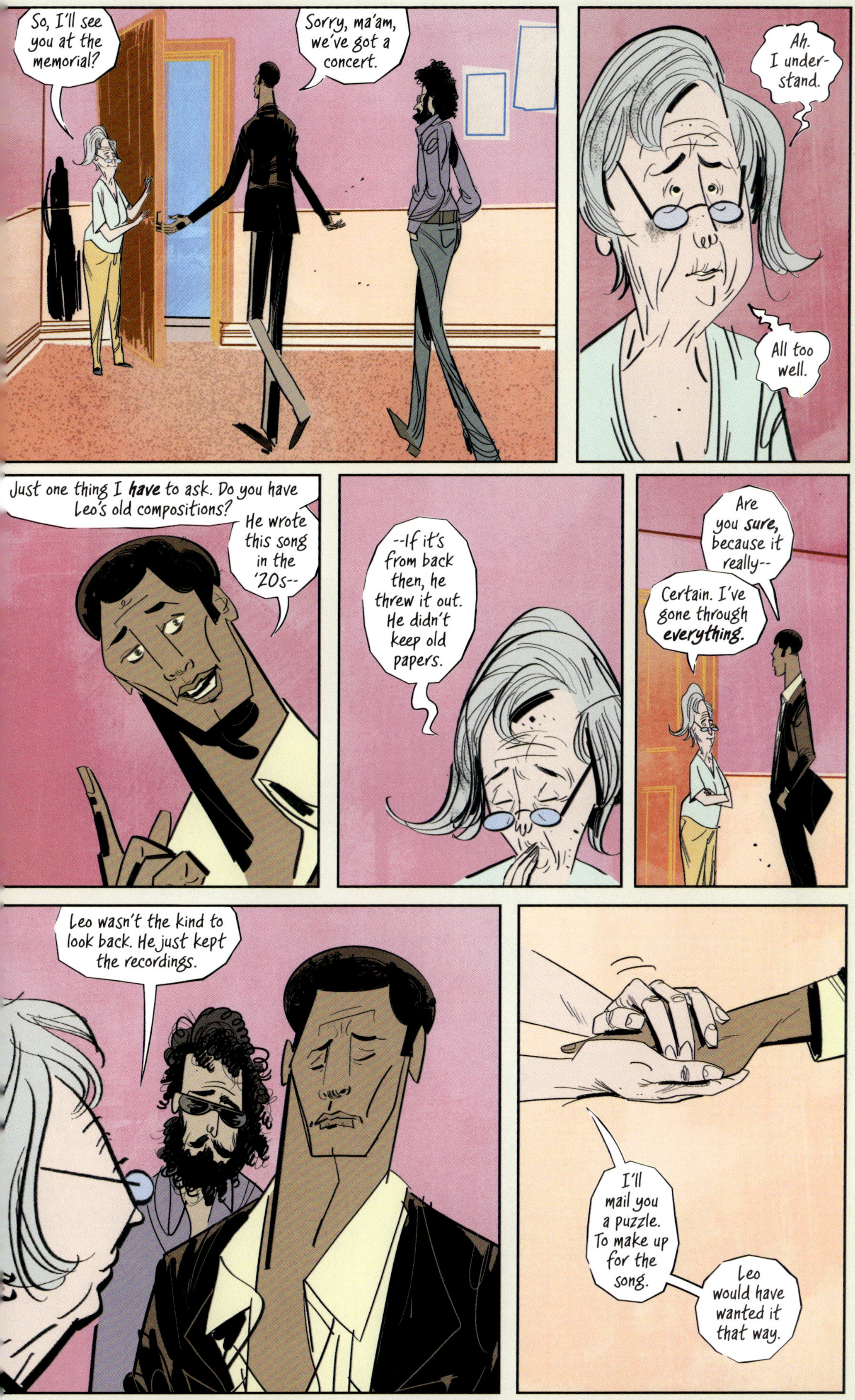
So, I'll see you at the memorial?
Sorry, ma'am, we've got a concert.
Ah. I under-stand.
All too well.
Just one thing I **have** to ask. Do you have Leo's old compositions?
He wrote this song in the '20s--
--If it's from back then, he threw it out. He didn't keep old papers.
Are you **sure,** because it really--
Certain. I've gone through **everything.**
Leo wasn't the kind to look back. He just kept the recordings.
I'll mail you a puzzle. To make up for the song.
Leo would have wanted it that way.

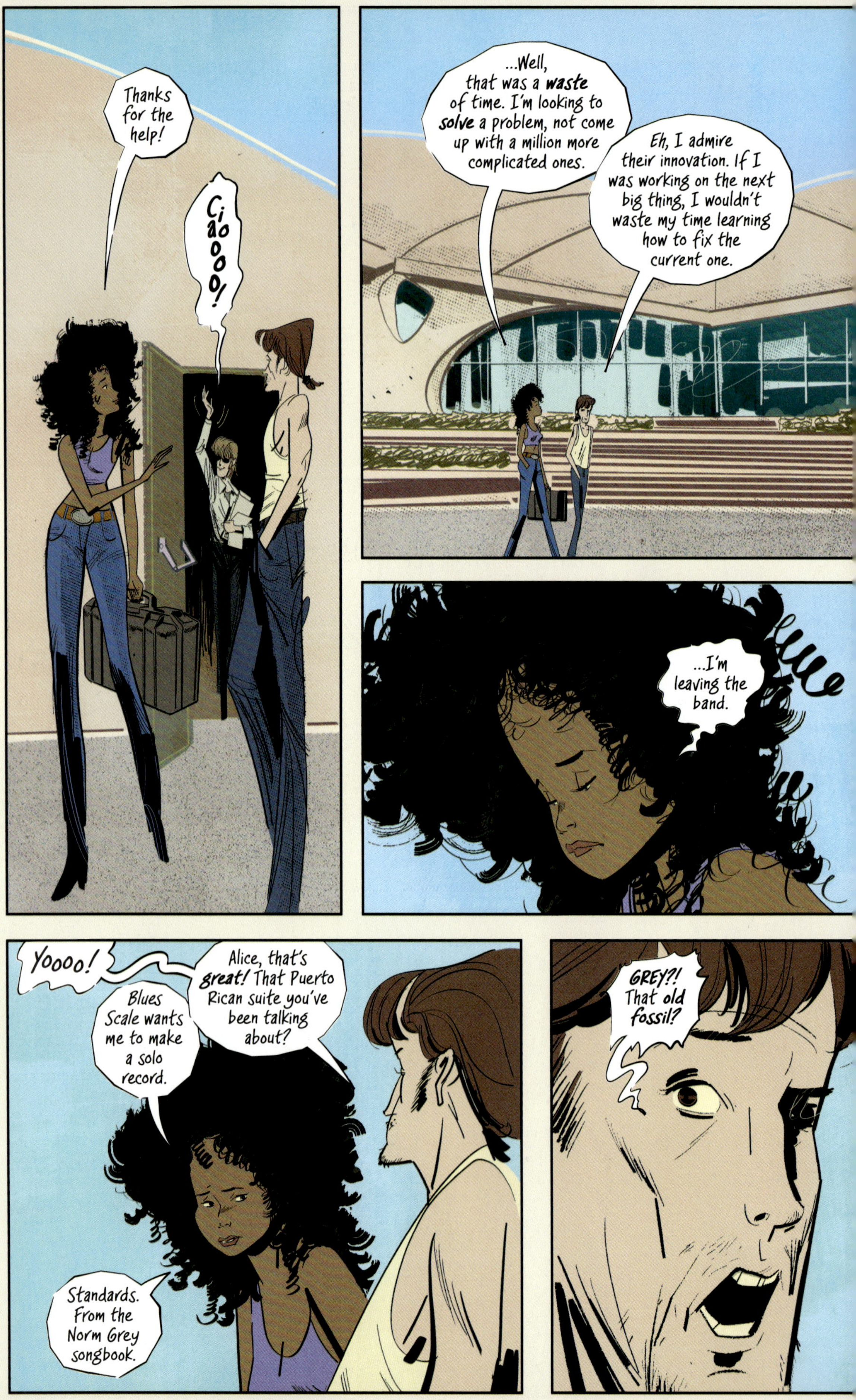

Thanks for the help!
Ciaoooo!
...Well, that was a **waste** of time. I'm looking to **solve** a problem, not come up with a million more complicated ones.
Eh, I admire their innovation. If I was working on the next big thing, I wouldn't waste my time learning how to fix the current one.
...I'm leaving the band.
Yoooo!
Alice, that's **great!** That Puerto Rican suite you've been talking about?
Blues Scale wants me to make a solo record.
Standards. From the Norm Grey songbook.
GREY?! That old **fossil?**

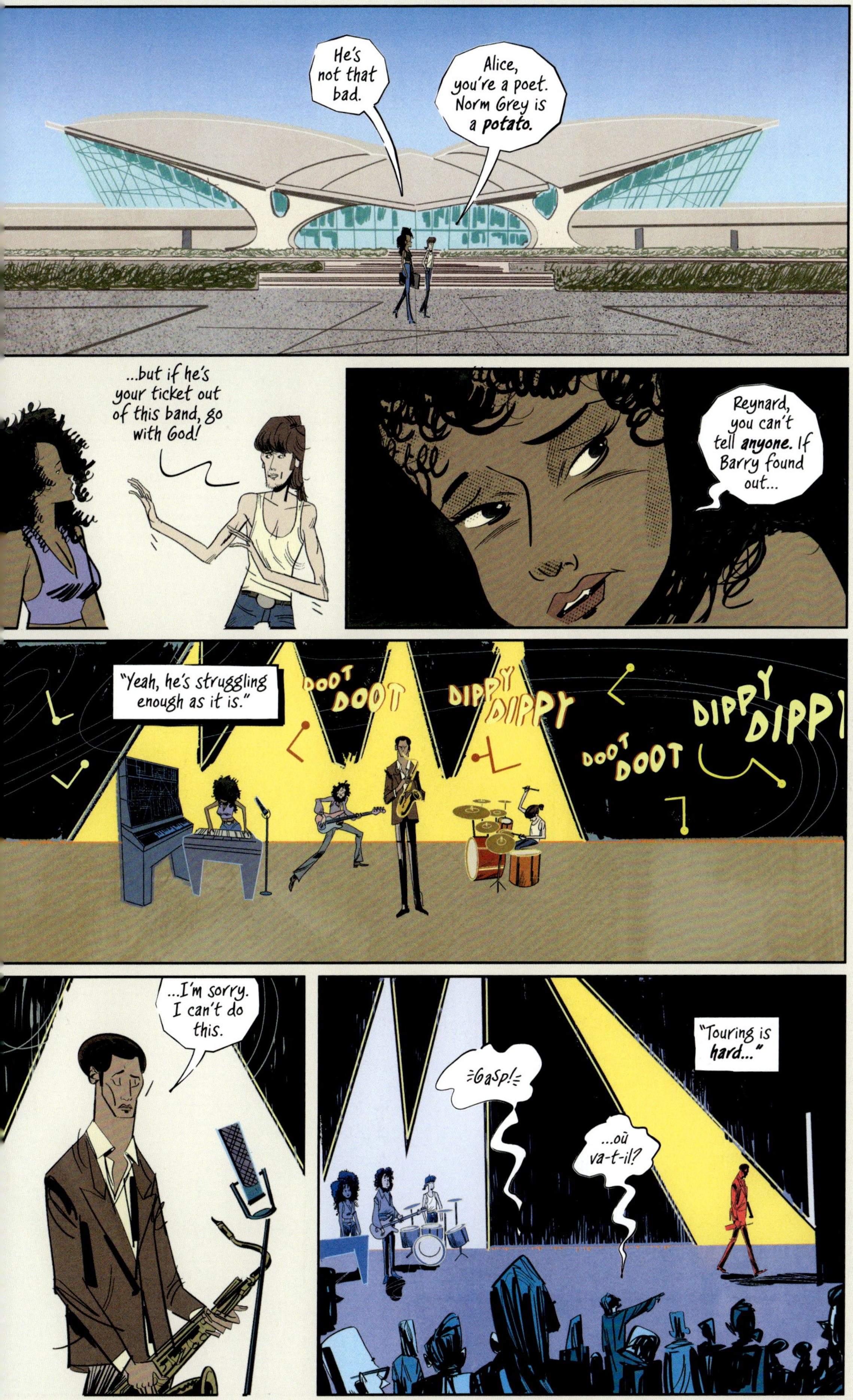
He's not that bad.
Alice, you're a poet. Norm Grey is a **potato.**
...but if he's your ticket out of this band, go with God!
Reynard, you can't tell **anyone.** If Barry found out...
"Yeah, he's struggling enough as it is."
DOOT DOOT
DIPPY DIPPY
DOOT DOOT
DIPPY DIPPY
...I'm sorry. I can't do this.
"Touring is **hard...**"
Gasp!
...où va-t-il?

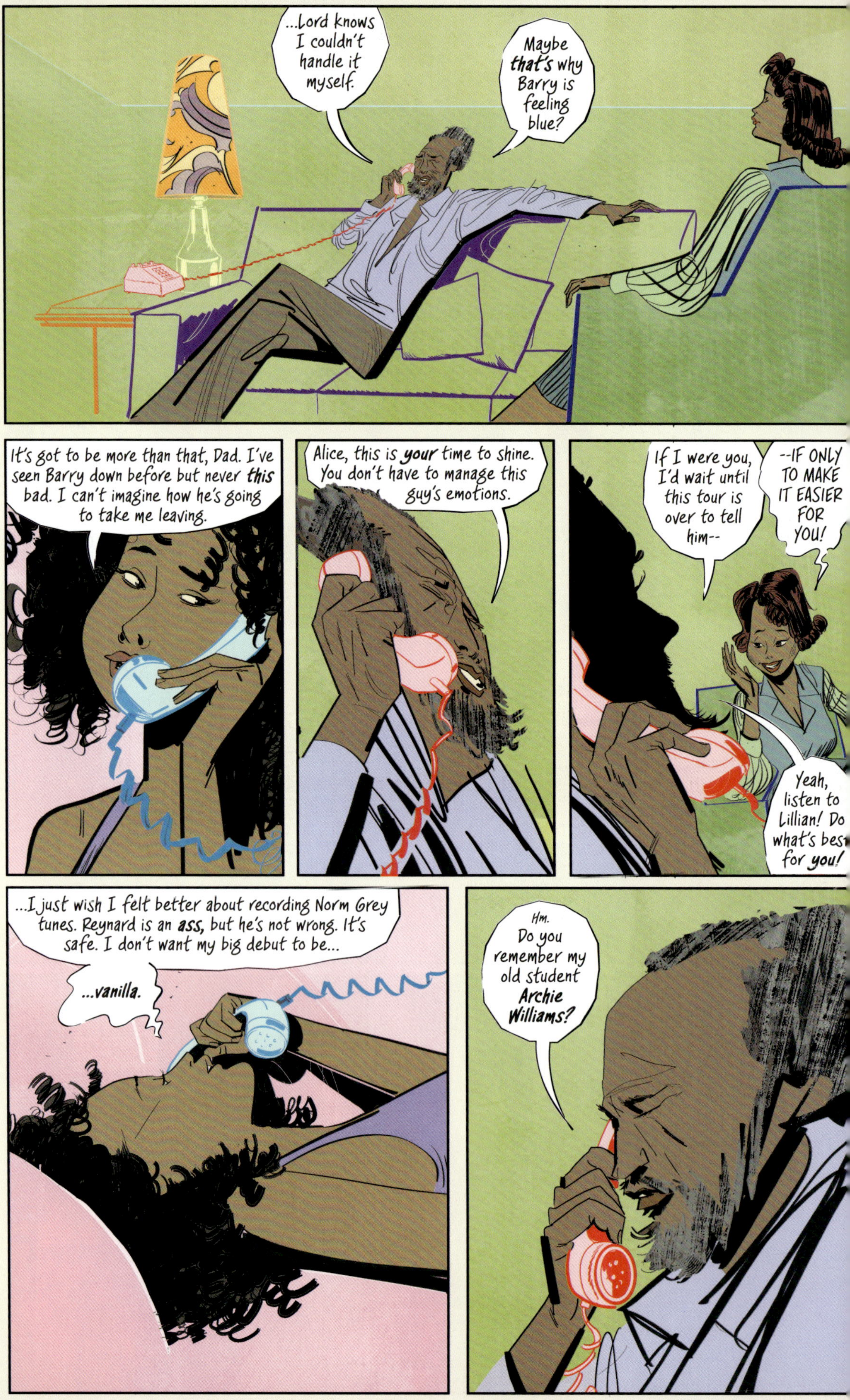
...Lord knows I couldn't handle it myself.
Maybe **that's** why Barry is feeling blue?
It's got to be more than that, Dad. I've seen Barry down before but never **this** bad. I can't imagine how he's going to take me leaving.
Alice, this is **your** time to shine. You don't have to manage this guy's emotions.
If I were you, I'd wait until this tour is over to tell him--
--IF ONLY TO MAKE IT EASIER FOR YOU!
Yeah, listen to Lillian! Do what's best for **you!**
...I just wish I felt better about recording Norm Grey tunes. Reynard is an **ass,** but he's not wrong. It's safe. I don't want my big debut to be...
...vanilla.
Hm. Do you remember my old student **Archie Williams?**

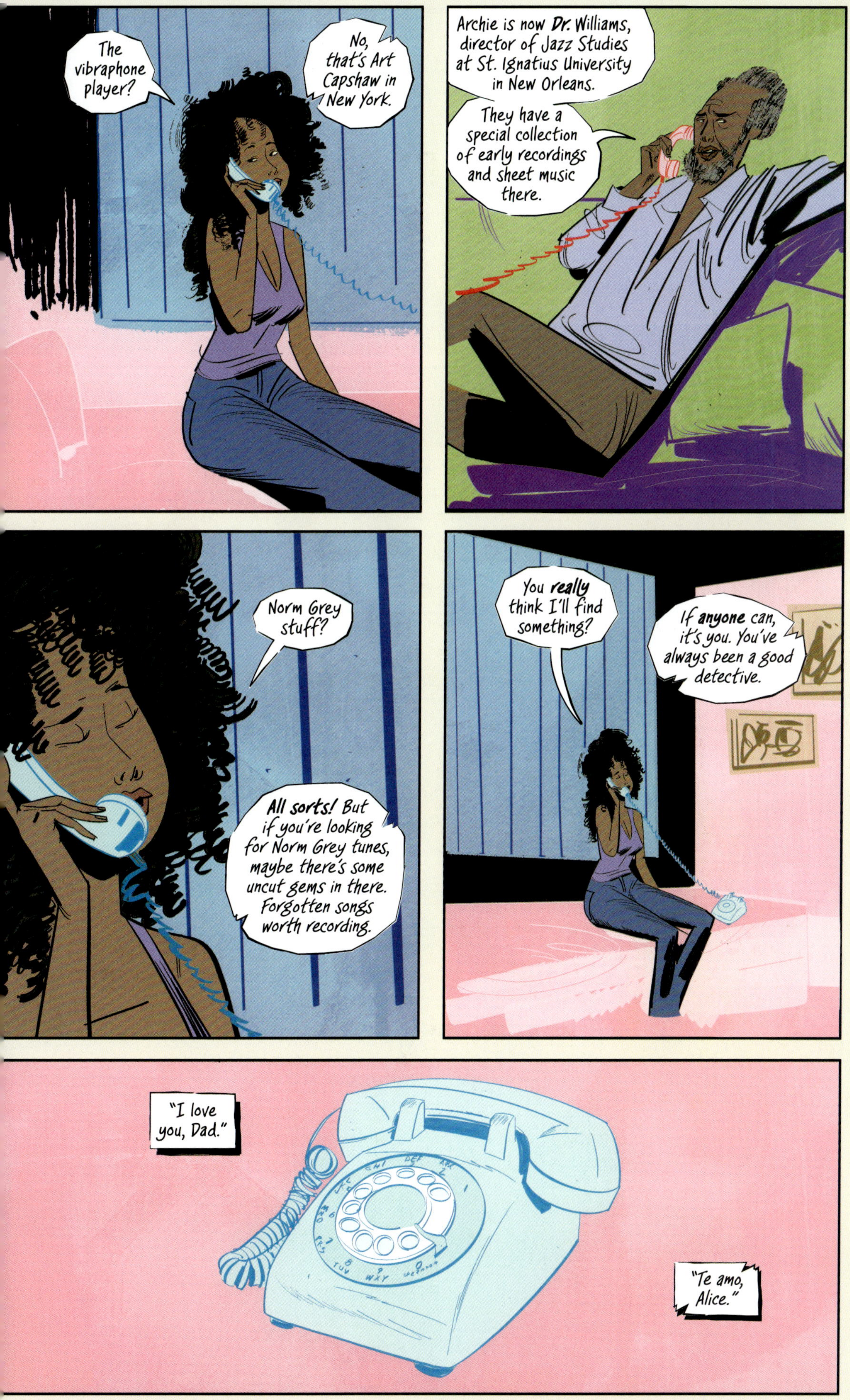
The vibraphone player?
No, that's Art Capshaw in New York.
Archie is now **Dr.** Williams, director of Jazz Studies at St. Ignatius University in New Orleans.
They have a special collection of early recordings and sheet music there.
Norm Grey stuff?
All sorts! But if you're looking for Norm Grey tunes, maybe there's some uncut gems in there. Forgotten songs worth recording.
You **really** think I'll find something?
If **anyone** can, it's you. You've always been a good detective.
"I love you, Dad."
"Te amo, Alice."

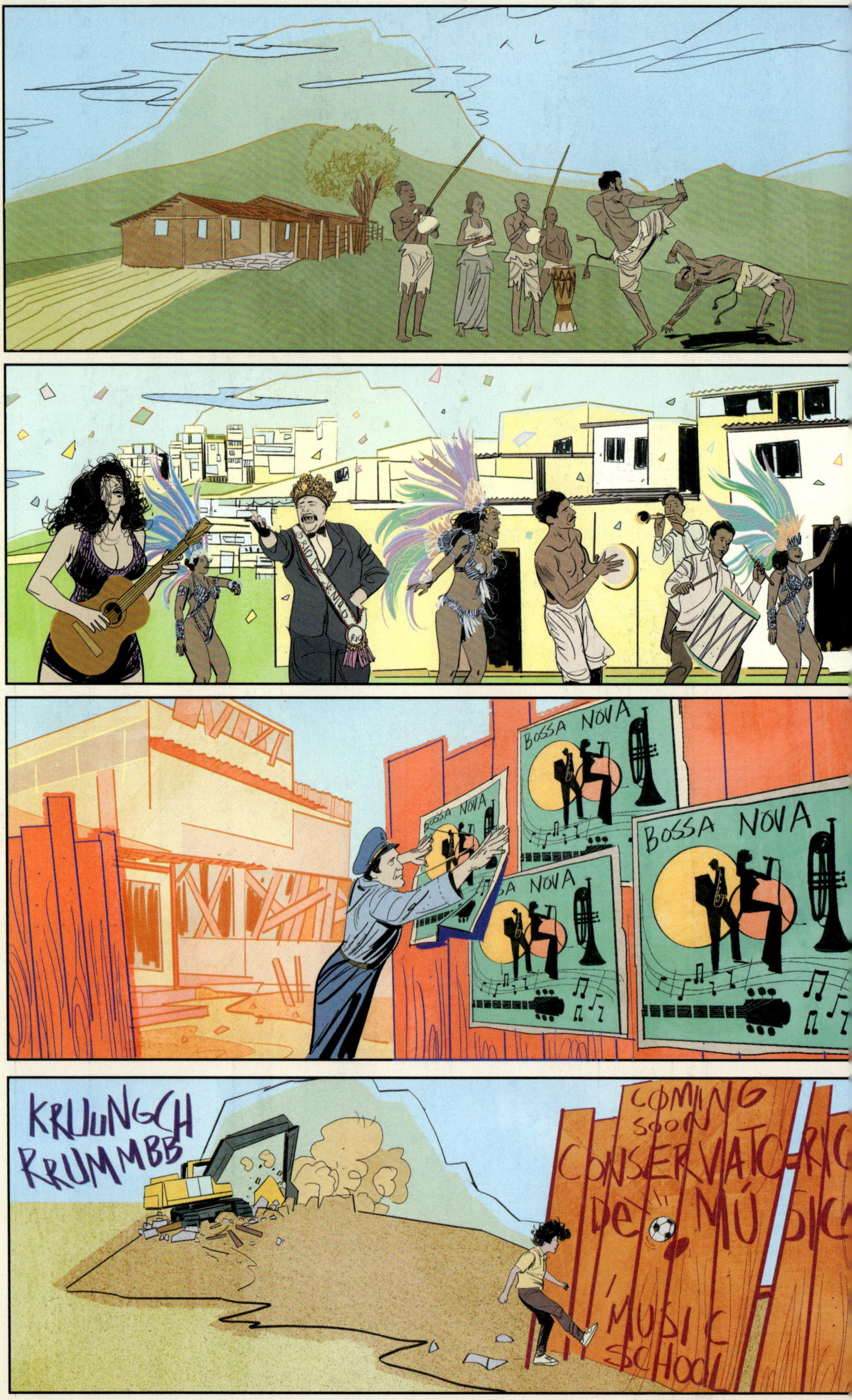
BOSSA NOVA
BOSSA NOVA
BOSSA NOVA
BOSSA NOVA
KRUUNGCH
RRUMMBB
COMING SOON
CONSERVATÓRIO DE MÚSICA
MUSIC SCHOOL

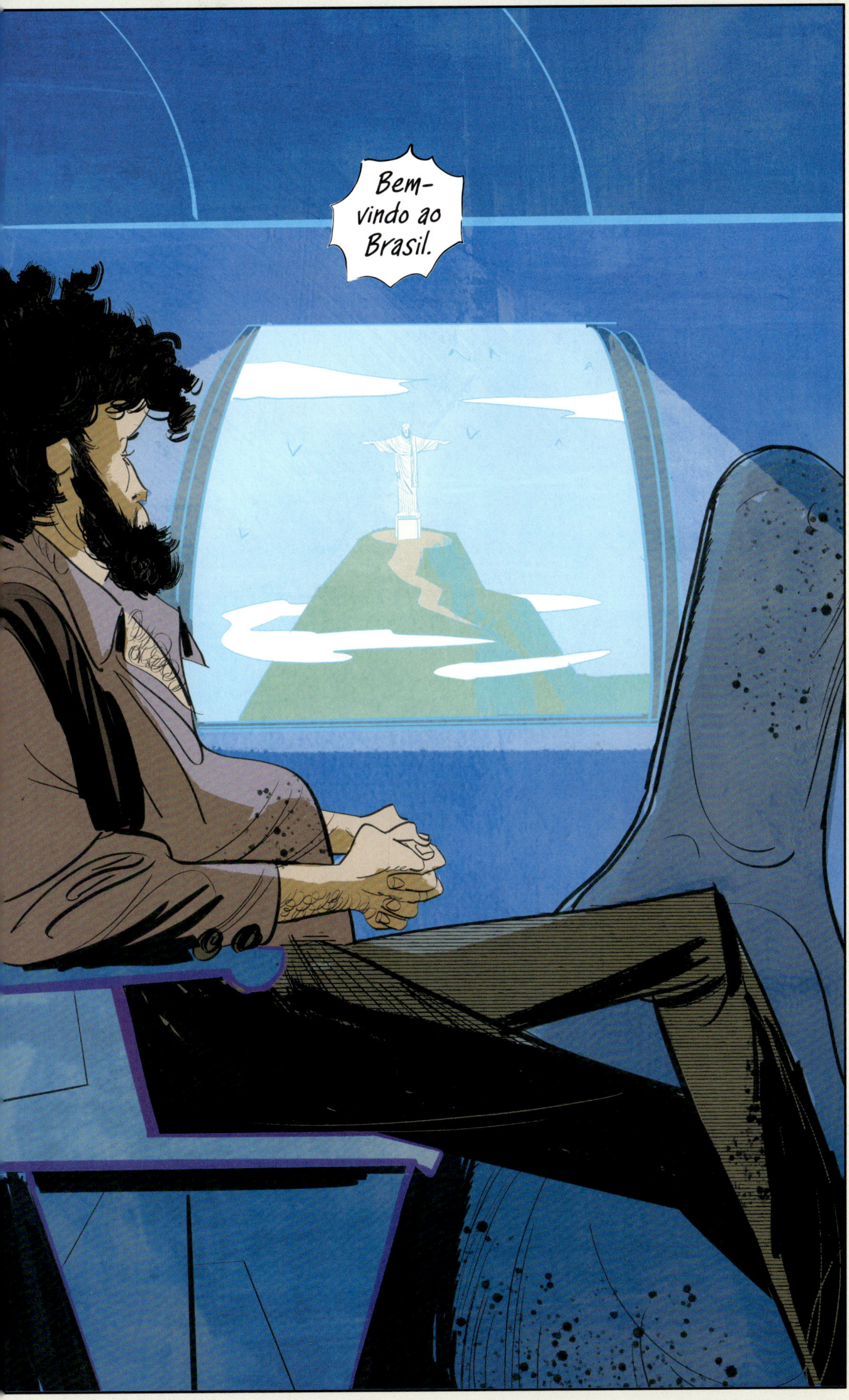
Bem-vindo ao Brasil.

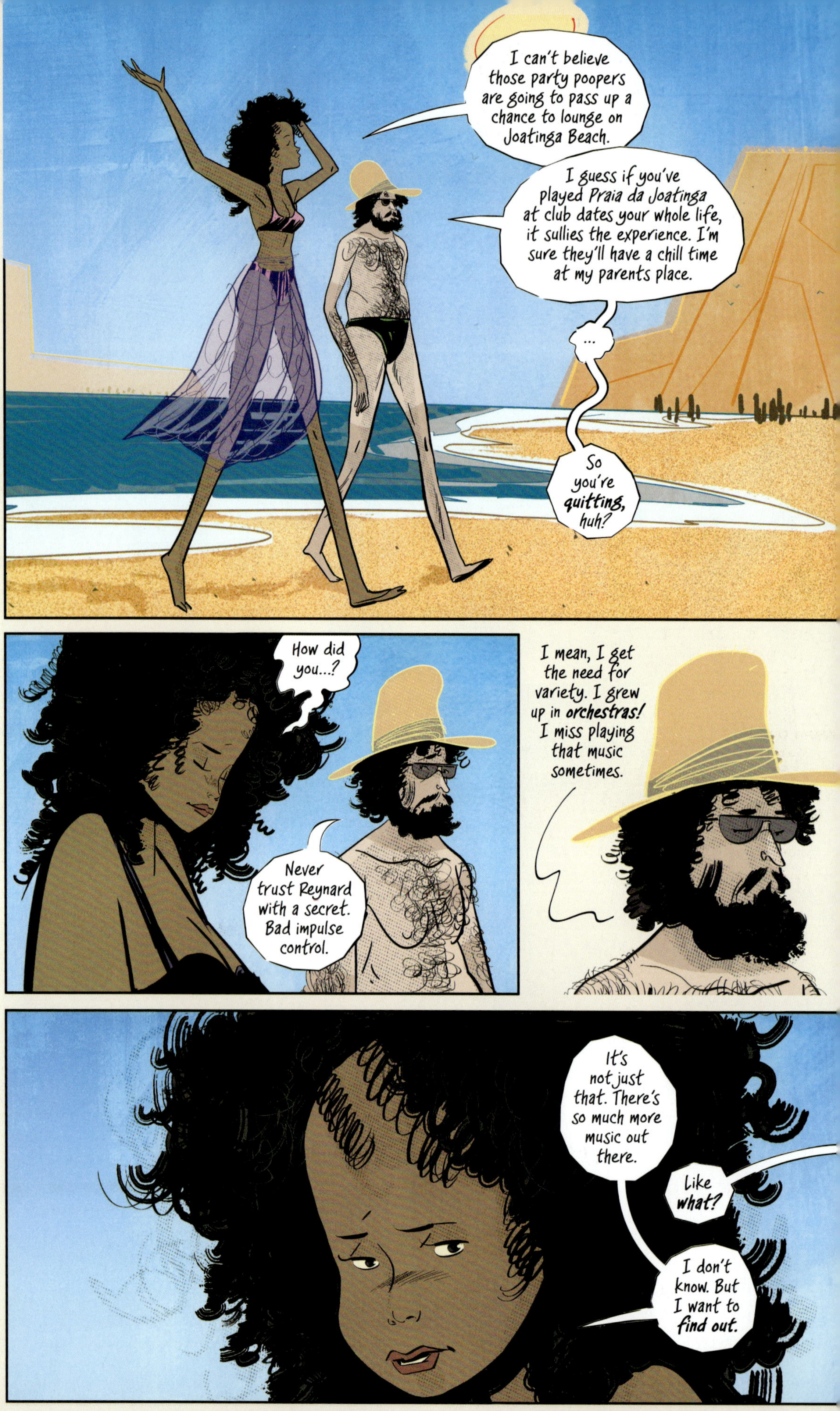
I can't believe those party poopers are going to pass up a chance to lounge on Joatinga Beach.
I guess if you've played Praia da Joatinga at club dates your whole life, it sullies the experience. I'm sure they'll have a chill time at my parents place.
...
So you're quitting, huh?
How did you...?
Never trust Reynard with a secret. Bad impulse control.
I mean, I get the need for variety. I grew up in orchestras! I miss playing that music sometimes.
It's not just that. There's so much more music out there.
Like what?
I don't know. But I want to find out.

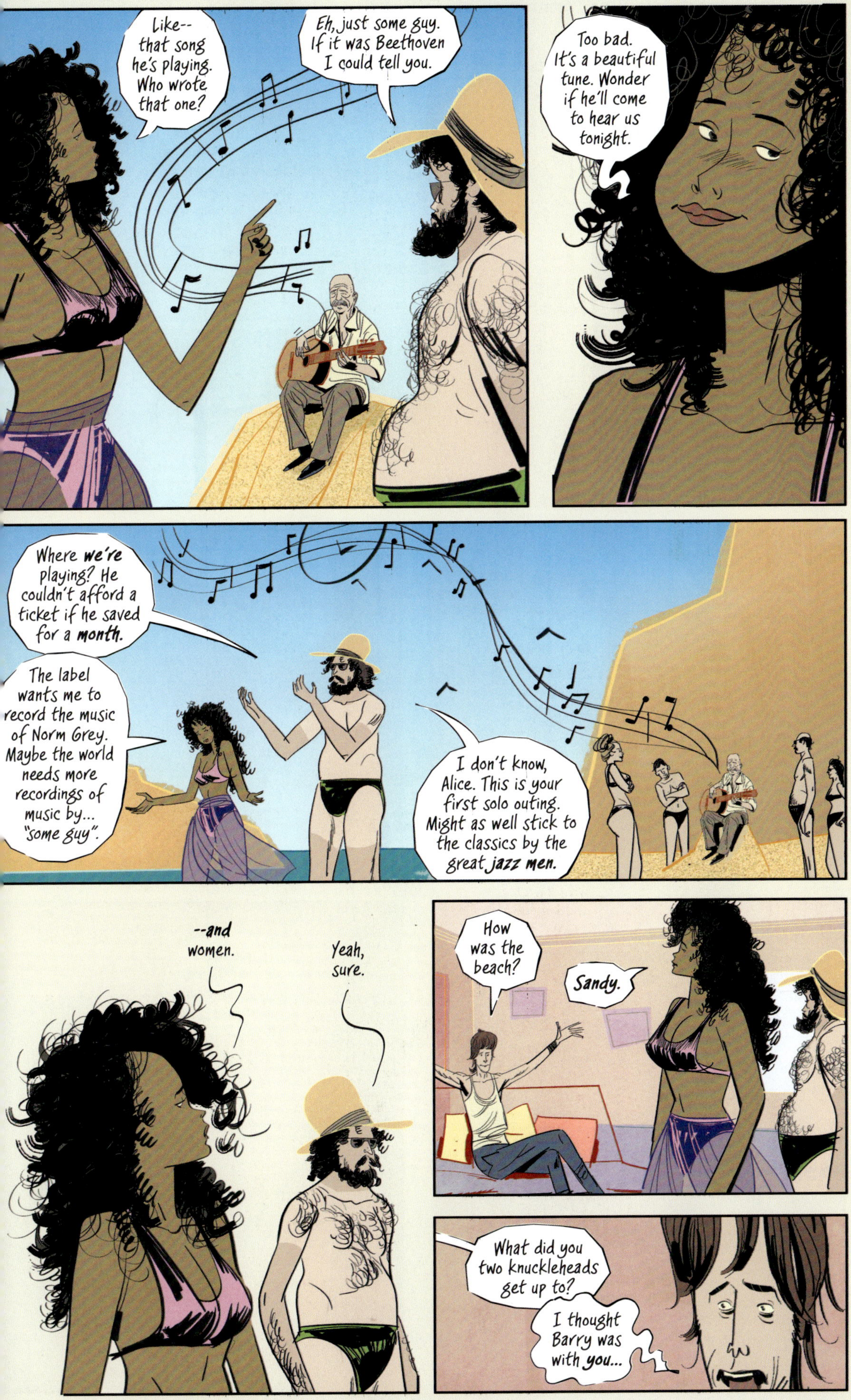
Like-- that song he's playing. Who wrote that one?
Eh, just some guy. If it was Beethoven I could tell you.
Too bad. It's a beautiful tune. Wonder if he'll come to hear us tonight.
Where **we're** playing? He couldn't afford a ticket if he saved for a **month.**
The label wants me to record the music of Norm Grey. Maybe the world needs more recordings of music by... "some guy".
I don't know, Alice. This is your first solo outing. Might as well stick to the classics by the great **jazz men.**
--**and** women.
Yeah, sure.
How was the beach?
Sandy.
What did you two knuckleheads get up to?
I thought Barry was with **you...**

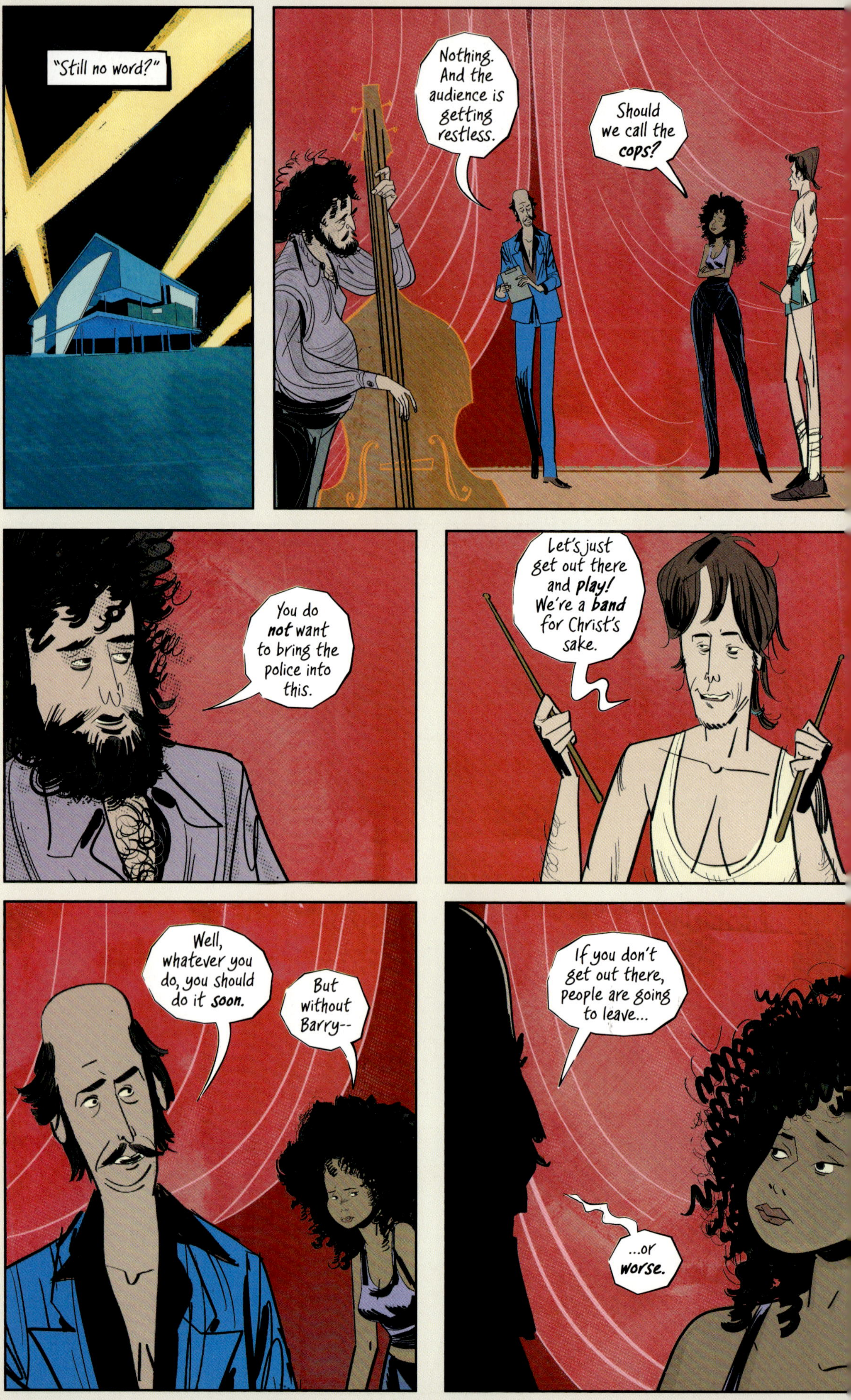
"Still no word?"
Nothing. And the audience is getting restless.
Should we call the cops?
You do not want to bring the police into this.
Let's just get out there and play! We're a band for Christ's sake.
Well, whatever you do, you should do it soon.
But without Barry--
If you don't get out there, people are going to leave...
...or worse.

DOOT DOOT?
DIPPY DIPPY?
WHADDER Y'ALL YAWWWNING FOR? THIS IS HOT SHTUFF!
YEEEAH! LET'S HEAR IT FOR 'EM! "THE UNKNOWN".
I USTTA THINK I KNEW. BUT WADDA I KNOW? NOTHIN'.
Barry! We were so worried--!
DISCOOOOooo
I guess... whadever.
NO, no. I'm good. Y'know what else is good?
Allll right, let's give the piggies their slop.
SQUEEEE

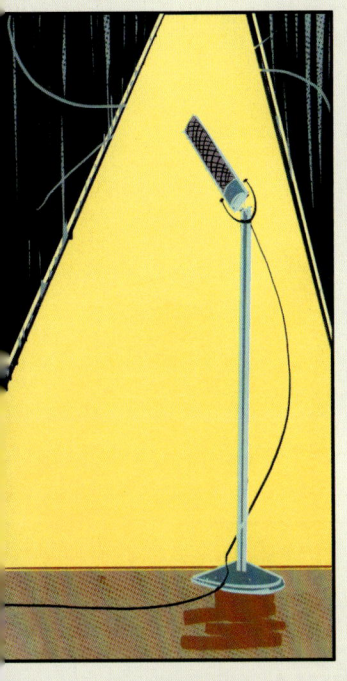

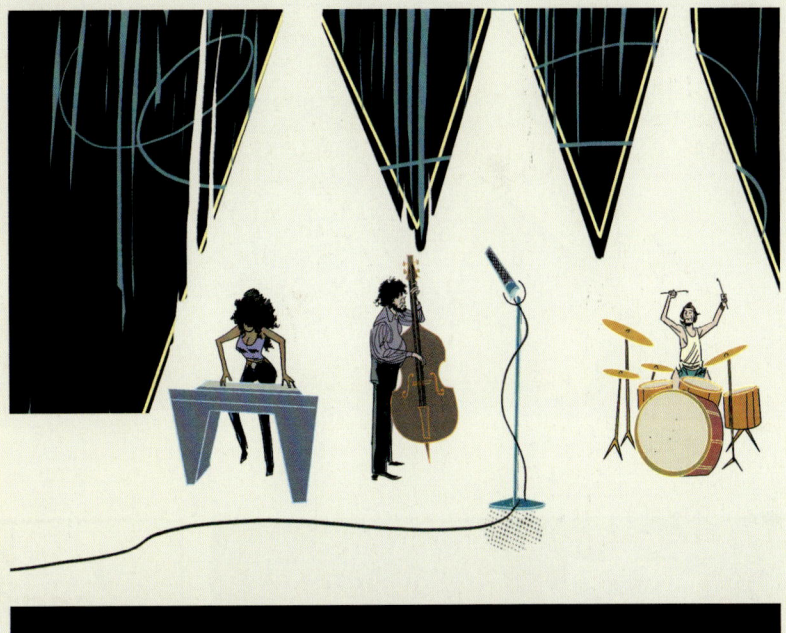

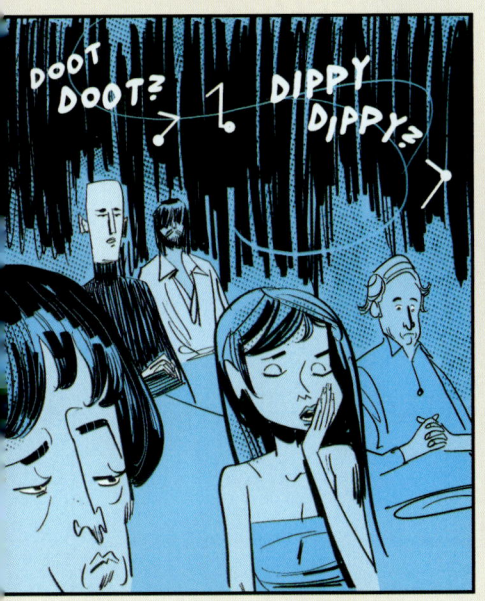

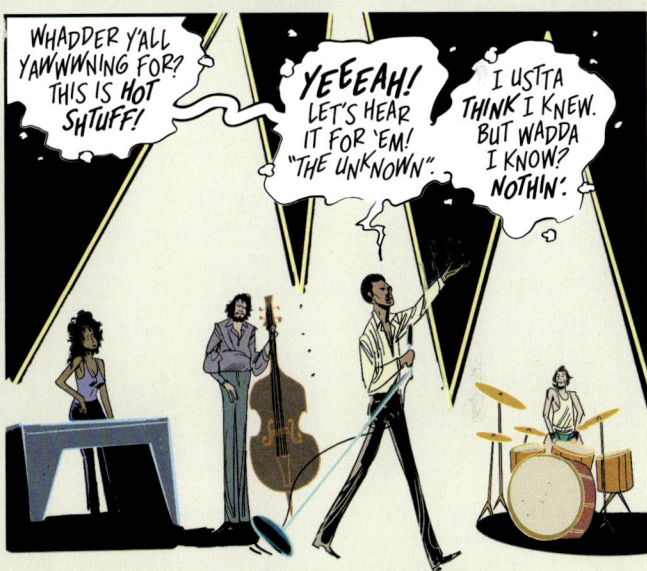

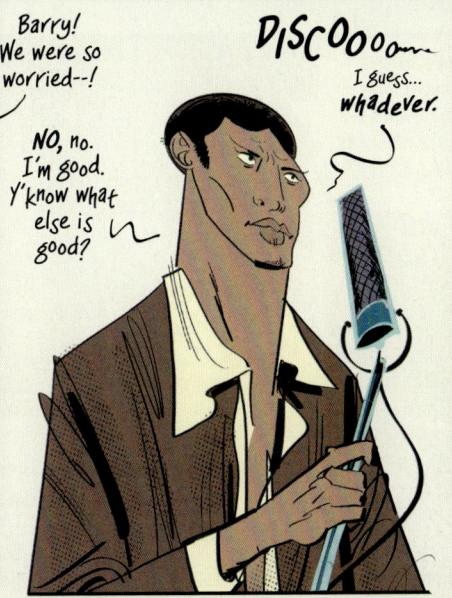

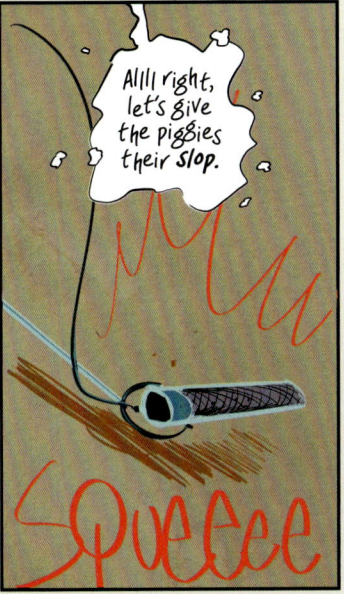

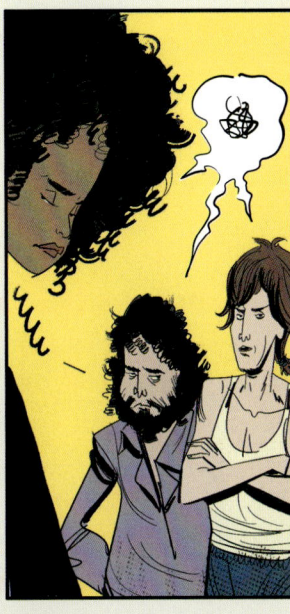

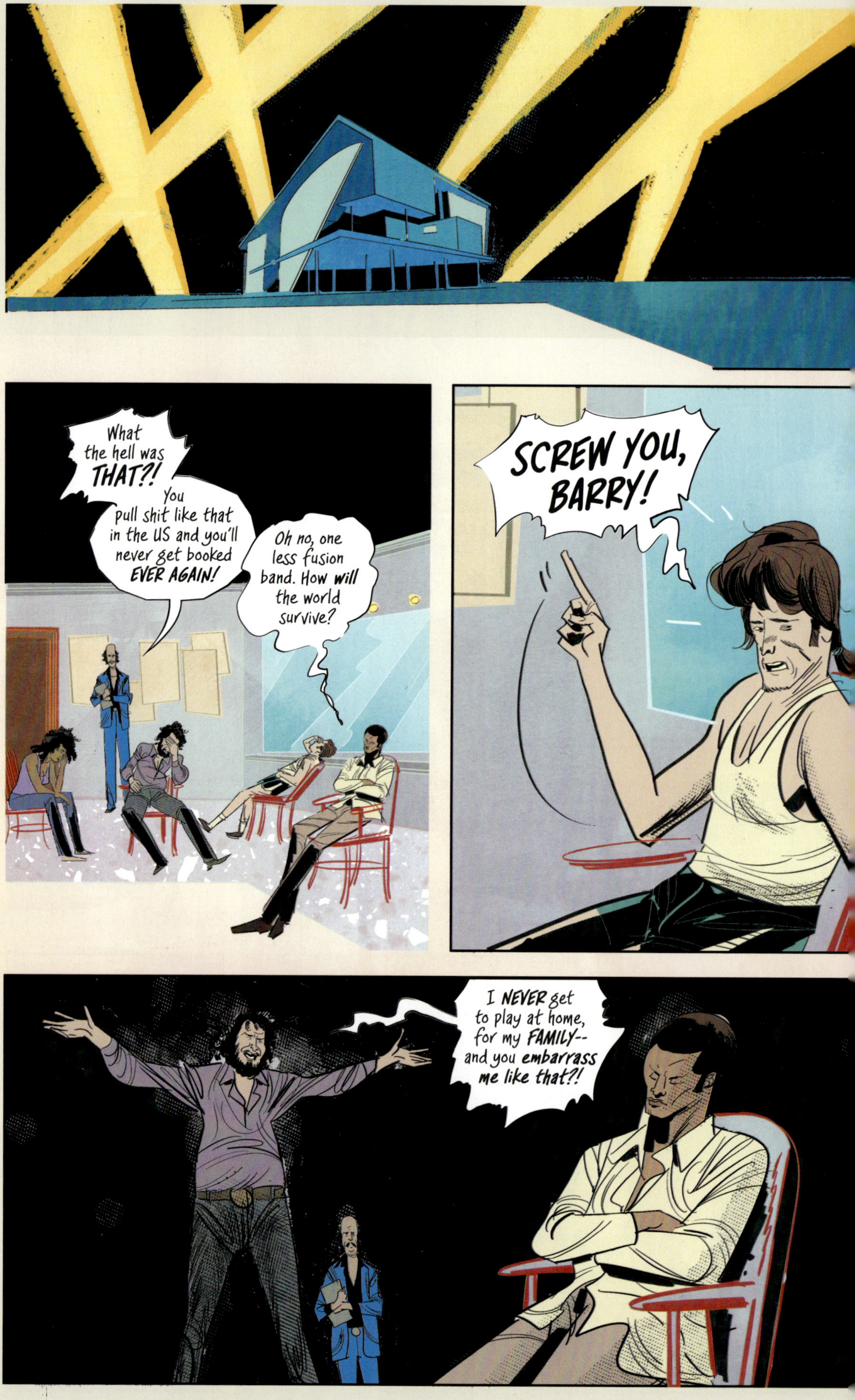
What the hell was THAT?!
You pull shit like that in the US and you'll never get booked EVER AGAIN!
Oh no, one less fusion band. How will the world survive?
SCREW YOU, BARRY!
I NEVER get to play at home, for my FAMILY-- and you embarrass me like that?!

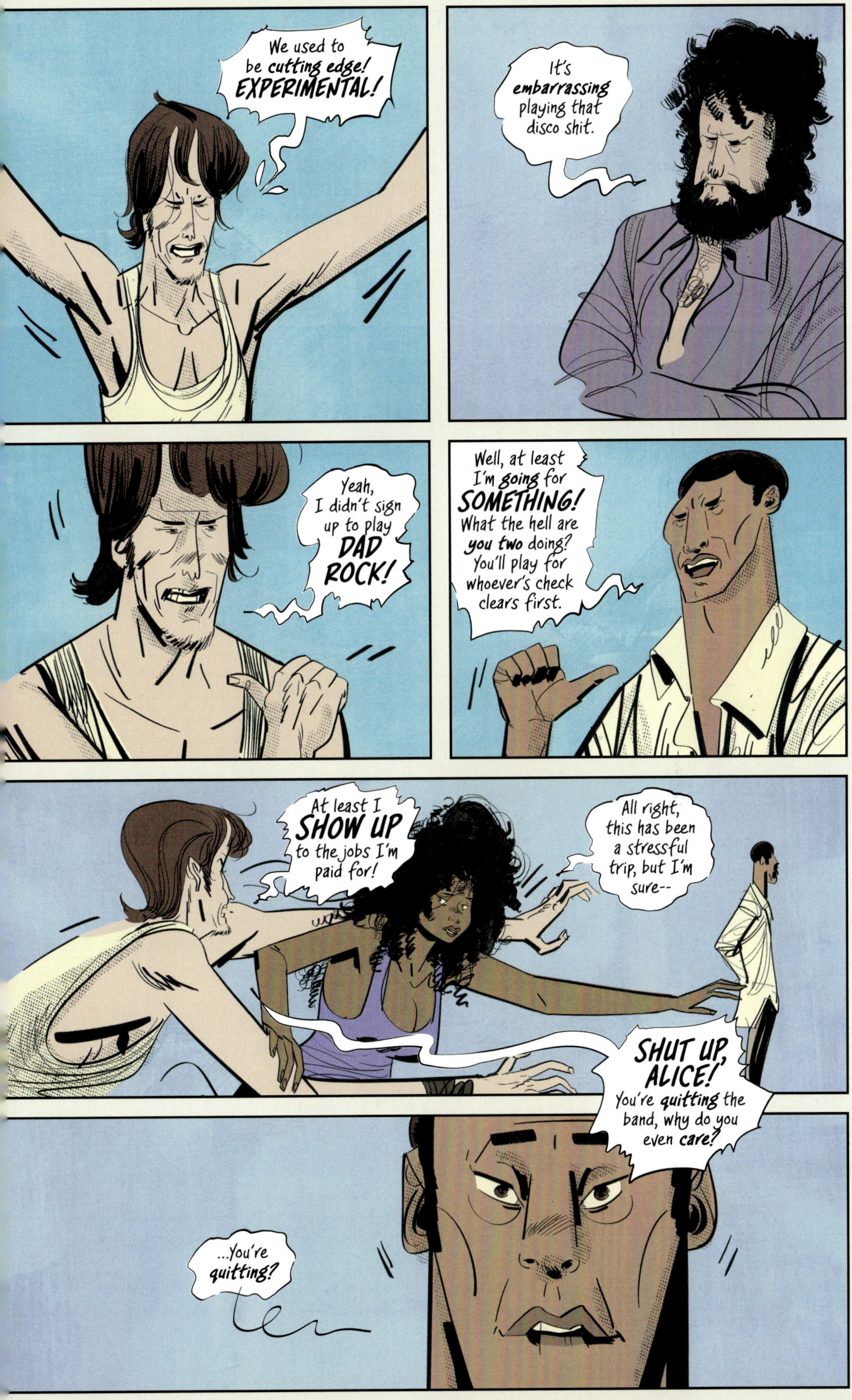
We used to be cutting edge! EXPERIMENTAL!
It's embarrassing playing that disco shit.
Yeah, I didn't sign up to play DAD ROCK!
Well, at least I'm going for SOMETHING! What the hell are you two doing? You'll play for whoever's check clears first.
At least I SHOW UP to the jobs I'm paid for!
All right, this has been a stressful trip, but I'm sure--
SHUT UP, ALICE! You're quitting the band, why do you even care?
...You're quitting?

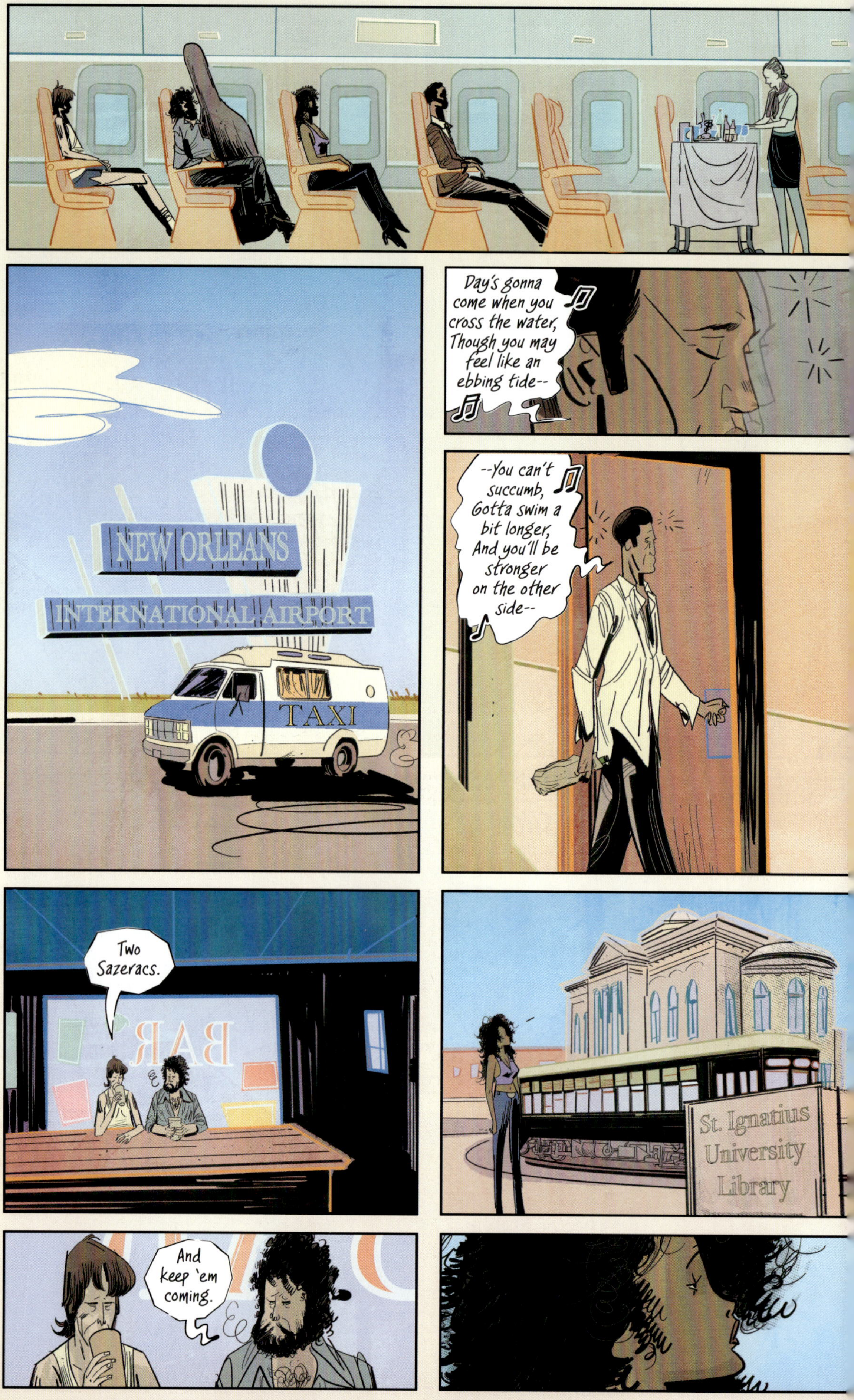
Day's gonna come when you cross the water, Though you may feel like an ebbing tide--
NEW ORLEANS
INTERNATIONAL AIRPORT
TAXI
--You can't succumb, Gotta swim a bit longer, And you'll be stronger on the other side--
Two Sazeracs.
BAR
St. Ignatius University Library
And keep 'em coming.

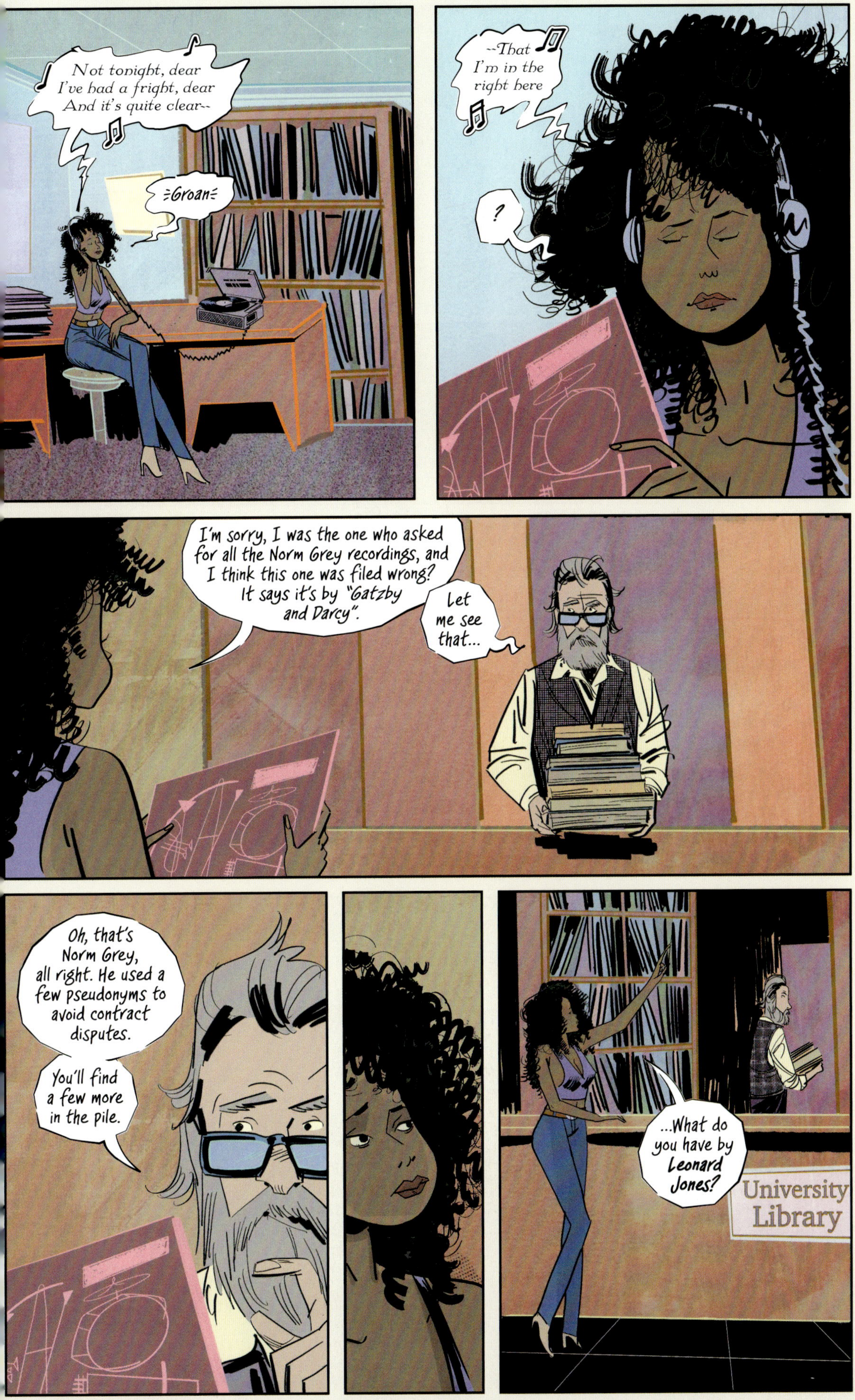
Not tonight, dear
I've had a fright, dear
And it's quite clear--
=Groan=
--That
I'm in the
right here
?
I'm sorry, I was the one who asked for all the Norm Grey recordings, and I think this one was filed wrong? It says it's by "Gatzby and Darcy".
Let me see that...
Oh, that's Norm Grey, all right. He used a few pseudonyms to avoid contract disputes.
You'll find a few more in the pile.
...What do you have by **Leonard Jones?**
University Library

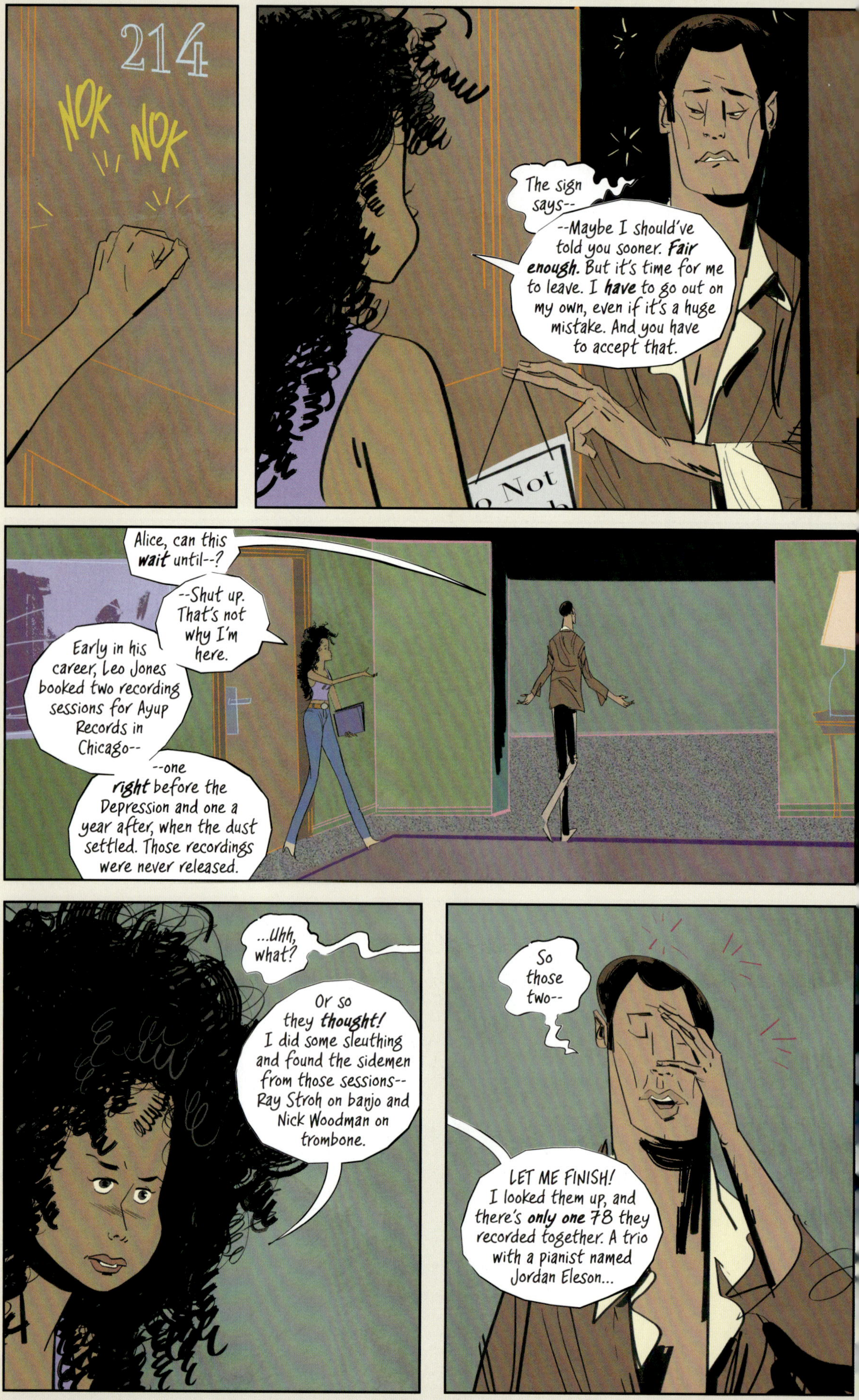
214
NOK NOK
The sign says--
--Maybe I should've told you sooner. **Fair enough.** But it's time for me to leave. I **have** to go out on my own, even if it's a huge mistake. And you have to accept that.
Not
Alice, can this **wait** until--?
--Shut up. That's not why I'm here.
Early in his career, Leo Jones booked two recording sessions for Ayup Records in Chicago--
--one **right** before the Depression and one a year after, when the dust settled. Those recordings were never released.
...Uhh, what?
Or so they **thought!** I did some sleuthing and found the sidemen from those sessions--Ray Stroh on banjo and Nick Woodman on trombone.
So those two--
LET ME FINISH! I looked them up, and there's **only one** 78 they recorded together. A trio with a pianist named Jordan Eleson...

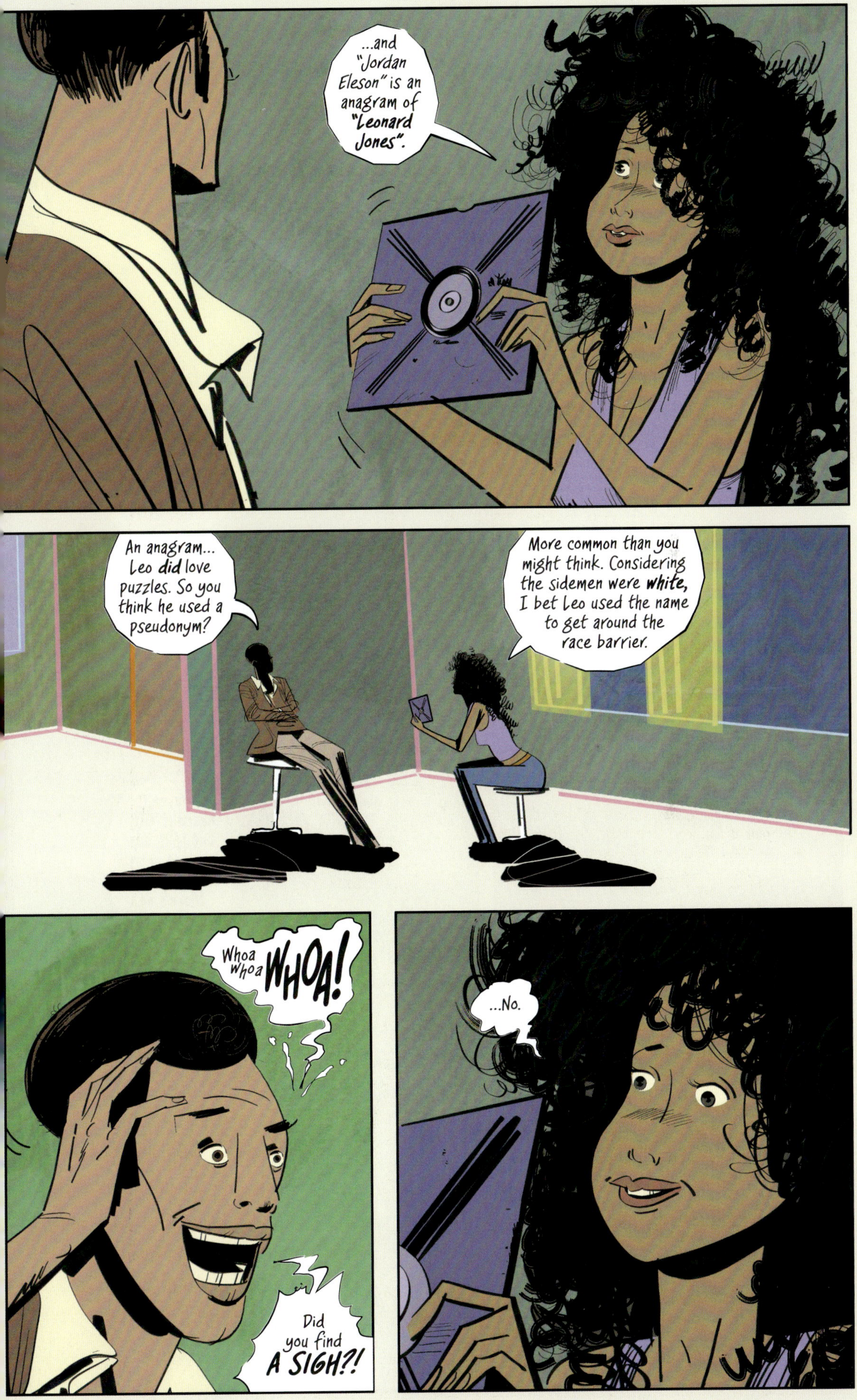
...and "Jordan Eleson" is an anagram of "Leonard Jones".
An anagram... Leo did love puzzles. So you think he used a pseudonym?
More common than you might think. Considering the sidemen were white, I bet Leo used the name to get around the race barrier.
Whoa whoa WHOA!
Did you find A SIGH?!
...No.

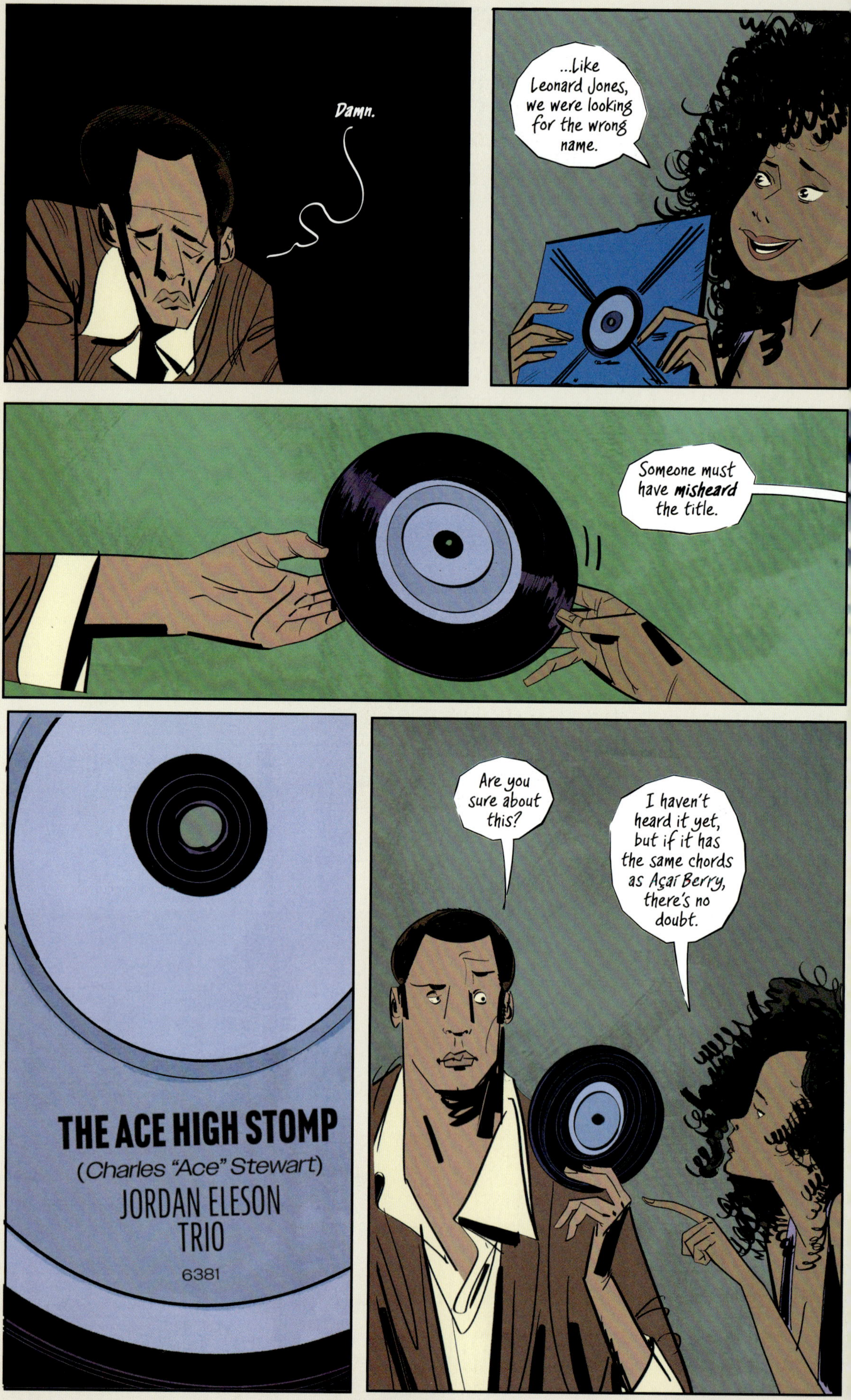
Damn.
...Like Leonard Jones, we were looking for the wrong name.
Someone must have **misheard** the title.
THE ACE HIGH STOMP
(Charles "Ace" Stewart)
JORDAN ELESON TRIO
6381
Are you sure about this?
I haven't heard it yet, but if it has the same chords as Açaí Berry, there's no doubt.

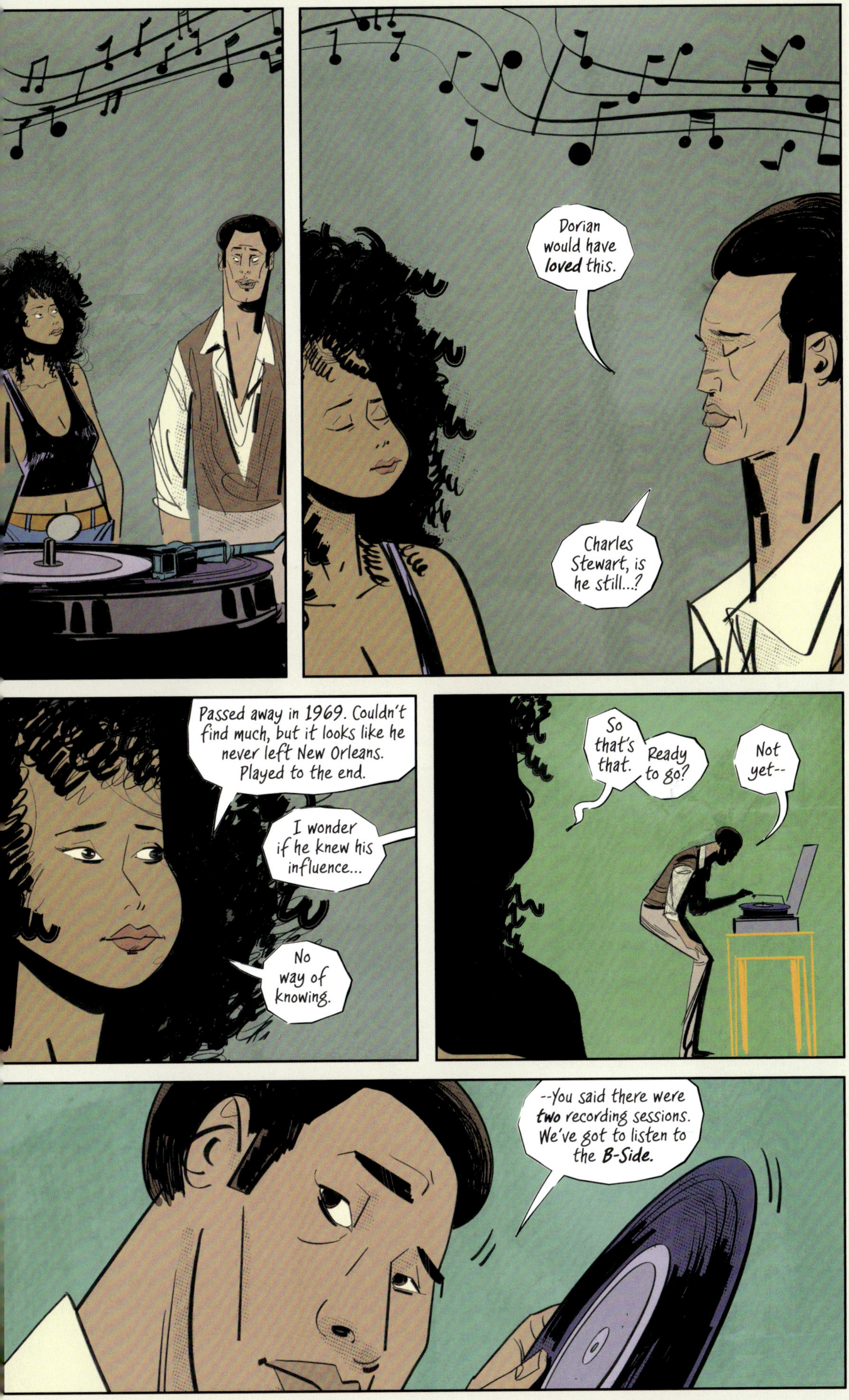
Dorian would have **loved** this.
Charles Stewart, is he still...?
Passed away in 1969. Couldn't find much, but it looks like he never left New Orleans. Played to the end.
I wonder if he knew his influence...
No way of knowing.
So that's that.
Ready to go?
Not yet--
--You said there were **two** recording sessions. We've got to listen to the **B-Side.**

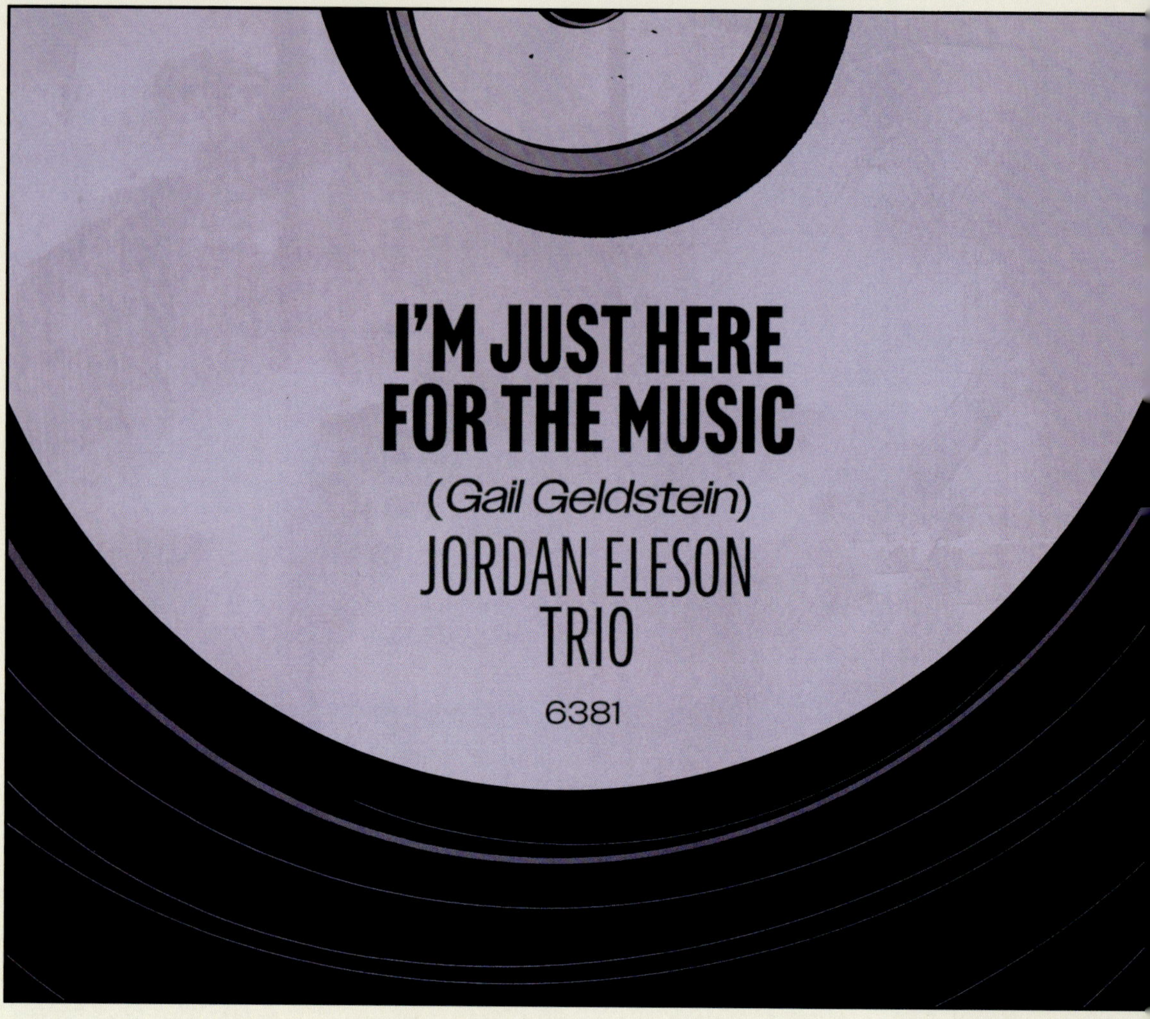
I'M JUST HERE
FOR THE MUSIC
(Gail Geldstein)
JORDAN ELESON
TRIO
6381

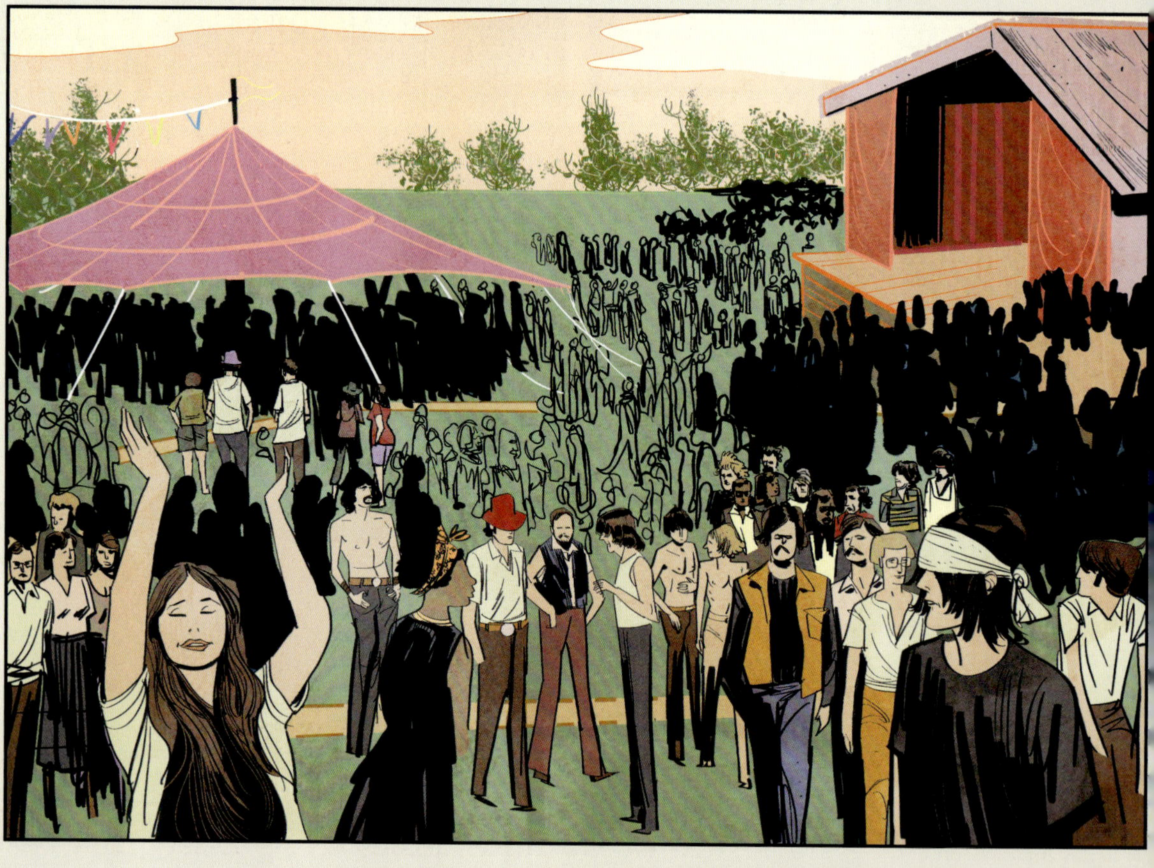

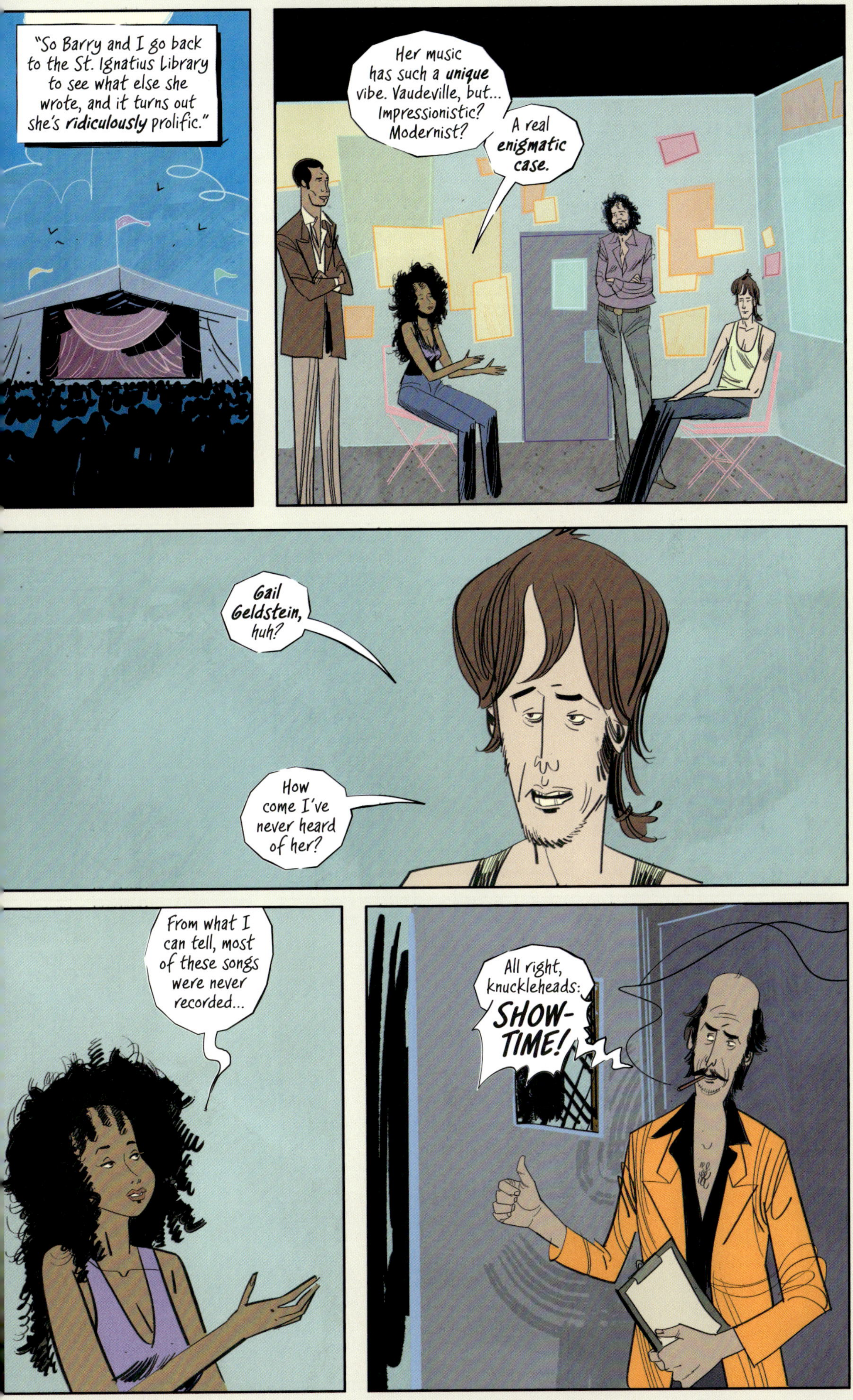
"So Barry and I go back to the St. Ignatius Library to see what else she wrote, and it turns out she's *ridiculously* prolific."
Her music has such a **unique** vibe. Vaudeville, but... Impressionistic? Modernist?
A real **enigmatic case.**
Gail Geldstein, huh?
How come I've never heard of her?
From what I can tell, most of these songs were never recorded...
All right, knuckleheads:
SHOW-TIME!

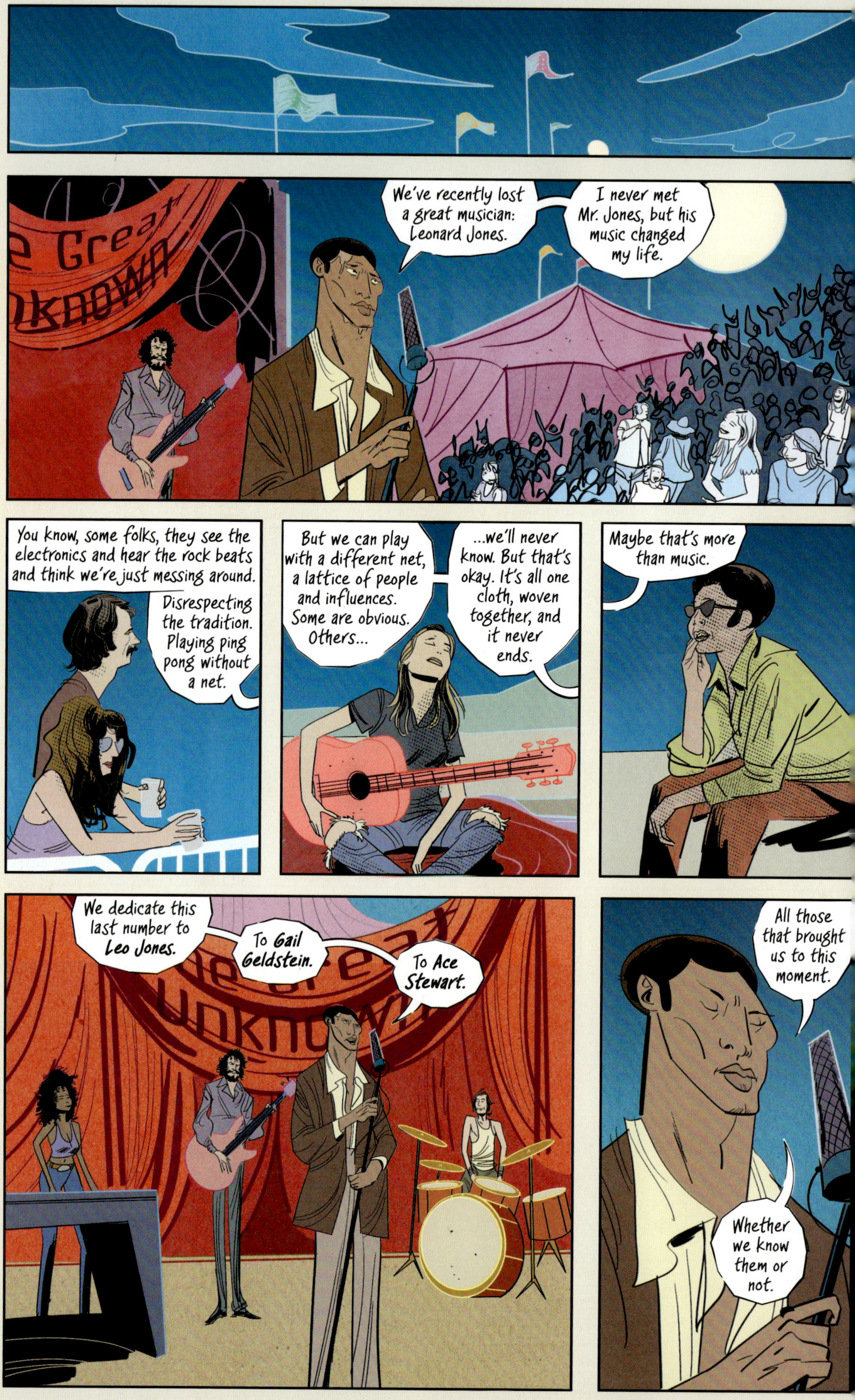

We've recently lost a great musician: Leonard Jones.
I never met Mr. Jones, but his music changed my life.
You know, some folks, they see the electronics and hear the rock beats and think we're just messing around.
Disrespecting the tradition. Playing ping pong without a net.
But we can play with a different net, a lattice of people and influences. Some are obvious. Others...
...we'll never know. But that's okay. It's all one cloth, woven together, and it never ends.
Maybe that's more than music.
We dedicate this last number to Leo Jones.
To Gail Geldstein.
To Ace Stewart.
All those that brought us to this moment.
Whether we know them or not.

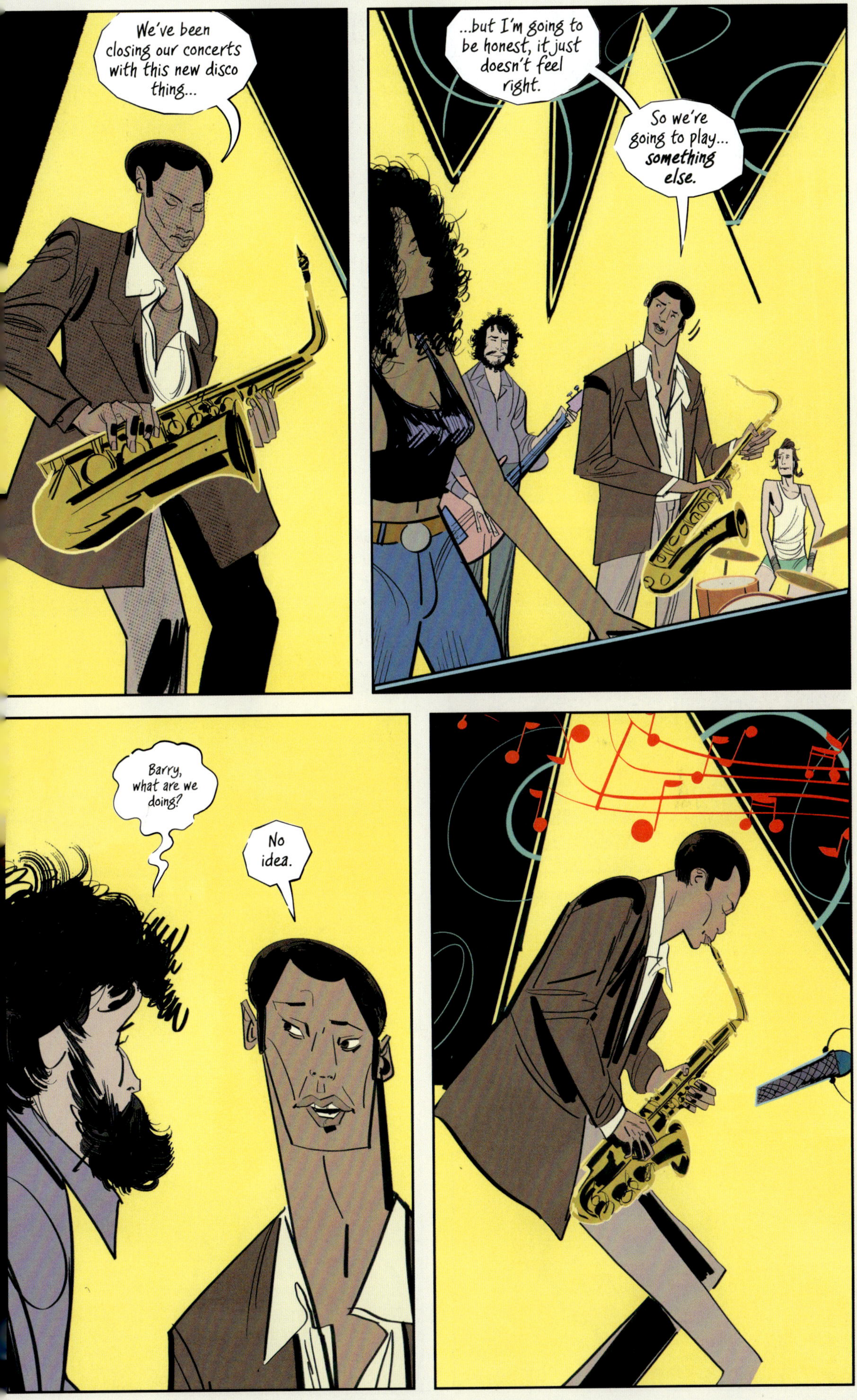
We've been closing our concerts with this new disco thing...
...but I'm going to be honest, it just doesn't feel right.
So we're going to play... **something else.**
Barry, what are we doing?
No idea.

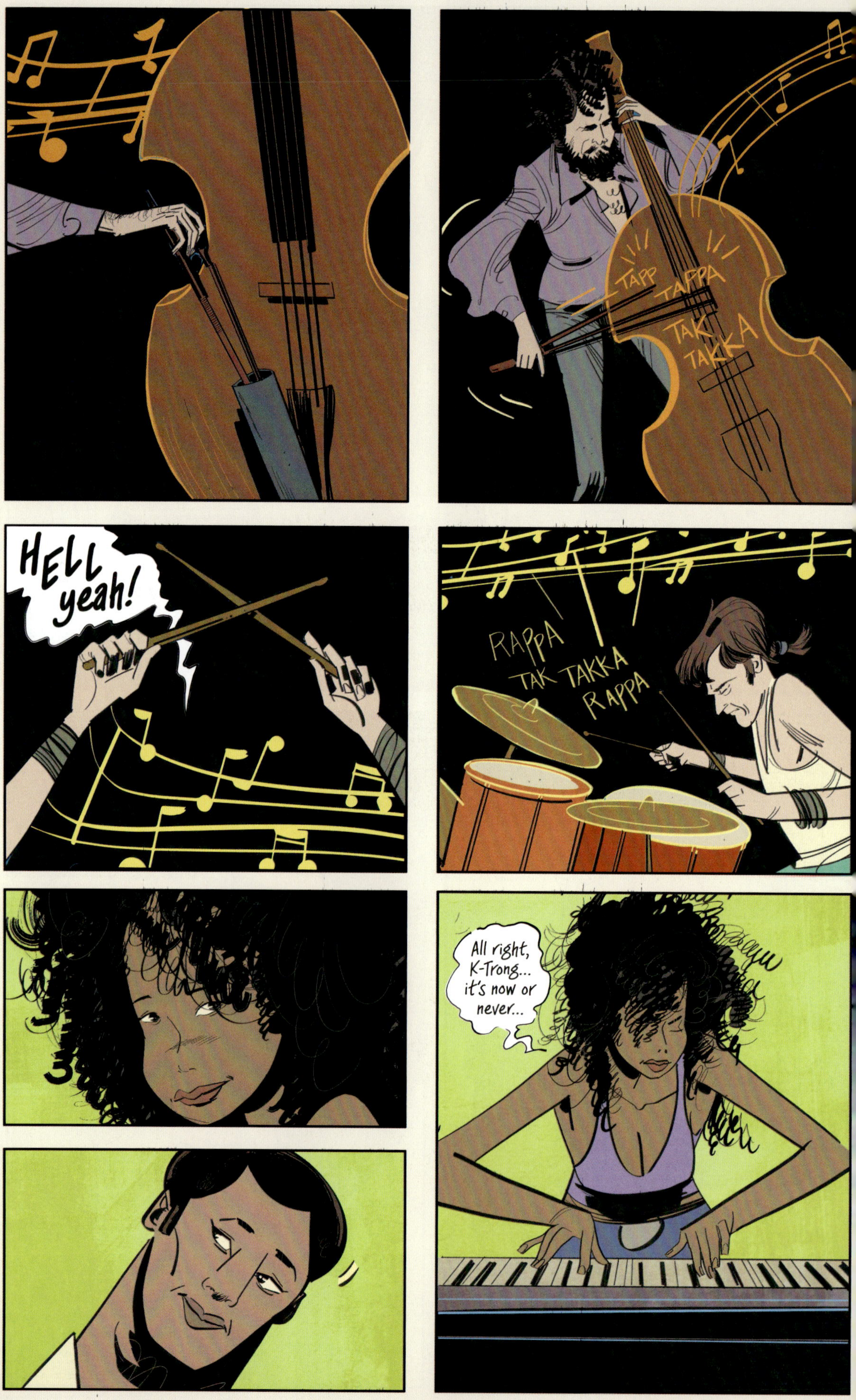
TAPP
TAPPA
TAK
TAKKA
HELL yeah!
RAPPA
TAK TAKKA
RAPPA
All right, K-Trong... it's now or never...

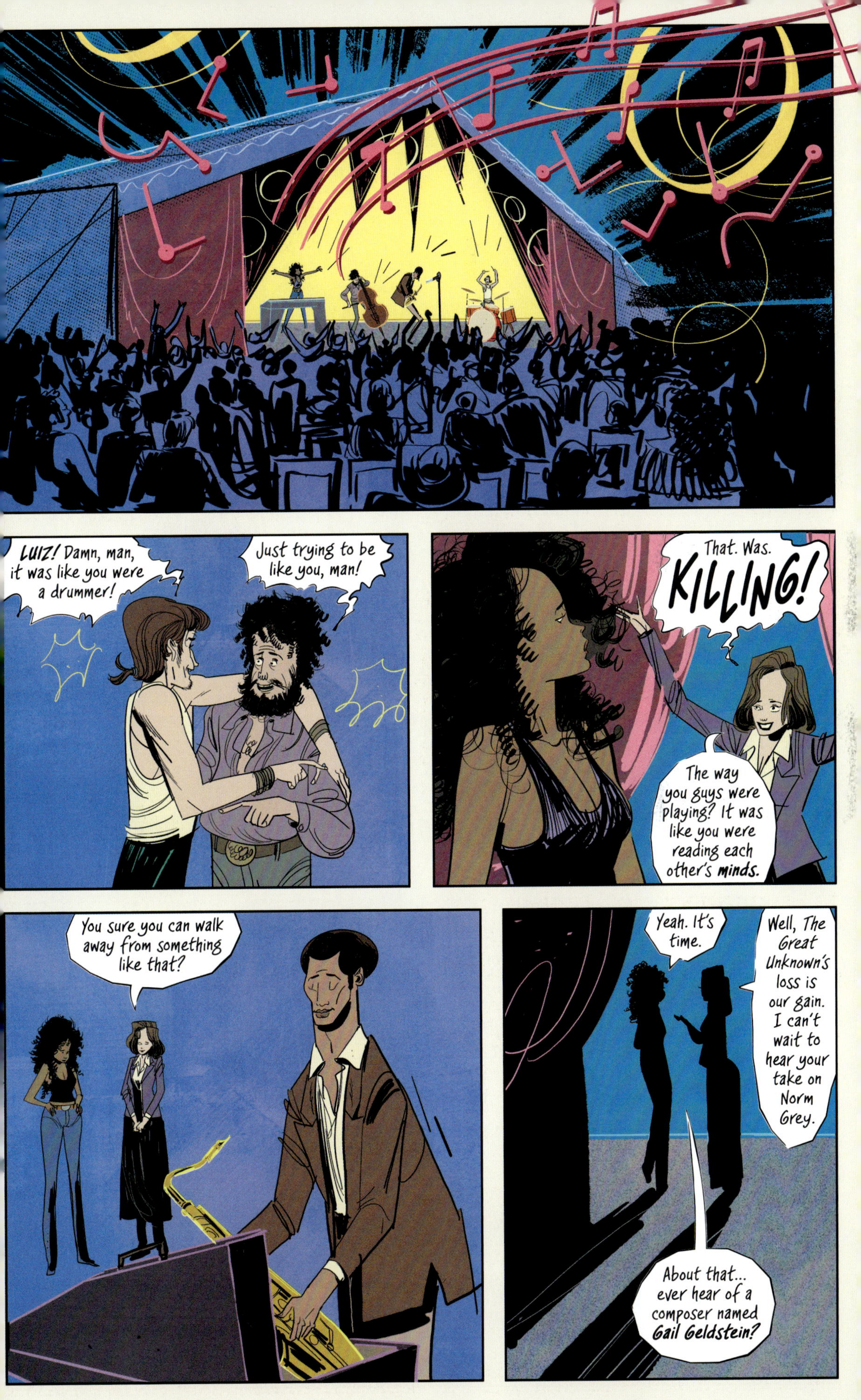

LUIZ! Damn, man, it was like you were a drummer!
Just trying to be like you, man!
That. Was.
KILLING!
The way you guys were playing? It was like you were reading each other's minds.
You sure you can walk away from something like that?
Yeah. It's time.
Well, The Great Unknown's loss is our gain. I can't wait to hear your take on Norm Grey.
About that... ever hear of a composer named Gail Geldstein?

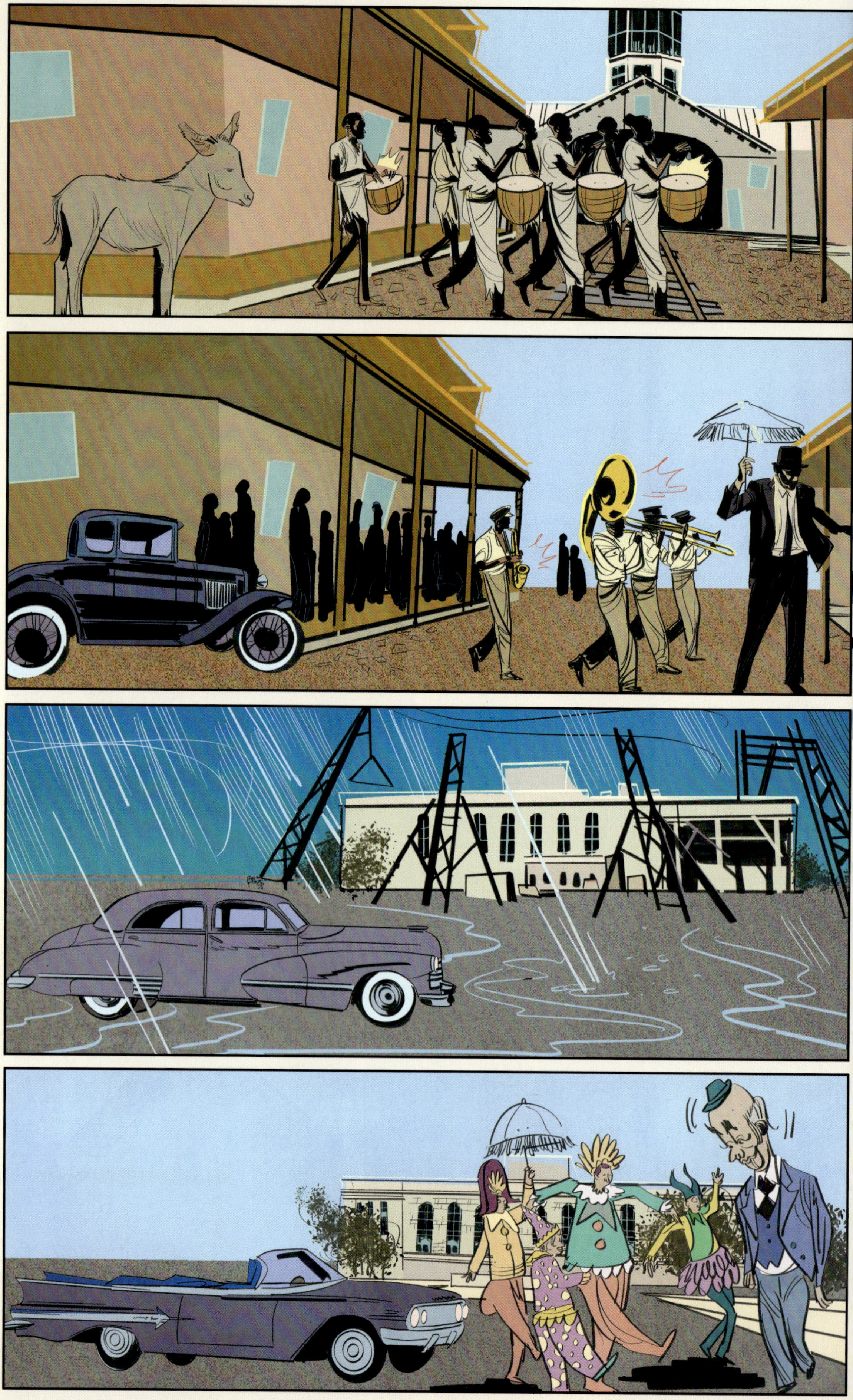

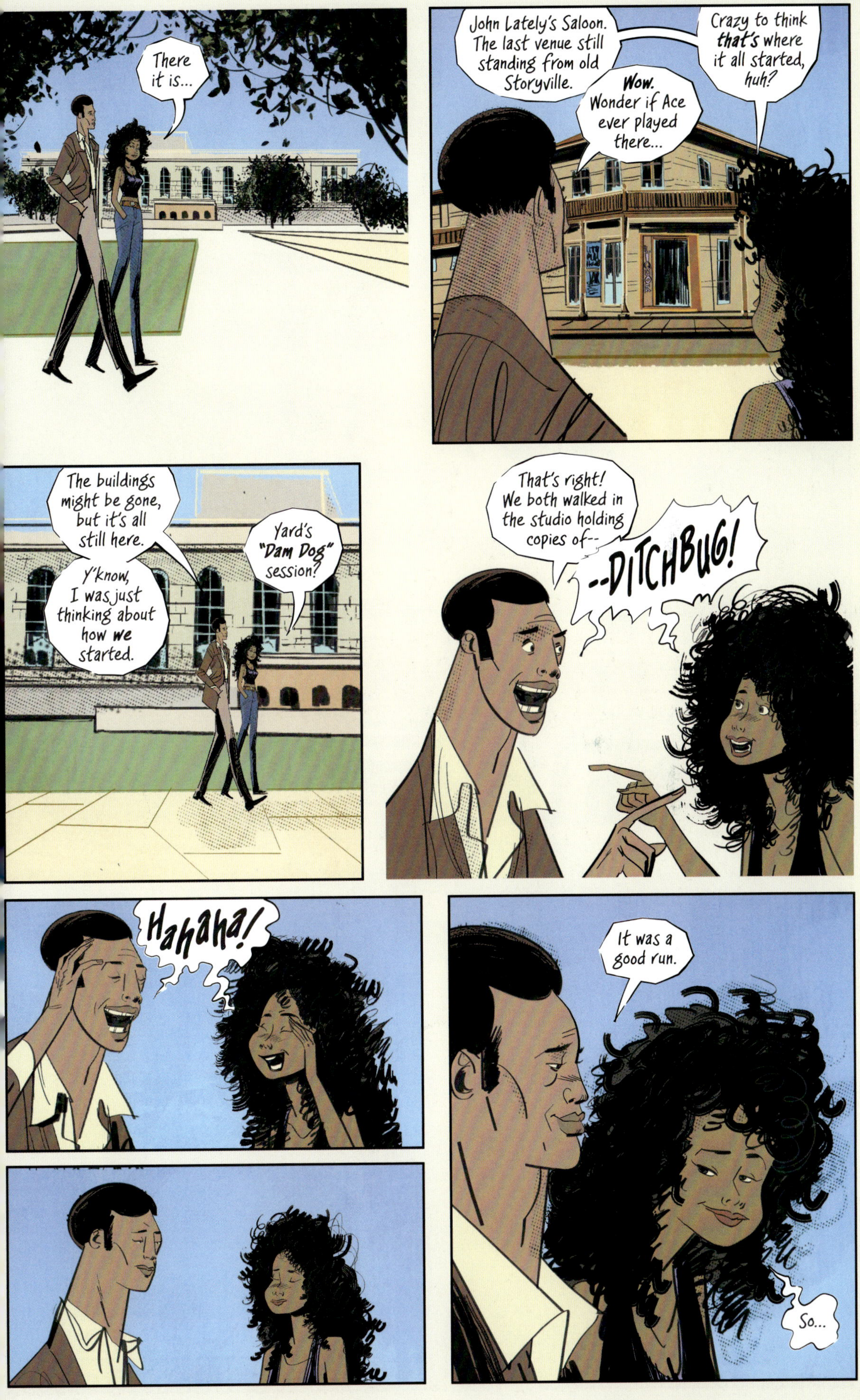
There it is...
John Lately's Saloon. The last venue still standing from old Storyville.
Crazy to think **that's** where it all started, huh?
Wow. Wonder if Ace ever played there...
The buildings might be gone, but it's all still here.
Y'know, I was just thinking about how **we** started.
Yard's **"Dam Dog"** session?
That's right! We both walked in the studio holding copies of--
--DITCHBUG!
Hahaha!
It was a good run.
So...

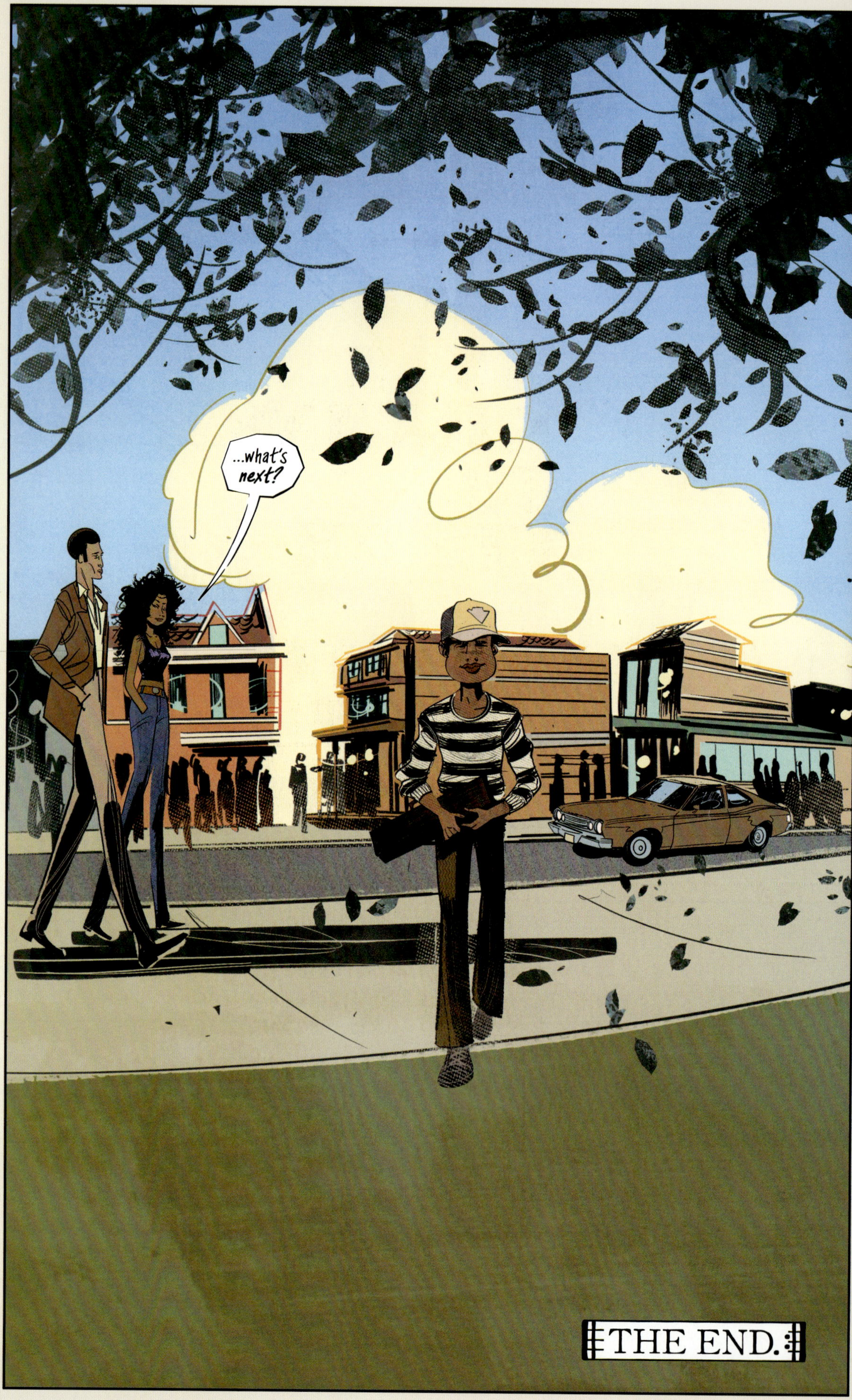
...what's next?
THE END.

DEEP CUTS

WORDS **KYLE HIGGINS & JOE CLARK**

CHAPTER 1 **DANILO BEYRUTH**

CHAPTER 2 **HELENA MASELLIS**

CHAPTER 3 **DIEGO GRECO**

CHAPTER 4 **RAMÓN K. PEREZ**

CHAPTER 5 **JUNI BA**

CHAPTER 6 **TOBY CYPRESS**

COLORS	**IGOR MONTI**
LETTERS	**HASSAN OTSMANE-ELHAOU**
PRODUCTION	**RICH FOWLKS**
DESIGN	**MICHAEL BUSUTTIL**
SPECIAL THANKS	Eric Stephenson Damon Stone Catie Hickey Daniel Sniderman Julia Filson Cantor Shelly Friedman Rabbi Marcey Rosenbaum Sara Neilson Roy McGrath and Herbie and Wayne

BLACK MARKET NARRATIVE

1—6.

COVER GALLERY

CHRIS BRUNNER & RICO RENZI

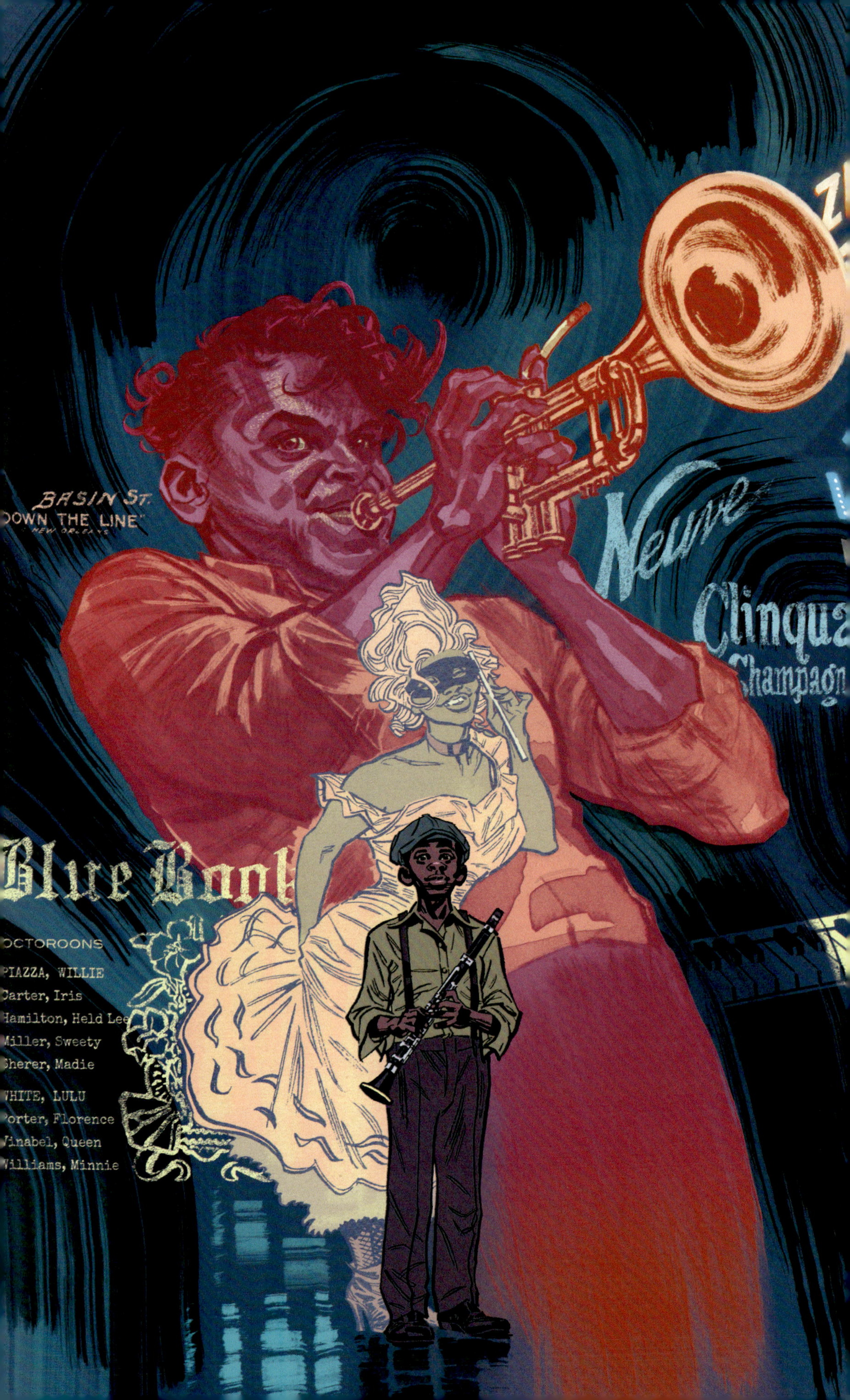
BASIN ST.
OWN THE LINE"
NEW ORLEANS
Neuve
Clinqua
Champagn
Blue Book
OCTOROONS
PIAZZA, WILLIE
Carter, Iris
Hamilton, Held Lee
Miller, Sweety
Sherer, Madie
WHITE, LULU
Porter, Florence
Vinabel, Queen
Williams, Minnie

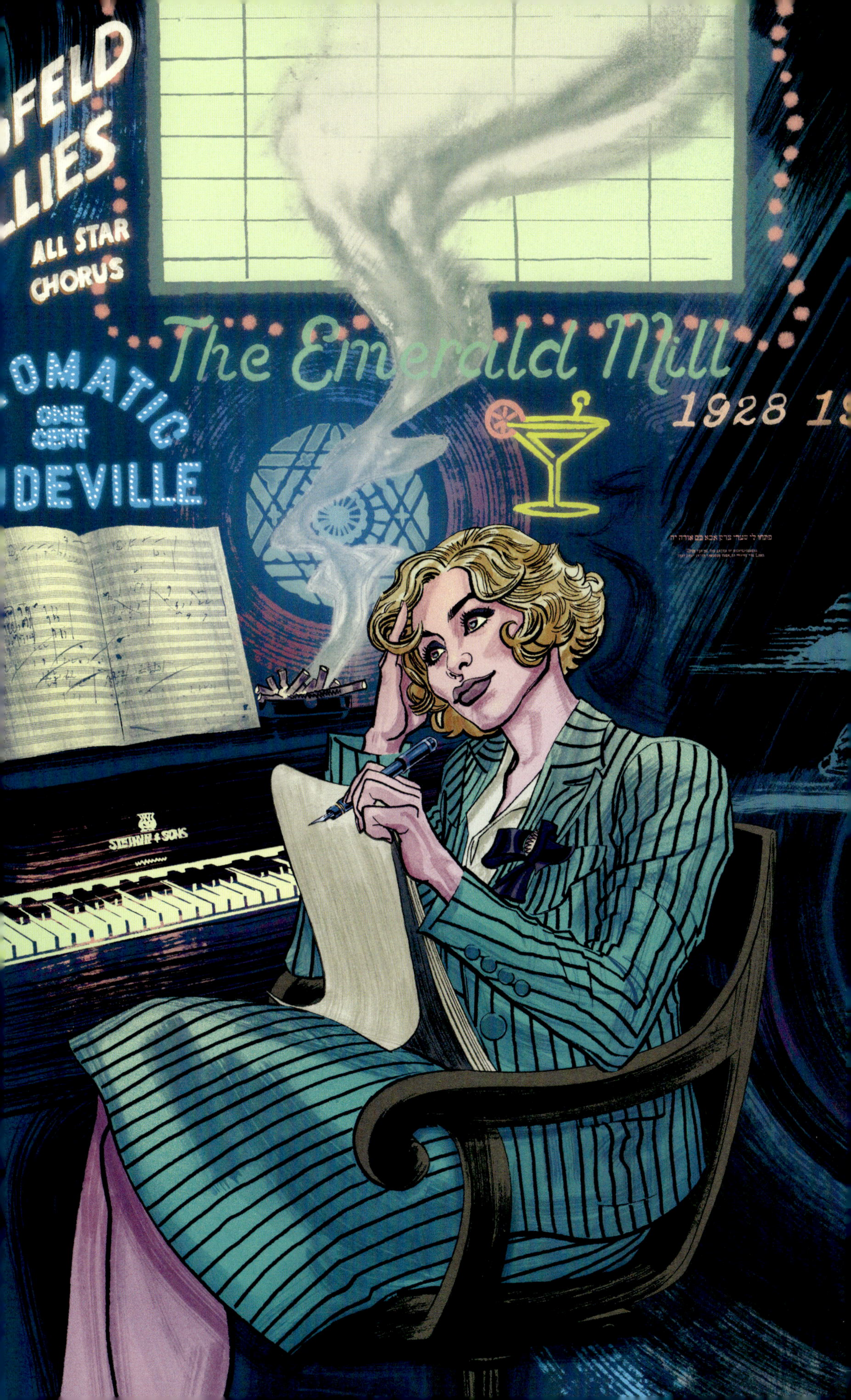

ALL STAR
CHORUS
The Emerald Mill
1928 19
ONE CENT
DEVILLE

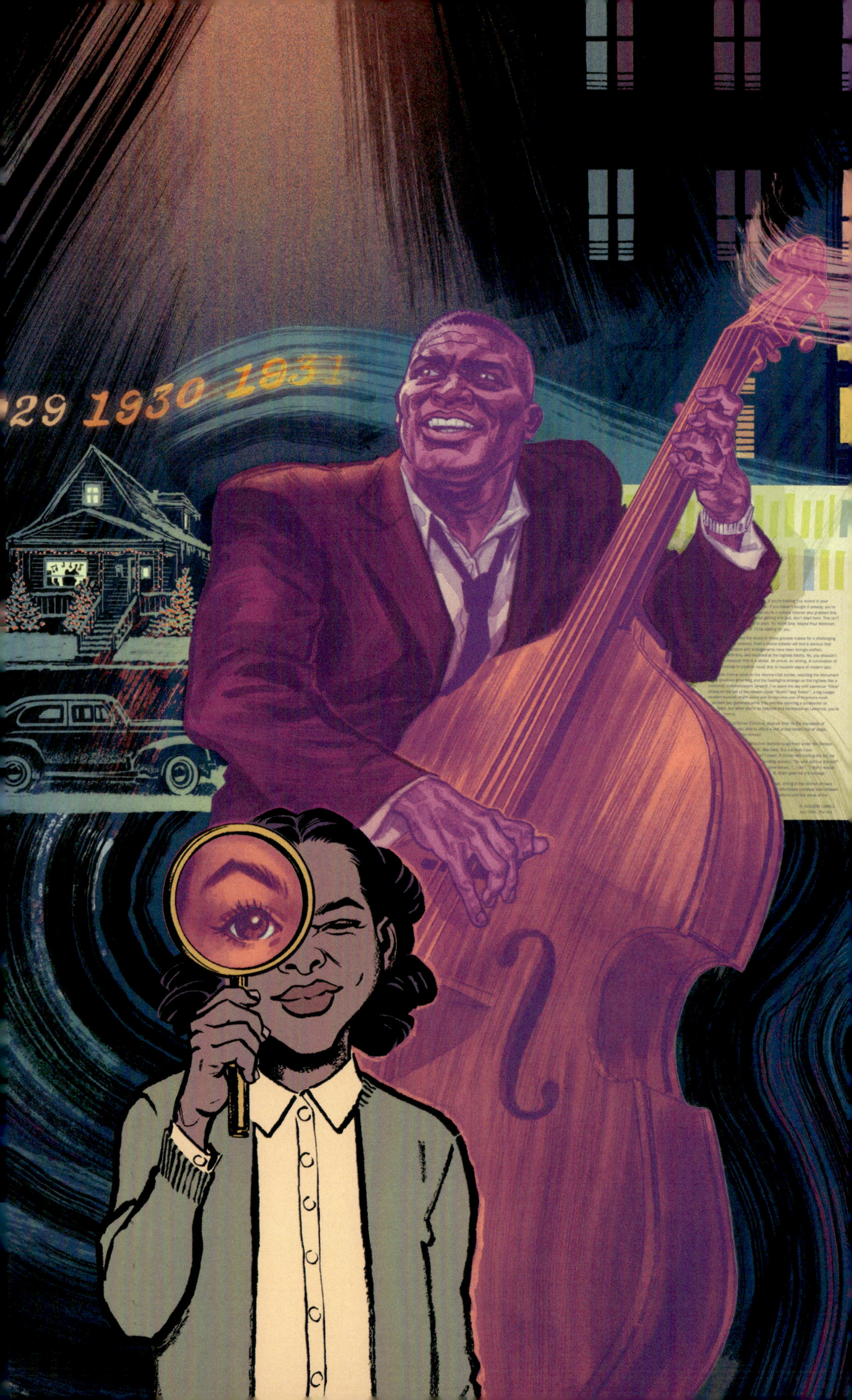
29 1930 1931

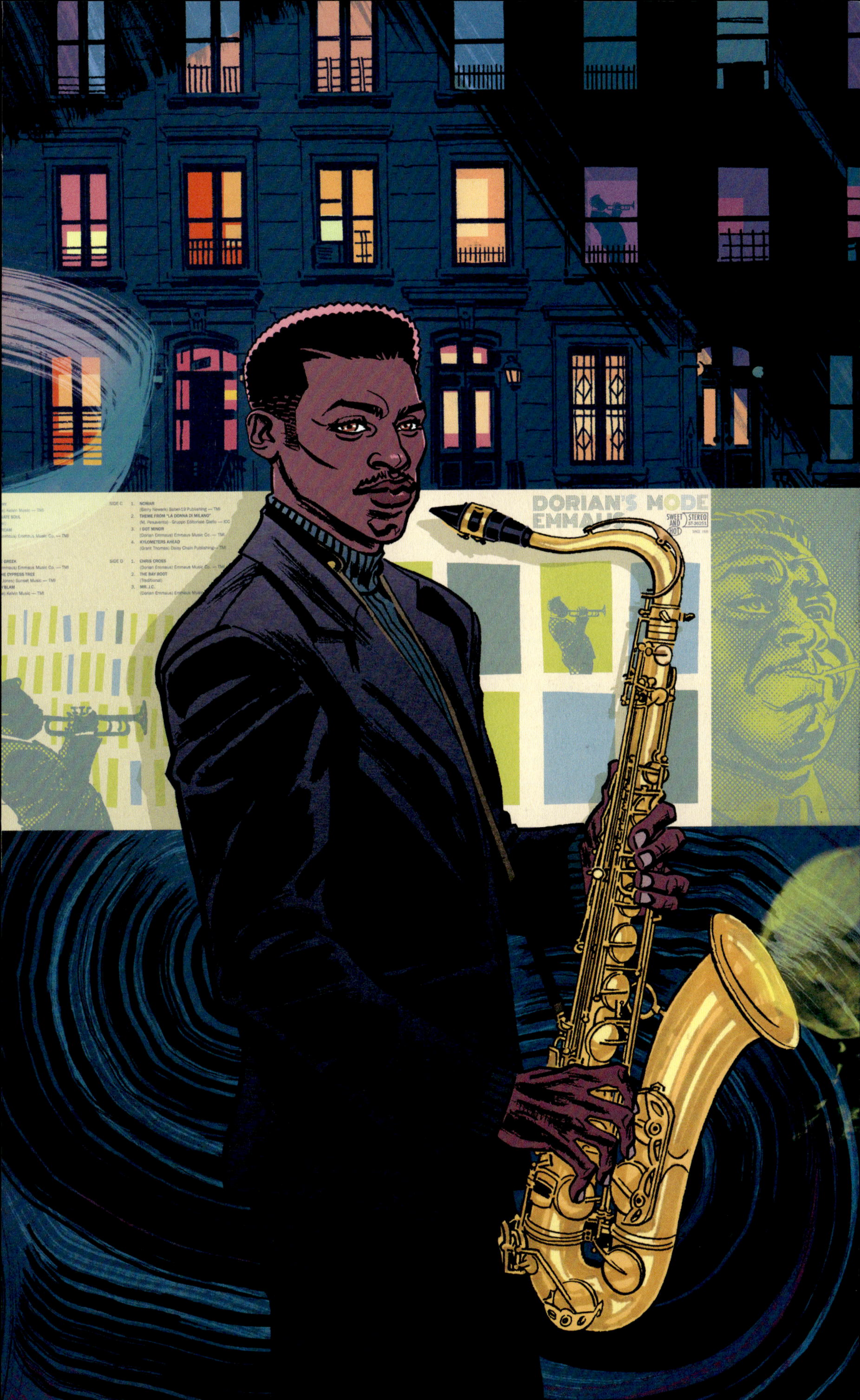

DORIAN'S MODE
EMMAUS
SWEET AND HOT
STEREO
ST-36251
SIDE C
1. NOMAR
(Barry Newark) Babel-19 Publishing — TMI
2. THEME FROM "LA DONNA DI MILANO"
(M. Pesavento) - Gruppo Editoriale Giallo — ICC
3. I GOT MINOR
(Dorian Emmaus) Emmaus Music Co. — TMI
4. KYLOMETERS AHEAD
(Grant Thomas) Daisy Chain Publishing — TMI
SIDE D
1. CHRIS CROSS
(Dorian Emmaus) Emmaus Music Co. — TMI
2. THE BAY ROOT
(Traditional)
3. MR. J.C.

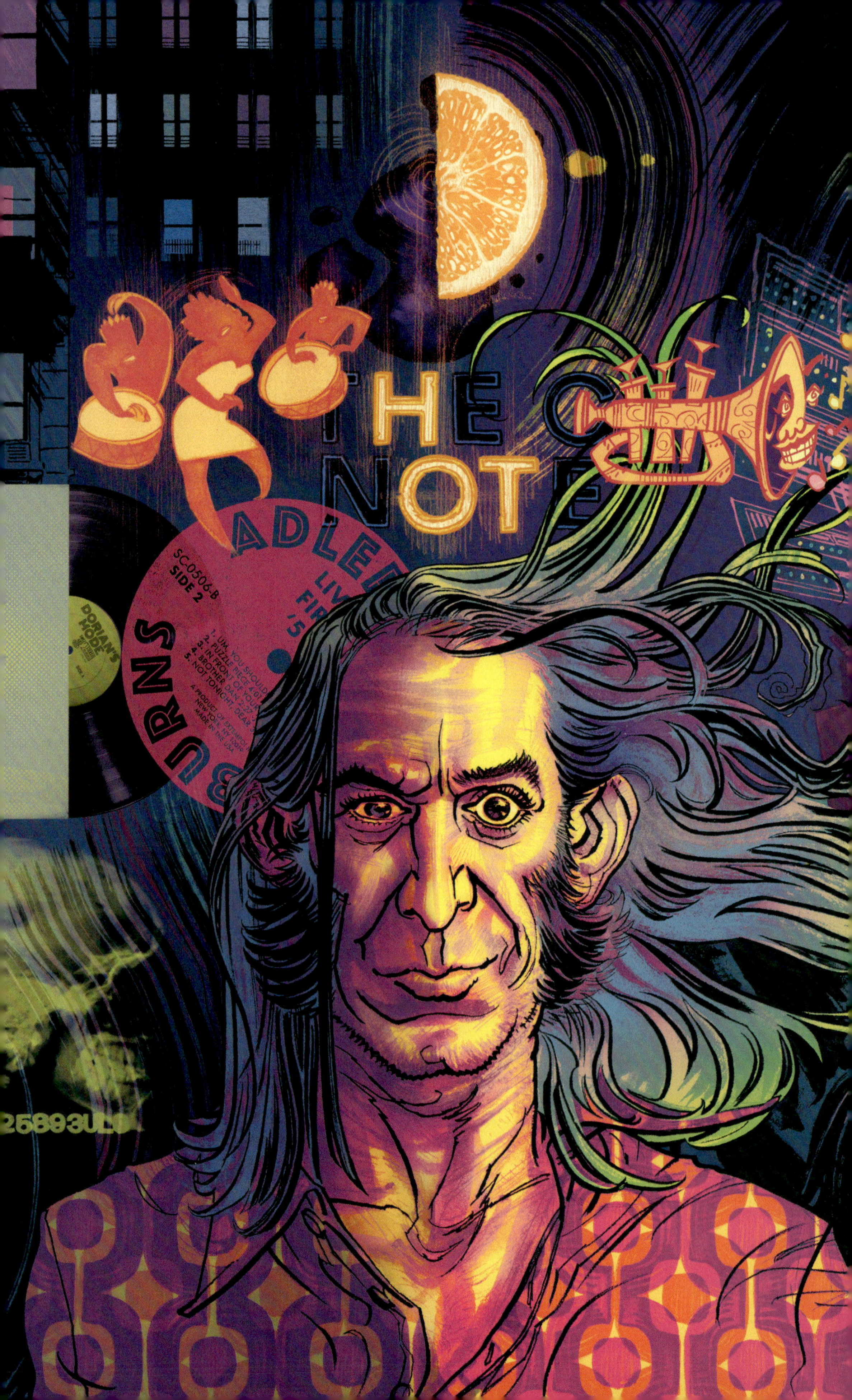
THE C
NOTE
ADLE
SC-0506-B
SIDE 2
URNS
1. UM, YOU SHOULD
2. PUZZLE PIECE
3. IN FRONT OF YOUR
4. BROTHER DAN 2:27
5. NOT TONIGHT, DEAR
MADE IN THE USA
DORIAN'S MODE
25893UL

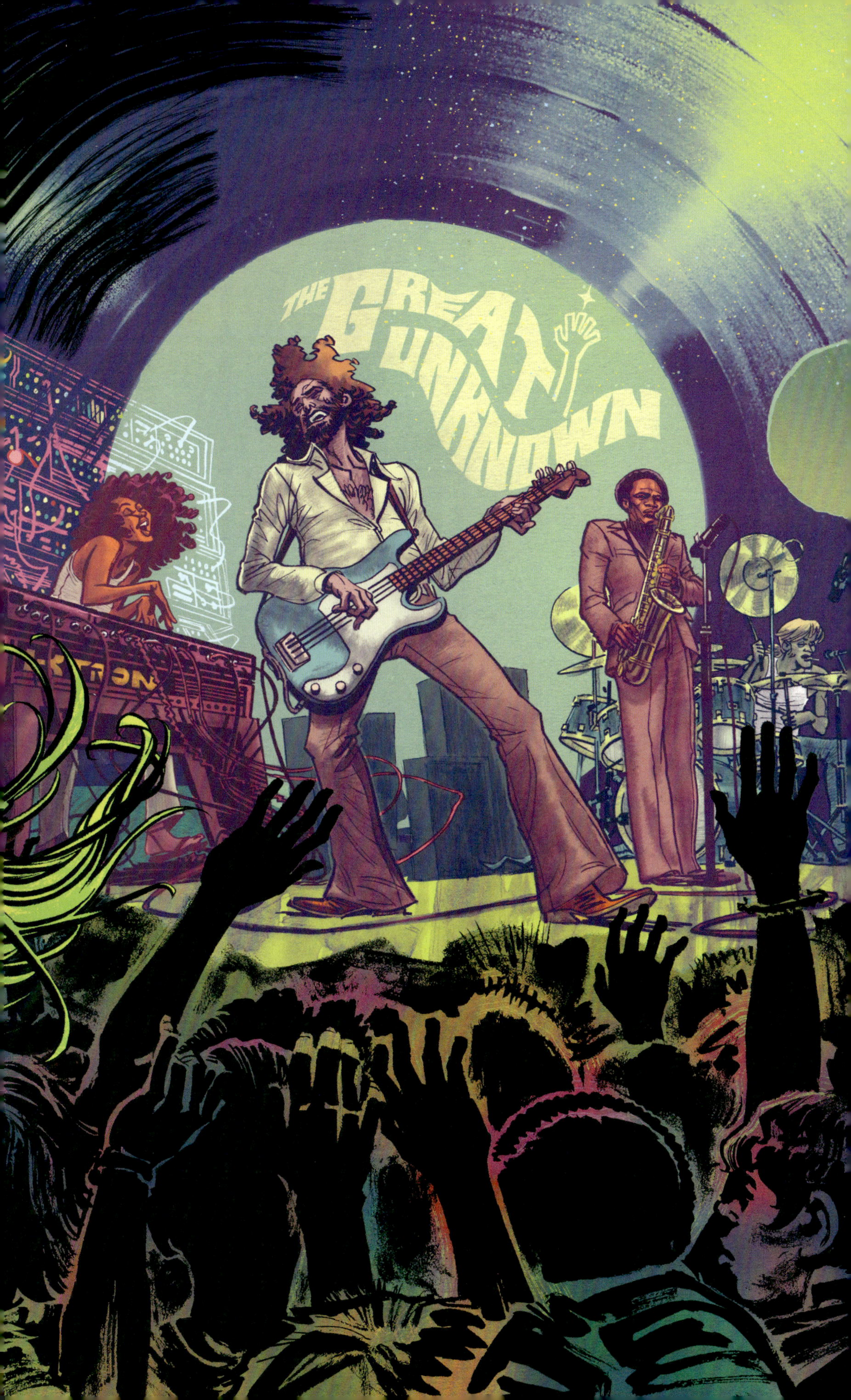
THE GREAT UNKNOWN

1—6.
LEAD SHEETS

THADDEUS TUKES
KATIE ERNST
QUENTIN COAXUM
MARQUES CARROLL
MAI SUGIMOTO
GREG WARD

Here We Go!

Thaddeus Tukes
For Deep Cuts #1

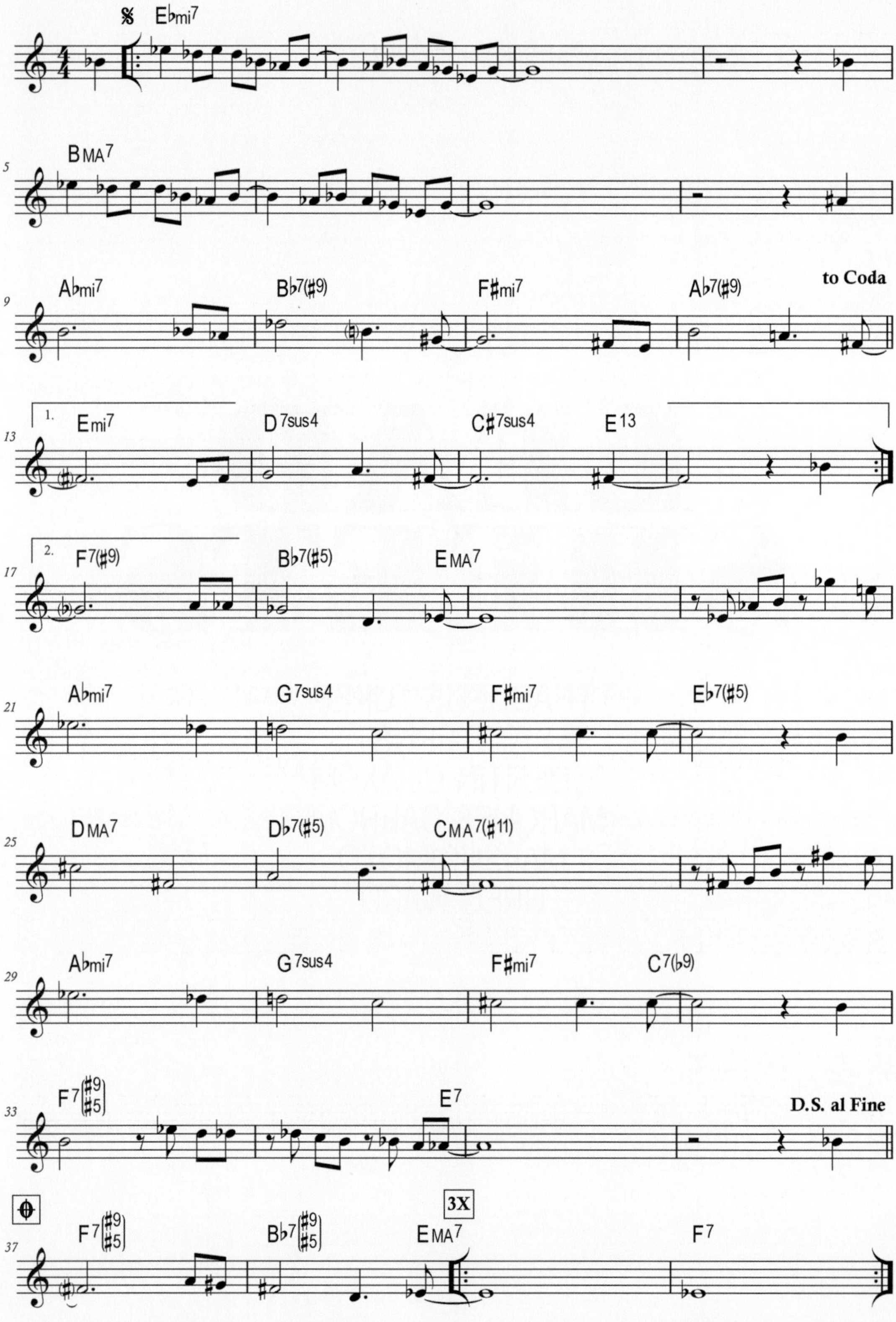
E♭mi7
BMA7
A♭mi7
B♭7(♯9)
F♯mi7
A♭7(♯9)
to Coda
Emi7
D7sus4
C♯7sus4
E13
F7(♯9)
B♭7(♯5)
EMA7
A♭mi7
G7sus4
F♯mi7
E♭7(♯5)
DMA7
D♭7(♯5)
CMA7(♯11)
A♭mi7
G7sus4
F♯mi7
C7(♭9)
F7(♯9/♯5)
E7
D.S. al Fine
F7(♯9/♯5)
B♭7(♯9/♯5)
3X
EMA7
F7

Epitaph

a postlude for forgotten fame

Katie Ernst
in response to Deep Cuts #2

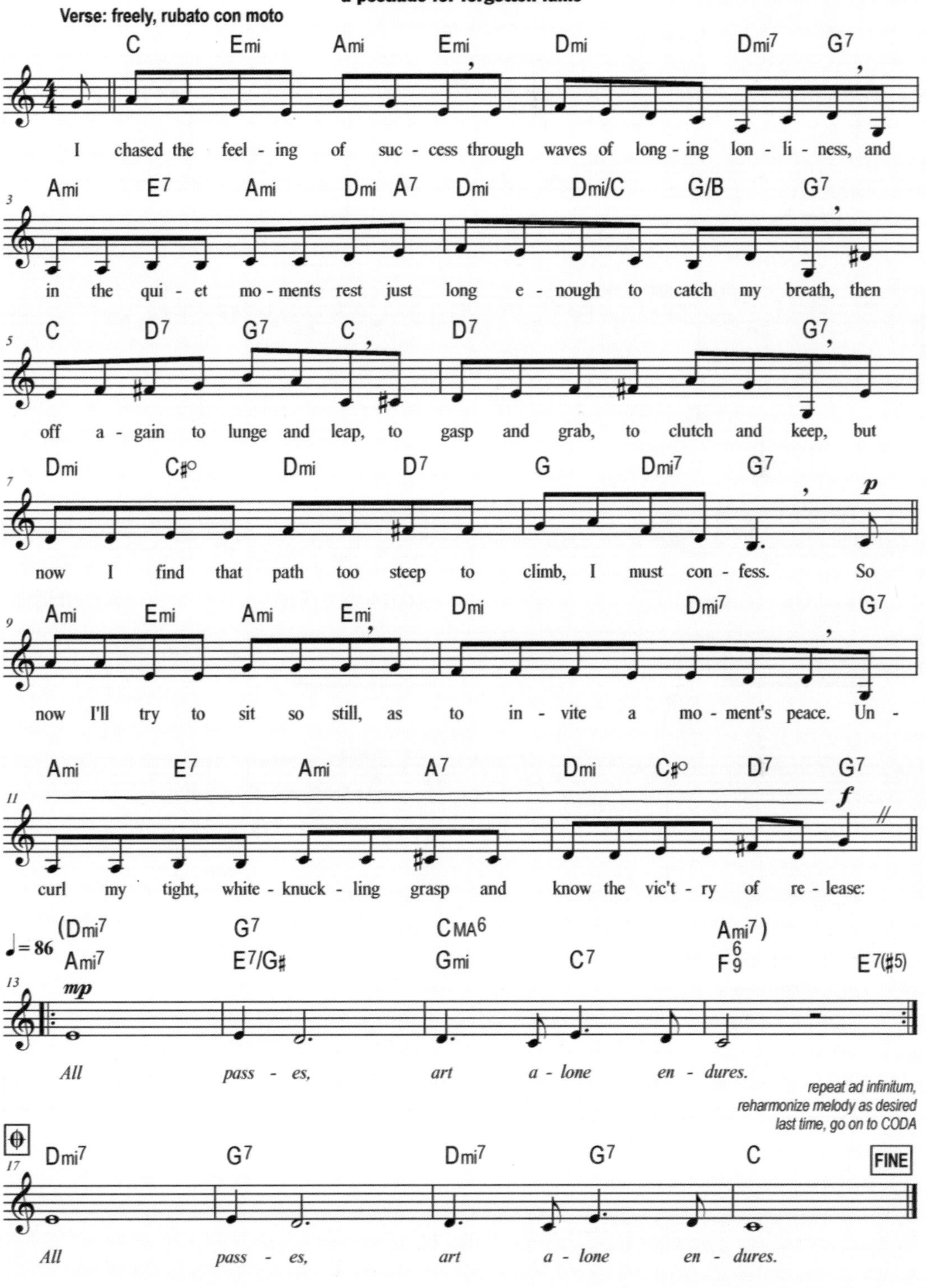
Verse: freely, rubato con moto
I chased the feel - ing of suc - cess through waves of long - ing lon - li - ness, and
in the qui - et mo - ments rest just long e - nough to catch my breath, then
off a - gain to lunge and leap, to gasp and grab, to clutch and keep, but
now I find that path too steep to climb, I must con - fess. So
now I'll try to sit so still, as to in - vite a mo - ment's peace. Un -
curl my tight, white - knuck - ling grasp and know the vic't - ry of re - lease:
♩= 86
All pass - es, art a - lone en - dures.
repeat ad infinitum,
reharmonize melody as desired
last time, go on to CODA
FINE
All pass - es, art a - lone en - dures.

1Cent

Quentin Coaxum
For Deep Cuts #3

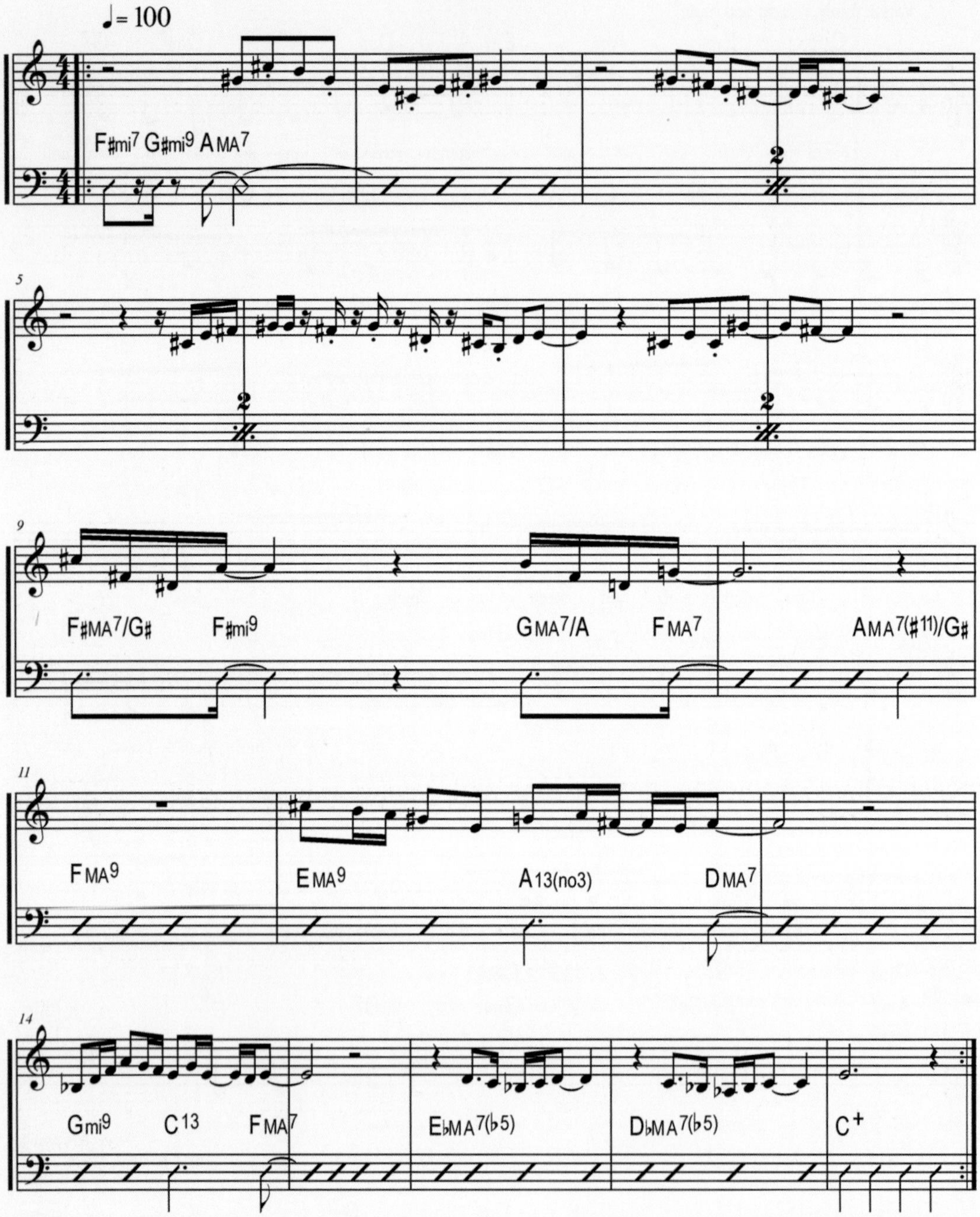
♩= 100
F♯mi7 G♯mi9 AMA7
F♯MA7/G♯
F♯mi9
GMA7/A
FMA7
AMA7(♯11)/G♯
FMA9
EMA9
A13(no3)
DMA7
Gmi9
C13
FMA7
E♭MA7(♭5)
D♭MA7(♭5)
C+

The Ancestors' Call Upon Us

Marques Carroll
For Deep Cuts #4

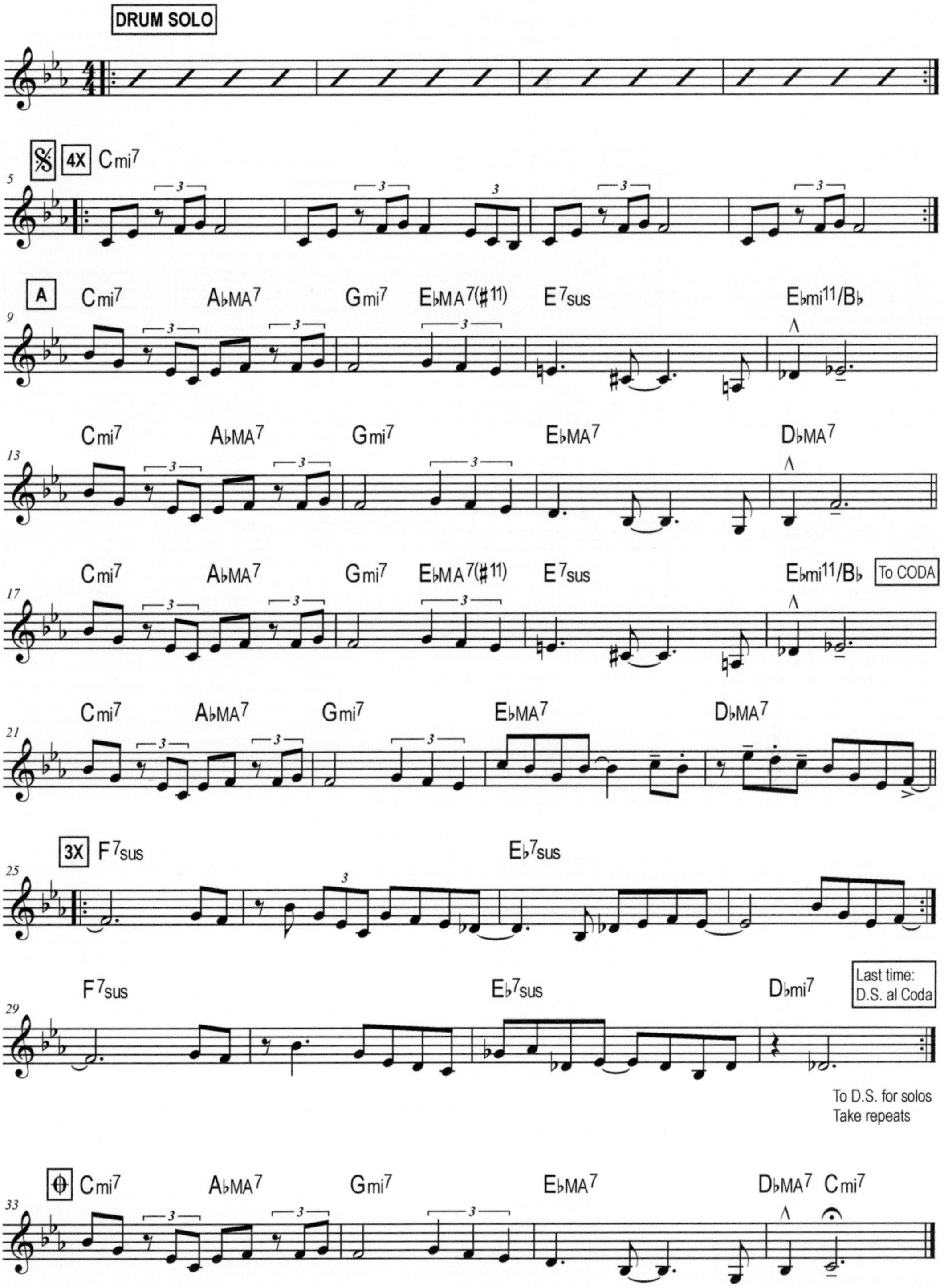
DRUM SOLO
4X
Cmi7
A
Cmi7 AbMA7 Gmi7 EbMA7(#11) E7sus Ebmi11/Bb
Cmi7 AbMA7 Gmi7 EbMA7 DbMA7
Cmi7 AbMA7 Gmi7 EbMA7(#11) E7sus Ebmi11/Bb
To CODA
Cmi7 AbMA7 Gmi7 EbMA7 DbMA7
3X
F7sus Eb7sus
F7sus Eb7sus Dbmi7
Last time: D.S. al Coda
To D.S. for solos
Take repeats
Cmi7 AbMA7 Gmi7 EbMA7 DbMA7 Cmi7

KIRA KIRA

Mai Sugimoto
For Deep Cuts #5

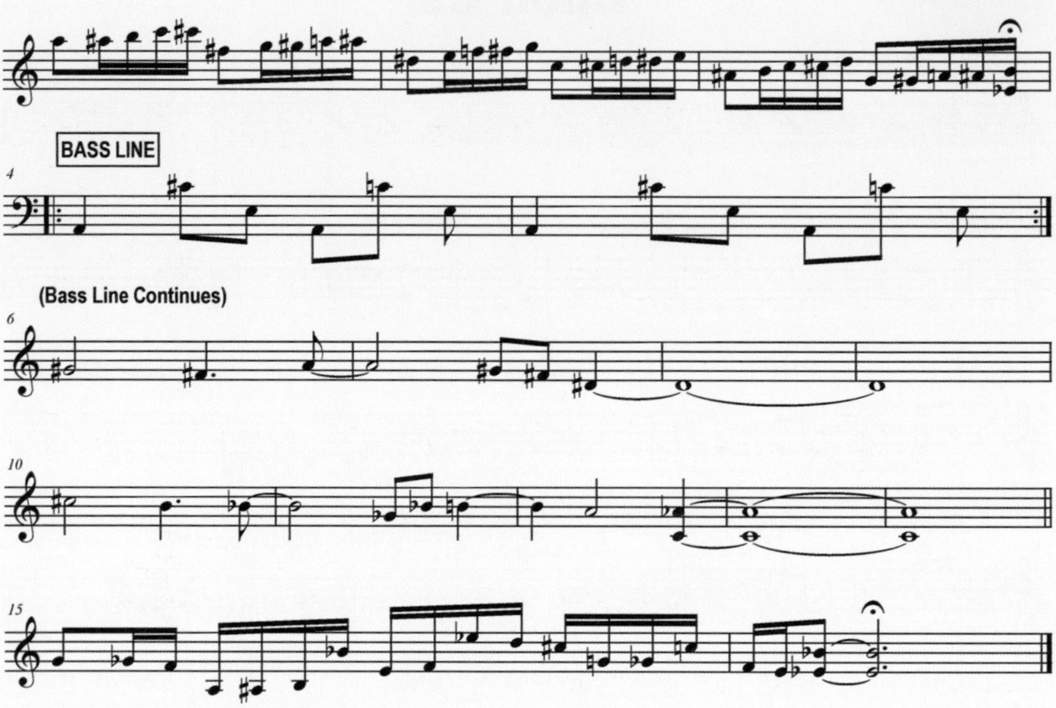
BASS LINE
(Bass Line Continues)

John Cotton

Greg Ward
For Deep Cuts #6

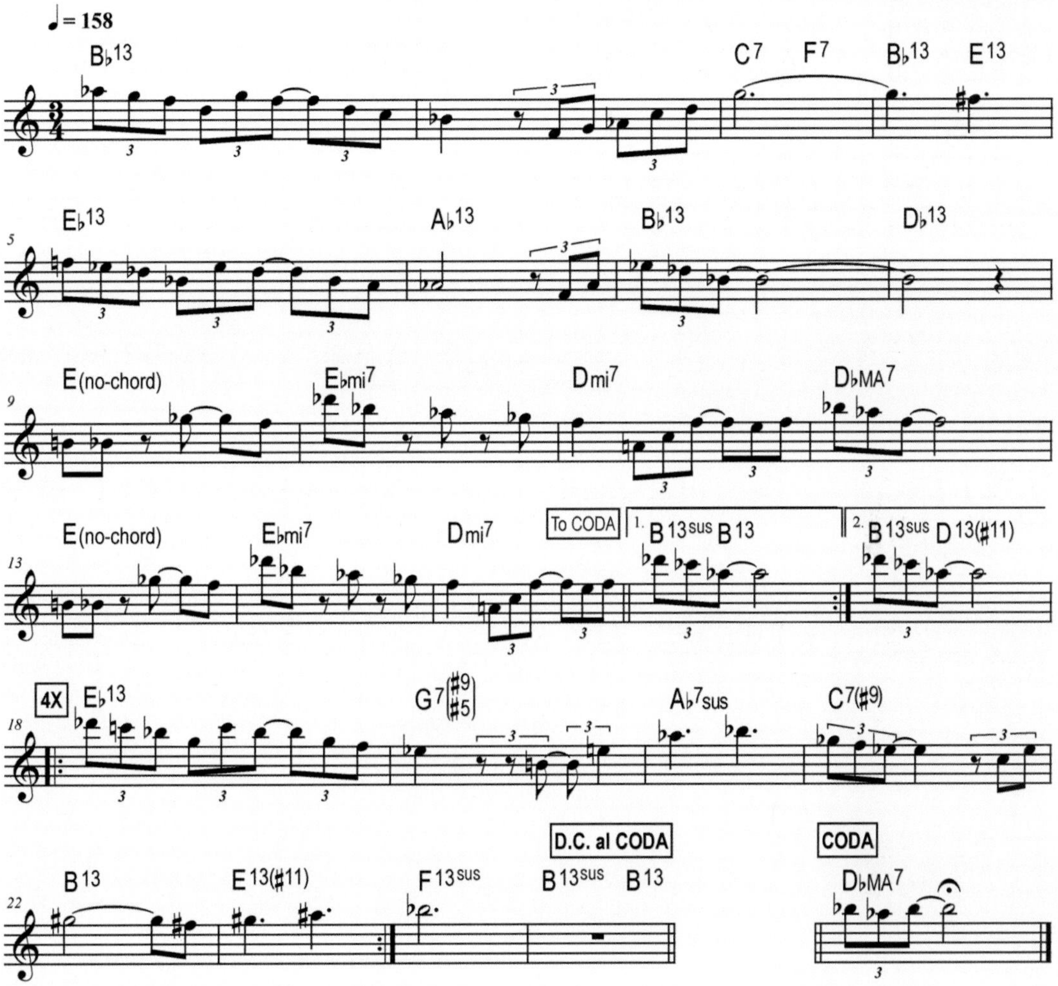
♩= 158
B♭13
C7 F7 B♭13 E13
E♭13 A♭13 B♭13 D♭13
E(no-chord) E♭mi7 Dmi7 D♭MA7
E(no-chord) E♭mi7 Dmi7
To CODA
1. B13sus B13
2. B13sus D13(♯11)
4X
E♭13 G7(♯9 ♯5) A♭7sus C7(♯9)
D.C. al CODA
CODA
B13 E13(♯11) F13sus B13sus B13
D♭MA7

IMAGE COMICS, INC. • Robert Kirkman: Chief Operating Officer • Erik Larsen: Chief Financial Officer • Todd McFarlane: President • Marc Silvestri: Chief Executive Officer • Jim Valentino: Vice President • Eric Stephenson: Publisher / Chief Creative Officer • Nicole Lapalme: Vice President of Finance • Leanna Caunter: Accounting Analyst • Sue Korpela: Accounting & HR Manager • Lorelei Bunjes: Vice President of Digital Strategy • Emilio Bautista: Digital Sales Coordinator • Dirk Wood: Vice President of International Sales & Licensing • Ryan Brewer: International Sales & Licensing Manager • Alex Cox: Director of Direct Market Sales • Jon Schlaffman: Specialty Sales Coordinator • Margot Wood: Vice President of Book Market Sales • Chloe Ramos: Book Market & Library Sales Manager • Kat Salazar: Vice President of PR & Marketing • Deanna Phelps: Marketing Design Manager • Drew Fitzgerald: Marketing Content Associate • Heather Doornink: Vice President of Production • Ian Baldessari: Print Manager • Drew Gill: Art Director • Melissa Gifford: Content Manager • Erika Schnatz: Senior Production Artist • Wesley Griffith: Production Artist • Rich Fowlks: Production Artist • IMAGECOMICS.COM

DEEP CUTS. First printing. May 2024. Published by Image Comics, Inc. Office of publication: PO BOX 14457, Portland, OR 97293. Copyright © 2024 Kyle Higgins & Joe Clark. All rights reserved. Contains material originally published in single magazine form as DEEP CUTS #1-6. "Deep Cuts," its logos, and the likenesses of all characters herein are trademarks of Kyle Higgins & Joe Clark, unless otherwise noted. "Image" and the Image Comics logos are registered trademarks of Image Comics, Inc. No part of this publication may be reproduced or transmitted, in any form or by any means (except for short excerpts for journalistic or review purposes), without the express written permission of Kyle Higgins & Joe Clark, or Image Comics, Inc. All names, characters, events, and locales in this publication are entirely fictional. Any resemblance to actual persons (living or dead), events, or places, without satirical intent, is coincidental. Printed in Canada. For international rights, contact: foreignlicensing@imagecomics.com. ISBN: 978-1-5343-9862-7.